EARTHCORE

Also by **Scott Sigler**

NOVELS
Infected (Infected Trilogy I)
Contagious (Infected Trilogy II)
Ancestor
Nocturnal
Pandemic (Infected Trilogy III)

THE GENERATIONS TRILOGY
Alive
Alight
Alone

THE GALACTIC FOOTBALL LEAGUE SERIES
The Rookie
The Starter
The All-Pro
The MVP
The Champion

THE GALACTIC FOOTBALL LEAGUE NOVELLAS
The Reporter
The Detective
Title Fight
The Rider

THE COLOR SERIES SHORT STORY COLLECTIONS
Blood is Red
Bones are White
Fire is Orange

EARTHCORE

SCOTT SIGLER

EMPTY SET ENTERTAINMENT

EARTHCORE
May 2017

Library of Congress Cataloging-in-Publication Data
Sigler, Scott
The MVP/Scott Sigler. — 1st ed.
p. cm.
1. Science Fiction—Fiction. 2. Fiction—Thriller.
Library of Congress Control Number: 2012932078

ISBN: 978-0-9831963-5-8

Book design by Donna Mugavero at Sheer Brick Studio
Cover design by Scott E. Pond at Scott Pond Design Studio

Published in the United States of America
by Empty Set Entertainment

For the dreamers, the fighters, the destined and those too stubborn to quit — never stop digging for treasure.

ACKNOWLEDGMENTS

I thank the experts who helped make this book as accurate as it could be.

Joseph Albietz III, M.D.
Dr. Daniel Baker, Ph.D. Pharmacology and Toxicology
Dr. Jeremy Ellis, Ph.D. Developmental and Cellular Biology
Robert W. Gilliland, Lieutenant Colonel, U.S. Air Force (Ret.)
Chris Grall, U.S. Army Special Forces (Ret.)
J.P. Harvey, Colonel, U.S. Air Force (Ret.)
Dr. Joseph Meert, Ph.D. Geology
A.B. Kovacs, Publisher
Dr. Phil Plait, Ph.D. Astronomy
John Vizcarra, Siglerverse Continuity Editor
Dan Stahl and Kevin Capizzi, designers of "the knife"

EARTHCORE

PROLOGUE

March 15, 1942

WILFORD IGOE JR. WRAPPED HIS FINGERS around the pumpkin-shaped rock, moved it a half inch to the left, then waited to die.

He held his breath, listening for further grinding sounds, for the sound of settling rocks—the sounds of certain death.

No sounds came. He let out a long sigh of relieved tension.

"Just a little more, Will," said his friend Samuel, who stood behind him in the cramped cave, watching for any signs of settling.

Will could only grunt in response. The light from Samuel's mining helmet jittered from side to side, up and down, bouncing all over the rough gray rock that filled Will's hands. Will's own helmet lay behind him and to the right—he'd had to take it off to squeeze into the narrow crawl space among the cluster of ancient... boulders.

The headlamps' illumination was the first light this pitch-black place had known in decades, possibly centuries. Sunlight had never graced the interior of the cave, not this far into the zone of perpetual darkness.

"Stop moving that damn light, Samuel," Will said, growling out the words. "If I move this rock the wrong way, we're all goners." Samuel's light stopped bouncing, but only for a moment, then began flittering about again, following the excited movements of his head.

Will fought down his irritation and tried to concentrate, which wasn't easy considering his position. He was wedged into the crawl space that he, Samuel and Douglas had made over the last three days. The space was part of a much larger tunnel that led steadily down into the mountain. Will's head was at the low end of that incline, his body lying in powdery cave silt. It felt like going down a slide headfirst, although he wasn't actually moving, especially if he couldn't budge that boulder.

But removing the rock wasn't the real problem. He had to move it *right*, he had to move it *just so*. The boulders surrounding him were remnants of an ancient cave-in. You couldn't tell how these rocks had settled against one another. Move out a "linchpin" rock—even a tiny one—and sudden settling would crush anything lying below.

"Come on, Will," Samuel said. His excited voice rang off the dead stone walls. "Try a little to the left."

"Up yours, Anderson," Will said. He wrestled with the chunk of limestone, his thick arms shaking with a combination of exhaustion and concerted effort.

Thousands of years ago this passage had housed a swiftly churning underground river. Now all that remained of the ancient stream was the tunnel itself and a floor of bone-dry silt, two inches thick and as fine as high-grade flour. That same silt coated Will's sweaty skin.

Sweat dripped from his face, the inverted position making it seem as if it ran up his neck, up his cheeks and into his stinging eyes. Will heard his own labored breathing as he wrestled with the rock, which had already split open two of his knuckles. His breath sounded loud—not because of the claustrophobically confined space, but because there were no background sounds. A hundred yards into the cave and all sound ceased. Not even the insects made noise, although that far down the insects were strange indeed: blind crickets with fragile antennae twice as long as their body; tiny beetles that burrowed ceaselessly into the sand; and ghostly white, long-legged spiders that had never felt the faintest trickle of sun.

"Sam, keep that fucking light still!"

To Sam, the opportunity to take the cave deep into the rock layers—to travel through the mountain as if they were a blood cell in the circulatory system of the very stone itself—was like heaven on Earth. Sam couldn't wait to get through this cave-in and continue exploring the tunnel. Will also wanted to know what lay beyond, but for the moment he didn't give a good goddamn about the tunnel or geology or the fact that he had to piss like a racehorse. His world narrowed to his hands, his arms and the damn stubborn pumpkin-shaped boulder streaked with his blood.

"Try a little to the left," Samuel said again.

"Yeah, thanks for the tip, Einstein," Will said. But for lack of a better idea, he pushed it hard to the left—it slid a good two inches.

"Oh, *shoot*," Samuel said. "Holy moley, it's moving!"

"Almost got it." He readjusted his grip, blistered hands searching for just the spot. He had it now. Oh, it wanted to fight him, but it was too late, he had that bastard of a rock and he wasn't letting go.

Will felt the thud of footsteps approaching from up the tunnel. Douglas Nadia moved with all the grace of a drunken elephant. Will always wondered how someone so thin could make so much noise.

"Where have you been, Douglas?" Samuel asked. "We've been working on this boulder for the last twenty minutes."

"What do you mean *we*?" Will said. He adjusted his body, wedging his hip against the tunnel wall to gain more leverage. He pushed again, felt his pumpkin-shaped enemy slide another inch. He listened for the sounds of settling rock.

Nothing.

"I did a little chiseling back up at the plateau," Douglas said. His thick Texan drawl betrayed his excitement.

Samuel sounded immensely annoyed. "Douglas, *please* tell me you didn't carve your name on the tunnel mouth."

"Hell no," Douglas said. "I carved *all* our names. Hey, you think we'll find any more cave drawings or maybe another goofy knife, like last time?"

"Who cares about that?" Samuel asked. "Once we're through, and if this tunnel continues to descend, I surmise we'll drop below the next sedimentary layer within fifty feet or so. That will give us a real good look at this mountain's composition."

Douglas's sharp laugh bounced off the rough, narrow walls. "You crack me up, Anderson. We've found some lost Injun tribe in here, maybe even with buried treasure, and all you can think of is geology. You're a screwball."

The two continued to babble, but Will tuned them out. The pumpkin-shaped rock didn't block the passage completely, just enough to make it impossible to crawl around. If he created a bit more space, they could squeeze through and continue on.

They'd found the opening while researching Samuel's PhD thesis. The Wah Wah Mountains were only a three-hour drive from Brigham Young University and yet were a wild and obscure treasure of geological wonders. The thick limestone mountains seemed to rise straight out of southwestern Utah's scrub-brush deserts.

Five months earlier, they'd been four thousand feet up the side of an unnamed peak when they discovered a small limestone plateau and a dark, cramped opening. The opening led into a slender tunnel that traveled down and in, well over one hundred yards into the mountain before dead-ending at the ancient cave-in. The tunnel wasn't listed on any maps — as far as the trio knew, they were the first modern-day people to discover it.

They kept their find secret while they gathered enough supplies for a long exploration. Douglas had been key for that, somehow procuring a box of old dynamite. Will hadn't been crazy about putting the stuff in the back of his '32 Ford coupe, but Samuel's enthusiasm had worn him down.

For the last three days they'd probed the cave-in, placing small charges to help break up the tightly packed rocks. Following each blast, they labored to clear loose stones. It had been three days of noisy, backbreaking work, but the intensive effort was all but forgotten as Will wrapped his arms around the pumpkin-shaped rock, adjusted his feet, and *pushed*. It resisted. He pushed harder, pushed until the muscles in his legs and arms screamed, until it felt like something was tearing along his left side.

Teeth gritted, breath held, Will dug deep and gave it one more bit of all that he had.

The stone moved a fraction of an inch, stuck, then finally slid loose with a horrible, grinding sound of protest. Will stopped, arms still wrapped around the rock like it was his lover.

He held his breath. He waited. They all waited, glancing upward, half expecting the suspended rockfall to give way and crush them all.

Nothing happened.

"Take that," Will said, his voice an exhausted whisper. "Take that, you piece of shit."

"Quit cursing," Samuel said. "Hurry up and get out of there, will you?"

Will wanted to squeeze out of the opening, sit up, then wring Samuel's neck, but he didn't have the strength. He couldn't even move. Samuel and Douglas each took an ankle and pulled, hauling Will out like a dead animal. His chin made a little trench in the silt.

Samuel rushed to the opening, laying flat and letting his light probe the newfound depths.

"How's it look?" Douglas asked, leaning on Samuel's shoulder and craning his head for a peek.

"Looks like a straight shot," Samuel said. "As far as I can see—at least another fifty yards!"

Douglas let out a yelp of triumph. A hint of an echo came back from the as-yet-unexplored passage beyond.

Will rolled to his back. He tried to wipe sweat off his face, but he only managed to spread a little more wet silt across his skin.

Douglas slapped at Will's thigh. "Get up, lazybones. Lookit Samuel— he's already crawling in."

Will remained on his back, breathing deeply, but turned his head to see Samuel's skinny body wiggle through the narrow opening. Will thought it looked like the rocks were a giant stone mouth with pursed lips and Samuel was a piece of slurped spaghetti.

"You go on ahead," Will said.

Douglas again whacked Will's thigh. "Get up, rich boy."

With effort, Will raised up on one elbow. "Doug, you hit me again and I swear I will murder you and leave your body here with the blind crickets."

Samuel's head popped back out. "Fellas, did you hear that?"

"Hear what?" Douglas and Will said together.

"That sound." A lock of Samuel's thin blond hair fell free from under his mining helmet, dangled on his high forehead. In the poor lighting, he looked like a talking guillotine victim perched on a wall of tan and red boulders.

"Sounded like sand blowing across the desert or something like that," he said. "Didn't you hear it?"

"No wind down here," Douglas said. "Unless maybe there's another opening?"

Will fell to his back again. He stared up at the ceiling of the limestone tunnel. Cracked rock, a few black marks left by small charges. His chest still heaved from the effort of moving that damn rock.

"Maybe," Samuel said. "Could be a connecting tunnel further in, which would be swell. Come on, fellas, let's see where this thing leads."

"I think rich boy is staying here," Douglas said, aiming a slap at Will's thigh but pulling back at the last second, avoiding contact.

Will said nothing, merely raised his hand, extended his middle finger, then let the hand *whump* heavily back into dry silt.

Samuel's head disappeared into the dark hole. Douglas followed him, headfirst, working his body through the confined opening.

Will lay motionless, eyes closed, listening to his friends' excited laughter fade into nothingness. He'd catch up to the goldbrickers in a moment, he just needed to rest. The cave was so peaceful, so still. He'd close his eyes for a few minutes, relax in the motionless, timeless caverns. Just a catnap, perhaps, and then—

His eyes flew open, yet he remained deathly still. He'd heard the faintest echo of a noise, a noise that somehow didn't belong. A faint clicking: the sound of metal tapping rock. And another sound, something he couldn't put his finger on, and yet it stirred recollections of Chicago, his hometown.

He strained to grasp the noise again, as if by concentrating his hearing he could tear free the thick veil of silence enveloping the tunnel. Not moving, not breathing, not understanding the cause of his sudden fear, he listened.

And heard the noises again.

click-click, click, click-click

Metal on rock, followed by a hissing, breathy, scraping sound. He immediately understood why the noise made Samuel think of a sandstorm, but that analogy wasn't quite right. Samuel had spent all twenty-two years of his life in the deserts of southern Utah. For Will, however, the sound brought back memories of Chicago's powerful weather.

That sound: dry, windblown leaves and loose paper hissing across concrete streets and sidewalks. But unlike steady gusts of Chicago wind, the new sound ebbed and flowed with a jerky, stop-start feel. It reminded Will of another noise, a noise he'd learned to watch out for since he'd started hiking into the mountains with Samuel and Douglas some three years ago—the malignant shake of a rattlesnake's warning.

Will fought down a creeping panic and a sudden, clutching stab of claustrophobia. His reaction to the strange noise was primitive, instinctive and raw.

He rolled to his knees. He reached out, found his helmet, put it on. He peered into the hole he'd labored so long to create. The helmet lamp's light showed more ancient silt, more ancient stone. Maybe fifty yards in, the tunnel angled down, out of sight. He felt a strong urge to run, but his friends were in there.

Will stared into the tunnel, listening to the bone-dry hissing-rattling grow and swell—until another, more recognizable sound overwhelmed it—a man, screaming.

It billowed up from some unseen place far down the tunnel. Will knew it was Samuel, although he'd never before heard Samuel scream. A high, piercing noise, almost feminine, full of agony and terror that transcended either sex. The scream lasted only a few seconds, faded to a single, mournful moan, then ceased.

Will forced himself to remain rooted to the spot. He couldn't summon the courage to cram himself into the narrow opening, to crawl deeper into the mountain's belly, but he could keep himself from a cowardly flight while his friends remained in the tunnel.

He saw a bouncing light before he heard the rhythmic pounding of heavy footsteps and the strained breath of a man running for his life. It was Douglas, pounding hard and fast up the sandy incline, blood smearing his face and covering his chest as if someone had splashed him with a great bucket of gore. Douglas fell hard. His helmet rolled and bounced like a decapitated head, clattering off the cave wall. He scrambled to his feet and ran some more, each desperate step kicking up fine silt that arced in the air behind him.

His friend didn't look like his friend anymore ... he looked like an animal, panicked and desperate, fleeing something that wanted to catch him, bring him down, eat him alive.

Will turned, started to run, stopped himself. His chest and stomach tingled, a glassy feeling that pulled at him, told him to get the fuck out of there. No ... he couldn't leave his friends. Will forced himself back to the opening.

"Douglas! What's happening?"

Douglas said nothing. He kept sprinting through the narrow tunnel, closing the distance. Will's light played off his friend's blood-smeared skin, his wide eyes.

And something else ... something *behind* Douglas. Strange lights, colors flowing across the stone.

Lights, and movement.

Douglas dove for the narrow opening. He tried to worm his way through the tight bottleneck, but panic slowed his efforts. His hands lashed forward, more like he was fighting against drowning water than crawling through a mountain. Knuckles burst open each time they slammed into jagged, unforgiving rock.

"Doug, calm down!" Will grabbed at his friend's flailing arms and bloody hands. "Let me pull you out!"

The man made noises that weren't words. Spittle flew from his wide-open mouth, splattering against his face, mixing with the blood that Will somehow knew once belonged to Samuel.

Will locked down on Douglas's blood-smeared right wrist, gripped it tight with both hands. Will pulled. Douglas started to slide through, but whatever had been chasing him caught up and pulled back — hard. Doug's free hand grasped desperately at the rocks, his fingers as taut and rigid as dry sticks scattered by desert wind. Douglas's eyes somehow grew even wider. His mouth let out a throat-ripping scream.

That glassy feeling exploded throughout Will's stomach, his chest, his throat, made him want to cover his ears — made him want to turn and run.

He didn't.

A smell billowed up, assaulting, unavoidable: cat shit, old pears, fish gone bad.

Will planted his feet, right foot on the stone mouth, left on the very pumpkin-shaped rock he'd worked so hard to move. He squeezed harder, refused to let Doug go.

The strange lights flickered inside the tunnel beyond Douglas, backlit his sweat-wet skin and terror-trenched face, cast strange, jerking shadows on Will and the stone around him.

Will arched his back. He pulled, pulled with everything he had, knowing that if he failed, that if he lost his grip, his friend would die.

From inside the opening, Will saw a flash of something silver. A sudden release of opposite pressure made him fall backward on his ass, as if his opponent in the tug-of-war had just dropped the rope.

Only it wasn't a rope he'd been pulling.

His two hands still clutched Douglas's wrist. Doug's fingers twitched. Split knuckles dripped red. Halfway to the elbow, shirtsleeve still attached, Doug's arm *ended*, severed with a cut as clean as that of a butcher's meat-saw. Will's headlamp light lit up the blood pattering down to the silt below. Doug's radius and ulna gleamed white, oozed gooey marrow.

Darkness seemed to close in.

But it wasn't *all* dark.

Flickers of colored light sparkled from the opening. Danced off the rough rocks. Burned brighter, growing in intensity. And then, more movement, a glowing shape that Will's mind couldn't identify, couldn't process.

He tossed Doug's hand aside, scrambled to his feet. That glassy urge to save himself finally controlled his thoughts, completely and without question.

Will *ran*.

Behind him, the scratchy rasp of something sliding through the narrow opening. Those strange colors lit up the rocks around him, cast ahead of him the long, jerking shadow of a man.

He didn't look back. He attacked the incline. Feet pounded into soft silt, legs drove him forward with strength he hadn't known existed. If he could just make it back to the opening, maybe he could escape.

The darkness ... that's where this thing lived. If he could make it to the tunnel opening, he knew he knew *he knew* he would survive.

He clung to that hope as he made his desperate dash. Chest heaving, limbs screaming white-hot from fatigue, he finally saw salvation: *sunlight*.

Will poured it on, ignored his exhausted body, forced himself to go faster. With a final burst of energy, he escaped the shaft and stumbled onto the small limestone plateau. The hot sun—the glorious, life-giving sun—instantly warmed his shadow-chilled skin.

He fell. For a moment, just one moment of lovely denial, he thought his legs had given out. Then the pain set in: slashing, slicing, piercing.

He smelled that horrid scent.

Something warm grabbed his ankles.

For the second time that afternoon, he was dragged along on his stomach. His eyes locked on a small, pale cricket. He saw it in utter clarity, saw each long, thin leg, saw the delicate antennae that were three times as long as the body.

It seemed so stupid that the cricket would survive while he would not. So unfair.

The cool darkness slid over him once again.

Article from *The Y News*, Brigham Young University
APRIL 4, 1942

GRADUATE STUDENTS MISSING

Presumed Lost in Caves

By **SHANNON CARMICHAEL**

TODAY POLICE DECLARED three Brigham Young graduate students missing. The three geology students were doing fieldwork in the southern Wah Wah Mountains in western Utah.

Samuel J. Anderson, 22; Douglas Nadia, 21; and Wilford Igoe Jr., 22, were doing research in the remote area. Officials became concerned when Anderson's parents contacted the university, saying that he was due home on March 27. Utah State Police hiked out to their last reported location, which sits at an elevation of 3,500 feet.

"It was difficult reaching the site," said Henry Isbey of the Utah State Police. "We had a plane fly over their last reported location, but couldn't find anything. We hiked up and found no sign of them, not even a campsite."

Police officials said the search could prove difficult because of the terrain, and because the students have been in the hills for almost a month with no contact. Isbey added that it's impossible to know exactly when the students ran into trouble.

It was the three students' second trip to the area, the first coming in October 1941. They discovered what appears to be a ceremonial metal knife. Shortly after returning from that excursion, Anderson donated the knife to the BYU Archaeology Department. It is unknown if their disappearance is related to the knife.

School officials said they would do anything in their power to help find the students.

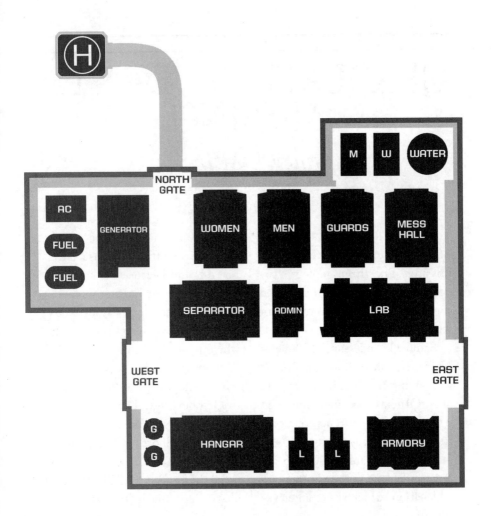

KEY:

AC = Air Conditioner

F   = Fuel Tank

L   = Latrine

M   = Men's Shower

W   = Women's Shower

G   = Gasoline

BOOK ONE
OPPORTUNITY

July 30

SONNY MCGUINESS CHECKED THE TIME on his cell phone. Goddammit—he'd spent thirty minutes now, sitting at a corner table, staring angrily at the long-haired Indian sitting across from him. The bar was dark with shadow despite noonday sun that blazed against shuttered windows. They had the corner of the place to themselves, not because there were only ten people there, but rather because both of them smelled as if they hadn't bathed in weeks. Sonny's shocking-white, unkempt beard framed a scowl that furrowed his deeply wrinkled, dark-black face. The skin around his eyes was somewhat lighter than the rest of his onyx complexion, giving him an odd reverse-mask appearance. He drank his beer as if it would douse his sudden burst of temper.

"Bullshit," he said. "You ain't found no Silver Spring."

"Hey, man, don't get hostile," said Dennis the Deadhead. He

drawled out the word *man*, making it sound long, smooth and mellow. "You said you were a prospector, so I just thought I'd share a tale with you. You believe what you like, man."

Dennis sipped his double shot of Red Star vodka.

The mention of the Silver Spring had caused the first conversational pause in over an hour. Sonny had entered the bar planning to drink alone, as he usually did, when he spotted a man with a telltale head of long, straight black hair. Sonny had introduced himself, then bet a beer he could guess the Indian's tribe on the first try. The Indian's name was Dennis Diving-Bird. Most people, however, just called him "Dennis the Deadhead." Dennis took the bet, Sonny guessed Hopi—Dennis bought the first round.

After forty years of prospecting in the American Southwest, Sonny prided himself on guessing any Native American's tribe. He liked Indians. They were, in fact, the *only* people he liked.

"The Silver Spring is just a myth," Sonny said. "I should know, I looked for it twenty years ago and didn't find squat."

Dennis the Deadhead shrugged. "Where'd you look?"

"I looked in the Snake, Black, and San Francisco ranges." Sonny finished his beer. "I didn't find nuthin'."

"Well, you were close," Dennis said. He took a puff from the latest in his nonstop chain of Pall Malls. "It's in the Wah Wahs."

Dennis's wrinkled face hid under long, dirty-black hair. He wore a tie-dyed shirt, a fringed leather jacket covered with Grateful Dead skull patches, and he stank. Not that Sonny minded the stench all that much; after two straight weeks in the scorching Arizona foothills, he knew he didn't exactly smell like flowers himself.

"The legends are true, man," Dennis said. "That spring is bubbling out of the ground into a little pool full of silver dust."

Which in itself was bullshit, or Dennis had been given misinformation. Silver was usually tied up in rock ores. Native silver was a rare thing, silver dust even rarer, and when it was found it was often tarnished—it didn't actually look "silver" at all.

The story was a lie.

So why did Sonny's gut tell him Dennis *wasn't* lying?

"So it's just sitting there," Sonny said. "Just waiting for someone to claim it?"

"That's right, man." Dennis took another small, slow sip. "It's just layin' there, pretty as you please. As long as no one's found it since I was there about ten years ago."

"Right. And that's why you're here, at the Two-Spoke Bar, drinking rotgut vodka instead of livin' high on the hog at the Hilton."

"Hey, man, just 'cause I didn't take it don't mean it ain't there."

Sonny slapped the table. "Then why the hell didjya leave it?"

That came out louder than he'd intended, loud enough to draw the attention of the other patrons. Sonny leaned over his beer, ignoring them until they turned back to their own drinks.

He wasn't mad at Dennis, only at himself. The Indian's story was pure bullshit, yet already he felt an uncontrollable part of him embrace the tale the way a girl's legs wrap around her lover. Some men suffer addictions to drugs, booze, women, money—Sonny's habit was curiosity. It was that little voice pulling his strings, the one that endlessly repeated: *Don't you wanna know?*

Dennis the Deadhead glanced around, as if to make sure no one was watching him. He leaned closer, spoke softly.

"I left it because that place is cursed, man."

"Aw, go fuck yourself," Sonny said, this time controlling his volume. "No curse ever stopped anyone from grabbin' the pot at the end of the rainbow. I'd lift the devil's sack and pluck treasure from his prostate, if that's what it took."

"That's 'cause you ain't ever been there," Dennis whispered. "The Hopi know enough to steer clear of that place. No one goes out there. No reason to *go* there in the first place. Nothing there but dirt and rock. I went there to see for myself, to test the legends, you might say, but I only went once. The devil lives on that mountain. You can *sense* him, man."

Throughout the beginning of their conversation, Dennis's eyes had sparkled with friendly laughter. Especially when he talked of the summers of '79 through '84, during which he'd toured with the Dead. Now, however, Sonny noted that Dennis's friendly emotion filtered away like the wisps of smoke from his Pall Mall. As he spoke of the Silver Spring and the Wah Wah Mountains, his eyes filled with fear. Every few seconds, Dennis looked from one corner of the bar to the next, as if the simple mention of the legend might summon some evil power.

"So if you know where this place is, how come you haven't told anybody?"

"No one ever asked," Dennis said. "Most people take one look at me and shy away. Can't remember the last time someone introduced themselves and offered to buy me a drink. In fact, I think you're the first."

Sonny nodded. "Yeah, but a secret like that can burn a hole in a man's belly. If no one has found it yet, you haven't really told anyone. Why me?"

Dennis stared at Sonny. He stared long, he stared hard.

"I don't know," the Indian finally said. His words slurred slightly. An hour's worth of steady drinking was beginning to take effect. "You're a man of the land. I can feel that. Maybe I told you because if you go there, I know you'll feel what I feel. Maybe because that place scares the shit out of me, and it won't scare you as much, so maybe you can do something with it. Maybe it's because I'm getting drunk. Who knows, man?"

"Could you draw me a map?" Sonny asked.

Dennis knocked back the rest of his vodka. "Buy me another Red Star and I'll draw it right on this napkin, man. But I warn ya—you won't like that place."

Sonny signaled the bartender again. When a vodka and a beer landed on the table, Dennis produced a red Crayola from a jacket pocket. He started drawing on a bar napkin.

The two men talked for another hour, during which they both got exceedingly drunk. Good conversation, sure, but Sonny wasn't really paying attention anymore. All he could think about was the possibility that the fabled Silver Spring—where silver poured from the ground like water from a bottomless well—was real.

Sonny wasn't some greenhorn straight off the bus. He knew the Southwest like a man knows his wife's body. He could hop in his Humvee, drive five or six hours to Utah, then hike into the Wah Wah Mountains and locate Dennis the Deadhead's mythical spooky G-spot. The trip might take a day. Maybe two, considering hiking speed in the unforgiving Wah Wahs. That wasn't much wasted time, and it would let him take his goddamned unrelenting curiosity and kick it dead square in its metaphorical nuts. He was already beyond his ability to control himself; the only way to get the brain-worm out of his head was to go out there and make sure Dennis was full of shit.

Sonny *had* to check it out, because as his sainted mother once told him: *An ounce of truth lined every old wives' tale.*

Sometimes, an ounce of truth paid off with an ounce of gold.

Or, in this case, maybe an ounce of silver—Sonny wasn't going to be picky.

2

August 1

SNOW CAME IN A NEAR-BLINDING WAVE, big wet clumps collecting on the windshield only to be swept away by the wipers. Headlamps blared off thousands of whipping white streaks that marked the wind's direction like tracer bullets.

Connell leaned forward and squinted, as if that could somehow help him see better. Visibility was a few hundred feet, at best. Rows of lights on either side of the winding driveway glowed with fuzzy halos of whipping snow.

"Maybe we should stay for a while, hon," Cori said. "It's still quite a bash in there. Although, I wonder how long it will last without Mister Life of the Party charming the pants off everyone."

Her hand reached out to touch his, which clung to the steering wheel in a white-knuckled grip. He threw her a glance, offering her a reassuring smile.

"Oh, I'm sure they'll find a way to celebrate without me," Connell said, holding her hand for a moment. "Besides, I'd rather spend at least some of the first day of the New Year with my wife, not a bunch of drunken coworkers."

She smiled, that same warm, melting smile that had caught his eye at another New Year's Eve party six years earlier. He grinned back.

"Don't worry, Pea," Connell said, returning the smile. "We'll be fine."

The storm was getting worse. He had no intention of spending the night at his boss's house, crashed on the floor somewhere with passed-out coworkers scattered about like victims of some party land mine. This was New Year's Eve, after all, the anniversary of the night he'd met the woman who would become his wife. He'd spend the night with her and her alone, in their bed.

Connell looked hard both to the left and to the right. He saw nothing through the almost solid swirl of snow. He pushed gently on the accelerator and eased the Lincoln out onto the road, tires crunching on the snow-covered driveway.

No squeal of brakes, no blaring horn, only a sudden, smashing impact and the impossibly loud cries of screeching metal. The Lincoln lurched to the left, back end whipping across slushy pavement, spinning almost a full 360 degrees before the rear end flew into the ditch. As suddenly as it started, it ended. Stillness. Total silence, save for the howling wind and the rapid clinking of a ruined motor cooling in the night's grip.

Connell blinked, hands still clutching the steering wheel. A dull throb pulsed in his neck. A stabbing pain lit up his right knee. His mind finally centered on a single word: *accident.*

He turned to look at Cori. Faint light strayed from the lamps surrounding the driveway. She was sitting next to him, far closer than she should have been, pressed near by a mangled monster of plastic and metal that had once been the passenger door. Snow blew through what was left of the window, melting where it hit blood.

She stared out at nothing. Her beautiful curls clung to her face, held fast by glistening red. Flecks of glass hung in her hair like glitter. Blood sheeted her scalp, her cheeks, her chin, pulsing down to stain her white coat.

She looked at him, eyes wide and unfocused.

"Connell?"

Her voice gurgled with wetness. She sounded weak. Fractured.

He knew, instantly, that she was dying. There wasn't time for panic or rage. Only moments remained.

A strange calm claimed him. So strong was their love, so powerful their fear that someday one of them would be alone, that they had often talked about dying in each other's arms. Far from now, far *far* from now—but *now* had come sooner than they thought. He would be there for her in those last seconds, he would make sure she didn't die alone.

"Take it easy, Pea," Connell said. "Help is on the way."

"Connell?" she asked again. A red bubble formed on her lips, popped, sent a droplet into her eye, made her blink rapidly.

She weakly lifted a bloody hand toward him. He took it, held it, felt the movement of tiny broken bones beneath her skin.

"I'm here, Pea," he said.

He felt tears welling up; he fought them back. She didn't need to see that. He held her ravaged hand against his cheek. He did the impossible—he forced himself to smile at her.

"I'm here, Pea. I'm here. I will always be here for you."

Her head lolled forward. Connell heard voices shouting over the whipping wind. Faces appeared around the car; coworkers and concerned friends peered in, asking if he was okay. His eyes remained fixed on his dead wife. Snow swept in.

He held her hand against his cheek. He held it there until her warmth started to fade.

CONNELL LURCHED UP, a scream locked in his throat. He was freezing—not from the dream-snow, but rather from sweat-soaked sheets turned icy by air-conditioning running full blast.

He tried to control his ragged breathing. He never knew when the dream would come. Sometimes he'd have it for weeks on end, every night a reenactment of the terror and the loss. Sometimes he'd go months between the dreams. When that happened, he wondered if he was finally getting over Cori's death.

But he knew better. He would never get over it. Never get over her.

He sat on the edge of the filthy bed, on sheets that hadn't been changed in months. As he stared out into the black mess of the room, he realized what he always realized—that car crash had taken his life as well.

His pulse slowly returned to normal. He steadied his breathing, fighting down the stabbing pain of losing her yet again. He looked at the clock—4:17 a.m. He'd overslept.

He dragged himself out of bed. He had work to do.

3

August 1

NO WIND. NO PEOPLE. NO NOISE. Just rocks. Rocks and the Utah sun—punishing, unforgiving, merciless.

Sonny adjusted his canvas backpack, the same one he'd used for decades. He stared at the tiny spring bubbling forth from the limestone mountain. It spilled cold water onto cracked rocks. Sonny's huge smile split his deep-black skin, revealing too-white false teeth.

Sometimes you just get lucky.

When he'd been thirteen, he'd taken a summer job helping out Mister Bronson, an old-timer who went into the mountains of Colorado to pan for gold. To this day, Sonny didn't know Bronson's first name. The man died just two weeks after Sonny had gone to work for him, killed in a rockfall. Two weeks, that was it, but in those two weeks, they'd lucked into a significant find.

By adult standards, that "significant find" didn't amount to much. About three hundred bucks. To a dirt-poor thirteen-year-old kid, though, it was a fortune. It hadn't just been the money, it had been that they had *found* the gold. Lying there, barely hidden, just waiting for someone to put in the work to find it. That thrill of discovery changed Sonny, instantly and permanently.

He had never been what one would call a strapping young lad. Even now he might tip the scales at 140 pounds, and then only if the weigh-in came after a big Thanksgiving meal. At thirteen, though, he'd barely been three digits, yet he had hauled Bronson's broken body out of the mountains, back to the man's car, and had driven him to the nearest town. Hauling a corpse around might have made most teenagers seek other means of employment, but not Sonny McGuiness. For him, it was too late.

He had the bug.

Fifty-four years later, he still hadn't shaken it.

He'd spent the rest of his thirteenth summer right back in the Colorado mountains, alone, learning his newly chosen career by trial and error. That was just the beginning. He'd spent five decades searching for gold and silver, a dozen other precious materials, following up on leads, rumors, hunches, and myths. Usually he got squat. For every valuable find discovered from such dream chasing, there were twenty or thirty searches that turned up nothing but dirt.

In his twenties, he'd learned that the best way to find riches involved a different kind of digging—libraries rather than mountains. And city halls. And university archives. Anywhere, really, that contained old newspapers and forgotten records that had yet to be scanned and digitized.

Turned out that it was much easier to find an old mine than to discover a new one.

A vein that "ran dry" in 1914 could be reworked with leaching or strip-mine techniques made possible by modern technology. If you found one of these old veins, bought up the worthless property and then sold it to a mining company, you stood to make a tidy profit. He wasn't the only one to use such tactics, but he *was* the best at it, if he did say so himself.

In the six months before he'd bought a Hopi Indian a few rounds of shitty vodka, however, Sonny's various methods had produced jack shit. After a fruitless season spent researching dead mines, lost mines, abandoned mines, and—yes—a summer spent hiking in the heat, of breathing dust, of digging and panning, he'd had nothing to show for his efforts but a dwindling bank account, big blisters, and the occasional paper cut.

All that futility, yet here he was, grinning like mad at the results of good old-fashioned dumb luck.

Dennis's Crayola map had proved amazingly accurate considering it was based on a ten-year-old memory. Those Hopis sure knew their land. The water burbled out of the rock, trickling slowly into an ages-old, mostly dried-up stream bed.

Water was scarce in these parts. Always had been. That should have made even a tiny spring a known landmark. So how come this one wasn't on any maps? How come no one came here? No logical reason, but Sonny guessed the reason had nothing to do with logic.

The devil lives on that mountain, Dennis had said. *You can* sense *him, man.*

Sonny sensed something, all right. Not the devil, of course, but there was something *off* about this place. He'd hiked and climbed for six grueling hours to get here. The first five hours, he'd felt nothing other than the sun trying to kick his ass. The last hour, though … he'd started to get the creepy-crawlies. Goose bumps and all that happy horseshit. There was something familiar about the vibe, but he couldn't place it.

The words of Dennis the Deadhead echoed in his head. So, too, did a line from one of his all-time favorite movies: *I've got a bad feeling about this.*

That feeling hadn't been bad enough to make him turn around, though. Not after a worthless summer. Not when he was so close to satisfying his curiosity. Sometimes bad feelings happened when you were the only person for miles around. Besides, other than a trickle of water, it wasn't like there was a reason for people to be up here. Nothing but rocks and sand, a few scraggly trees fighting a decades-long battle for survival. The nearest town, Milford, was over an hour away.

So it felt spooky, so fucking what? Wasn't like that was the reason no one had built a Starbucks.

Sonny's lucky pie tin hung from his belt, dangling from a short rope like a six-shooter dangling from an outlaw's hip. He unhooked the pan, used it to scoop up some silt and water from the stream bed. He swished the contents around, a circular motion carrying the fine silt over the edge to splash against the mountainside. After two minutes of panning, all that remained was a fine, white, metallic dust.

A whoop escaped his lips, a yell of joy that bounced off the mountain and into the dry summer air. Sonofabitch — that stinky, long-haired, wrinkled-up old Indian hadn't been full of shit at all. Sonny wanted to kiss that Pall Mall–blackened mouth. With tongue, even, because fuck it.

Sonny pulled a small vial from the leather bag he took everywhere, poured in the watery dust and sealed it tight. He carefully placed the vial back in the bag, right between the beat-up cases of his binoculars and his compass, both of which he'd had for more than thirty years.

Six hours of mountain stood between him and his Humvee. The chances of someone else finding this spot were slim and none — and Slim had just left town — but Sonny covered up his tracks and any evidence of his visit anyway.

Couldn't be too careful. Especially not now.

He'd found silver a couple of times in his career. The spring didn't contain enough dust to cover a summer's worth of prospecting, but that wasn't the way things worked anymore. Nowadays you made far more money finding the stuff, then selling the location to a big company. Let some mining corporation suck the minerals from the ground. Sonny, meanwhile, would spend the winter in Rio with a bronzed little piece of fluff a third his age bringing him drinks and keeping him warm at night.

He started down. That spooky feeling hadn't let up. He felt the skin on the back of his neck crawling, prickling.

Sonny stopped walking. He stared out, taking in the stunning view of empty desert. Maybe fifteen miles northwest, across a flat valley, he recognized Frisco Peak. He couldn't quite make out Route 21 that ran between where he was and the Frisco Range, but he knew it was there. If there had been a car on it, maybe he would have detected the motion.

It hit him. That spooky feeling, it didn't come from the mountain, it came from what was on it.

Or rather, what *wasn't*.

No animals. No birds flying overhead. No jackrabbit tracks. No rodents. No chewed branches or seed husks. No droppings of any kind. There should have been wildlife, at least *signs* of wildlife, all over.

But there was nothing.

So damn *still*. So damn *quiet*.

This mountain, the vibe of the place ... he finally nailed it. Yes, he'd felt this feeling before, the sad sense of darkness, of loss.

It felt like being at a funeral.

The fingers of his right hand traced the bracelet on his left wrist. His most-prized possession: a genuine Sikyatata. Over a century old. Sonny knew that most people would find it ridiculous that a man of his color—as black as black gets—would wear a silver bracelet engraved with a black swastika, but the Hopi had used that symbol long before fucktard Hitler did. To the Hopi, it represented the center of their land. To Sonny, it acted as a ward of sorts, something he believed protected him against evil.

He rubbed at the bracelet, hoping the mountain's evil feeling would fade.

It didn't.

He started down again. Faster, this time. Much faster.

As darkness claimed the desert, Sonny finished his long hike back to the Humvee. He took a thirsty look at the blazing sunset, a picture that grew more and more beautiful as the years wore on. He felt a sense of relief that the mountain would soon be behind him. He'd mapped the location extremely well and could give exact coordinates to the spring. He wouldn't have to come here again, and that was good—he hated funerals.

He checked the bag one more time, just to make sure the vial was still there. His leathery face split by a wide smile, Sonny headed for Salt Lake City.

4

August 3

AS SOON AS THE METALLURGY RESULTS came back, Herbert Darker knew he was going to betray Sonny McGuiness. He felt bad about it, but business was business. It wasn't like Sonny would come out of this with nothing. That wasn't how Herbert's contact worked. Most of the time, anyway.

Sonny sat on the other side of a black lab table. A tablet lay flat in front of him, test results glowing on the screen. Both men perched on stools. Herbert liked talking to Sonny, because it was one of the few times he could actually look eye to eye with another man. Most people Herbert dealt with were taller than he was. Hell, other than his children, *everyone* was taller than he was. Even his wife.

Sonny stared at the results. Herbert sat quietly, waited, looked out his lab window at the breathtaking backdrop of the Wasatch Mountains.

He'd been born in Salt Lake City, gone to school here, got married here, started his own business here. Aside from the few GSA and MMSA conferences he attended, he didn't even like to leave the state.

Sonny finally looked up. "You sure about this, Herb?"

Herbert nodded. "Positive. You can see the numbers yourself."

Sonny's dark black fingers slid into his bright white beard. His fingers pulled gently, straightening the hair before sliding free.

"Yeah, I can see it." Tangle, pull. "I just didn't expect it is all." Tangle, pull. "There ain't any platinum veins in Utah."

"Did this sample come from Utah?"

Sonny grunted. That was the closest the man would ever come to saying *yes* about the location of a find. He never told Herbert any details. Real prospectors never told *anyone* details, really, at least not the prospectors who wanted to keep their claims.

While Herbert had no idea exactly where Sonny's find came from, the mention of Utah surprised him. Untold fortunes had been torn from beneath the state: gold, iron ore, molybdenum, potash, magnesium, beryllium, Gilsonite. All those things and more, but in Herbert's twenty years of experience he'd never heard of Utah holding such a concentrated source of platinum.

"It looks like a very rich find," Herbert said. "Your sample is almost pure. That's unheard of. And the only impurity is iridium, which is valuable in itself. This is an *amazing* discovery, Sonny."

Tangle, pull.

A smile slowly made the thousand lines on Sonny's face crinkle, deepen.

"Herb, are you telling me this is my biggest find yet? Bigger than the Jorgensson Mine?"

Herbert shrugged. "Well, it's the biggest find *I've* analyzed for you, anyway."

Sonny slid off the stool, reached across the table, grabbed Herbert's shoulder and gave an overly enthusiastic shake.

"Shut up, you old bastard," Sonny said. "You know damn well you're the only one I let touch my samples for going on, what... has it really been *fifteen years?*"

Herbert looked away for a second—away and *down*. Then just as quickly, he glanced up, looked Sonny in the eye and forced a smile.

"Sixteen years, actually," he said. "And in all that time, you haven't brought me anything like this. There hasn't *been* anything like this. Anywhere. After the results came back, I read up a bit. From what little I saw—" his voice dropped to a breathless whisper "—you might have the purest vein in the *world*."

THIRTY MINUTES LATER, Herbert Darker sat on the same stool, a cell phone in his hand. Sonny had left, visions of untold fortunes fixing him with a crinkled perma-smile. Herbert had waited as long as he dared—just enough to be sure Sonny was gone and wasn't coming back—before making the call.

"This is big, Mister Kirkland. Really big."

"Just tell me the ore grade."

"He didn't bring in an ore sample, just the dust he panned. For there to be that much dust and have it be that pure, though, it would have to come from a concentrated source. The only impurity is iridium, at about thirty percent. I could only guess at the ore grade."

"Then guess."

Herbert hated guessing. And when it came to Connell Kirkland, he hated saying anything that he wasn't completely sure of.

He also hated the way he sounded when he talked to the man. Higher pitched than usual. Kirkland made Herbert nervous, made him think of nature shows about lurking predators and oblivious prey: the mouse squeaks, while the snake makes no noise at all.

"If I had to guess…I'd say at least ten ounces per ton. Maybe higher."

"Bullshit. If you think you can shake me down, you won't like the results."

Sometimes you can hear a smile in a person's voice. If Kirkland smiled like that, he'd never done it while talking to Herbert. If not for overtones of anger and a constant hint of annoyance, the guy could have been a fucking android or something.

"I'm not shaking you down," Herbert said.

"Claiming this find produces ten ounces per ton of ore? There is no platinum vein that rich, not anywhere."

"You think I don't know that? Why do you think I called you so quickly? And I'm not *claiming* anything. You told me to guess, so I guessed."

Herbert's eyes scrunched tight. He needed a Tums. The last thing he wanted was to piss this guy off. Maybe he shouldn't have called Kirkland, but now it was too late. He had to ride this out.

Kirkland was all the things that Herbert was not: tall, lean and handsome, with a full head of thick, black hair. Herbert had met the man only once. Once was enough, though. Kirkland's gray eyes didn't look at you like one person looks at another. They looked at you like you were an asset to be used and discarded, no better than a piece of mining equipment or a chunk of rock that might or might not have some limited value.

"Let's assume you're not stupid enough to lie to me," Kirkland said. "Where did he get this sample?"

"Hell if I know. He's a crafty old bastard."

"How can you not know, Herbert? It's got to be in the area, right? I mean you're in Salt Lake City, and he came to you."

Herbert took a breath. The pain in his temples throbbed in time with his heartbeat.

"McGuiness always comes to me. He does it so no one can guess the location of his finds."

It had been that way for sixteen years. No matter where Sonny found samples, he brought them to Herbert. From Wyoming, from Colorado, from California. From Mexico. From Canada. Even Brazil. Sonny trusted Herbert and no one else. That made this Sonny's own fault, really—if he'd developed more business relationships, maybe he wouldn't have brought the sample to Herbert in the first place.

"But you think it came from Utah," Kirkland said. "Why?"

"Most of his finds come from there. He's an absolute expert on the state's mining history. I've seen him come up with finds just from reading old newspapers, letters, records, that sort of thing. I don't know if that's how he discovered this one, but that's my guess."

"A history buff as well. Fascinating. I need to talk to this man. Give me his name and number."

Herbert's free hand cupped the phone. He spoke in a hissing whisper, even though there was no one else in the office, no one else in the building.

"I can't do that!" Herbert heard the whine in his voice, but he couldn't help it. "That's not the way it works and you know it."

"That's the way it works now."

"No, you have to wait. He's only been in town for a couple of days!"

"You're a real piece of work," Kirkland said. "This might be the richest find of the *century*, you don't know where it came from, and you're telling me I shouldn't call him?"

"He only found out about the platinum quality thirty minutes ago! He'd know I gave you the information!"

"I give a fuck, Herbert. I really do. I want his name, I want his number, and I want them now. I'll give you an extra ten grand, on top of your usual fee."

Herbert fell silent. He could still back out and protect Sonny's find, at least for a while. Perhaps give Sonny time to properly sell the claim. Kirkland was ruthless and would find a way to own the site within days. Sonny might very well wind up with nothing.

"Silent treatment, Herbert? All right, if you're going to play hardball, so will I. The moment I have a chat with Sonny McGuiness, my courier will deliver your usual fee plus twenty-five grand extra. This is a one-time offer. I need a decision right now."

Herbert's head throbbed. So much money in one shot, but only if he served up Sonny on a plate. Kirkland didn't make idle threats; it was now or nothing.

College was getting more expensive every year. Herbert's youngest son was in the fourth grade, his oldest already in the seventh. Everything since they'd been born seemed a blur. The time went by so fast, and before he knew it, they'd be off to begin their own lives. Yes, he was selling Sonny out, but Sonny didn't have kids, and even if he did, that wasn't Herbert's problem—he had to look out for his own family.

"Well, thanks for wasting my time," Connell said. "I'll get my information elsewhere."

"Wait! I'll give it to you."

Herbert wasn't stupid. As powerful as Kirkland was, he'd just get Sonny's contact information somewhere else. Sonny would still be screwed, and the college fund would be out twenty-five grand. How did that make any sense?

It didn't.

The mouse squeaked.

The snake listened.

"Smart man," Kirkland said. "I also need any information you can give me on Sonny himself. What other sites has he discovered? What companies does he usually work with?"

The spot of heartburn flared up, intensified. Herbert winced as his body turned stress and anxiety into a rumbling lava pit of stomach acid.

"No," he said. "And this time, I mean it, Mister Kirkland. You pay me to tip you off to big finds, that's it. How you steal them is up to you."

Herbert wanted to take those words back as soon as he said them. The silence on the other end of the line seemed to hover, seemed to sway—a cobra waiting to strike.

"It took balls to say that to me," Kirkland said. "I didn't think you *had* balls. I'm impressed. But that doesn't change anything. I want everything you have on McGuiness and I want it now. I'll double my offer—fifty thousand dollars."

The lava pit's bubbling increased, sending acid straight into Herbert's throat. Fifty grand? So much, for just one little betrayal when Sonny was going to get screwed anyway. But there was screwed and then there was *fucked*. If Sonny could negotiate for himself, he could come out of this with something. Maybe. Hopefully. If Kirkland went into that conversation armed to the teeth, Sonny might come out with absolutely nothing.

"My answer is still *no*."

"You listen to me, you little squirt of piss. You give me everything you have on McGuiness, right now, or you're out of the stable. No more payoffs."

Herbert just wanted to get off the phone. He couldn't take any more. It wasn't fair. He'd done his job, he'd given Kirkland the tip-off... how had it come to this?

"Mister Kirkland, I've given you good information. I know of three mines that you have because of me. That's millions of dollars. You wouldn't cut me off over something like this."

"You think you're the only one on the payroll? You think I do this shit for my health? I have a system, a system that gives me major finds. If you're not *part* of that system, you're out of that system."

Herbert paused, then clenched his teeth. His head felt hot. This time, he'd bitten off way more than he could chew. Kirkland had never been so aggressive. Things were escalating. Herbert wanted out of this quagmire before it sucked him in even deeper.

"I'll take my twenty-five thousand and call it finished."

This time it was Connell's turn to pause.

"When you're out, you're out for good," he said. "You understand that?"

Herbert's belly tightened, turned.

"I understand."

"I won't forget this," Kirkland said.

Herbert hung up the phone just as the lava pit became a volcano he couldn't hold back: stomach-acid vomit erupted all over his desk.

All he'd wanted to do was make a little extra money for his family. What was wrong with that? He'd tried to protect Sonny—had doing so earned him an enemy?

Not just any enemy: *Connell Kirkland*.

The mining industry had a nickname for Kirkland: they called him "cutthroat."

The volcano erupted again.

CONNELL'S FINGERS DRUMMED the desktop, *ba-da-ba-bump, ba-da-ba-bump*.

He hated Herbert Darker. Connell hated any whiner, and Herbert was a whiner of the highest degree. In business, if you had to sell someone out to make money, that's what you did. You didn't bitch about it. You didn't rationalize it or try to justify it in order to assuage your guilt.

Guilt: if you felt that worthless emotion in the first place, you didn't belong in business.

What about the guilt you *should feel? Murderer.*

The thought jolted him, made his face flush hot.

"I didn't murder anyone," he whispered.

Which was bullshit. He hadn't pulled the trigger, sure, but his money had fired the bullet. A public service. Why should that man have lived when Cori was six feet under? When it turned out Cori's wasn't the first life the drunken maniac had taken?

A decision made in rage, in heartbreak. Two dead instead of just one.

Blocked it out for so long. Mostly, anyway. So why think about it now?

He knew why: he hadn't pulled that trigger, but he needed to use the person who had.

Connell rubbed his face hard, used his mental discipline to put those thoughts away. This had nothing to do with what happened back then. This was *now*.

A problem needed to be solved.

Dozens of agents performed the same task as Herbert Darker. Connell referred to the numerous informants as his "stable," as if he were a street pimp. He'd created the network four years ago with only three people—two in America and one in South Africa. The system was illegal but highly profitable, so he'd gradually added to the roster. His "whores" now included twenty-seven geologists, metallurgists and environmental analysts from all over the world. They all knew reporting a potential find could earn them a fast ten grand.

Those reports usually amounted to nothing. Sometimes they were outright bullshit, people trying to scam him. Sometimes he *let* them scam him, just to keep people interested. The risk/reward was so damn low: getting taken three or four times for ten large paled in comparison to a find that eventually generated millions in profit.

Herbert Darker had never tried to run a scam. That was the one thing—the *only* thing, perhaps—Connell liked about the man.

Darker never called with low-grade sites. He never called with finds that amounted to nothing, and he never, *ever* called with erroneous data. Each time Connell took a call from Herbert, it merited special attention. Herbert was a little fuck, sure, but he was a *meticulous* little fuck. He triple-checked things before ever picking up the phone.

This time, however, Herbert had called after only one test, and less than three hours after completing it. Very amateurish. Or at least it would have been from anyone but him. It meant Herbert had almost pissed himself from excitement. Ten ounces of platinum per ton of ore would do that to a fella.

That was four times the quality of the richest platinum ore ever found.

It was probably a false lead. Someone sold this McGuiness character the land, perhaps, maybe gave him a trumped-up sample to hook him. Or, maybe, McGuiness already knew of Herbert's connection to Connell, and had trumped up the sample himself—to hook *Connell.* Unlikely, but still possible.

Connell paced his office, staring out his window on the fiftieth floor of the Republic Plaza building. Denver looked dank and drizzly, thick clouds blotting out the stars. It hadn't been raining when he'd come in that morning. He hadn't been outside since.

A false lead. Had to be. Ten ounces per ton? A shot in the dark, sure, but if it was even *half* that quality, it was still the highest concentration ever found. If that vein existed, and if it was *big*, it would be one of the richest sites on the face of the planet. It would definitely be EarthCore's biggest asset.

An asset that someone could grab before Connell did.

McGuiness could be on the phone, right then, offering his claim to another company.

At that moment, Connell knew he had the edge. That moment wouldn't last long. He had to get to Sonny McGuiness and he had to get to him fast.

First, however, he had to inform the boss.

"CONNELL, SWEETIE," Barbara Yakely said through a cloud of cigar smoke. "Come on in."

He wore a button-down gray shirt, black jeans and black cowboy boots. So long and lanky the boy was, but that *swagger*—throw in a Stetson and gun belt, and he could have been strutting down a dirt street in some '60s western.

Connell didn't know he was swaggering. He just did it. Men who have that thing, that inexplicable *thing*, never thought about how they walked, how they projected. They just lived their lives, and when they did, the world around them watched.

So much like her Rocky. A little bit like Charles Jr., too, but Connell was closing in on forty. Junior hadn't made it far enough to really come into his own as a man. He'd died at thirty-two, in the same plane crash that had killed Charles "Rocky" Yakely—Barbara's husband, the only man she'd ever loved.

Connell sat in the chair in front of her desk. Sure, he had that leading-man swagger, but no leading-man warmth in those gray eyes. And the shirt and jeans ... he'd worn the same thing yesterday. Maybe the day before, too.

"Got any big plans for the weekend, honey?"

"I'm heading to Utah tonight," he said. "I've got a lead on something big."

"I meant plans that don't involve work."

Connell shook his head.

No surprise there. He never did.

He hadn't always been like this. She still remembered the smiling young man she'd hired ten years earlier, not long after Rocky and Junior passed, not long after the entire company fell to her. Back then, she was the one who needed work to distract her from a bottomless well of grief. It had helped. Some, anyway. Now Connell was the one who used work as a shield, to keep him from thinking about what he'd lost.

After that horrible car accident, she'd watched him change from a gregarious, wide-smiled person into a hard-faced, hard-hearted man. Once upon a time he'd been friends with almost everyone in the company. In the last four years, those friendships had crumbled. Connell Kirkland got shit done—woe be to those who didn't move fast enough or work hard enough for his taste. Sometimes, he drove those around him a little too hard. Barbara had often thought about saying something to that effect, but Connell's drive made the company money. A lot of money. And wasn't that the point of being in business in the first place?

She took a puff of her cigar. Rocky had always smoked cigars. Barbara liked the smell of the things. They reminded her of her husband. And, to be honest, smoking big cigars was the kind of thing bosses did. She was the boss. When in Rome ...

"Connell, it's Friday night. It's nine thirty, honey. What are you still doing in the office?"

"You mean other than not trying to give myself lung cancer?"

The smart-ass was always trying to get her to give up the cigars.

"Yes, other than that."

"Same thing you are, apparently."

"If by that you mean *not getting laid*, you're right. That's fine for me,

I'm sixty-seven. The last time I had a tingle to tangle you were probably thrilled if you could cop a feel in the back of your mom's car. You're thirty-eight. When's the last time you got some?"

He raised an eyebrow. "Are you harassing me again, Barb? Because I know the HR manager on a first-name basis."

She made a smoke ring, then another, watched them float away.

"Honey, if I wanted your wedding tackle, trust me, you'd know it."

He laughed. A rare sound, one he only seemed to make with her. The laugh didn't last long.

"Barb, if this is the part where you tell me it's time to *move on with my life*, can we skip it? I'm not in the mood. And when it comes to moving on, you're a fine one to talk."

He was right about that. He'd been alone for six years. She'd been alone for twelve.

"You're a real smart-ass," she said.

He nodded. "That I am. May I continue?"

Such a waste. A beautiful man, dedicated, loyal as hell, and here he was, all work and no play. It made Barbara sad for all the lonely women in Denver who would never see how special Connell Kirkland really was. Or, at least, how special he could be if he ever decided to get a life.

"By all means, honey. Continue."

"I've got a lead on a platinum deposit. Probably in Utah."

"Platinum? That's new for us."

He nodded. "It would be, sure. But if this turns out to be for real, it could dwarf everything else we have combined. Ore grade for platinum is usually low, in the range of one ounce per ten tons ore. That's about what the Russians and the South Africans get from their deposits, although most people think the Russian sites have run dry or will do soon. Stillwater Mine is the biggest producer in the U.S. They claim their ore produces eight-tenths of an ounce per *single* ton of ore."

Connell leaned forward. He lifted a framed picture of Rocky off her desk. An old picture, of Rocky when he was ten years younger than Connell was now, when Junior had been just a baby.

"This find is something else altogether," Connell said. He put the frame back in its place, gently, almost reverently. "If my sources are right, we may be onto a site that possesses a vastly higher ore grade. In fact, we may be onto the richest platinum vein in history. The prospector who discovered it is in Salt Lake City. I need to buy him now, before a bidding war erupts."

A bidding war that EarthCore could not win. The company made plenty of money. It had made Barbara a rich woman, sure, but compared to the big-timers, EarthCore was barely a blip on the radar. A company like Xstrata or BHP Billiton could buy EarthCore twenty times over in the blink of an eye.

"This prospector," Barbara said. "He's new enough to take the first offer he gets?"

Connell said nothing. He just stared with those dead gray eyes.

And then Barbara understood the reason for his visit.

"You want to use Farm Girl."

His left eye always twitched a bit when he heard that name. He kept on staring.

Barbara stabbed her cigar into an ashtray.

"We discussed this," she said. "You promised me we weren't going to use her anymore."

Connell nodded. "That was then, this is now. I don't know if the prospector will play ball."

"So throw a gob of money at him. If your hunch is that strong, take a chance. I'll authorize a million."

"Don't know if that will be enough," Connell said. "You asked if he's new to the game. He's not. An old-timer. If he understands how valuable this find might be—and I think he already knows—he won't even blink at a million."

"You know his name?"

"Sonny McGuiness."

Barbara leaned back in her chair. "Well, shit."

"You know him?"

"Not personally," she said. "Rocky met him a few times, I think. When we were young."

When she and Rocky had been in their twenties, just starting the company. McGuiness had been the same age, maybe. Everyone full of fire and brimstone, everyone ready to take on the world and live forever. She didn't know McGuiness, but she didn't have to—anyone who had been in the mining game for that long would know what he had.

"You're right," she said. "A million won't faze him."

She thought of authorizing more, but what was the point? Unless McGuiness was a drunk or had a mental disorder, he would contact every conglomerate, then sit back and wait for the offers to pour in.

"We only have one shot," Connell said. "I think an opportunity like this comes along once in a lifetime. McGuiness got his sample analysis today. Just a few hours ago. Maybe he's celebrating. Maybe he'll start making calls first thing tomorrow morning. If we don't lock him up now, Barb, we might be missing our chance at *billions*. I think Rocky would have liked knowing his company was worth ten digits."

The mention of his name made her eyes flick to the picture on her desk, then to the larger one on the wall. On the desk, Rocky was young, with rolled-up sleeves showing coal-streaked, muscular arms. That smile, that mouth. The one on the wall was from two decades later—Rocky in a suit and tie, looking serious and official. He'd gotten even more handsome as he'd grown older, and he'd been damn fine to begin with.

Connell was playing on her emotions. He knew it, she knew it, and they both knew that kind of tactic worked. EarthCore had been Rocky's dream. It had been *their* dream, together. That was why she was still working when she could have retired long ago. EarthCore wasn't just a company: it was *Rocky*, still alive, still kicking, always hungry for more, more, more.

"She's a psycho," Barbara said. "She put that Crittenden Mines rep in a wheelchair."

"Allegedly," Connell said. "She was acquitted."

Did he actually believe what he was saying? Or, as long as he got what he wanted, did he just not give a shit that some man would never walk again?

"For fuck's sake, she was kicked out of the NSA," Barbara said. "Ever wonder what she had to do to get booted from there? Ever wonder if it was even worse than crippling someone?"

"You don't pay me to wonder," Connell said. "You pay me to acquire new projects and properties. To do that, this time, I need her."

Barbara looked off. She stared absently at her cigar, at the smoke curling up from it.

"I don't like it," she said.

"You like the copper mine in Moyobamba. And the bauxite site in Queensland. We have both of those because we used Farm Girl, remember?"

Of course Barbara remembered. Those two sites now produced 36 percent of the company's revenue. Without them, EarthCore would have gone under.

"Don't forget O'Doyle and Takachi," Connell said. "Remember the security problems we had before Farm Girl told me about them?"

Barbara remembered that, too. Competitors kept beating EarthCore to the punch. Turned out there were people on her payroll who were also in the employ of other mining companies. Hackers, spies... Barbara hadn't seen any of it coming, hadn't understood it was happening. Connell did, though. He hired help: Cho Takachi and Patrick O'Doyle. Ex-military. Takachi had broken into the culprits' homes, apparently, looking for dirt, while Farm Girl did some computer stuff—maybe legal, maybe not. Connell had told Barbara she didn't want to know what was being done; she'd taken his word for it. In the end, the new "security division" found three people who had betrayed her trust. She and Rocky had always treated employees like family. Another nail in the coffin of Rocky's legacy, maybe, but Barbara acted instantly. She called the entire staff together so they could see that scarred-up freak O'Doyle show those traitors the door. Since then, no problems—no one wanted to even talk to that man, let alone have him escort them out of the building.

"All right, Farm Girl did some good things for us," Barb said. "But last time she went too far. She's a liability, Connell. Close the deal without her."

"I can't. You know I can't."

He stood. He put his hands on the desk, leaned over it.

"This is the one, Barbara. This is the one. You've helped me through some tough times, but I've also helped you. I know you better than anyone. This is the one, and if you don't let me do what I need to do, it will haunt you until the day you die. Just ask yourself one question— would Rocky have let me use Farm Girl?"

Barbara glanced at the picture on the wall again, at the love of her life in his prime as a captain of industry. She glanced at the photo on the desk, when he was full of dreams, when he was too dumb to listen to the old people around him who told him it couldn't be done. Together, they had built this company—and sometimes, they hadn't played by the rules. When they'd been younger, they'd done a lot of things she wasn't proud of.

When they'd been younger... when they'd been Connell's age.

"You're right," she said. "Rocky would have liked ten digits."

He stood straight. "So I have your permission?"

Barbara wondered if someone else might wind up in a wheelchair. Or worse.

"Yes," she said.

"Thank you. I also need to get Angus and Randy on this right away."

No matter how sour her mood, the mention of those names managed to make it worse.

"They're on vacation," she said. "*Again.*"

"I know. When they see what I have, though, they'll come back."

"If you can get them to answer their phones. Which I doubt. I know you approved Kool's work on that laser drill head sci-fi beam-me-up-Scotty crap, but have you seen what that prototype has actually *cost* us?"

Connell shrugged. "It will pay off for us, Barb. His inventions usually do."

No, they usually didn't. The ones that did pay off, though, paid off well enough to offset the ones that did not. By a wide margin. But it was just like Connell to only remember the wins.

"I'll take care of getting Angus and Randy back on the job," he said. "Unless you have more questions for me, I need to get going. My flight leaves in two hours."

She had hundreds of questions, but few of them involved this mysterious new find.

"I'm good for now," she said. "But you be careful. You taking O'Doyle with you?"

He shook his head. "Not this time. I'm taking Takachi."

"You always take O'Doyle. Why the change?"

Connell smiled. "Because I'm sending him to make sure Angus and Randy answer their phones."

Barbara paused. What a mental picture that created. She wished she could be there to see it.

"Crafty," she said. "You really think this find is *that* important?"

"I do," he said. "No question."

She waved dismissively.

"Well, then get out of here, already. You aren't making me money standing here with your thumb up your ass."

He headed for the door. She stopped him just as he was leaving.

"Connell?"

He turned, waited.

She glanced at the picture of Rocky—God, did she miss that man—then back at her handsome young bulldog.

"Be smart," she said. "No crazy risks, okay?"

He nodded, grinned. "Of course. I'll be safe."

And with that, he left.

Safe. She'd heard that one before, from two different men—men that were now gone forever.

"Just don't do anything stupid," she said quietly, knowing full well that a man Connell's age, with his drive, would rarely know what *stupid* really was.

HE CALLED FOR THE FIFTH TIME. One after another, the calls went to voicemail.

Time zones. They're a real bitch when you want to get work done.

It went to voicemail again, so he dialed again.

A hair after nine thirty p.m. Denver time. In London, that was … what, four a.m.? Connell wasn't sure. And was she even in London to begin with? He had no idea. And, frankly, he didn't give a shit what time it was for her—when he called, she needed to answer.

She finally picked up, her voice groggy from interrupted sleep.

"Whoever this is, you suck syphilitic pig cock, and this had better be good enough to turn my shit into nuggets of solid gold, or I will fucking find you."

That voice. He thought of the news reports. A man shot to death outside a bar. Connell found it hard to believe he'd been *happy* to read that news, but he had.

No point in thinking about that anymore, not now.

"Definitely solid gold," he said. "With diamonds in it."

He heard a rustling, the sound of someone sitting up, coming fully awake.

"Mister Kirkland," Kayla Meyers said. "Sorry about that."

"Like I pay you for apologies. You ready to listen?"

Another pause. More rustling. He imagined her naked, nothing but silk sheets clutched to her chest as she got out of bed and walked to a desk. Hard not to imagine such things with Farm Girl—Connell was grieving, sure, but he wasn't a eunuch.

"Yes sir," she said. "I'm ready to listen."

"Is this line secure?"

"It's a good thing I like you so darn much," she said. "Ask a girl like me a question like that? It's almost like you've forgotten what I do for a living."

He didn't often feel stupid, but at that moment, he did.

"My bad," he said. "I need dirt on a man and I need it now. The name is Sonny McGuiness. He's a prospector. He's staying at the Grand America in Salt Lake City."

He heard Kayla scribbling furiously.

"Permanent address or phone?"

"Don't have that. He operates out of Salt Lake City and vacations in Rio. That's all I know."

"What else?"

"I said that's all I know."

"You've got to be fucking shitting me."

Connell smiled. Farm Girl swore nonstop. She tried to cut back when talking to him, but all it took was a tiny bit of annoyance to open the cursing floodgates.

"I shit you not, Miss Meyers."

"You are aware that there are limits even to my incredible talents. In other words, that's not much to go on."

The sleepy tone had faded, replaced by a wicked purr that would strum the strings of any hetero male who could still get it up—and probably even a few who could not. Connell knew she did it on purpose, used it as a way to get a leg up on men. Knowing her tactic, however, didn't change the effect it had on his body.

"That's all I have," he said. "Do you want the gig or no?"

"You told me we were done. I remember, because I cried myself to sleep that night. My pillow was all wet."

"Things change," he said. "I've got a plane to catch. You either take this job and get me what I want, or we're done for good. And when you're out, you're *out*."

"Such language," she said. "Does that Big Daddy bullshit actually work on other people you know?"

He laughed. "Yes, it does."

"You need to hang out with a higher caliber, Mister Kirkland."

"Which is why I called you. Are you going to take the fucking job or not?"

"Not unless you give me something I can actually use," she said. "I like money just fine, Mister Kirkland, but I draw *pleasure* from doing a job right. You might say that's what gets me off. One of the things that does, anyway."

He smiled, and was glad she couldn't see it. The way that woman *talked*—it could make a gay guy spring wood. Of course, Connell would rather stick his cock in a six-foot-tall black widow than put it in Kayla Meyers.

Still, she had a point. You can't make an omelet without breaking a few eggs.

"McGuiness has his samples analyzed at Darker Incorporated, a Salt Lake City company run by a man named Herbert Darker. Darker may be your best source for leads."

"You know the Darker guy? He'll cooperate?"

Cooperate? If he'd have done that in the first place, Connell wouldn't have had to call Kayla at all. Backstabbing little shit, pretending he was having some moral crisis. If that charade continued, it would cost time. Connell couldn't afford to lose a single minute.

"Do what you have to do. Just get me something I can use on McGuiness." Images of a man in a wheelchair flashed through his thoughts. "But keep it under control this time. No more crowbars. No more anything *like* crowbars, either. Got it?"

"I'm always under control," Kayla said. "I'm always under *something*, anyway. Or up on top of it. Depends on my mood. Hopefully, this Darker fella is on the winning end of that."

Connell heard the smile in her voice. He wondered what Herbert was in for, then decided he really didn't care. Darker had made his bed—now he'd have to sleep in it.

"I need the information sooner rather than later," Connell said. "And by *sooner*, I mean *yesterday*. Got it?"

"I may have to go see Darker in person. Getting there will take time. I'm in D.C. right now."

"I thought you were in London."

"Awww, how sweet," she said. "Are you trying to keep tabs on where I rest my pretty little head? I didn't know you were that obsessed with me, Mister Kirkland."

Her sex-kitten routine got old, fast.

"I don't care where you are. I need a yes or a no—can you get me something I can use by tomorrow afternoon, or is that beyond your meager abilities?"

Another pause. This time, he didn't envision her covered in silk sheets—he imagined her loading a handgun.

"You shouldn't talk to me like that," she said, the sultry purr forgotten. "I've done a lot for you."

Sometimes her words aroused him. Other times—like *this* time— they made his balls shrivel up and head for higher ground.

"I'll pay triple your normal rate," he said. "And I'll cover travel expenses. Book whatever you need to book to go wherever you need to go. Fair enough?"

"Sure, that's fair," she said. "Anything else?"

"No." Connell hung up.

She didn't sound happy. Knowing her record, that should have made him afraid. But to be afraid of death, you first have to give a goddamn about living. He didn't.

Kayla would get him what he needed. She always did. She was like him in that way—when you've gone through enough bullshit in life, there is the thing you do and there is nothing else. Kayla played to win.

She would find something, she would find it fast, but would it be enough?

5

ABOARD A PRIVATE CHARTER from Dulles to SLC, the woman traveling as Miriam Van Doren split her time between sipping a pisco sour and working her computer. On her screen, a recent Nevada DMV photo of Sonny McGuiness smiled back at her. Blazing white teeth, clearly false. An even more blazing white beard that seemed electric against his pitch-black skin.

You're a real pain in the ass, Sonny-boy.

It had taken Kayla well over an hour to dig up information on Sonny. That was twice her normal search time. She had, however, finally tracked down his Social Security number. For any American, those nine digits were a key that opened many locks: credit ratings, medical histories, tax info, houses and vehicles, so much more. If people really knew how *not* private their private information was, they would realize a Social Security number was the modern equivalent of a concentration camp tattoo.

"Must be hard to type with those long nails of yours."

She looked up to see the private jet's only male passenger leaning close to her seat. Six-two. Receding hairline. Practiced grin that probably worked wonders in whatever boardroom this rich bastard frequented. Fifteen pounds overweight, if she was being generous. And as long as she was being generous, she'd call him an even twenty years older than she was.

In a smooth, unhurried motion, she closed her laptop. She stared at the man. Her red fingernails slowly *bop-bop-bop-bopp*ed a pattern on the computer's plastic.

"You're a fine-looking woman," he said. "I don't usually go for blondes, but in your case, I'll make an exception. How about when we land, you let me buy you a drink?"

"I already have plans," she said.

"Plans for the entire day? Or, should I say, for the entire *night*? Because that little low-cut number of yours is driving Daddy crazy."

Daddy. She hated it when they said that.

Kayla could have dressed down for the trip, sure, but that wasn't how "Miriam Van Doren" rolled. Knee-length white skirt tight to her thighs, white pumps, a white top that left her belly exposed. And why shouldn't she leave it exposed? She worked hard enough on the damn thing and ate like a rabbit.

"Not interested," she said.

The man's grin faded.

"What's the matter, someone already paying you? Trust me, darlin', I can double it."

Bop-bop-bop-bop.

"For an out-of-shape piece of shit like you, all the money in the world wouldn't get you laid," she said. "At least not with me. You want a fuck? How about you *fuck off*? Then we both get what we want."

He stood straight. He stared at her like he wanted to hit her. She hoped he would.

"You should smile more," he said.

"At the moment, there's nothing to smile about."

His eyes narrowed and his face reddened. "If you don't want men to talk to you, you shouldn't dress like a slut."

She nodded. "Thank you for telling me what I should and shouldn't wear. I'll be sure to make a note. Now run along."

The red-faced man walked back to his seat.

Eight seats in the jet. Five empty. The other passenger—a middle-aged woman—was sleeping. It had been pricey for Kayla to buy into this flight, but hey, it wasn't *her* cash.

She watched the man sit and buckle in before she opened the computer again.

Sonny's DMV history showed he currently owned a Humvee, a Grand Cherokee and a classic '79 Corvette. A cross-reference to his credit rating showed all three vehicles were paid off.

She again cross-referenced his credit rating to find mortgage information. One residence: a $700,000 home in Reno.

Looks like a bum, lives like a king.

With a few keystrokes, she back-hacked from his credit report into his bank account. Interestingly enough, he showed only thirteen grand to his name. She'd have expected more from a man with such expensive tastes.

How about tax evasion?

Kayla accessed sleeper programs she'd planted in the IRS system a few years ago, back before her boss decided she was ... how had he put it ... *no longer NSA material.* Vogel. That stupid fuck. She wanted to gut that man. Or blow him, if that's what it took to get her job back.

She pushed the past from her thoughts, focused on the now. As she waited for her program to get Sonny's info, she thought of Connell's sense of urgency. He'd hired her four times before this. For those four gigs, he'd been calm, methodical. She'd tried to drive up his offered price. She'd failed. This time, however, he'd been in a hurry. He'd paid her triple. Why the change in behavior? Maybe McGuiness was onto something big, so big that Connell knew he had to act fast before someone took it away from him.

Thirty years of McGuiness's tax info started scrolling across her screen. She scanned, piecing together his financial picture. In the past twenty years, he'd reported an income of $7 million. Not bad for an old geezer. Seven million and now only thirteen grand in savings? Sonny McGuiness apparently spent it almost as fast as he made it.

She activated another program, a tax-fraud sniffer made by some of her former NSA coworkers. As it ran, she glanced down the aisle at the man who had hit on her. He was staring out the window, trying to act like being shot down in flames didn't bother him. What a prick. Maybe she would get his number after all. Maybe a little late-night visit could prove to be fun. For her, at least.

You want to be my daddy? Sure, you can be my daddy.

The sniffer program came back blank. Sonny McGuiness actually *overpaid* the IRS. He was honest, at least when it came to taxes.

His exemptions and records painted a rather detailed picture of his life. For one thing, McGuiness appeared to be quite the philanthropist. Over the years he'd given $100,000 to both the United Negro College Fund and the Wildlife Fund, $200,000 to the Paralyzed Veterans of America, $100,000 to the University of Utah and over $200,000 to Brigham Young University's Archaeology Department.

Kayla's anger grew. She checked her watch — 5:12 a.m. She would land in another hour. She was running out of time.

While the financial picture was notable, it didn't give Connell anything to work with. He needed a negotiation lever, if not outright blackmail information.

Nothing to be had on McGuiness. Nothing *real*, that was. She didn't need facts, she needed a threat of charges that would stick.

Could she get that from Darker?

She set the tax-sniffer program to look at Darker's records. While it ran, she checked Sonny's criminal record. A felony conviction. That was good. From three decades ago. That was bad.

The old prospector had served a two-year stint in Rikers for assault and battery. That wasn't leverage in itself, but if she could come up with something else illegal — or that lawyers could *present* as illegal — Sonny's criminal record mattered.

The felony wasn't the only mark on his rap sheet. Several arrests, all for solicitation. For a man who listed his legal residence in Reno, Nevada, she didn't think a patronage of the world's oldest profession would provide adequate blackmail material.

There just wasn't enough. Aside from hookers, Sonny McGuiness seemed to be a straight shooter.

The computer beeped, indicating it had finished searching Herbert Darker's file. She read through the information.

Her anger subsided. There, she finally had something to smile about.

HERBERT STOOD at the bottom of the stairs, looking into his kitchen.

"Honey, hurry up or the boys will be late for school."

His wife, Angie, quickly stuffed Tupperware containers into cloth lunch bags. Herbert's company had grossed almost a million dollars that fiscal year, but he still couldn't bring himself to buy lunch. After ten years of struggling to build his own business, frugal habits established in the early days were impossible to break.

A high-pitched scream of attack ripped through the house; Herbert braced himself as his youngest son launched off the third-to-last stair and landed on Herbert's back. Herbert let out a small *whuff* and stumbled forward. Luke was getting bigger and stronger every day; pretty soon the daily Attack from the Stairs would send Herbert sprawling across the entryway's Spanish tile floor.

"Take it easy, Luke. You're going to kill your pops one of these days."

Luke squeezed Herbert's shoulders tightly. "I wouldn't kill you! I *love* you!"

Herbert smiled and lowered his youngest son to the ground. Luke was at the age where he had no problem declaring his love for Mom or Dad. Soon he'd be in the fifth grade, then the seventh, and that kind of unabashed expression would fade. Herbert had already seen it happen.

Thomas, his sullen and surly oldest, thumped down the stairs. Only in the seventh grade and already the tallest one in the house. He had Angie's genes. Herbert was grateful for that—he'd been the smallest boy in school, and that had sucked—but there was still an odd feeling at having to look *up* to meet the eyes of someone you used to cradle in one arm.

"Morning, Thomas," Herbert said. "Ready for a big day at school?"

"Whatever, Dad."

Angie hurried over with the three sacks, one for each of the Darker men.

"Thanks, honey," Herbert said, giving her a kiss. "Come on, boys, let's go."

Angie's cell phone rang just as Herbert reached the door. She held the phone toward him.

"It's for you. It's a woman."

"Who is it?"

"How should I know? Are you going to answer it or not?"

Herbert looked at the phone. How odd. A woman his wife didn't know? Did he even *know* a woman that wasn't one of his wife's friends?

He came back inside and took the phone.

"Hello, this is Herbert speaking."

"Hiya, Herbie." A woman's voice, yes, all slow and sultry. "On your way to work?"

"Yes, I am, and I'm going to be late. Can I help you?"

"I sure hope so," the woman said. "I need to meet with you. Immediately. I've got some tax information you might be interested in."

Herbert froze. Angie stared at him, arms crossed, waiting for an explanation: Who was this strange woman calling on *her* phone for *her* husband?

"I know about your taxes, Herbie," the woman on the phone said. "I know everything."

"Ah, Professor Adams," he said. "I didn't recognize your voice. Hold on a moment, please." Herbert pressed the phone to his chest, smiled at his wife. "Sorry, honey, it's something for the Geological Society of America."

A fast lie, a good one, and yet Angie didn't seem fully convinced.

"Why did they call *my* number?"

He shrugged. "I don't know. I'll find out. Just watch the boys for a moment while I answer her questions, okay?"

Angie stared a moment more, then walked out the door. Herbert shut it behind her before speaking.

"Who *is* this? How *dare* you call my wife's phone!" Then he remembered the threats made the day before, he remembered his new enemy: *Cutthroat.*

"Did Kirkland send you?"

"Does it really matter? You need to meet with me. Now."

Herbert's stomach started to burble. Was Kirkland really coming after him?

"I can't meet now. I have appointments."

"Pioneer Park, fifteen minutes," the woman said.

"But I just told you that I—"

"Have Angie drop Tom and little Luke at school, Herbie. Trust me—you do *not* want to be late."

This woman, this *stranger*, she knew his wife's name and number. She knew his children's names. His chest felt tight. The first few drops of acid set up camp behind his sternum. His *family*.

Kirkland...he *had* to be behind this.

"Lady, you tell that boss of yours—"

"Now it's fourteen minutes," the woman said. "I'm easy to spot. Look for the white van. If you're not there on time, my next call is to the IRS. I'm sure your wife would *love* to hear where your money has come from over the past few years, and why you chose not to report those little bonus payments."

The burning rose from his chest to his throat. Angie knew nothing— Herbert was going to keep it that way.

"I'll be there," he said.

"I know you will. See you soon, Herbie."

THE HOTEL ROOM PHONE'S RING jerked Sonny awake. He opened his eyes, closed them, actually managed to fall asleep again before a second ring made him jerk awake anew.

His body told him to ignore the phone. He needed sleep. Good *God* did he need sleep, after what the exquisitely talented Chloe had done to him the night before. That's what he got for hiring a twenty-year-old instead of someone at least *half* his own age.

The phone rang a third time.

He looked at Chloe, still asleep, tangled up in sheets that hugged her curves, and hoped the ringing would stop.

It did not. He answered.

"Yes?"

"Mister McGuiness?"

Sonny had told only one person—Herbert Darker—where he was staying. The voice on the other end wasn't Herbert Darker.

"If this isn't the front desk telling me I'm getting free room service and a complimentary rim job from the manager, then whoever you are, you and I have a problem."

"My name is Connell Kirkland," the man said. "I represent a company that would like to talk to you about your find."

That name. A longing desire to be unconscious again made Sonny's brain miss gears. Kirkland ... Kirkland ... did he know that name?

Oh, he did know it. *"Cutthroat"* Kirkland.

Sonny sat up, leaned back against the headboard. He'd heard things about this guy. *Bad* things. Kirkland worked for a smaller company. Sonny tried to remember which one. Earth-Crack or something like that. Digger Yakely's old outfit, maybe? Shit, Sonny hadn't thought about Digger in years. No, not Earth-*Crack* ... Earth*Core*. Yeah, that was it.

"You woke me up, asshole."

"I seem to be making a bad habit of that lately," Kirkland said. "Sorry. But since you're up, I'd like to meet."

Sonny's fatigue faded, instantly replaced by disappointment, by cold anger. Had Darker sold him out? Couldn't trust anyone anymore. But had Sonny *ever* been able to trust? No. This phone call was a perfectly good example why.

"Listen, Fancy Pants, I don't want to waste your time and I don't like having my crank yanked if I'm not going to get off. I'll be talking to companies a bit larger than yours, know what I mean?"

"I know what you mean," Kirkland said. "But you have to admit, if the right person is doing the yanking, it can be a pleasant way to pass the time. Meet with me. Today. I assure you, it is in your best interest. You don't like what I have to say, by all means, do what you were going to do anyway."

Sounded harmless enough. And Sonny needed to know what information Kirkland had. He couldn't have much, because Sonny hadn't given Darker much. *Darker* ... had that little asshole really sold him out? Maybe there was another explanation for it. Sonny hoped there was. The older he got, the more alone he felt—trusting Herbert *mattered*, even if Sonny only saw him once or twice a year, even if Sonny paid the man to do a job.

And then there was the financial aspect. EarthCore would offer whatever they could. Sonny could use that number as a jumping-off point when he talked to the big-timers.

"Gibson Lounge, five o'clock," he said. "It's in my hotel. Drinks are on you."

"My pleasure, Mister McGuiness. See you then."

Sonny hung up. He made the meeting for later in the day so he'd have time to go to Darker Inc. and confront that little weasel himself. Kirkland had info? Well, shit, Sonny could get info, too. Herbert's office was only a twenty-minute cab ride from the hotel.

Yeah...he had to know if Herbert had sold him out. Hopefully, there was a mistake or something, and Herbert hadn't done anything wrong. Sonny rapped his knuckles three times against the nightstand: knock on wood.

He started out of bed but stopped when a hand with long, purple fingernails lightly scraped his back. He turned to see Chloe smiling up at him, her light-brown skin beautiful against the white sheets, her lush lips slightly parted, her black eyes glinting with sex.

Sonny's anger dissipated, replaced by morning lust. He had all day, after all—Herbert wasn't going anywhere.

KAYLA SAT AND WAITED. The park took up a full city block. She'd parked the white cargo van along the curb, under some trees that grew up from between the sidewalk and the street. Thick branches and plenty of leaves provided a nice, shady overhang. It made for an ideal spot. A public place, four lanes of traffic, businesses on the other side of the street. Pretty safe, right? That's what Darker would think.

"Public" is only "public" if someone is looking.

Connie Browning had rented this van. Kayla liked her Connie character. A little dirtier than Miriam, a little sluttier. And *weaker*—an important thing with most men.

She checked her makeup in the rearview mirror. She used her fingers to tease out her blonde hair a little more, giving it volume, letting it hang past her shoulders. Connie preferred heavy eyeliner, fake lashes and thick, colorful shadow. Never red lipstick for Connie—too traditional. Dark pink. That was how Connie rolled.

Despite snagging only a catnap on the flight out from D.C., Kayla had to admit she still looked damn good, if she did say so herself. The bags under her eyes showed through the makeup, but only slightly.

Five years ago, a little concealer and *boom*: no problem. Five years ago, though, her age had still started with the number *two*. It was getting harder to look young. Soon, maybe, she'd have to permanently move her cast of characters into MILF-land.

For now, though, the Great Distractors would see her through. She unbuttoned an extra button on her shirt, angled the mirror down to see the results. Black lace bra barely visible, but *visible*. The girls on display. Yeah. That would do it. As long as Herbert wasn't secretly gay. And even then, he'd still have a hard time not looking.

Sonny McGuiness might have nothing to hide, but Herbie had a closet full of financial skeletons. He'd pulled in $210,000 from Connell, one rat-out at a time. If the IRS discovered that unreported sum, Herbert would be looking at prison time. If she was going to come up with something on McGuiness, she'd have to fabricate it—Darker was the only person who could help her do that on such short notice.

At this early hour, there was plenty of open parking along the curb. A black Cadillac drove up into the space behind her. Jesus, he wasn't even bright enough to park a ways away and slowly walk up? Maybe take a look around as he did? Just more proof of that old adage: book smarts and street smarts are two different things.

In the van's driver's-side mirror, she watched him get out. Five-foot-five, maybe 140 pounds. All the muscle of a Dachau victim. No visible weapons. Poor coordination.

An easy mark.

He walked up onto the sidewalk and waited.

Kayla slid off her seat, smoothing her cotton skirt as she did. She adjusted her purse—she was never without a bag, although this one was smaller than she usually carried. Enough room for the essentials: lipstick and mascara, IDs, Springfield X-DS 9 mm, a compact to check said lipstick and mascara, Strider SNG knife, a granola bar in case she got hungry. The usual stuff for the girl on the go. And, of course, her three signature tools of the trade that she never left home without.

Kayla opened the van's sliding side door and stepped out. The three-inch heels on her black pumps slid into the grass, but only a little. She saw Herbert's eyes widen. She couldn't blame him. The skirt barely hung below her ass, showing off strong legs. With the pumps, she stood at six-foot-two, towering over him.

Darker stared at her face. Then, as predictable as the sun rising in the morning, his gaze drifted down to her tits. The Great Distractors were doing their job.

"Thank you for coming," she said. "I wasn't sure if you would."

Connie had a wavering voice. Kind of a *girl just off the bus from the farm* thing. Truth be told, it was very close to the way Kayla had sounded back when she'd first left home. When she'd left Daddy and her sisters.

With some effort, Herbert looked her in the eyes again.

"I have a message for Kirkland," he said. "You tell that asshole he crossed the line when you called my *home.*"

So tough, this one was. She wondered if he'd have that brave voice if Kirkland were standing here instead of her. Of course not. If he were facing a *man*, Darker would be wheedling and whining. But not for a woman. Oh, hell no.

Kayla glanced across the park. A few new moms with strollers sitting and talking, but far enough away they weren't paying attention to anything but themselves. A few homeless people camped out, lost in their own worlds. A weekday, so no schoolkids.

"He made me do this," she said. "You have to believe me. He's an *awful* person."

The look in Herbert's eyes showed he instantly, desperately wanted to believe that. Women who looked like her weren't supposed to be bad people.

"You didn't sound like this on the phone," he said.

"I'm sorry about that. I had to get you out here. I didn't want your family to see, you know?"

I'm just doing you a favor, pal. I'm really on your side.

Darker crossed his arms. "So what is it you supposedly have on me, anyway?"

Kayla gestured to a cardboard file box sitting on the van's empty floor.

"Some paperwork or something," she said. "He told me you'd know what it was."

Darker took a step closer. He leaned forward, still wary, and peeked into the van.

Close enough, dumb-ass.

"Here, let me get it for you," she said.

She bent at the waist, reached in for the box. So predictable: he took another step closer, ready to help her in case the box was too heavy. She lifted the cardboard lid. There wasn't any paperwork inside. It held other things, things she needed for this job. She reached in and grabbed the Taser.

Herbert's eyes widened slightly, but before he had time to run or call out in surprise, ten thousand volts coursed through his body. Kayla watched him shudder and jerk.

She cut the power. He fell forward. With practiced ease, she caught him on the way down, flipped his short, light body over her shoulder. She tossed him into the van, jumped in after him and slid the door shut.

Bagging him had taken maybe three seconds. Three silent seconds.

She quickly rolled Darker onto his stomach. From her purse, she pulled the first of her favorite things: a small spool of thin copper wire. She used it to tie his hands and feet behind his back. He started to moan, already recovering. He'd be yelling for help within seconds. Fortunately, her purse contained the second of her favorite things. She pinched his cheeks, forcing his mouth open wide enough for the ballgag to fit. He seemed confused, tried to pull his hands and kick his feet as she buckled the leather strap behind his head.

"You can scream if you want," she said. "I don't mind."

Kayla slid into the driver's seat and gunned the engine, smoothly pulling away from the curb and down the street. The homeless people didn't even look up. What was another car or van or truck to them? The mothers remained focused on their strollers and on each other.

A public place. Safe, right?

Still, you didn't hang around for something like this. For the next step, she needed privacy.

They drove. Herbert started mumbling. The words seemed incomprehensible through the ballgag, but Kayla had done this before.

"You want to know where I'm taking you, sugar? Somewhere we can be alone. Gotta ask you a few questions."

He mumbled louder. Sounded like begging. Already? Kind of early for that, but to each their own.

While she didn't know Salt Lake City, she'd scouted the area before setting up the meeting. A vacant factory sat less than two minutes' drive from the park. She pulled in to the empty, weed-choked parking lot and drove behind the building, out of sight from the road. It wasn't a great hiding place, but she only planned on a fifteen-minute encounter.

She killed the engine. Time to get to work.

There was still one more favorite thing in her purse. Herbert wasn't going to like that one. Not at all.

Kayla slid out of the seat. She squatted in front of him, knees wide, her fingertips gently stroking her inner thighs.

He stared, bug-eyed, head cranked up uncomfortably so he could see what was in front of him. He had probably jacked off a thousand times to visions of a woman that looked like Connie, but Kayla was pretty sure none of Herbert's fantasies involved him kidnapped and tied up with copper wire.

She guessed, anyway. You never knew with men.

Spit already coated the rubber ball. Snot dripped from his nose. His eyes teared up. A little blood trickled from his left wrist where wire had cut into the skin.

"You and I are going to have a little conversation," Kayla said. She reached out, tenderly stroked his hair. "I need information from you. If you're good, I'll let you go. If you're not, I'll kill you."

He said something—shouted it, really—but the red ball blocked his words.

Kayla slid around behind him and straddled his back, resting her crotch on his ass.

She reached into her purse and pulled out a pair of rust-speckled pliers. She could, of course, afford to buy new pliers, but these had sentimental value. Back when the NSA still looked upon her as a fair-haired child, she'd put the pliers to good use in Honduras, Kuwait, Paris, Afghanistan. Even in D.C. once.

She couldn't think of her old job without thinking of her old boss. André Vogel, NSA director, had sacrificed her for political gain, made her a scapegoat in order to advance his career. If it had been a man involved in the Genada incident, would Vogel have reacted differently? Of course he would have.

We'll make an example of you, he'd said.

You're no longer NSA material, he'd said.

All bullshit. Vogel found a way to get rid of her because her continued success and unfailing patriotism undermined his control—if it hadn't been for Genada, he would have created some other fabrication.

She had loved the NSA. *God* how she had loved it. She'd made it her life. And now she put her pliers to use in the private sector. Not for God, not for Country, but for *money*. It was so unfair. Her life felt so empty.

But still, a girl's gotta pay the bills.

She knew the pliers, knew every nook and cranny, every rust spot, every scratch. The engraved words *kmart drop forged (japan)* showed on the handle. The tips were good for things like ripping lips off faces or pulling tongues from throats.

The pliers' best feature, though, if she did say so herself, were the four pointed "teeth" just behind the tip. The teeth let you get good grip on nuts and bolts. They also happened to fit nicely around fingers.

Around knuckles, to be precise.

She slid the cool pliers around the last knuckle of Herbert's right pinkie. Without a word, she squeezed with practiced strength. A loud crunching sound ripped through the van, like a tree branch breaking under the weight of wet snow.

Herbert Darker threw his head back and screamed.

His thrashing sent a tingling jolt through her body. Her skin felt electric, so sensitive she could feel her skirt sliding across her thighs. She felt that *tingle* building down there. He was more of a turn-on than she'd thought he would be.

Herbert pulled at his restraints, but the wire only dug further into his skin. He stopped moving. He kept screaming, though. His body trembled with fear.

Her breathing came in short, shallow pants. She felt her blood coursing through her body.

Kayla stroked Herbert's hair. He sounded loud, but she knew from experience that such screams were practically inaudible outside the van. He cried. He mumbled.

Sounded pathetic. It sounded *delicious*.

The tingling's intensity built slowly, steadily.

He repeated a single syllable, over and over again.

"Why?" Kayla said, echoing his question as she slid the pliers down his pinkie to the next knuckle. "I'll tell you soon enough, sweet thing."

With a snarling smile and a sigh of passion, she squeezed the pliers until she heard the *crack*. Herbert thrashed his head. His throat-tearing screams filled the van. He wiggled—yes, he *wiggled*—in just the right way, in just the right places.

She moved the pliers down to the pinkie's base knuckle. That one was always the best, always took the most strength to break, always made them scream the most.

Herbert finally started to fight, to jerk and kick.

God, could he be any sexier?

"That's it," Kayla said, feeling the *tingle* turn into a *buzz*, strong and building fast. "That's it... let me see you fight. Don't let me do it to you. Give momma some *sunshine*."

He cried, begged, thrashed, wiggling this way and that, trying in vain to throw off her weight. The way he *moved*... The buzz started to overtake her, growing in her head as well as down below. She tried to lock the pliers on his knuckle, but her hands seemed to lose strength, lose coordination.

He screamed. And when he did, she screamed with him.

The pliers slid from her fingers, clattered against metal. She breathed in deeply, body rejoicing in it after suffering through so many short, tiny breaths. The buzzing in her head slowed, settled.

The only sound was his steady whimper, still muffled by the ballgag.

Kayla opened her eyes.

"That wasn't so bad, was it?"

She unwrapped the wire from his wrists, rolled him over like a limp rag doll. He tried for her throat, but one grab and shake of his broken, swollen pinkie ended all thoughts of resistance. As his face screwed into a mask of agony, she calmly rewrapped the wire, binding his hands over his stomach.

Tears and snot streaked his face. Bleary eyes gazed up with mindless incomprehension. In less than fifteen minutes, he'd gone from a meeting in a sunny park to a helpless torture victim.

She straddled him again, then reached down and unsnapped the ballgag. It popped from his mouth and hung off his left cheekbone, a thick strand of spit running from the rubber to his lower lip.

"Please *stop*," he said. "*Please!*"

Kayla stroked his hair, used her thumb to gently wipe the tears from his eyes.

"I need some dirt on Sonny McGuiness."

Herbert's face: confused, disbelieving.

"I need to blackmail him," Kayla said. "I know you've got something I can use."

"Use? B-b-blackmail? I don't... I don't know anything like that."

"You'd better come up with something," Kayla said sweetly. "Or I'll start in on your ring finger next."

Sobs racked his voice, each word following a sharp, snot-filled intake of breath. "You... crazy... fucking... *bitch!*"

Kayla picked up the pliers, held them in front of his face so he couldn't help but look at them. His crying ceased.

"Hold on a second," he said. "Just give me a second, okay? I've got something, I swear."

Kayla waited, letting Herbert think. She watched him blink furiously, as if his eyelids were mental speedometers.

"Okay-okay-okay," he said in a rush. "There was this mine a few years ago. The Jorgensson Mine. Sonny discovered it and sold it but it went bust. You could say he knew it would run dry but he sold it anyway."

Herbert babbled for several minutes, the sound of a broken man begging for his life. His subservient tone caressed Kayla, adding to the energy still simmering through her body. She pulled a notebook from the file box, scribbled down the information, smiling the whole time.

"That's exactly what I needed," she said. "Now, I want something else. Whatever Sonny found, people are all fired up about it. Tell me everything you know about his latest discovery?"

Herbert talked. He talked so fast she had to make him go back and repeat things. One phrase, in particular, he repeated over and over—*billion-dollar find.*

Oh, Connell... something like that floating around out there, and you only pay a girl triple her normal rate?

Kayla placed the notebook back in the box. When she finished with Herbie, she'd research the Jorgensson Mine, find all the relevant details. Connell would get the information he wanted, and get it by his ridiculous deadline.

Damn, girl ... you're good.

She stroked his hair one more time, then slid into the driver's seat. The white van pulled away from the empty factory.

KAYLA PARKED BEHIND Herbert's Cadillac, then cut the copper wire around his wrists and feet. She handed him a white towel to clean up the blood; aside from the broken pinkie, he had only minor cuts on his wrist. All in all, it was a pretty clean job, one that wouldn't draw an ounce of suspicion when Herbert went to the doctor and made up some excuse for the damage to his finger.

True to her word, she hadn't put anybody in a wheelchair.

She opened the van and helped him out. His shoulders slumped. His head hung low. He reminded her of an old balloon, saggy and half-deflated.

This was the true essence of any man.

"I'm letting you go," she said. "You're going to keep your trap shut. If you don't, the IRS will be the last of your worries, because I'll come for your sons."

Herbert's head snapped up, pain suddenly forgotten, the spark of defiance back in his eyes. Perhaps there was a backbone in there after all.

"That's right," Kayla said. "Let's just say little Tommy and little Lukey will never play the violin again." She slowly opened and closed her pliers. The metal squeaked like a baby bird calling for food. "You understand me, Herbie?"

He nodded quickly.

She always threatened the kids. They were better than the wife or the husband; you never knew who would actually prefer their spouse tortured and dead. Threaten the children, though, and people listen. In ten years using that theory, she'd only had to keep her promise once.

She knew fuck-all about mining, but she knew the word *billion*. A big word, a big number. She needed to find out more. Maybe there was a way for her to get a little piece of the action.

Because even a little piece of a *billion* was pretty damn big.

• • •

ANOTHER BAR, ANOTHER NEGOTIATION, but this one so different from the Two-Spoke. That place had been a dirty, broken-down dive. *Well-worn* was a better way to put it. This place? The wood walls didn't have any scratches, or dents from someone's head being *thonk*ed into them. The leather chairs were padded and looked brand-new. And they were teal. *Teal leather,* for fuck's sake. The Gibson Lounge had all the personality of a fake tit. That's what you got for a hotel lounge.

The last time Sonny had drunk, he'd really enjoyed the company. Dennis the Deadhead was good people. This time? Sonny wished he'd brought his gun.

He'd heard about Kirkland, sure, but never met him. Spooky eyes, gray and hollow. He looked at you like a Doberman looks at a T-bone. And he was much younger than Sonny had expected. The older Sonny got, the more irritated he was with young men doing well in his field. Made no sense—he'd been quite successful himself as a youth, and older men had hated him for it—but it was what it was.

"I do thank you for seeing me on such short notice," Kirkland said. "I'm sure you have quite an agenda lined up."

They sat in comfortable chairs—yes, *teal*—and spoke to each other over a small, knee-high marble table. Kirkland sipped his bourbon. On the rocks, even, like some kind of pansy. Sonny couldn't remember what kind of bourbon it was, exactly, and he didn't give a shit. He didn't give a shit about any liquor save for his favorite: Old Overholt.

"Got people I want to talk to, if that's what you mean," Sonny said. He took a sip of his own drink, felt the pleasant burn. "So, let's get to gettin'."

Sonny had expected someone in a suit. The stuffy kind, the board-room kind. If that was Kirkland's true nature, he wasn't showing it here. Dark gray sport coat over a blue button-down shirt, jeans, and well-worn cowboy boots that gleamed despite years of obvious use. His leather briefcase sat on the table between them.

Kirkland drained his glass. He nodded at Sonny's.

"You want another?"

"You trying to get me drunk? Think that's going to make this easier for you?"

"Mister McGuiness, if it comes to a drinking contest, anyone in this bar could beat me. I've had a long day and I want another drink. You want one or not?"

Sonny stared at those gray eyes, tried to get the feel of the man. Skinny, but not *that* skinny. Looked like the kind of asshole that ran five miles every day just for the sake of running.

"Sure," Sonny said. He polished off his drink.

When the bartender brought over the second round, Kirkland raised ice-clinky bourbon.

"To your find," he said. "And to hopes of doing business together?"

Kirkland waited for Sonny to clink glasses. Sonny did not. Kirkland shrugged, took a sip.

Maybe Sonny wasn't mad at Kirkland. Maybe he was just *mad*, his mood fouled by Herbert's apparent betrayal. Greed. Always gumming up the gears. That was the very reason Sonny hid his finds and always had his samples tested at the same place. Apparently, that strategy had paid off. If Sonny had given Herbert the find's location, Kirkland and his company would already be greasing the local politicians and buying up property rights.

Sonny had gone looking for Herbert. Hadn't found him. Herbert's office said he'd called in sick. A fall at home or something. How convenient.

"Interesting that you know of that find, Mister Kirkland. I haven't told many people about it. How'd you come across it?"

Connell stared hard for a moment. Gray eyes. *Dead* eyes.

"Let's cut the bullshit, Mister McGuiness. I'm not going to play games with you and I hope you're not going to play them with me. You know damn well where I got the information. How you handle that is up to you. I really don't care. The important thing is that I know of your find, I want it, and I want it before anyone else finds out about it."

Kirkland's abruptness surprised Sonny. Company men were usually smiles and compliments and bullshit. This guy was all business. He struck Sonny as the kind of man who'd sell his own mother to a Bangkok whorehouse if she could turn a regular profit.

"What we want and what we can have are often two different things," Sonny said. "And what you want will be expensive."

"How expensive?"

Sonny took another sip of rye. Still delicious, still perfect, but the second glass never tasted quite as good as the first.

"You want me to make the first offer," Sonny said. "Read that in some negotiating book, did you? Well, college boy, let's light this candle. I'll take fifteen million, up front. And twenty percent of the net for the first ten years."

Kirkland smiled. There was no real humor in it.

"Wow, Mister McGuiness—only a decade's worth of the profits?"

"I'm feeling generous," Sonny said. "Because I'm old and who knows if I'll be around in another ten. And I get full accounting access. All day, every day, not just quarterly. Someone so much as steals a Sharpie from the mine's supply cabinet, I want to know. I wasn't born yesterday."

"No? But your cheeks have that rosy glow of youth."

"Fuck you," Sonny said. "You should be so lucky to get as old as I am. That's my offer, take it or leave it."

Kirkland stared. He stared some more.

Sonny felt uncomfortable. It was okay, though, because that was how these bossy fuck-nuts operated. Something about *embracing silence* or some horseshit like that, waiting for the other guy to stammer and yammer to fill the space. Like Sonny was going to lower his offer just because this emotional zombie kept his trap shut? Hardly.

"Pricey," Kirkland said, finally.

"No shit," Sonny said. "And if you keep putting them long sentences together, I'm going to have to go fetch a notebook and a dictionary."

Another smile. A cold one, but Sonny thought maybe he detected a tiny bit of sincerity in that one, a glimmer of an actual sense of humor. Then, it was gone. The gray eyes once again held sway.

"Perhaps if you owned the land and the mineral rights, we'd play with that number," Kirkland said. "You own neither."

"Oh, is that right?"

"That's right," Kirkland said. "Mister McGuiness, I know everything that you own. You don't own any mining properties. The seventy-nine 'Vette sounds bitchin', though. Sweet ride."

How did he know about the Corvette? Just what the fuck was going on? Maybe Sonny hadn't been mad at Kirkland before, but he was now.

"Negotiation is *over*, shit-bird. You've been snooping around in my private business."

"When I want what you've got, your business *is* my business," Kirkland said. "You don't own the land. If you try to get it, we'll outbid you instantly and you'll be left with dick. Let's not bother talking about claim-jumping and other legalities, because this is the game and you're already playing it. Since our relationship has been so delightful right out of the blocks, I'll make a counteroffer. We'll give you one million dollars for the location. No back-end. You take your mil and you walk the fuck away so I don't have to look at your wrinkly old ass ever again."

Sonny stared. Not for effect, like Kirkland, but rather because he had no idea how to react. *He* was the one with the location, *he* was the one holding all the cards. Didn't this guy realize that? Sonny wanted to flip this asshole off and walk out... but he wanted to put him in his place even more.

"You listen to me, you little fuck. You wanna play tough? I'll go to a dozen other companies with what I've found and start a bidding war that will make you bend over, grab your ankles and beg me to fuck your ass if I give you the original price. I figured you'd counteroffer, but since you didn't, it's fifteen million and that's that. Someone is going to write me that check. If that's not you, tough shit. Think you can swing your big imaginary cock around and I'll just fall to my knees and beg to gobble it down? I've been handling people like you since before you was an itch in your daddy's little pecker."

Kirkland sipped at his bourbon, pansy-ass ice cube swirling and clinking as he did.

"Mister McGuiness, you've *never* dealt with someone like me."

Sure, Sonny wanted to put this arrogant pup in his place, but it was beyond even that now. There were only two options left to Sonny: leave that very moment or shove his glass right into that emotionless face.

"Fuck you," Sonny said. "The only person who will know the location is the one who pays the most money, so your lawyer friends won't have any chance to jump the claim. And you know what? Now that I think about it, I bet you *don't* make it to my age. I hope you die of dick cancer first."

He stood up, drained his drink and set it down hard enough on the table to draw a look from everyone else in the shitty, fake lounge.

Kirkland opened his briefcase, pulled out a piece of paper. "Before you go, Mister McGuiness, there's something you should see."

"Whatever it is, I don't care."

Kirkland's eyebrows rose. He nodded slightly.

"I see. Well, do you care about being sued into the Stone Age? Losing your house, that pitiful excuse of a savings account and—I'm sorry to say—that classic Corvette?" He held the paper up by one corner, rattled it. "You'll see that your friend Mister Darker was very helpful to us. You sold a location to the Jorgensson Cooperative. You know, the one that netted you a half a mil? The one that went bust when the initial high-grade ore gave out after only a month of mining?"

Sonny stood there, unable to turn away. He felt eyes on him, other people in the lounge glancing his way, wondering why he was standing there with his fists clenched.

He wished he'd brought *two* guns.

"I don't guarantee my finds," he said, forcing himself to speak quietly, slowly. "Everybody knows I get paid for a location, and *only* a location. What happens at that location isn't my problem."

He had been doing business that way for twenty-five years. Some finds panned out, some didn't. He was always exceedingly clear about what he was selling. Sonny knew he was in the right, both legally and morally—so why did he have such a sinking feeling about that bullshit piece of paper?

"I'm sure you're as pure as the driven snow," Kirkland said. He gave the paper another small rattle. "But this statement—provided by a man who has known you for sixteen years, I might add—says that you *knew* the vein was small and that the ore grade was too low to be profitable beyond the first hundred thousand tons. According to him, you had *full knowledge* the find was a total lemon, yet you sold it anyway, for far more than it was worth."

Sonny hadn't wanted to hit someone this bad in a long, long time. He'd been in the business most of his life; he'd never had anyone try to strong-arm him like this before. It infuriated him. It terrified him. Could EarthCore really get away with this?

"I didn't know any such thing," he said. "Herbert Darker is a lying sonofabitch, and when I find him, I'm going to take this out of his hide. The ore I found near the surface was very rich." The ore that Herbert analyzed, Sonny couldn't forget. "The Jorgensson people did their own analysis. They agreed with my findings and that's why they bought the location."

Kirkland let the paper drop to the table. It slid a little, stuck on a bead of water that had fallen from the outside of Sonny's glass.

"That's not what Mister Darker will state in court," Kirkland said. "And after I pass this information to my friend at Jorgensson—Bob Kitchum worked for EarthCore before moving on, we used to play golf together, great guy—you will *definitely* be in court."

He leaned back in his chair, took another slow sip. All the while, those wax-museum eyes of his stared.

Sonny knew he had to calm down. He couldn't think straight. These motherfuckers were stealing his find. *Stealing* it. Sonny's jaw felt tight. He was shaking. If he'd been twenty years younger, he'd have come right over that table and hit Kirkland. And hit him again. And *again*.

Kirkland gestured to Sonny's chair.

"Please, have a seat. We can work this out. I've got the upper hand, but that doesn't mean you're not going to get paid."

Sonny knew he shouldn't have taken this meeting. He shouldn't have assumed he could use Kirkland to find out about Herbert's actions. He should have got on the first plane out of SLC and gone where he couldn't be found. He hadn't done any of those things. Instead, he'd walked right into this, blind, without a shred of research or preparation.

He didn't know what to do. So, he sat.

Kirkland signaled for the bartender to bring another round, then leaned forward, elbows on knees.

"I'm not going to use this on you unless you force my hand," he said. "We both know Darker's statement is bullshit, but that doesn't matter. It wasn't just the purchase price—Jorgensson shelled out millions for equipment and labor." He tapped the piece of paper. "If they get this, they'll come after you with both barrels blazing. Maybe they'll win a suit against you, maybe not, but the best you can hope for is to spend money you don't currently have on lawyers. The worst you can hope for? With Darker's testimony, and with your record, you could wind up in jail."

The concept of prison brought the situation home. Sonny would do anything rather than risk another stint, locked away from open skies and sprawling landscapes.

"Why are you doing this to me?"

The bartender dropped down two fresh drinks, took away the two

empty glasses. Sonny didn't think Kirkland's ice cube looked all that
pansy anymore.

"Because I can't afford to let you put this on the open market," he
said. "It's that simple. I want what you have, I don't have the money to
buy it, so I found another way."

He made it sound so simple. So basic. So primitive ... so *cutthroat*.

"Mister McGuiness, we both know your demand of fifteen million
was ridiculous."

Sonny picked up his drink. He drained it. He didn't taste any of it.

"It was," he said. "Not as ridiculous as *one* million, though."

Kirkland nodded. "True, true. Since we've established that EarthCore
is going to get the claim, we—" He stopped, raised one eyebrow. "We
have established that, have we not?"

Sonny wanted to say something smart. He wanted to insult this prick.
Instead, he simply nodded. As his mother had always told him, *a smart
man knows when he's whooped*.

"Good," Kirkland said. "Here's what I think we should do. One
million up front for you. Cash. No obligation. And, two percent of
revenue. For *life*, to be passed on to your heirs or whatever charity you
choose. And that's two percent *gross*, not *net*, so we won't be able to
cut you out by shuffling the numbers around to make it look like we're
losing money."

Sonny didn't understand what was happening. This wasn't some
pity offer: it was generous. He'd pulled the 20 percent number out of his
ass—just to be a dick, really. Two percent of the mine's profit, for life?
If there was any size to that find, any size at all, that percentage would
wind up making fifteen million look like monopoly money. Sonny could
wind up being rich beyond his wildest dreams.

And he was a man that didn't dream small.

"What's the catch, Kirkland?"

"Catch?"

"You've got my balls in a vice," Sonny said. "You could just take the
damn thing and cut me out altogether, so there has to be a reason for
this sweetheart deal."

Kirkland sipped, nodded. "Ah, *that* catch. Of course. Well, the
million is yours. No strings. But to get that two percent, I need you
on-site for the next year. That will give us time to probe and figure out

the best place to begin. You found it. You know the area. Having you there saves me time and money."

Sonny's anger faded, pushed aside by a creeping sensation—the same feeling he'd had on that mountain. If he wanted to get rich, he'd have to go back. Go back and *stay*.

Stay for a year, in the place that felt like a funeral.

"Mister McGuiness, this is a good deal. You know it is. I want this to be a success. I think I need you there for that to happen. So I got the better of you this time, so what? Forget it and join me."

Kirkland again held up his glass. "What do you say, Sonny? Let's get rich."

Sonny McGuiness felt overwhelmed, completely confused. He'd just gotten his ass kicked, sure, but wound up with one *hell* of an upside.

And, maybe, he was getting tired of going into the mountains all by himself. The lone-wolf act was great for a young man. He wasn't a young man anymore. Not even close.

He clinked Kirkland's glass.

"I'm in."

Kirkland grinned. When he did, his eyes crinkled. Well, what do you know... there *was* an actual human being in there after all.

The two men finished their drinks. Then they finished another.

An hour later and drunk off his ass, Sonny stumbled back to his room. Hotel lounges sucked, but they did offer a proximity advantage when you were so crocked you could barely walk.

He dropped into bed without even taking off his clothes. He fell asleep almost immediately. *Almost.* Before the blackness claimed him, he had a brief realization.

He was going back. Back to that lifeless place where animals had the good sense not to tread.

6

August 5

HE TURNED SIDEWAYS, long legs hanging off the side of the hotel bed. In his sleep, he smiled. A real smile, the kind that grabbed up every inch of his face, the kind people who knew him hadn't seen in five years.

A smile for his wife.

He twitched. He jerked. His legs drew toward his chest. His face shifted from all-encompassing smile to twisted snarl of horror—two expressions that are almost indiscernible from each other in a snapshot, but in real time, there is no mistaking the opposite emotions that drive them.

Feet kicked at sheets and blankets. Fingers curled and stretched, as helpless to stop death now as they were five years ago.

"No," he said. "No-no-*no-no*."

The words shifted to a scream. He lurched up, hands flailing, knocking a bedside lamp across the room, where the porcelain shattered against the wall.

Connell Kirkland sat up, stomach heaving with clutching breaths. He stared into the dark, silent room. No light save for the clock's glowing red numbers: 3:02 a.m.

He felt exhausted. He always felt that way, truth be told, almost like an unseen crack somewhere on his body slowly leaked the intangible energy that kept people moving day after day.

He could go back to sleep, try for another hour or two.

Sure ... and if he succeeded, he could see the love of his life die all over again. Lucky boy.

He wanted that goddamn memory to go away. He'd grieved, hadn't he? Wasn't that the way it was supposed to work?

Doting husband stands over the grave of his beloved. Gray clouds drop a steady mist, enough to make umbrellas blossom but not enough to drive people away. Doting husband stands there, somber but resolute, one hand holding a rose, the other a fistful of dirt. People leave, one by one, all approaching doting husband—reaching out to him, perhaps—but leaving without touching him, without speaking to him. Doting husband doesn't leave. Doting husband is left alone, standing next to the grave. Doting husband tosses the dirt down. It clatters against the curved wood, a symbol of letting go.

Doting husband carries the loss ... for a while, then life moves on. The sun rises in the morning. He meets someone new. The pain never vanishes, but it recedes, drowned out by new happiness, only to be seen again on a certain birthday, the anniversary of when they first met, or when they married, when moving and pictures go into or come out of boxes.

That was how it was supposed to work. In movies, in books. In poems, probably, but Connell wouldn't know—the last time he'd read that sappy bullshit was in the sixth grade. Life wasn't a poem. Life wasn't a book. Life was waking up every day and wondering, *why do I bother?*

The room's air-conditioning cooled the sweat sheeting his skin, making him shiver. He reeked of fear, of weakness.

A shower, then he'd get to work. He'd landed Sonny McGuiness, but there were many more pieces to put into play. First things first: a list of tasks for McGuiness. Once that was done, Connell would move on to the next piece — Dr. Angus Kool.

THE WAKE-UP CALL had come at seven thirty a.m. The grade A bitch of a hangover was already there, ready to spring, just waiting for Sonny to stop sleeping.

Kirkland had arranged the wake-up call. He'd also had room service deliver breakfast: steak and eggs, hash browns, toast, a pot of coffee, two bottles of water and one of Excedrin. Sonny could only hope that dead-eyed asshole was also suffering from several rounds too many.

With breakfast came a package and a sealed note. Inside the package: a new cell phone.

He read the note:

> You work for me now. No sleeping in. Keep this phone on you at all times. When I call, you answer. When you call, I answer.
>
> Begin by researching the area's history. I want to know everything.
>
> Be out front at 08:30 sharp. Your escort will be waiting for you.
>
> —CK

Sonny had a sneaking suspicion this would not be the kind of "escort" he was used to.

He reread the note. Bossy as hell. So this was how the next year would be? Go team.

"C-K, the asshole signs it," Sonny said. "Sound it out, and it's *cock*. Kinda appropriate."

Breakfast was delicious. The coffee helped the hangover, as did the water and the Excedrin. Sonny felt somewhat human again when he stepped out of the elevator and walked through the Grand America's fancy-ass lobby. Just outside the hotel's brass and glass doors, valets were busy moving cars in and out.

A man waved, caught his attention. Asian guy, leaning against a black Lexus SUV. Dangerous looking. Jeans, black blazer, shaggy hair, aviator sunglasses. He could have been an extra from a low-budget action flick.

Sonny walked over.

The man checked his watch—looked like an expensive thing, obnoxiously large and shiny—then shook his head.

"Eight thirty-three," he said. "Mister Kirkland likes people to be on time."

"Mister Kirkland can toss my salad. I take it you're my escort?"

The man nodded. "I am."

"A shame," Sonny said. "I was hoping for bigger titties."

The man smiled wide, a real smile, a welcome departure from Kirkland's vacant grin.

"Cho Takachi," he said, holding out his hand.

Sonny shook it. "And what does an *escort* do for me? Drive the car?"

"If you like. I'm here to protect you and assist you any way I can."

Sonny huffed, held out his hand. "Give me the keys, errand-boy. I'm driving. And I don't need any *assistance*."

Cho shrugged. "Suit yourself," he said, and handed Sonny the keys. When he did, his blazer opened a bit: Sonny saw a pearl-handled .45 gleaming from a shoulder holster. Flashy, just like the watch, just like the sunglasses.

"Assistance or no assistance, I get paid either way," Cho said. "More than happy to sit on my ass and do nothing." He glanced away, scratched his head, made a show of acting like he was trying to remember something. "Oh! I almost forgot. I also get paid to make sure you don't back out on your deal with EarthCore."

Not the kind of thing Sonny wanted to hear from an armed man. Kirkland kicking his ass, the hangover, and now this? And to think: last night he'd actually thought working with other people might be a nice change of pace.

The two men got into the SUV.

"Do whatever you like," Sonny said. "Just stay the hell out of my way, got it? I don't trust slant-eyed gooks that pull their pud to old Bruce Lee flicks."

Cho reclined his seat, adjusted himself as if to start napping immediately.

"No problem," he said. "I don't trust dirty, wrinkled-up old mother-fuckers with surly attitudes and a complete lack of manners, so I empathize with your situation."

Sonny blinked a few times in surprise, then put the car in gear and smiled.

He liked this Cho Takachi already.

Cho crossed his arms and settled in.

"So, pops—where are we going? Off to do some digging in the dirt?"

"We'll be digging, all right," Sonny said as he started the SUV. "But not in the dirt. Stick with me, kid, and you'll learn something new."

THE LAWYERS WERE ALREADY doing their thing, subtly inquiring about mineral rights in the area surrounding Sonny's find. There was quite a bit to that job—find out who owned what, what belonged to the government, and so on. Ask too many questions in too short a time and red flags would go up. The last thing Connell wanted was for other mining firms to get wind that EarthCore was sniffing around. Locking up the land took subtlety: admittedly, a trait Connell didn't exactly possess in spades.

The legal geeks would get the job done. Aside from red beryl emerald and a few nearly tapped-out iron prospects, there was little demand for the southern Wah Wahs. Antimony, zinc, copper, manganese, molyb-denum, lead, cobalt, vanadium … all present in trace amounts, but not enough to draw any attention.

The Wah Wahs: one giant-ass lump of worthless rock.

Let the lawyers do lawyerly things. His time was better suited putting the rest of the pieces into play.

Sonny's "Silver Spring" wasn't the actual source of the platinum. It was a placer deposit, where eroded platinum particles accumulated after being carried along by water. Probably from some place deep within the mountain. Finding that source—or sources—was the most important part of the operation. Connell trusted only one man to properly execute that vital task.

Unfortunately, the man in question was a complete and utter flaming asshole.

Angus Kool had acquired undergrad degrees in geology and

material sciences, as well as a PhD in metallurgy, before he was even old enough to legally drink. The word *smart* didn't even come close to describing Angus. Connell had hired him right out of MIT. Other companies had wanted Angus, of course, and from a variety of fields—particularly the defense sector. Lockheed Martin and SAIC had recruited him. Northrop Grumman offered him a king's ransom of a salary. EarthCore shouldn't have been able to compete for his services, but Connell's instincts had won the day. Angus had been nineteen at the time. Connell, twenty-nine. A decade apart, but close enough to understand the two things Angus really wanted: complete ownership of his research and an obscene amount of paid vacation time.

Those were two perks big contractors simply didn't offer. You invented a weapon for Raytheon, Raytheon owned that weapon. Too bad for the big contractors. As long as EarthCore got full use of any invention, and as long as Angus fulfilled all analysis duties required of him, Connell didn't give a shit about who owned what.

It had been a great hire. Depending on how you looked at it, of course. And, Connell had to admit, depending on if you were Angus's boss, or he was yours. Under Angus's control, EarthCore's small research department clicked like a finely tuned machine—though perhaps a well-disciplined Nazi SS squad was a more fitting analogy. Kool ran the lab with a dictatorial hand and demanded perfection from his underlings, some of whom were more than twice his age.

McGuiness's find required immediate analysis, which meant Kool needed to be in the lab ASAP. Connell called up EarthCore's master personnel schedule; what a surprise, Kool was on vacation. Again. This time, caving in Kentucky. The man didn't just study geology, he lived it, a dedicated spelunker who traveled to all corners of the world exploring cave systems.

The itinerary showed that Kool was on vacation with Randy Wright, another of EarthCore's big-brained scientists. Randy was Angus's adrenaline-addicted sidekick. He'd been with the company a good ten years—five of those years before Angus was hired. Connell had always given Angus plenty of rope, knowing that someday he'd have to reel the man in. That day had come—hopefully, Wright could share some wisdom about what would happen if Angus didn't snap to.

Whatever it took, Connell needed both men back at the EarthCore lab in Denver by tomorrow morning.

Come to think of it, there was one way to make sure that happened. He suspected Angus wouldn't like it. Not one bit.

RANDY WRIGHT COULD BARELY MOVE his legs. His arms weren't much better. Every muscle screamed at him to stop. Two hours crammed into a crack in the earth so narrow that he couldn't even rise up on his hands and knees. Above him, rough rock, digging in and scraping. Beneath his belly, more stone, this covered by a sheen of water and two inches of thick mud. He had so many kinks in his back and neck it would take a week of yoga to straighten himself out.

Wouldn't that be just the thing? Some Enya on the sound system, a little incense, and a good hour of uninterrupted stretching. After a shower, of course—he smelled like a dead animal.

At least he wasn't cold. The bodysuit Angus had invented kept the ice water out, regulated Randy's body temperature. Gloves made of the same thin, tough material let him reach and grab normally, use tools or rope without difficulty. Only his face—this suit's sole exposed area—felt the water's deep chill.

"Hey, pussy," a voice called from up ahead. "You stop for a fucking grease-down and a shiatsu or something?"

Randy sighed. He closed his eyes, wished Angus would be quiet for once. That rarely happened.

"I'm right behind you," Randy said.

"*Behind* is a relative term. Move your ass, because I see the outside."

Sunlight? There was an *end* to this torture?

"I'm coming, I'm coming."

Randy kept pushing, kept sliding along like he was the moving meat of a rock sandwich. He looked forward as best he could, but all his helmet light showed up ahead was a pair of small, mud-coated boots. And then, he saw it, too—the soft glow of fading daylight.

"Oh my gosh. I can't believe we made it."

"Let's just hope we fit," Angus said.

Well, there was that small detail. After six hours in a cave that no human being had ever entered before, they had finally reached an opening—and if they didn't fit, they'd have to turn back. Maybe Randy would opt out. Maybe he'd just die here, become a fossil that some paleontologist would find millions of years from now.

Randy stopped. He watched Angus's boots. They pushed, they kicked...and then they were gone. Where they had been, a rough oval of green and brown.

He wriggled and pushed, ignoring his body's complaints. He slid through the narrow opening, mud lubricating the way, and into a tangle of creepers and tree roots. He landed in a heap, so happy to smell dry earth beneath him he didn't want to get up ever again.

"Get up," Angus said. "Can you at least *try* not to be such a little bitch?"

Randy stood on wobbly legs. Six hours below ground, where the only light came from their helmets, and now he was surrounded by the lush greenery of untouched Kentucky woods. The setting sun lit up the leaves, making them glow like soft green neon.

He pulled his Rec Specs down, let them hang from his neck by their thick elastic band. From a thigh pocket, he pulled out the hard case for his glasses. He put on his normal, heavy black frames, blinked a few times, opened his jaw wide and scrunched his face the way people who wear glasses sometimes do to settle them into place.

"I can't believe we did that," he said. "You really think we're the first ones in there?"

Angus stripped off his suit's mud-slimed gloves, unzipped a side pocket and fished out his cell phone.

"Checking GPS," he said. His thumbs flashed on the touchscreen. He looked up, grinned. "This spot isn't recorded in any cave database. We're the first."

Randy wanted to shout triumph to the sky, but he just didn't have the energy.

"We did it," he said.

"*Fuck yes*, we did," Angus said. "You should have never doubted me."

Randy often doubted Angus. He was often wrong to do so, a fact that Angus never hesitated to mention.

He felt a buzz from his own side pocket. He had two cell phones zipped into his suit, each in an airtight case. The suit kept out all water, but you could never be too careful. The phone in the left pocket was his personal cell. The buzz came from the one on his right—from the phone once handed to him by Connell Kirkland.

Randy stripped off his gloves and unzipped the pocket.

"Ignore it," Angus said.

Randy's hand froze halfway in. The phone kept buzzing. Randy felt it there, each vibration seeming to screw into him a little bit.

"But he's our boss. We have to answer."

Angus looked up from his phone. Mud covered his face, which was the only way his skin would ever be any color other than *pale*. Green eyes glared out from beneath a mining helmet covered first with stickers of Snoopy and other Peanuts characters, then with wet muck collected from hundreds of feet below the surface. Short and thin, Angus's body seemed to have been specifically engineered to crawl through narrow spaces for hours on end.

"Randy, the word you're looking for is *bossy*," he said. "We do what we want. Fuck him."

"Well, I don't want to get in trouble."

Randy pulled out the cell phone. One glance at the screen showed Kirkland had been trying to reach him for hours. No signal could penetrate the rock: now that Randy was back on the surface, missed calls and texts hit all at once.

Answer your phone.

Call me.

Call me.

You are making me angry.

The last one was the worst. Randy hated to disappoint Angus, *hated it*, but Connell was his boss.

Randy started to dial.

The phone was ripped from his hands.

Angus held it up. He stared at Randy, eyes narrow with disgust. Randy hated that, too.

"Jesus, man," Angus said. "Would you grow a pair?"

He turned and whipped the phone at the cave entrance. It smashed against the rocks, breaking into a dozen pieces.

Randy stared at a bit of black plastic.

"Angus, you're kind of a dick."

Angus laughed, a snorting, nasally thing that always made Randy wince a little—Angus laughed like some evil clown from a bad horror movie.

"That I am," he said. "Come on. It's about a two-mile hike to the Jeep. I want to get back to the hotel and clean up. We need to talk about what we're naming this entrance and make plans on what to explore tomorrow."

BY THE TIME ANGUS KOOL strode into the lobby of the Super 8 motel, most of the mud coating his bodysuit had dried. Not all the way, but enough to flake off as he walked, leaving a trail of damp brown clumps in his wake.

At the reception desk, a balding fortysomething man glared at him. Angus waved. "How's it hanging, Bob?"

The man pointed to the dirty floor. "Couldn't you knock that off outside? You did the same damn thing yesterday and I asked you not to."

Angus kept walking. He smiled and shrugged.

"Yeah, musta forgot about that. Thanks for cleaning up, though—wouldn't want this place to get less classy, now would we?"

Like that dipshit had anything better to do. If he didn't want to perform the basic janitorial services inherent with working at a hotel in the middle of bum-fuck nowhere, maybe he should have made better choices in his youth. Some people got all worked up about things that didn't matter, and when they did, Angus liked to rile those people up a little. Just his way of helping others see the brighter side of life.

After all . . . not everyone got to be a genius. The world needed ditch-diggers, too.

He reached the end of the lobby, realized he was alone. He turned to see Randy at the entrance, on one knee, scooping chunks of mud off the floor and into his mining helmet.

For fuck's sake. That guy.

"Randy, come on," Angus said.

Randy looked up, eyes ringed by those black frames, magnified by the thick lenses. He had that *what did I do now?* expression. Brown hair all tousled from being held down by the suit's hood.

Angus tilted his head toward the reception desk.

"Bob there gets paid to clean up. Don't go imposing on a man's right to work."

Randy stood and hurried over. Good boy. They'd been hanging out for years, ever since Angus had joined EarthCore. Randy was okay, but man, did he ever need to lighten up. Why be nice to people who don't give a shit about you? No, correction, who probably *hate* you because you're so much smarter than they are.

He and Randy headed for their rooms.

"You're always worried about those fucking muggles," Angus said. "If you don't want to be a bitch, Randy, stop acting like a bitch."

"I'm not acting like a B, Angus."

The guy never swore. It was kind of ridiculous.

Angus shrugged. "Walks like a bitch, squawks like a bitch."

"Lay off," Randy said. "I just want a shower."

"Whatever. Come to my room for a minute first. I want to map out tomorrow's spelunk."

Angus felt so excited. An undiscovered entrance. So, so rare. His fourth, but his first in the massive Mammoth Caves system.

He unlocked the door and stepped into his room.

And stopped when he saw a man sitting on his bed.

A big man.

"Hello, Doctor Kool," the man said. "Welcome back."

Angus stared. For once, he didn't know what to say.

"Holy crap," Randy said. "What are you doing here, O'Doyle?"

If Randy hadn't sounded like a bitch before, he certainly did now. Angus couldn't blame him—just one look at O'Doyle sparked up a flare of fear that made Angus feel like a bit of a bitch himself.

O'Doyle had the look of a linebacker two decades past his glory days. Big and thick, in the ballpark of 275 pounds. His burgeoning beer belly stood as the only blemish on an otherwise muscular frame. Each time O'Doyle moved, Angus saw both the twitch of muscle and the jiggle of gut.

He looked old enough to be Angus's father. A thinning blond crew cut covered a pinkish scalp. A mass of scar tissue clung to where O'Doyle's right ear should have been. Wrinkle-free khaki button-down long-sleeve over a white T-shirt. Black slacks, also wrinkle-free, black shoes gleaming. It was like a uniform with all insignia removed. O'Doyle gave Angus the impression of a two-legged, thick-necked, one-eared bulldog.

That bulldog smiled at Randy.

"Hello to you, too, Doctor Wright."

The guy was big, sure, and scary, but this wasn't a military base in some war zone. Angus was on vacation: Kirkland's security thug had no right to be anywhere Angus was, *particularly* in his room.

"Randy asked you a question," Angus said. He had meant to say, *Randy asked you a question, fuck-nuts*, but the last two words just hadn't come out. "What are you doing here?"

O'Doyle reached into his breast pocket: he pulled out a cell phone.

"I'm here to make sure you answer this. Mister Kirkland gave you one just like it. You know, the one you're supposed to answer whenever he calls? Yours must be broken, because surely you would want to hear what your employer has to say."

Angus reached into his suit's side pocket and pulled out his own phone.

"Nope, not broken at all. Watch, I'll show you." He started texting, speaking as he typed. "Miss...ter...Kirkland. Having...fun on...vacation. See...you...in two...weeks. Until then...go...fuck...yourself."

He hit *send*, then held up the screen toward O'Doyle.

"See? Works like a champ."

O'Doyle's lip twitched, just a touch, the start of a curl that didn't quite make it to a snarl.

He stood. Angus managed to stop himself from taking a step back. O'Doyle held the phone out.

"If you could just read this, sir, Mister Kirkland said you would understand."

Angus dropped his own phone to the carpet. He raised a muddy boot and stomped down on it. It didn't break, which infuriated him. He had to stomp a second time to make the glass crack.

"What part of *I am on vacation* do you not understand, you retarded mountain of washed-up grunt?"

This time, O'Doyle didn't sneer, or even start to. This time, he smiled—a smile that made Angus's skin crawl.

"See, now you've gone and made me happy," O'Doyle said. "Mister Kirkland told me I had to make sure you read the message. I said I didn't think you would. I asked him, *Mister Kirkland, if he won't read it, can I make him read it?* He said, *if you have to.*"

O'Doyle put the cell phone back into his breast pocket.

"Well, sure looks like I have to."

Did this lummox think he could push Angus around? O'Doyle wasn't going to do a damn thing. EarthCore relied on Angus's talents far too much to risk pissing him off.

The big, scarred man took one step closer: a burst of fear washed up from Angus's belly.

Randy stepped between them.

"I'll read it," he said. He held out a hand. "Please, give it to me."

Without looking away from Angus, O'Doyle took the phone out and handed it to Randy.

Randy read, scrolling through the screen. Angus watched him.

What the hell was this all about? Kirkland and Yakely had always let him do whatever he wanted. Now they were sending an ex-military goon after him?

"Holy crap," Randy said. He held the phone toward Angus. "Metallurgy analysis. Just read it."

Angus took the phone. He read. In a few lines, everything became clear. He understood O'Doyle's presence, as well as Kirkland's urgency.

The report's numbers shocked Angus. A platinum/iridium compound. Multiple mass specs on multiple parts of the sample produced identical numbers: 80 percent platinum, 20 percent iridium. No variation. There was always variation within a sample. Always. For it to all be the same, it had to have come from the same chunk of metal—a *big* chunk.

"Where is this from?" Angus said. "This sample . . . where?"

"Utah," O'Doyle said.

"How deep? How big is the lode?"

"Unknown," O'Doyle said. "That's why I'm here. I'm to make sure Doctor Wright gets on a plane to manage on-site data-collection efforts, a large-scale examination of the area to pinpoint the deposit's source."

"But I need to organize crews," Randy said. "I need to—"

"Already in process," O'Doyle said. "Helicopter contracted and en route. Crews will be there before you will." He turned to Angus. "You,

Doctor Kool, are to return to the Denver lab immediately for further sample analysis and to prepare for mining operations."

Angus nodded as he read the information a second time. They would use his new method to search for the sample's source. Randy could handle it. Kirkland knew that, of course—that's why Randy was going on-site while Angus was returning to the lab.

"Right, back to Denver. I can see the need for that."

He started to put the phone in his pocket.

O'Doyle cleared his throat.

"I have to keep that," he said, and held out his hand. "Mister Kirkland requested absolute operational security."

Angus looked at the large hand for a second: thick fingers, gnarled knuckles, several tiny scars.

"Oh," he said. "Right. This is top secret?"

"You're to tell no one," O'Doyle said. He slowly reached out, took the phone from Angus's hand. "Get dressed. I'm to take both of you to the airport. Doctor Wright will travel alone. Doctor Kool, you and I will travel together to Denver."

Angus nodded absently. "Sure. Fine. Whatever you say, big man."

Big man. How about *giant fucking troglodyte*? That was more accurate. So Kirkland had sent his pet gorilla to bully and intimidate? Well, goody for him. As soon as Angus got back, he'd storm into Barbara Yakely's office and demand that she fire O'Doyle. This ugly-ass, past-his-prime grunt would find out what it meant to fuck with Angus Kool.

Knowing that mollified his anger, at least somewhat. And when the anger receded, the enormity of the situation settled in. If there was any size to this find—any size at all—the monetary value would be staggering.

And that 80/20 percentage consistency... that had lodged in his brain and wouldn't leave.

It just didn't make sense.

He knew he'd be able to think about little else until it did.

THE SUV PULLED IN to the parking lot and stopped.

"Here we are," Sonny said.

Cho lowered his sunglasses, peered over the top of the silver frames.

"A fucking *library*? Wow, old man, you really know how to swing."

"Let's go, smart-ass. If you're with me, you're going to work."

Cho used the tip of his pointer finger to slowly slide the glasses back into place. Sonny had to admit, that looked kind of cool. Everything the kid did—from the glasses to the slouch against the car to the way he smiled—seemed like he practiced it in front of a mirror. Vain as hell.

Sonny could roll with it, though. The drive from the hotel to the Marriott Library at the University of Utah took only about fifteen minutes. During that short time, however, Sonny learned something that instantly changed his attitude toward Cho Takachi: the young man had served eight years as an army combat medic. Sonny had never served in the military but had a healthy appreciation for those who did. Cho had deployed three times, all in idyllic vacation spots with lots and *lots* of sand.

"What are we doing at a library, old-timer? You need to check out *Clifford the Big Red Dog* for your bedtime story?"

"I've got a big red dog for ya," Sonny said, grabbing his crotch and giving it a shake. "But it's for your mom's bedtime. Puts her right to sleep."

Cho laughed as he got out of the car.

"You know, Sonny, when I first met you, I thought you were ugly and had Alzheimer's. But I don't think you have Alzheimer's at all."

It was Sonny's turn to laugh. "Clever. Just hope when you're as old and ugly as I am, you've still got enough money to interest the young ladies. Because I do."

"Fair enough," Cho said. "But seriously, folks—what are we doing at a library?"

"I told you you'd learn something, and here it is. It's easier to find an old mine than it is to dig a new one."

"They even going to let you in? You aren't exactly college age, if you know what I'm saying."

"That's another thing you can do with money," Sonny said. "You can donate it to universities, then sit back and enjoy the ass-kissing that comes your way."

PROSPECTING FOR INFORMATION was nothing new to Sonny. He'd researched hundreds of old mines and depleted areas in his day. The United States had been picked over with surprising thoroughness during the various "rushes" that hit in the late nineteenth and early twentieth centuries. It was valuable to know who found what, how they found it, as well as how long it lasted and what extraction methods were last used. A vein that "ran dry" in 1914 could be reworked with leaching or strip-mine techniques made possible by modern technology. If you found one of these forgotten, abandoned veins, bought up the worthless property and then sold it to a mining company, you stood to make a tidy profit.

"Paper prospecting," as he called it, required paper. The kind of paper in historical archives. Today's youth rarely ventured past their computer keyboard. If it wasn't on Google, if it wasn't in Wikipedia, it just *wasn't*. He wasn't sure if anyone under thirty-five even knew that library archives existed.

Sonny had donated a shit-ton of money to the Marriott Library. While that was altruistic on the surface, he had quietly made it clear that the money gave him permanent access to historic archives. He never asked to take anything out of the library, and he always obeyed the rules on what could and couldn't be touched, but to him, nothing was off-limits.

In researching his mountain, he started with the computer indexes, everything from books to periodicals. He didn't find diddly-squat. It was almost as if that particular peak of the Wah Wahs didn't exist to the general public. It didn't even have a name. Tourists didn't visit. There was no water; nothing but rocks, sand and devilish terrain. Only experienced campers ventured into the hills.

Cho leaned back in his chair.

"This is a waste of time, gramps," he said, lacing his fingers and stretching his arms up. "Three hours and we haven't found a squirt of piss about your little G-spot."

Sonny nodded. "So it seems. Plenty more for us to look through, though. Buck up, little camper—more digging to do."

The University of Utah had a massive collection of old newspapers. The late 1800s saw mining booms that sparked, burned bright for a few years, then flamed out when the ore ran dry. These booms inevitably gave birth to new towns that followed the same cycle. The University had an active program to digitize these old papers, but their collection was so large it would be decades before they scanned what they already had in their possession—not to mention the donated documents that seem to come in every other day.

As big as the collection was, though, many papers were gone forever.

The entire history of some towns was represented by one, maybe two crumbling issues. When people flee dying places, they rarely think about preserving history.

Sonny sorted through bound volumes.

Cho peeked over his shoulder. "What are we looking for?"

"To see if anyone mined the area of the find," Sonny said. "The site isn't that far from a couple of ghost towns, Newhouse and Frisco."

"Like *San Francisco*?"

"No, like the *Frisco Mountains*, here in Utah," Sonny said. "Place was a boomtown. Made a lotta people a lotta rich. Supposed to be pretty violent, pretty crazy place."

"What did *pretty crazy* mean back then?"

"Well, at one point, the town had twenty-three saloons."

Cho did the peeking-over-the-sunglasses thing. "Twenty-three bars? My kind of place."

Sonny grunted in agreement. "Hey," he said, "anyone ever tell you that people who wear sunglasses inside look like jackasses?"

With his fingertip, Cho pushed the frames back into place. "Nope. When you say *rich*, what are we talking?"

"For Frisco? People pulled somewhere around twenty million dollars' worth of zinc, copper, lead, silver, and gold outta the ground."

"Twenty *million*," Cho said dreamily. "That in old-timey money or delicious modern dollars?"

"Old-timey. By today's standards, it's about a half a billion."

This time, Cho took the sunglasses off.

"Jesus H. Christ, and the *H* stands for *His-Holy-Ass-Is-Made-Of-Money*. Half a *billion*?" Cho pretended to dab at his mouth with the sleeve of his blazer. "Oh, sorry, I just started to drool there for a minute. This Frisco place still making that fat bank?"

Sonny laughed. "Not for about the last century, no. It's gone. A few ruined buildings remain, but that's it. Whole town lasted only about ten years. Frisco Mine collapsed in 1885, which pretty much killed the town. Early on they built a smelter, though, that's why we're looking for newspapers from there. Once the smelter went up, people brought in ore from all over the area to see the value of what they had, or what they thought they had. Newspapers reported on shit like that back then."

Sonny found the bound volume he was looking for.

"The *Southern Utah Times*," he said. "One of Frisco's papers. Looks like they have a bunch, maybe we'll get lucky."

Cho pointed to a sticker of the letter *D* on the cover's lower right corner.

"What's that mean?"

"Oh, that means they scanned it or whatever. We can use a web browser to search for all the stuff inside. That helps a bunch."

"Wait a minute," Cho said. "This shit's all digitized? We could have done this from your computer."

"Don't own a computer," Sonny said.

"The hotel does. Shit, we could have done this on my cell phone."

"And missed spending quality time together? Shut your trap and let's get to work."

Sonny carefully returned the volume to the shelf, then moved to a computer and started up a browser. He called up the university's digital newspaper project, began by searching for *Wah Wah*. Results came up immediately.

"Well, lookee here," he said. "I think we have a winner."

The article was dated May 10, 1883.

BENJAMIN STAKES CLAIM IN WAH WAH AREA

By STOSH WITTENDON

WILLIAM BENJAMIN, who produced very successful claims in Nevada and in the Wasatch Mountains, has staked a claim in the remote Wah Wah Range.

We see claims staked everywhere these days, but this reporter was surprised to see a claim in the southern Wah Wah Mountains. There have been only two or three decent prospecting excursions to that area, and nothing has ever turned up. Many think that Benjamin may be onto something. The town holds its breath waiting for him to return with the first cartloads of ore. Some motivated prospectors have already headed out to that area, hoping they can get a jump on the competition should Benjamin's hunch prove right.

If Benjamin discovers anything of substance, it might require construction of a new town. Benjamin's claim is 18 miles west of Frisco, too far for transportation of ore, and there are no trails or decent areas on which to build them.

———

The story surprised Sonny. Eighteen miles west of Frisco would have put Benjamin within a mile of where Sonny discovered the Silver Spring. In fact, *less* than a mile. Platinum was almost unheard of in those days. It often occurred alongside gold deposits, but many miners threw away the platinum because they didn't know what it was and only wanted the gold. Before 1900 or so, most recovery processes lost up to 99 percent of the ore's value, and often lost all the platinum group metals.

The more he thought about it, however, the more it made sense. If the spring Sonny discovered was bigger back in 1884, there would have been a good-sized stream to pan. Benjamin may have found that very same spring—or one similar to it—and staked a claim.

Sonny found the next entry regarding the mine on August 24, 1885. Benjamin had apparently returned to Frisco with a bag of dust, only to find his treasure trove wasn't as it seemed.

———

WAH WAH SITE FULL OF "FOOL'S SILVER"
BENJAMIN CLAIM A WASH
WILL CONTINUE TO DIG THE AREA

By STOSH WITTENDON

ALL THE SPECULATION surrounding the mysterious Wah Wah site staked by William Benjamin has come to an end. Benjamin arrived in town yesterday with 10 pounds of dust, which he took to local chemist Elron Wyrick for analysis. Wyrick told a disappointed Benjamin that the dust was not silver, as Benjamin had thought, but platinum. Wyrick commented that it's rare to find such high quantities of platinum.

Benjamin declined to comment on the development, which is no surprise, considering that he wants to keep his site secret. Benjamin has worked his claim for three months, and rumor has it he has killed two men defending it. Mining parties are already forming, bent on probing the Wah Wah Mountains for similar platinum deposits.

Wyrick is sending a cable east to find a buyer for the platinum. Such a large amount may bring a tidy sum, but, unlike gold, demand for platinum exists only in the metropolitan centers of the East. Wyrick advanced Benjamin money to buy equipment, dynamite and lumber for square-set supports of a future underground mine. Benjamin also hired a crew of ten men to work the site.

———

Sonny's mouth went dry.

"A ten-pound bag?" Cho said. "How much would that be worth today?"

"Oh...a bit over three hundred grand. Give or take."

Cho let out a long whistle. Sonny kept searching through the list of stories.

When he found an entry dated November 30, 1885, the story of the Benjamin Mine suddenly changed from minor coverage to front-page news with thick, black, screaming headlines.

———

MURDER AT BENJAMIN MINE

TWO DEAD, EIGHT MISSING,
VICTIMS OF MADNESS
BENJAMIN TO HANG TOMORROW MORNING

By STOSH WITTENDON

IT SEEMS THAT mining madness ran amok last week, claiming more than its usual share of victims. William Benjamin butchered at least two of his own men. Eight more men are missing and presumed dead.

Chuck Wierenski of Chuck's Feed & Grain was on his normal supply run to the Benjamin Mine. Wierenski found Benjamin wandering in the desert, about three miles from the mine.

"Benjamin was ranting on and on about monsters," Wierenski said. "He said demons killed his crew. He had a pretty bad cut on his arm and was bleeding all over the place. He was clutching this strange knife in his hand."

Wierenski brought the madman back to Frisco, where Sheriff Tate took over. Tate locked Benjamin in the jail and mounted a posse to head out to the mine. Tate returned this morning, telling a grim tale of murder and insanity.

"There were no monsters, only dead men," Tate told me when he arrived. "Benjamin must have killed them. We found two bodies. They'd been hacked up a bit before they ran out into the desert, where they died."

Tate was unable to locate Benjamin's mining camp, and now speculates that Benjamin lied on his official claim registry to protect the location of his mine. Tate said he found nothing at the official campsite, and no evidence a camp ever existed there. Wierenski refuses to travel to the mountain ever again, due to fears of an Indian curse.

This reporter has rendered pictures of the strange curved knife below. The knife is a solid piece of metal. Its maker is unknown.

———

The sketch showed the curious murder weapon: two pointed, curved blades, each about seven or eight inches long, their bases seamlessly affixed to a center ring. The blades curved in opposite directions, like two big commas sharing a hollow dot.

"Never seen anything like that," Sonny said. "You?"

Cho shook his head. "Nope. Weird, though. How the hell are you supposed to hold that? By the ring in the middle?"

"Do I look like an expert in fucked-up knives?"

"You look like an expert in adult incontinence. Can I fetch some Depends for you?"

Sonny flipped Cho off, continued to stare at the drawing of the knife. So peculiar. An Indian knife, maybe? No, not with metalwork like that.

The murder weapon was odd, sure, but not the murder itself. Tales of murder in the golden age of mining were so common that many killings barely merited a paragraph in the local paper. In some towns—Frisco, for example—things grew so out of control that there was at least one murder a week. Men often killed in the hills, either to protect a mine or because they just went crazy. Months in the desert, feverishly digging through the rocks, running out of food and water, fending off attacks by Indians and, more often, by claim jumpers—all of these things often drove men over the edge.

Sonny finally closed out of the article. He scrolled through the list: hundreds of old stories of the Wah Wahs. On water, mostly, or the lack thereof. He tried combinations of *Silver Spring* and *Wah Wahs*, found nothing. He didn't find any other stories about platinum, either.

"Try *knife* and *Wah Wah*," Cho said.

"Why?"

The man shrugged. "Well, you have a weird knife, and you have ten pounds of platinum dust, both related to the same guy. If someone else found a knife like that, couldn't it be a clue to more info on the platinum?"

Sonny nodded. He should have thought of that.

He typed in the keywords.

The search produced only one story. The headline read: GRADUATE STUDENTS MISSING: PRESUMED LOST IN CAVES.

"Bingo-bango-bungo," Cho said.

Sonny clicked. An article from the Y *News*, the school newspaper from Brigham Young University.

He and Cho read about the disappearance of Samuel J. Anderson, Douglas Nadia and Wilford Igoe Jr. They read about a ceremonial metal knife.

"Holy shits and giggles," Cho said. "Think it's the same kind of knife Benjamin used to carve up his homies?"

"Could be. I might know how to find out. Let's get out of here."

"Where we going?"

"Provo," Sonny said. "Brigham Young University."

7

August 6

ANGUS KOOL ENTERED EARTHCORE'S MAIN LAB and slammed the door behind him. He slammed it *hard*. He was angry and he wanted these stupid fucks to *know* he was angry.

They knew.

Katerina and Achmed had frozen in mid-task. They stared at him with that look he hated, a blank-faced combination of fatigue and annoyance. If it weren't for the tiny bit of fear mixed in, he would have guessed they thought they were better than him. But they weren't. He knew it. They knew it.

"Welcome back, boss," Katerina said. "You're early."

They didn't know why he was here? They didn't know about the new find? No, of course not, not yet. Only the important people had been told, Angus was quite sure.

She smiled that cherub-cheeked smile of hers. That smile annoyed him. If only he'd been here first, he would have never hired her. He wouldn't have hired that kiss-ass Achmed, either. As far as EarthCore's science staff went, Angus would have kept Randy and shit-canned everyone else, started from scratch.

"Get back to work," he told them, and walked to his office. He slammed that door, too.

He couldn't control his anger. First, that gorilla O'Doyle invading his privacy, *stalking* him, all but threatening to kill him to get him back to Denver. And then, once *in* Denver? Angus had stormed into Barbara Yakely's office and demanded O'Doyle be fired.

She'd puffed on that obnoxious cigar, then told him to (a) shut the fuck up, (b) get the fuck out of her office, and (c) get the fuck back to work. Oh, he didn't like that? Well, then he could quit—and forfeit all his stock options, which might be about to rocket from damn near worthless to so valuable they would make him a millionaire a dozen times over.

Angus sat at his desk. He gripped the edge of it. Gripped and *squeezed*. He squeezed until his hands hurt.

These assholes, these *stupid people*, they were going to tell *him* what to do?

Well, they would learn. On this job—especially this job—he'd find a way to rub their nose in it.

By the time this was over, he'd make sure everyone knew who was the best.

He'd show them all.

8

August 7

THE CH-47C CHINOOK HELICOPTER buzzed through the night sky over the Wah Wah Mountains, back and forth, back and forth, each pass another tenth of a mile south. Wide antenna arrays fixed to the bottom of the helicopter fired powerful radar signals into the ground and recorded their reflections.

Randy Wright sat in the Chinook's cargo bay. Data scrolled across his laptop screen, showing the growing picture of the area's underground composition. The night before they'd completed the north-south lines of the grid, and in another two hours or so they'd finish the east-west lines. It was quite an accomplishment: a twenty-five-mile grid knocked out in twenty-four hours' worth of flying.

He had a crew on the ground collecting soil and plant samples from all over the area. Another crew was preparing a series of charges. Like the ground-penetrating radar, shockwaves from the explosions would bounce back from underground formations. Seismometers would record that information, adding to the overall picture.

The big boom was the big finish. After those charges detonated, Randy would head back to Denver.

A one-day data-collection sprint, the scientific equivalent of a commando raid. With the technology at his disposal, however, one day was all it would take to provide Angus with everything he needed.

"DUDE," CHO SAID, "this is kinda trippy."

Sonny couldn't argue with him. There was something surreal about holding the doctoral dissertation of a man gone some seventy years, a man who vanished before Sonny had even been born, and yet was a third of Sonny's age when he disappeared. It made for a clash of feelings. Just a paper, sure, and by a guy no one had ever heard of, but seeing the old-school typeface—obviously made by a manual typewriter—changed Samuel J. Anderson from a name in a story to an actual person. Anderson had held these very pages. He'd poured his heart into them.

The title: *Tunnel Systems in the Lower Wah Wah Mountain Range.*
The date: October 1941.

"Wasn't there a war on then?" Cho asked. "The Russians or something?"

Sonny shook his head. "And people say education budgets don't matter."

It had taken them a little while to find the paper. They'd started in the Geology Department. Sonny wished he'd had a camera to see the reaction of the people there when he'd asked for PhD papers from the '40s.

One person passed them on to the next, who passed them on to the next. Three hours later, they found a file cabinet in a storage building. In it, doctoral papers from the '20s through the '50s. And in there, gold; the paper version of it, anyway.

Sonny flipped through Anderson's report. Cho leaned in. A little too close for comfort, maybe, but the kid was excited. That excitement was contagious. Turned out it was fun to share this hunt with someone else, even if the guy was almost a complete stranger.

"They found *tunnels*," Cho said, reaching to stab a finger on the yellowing paper, then stopping an inch short as if afraid he might accidentally punch right through it. "Bond villain shit. That's so pimp!"

If there weren't tunnels, the paper's title wouldn't have made much sense, but Sonny let it slide.

A few more pages, then Sonny found the information that really mattered: coordinates.

"Sonofabitch. The tunnel they found is about a quarter mile from the Silver Spring."

"No way," Cho said. "How about Benjamin's mine? Close to that, too?"

"We don't know the exact location of Benjamin's mine, but I figure it's close."

The paper detailed Anderson's discovery of a natural tunnel entrance located about five thousand feet up the unnamed peak. He and his fellow students followed that tunnel for around four hundred feet before hitting an old cave-in that blocked further access. Anderson surmised that primitive people had once lived in the caves. He based that theory on a tool discovered deep in the tunnels.

Sonny's blood chilled as he read more on the tool. Anderson thought it worthy of little more than a footnote compared to the geological formations, but it did strike him as odd enough to list a brief description.

> Approximately seventy-five yards into the cave, we found a primitive tool. It appears to be a scraper, perhaps, or possibly a weapon. It is a metal blade, obviously made by a skilled craftsman, measuring 14.5" in length and 3.75" at the widest point. The culture that created this tool was obviously very skilled at working metal. It appears to be steel. The blades are very sharp. The quality of work seems excellent, but not being an anthropologist, I'm sure that artifacts such as these are nothing out of the ordinary. I'll turn it over to the Anthropology Department.

Anderson's paper included a crude sketch of the blade. The nasty-looking, double-crescent shape looked exactly like Benjamin's murder weapon.

In the report, Anderson had written the number 32 next to the knife. A footnote reference. Sonny looked at the footnote and found another number.

"I think this is a catalog number," he said.

"Like something you can order?"

"Not that kind of catalog. A museum catalog. It's how they keep track of the stuff in a museum. That newspaper article said he turned the knife over to the Anthropology Department. I wonder if it's still around."

"Oh, come on," Cho said. "That was seventy years ago, pops."

Sonny nodded. "Yeah, but old museums are all the same, especially at universities. They've got more stuff than they can deal with. New things are always coming in, and many times students are the ones tracking stuff. Students get in a hurry, they make mistakes, they aren't thorough. Years pass, people leave, things get put in boxes before they're properly recorded. You'd be surprised—oftentimes a museum is a giant cluster-fuck. Sometimes they don't even know everything they've got. *Especially* if it came in a long time ago. Say, seventy years or so ago. We might as well see if we can track it down."

"Let me guess," Cho said. "You're a big-time donor here, too?"

Sonny smiled. "Money well spent. Especially if we get lucky and this catalog number leads somewhere."

Cho took off his sunglasses. He pulled a small cloth from his pant pocket, slowly cleaned the lenses.

"It would be cool to see one of those knives for real and all, but we're supposed to be looking for info on the Silver Spring, you know? I'm supposed to keep you on task. What's the knife itself got to do with mining?"

Sonny scratched absently at his beard. It was a good question. What did the knife of some long-gone Indian tribe have to do with the platinum find? Probably nothing. But his curiosity was up, blazing bright. He knew more about southwestern Utah than probably anyone alive. He'd spent decades meeting people, researching ancient cultures, getting to know people from paleontology departments ... anything that might give him a leg up finding some old site that history had forgotten. He knew his history. He knew his tribes. But in all the time he'd spent gathering information, he had never seen a knife like that. As far as he knew, no one had. Now it had popped up not once, but twice, both in proximity to the place where he'd discovered a possible mother lode.

"Can't say for sure," he said finally. "Just feel like if we *can* find the knife, we need to find it."

He finished scanning Anderson's paper. It concluded with detailed plans for another excursion, scheduled for March 1942.

"That was the one they never came back from," he said.

"Maybe they came back after that article was written," Cho said. "We don't know, maybe there's another article in the same school paper."

Unlike the newspapers of long-dead ghost towns, back issues of BYU's student paper were well organized, complete and fully digitized. The two men searched for additional articles on Anderson and his friends.

From April 1942 on, accounts of the missing students were in every issue. Articles chronicled the continued search for the three boys. As time went on, the articles grew smaller and smaller. The last article Sonny could find was dated June 30, 1942 — it simply said that the students were presumed dead.

Cho absently ran his fingers through his black hair.

"First Benjamin's murder spree, then these kids," he said. "Combine the miners and Anderson's crew, that's thirteen people either dead or never heard from again. This peak doesn't have a name? Maybe we should just call it Funeral Mountain."

A sense of dread made Sonny shiver. He remembered the feelings he'd had at the Silver Spring. *Funeral Mountain* was the perfect name for that place.

Thirteen people gone. Thirteen. One bastard of an unlucky number.

Maybe there was a very good reason this platinum find had gone unnoticed for well over a century.

He couldn't back out, though, not yet, not with 2 percent of the mine's future on the line. Sure, he had a million bucks, but that 2 percent had the potential of making a million bucks look like chump change.

Sonny had promised Connell a full year. If he wanted that 2 percent, he had to see this thing through.

This research was just the beginning. Soon Connell would want him on-site. Sonny had no doubt of that, because had their positions been reversed, he'd have demanded the same thing. Sonny would be back on that unnamed peak—back on Funeral Mountain—with that clammy feeling of darkness creeping up his groin and tickling his balls. He should fly to Rio right now, have his balls tickled by something much more hospitable than that desolate, dead mountain.

Cho's sunglasses slid down.

"Pops, you all right? You're kind of spacing out on me here."

Sonny snarled at him. "Mind your own business, boy."

The sunglasses slid up. "You *are* my business, you fucking raisin."

Well, that was true.

Sonny went through Anderson's paper again, taking notes, being careful to double-check all the locations. He needed to internalize this info. For Connell, sure, but also—Sonny hated to admit it, *hated* it—for himself.

Because that little voice was eating at him again.

Don't you wanna know what's there? Don't you want to know about the knives? Don't you?

He did want to know. And he had an awful, nagging feeling that when he finally found out, he really wouldn't want to know at all.

9

August 9

CONNELL DROVE NORTH on Downing Street. Only a five-mile drive or so, but traffic was bumper to bumper. Maybe he should have taken Colfax. It was more than a little embarrassing to admit, but he'd spent most of the last five years at the office or his apartment—he didn't drive enough to know the fastest route.

It probably didn't matter which way he went. All the roads were packed. Had been since the terrorists took out the 87-85 interchange a year and a half ago. All told, Denver hadn't suffered extensive damage in the Pandemic, but a few crazies had organized early, managed to destroy a huge amount of roadway before anyone was onto them. The interchange was mostly repaired and supposed to be active again soon. *Any day now* was what he'd heard on the news, but the news had been saying that shit for three months running.

The traffic didn't bother him much, though, because he was already plenty bothered by the person on the other end of his phone call.

"What are you telling me, Sonny? Are you saying we need to scrap the whole project because there's some bad history in the area?"

"Don't think you can classify multiple murders and missing persons as simply *bad history*, Kirkland," Sonny said. "I think that mountain is cursed."

"Cursed? Oh, come on, Sonny, don't tell me you're superstitious."

"Goddamned right I am. Hell, I'm the *poster boy* of superstitious."

At least he was honest. Say one thing for Sonny McGuiness: what you saw was what you got, and he didn't give a damn what you thought about that.

"So, what I'm gathering is that, in your professional opinion, we need to stay off that mountain because you got some voodoo heebie-jeebies?"

"*Voodoo?* That a racist comment?"

"No. Now answer the fucking question. Are you saying we should walk away from this?"

Sonny paused a moment. "Don't know if I'd go that far."

"That's what I thought," Connell said. "Look, you found prior evidence of a find in that area. That's a big indicator we're on the right track. I'm on my way to see what the lab geeks have come up with. The camp is under construction as we speak. Be there tomorrow. Unless maybe you want to give up your two percent and hurry along to your nursing home?"

"Was that an ageist comment?"

"Yes, it was. Will you be on-site tomorrow, or not?"

Sonny sighed. "I'll be there."

Connell disconnected, then exited off the highway. Single-story buildings, strip malls and industrial parks. A different look and feel from downtown Denver, and something he hadn't really seen for … what … four years?

No, not four—*five*.

He hadn't been to EarthCore's lab since Cori's death.

Five *years* since he'd stopped by just to see how everyone was doing? There had been a time when he didn't let a week go by without visiting the lab to touch base, talking to the technicians, getting the scoop on the latest research techniques, the latest family news, the latest company gossip. Of course, there was also a time when he gave a shit about that worthless garbage.

He accomplished far more for the company by staying in his office. His apartment was only a block from there. Aside from traveling to prospective sites, those were the only two places he spent any time.

Connell pulled in to the parking lot. A nondescript one-story industrial building. Looked the same as it had the last time he visited. A surreal feeling washed over him, that he'd just been here, just yesterday, maybe. Maybe he'd pulled in, nodded off, dreamed the whole thing.

Maybe she wasn't really gone.

He closed his eyes.

Please ... please let it be a dream.

He opened his eyes. Same building. Same car—a car he'd bought just six months ago.

"Fucking idiot," he said, then got out.

The building had no signage, which was status quo for any EarthCore facility. Barbara didn't believe in flashy. Of course to her, "flashy" included branding, advertising and just about anything that required the presence of a logo rather than a handshake, a cigar and a beer.

He quietly entered the lab. The staff wore white lab coats. He didn't remember them wearing those before. The people closest to the door looked up, saw him. Jaws dropped. Work slowly ground to a halt. He knew some of the faces from when he'd been more ... social. Others he knew only from pictures in personnel files.

A man approached, smiling wide. Connell remembered the face, and the thick, black mustache that the man was so proud of. He remembered how everyone teased the man for being a wannabe '70s porn star. But the name ... the name wouldn't register.

"Connell, it's so good to see you again." The man started to extend his hand, then paused, as if he wasn't sure a handshake was the right thing. "It's been a long time."

Achmed. His name was Achmed. Connell hadn't seen him since ... since ... well, since the night Cori died. Connell and Cori had actually gone to dinner with Achmed and his wife before that fateful New Year's Eve party. The four of them had been friends. Connell hadn't spoken to the man since that night. Not even once. He remembered sympathetic voice mails from Achmed, consolation cards, supporting emails – all of which had been ignored.

"Yeah, a long time," Connell said. He reached out, shook the man's hovering hand. "How is…"

His voice trailed off. He couldn't remember Achmed's wife's name.

Achmed's smile remained in place but shifted from genuine to forced, the kind of smile you put on to try to make someone else feel not-as-bad.

"She was in Chicago," he said. "During the Pandemic."

Chicago. Where the worst of it had gone down.

The emotion that washed over him felt so alien, so unfamiliar, that it took Connell a second to place the skin-prickling, stomach-wavering sensation: *guilt*.

When Connell's wife had died, Achmed had reached out dozens of times. When Achmed's wife had died, Connell hadn't even known.

"I'm so sorry," he said.

This time Achmed's smile was a sad thing, a time capsule of fond memories forever locked away.

"Thank you," he said. "We deal with our grief and make the best life we can, no? I'd better get back to work. Angus is very demanding." He walked back to his station.

If the closing-his-eyes-and-wishing thing actually worked, Connell would have at least used it to erase that conversation.

He saw O'Doyle approaching. Connell welcomed the distraction. He hadn't known O'Doyle… *before*. No past friendship here. No pleasantries forgotten. Just work.

"Mister Kirkland, welcome."

Connell had called ahead. His visit was a surprise to everyone except for his chief of security, who had been assigned to watch the science staff and provide anything they needed during the analysis blitz.

"Thank you," Connell said. "What's with the lab coats?"

"Doctor Kool's requirement. Everyone in the lab has to wear one."

Connell glanced at O'Doyle's clothes: black slacks, long-sleeve black shirt buttoned up to his neck.

"He didn't ask you to wear one?"

"He did," O'Doyle said. "I told him, *I would prefer not to*. He didn't ask again."

Connell couldn't blame Angus for that.

"You've been here the last three days?"

O'Doyle nodded. "As you requested. And Doctor Kool has been here the entire time. I'll be honest, Mister Kirkland—I've never met anyone who can get by on less sleep than I can. If he's not snorting cocaine when I'm not looking, you should have someone dissect him, find out what makes him tick and patent it. That would be worth more than all the precious metals in the world combined."

Connell shrugged; wasn't the first time someone had mentioned dissecting Angus Kool.

"And the computer system remains isolated?"

"Completely," O'Doyle said. "I followed protocol to the letter. Computers working on internal databases only, all connections to the Internet shut down. I confiscated . . . I mean . . . I *requested* everyone's cell phones when they entered. No one can even open an email that might allow a worm in. But may I speak freely, sir?"

"This isn't the military, O'Doyle. I'm your boss, not your commanding officer."

"The only difference between those two, sir, is how you fire someone."

O'Doyle waited.

"I don't get it," Connell said.

"It's a firing-line joke. Execution for dereliction of duty."

"Hysterical. You're very funny."

The big man nodded. "That's what my men always told me, sir."

"Perhaps you could move on to the *speaking freely* part?"

"Right," O'Doyle said. "I know computers, but I'm not an expert. Maybe you should have a certain female who might or might not be involved in the farming industry check things out, just to be sure?"

Connell shook his head. Like he was going to tell Farm Girl about any of this. She was only as loyal as the highest bidder, and for what this find might become, other companies would bid *very* high indeed.

"She's one of the reasons I have everything isolated in the first place," he said. "Some people just can't be trusted. How's the rest of the lab staff doing?"

"They're tired, but working. Doctor Kool is a slave driver. If it wouldn't be an insult to my old drill sergeant, I'd say he reminds me of my old drill sergeant."

The mention of the word *tired* made Connell take another look around. Ten staffers. They all looked exhausted.

"Angus is pushing them hard?"

"Nonstop," O'Doyle said. "Nothing they do satisfies him."

Angus stood on the other side of the large lab, oblivious to Connell. He moved like he was made of caffeine.

"You call these results?" the little man said, practically screaming at a small, black-haired woman, a sheaf of computer printouts clutched in his hands. Connell vaguely remembered the woman's name—Tina something-or-other. He remembered hiring her shortly before Cori's death.

Lab workers flinched as Angus's arrogant, nasal voice filled the room.

"I said, do you call these results, Katerina?"

Katerina. That was it. Katerina Hayes.

She glared back at Angus, her expression fierce despite the tears brimming in her eyes.

"I've double-checked the metallurgical analysis," she said. "It's consistent."

Angus threw the report. The pages spread out like a flock of birds, then fluttered to the ground.

"Do it again! That work isn't fit for an undergrad, for God's sake! Do it again! And make it quick—this repetitive work is making you fall behind."

O'Doyle spoke quietly.

"He picks on her the most. I looked at her files. IQ of one hundred and fifty-six. I wonder how Doctor Kool would treat a dumb old soldier like me if I worked under him."

"You're far from dumb," Connell said. "And besides, if he were your boss, I imagine you'd have already strangled him."

O'Doyle shook his scarred head. "Oh, *no sir.* I'd use a knife."

Connell laughed and was a little surprised to hear the noise escape his lips. Did he laugh so rarely that it sounded strange to him? No way to live a life, really. Then he remembered sitting in his car, closing his eyes and wishing that the last five years hadn't happened—all traces of humor faded away.

"Your prep for security at the dig," Connell said. "Any problems?"

"No sir. I'm drawing personnel from five other EarthCore sites. I've hired a different temp security agency to fill the vacancies at each of those five sites, so we should avoid word getting out that we've pulled all of our experienced guards at the same time."

"Smart," Connell said. "And your equipment needs?"

O'Doyle grinned. The missing ear was disturbing enough, but that smile was a close runner-up.

"Your budget was quite sufficient, Mister Kirkland. I felt like a kid in a candy store."

"Good. Keep me updated."

Connell walked toward Angus. O'Doyle trailed a step behind. Angus saw Connell coming. Surprise — then haughty anger — spread across his face. He straightened his lab coat. Charlie Brown, Snoopy and Pigpen pins decorated his lapel.

"Well, if it isn't the king himself," Angus said. "Come down from your ivory tower to watch your lowly serfs toil?"

Connell wondered how anyone could work day in and day out with this jackass and not punch him in the face.

"Doctor Kool, I hope you've got something for me other than a surly attitude."

Angus nodded, making his wild red hair bob.

"I've got something, all right. We've been processing the data Randy collected. We discovered a rather large anomaly of extremely dense material, about three miles underground."

Connell felt that spark of excitement, the one that came when his efforts finally paid off. It was the only thing that thrilled him anymore.

"So you found it," he said. "We're in business."

Angus waggled a finger side to side.

"Not so fast. While I would love to render unto Caesar and all that jazz, there are still many questions. Up on the surface, we haven't found anything indicative of a large platinum deposit. With the dust McGuiness collected, I expected to see biogeochemical evidence of a deposit. The roots of some trees and plants gather elements from the ground and transmit them to the leaves. Juniper bushes, for example, which are common at the Wah Wah site, can send roots as far as a hundred and sixty feet below the surface."

That thrill of discovery ratcheted back, like a rushing junkyard dog reaching the end of her chain just before biting into the trespasser.

"You're telling me the biogeo turned up *nothing?*"

Angus grinned, shrugged. He enjoyed being the bearer of bad news.

"Not a damned thing," he said. "Some iron deposits but no platinum. Or any other valuable mineral."

"What about metallogenic?"

O'Doyle leaned in. "I get *biogeo,* but what does *metallogenic* mean?"

Angus sneered. "*You* know what biogeochemical analysis is?"

The scarred solder smiled. "I've been here three days. I've paid attention."

"Well, whoop-de-fucking-do for you, Rhodes scholar," Angus said. "I'm afraid I left my gold stars in my other pants."

"Knock it off," Connell snapped. "You should be nicer to O'Doyle, Angus."

The little scientist crossed his white-sleeved arms.

"Why's that? Did I miss a Miss Manners clause in my contract?"

"Because Mister O'Doyle is going to be on-site with you," Connell said. "He'll be protecting you day and night. You know, with lots of guns, that sort of thing."

The snotty grin faded. Angus glanced at the big man.

"That's right," O'Doyle said. "Even while you sleep."

Angus nervously licked his lips.

"Ah, well, then I'm sure we'll all be quite safe. You were asking about metallogenic analysis?"

O'Doyle nodded. "I do love to learn."

"Metal ores often appear in groups," Angus said. "Various minerals in a given area can reveal probable locations of undiscovered deposits. Platinum can be found mixed in with copper, nickel and palladium, for example. The trouble with the McGuiness discovery is that we've found absolutely *zero* elements commonly associated with a platinum deposit. In addition, ore deposits can leave surface discolorations. Randy saw none of those in his surface flyovers."

This wasn't the picture Connell had been hoping for. Not even close.

"You have something else, then," he said. "If the site was a bust, I know you'd revel in being the one to tell me."

Angus put a hand to his chest.

"You wound me, sir, to think that I would feel schadenfreude at such a thing."

"I won't even pretend to know what the fuck that word means," Connell said. "You're the smartest kid in the class. We get it. I want to know if you found something we can use or not."

Angus smiled his self-satisfied smile.

"We do have some good news, thanks to advanced tomographic techniques I've developed."

"*Tom*-ographic?" O'Doyle said. "Do you mean *top*-ographic?"

Connell winced. He'd made a similar statement a few years back. Angus loved it when people thought he had made a mistake.

"No, Mister O'Doyle, I do not," Angus said. "*Topography* is mapping the surface. *Tomography* is mapping the ground itself, the shape and the contours of various substances and densities. Here's an easy trick that even you can remember—the *top* in *top*ography means up *on top*. Get it?"

O'Doyle didn't answer.

Connell longed to wipe that arrogant sneer from Angus's face.

"Angus here is an expert on tomography," he said. "You're standing in the presence of greatness, Mister O'Doyle."

"Ah, that's what it is," O'Doyle said. "And here I thought someone farted."

Angus ignored the remark.

"Ground-penetrating radar, known simply as GPR, can map the contours of solid ground by sending radar waves into the earth and charting the time of their echo, much like you might use standard radar to locate a plane in the sky. Current GPR techniques allow a maximum of a thousand-foot penetration below the surface. My new method, however, allows you to penetrate up to sixteen thousand feet—over three miles. That's *eight times* better than anyone else in the world, I'd like to note."

It was moments like this that Connell reminded himself why he put up with the horrible attitude. Angus thought of himself as *the shit* because that's exactly what he was.

"Just show us what you've found," Connell said.

Angus turned to a computer terminal and called up a graphic of tightly packed vertical lines of varying height.

"This peak here is our anomalous dense area." He pointed to the longest line on the graphic. "Notice how much higher it is than everything else? That's because it's dense. *Really* dense, much more so than the surrounding rock, which indicates that if it's metal ore it's very high-grade."

"*If*," Connell said. "You can't tell me with certainty that we have ore at all?"

Angus shook his head. "No, not with certainty. Part of the problem is that we had a lot of noise in the signal, like very weak, very soft areas throughout the mountain. To bolster our data, we took geophone readings. We detonated high explosives throughout the area and measured the echoes. It's just like taking a CAT scan except we measure the travel time of the seismic waves resulting from the explosions rather than X-rays sent through the patient. I combined this with the GPR readings to map the whole area."

Angus called up a three-dimensional image. The picture showed a solid green mass at the center, clearly oblong in shape but broken up in many places. A bright yellow envelope surrounded the green mass. Faded yellow vein-like branches extended in all directions, but mostly up and away from the mass. Only one straight, thick yellow vein pointed down, protruding from the center of the green mass until it fuzzed and faded to nothing. The picture gave the overall impression of a neon-green sea anemone waving hundreds of thin yellow tendrils through the water.

Connell was used to seeing similar pictures, courtesy of Angus's cutting-edge talents, but normally the screen was also dotted with a plethora of colors and shapes representing myriad rocks and minerals. Even the most concentrated deposit images showed at least a dozen significant changes in color. The yellow branches were new as well.

"What am I seeing here?"

"Well, the green is what I call the *Dense Mass*. Whatever that chunk is, it's all the same density."

"So the same material," Connell said. "Why are you only showing that? Usually these images show other mineral deposits."

"It doesn't show any because there *aren't* any." Angus shrugged. "That's what's so strange about all this. That mountain is a big, solid, worthless chunk of limestone. There's some low-grade iron ore, but that's it. I filtered it out of the map so we could really see what's there—limestone, and the Dense Mass."

Connell wanted to touch the green image. He kept his hands at his sides. His fingertips brushed against his thumbs.

"You think that's platinum ore, don't you?"

"I don't think it's *ore* at all," Angus said. "I think the Dense Mass is the same platinum/iridium compound that makes up Sonny's dust."

"Fuck me," O'Doyle said.

Connell stared at the image. Part of him wanted to slap Angus for the slow reveal. Why hadn't the jackass just come right out and said *we're onto something so big it could change the world's economy?*

"How big, Angus?" Connell's fingertips moved faster.

"About four miles long." The little man's arrogant smile was gone. He stared at the image just as reverently as Connell did. "Four miles long, a little over a half mile wide. We don't know how deep because it goes below the bottom of my equipment's max range."

If that really was platinum/iridium, a fucking solid *chunk* of it... the value wasn't even calculable, because it had the potential to dwarf the world's entire supply of the stuff.

O'Doyle grunted in amazement, an *mmm-MMM-mmm* that made him sound oddly like an old Southern man seeing some newfangled invention for the first time.

"Just one big chunk," he said. "That can happen? It's like the world's biggest nugget or something?"

Angus stared into the image, right hand rubbing slowly at his cheeks and jaw. If he'd been capable of growing a beard, he would have been stroking it.

"Platinum can form naturally, sure," he said. "You can find a nugget of it just like you can find a nugget of gold or silver or copper. That's rare, though. Most often metal is locked up within rock. A *nugget* that's four miles long? It was a crazy day in Earth's history when that bauble got coughed up from down below."

"Maybe it's an asteroid," O'Doyle said.

Angus nodded. "Could be, but something that big would likely have broken up into several pieces. Doubtful it could stay in one chunk. And the crater would have been massive. There'd still be some evidence of it, even if the impact was a billion years ago. There's no indication of such a crater."

Connell glanced around the lab, seeing if anyone was looking. Did the rest of the staff know this already? If so, had they told spouses? Kids? Was word already out?

"It gets odder," Angus said. "The yellow lines—the soft stuff I told you about—it's not rock. It's not anything. As near as I can tell, those are caves."

Connell stared at the image anew. Tunnels. Some of the yellow lines seemed tiny, threadlike, while others were thick and solid, connecting yellow blobs that had to be caverns.

"It's the largest cave system in the world," Angus said. "To date, the largest individual cavern ever found, located in Nevada's Carlsbad Caverns, covers over fourteen square miles with a ceiling as high as two hundred and fifty feet. These Dense Mass Caverns are much bigger than that. There's one kidney-shaped cavern at the GPR's bottom-edge range that may be as big as twenty-five square miles, with a ceiling over a thousand feet high. On top of that, the Dense Mass Cavern itself is roughly another ten square miles. I've never seen anything like this—no one has. We've made one hell of a discovery here. So far, the longest known system is the Flint-Mammoth Caves in Kentucky with over three hundred miles of known tunnels. I estimate the Dense Mass cave system covers *six hundred fifty miles* of tunnels, and about three hundred fifteen total square miles of cavern."

O'Doyle let out a long, low whistle of amazement.

"This is all good and fine," Connell said. "But it doesn't mean anything until we confirm that the Dense Mass is worth digging up. How long until we get a sample?"

"A diamond rig is on the way to the site," Angus said. "Randy will handle it. Although at that depth, it's going to take us at least two weeks to get all the way down."

Connell nodded. "That's fine, as long as we're moving forward."

Now came the million-dollar question. Or, in this case, the billion—or *trillion*—dollar question.

"Deepest mine in the world is Ventersdorp," Connell said. "Two point eight miles. They've been digging that for twenty years. We don't have twenty years, Angus, so I have to know. Don't bullshit me, don't pad the truth, don't show me how smart you are, just tell me—can your laser drill go deeper than that?"

The redhead's eyes lit up, crinkled with aggressive pride.

"Goddamn right it can," he said. "I've been waiting years for a chance like this. My drill will change mining forever."

Connell nodded. That was probably true. And if it did, Angus would sell his patented technology to every company that wanted it. That was in his contract, that was his right, and Connell didn't care. Angus could have all that money and more. If that Dense Mass turned out to contain platinum, EarthCore would instantly become the richest company in the world.

The richest company in *history*.

"My drill can punch that hole," Angus said. "But that far down, geothermal heat changes the game. No one in EarthCore has managed a mine even half that deep. Getting to the Dense Mass is only half the battle—you have to find someone who can bring it back up."

"I've got someone in mind," Connell said. "I need you on-site tomorrow to manage the core sample and make sure the drill setup goes off without a hitch."

Angus nodded, so hard his stiff red hair flipped back and forth.

"Don't you worry your pretty little head, Boss Kirkland. I'm on it like a priest on a choirboy."

Connell saw a gleam in Angus's eyes, a gleam he didn't like at all. The little man was probably dreaming spelunking dreams, planning on exploring the vast tunnels beneath that Wah Wah Mountain. Connell would have to make sure someone had eyes on Angus all the time, lest the wee genius skip off to do some exploring.

"Get me that sample," Connell said. "You don't mind if I use your office, do you?"

Angus bristled, then forced a smile.

"*Mi casa es su casa, señor.*"

Connell glanced at O'Doyle.

"A word, please?"

They entered Angus's office. O'Doyle shut the door.

"You want me to lock the lab down," he said. "No one leaves, right?"

Connell nodded, impressed. "How did you know?"

"Like I said, Mister Kirkland, I'm a fast learner. While Angus has been whipping the backs of everyone here—everyone except me, of course—I've been studying. The South Africans and the Russians mostly control the world's platinum supply. Zimbabwe's Darwendale is producing well, but since the Russians run that, same difference. Forced scarcity keeps prices high. We introduce a massive new supply, and prices go down. Know who doesn't like prices to go down?"

"Russians and South Africans," Connell said.

"That's my guess. So, if word gets out about what we might have, and those guys get wind of it...let's just say EarthCore isn't the only company to employ people like me."

People like me. Connell had hired O'Doyle because Kayla Meyers said he was the man for the job, yet Connell still knew so little about him.

"You hit the nail right on the head, Mister O'Doyle. Fantastic initiative."

The big man beamed.

"Thank you, sir. I'll inform the staff they can't leave. I assume I have a discretionary budget to provide them with anything they want that will make this stay easier?"

"Sure, good idea." After all, what did additional expenses matter? He was precariously close to putting all of EarthCore's eggs into this one basket. It was coming to a head very quickly: EarthCore would be either broke or sitting on a mountain of money.

"And reassign non-lab staff to help them," Connell said. "Pay for family members to come to Denver. Uncles, aunts, grandparents, that sort of thing. Make sure the kids have someone who knows them taking them to school. Hire cooks and drivers and cleaning ladies, et cetera. Can you handle all that?"

O'Doyle nodded.

"Absolutely, Mister Kirkland. If you don't mind me saying so, bonuses would be the sugar that helps the medicine go down."

Bonuses. Why not?

"Triple their prorated salary for as long as this goes on," he said. "That should do it."

"I'll start immediately. I'm sure I can have everyone situated in the next twenty-four hours, before I head to the site myself."

Not counting Angus, there were eleven staffers in the lab. O'Doyle was going to manage setting up care for all their families? In a single *day*?

"Mister O'Doyle, just what kind of soldier were you?"

The big man's smile pulled at his scar tissue. "The kind that can think on his feet, sir. Other than that, you know my background is—"

"Classified," Connell said, nodding. "I know, I shouldn't have asked. Just get this done for me."

O'Doyle reached out, opened the office door and held it for Connell.

"Absolutely, sir."

Sometimes, you hired people who turned into flaming assholes. Other times, you got the right person for the job.

"See you in Utah," Connell said, then headed to his car.

"BE CAREFUL," SONNY SAID. "It's a sharp sonofabitch."

Dr. Hector Rodriguez lifted the heavy, double-crescent-shaped knife by the hole in its center. There really wasn't any other way to pick it up. No handle, just the two curved blades, each finely edged on both sides. He could only fit two chubby fingers inside the ring.

"Around twelve pounds, maybe," he said.

"Fifteen," Sonny answered. "Fifteen pounds, one ounce."

Hector tried to adjust his grip on the metal ring. When he did, the smooth metal slid across his skin—the knife turned. The tip grazed a finger.

"Oh my," Hector said, looking at the red rivulet cascading down his wrist. Blood drops splattered the layers of paper that covered his desktop. He grabbed a handful of Kleenex and squeezed it around the fresh wound.

"Shit, Hec," Sonny said, standing and leaning forward. "You okay?"

"Oh, sit down, Sonny. Just because I'm a professor doesn't mean I'm a wuss. It's just a little cut. I can't believe how sharp that thing is. What idiot would sharpen an artifact?"

"Don't think anyone sharpened it," Sonny said. "Don't think it's been touched since they put it in storage."

Hector let out a small *harrumph* and looked at the knife sitting on his desktop. A smear of blood streaked to the jagged edge.

Sonny pointed to it. "So you don't recognize it?"

"I'm afraid not," Hector said. "I've never seen anything like this. And you're sure this came from our archives?"

"That's right. Was in a metal box. Hasn't been touched in so long the lock was rusty. I don't think anyone's opened the sucker in decades, but it was right there, on a shelf. Anyone could have grabbed it."

Hector shook his head, marveling that such a beautiful object had been forgotten. There was an enormous amount of material in the anthropology archives, to be sure. Most material was tagged, cataloged and carefully stored on a shelf or safely in boxes. The thing was, there was just so *much stuff*—boxes and boxes of artifacts brought in by staff and students in the '40s, '50s, '60s and on. Even cataloged material could be forgotten. University basements and storage buildings bulged with the stuff.

That didn't mean missing something this unique wasn't embarrassing, though. At least it wasn't as bad as some places. He'd read about a new sauropod species that had sat on a shelf of London's Natural History Museum for over a *century* before a computer programmer and part-time paleontologist discovered what decades of professionals had simply overlooked.

"Come on, Hec," Sonny said. "You gotta know what tribe made this."

Sonny McGuiness was such an interesting man. Aside from the fact that he was a *huge* donor to the Anthropology Department, his wrinkled, brightly bearded face could light up with the energy of a six-year-old staring at a mountain of birthday presents.

Hector just didn't recognize it. But … was there something about it that seemed familiar?

"Maybe I've seen that shape somewhere," he said. "I just can't place it. Whatever it is, it's obscure. Not part of any peoples or cultures from the Southwest."

They sat in Hector's tiny, disaster-area-messy office buried in the Archaeology Department's basement. Sonny's face was very familiar to the staff, who were always eager to provide him any help he requested. This time, however, Sonny came in with another man, a dangerous-looking Asian fellow named Cho something-or-other. Perfect hair. Insisted on wearing his sunglasses indoors.

The shape of the knife … that *shape* … where had Hector seen it before?

"How long has it been down in the archives?"

"Since 1941," Sonny said. "A graduate student found it, in an area I'm currently prospecting."

Hector peeked inside the ball of Kleenex pressed to his finger. Blood welled up instantly, and he squeezed back down again.

"Gonna need stitches," Cho said. "Trust me, I know cuts."

He smiled. The smile made Hector nervous.

Hector turned his attention back to Sonny. "How did you come to find a box that we … wait … you said the box was locked?"

"Yes, *was*," Cho said. "Tenses, man. Grammar is important."

Hector decided he'd rather not ask why the two men had opened up locked university property.

"Anyway," he said, "how did you find out about it?"

Sonny reached out, pressed the flat of his finger against the flat of the gleaming blade. He lifted the finger, leaving a visible print.

"Research," he said. "Y'all don't even know what you've got around here. More stuff in that library and that museum than you'll ever know, Hec."

Hector sighed. "Tell me about it. Just not enough hours in the day. I remember when—"

He stopped in mid-sentence, the image of the knife's shape finally crystallizing in his mind.

Sonny smiled: too-white teeth, the same shade as his beard.

"You got something?"

Hector turned to the impossibly overstuffed bookshelves and riffled through reams of loose papers. "I recall that shape. A former BYU student found something similar. In the Andes, I think. A Doctor Veronica Reeves from the University of Michigan. Her father works in the Biology Department. I've got the article here somewhere. A blurb in *Scientific American*, maybe."

Hector sifted through his endless morass of papers. No, not that pile. Maybe the pile by the window. No, not there, either. Maybe the pile up on the shelf …

Sonny stood. "Hec, if you figure it out, call me. We need to get going."

He reached for the knife.

Hector's hand shot out before he even knew he was moving. The Kleenex flew free as he laid his fingers against the flat of a crescent blade. Blood streamed from his cut, beading up on the gleaming metal.

"You can't take that."

Sonny's hand was still halfway to the knife. His white eyebrows rose.

"Sorry," Hector said. He forced a smile, cognizant that the blood from his finger was pooling on his desk, already soaking into a pile of midterm reports. "University property, Sonny. I appreciate you bringing this to our attention, but you can't take it with you. You understand."

Sonny seemed poised to argue. The Asian man stood by quietly, calmly, eyes hidden behind his sunglasses.

"Of course," Sonny said. "Yeah, of course."

Cho slowly shook his head.

"Mister Kirkland will want to see that knife," he said. "We should take it with us. You don't mind, do you, Hector?"

Nice words, nice words that carried a not-so-disguised threat.

"I most certainly *do* mind."

Sonny held up both hands, an *everyone calm down* gesture.

"It's fine," he said. "Of course we'll leave the knife here."

Cho's head swiveled to Sonny.

"I repeat—Mister Kirkland will want to see that."

"Heard you the first time," Sonny said. "And what *Mister Kirkland* wants doesn't matter. Let's go." He tipped his head toward the door.

Cho glanced at Hector, at the knife, then back to Hector. He pointed to Hector's finger.

"Stitches," he said. "Sooner is better than later."

Hector nodded. "I'll get right on that."

Cho's lips twitched to the left, stayed there, then he shrugged and walked out.

Sonny spread his hands apologetically.

"Sorry about that, Hec. Kids these days."

Hector picked up the bloody Kleenex, again squeezed it tight on his wounded finger.

"Sonny, it's not my business, but how well do you know that man?"

"Couple of days is all. I'm working with a new company. He came with the deal."

As far as Hector knew, Sonny had always operated alone.

"Just be careful," he said. "We wouldn't want anything to happen to you."

Sonny grinned. "You know me, Hec. I'm bulletproof. Get that finger fixed and call me if you figure out where you saw the knife, okay?"

Hector nodded. He was glad Sonny was bulletproof... but was he *knife* proof?

The knife... that shape...

Hector squeezed tighter. He probably did need stitches, dammit. Blood all over his desk. But that article, it was here somewhere. As soon as he found it, he'd go get the finger looked at. He tore off a big strip of Scotch tape and wrapped it tightly around the reddening Kleenex. Good enough for now, anyway.

Twenty minutes after Sonny and Cho left, Hector found the magazine in question. Dr. Reeves's Andes find wasn't some obscure article, and it wasn't in *Scientific American*. A double-crescent knife — exactly like the one sitting on his desk — graced the cover of *National Geographic*.

Hector dialed an office in the Biology Department. It was answered by a man with a thick Indian accent.

"Doctor Haak speaking."

"Sanji, Hector Rodriguez in Archaeology."

"Ah, Hector! How can I help you this fine afternoon?"

"Is Veronica still up in the Andes? Can you reach her?"

"She is still there, yes," Sanji said. "Not many phones where she is, but she checks in regularly enough. I can reach her. Why?"

Hector stared at the knife as he talked. The center ring reflected his face, distorted and curved against the metal.

"You better come to my office," he said. "You're not going to believe this."

"I'll be right down."

Hector hung up and stared at the magazine, amazed he hadn't instantly made the connection. After all, it wasn't every day that a BYU alum's work graced the cover of *National Geographic*.

The cover showed a well-lit double-crescent blade gleaming against a black velvet background.

White block letters read:

MOUNT FITZ ROY:
FORGOTTEN UNDERGROUND METROPOLIS

10

August 12

NO MATTER HOW MUCH AIR they pumped down the shaft, there was no escaping the geothermal heat generated by the Earth's core. Such heat is unnoticeable on the surface, but at 2.8 miles down, it bakes you. Without constant—and horribly expensive—air-conditioning, the bottom of the Ventersdorp Mine hovered around sixty degrees Celsius.

Mack Hendricks wished there was some trick he hadn't found yet, some way to further cool the mine. The best he'd managed so far was to bring the temp down to twenty-nine degrees Celsius. Lying on a beach and doing nothing, that temperature might be very nice indeed. If you were running heavy machinery, moving rocks, planting charges, engineering support structures, though, it drained you in a matter of hours.

But such was the cost of gold.

The trip back up to the surface was a time of contemplation for some. From the very bottom of Ventersdorp, a ten- or fifteen-minute walk to a cart that would take you to the first cage, which lifted you one mile to the second cage, which would take you back up to the surface. Twenty minutes at least, sometimes thirty, depending on the time of day and how many people were moving back and forth. Contemplation for some, but not for Mack.

He spent every minute of travel talking to one engineer or another, covering details on current excavations, exploratory drills, equipment, supplies, injuries and more. As the man who ran the whole thing and managed five thousand miners and staff, his time was always in demand. Thirty minutes from the top to the bottom or the bottom to the top? Well, those that wanted face time knew that was a good chance to get in front of him.

But this trip up, none of that—his mother was sick.

She was always sick, truth be told. A lifetime of smoking had caught up with her. Mack had been at the bottom of the mine—the *very* bottom, where grinders chewed on rock that had laid untouched for millions of years—when a runner had told him there was a call from Royal Perth Hospital: his mother had been readmitted.

So for once, no one talked to him. The cage rose. The minutes dragged on. Mack coughed out rock dust that always got around whatever mask he used. In a way, he was damaging his own lungs just as bad as his mother had damaged hers. Maybe he'd go out the same way: sucking each breath courtesy of a ventilator, a shitty hospital gown the last thing he would ever wear, a hospital bed the last place he would ever lay.

The cage rattled to a halt. Mack was the first out. An assistant was waiting with a phone. Mack grabbed it, already heading for his office.

"This is Mack Hendricks."

"Are you somewhere we can talk?"

The accent—American. He didn't remember any of his mother's doctors being American.

"Who am I speaking to?"

"Connell Kirkland."

Mack stopped walking.

"I know who you are," he said. "You want to explain to me why I just came up from almost three miles down to hear about my sick mother, and the person on the other end isn't a doctor at all, but rather some wanker who styles himself a *cutthroat* pirate or some such bullshit?"

"*Styles himself,*" Kirkland said. "Such a way with words. I asked you if you were somewhere you could speak. Are you?"

Not exactly a question someone asked if they wanted to talk about the weather. But Mack didn't want to talk about the weather, or anything else this man wanted to discuss.

"Don't know what you're playing at, but I'm not happy," Mack said. "And while I'll probably never see you face to face, you better pray that I don't, because using my sick mum to get me on the phone is—"

"We're breaking the three-mile barrier."

Three miles. Just under five kilometers.

"Bullshit."

"Truth," Connell said. "We're doing it, we're doing it fast, and I want you to run it. Come work for me."

The *balls* on this guy.

"You're crazy," Mack said. "You pull this stunt to get me on the phone because you know if you came after me through normal channels, either I wouldn't talk to you or Euromine wouldn't *let* me talk to you. I can't just walk away—I run the deepest mine in the world."

"Not for long. We're going deeper. I want you because you're the best. But the guy right behind you ain't too bad, either. If you're not in Denver tomorrow, I know Klaus Honneger would love to break your record."

The mention of that name kicked off storm clouds of anger and jealousy. Honneger ran the Mponeng Mine. At four kilometers deep, it had held the world record—until Mack had convinced Euromine to let him add another kilometer to Ventersdorp. But there was no financial benefit to taking Ventersdorp any deeper. If Kirkland was for real, and Honneger went that deep, Honneger would hold the record—possibly for good.

"What's your answer, Mack?"

"Just hold on a fucking second. I'm willing to listen, mate, but slow down! You haven't even given me a chance to think about this."

"I'm in a bit of a hurry here," Kirkland said. "If you're not in my office tomorrow, Honneger will be."

Which could be total bullshit. Kirkland clearly had no trouble lying to get what he wanted. Would Honneger fall for the same line of high-pressure horseshit?

"At least tell me what you're digging for."

"I'll tell you tomorrow. In person."

"So you want me to quit my job and come see you without knowing any details? Are you just screwing with me?"

"Jesus and Mary. Are all Australians such fucking babies?"

Now Mack really wanted to make that trip. Not just for the possible job or the world record, but so he could flatten Kirkland's nose.

"You must instill such loyalty in your employees."

"I do," Kirkland said. "With money. And a permanent percentage. Euromine didn't give you that, but I will."

A permanent percentage? No, Euromine had not given him that. It wasn't like they didn't pay well—by the standards of Mack's youth, he was a rich man—but they could shit-can him anytime they liked. He'd designed the world's deepest mine, yet he didn't *own* anything but the record.

"You don't have to quit," Kirkland said. "Are you telling me it's not worth burning a few sick days just to find out if I'm real?"

Mack didn't know Kirkland, didn't know what kind of a man he was. How had he found out about Mum? How had he known Mack would stop everything he was doing if a call like that came in? How had he known about Mack's compensation?

"You're an arrogant fuck, you know that, Kirkland?"

"Come on, Mack. What I said wasn't arrogant. *Arrogant* would be something like, oh, I don't know—my private jet is sitting at Klerksdorp, right now, waiting for you, because I already knew you were going to say yes before I even bothered to pick up the phone."

Cutthroat. Maybe that was a good nickname after all. Why get into business with a man like this?

Because of the record.

Of all the people in all the world, no one had ever done what Mack had done. He was the best in history. They called him "King of the Deep." That title would last right up until someone went just a few feet deeper.

"I assume someone will be waiting for me at the airport?"

"Your house, actually. See you tomorrow."

Kirkland hung up. Mack looked at the phone as if it had some strange power.

"Just a couple of days," he said to himself.

Call in sick. Not that big a deal, really. A couple of days in the States. What could it hurt? And if it didn't work out, at the very least, he could show Kirkland just what a good Australian lad thought of being called *a fucking baby.*

IN THE MODERN AGE, smart companies paid whatever it took to keep their computer systems secure. But even the smartest of that bunch could forget one small detail—the person you hire to build those walls is the best at finding ways around them.

After ten hours of probing, Kayla finally cracked EarthCore's security programs. It should have only taken her two hours, but Kirkland had hired someone *after* hiring her, trying to make sure she couldn't get in. Paranoid fucker. Was there no trust in this world anymore?

The other firm he'd hired had done a bang-up job. A whole helluva lot better than Euromine's security, at least. EarthCore's firewall was top-notch, enough to keep out the world's best black hats. But Kayla—former darling of the National Security Agency—wasn't some off-the-shelf Doritos-munching fat boy hiding in his mama's basement.

The NSA's mission revolved around protecting U.S. communications or intercepting foreign communications. She'd spent countless hours training in COMSEC, which was military parlance for "communications security." Part of her job entailed making sure U.S. communications were free from the prying ears of foreign intelligence operations. The other end of the NSA mission was just the opposite—SIGINT, or "signals intelligence."

SIGINT involved intercepting messages from foreign governments and exploiting such information as needed for national security purposes. She'd been trained to pick off signals sent by phone, radio, microwave, laser or—especially—computer. The NSA had turned her into a communications expert, an artist in data espionage and a hacker extraordinaire.

The interrogation parts of her job? She'd learned those skills on her own.

Daddy would have been so proud.

Kayla pushed away any thoughts of that bastard. She'd come far in life, didn't need his bullshit haunting her anymore.

She carefully worked her way through EarthCore's confidential files. Plenty of goodies in there, for sure, but she'd already seen most of that info. She was looking for something new. A *billion-dollar find*. All she had was that phrase and a name: Sonny McGuiness. Not what people in the trade would call "actionable intelligence."

Kayla looked. And looked. And looked. The longer she spent on it the angrier she became. A creeping suspicion: she couldn't find any files because there *weren't* any, because Connell hadn't made any.

The new project: as far as EarthCore's computers were concerned, it didn't exist.

There was paranoid, and then there was *paranoid*.

She had to wonder—was that because of her?

The thought stuck for a moment, then she shook it away. Of course not. If he was really onto something that big, the major platinum producers wouldn't like it very much. The South Africans, in particular, seemed to take it almost personally when platinum was discovered in other countries. And the Russians? You did not want Sergei Berehzkov to think his oligarchiness was in such jeopardy that a glut of platinum would gut the per-ounce price. In platinum, at least, supply and demand ruled.

The shit was rare.

Rare enough to make Connell Kirkland follow a different level of secrecy.

"Naughty boy," Kayla said. "You didn't send me my decoder ring."

Acting on a hunch, she switched tactics and slipped into Accounting's travel records. Any company's accounting files often provided a warehouse of knowledge if you knew what to look for, knowledge that few companies spent much effort protecting. After all, who gives a crap if the competition sneaks a peek at your travel logs or expense reports?

Connell's company jet. Recently, just one trip to Johannesburg. Well, that made sense; most of the world's supply of platinum came from South Africa. APA to KXE and back. Was Connell dumb enough to think he could start a new dig on South African soil?

Was he paranoid? Maybe. Was he sexy? Certainly. Was he dumb? Not even close.

Kayla called up all purchase orders Connell had authorized in the past two weeks.

Bingo.

Over $10 million of state-of-the-art mining equipment told her she was on the right track, but that wasn't the real find. What made her smile was the $356,312.35 paid — in advance — to Southern Air Freight of Phoenix.

She exited EarthCore's system, erasing all evidence of her presence, and quickly hacked into Southern Air Freight's system. Air Freight's computers had off-the-shelf protection, which held her up for all of fifteen seconds. She called up the customer account for EarthCore. Southern's big cargo planes were scheduled to make deliveries to Milford Municipal Airport, in Utah. From there, the company force of five freight helicopters was scheduled for a day and a half of work shipping those deliveries to a specific, roadless area. Kayla noted the delivery coordinates: 38 degrees, 22 minutes, 50 seconds north latitude; 113 degrees, 35 minutes, 19 seconds west longitude.

A spot in the southern Wah Wah Mountains.

BOOK TWO

CAMP

11

August 13

RANDY WRIGHT SAT IN THE BACKSEAT, sweating like a pig. Despite the air conditioner's valiant efforts, a slimy film covered him from head to toe. He could almost hear the Land Rover's paint bubbling under the angry sun. They'd reach the camp soon, and they'd have to get out—an act his mind ranked as slightly more fun than having a wisdom tooth extracted.

He looked out the back window. Dust billowed up behind as if the Land Rover were a bi-wing crop duster, swooping in low over the ground to drop clouds of noxious pesticide. The view out the front wasn't much better—an endless vista of brown and yellow, dotted every now and then with scrub or other vegetation so tough it looked as if it would flourish on the surface of the moon.

They'd left Milford Municipal Airport an hour and a half ago.

Thirty-five minutes on State Route 12, then almost an hour on an inhospitable, unnamed road that was nothing more than two tire tracks in the
dirt—and they still had another twenty minutes of driving where there
weren't any roads at all.

Welcome to the middle of nowhere.

He pushed his glasses into place for the hundredth time; the rough,
catapulting ride had the frames constantly sliding down his sweat-slick
nose. He didn't mind the constant bouncing in the seats, but this heat
could suck the fun out of a clown.

The bumpy ride bounced Randy in all directions, but it didn't seem
to bother the Rover's other occupants. The driver, a stocky, serious
brunette named Bertha Lybrand, took the bumps without complaint.
O'Doyle sat in the front passenger seat. He didn't seem to have any
problem with the ride – it would take a wrecking ball to jostle that man.

The camp's helicopter landing pad wasn't ready yet. Maybe tomorrow, the contractors said. Until that was done, the way in and out of the
camp was to drive. Drive, then hike—construction on roads directly to
the site wouldn't even begin until Angus verified that the Dense Mass
was, indeed, platinum ore.

Randy had driven one Land Rover out from camp, Cho Takachi
another. They'd gone to Milford Municipal to pick up the latest
arrivals: three security guards, along with Angus and O'Doyle. The
guards all looked like serious business: Lybrand; a tall, skinny, coal-
black man named Lashon Jenkins and Bill Crook, fair-haired and
so fair-skinned it looked like his skin was burning after just fifteen
minutes in the sun.

Takachi had taken Jenkins and Crook with him. O'Doyle told
Lybrand to drive Randy's Rover, made Angus and Randy ride in back.

Angus, of course, had immediately started whispering, making fun
of the two people in the front seat. Randy was caught between trying
to ignore Angus—something that was just not done—and being part
of a catty conversation about people he barely knew. When Angus had
called Lybrand a "linebacker factory," Randy had raised his eyebrows
and nodded, like an idiot, hoping that mean name would be the last of it.

Fortunately, Lybrand didn't seem to hear. Neither did O'Doyle. Not
that they could hear anything over their own rapid-fire conversation.
They'd both served in the same area overseas, apparently. Randy didn't

want to be part of that discussion, either. The more he could avoid O'Doyle, the better. Rumor was the big man had served in some secret Green Beret infiltration unit. Rumor also had it he'd once killed five men with his bare hands.

Angus tapped Randy on the shoulder, waved him closer, that mean grin on his face again. Randy did *not* want to hear this. He glanced forward: O'Doyle babbling away, Lybrand listening and driving.

Randy leaned in.

"Changed my mind," Angus whispered. "That right there is a gorilla with tits."

Randy's face flushed hot. He leaned away, stared out the side window, not knowing what else to do. Lybrand was *right there*, for crying out loud.

Angus tapped on his shoulder again.

This time, Randy shrugged his shoulder away, continued to stare out at the desolate landscape.

"Oh my God, Mister Politically Correct," Angus said. "Why don't you go blog about your feelings and how fucking offended you are?"

Sometimes it was hard being friends with Angus Kool. He could be kind of a jerk. Randy had gotten over the weirdness of having a boss that was almost ten years his junior. Angus was in charge, had been for a few years, and he was still the youngest guy in the lab. That rubbed some people the wrong way, but Randy didn't mind so much.

Yeah, it was hard, but being friends brought fringe benefits, more than just preferential treatment at work. Angus was a genius. Not the *hey, my friend is really smart* kind of genius, or *my kid is already in the upper third percentile* kind of genius, but rather the textbook definition of the word. Randy had never met anyone like Angus. Watching Angus do what he did—invent things, figure things out, see things no one has seen before—it was shocking and thrilling. Sometimes Randy wondered if he knew exactly how Thomas Watson had felt when he was Alexander Graham Bell's assistant.

And that was just the stuff in the lab. The *real* thrill was spelunking. Together, they had discovered new caves. They had literally been the first human beings to ever set foot in those places. Angus invented tech that gave him the edge over more experienced cavers.

That same tech was about to be put to use in the world's largest cave system. Angus—and Randy with him—would be the first people to see much of it.

Sure, being friends with Angus was hard, but they *were* friends. Randy hadn't known many of those in his thirty-five years. Among the few that he'd had, not one of them would have done something like this, something so *special*. Not one of them would have taken him along on a trip of pure discovery. This wasn't just finding a small branch of the Mammoth Caves that no one had seen—this was on another level altogether.

Angus and Randy would be the *first*. They would know the feelings of Columbus, Magellan, Armstrong, Lief Eriksson. They would know what it was like to *discover* something no one had ever seen, something that essentially *wasn't there* before they found it.

There was power in discovery, a form of immortality. In this case, his immortality would be on a map—part of that subterranean maze would be forever known as "Wright Cavern." That thought brought a smile to Randy's lips.

So was something like that worth putting up with occasionally immature behavior? With the attitude and the bloated ego?

In a word: yes.

"Oh my *God*, Randy," Angus said. "What did you eat?"

Randy opened his mouth to ask what Angus was talking about, but as soon as he did, he smelled it. He *tasted* it.

"Oh, *wow*," Randy said, waving his hand in front of his face to chase away the fart. He glared at Angus, who was pinching his nose and silently laughing.

O'Doyle turned in his seat, glared at Randy.

"Something's wrong with your ass, boy," he said. O'Doyle shook his head in disgust, then faced forward.

Angus shook with laughter.

Randy sighed.

Yeah, friendship with Angus was hard. And some of those times were harder than others.

12

August 15

VERONICA REEVES HELD THE SATELLITE PHONE to her ear, although she was barely aware it was still in her hand. Part of her still tracked the cold, the mountain wind, the warmth of her jacket and the chill in her toes that never went away no matter how many pairs of socks she wore.

He'd said six words. Six words that had scrambled her thoughts.

"Veronica?"

That voice on the phone. Was she holding a phone? Yes, she was. That hand was cold, because it wasn't wearing a glove. Her other hand was wearing a glove. Why was one glove on and one glove off? And that voice...was that her dad? Yes, Sanji Haak, that lovely, lovely man who had raised her like she was his own flesh and blood.

"Veronica, are we still connected?"

"Uh, yeah. Sorry, Dad. I just came out of the caves, maybe I heard you wrong. I...can you say what you said again?"

"What, the part about us being connected?"

"No," Veronica said. "The part before."

"Oh. Of course. I said, *they found a knife in Utah.*"

Yep, the same six words. Words that made no sense.

In the past seven years, the word *knife* had lost its conventional meaning. She now associated it only with the double-crescent weapons she and her team had found scattered in and around Cerro Chaltén—the local name for the peak also known as Mount Fitz Roy. The knives were evidence of a unique culture that had likely dominated the southern tip of the Andes around 5000 BC.

Six *impossible* words.

"Are you sure it's the same? It *can't* be the same. Is it the same?"

Couldn't be. The Cerro Chaltén knives were completely unique in all the world's history—a highly crafted platinum-alloy blade made at a time when humanity still struggled to master flint arrowheads.

"It is," her father said. "Would I have called you if I hadn't verified it myself?"

Sanji's voice: calm, measured, patient. A voice she knew almost as well as her own.

Of course he'd verified it first. As best he could, anyway. He was a scientist, yes, but a *biologist*—this wasn't his area of expertise.

He was wrong. Had to be. Because if he wasn't...well, the significance of a knife that far north was just...well, it was impossible.

"Has to be a fake," she said. "Someone saw the *Nat Geo* article and is trying to screw with me, or the university. You know, 3-D modeling, metal coating, and—"

"Ronni, I am holding it right now."

Ronni. His pet name for her. He'd called her that the first day she'd gone to live with him. He was the only one who called her that.

"I weighed it," he said. "Identical to the ones you've found. Dimensions are also a perfect match. And to make sure I didn't waste my dear girl's time, I had Kilman in Chemistry take a look at it. She said it's a platinum alloy, no question."

Veronica's brain was a broken record spinning only one phrase: *that's impossible.* The world at large knew about the knives she had found but did not know their composition. She'd kept that fact hidden from all but a few trustworthy colleagues.

"Where, exactly, did you find it?"

"In a box on a museum shelf," Sanji said. "It's been there since 1941, apparently. With verified documentation of the check-in date. This is real, and it predates your find by over seventy years."

Her breath felt short. The cold mountain air bit at her face. She needed to get out of the wind, soon.

"There's more," he said. "It was found by a BYU student, in a cave in the Wah Wah Mountains. Right here in Utah."

Her legs sagged. She sat. A sharp rock dug into her butt cheek. She made no effort to move.

"Glyphs," she said. "This student … did he report any glyphs?"

"I don't know. All I know right now is that the knife came to our attention because of a prospector. That's why I called you as soon as I knew it was real—my colleague thinks someone may be preparing to mine the area."

Veronica's blood simultaneously chilled and boiled. *Miners.* She hated that word, hated what those soulless people could do to invaluable archaeological sites, not to mention the irreparable damage they inflicted on the environment. That was why she'd always hidden the fact that her knives were made from platinum; if that had ever become known, miners and treasure seekers would have descended like locusts, torn the mountain apart with explosives, strip mines and leaching compounds, turned the entire area into a wasteland.

If she didn't do something, fast, that's exactly what would happen in Utah.

"I'll be on the next flight out," she said. "I'll call with the details. I love you, Dad."

"I love you, too, Ronni."

She disconnected. Her legs still didn't work. Just a moment sitting here, thinking, but only a moment—being high up in the Andes meant it was an adventure just to reach the nearest airport. A *long* adventure.

A knife.

In Utah.

If it was real, if this wasn't a hoax, prank or a mistake, then that knife—combined with the ones she found—was the archaeological find of the century.

And some money-grubbing mining slime might ruin it all?

We'll see about that, you vampires. We'll just see about that.

13

August 21

KAYLA MEYERS LOVED THE HEAT. It reminded her of home.

She had to hand it to the designers: the EarthCore camp, while not quite finished, was quite the piece of work. From start to finish in less than two weeks, in some seriously inhospitable territory.

They'd expanded a natural plateau notched at the intersection of two tightly packed peaks. Slanting walls of limestone rose up on either side of the camp, and behind it as well, the mountain's main peak rising up to the Northwest. Scrub brush fought for survival on the west-facing slopes, while scraggly pines had slightly more success on the east sides. From the air, Kayla imagined the camp looked like a three-masted ship bobbing amid a frozen tan-green tidal wave.

Several blue sheet metal buildings were already in place, with more under construction. Lab, administrative office, generators, fuel storage ... all the things that would let over a hundred people stay in relative comfort despite being on the side of a sunbaked mountain in the middle of a desert.

Four small Quonset huts housed camp staff: one for the mining crew, one for security, one for male staff and one for female staff. Large canvas tents were pitched over the Quonsets to keep sunlight off the corrugated metal. A larger hut, the size of a small airplane hangar, housed vehicles and large equipment—Jeeps, Land Rovers, the continuous mining machines that dug the horizontal tunnels, the squat diesel trucks that hauled out loose rock. A sixth hut served as the mess hall.

Chain-link fence topped by concertina wire surrounded the camp. Just three entrances in that fence, all sliding chain-link gates; one on the north fence that led a few hundred feet to the helicopter landing pad, a sliding gate on the west side and a matching one on the east. A straight road running between the east-west gates. To the east, the road ran downhill to where construction crews were expanding it so that it would eventually connect with existing roads that ran to State Route 21.

From the west gate, the road ran up the mountain in sharp switch-backs until it ended at the adit entrance. *Adit* was a new word she'd learned during research: a horizontal shaft that ran into the mountain, providing access to the vertical shaft that led down to the ore body. Looked like about a five- to ten-minute walk from the camp up to the adit entrance.

The "three masted" impression came from three tall light poles, which were evenly spaced in a straight east-west line. The middle pole held a speaker, for camp announcements and for a klaxon alarm.

She didn't see much wrong with the camp design. A couple of weak spots: the generator and the big diesel fuel tank for it in the northwest corner, and a pair of auto fuel tanks in the southwest corner. Possible boom-boom hazard. She'd have buried those, not put them above ground. And the armory—the only brick building other than the lab— was in the southeast corner; she would have put that right in the middle, to make it as hard as possible for any attackers to reach it.

The air conditioners peeking from every building in the camp made her want to laugh with contempt. She'd grown up in South Texas; the scorching sun was an old, dear friend. Growing up isolated—and dirt-poor—she'd had few friends.

Her father saw to that. Kayla and her two older sisters all suffered his abuse, his beatings, his touch. Mary and Shelly suffered the most, succumbing to his will, stepping and fetching whenever he walked in the room. They did anything to avoid a beating.

Or, far worse, the loving.

When Kayla turned eight—or maybe nine, she couldn't remember—Cyrus Meyers came for her, too. Their tiny ranch lay in a solitary strand of barely arable farmland.

She could still remember those nights he came home hammered. Slurred words, binge-drunk voice screaming at the top of his lungs as he lurched out of the rust-eaten Dodge long-bed truck, bar smoke clinging to him like stink on roadkill.

"Wake up, girls!" Cyrus would scream as his daughters cowered in terror. "Get your fingers out of the tuna bowl and come give yer daddy some biscuits 'n' gravy!"

He'd stumble into the house. He could barely walk, but somehow he kept just enough balance to make it to Mary's bed. Then Shelly's.

Then Kayla's.

Cyrus didn't like to hear any noise when he visited his daughters. The sisters would choke back cries as tears trickled down their faces onto threadbare pillowcases bought by a mother Kayla had never known.

Sometimes the girls got hurt worse than others. Sometimes the cops came. Sometimes teachers or school administrators asked questions. At all times, the sisters kept their mouths shut. The things their father did to them were horrible, and yet they all knew that if they said anything, he would do far, *far* worse.

Mary and Shelly wordlessly suffered his touch, succumbing to his perverse will. But Kayla was different. She'd always been different, preferring the boys' roughhouse schoolyard games to dolls and tea parties. Watching her sisters had taught her at an early age that girls were weak: boys were tougher.

For the five years that Cyrus molested her, sodomized her, beat her for reasons Kayla could never quite fathom, a quiet rage steadily grew. Fear and guilt dominated her sisters, which seemed to be exactly the emotions Cyrus wanted, but Kayla was made of different stuff.

Cyrus seemed to sense that. He was an abusive drunk, but he wasn't blind—he knew of the rebellion bubbling in Kayla's soul. He tried again and again to break her spirit.

He failed.

Her father followed a pattern: first Mary, then Shelly, then Kayla. For years, Kayla cowered in her bed, furious at herself for being so helpless. He *touched* her. What could she do to stop him? He was so much bigger, so much stronger. He was a grown-up. He was her *father*, and she was expected to obey.

All of that came to an end on a god-awful hot July evening.

Cyrus had come home drunk. He'd shouted as he stumbled into the house, whooped and hollered as he entered Mary's room. A while later, he stumbled to Shelly's room.

That was when Kayla walked to the kitchen, grabbed a butcher knife and brought it back to her bed.

Cyrus came into her room: stinking, staggering, bragging.

Kayla let him sit down on the bed next to her. Then, she buried that rusty knife in his heart.

Thirteen years old. Her first murder. It sure as hell wasn't her last. As their father lay dead on the worn, yellow shag carpeting of Kayla's bedroom, Mary and Shelly didn't know what to do. The older sisters seemed caught between the violent horror of a murdered father and the unfathomable relief and freedom brought on by Kayla's brutal act. They didn't know what to think, so Kayla did their thinking for them. The three sisters spent an hour arranging things. Even then—at thirteen—Kayla possessed an uncanny knack in accounting for every detail.

She had Mary call the police. Of the three of them, Mary was the best actor.

The police came and all three girls gave a convincingly hysterical report of a burglary gone wrong. Kayla knew the cops saw right through her story; the Meyers family didn't have anything worth stealing in the first place.

Even the most stolid, die-hard, live-by-the-law cops didn't pry into the matter. If Cyrus's sickening treatment of his daughters finally got him killed by their hand, well, no one was going to miss him. It wasn't like the town sheriff and his deputies hadn't wished they could do the same thing more than once when they saw the Meyers girls bandaged, bruised and laid out in a bed at County General.

When Cyrus died, Mary inherited the house. She was old enough to become Kayla and Shelly's legal guardian. Kayla lived with the two of them for another five years. Happy time, if happiness is measured in the sheer joy of no one molesting you.

Without the presence of her father, Kayla flourished in school.

When she graduated high school, she joined the marines. There she excelled; her killer instinct was encouraged and honed. Ironically, she never got the chance to kill while in the corps.

Instead, her entry into the service marked the first time anyone had bothered to find out how smart she was. And she was smart indeed, smart enough to excel as an electronic warfare operator. And also—who would have known?—the dirt-poor girl from South Texas who grew up being abused had a knack for languages. An insane knack. In four years, she learned Mandarin, Arabic and Russian.

Kayla blossomed. For the first time in her life, she had support, she had direction—she had a *purpose*.

And she had something else: looks.

Hence the transition from the marines to the NSA, where her combination of drive, brains and beauty put her in human intelligence—HUMINT—and in the Sentry Osprey program. While men from different cultures might kill each other over religion or politics or nationalism, the vast majority of hetero boys have at least one thing in common: a driving interest in pretty girls.

Four years in the marines, two years of concentrated NSA training, and twenty-four-year-old Kayla Meyers became an actual spy for Uncle Sam. She infiltrated tech companies. She developed moles, both in business and in foreign agencies. Sometimes, things got violent. She hurt people. She killed, but only to stay alive.

At least that's what she told her superiors. They believed it.

God, country, career, purpose ... the only thing she didn't have was money.

Infiltrating some of the world's richest companies opened her eyes to just how *much* money was out there. When she found information that people might want, she sold it. Nothing the U.S. government needed, mind you. No secrets. Nothing like that.

Not at first, anyway.

That little habit of selling info wound up costing her everything. In retrospect, she should have stayed away from the Department of Special Threats, a shadow organization that barely existed on paper. The DST looked into weird biotech shit. Kayla's instincts had told her to leave that group alone, but one of her contacts wanted as much info as he could get on them, and he was willing to pay for it—Magnus Paglione and his company, Genada, had no shortage of cash.

So much money for a few bits of harmless information.

Kayla had assumed she was smarter than everyone around her. Smarter than the NSA, in fact. She'd been wrong.

Who caught her? She still didn't know. Maybe that DST colonel, Paul Fischer. All she knew was André Vogel had called her into his office, told her she "wasn't NSA material" and had armed guards escort her not just out of the office, but back to her home, where they took every piece of equipment the agency had given her. Even the stuff she'd built herself.

Discarded.

That was how she'd felt. She'd wanted more money, sure, but really, it had all been about God & Country. Vogel had taken that away from her, left her hollow.

Good thing she had a certain set of skills that helped her make a living.

That certain set of skills had led her here, to a small, camouflaged pit high up the side of a mountain, overlooking the EarthCore camp. Mister Paranoid—aka Connell Kirkland—was coming soon. When he arrived, it was only a matter of time before Kayla finally discovered what this was all about.

Whatever it was, someone would pay her to know that information. Pay her a *lot.*

Far off in the distance, over the sound of the camp generator, over the sound of construction crews building roads, she heard the *thump-thump-thump* of approaching rotor blades.

"Right on time, sugar," she said.

She knew Kirkland's ways. He had no idea, but right from the first time he'd hired her she had watched him, studied him. In another world, maybe she and Kirkland could have been a thing. Maybe, but he was too much of a momma's boy for her taste. Not his birth momma—she had died when Kirkland had been six years old—but the woman that had eventually filled that role for him: Barbara Yakely.

Kirkland would swoop into the camp like a field general. He'd boss people around. And as soon as that was done, he'd call Barbara Yakely and report in like a little boy coming home from his first day at school.

Kayla was ready for him.

She raised her binoculars and looked to the East.

CONNELL CAME IN by helicopter.

He hadn't been on-site at a dig in years. Since Cori's death, he'd run things from his office in Denver. But this one was too damn big to leave to chance. He'd hired the best in Mack Hendricks. Mack could run things as he saw fit, but Connell had to be there, watching, monitoring, ready to solve any problem that might jeopardize this once-in-a-lifetime find.

So odd: when he'd been with Cori, he'd spent so much time away from home, away from *her*, because his career had been so important. Since her death? He barely left home at all.

Time wasted then, time wasted now.

Mack Hendricks waited at the edge of the landing pad. He fit every American's stereotype of Australian men—blond, square jaw, solid shoulders, the skin around his eyes wrinkled from constant laughter and too much time in the sun. Mack smiled freely and looked like he could quickly acclimate himself to any social situation, whether that situation called for black-tie or biker jackets.

In their first meeting a few days earlier, Connell thought Mack was going to take a swing at him. Fortunately, Connell had Herbert Darker's metallurgy analysis ready, as well as Angus's mass-spec results and a map of the Dense Mass. That one-two-three punch had defused Mack's anger, had him signing a contract a few minutes later.

Connell stepped off the chopper and into the desert's blowtorch heat. The helicopter's still-spinning rotors kicked up clouds of dust. He raised his briefcase over his head to block the sun.

"G'day, Mister Kirkland," Mack said, reaching into the helicopter to grab the large duffel bag that held Connell's clothes for the next month. "How was the flight in?"

Connell spat, trying to clear the dust from his mouth.

"I made it, that's how it was. How far have you got?"

Mack's smile faltered slightly.

"You always so good with the pleasantries, mate?"

"Maybe I'll be more pleasant if you get me out of this fucking heat."

The smile brightened again. "Doubt that, but let's give it a try. Angus has the core sample results. Said the info was for your eyes only. Truth be told, your scientist is a bit of a shit."

No surprise there.

Mack led them away from the landing pad and into the camp proper.

"We're a hair over thirty-six hundred feet in our first three days of actual digging," he said. "Now that we've got Angus's laser drill properly dialed in, we're breaking every world record there is for digging speed. It's amazing to see, Mister Kirkland—that thing is *vaporizing* solid rock. With three shifts running around the clock, we're capable of more than two thousand feet a day."

"How far to the ore body?"

"We're eighty-four hundred feet from what Angus says should be the first large tunnel," Mack said. "That tunnel runs near a huge cavern. On the far side of that cavern is another tunnel that leads all the way to the ore body. The cavern is about fifty-two hundred vertical feet from the planned shaft bottom, but we'll be following horizontal tunnels, so it's more like ten miles of rough walking and some crawling. I figure with all the switchbacks in the caverns it's at least a day's hike from the vertical shaft bottom to the Dense Mass. We'll be under for quite a while."

A day there and a day back. Two days underground just to *see* the Dense Mass. The time estimate gave Connell a true appreciation for the tunnel complex's massive breadth.

Sweaty people bustled through the sandy camp. The air rang with the pulsating sounds of the large diesel generator that provided electricity. As he walked, Connell recognized the buildings he'd signed off on: the Quonset huts, the administration trailer that sat between the separator shed and the lab, the big hangar for the vehicles.

And, finally, the lab. Cinder block instead of corrugated metal. Sun blocked by a real roof instead of canvas. Aside from the laser drill, this was the camp's most important building.

The lab's interior seemed as icy cold as the desert was scalding hot. The sudden temperature change made his head hurt almost instantly.

The lab was a tiny maze of expensive, humming equipment. Angus's wild red-haired head popped up from underneath a machine. A smile broke over his small face. He hustled over to greet Connell.

"Mister Kirkland! I'm glad you made it out safe."

Ah, putting on the happy face already? Of course Angus was happy— he probably thought he'd be spelunking any day now, whether he had permission or not. O'Doyle had already been instructed to keep a close eye on the man. Connell wasn't about to let *anyone* go near the caves until safety had been assured.

"You seem in good spirits, Doctor Kool," Connell said, shaking the hand that was offered.

"As good as can be expected, considering." Angus looked off sharply. "Oh, sorry, one second." He extended his pinkie and thumb, held them to his mouth and ear like a fake phone. "Hello? Hello? What's that, Mom? You can't call your lovely, intelligent and oh-so-caring son because some fucking one-eared ogre took away my cell phone? Yes, that does seem like a weird thing for a successful company to do, I agree. You—"

"Knock it off," Connell snapped. "I think you can make it a few weeks without your phone."

"Sure, Mom. Love you, too. Buh-bye."

Angus made an exaggerated, slow, downward arc with his arm. His *hanging up the phone* pantomime was meant to be annoying, and it worked.

"Good God, mate," Mack said to Angus. "Could you be any more of a poofter? I gave up my cell and you don't hear me whining all fucking day about it."

Angus put his hands on his hips. "Oh, Mack…you're just so *butch*, you big galoot."

Connell found himself wishing it was legal to beat employees with a belt.

"No phones, no exceptions," he said. "We're not going to have someone goof up and accidentally give this location to the competition."

Angus pointed at Connell's left pant pocket.

"No exceptions, except for you, right, boss man?"

Connell nodded. "That's right. Because I'm special. Enough with the theatrics. I was told you've got core sample results back?"

The redhead's face lit up, instantly switching gears from conceited little snot to unabashed lover of discovery.

"It's amazing," Angus said. "It's even better than what we expected."

He reached into his pocket and produced a sealed foil envelope. It resembled a small condom wrapper. He opened it and pulled out a thin dot of plastic the size of a watch battery.

"If you could turn around, Mister Kirkland, I need to attach this."

"What is it?"

"It's a homing device I invented. I call it the *Marco/Polo System*. The tunnels are so extensive that if someone gets separated, we might not find them. It's that big. I programmed this micro transceiver with your name. The finder unit—I call it a *Marco*—sends out a signal. Your unit receives the signal and responds with a message containing your name. This dot of plastic is the *Polo*. That way if you're lost or get injured or knocked out, search parties can locate you. The Marco unit detects body temperature, pulse and alpha waves along with distance and altitude."

"What's the range on it?"

"In open air it's a couple of miles." Angus pressed the dot against the base of Connell's skull. "Underground, depends on how much rock comes between you and the Marco unit."

"Safety first," Mack said. "Everyone in the camp has a Polo. They've all been told that if they get separated or lost, they need to just stay where they are. As long as they don't keep wandering, we'll be able to find them fast."

Angus removed his hand. Connell turned his head from side to side but felt nothing.

"Did it fall off?"

"Nope, it's still there," Angus said. "It's attached with artificial skin that breathes just like the real thing. It will stay on until it's removed. Now, take a look at this."

He turned to a monitor that showed a horizontal line with intermittent vertical spikes.

"This whole line is a breakdown of the core sample's mass spec results. We took periodic samples every hundred feet down to sixteen thousand. That distance is, by the way, deeper than anyone has ever drilled in one shot, which gives me yet another world record. No big deal, right?"

Connell nodded. "I'll be sure to call the Guinness people in the morning. Because world records matter so fucking much."

Mack grunted. "Speak for yourself, mate."

"Don't mind Connell, Mack," Angus said. "Those that can't set records rarely understand the drive of those that can."

Connell crossed his arms. "And those of us that sign payroll checks would love to hear about some *actual goddamned results.*"

"Oh, sure," Angus said. "Let me get that for you."

A mass-spec result came up on a display. A series of peaks, under which were labels like $KFe3(SO4)2(OH)6$ and $CUs(AsO4)(OH)$. The only compound Connell recognized, $CaCO3$—limestone—sat under the biggest peak. The second-highest peak read only Pt, and the third read $Pt60Ir12(?)$.

"The whole mountain is basically Cretaceous Period limestone and limestone compounds," Angus said. "The second spike is a control sample of pure platinum, highly refined. This third spike—" Angus paused, smiled and looked directly at Connell "—this third spike is a flake of what we found at 16,340 feet, the absolute bottom range of the drill sample."

Connell's stomach fluttered.

"Doctor Kool, are you telling me that your core sample came back with *solid* platinum?"

Angus shrugged and nodded at the same time. "Platinum-iridium, actually, but sure."

It wasn't a knockout punch, not yet, but the fighter had taken a hard right hook and was on his way down to the canvas.

"And where does this particular sample match up with your data on the Dense Mass inside the mountain?"

Angus brought up the now-familiar schematic of the green mass and surrounding yellow tunnels. A dozen vertical red lines appeared surrounding the green.

"We ran drilling and bulk sampling where you see all of the red lines," he said. "Eleven of the samples turned up nothing but worthless rock. Not a trace of platinum. Only one drill sample gave us the results I just showed you. This one."

Another red line appeared, glowing bright orange where it intersected with the green mass.

The three men stared at the display for a moment. Just stared, as if talking about what they all saw plain as day might make the numbers change, might twist reality and let this slip away. *You jinxed yourselves, boys, and now it's all gone.* Connell couldn't avoid that feeling, even though it felt just as stupid as sitting in a car wishing to travel back in time.

"It's real," Angus said, finally breaking the silence. He sounded like a pilgrim seeing some rumored holy relic for the first time. "It isn't *ore,* Mister Kirkland. I'm convinced the entire Dense Mass is of the same composition as our drill sample. We are standing above a four-mile-long, half-mile-wide chunk of *solid platinum.*"

More silence. It was real, all right, at least as real as it could be until they got down there and brought some back up.

Connell pointed to the Pt60Ir12(?) symbol on the display.

"What's with the question mark?"

"Nothing to worry about," Angus said with a dismissive wave of his hand. "The platinum-iridium compound appears to be something uncalibrated on the SIMS."

"English, please," Connell said.

"*Secondary Ion Mass Spectrometry,*" Angus answered. "We bombard the target material with positively charged ions. The bombardment transfers that positive charge to the target material, which in this case is the core sample. That positive charge makes an atom break free, causing fragmentation. Because fragmentation patterns are distinct and reproducible, we can precisely identify the trace elements of any solid material."

"If it's so precise," Connell said, "then why the question mark?"

"Because the platinum-iridium alloy is something nobody has ever seen before. In effect, the computer is taking an educated guess. The ion bombardment produces platinum and iridium atoms, and the computer is guessing how those elements are combined. It's just an unusual compound, that's all."

"But there's nothing wrong with it," Connell said. "We can process it?"

Angus smiled and shook his head, like he was enamored with a child's stupid-but-cute comment.

"Can we melt it down and separate the platinum from the iridium? Yes, Mister Kirkland, I'm sure someone, *somewhere,* has learned how to melt metal."

Another jibe, but Connell didn't care. His gaze remained fixed on the display. Platinum never occurred naturally in a large solid mass, and yet there it was. A find so big that EarthCore could dictate supply for at least the next fifty years, if not the next century.

It was worth trillions.

"I want two more drill samples. Make sure they intersect different areas of the Dense Mass so we confirm you didn't hit a sweet spot or something."

Angus shook his head. "No can do. Our drill bit was destroyed when we tried to core deeper into the Dense Mass."

Connell frowned. "I thought that diamond bit could slice through anything."

"It can," Angus said. "But this platinum-iridium alloy is unusually hard, perhaps almost as hard as the diamond itself. The alloy ground the diamond bit down to nothing. There may be some serious commercial applications for this compound. It's very unusual. I wouldn't worry about it—we've gotten plenty of data and the shaft is already under way."

A multimillion-dollar piece of equipment destroyed, and Angus didn't bat an eye. Of course he didn't—people like Angus Kool didn't concern themselves with the cost of their toys, not when someone else footed the bill. And, Connell had to admit, losing the drill didn't make any difference. The tunnels meant Mack's people would be at the Dense Mass in a few days. Why spend money on another core sample when people were going to see it firsthand?

"Excellent work, Doctor Kool," Connell said. "Gentlemen, I'll let you get back to work. I'll be in the admin trailer if you need me."

IT WAS A QUICK WALK from the lab to the admin trailer, but even three minutes outside was enough to make Connell start sweating again.

He walked into the administration shed and wearily shut the door behind him. Even that short time in the heat had drained his body. He needed a drink and a nap. He went to the desk that would be his home for at least the next two weeks. He pulled a framed picture from his briefcase.

A picture of Cori.

He stared down at his wife's smiling face, feeling the familiar hurt worm its way through his guts. He set the picture on his desk so her image could watch everything he did.

Also from his briefcase, he pulled out the blocky satellite phone. The matching set had cost a fortune. Barbara Yakely had the other one back in Denver. Barbara's was the only phone that could decipher the scrambled signal sent out by Connell's, and vice versa. State-of-the-art stuff, secure, encrypted—impossible to crack.

If Kayla Meyers thought she had a monopoly on his communication needs, she had another think coming.

He punched the "connect" button; Barbara answered almost immediately.

"HELLO, SWEETIE," Barbara said. "So happy to hear from you."

And she was. She knew saying things like that made her sound like a grandma, but she didn't care. She was the boss: anyone who didn't like how she talked could kiss her fat ass. And besides—she *was* old enough to be a grandmother.

"Hi, Barb," Connell said. "Can you hear me okay?"

"A little scratchy, but not bad."

"So it sounds like I smoke ten cigars a day, then?"

She glanced at the cigar in her hand. Wait a minute ... was that a dig on her?

"Connell, did you just make a joke?"

"Tried to," he said. "How'd I do?"

A joke. He hadn't cracked a joke in ... in she didn't know how long. Things had to be going well.

"Don't quit your day job," she said. "But seriously, folks, speaking of day jobs ..."

His throat made a noise, as if he started to talk, then stopped before the words could come out.

"Out with it, honey," she said.

"All right. It's ... it's bigger than we thought."

Oh, how she hoped that was accurate. He'd already invested heavily in this dig. So much so that if it didn't pan out, she'd wind up a permanent resident of a state she didn't even want to visit: the state of *retired*.

"You have core samples?"

"Yes, and they're better than we estimated."

His voice sounded thin through the handset, but not enough to dilute his excitement.

"Connell, what kind of potential are we talking, here?"

"I'd rather not discuss it over this line."

She held the bulky phone away from her ear, glanced at it. He'd paid a fortune for these things, and he didn't trust them? How big was the find if it made him this cautious?

"Be careful," she said. "And can you at least *try* to keep costs down? These purchase orders are giving me hemorrhoids."

"I hear cigar smoke causes those."

"Only if you shove them up your ass," Barb said. "Which I suggest you do."

"Now who's the comedian?"

"The difference between you and me, honey, is that my one-liners are actually *funny*. Be careful, okay?"

"Always, Barb. I'll be in touch."

He disconnected. She set the strange phone down next to her picture of Rocky.

"I mean it, Connell," she said. "Be careful."

Barb had already lost one son, the biological one. If she lost Connell, too?

That would be more than one mother could bear.

CONNELL KIRKLAND WAS starting to piss her off.

Kayla thought it was cute that he'd bought a set of banded/encrypted phones. It had taken her all of thirty seconds to intercept those signals and crack them.

Hauling the compact but heavy JM-251 Harris SIGINT manpack from her hidden Jeep Wrangler to her little hideaway had been a grade A bitch, but with it she could pick off any communications coming in or going out of the camp—even from Connell's "secure" little toys.

It wasn't that he'd bought gear from someone other than her that made her mad. What pissed her off was that—even with his fancy gear—the paranoid fucker still hadn't given up any real actionable intelligence.

I'd rather not discuss it over this line.

Asshole.

He was making more work for her. A lot more work. Unless he was going to suddenly connect the lab's isolated computer systems to the Internet, if she wanted real intel, she was going to have to physically enter the camp.

Thanks to the presence of one Patrick O'Doyle, that was a rather unappealing option. How could she have known connecting that man with Connell would come back to haunt her?

A little more than a year ago, Connell had come to her asking for a first-class security man, someone with military experience, the real deal. She'd hacked into Defense Department black files and discovered O'Doyle. He was beyond special ops. He was a fucking *assassin*, the kind of guy you dropped into enemy territory and let take out whatever asset needed taking out. Most of what he'd done had been so classified—or so *illegal*, depending on how you looked at it—that there weren't even computer records for those ops.

O'Doyle had recently been retired from service. Maybe his scarred-up face had become too well-known, or maybe he'd committed the ultimate sin of getting "too old." At any rate, he'd become a free agent. She had given his info to Connell, who had hired the man after a single interview.

So Kayla had played matchmaker, and now O'Doyle's skills and smarts were going to make life hard for her.

The rest of the EarthCore security staff wasn't up to his caliber, but they weren't pushovers, either. Kayla had looked up their records. All ex-military. O'Doyle had combed through EarthCore's personnel and found a dozen people with combat experience.

Awesome. Fun for the whole family.

And he'd armed them well. They carried Glock 21s—.45 caliber with thirteen-round magazines. And a dozen Mark 14 EBRs. The "Enhanced Battle Rifle" had an eighteen-inch barrel, fired 7.26 x 51 millimeter NATO rounds. Accurate at five hundred meters, up to eight hundred with the right optics. Twenty-round mag. Selective fire with full auto option. A U.S. Military weapon, which meant Patrick O'Doyle still had plenty of contacts in the service.

Experienced guards. And well-armed. She'd have to be careful.

Or, maybe she should just pull up stakes and get the fuck out of there? There wasn't a payday in getting shot.

She *might* leave … but not yet.

No, she would continue to watch, to gather information. Document the guards' patterns, look for a way in. People—even well-paid, well-trained people—get complacent. The concertina wire and fence she could handle, as long as someone wasn't paying attention.

EarthCore was betting the house on this dig. Whatever was down there, it had to be worth that gamble.

Kayla wasn't worried about someone finding her perch. Unless O'Doyle started sending patrols into the surrounding mountains, no one would see her, and even then they could walk within three or four feet of her hiding spot and pass right by without noticing a thing. She'd been trained for this. She'd done this before.

She would wait. She would watch.

What could a few more days hurt?

FOR THE FIRST TIME since arriving, Randy Wright found himself alone in the lab with Angus Kool.

The rest of the staff had knocked off for the night. Some headed to their bunks, some to the mess hall to join the impromptu party that seemed to spring up every night. Mack didn't let anyone get so drunk they would miss work the next day, but he was too smart to ask everyone to be teetotalers. Lots of music, plenty of beer, plenty of wine, plenty of food.

Randy had partaken a couple of times. The people were nice, mostly. He didn't really know how to talk to the miners. Or the security guards, or the other staffers that didn't work in the science lab. He could talk to Angus, but Angus worked all day and most of the evening as well. As far as Randy could tell, Angus was getting by on three hours of sleep a night. Maybe less. Yet he didn't seem slightly the worse for wear.

Angus walked to the lab door, peered out the small window. He turned around, all smiles. He rubbed his hands together.

"Talk to me, Dirty Randy."

Angus loved using that nickname. Randy was as far from *dirty* as a guy could get, probably, but he liked it.

"We're all set," Randy said. "Everything is ready. Custom webbing and climbing harness rigs are wrapped in plastic, buried fifty meters past the north fence."

Angus rubbed his hands even faster.

"What's the total weight?"

"Just over ten pounds," Randy said.

"That's good. And we got it all? Motion detectors?"

Randy nodded.

"The floodlights? Oxygen? First aid?"

Randy nodded.

"Titanium cams, the graphite-strand rope? *Everything* came in?"

Randy nodded.

Angus's face lit up in a maniac smile of bright teeth and wide eyes. He grabbed Randy's shoulders and *shook*.

"You are a *pimp*, Dirty Randy. A *pimp*."

Randy laughed along with his friend. He did feel a bit like a pimp. Well, *maybe*, because he wasn't sure how pimps actually felt, but if they felt like this, being a pimp had to be cool.

As soon as Angus started processing the data Randy had collected, he'd known Connell would sequester the lab staff. He'd started ordering gear and having it shipped out to Randy in Milford. Angus had false names, false accounts, all kinds of cool stuff. Some of the gear was off-the-shelf, but most were items Angus had invented himself. All Randy had to do was pick up the shipments and put the gear together. Things got harder when Mack arrived, but before the fence went up Randy had plenty of opportunities to slip away and bury the prepared equipment.

"I even preassembled the thumpers," Randy said. "Extra gear is stashed inside the second entrance."

The entrance Angus had conveniently left off the map he'd shown Kirkland and everyone else. Would that knowledge have saved EarthCore about, oh, say, three or four million dollars? Kind of. Mack could have used the entrance to get into the cave system without drilling at all, but a deep vertical shaft and a powerful elevator were still required to bring ore to the surface. Hiding the tunnel entrance just delayed Kirkland reaching his goal by a few days. No big deal, Angus had said.

Those few days would give Angus and Randy the opportunity to use the second entrance, to enter the tunnels long before anyone else.

In the game of exploration, the only thing that mattered was being *first*.

"You did great, buddy," Angus said. "Really great."

Randy felt a flush of pride. He couldn't hide his smile.

"Thanks, but there's two parts you haven't told me yet. There's no KoolSuits. You couldn't get the fabricators to make them in time?"

"They wouldn't make them at all," Angus said. "When Kirkland paid for EarthCore's suits, he told them if he found out they made more than he ordered, he'd run them into the ground. When I called, they wouldn't play ball. They agreed to not tell him I called, though, so there's that."

"But without suits, we can't go into the deep tunnels," Randy said. "What's the point of all the other stuff if we can't go?"

Angus smiled wide. "Dirty Randy, my friend, don't you worry your pretty little head about it. I have the suits covered. I'm guessing the other part you want to know is how we get out of camp?"

Randy nodded. "I got the stuff out before they built the fence. O'Doyle has guards at the gates twenty-four hours a day. How are we going to get out without being noticed?"

"I'll handle that," Angus said. "I have a whoop-ass plan. Trust me."

Randy did trust him. His friend would find a way to get them out of the camp and into the caves. And when they did, they would explore like no one in history.

14

AFTER SO MANY MONTHS in the frigid mountain air, Veronica Reeves reveled in Utah's heat. No down jacket. No heavy boots. Her toes and fingers weren't cold. She wore a hat, sure, but one made of straw — not wool.

Sanji's Rav4 rumbled along, trailed by a cloud of dust. Veronica stretched out in the passenger seat, happy to let him drive. By American standards, this road was horrible. By the standards of remote Southern Argentina, however, it might as well have been a four-lane highway, blacktop as flat as glass.

She'd grown up with Sanji in Provo, only about four hours sortwest of here. Too long since she'd been in Utah. Too long since she'd seen her father.

He understood, of course. Any scientist would. When you catch a tiger by the tail and your work draws major attention, you don't let go. She'd spent the last three years in the Andes, studying the strange culture of Cerro Chaltén. That effort didn't leave time for things like family. Or dating, for that matter.

All work and no play makes Veronica a dull girl.

The wind pulled at her ponytail. Strands of thin blond hair tickled her face and neck. Even in perfect conditions, she couldn't get it all to stay put. In a car with the windows open? Forget about it.

She enjoyed the drive, the heat, being back in Utah, being around her dad for the first time in years, but as great as those things were, they took a backseat to where this drive would end: at the EarthCore mining site.

When Veronica had landed in Salt Lake City, Sanji had been waiting for her, greeted her with a big, crushing hug—a hug that made everything right, a hug that said *I'm always here for you.* The first time she'd felt that hug, that unspoken promise of infinite support, had been at the age of five when her parents died.

From the airport straight to BYU. A meeting with Hector Rodriguez. He had shown her the knife. Yes, it was real. No question. A call to the state mining board. Her celebrity as an archaeologist getting her info that might have been denied to most—the name of the mining permit holder, the location of that company's site.

Veronica glanced at her adoptive father, who grinned back before returning his eyes to the crappy road. He'd gained weight in the three years since she'd last seen him. A *lot* of weight. Less hair than before, and what remained had gone mostly gray. Sure, she video-chatted with him once every other week or so, was aware he was getting older, but in person the changes seemed dramatic.

"Pops, you been working out?"

Sanji laughed, that bright, belly-born sound that made his eyes crinkle.

"Still the same as ever, Ronni? You always lead with tact. Then if you don't hear what you want, you hit me over the head with a verbal hammer. Let's save some time—no, I haven't been working out, which you can plainly see."

"Why not? You're not getting any younger, you know."

He shrugged. "The same as always—work."

"Know where you can't do work? A fucking coffin."

"And it's hammer-time," he said, smiling wide. "Still the same as you were when you were little. Of course, back then you didn't have such a filthy mouth. How interesting you grew up to have a vocabulary like your father's."

By that, Sanji meant her birth father. Veronica had only been five when the plane crash took her mom and dad. No aunts, no uncles, no grandparents. Like her, both of her parents had been only children. One accident, and suddenly she'd had no one.

She did, however, have Sanji.

Her father, also a biologist, had worked closely with Sanji at BYU. As far back as Veronica could remember, Sanji had been a part of the family in all but name. Her parents' will listed him as her legal guardian, a responsibility he honored. It was a debt of friendship he treasured more than his own life. She often wished she could have known her parents, known what kind of people they were to instill that level of loyalty in their friends.

Sanji proved as good a father as any little girl could ask for. With no family of his own, he doted on her. She grew up deeply loved and cared for, encouraged in everything she did, every dream she chased. One of those dreams became her driving passion, then her career, then her entire life.

When she was eight years old, she saw a documentary on the ancient Mayan city of Tikal and had been mesmerized by the tall towers, the ziggurats, a jungle that had swallowed the city up a thousand years earlier. She'd begged Sanji to go. He'd been surprised, but as a man of science, he'd taken the opportunity to show his daughter one of the world's true wonders. When Veronica had experience that place for herself, it was over—she knew what she wanted to do.

They took many more trips together. All over the world, Veronica saw the greatest places of many lost civilizations: Sukhothai, Hatra, Persepolis, Angkor Wat... so many more. While other kids spent school vacations worrying about clothes or jobs or romance, she planned trips on Sanji's limited budget.

Undergrad at BYU, of course. More travel, more study. The ruins of Aztecs and Mayans, Olmecs, the Anasazi. A few published papers. She could have chosen any graduate school she wanted, including

BYU, but the time had come for her to go out on her own. She chose the University of Michigan, leaving home for the first time in her life.

Sanji had cried when he sent her off. Far more tears came, though, when she left for Argentina, to chase reports of a strange knife tip found embedded in an ancient femur.

There was confusion about the find—the few artifacts found among the human remains seemed to indicate a person that had lived around 2000 BC, yet the metal embedded in the bone appeared to be steel. Experts pooh-poohed the report. Someone had used a modern weapon to try to dig up remains, perhaps. It certainly wasn't three thousand years old. Steel? In South America, when the Middle East was just beginning to develop bronze? Ridiculous. Not worth anyone's time.

Except, of course, for an ambitious graduate student seeking something that would set her apart.

Veronica acquired the bone. American dollars went a long way in the remote southern Andes, and the man who had found the bone was as remote as remote got. She was the first to have the bone carbon-dated, which validated the artifact-based estimate—in the ballpark of three thousand years old.

She had the tiny bit of metal analyzed. Not steel at all, but rather a hard alloy of platinum.

She bought the man's land. She started digging. What she found shocked her. Evidence of an ancient massacre. Men, women and children alike butchered, chopped to pieces. Buried along with their belongings—clothes, tools, pottery, even food—as if the attackers despised every last trace of their victims.

Veronica knew she was onto something. She spent the next two years searching the surrounding area, looking for signs of civilization, anything that might point to a reason for that massacre. She got to know the locals, became part of the dispersed community. It was that community that eventually led her up the slopes of Cerro Chaltén, to a small cave filled with ancient, chopped-up bones, bones that she carbon-dated to around 2,500 years old.

She explored that cave, that mountain, found another cave, one that entered into a subterranean complex. Some of the tunnels were natural, but most were man-made, chipped out of solid rock. Crude drawings and glyphs on those tunnel walls, forever protected from the elements, forever preserved. And far back in one of those tunnels, she found it—a double-crescent knife.

It all combined as evidence of a culture at least three thousand years old, a culture with metalworking skill vastly ahead of its time. In an era when basic agriculture and herding were still relatively new concepts, the Chaltélians made weapons superior to anything on the planet, and that would remain superior for at least the next two millennia.

The caves turned out to be outlying branches of a massive subterranean complex that sprawled out for miles, both outward and downward. The complex ran deep. So deep, in fact, that temperatures in the lower regions made exploring nearly impossible. She'd been treated for heatstroke twice so far. Much of the complex had yet to be traversed.

She wrote her first paper. Shortly afterward came the article in *National Geographic*. Everything changed. She applied for grants, got them easily. She hired staff. They studied and explored.

Veronica focused on the glyph language. Many of the symbols were recognizable: stylized versions of the sun, insects, people, various animals. One unique factor set the Cerro Chaltén language apart—the use of color. A full spectrum, with subtle shades and hues. She hadn't cracked the language, but she knew color was as important to the Chaltélian written word as punctuation was to English.

Without some equivalent of a Rosetta Stone, however, she had little hope of understanding what she'd found. There was nothing like it in the area, nor anywhere in the world.

The one thing she had nailed was their numerical system. Unlike modern base-10 counting systems, the Chaltélians used base-12. The modern term for that was the "Dozenal System." It was supposedly superior in several ways to base-10, although she hadn't spent much time learning why. Primitive cultures sometimes picked weird multiples— the Mayans sometimes used base-20, and the Babylonians got wild with base-60. The Chaltélians used base-12: just one more "weird factor" that Veronica couldn't explain.

Knowing their numbers had given her some insight to their calendar system as well. She'd identified a "zero year," the point from which their history seemed to begin. Although she didn't know where the zero year fell upon the modern historical record, it helped her make estimates about the culture's duration—she didn't know *when* it existed, exactly, but she had guesses for *how long* it had.

It had lasted for thousands of years, possibly longer than any human culture in history.

But at some point, the Chaltélian culture had simply died out. She didn't know why, or when. Other than the glyphs and a few knives, the caves held no artifacts—no bodies, no clothes, no pottery, nothing that could be dated.

And now, that mysterious culture had turned up seven thousand miles away. The knife McGuiness had rediscovered left zero doubt: the Utah culture was directly related to that of Cerro Chaltén. Even if the weapon had traveled that far because of a trade route, it was a monumental discovery, but Veronica felt in her soul it was more than that. Much more.

The Rav4 lurched, bounced upward by an unexpected pothole.

"Sorry," Sanji said. "Are you all right?"

Veronica laughed. "You must think I'm fragile, Dad."

"Ronni, I stopped thinking you were *fragile* when you were ten and hiked to the top of Machu Picchu. Doesn't mean I don't worry about you."

She reached out, squeezed his shoulder.

His forehead furrowed, the way it did when he had something difficult to say.

"What is it?"

He glanced at her, surprised.

"Am I that obvious?"

"You always have been. Tell me what's on your mind."

He slowed the vehicle, took another pothole with far more care, then sped up again.

"I'm wondering if you've given any thought to the distance between the finds," he said. "There wasn't any material on the Utah knife for carbon dating, but if it's from the same time period as the Cerro Chaltén knives…"

His voice trailed off.

"Yeah," Veronica said. "I've thought about the size."

She hadn't been able to *stop* thinking about that. The knives were nearly identical, clear evidence of a common culture. If they were from the *same* culture, though, at the same period in history, it meant the possible existence of an empire that stretched from the tip of Tierra del Fuego into what was now the southern United States—an area that dwarfed the amount of land controlled during the height of the Roman Empire.

"I think we're close to the mining site," Sanji said. He pointed to a dust cloud up ahead. "Construction machines, looks like they're making a new road."

"Can you cut in behind them? Head up to the camp?"

Sanji nodded. "Let's find out. Hold on, this will get bumpy."

CONNELL SAT AT HIS DESK in the air-conditioned administration trailer. Mack sat opposite him, finishing up the day's progress report.

"Let me get this straight," Connell said. "You've done fifty-eight hundred feet in four days, and now you're telling me the last sixty-two hundred feet will take a week, maybe more? Bullshit, Mack. Unacceptable."

Mack wore blue jeans and a white shirt, although both were closer to tan gray thanks to the dust that coated him from head to toe.

"The men are working overtime as it is," he said. "If they get careless, we'll have accidents. I don't have accidents at my sites."

"It's not *your* site, it's *mine*. A week is unacceptable. I want it done in three days. This operation is over budget. We need to know what's down there."

Mack stood, leaned his fists on the desk.

"You keep pushing this hard, and somebody is going to get hurt. This is dangerous work."

"I know that, you know that, and so do they," Connell said, gesturing in the direction of the mine. "The crew understands it's called *hazard pay* for a reason. I want that tunnel reached in three days. Make them work harder."

Mack stood up straight. Cuts, scrapes and scars covered his balled fists.

"When you first called me, you asked if I knew who you were. I did, but by reputation only. People call you *cutthroat*. Now that I know you face-to-face, I think *heartless prick* might be better."

He stormed out of the office, slamming the door hard enough to shake the thin trailer.

Connell sat in silence, feeling the weight of Mack's words. Maybe he was pushing too hard.

Maybe.

Connell rubbed his eyes. He managed only about three hours of sleep a night. He slept on a cot in his trailer, away from the barracks, away from everyone else in the camp. He even ate his meals here, separate from the mess-tent laughter. When he did sleep, sometimes he dreamed about Cori. Sometimes he didn't. Either way, good rest was hard to come by.

A walkie-talkie on his desk let out a burst of static.

"Mister Kirkland, come in."

He picked it up.

"Kirkland here."

"This is O'Doyle. I'm at the east gate. We need you here immediately."

"What's going on?"

"We have visitors."

"I'll be right there."

It was bound to happen sooner or later. Even though the site was remote, people were bound to start showing up. A curious hiker, hopefully. Maybe a local cop, checking things out. As long as it wasn't the competition.

Or, worse, an environmentalist.

Connell put on his sunglasses and a white hat to block the sun, then headed out into the heat. It hit him like a poking slap, enveloping him, actually making his body shiver a little bit as he shifted from air-conditioned cold to desert sun.

The east gate was directly to his left, at the end of the road running east-west through the camp. People were busy at work, moving about for one task or another. When they saw him, they gave out the obligatory *Hello, Mister Kirkland.* He returned this with a nod.

The sliding gate was open. A green Jeep waited just outside of it—an EarthCore vehicle—as did a purple Rav4 that did not belong to the company. Concertina wire sparkled in the sun. He saw two security guards outside the gate, a few staffers inside it, watching the scene.

One of the guards was clearly O'Doyle—his size gave him away even at a distance.

Connell picked up the pace. The staffers turned, saw him coming, hurried away to their assigned jobs.

He recognized the other guard, too: Bertha Lybrand, the only female guard on staff. She held a squirming blond woman in a tight hammerlock, making her bend at the waist because of the pressure on the arm bent up behind her. A beat-up straw hat lay in the sand. The woman wore a ponytail, but that didn't stop clumps of her blond hair from sticking out in all directions.

The other trespasser, an overweight man, was on his knees next to the Rav4, his hands cuffed behind him. He was fat, obviously out of shape, and didn't seem that interested in fighting. Sun gleamed from the brown skin of his thinning scalp.

"Mister O'Doyle," Connell said, stepping through the slightly open gate. "What's going on here?"

Lybrand answered. "These people tried to trespass. I told 'em to wait, but they insisted on coming in. I detained 'em until you could be notified."

The hammerlocked woman lifted her head, glared at Connell.

"You the asshole in charge here?"

She was cute. Or would have been, maybe, had her face not been so furrowed with fury.

"I am. I'm Connell Kirkland."

"Then you tell this bitch to let us go, now! You're already facing one hell of a lawsuit."

She tried to rise up. Lybrand casually applied more pressure, forcing her back down again.

"Just calm down, ma'am," Lybrand said. "We'll get everything worked out."

Connell was impressed. Lybrand was a big woman, and obviously at least some of that size came from muscle. An image of Kayla Meyers flashed through his head—she went by the name *Farm Girl*, but Lybrand had the body of a girl that had actually grown up working on a farm.

"I told you my name," he said to the blond woman. "What's yours?"

"My name is *go fuck yourself*," she growled.

The man on his knees cleared his throat.

"Ronni, perhaps less hammer, more tact," he said in a thick Indian accent.

That seemed to get through to the blond woman. Face flushed and furious, she kept glaring but said nothing else.

Connell knew her kind: used to everyone doing whatever she told them to do, used to being in charge of any situation.

Same as him.

"I'm sure this is a misunderstanding," Connell said. "If Miss Lybrand there lets you go, do you both promise to behave as proper guests?"

The Indian man lifted his head "—I promise—" and set it back down again.

"Halfway home," Connell said. "And you, ma'am?"

The woman's jaw muscles flexed.

"Sure," she said. "I promise."

Connell nodded to Lybrand, who released the woman and took a step back, hand resting on the grip of her sidearm. Connell made a mental note: even when in clear control, Lybrand was cautious, didn't underestimate anyone. Clearly a good acquisition on O'Doyle's part.

O'Doyle put a hand on the man's shoulder.

"I let you up, you'll be cool?"

"As cool as the other side of the pillow," the man said.

O'Doyle gently pulled on his shoulder, helped him stand upright. He unlocked the cuffs and took a step back, hand on his sidearm just as Lybrand had done.

Connell spread his hands in a *what can you do* gesture.

"I apologize for this treatment," he said. "However, I'm sure Miss Lybrand was very clear in her request that you stop. This is private property. May I ask your business here?"

The woman rotated her right arm, left hand gripping her right shoulder. That glare hadn't left her eyes.

"I'm Doctor Veronica Reeves," she said. "This is my associate, Doctor Sanji Haak. We're here because you're drilling into what will be the next UNESCO World Heritage site."

A chill spread through Connell's chest, down into his stomach. If she knew what she was talking about, she was bad news. He didn't believe her, though. Not just yet. He'd twice used Kayla Meyers in a similar fashion, sending her to gather information on the sites of rival companies. The first time it had worked like a charm. The second? Well, that had been the Crittenden Mine incident. A man in a wheelchair was the exact opposite of *worked like a charm*.

"There's nothing on this mountain that could make it a site of historical importance," Connell said. "And I assure you, if there is and we find it, we'll treat it like the treasure it is."

She rotated her arm one more time, then the glare turned into a sneer.

"It's not what's *on* the mountain, you lying sack of shit. It's what's *inside* it. Or rather, what's inside the tunnel complex. Find any interesting cutlery yet?"

The cold feeling spread to his balls. She knew about the tunnels. And about the knife, obviously.

A leak. There had to be a leak. Someone on the science staff, maybe. Sonny getting drunk and shooting off his mouth? Maybe even Kayla herself.

"I told you this is private property," Connell said. "Leave. Now. If you don't, Mister O'Doyle will detain you until the police get here, but you should know that will take the better part of a day."

The woman walked toward him. She strode like a prize fighter— not arrogant, not with a swagger, but rather with the cold confidence of someone who knows exactly what is going to happen when she reaches her foe.

Veronica Reeves stopped in front of him. If he hadn't been a full foot taller than her, they would have been nose to nose.

"You listen to me, Kirkland." Her voice: calm. Her eyes: angry, narrow slits. "Since you don't recognize my name, I'm guessing you don't read much beyond quarterly reports and brochures on your next luxury yacht. Because if you gave a greasy rat shit about science or anything remotely educational, you might know who the fuck I am. Here's the short version—when I make a call, people *answer*. In six hours, I can have the governor of Utah on the phone. I'll tell him that you are knowingly despoiling a national treasure. Then I'll let the press know about this big-business land rape. Once the governor hears the press is on this, he'll be in your shorts like the sweat that's pouring down your back. Then I'll get the National Geographic Society's lawyers to throw every injunction and blocking measure they can think of. They've dealt with your kind a thousand times. In ten hours the press will be swarming over this place and your cozy little hideaway will be national news. You do realize the governor can delay your operations immediately, don't you? Of course you do, it's your business to know such things. In fourteen hours—"

He held up a hand, cutting off her diatribe.

"That's enough," he said. "If you and Doctor Haak would be so kind as to come to my office, we can discuss the situation further."

Veronica flashed a winning smile.

"How hospitable of you, Mister Kirkland. A *discussion* would be lovely." She glanced back at her friend. "Let's go," she said. She walked past Connell and through the open gate. She stopped, crossed her arms and waited.

The Indian man walked by, an apologetic smile on his face.

"I'm sure we can work this out," he said quietly.

Connell nodded. "She seems rather insistent."

Doctor Haak sighed. "Oh, you really have no idea, my friend. But if you play your cards right, you won't have to find out. And that would be better for everyone."

If Reeves could do even half the things she claimed, she could delay the dig for weeks, if not shut it down altogether.

"Of course, Doctor," he said. "You'll find I'm very good at playing the right cards."

ONCE HE HAD HIS GUESTS in his office, Connell immediately checked their credentials. Haak claimed to be a professor at Brigham Young, while Reeves's claims were a bit more grandiose. He called the EarthCore offices in Denver and had his people contact BYU. No computer or cell phone in the camp had Internet access—except for his. While he waited, he Googled Reeves's name, hoping the search would come up blank.

It didn't.

Hit after hit after hit: her name associated with a cave system in the Andes. A cave system where she had found knives just like those Sonny had uncovered. Articles in *National Geographic. Popular Science. Scientific American.* Discovery Channel. PBS.

A mountain sometimes Monte Fitz Roy, or sometimes Mount Fitz Roy, and other times Cerro Chaltén. A huge tunnel system, with most of the tunnels man-made rather than natural. Double-crescent knives. He couldn't believe it; an almost identical find to what Sonny, Randy and Angus had uncovered. Was there platinum at Mount Fitz Roy as well?

Connell was facing the worst enemy possible: a zealot, and a powerful one at that.

He sighed and put the phone facedown on his desk.

"I'll assume you weren't checking the scores," Veronica said. "Or looking for untouched rainforest to burn."

She and Sanji both sat in folding metal chairs in front of his desk. The air conditioner cranked full blast. Sanji sat right under the air outlet. His eyes were half narrowed in pleasure and relief: he looked like a balding, overweight cat soaking up a sunbeam.

"Baby harp seals, actually," Connell said. "Checking Amazon to see if my Louisville Slugger came in."

Reeves smiled. Again, that look of a brawler, grinning at a shit-talking lesser opponent right before the fists flew.

"Funny," she said. "You must be onto something big here, or think that you are."

He had dealt with tree huggers before, many times, but no one of her apparent caliber. He was out of his element, floundering for a way to gain control.

"As I said, Doctor Reeves, this is private property. We have the legal right—"

She cut him off with a wave. "I don't give a damn about your businessman speak. What I do give a damn about is that this area could be vital to human history. Your mining might destroy artifacts that could rewrite the way we look at ourselves. Tell me about the knife."

Connell shrugged. "Knife? We haven't found any knives."

She stood, put the sole of her boot on the edge of his desk. She slid up the leg of her jeans, revealing a flat, leather bundle strapped to her foreleg. She tugged it free, tossed it on his desk, where it landed with a too-heavy *clunk*. She put her foot down, then flipped open the leather to reveal a long, wicked, crescent-shaped knife.

Connell stared at the gleaming metal. He'd looked at Sonny's cell phone pictures of it, but hadn't seen it in person. He'd been furious Cho hadn't taken it away from that professor.

"I take it Lybrand didn't frisk you for weapons."

"Good guess, genius," Veronica said. "This—" she pointed to the knife "—was found—" she pointed toward the mountain outside "—on that peak."

Connell shrugged. "Like I said, we haven't found anything like that here."

Which was accurate: *EarthCore* hadn't found anything. The decades-old discoveries of some graduate student didn't matter.

Sanji raised a finger. "But you knew about it. Sonny McGuiness discovered it in the Brigham Young University archives. Please, Mister Kirkland, if you tell the truth, this will go faster."

"*Much* faster," Veronica said. "There's a great deal of importance attached to that knife." She set her other foot on the edge of his desk, slid up her other pant leg, and pulled out a second leather bundle. "And this one as well."

She dropped it on his desk, opened it. Two curved, gleaming, platinum knives sat side by side.

This woman had walked in concealing a *pair* of fourteen-inch knives. Connell was going to kill O'Doyle.

"I found the second knife on Cerro Chaltén, a mountain in the southern Andes," Reeves said. "I've worked there for the past seven years on an archaeological dig. The knife comes from a lost culture that may have dominated the Tierra del Fuego area some nine thousand years ago. You see the similarity of the knives. There are only two logical conclusions to such similarity. Want to take a guess as to what those are?"

Connell shrugged. "Happy Meal toys used to be a whole lot better than they are now?"

Sanji winced.

"Funny," Reeves said. "Anyone ever tell you you should be a comedian?"

"Just yesterday, in fact."

"Then that person is stupid," she said. "The first possibility is that seventy-five hundred years ago, someone carried a knife from Cerro Chaltén to this distant peak in Utah, a trip of some seven thousand linear miles, where it lay in a tunnel for several millennia, waiting for some geology student to find it. The other conclusion makes more sense and is also harder to believe—that beneath us lies an underground city belonging to *the same culture* as we found at Cerro Chaltén. If that's true, we're looking at a culture that spanned two continents and constituted the largest premodern empire in history."

So much energy in her words. Joy and intensity writ large on her face. Veronica Reeves wasn't *cute*—she was *beautiful*.

Connell glanced at the picture of his wife, chased away those thoughts.

Veronica leaned her fists on the desk, the same way Mack had a few hours earlier.

"You fucked with the wrong girl," she said. "You think it sucks to have someone twist your arm behind you like a pretzel? It does. And when I'm finished using the media to twist *you* around, you're going to wish our places were reversed."

His phone rang.

He gave a fake smile and held up a finger—*just one moment, please*—and glanced at the screen. Barbara Yakely. Shit.

He answered.

"What have you got for me?"

"Hello, honey. Do I need to tell you how bad this is, or do you already know?"

"I have a pretty good idea," he said, still countering Veronica's scowl with his grin.

"Then flash those pearly whites of yours and make that woman happy."

Connell's fake smile faded.

"I disagree," he said. "We should pursue something more ... authoritative."

"Honey, you strut around like a peacock with a ten-foot feathered dick, and that's all good and fine, but do I need to remind you who is in charge of this company?"

Connell stared at Veronica as he talked. Everything had been going so well, going *perfectly*, then this arrogant blond ass-hat had stormed in and started kicking his house of cards. Sanji had spoken of a "hammer"— Connell wanted to show Veronica Reeves what that word really meant.

"We have people on retainer," he said into the phone. "Why pay them if we're not going to use them when we need them most?"

He heard Barb's heavy sigh.

"You want to talk to me about *money*? You mean that green stuff we'll be *out of* if you don't make your dig work? I know you can't stand to lose—ever—but if Reeves makes trouble and shuts the mine down, you're out of a job. You put all of our eggs in one basket. Make sure she doesn't break those eggs. Call me when you have a solution."

Barb hung up.

Fired? She would *fire* him?

Still leaning on the desk, Veronica smiled down. "You look like you swallowed a turd, Kirkland. Home office bring you bad tidings?"

Fired. EarthCore was all he had left. *Barb* was all he had left.

"Um ... no, everything's fine."

He realized he was still holding the phone to his ear. He set it facedown on the desk, gave it a last glance as if it were some alien object that couldn't possibly be real.

Fired. *Him?* No, not in this lifetime. The brief shock was wearing off. Barb was right—he had invested most of the company's reserves in his pet project. She had every right to demand he solve the problem.

Connell gestured to the empty chair behind Veronica.

"Please, Doctor, have a seat. Let's discuss this."

She stood up straight. "I think we both know this is over, Kirkland. How about you tuck that devil's tail between your legs, pull up stakes and get the hell off this mountain?"

Connell had a flash memory of that dinner with Sonny, the look on the man's face when he realized that Connell had won. Maybe Veronica Reeves was a kindred spirit—and if so, Connell didn't like that spirit one goddamn bit.

She wanted to win. Sure, he got that. But there had to be something else she wanted even more. The Cerro Chaltén culture—whatever the fuck that primitive shit was—was this woman's claim to fame. He had to play to that.

"How long were you in the Andes, Doctor Reeves?"

She crossed her arms. "Seven years. Wondering if I'll stick to my guns here, Kirkland? Don't bother. Sanji, tell him."

"Lots of guns," the man said. "Lots of sticking."

"That's not what I mean," Connell said. "Seven years, and how deep did you get? A thousand feet, maybe?"

She hadn't been expecting that question. Her expression became guarded, suspicious.

"That's none of your business."

He shrugged. "I'd like to make it my business. You couldn't go deep because you didn't have the equipment? Or was it because of the heat?"

Her eyebrows raised slightly. *Bingo.*

"Ah, yes, the heat," he said. "What would you say if I told you I had a solution for that? What would you say if I told you I can not only take you safely to the bottom of *this* cave complex, but *yours* as well?"

Connell again gestured to the empty chair.

"Please, sit. Let me make you an offer. If you don't like it, by all means, rain down the righteous thunder of the liberal media on my evil, capitalist ass. But I warn you, Doctor...you might like it. You might like it a *lot.*"

She stared at him, then glanced back at Sanji. She was looking to him for guidance. Ah, their relationship wasn't what Connell had assumed it to be.

Sanji nodded.

Veronica sat.

"All right," she said. "I'll listen to what you've got to say."

Connell smiled at her. This time, there was nothing fake about it.

BERTHA LYBRAND SAT IN THE CAFETERIA Quonset's air-conditioned comfort, poking at her can of Pepsi. O'Doyle sat across from her, staring at the white tabletop, toying with his own can. A few miners sat at other tables, their shift just ended. The cafeteria was large enough to hold a hundred people in comfort. With only a handful of people there, the place felt empty, and she felt exposed.

Maybe she'd overreacted. She shouldn't have laid hands on that woman, but the snooty bitch had tried to walk by like Bertha wasn't even there. Like she was an afterthought. Like she *didn't matter.* That happened a lot. Too goddamn much.

Still, everyone in EarthCore knew the rules: use force only to protect yourself, to protect other EarthCore employees or as an absolute last resort. A push from a woman that weighed a hundred bucks soaking wet didn't exactly qualify for any of those categories.

Bertha hadn't thought, she'd just *moved*. And for that, she was probably going to lose her job. No wonder O'Doyle had that sad-sack look on his face—Kirkland probably hadn't given him any choice.

"Listen, sir," she said. "About what happened…I know I should have used more restraint."

O'Doyle looked up. "Restraint?"

Was he going to talk to her like she was some newbie? Repeat her words so she could hear how ridiculous they sounded? Well, screw that. Maybe she'd be out of a job, but she wasn't going to sit here and eat shit.

"Yes, *restraint*," she said. "If you're going to fire me, can you get it over with so I can get the fuck out of this hellhole?"

He leaned back, confused.

"Fire you?"

Repeating again? What an asshole. Some people just got off on power.

"I don't need this shit," she said. "Know what? You can take your holier-than-thou attitude and stick it straight up your—"

He held up both hands, palms out.

"Hold on a minute. I'm not going to fire you."

"Then why did you call me in here?"

"To say you did a good job," he said. "I gave orders that no one was to enter the gates without permission, and you followed orders."

He looked down at his can again, moved it around in slow circles.

She had overreacted. That happened a lot, too.

"Oh," she said.

She waited for more, but he didn't say anything. He'd rolled his sleeves up just below his boulder biceps. Arms knotted with muscle, skin lined with wicked scars. On the inner left forearm, a faded eagle tattoo. A tattoo on his left bicep, too, although mostly covered by his shirtsleeves—a rectangle of some kind, blue with a horizontal white stripe. She couldn't make it out.

They sat in silence. She had no idea what was happening. This dude was normally all confidence and swagger, yet here he was almost shrinking in on himself.

"So if you're not pissed at me, sir, mind telling me what this is all about? If you wanted to say I did a good job, you could have done it out at the gate."

He cleared his throat. "I read your file. You got this detail because of your combat experience. Then I met you face-to-face. I thought we could … you know … maybe talk? Swap war stories, or whatever."

Bertha huffed. "I'm not too hip on those. Rather not remember any of it. To be honest, sir, I'm not too good at soldier-to-soldier stuff. I'm not really one of the boys."

O'Doyle shifted in his seat. He wouldn't look her in the eye.

She been with EarthCore for a couple of years, true, but she'd worked at a small gold mine in Southern California. Not the good part—LA, San Diego and such—but rather the Death Valley part. Why did every job she'd had since basic seem to involve a fucking desert? Until she'd been transferred here, she'd never met Patrick O'Doyle. She'd heard about him, though. When he'd been hired, rumors had flown: he'd served in some secret unit, he'd won the Bronze Star, that kind of thing.

Since she'd arrived here, the man had acted like a consummate professional solider and all-around badass. Bertha wouldn't want to make him angry, and she was a girl who had been through some serious shit in her day and could handle her business. Now he was fidgeting like a shy high school boy trying to ask a girl on a date.

He cleared his throat again. He still wouldn't look up.

"Didn't really mean like one soldier to another," he said. "Maybe more—you know—like man to woman."

Bertha stared. She felt the blood rush to her face.

He'd just said … no, that couldn't be right. Patrick O'Doyle was interested in *her*? No one had been interested in her in *that* way since high school, and she hadn't been interested in anyone since she'd killed those men in Afghanistan. Why would O'Doyle be interested in her? She was ugly. She knew it, and so did everyone else. Nothing wrong with being ugly, but it was what it was. An ugly killer. She didn't deserve attention from anyone. She …

No.

No, she wasn't going to do this to herself anymore. She wasn't going to let those thoughts engulf her, make her turn away from anyone and everyone. Over there, she'd done her job. She'd taken life to save lives.

It wasn't like anything real was going to happen, anyway. Not with someone like Patrick O'Doyle. Maybe he just wanted some fun. Maybe he only wanted her because there weren't a lot of women in camp.

If that was the case … so what? So *fucking what*. If anything, that made it easier. That made it better.

What was wrong with a little fun?

"That sounds cool," she said. Her voice cracked when she said it, but only a little.

He started moving the can again, staring at it like he was asking *it* out.

"It's very unprofessional of me to discuss this with you," he said. "Just so you know, I'm not one of those guys who *expects* you to be interested. I don't want to create any kind of sexual-harassment situation, considering I'm your boss and all."

Bertha shook her head. "No, it's okay. Just so long as whatever happens doesn't affect our working relationship. I've never asked anyone for favors, and I don't expect to start now."

He nodded. "I understand."

Still red-faced, she smiled. She smiled despite her self-consciousness about her poorly spaced teeth, sweaty blue uniform and muscular body. Patrick didn't seem to notice those things.

He finally looked her in the eyes—and smiled back.

15

ANGUS RELISHED THE RELIEF brought by the midnight breeze. The moon hung in full splendor, turning a desolate, brown terrain into a silvery landscape of beauty and mystery.

He turned his attention back to the task at hand and activated his newest invention. The foot-tall, pyramid-shaped device contained a ten-pound steel rod that slammed into the dusty soil with an irregular rhythm. Dubbed a "thumper," the unit sent small seismic waves into the earth.

Angus checked the satellite feed to his tablet computer, read the location and programmed it into the thumper. The thumper's small, green screen showed the input: 38.384151, -113.588092, 1821m. He unplugged the cable connecting the thumper to the tablet.

He pulled another small machine from his pocket. It resembled a calculator with a spike protruding from the bottom. He called it a "locator." The sensitive receiver picked up the rhythms from the various thumpers, calculated the time difference between the signals and used those differences to triangulate location. Angus pushed the locator's spike into the sand and waited. The locator's black display numbers showed clearly against the LCD screen's eerie green background.

The thumper unit he'd just programmed constituted one point of a six-mile-wide hexagon. Thumpers had already been placed at the other five points. He'd programmed the thumpers to go off at 3:00 a.m., 3:05 a.m. and 3:10 a.m. in order to calibrate and test the system. He checked his watch; at exactly 3:00 a.m., the thumper's rod pounded a complex rhythm into the ground. The message was a simple binary language code — the same language used by computers — announcing the thumper's ID number and location coordinates. Binary translated easily to seismic signals. Thumps were measured in tenth-of-a-second increments: a single thump stood for a *one*, while two thumps in that brief time span stood for a *zero*.

Angus eagerly checked the receiver's screen, waiting for it to receive and process seismic signals from all six thumpers.

The locator's display flashed numbers: 38.384151, -113.588092, 1821m.

He pulled the receiver from the sand and sprinted away from the thumper. He ran hard, heading south and down the mountain slope, slowing four minutes later to push the locator spike back into the ground. He was too far from the thumper to hear it go off at 3:05 a.m., but the receiver picked up the tiny seismic vibrations. Angus smiled as the locator display read: 38.383800, -113.587820, 1784m.

It worked perfectly, giving longitude, latitude and elevation in meters.

Angus pulled a walkie-talkie from his webbing. He'd modified it to encrypt the signals, using a new key every ten seconds. Randy's walkie-talkie, fitted with an identical encryption pattern, was the only thing that could read the signal. The shifting encryption pattern was impossible to break, providing totally secure communication.

Sometimes Angus amazed even himself.

"Woodstock, this is Snoopy, do you read?"

Sneaking around almost under the nose of security people with guns, exploring the mountainside looking for tunnel entrances ... Angus couldn't help feeling a bit like James Bond.

The walkie-talkie squawked with Randy's mild voice. "Snoopy, this is Woodstock, I read you loud and clear."

"What's your locator reading?"

"It reads 38 degrees, 39 minutes, 57 seconds North," Randy said. "And 113 degrees, 58 minutes, 34 seconds West. Elevation 2,034 meters."

Randy was reporting from his perch 250 meters higher up the mountain and over a mile away. Angus smiled; the system proved even more accurate than he'd hoped.

Each thumper was theoretically capable of sending signals through several miles of solid rock, more than enough to fix a location inside the deepest part of the Wah Wah caves. As long as the locator read signals from at least two thumpers, it could calculate distance and give a fixed coordinate.

Angus planned on being underground a long time. He wasn't taking any chances on getting lost. He needed accurate measurements to fully explore the tunnel system.

He'd even accounted for EarthCore's seismometer, which recorded any seismic activity in the area. The staff would be in for a surprise when the machine cut out every six hours or so: the cut-out times conveniently coordinated with the automated thumper cycles. He couldn't have them picking up thumper signals and coming out to investigate the source. Since he would be the first person called upon to fix the problem — and Randy the second person — that problem wasn't going to get fixed anytime soon.

The system worked the other way, too. He and Dirty Randy would carry portable thumpers in their gear. If they needed to, they would use them to send signals to the units on the surface, which could then broadcast pre-programmed messages — a critical ability in case of cave-ins, injuries, or about a dozen other possible scenarios Angus had thought up.

"Woodstock, get back to the Doghouse, Lucy's time is up soon."

"Got it, Snoopy. En route."

Angus had paid a guard to look the other way while he and Randy slipped in and out of camp, but the guard's shift would soon be over. Angus checked his watch; if Randy hurried, they'd be back in the lab with a few minutes to spare.

That idiot Kirkland had no idea what was going on under his nose.

Everything was in place. Supplies, equipment, intel, logistics... He and Randy had everything they needed. Only one part of the plan remained, and that part had some *serious* style to it.

Angus could hardly wait.

FROM A MILE AWAY, Kayla watched two bright green blobs descend a pale green mountainside.

Snoopy and Woodstock. They gave each other little code names, for God's sakes.

She flipped up her night-vision goggles. She looked at the JM-251 Harris SIGINT unit. Her fingers tapped out a random pattern on its rough, black casing.

"What kind of shit are you two trying to pull?"

She'd picked off the walkie-talkie signals of Angus Kool and Randy Wright. Angus's little encryption pattern was good for an amateur, far better than the shitty satphones Kirkland used. But the key word was *amateur*. Kayla had broken the code within the first twenty minutes.

Breaking their code, however, didn't mean she knew what they were up to. They were testing underground mapping equipment, that much was clear. She figured they hoped to sneak away and start exploring the caves. But why were they skulking around so far up the mountain? What did they have up there? What were they looking for?

When she'd first seen them slip away from camp, she'd pegged them as homos, out for a midnight hole-poke away from prying eyes and perky ears. But it wasn't that. Well, she didn't *know* it wasn't that as well (if it walks like a duck and squawks like a duck ...) but they were obviously up to something else.

Something Connell wouldn't like.

If *Snoopy & Woodstock* snuck out again tomorrow night, she'd follow them. That would be a risk. The mountain was so quiet. What if they heard her? Kayla knew how to track, she knew how to move almost silently, but if she made a mistake, the two butt-buddies might run off and tell Patrick O'Doyle they thought someone was out there, out in the dark, watching them.

Angus and Randy she could handle: Patrick O'Doyle she could not. Not without putting a bullet between his eyes, anyway.

All of her camouflage would pass a casual search, but if O'Doyle had an inkling that someone was out here and he *really* looked, he might find a trace she'd missed. After that, it would only be a matter of time until she'd have to leave.

Snoopy & Woodstock. What were they up to?

Maybe tomorrow night, she'd slip west, put the mountain range's ridge between her and the camp, then circle north, slide back over the ridge and track down the coordinates the pillow-biters had mentioned.

Their intentions were an unknown variable. Kayla didn't like unknown variables. Out here, with well-armed guards and an ex-government assassin, unknown variables could get a girl killed.

She had to know.

Angus Kool and Randy Wright were almost back to camp.

She watched them.

SONNY MCGUINESS SAT CROSS-LEGGED in the lab building's shadow, a blanket over his shoulders to ward off the night's chill. No hurry, no rush—he knew Angus and Randy would soon return.

Those boys were out to get a little piece of their own, he figured. They'd mapped the damn thing, after all. Maybe they knew the location of a bit of accessible ore, had kept it to themselves. Sonny couldn't blame them—capitalism is a grand thing. If he weren't getting 2 percent of the whole operation, he'd probably be out panning right now, getting as much as he could for himself before EarthCore took it all.

But he *was* getting 2 percent. That had changed his perspective on things. If the mine failed, his 2 percent equaled zero. Angus and Randy were the fair-haired bright boys of the operation. Their dicking around might cause problems. Sonny empathized with the boys' desire to get paid—as long as that didn't interfere with *him* getting paid.

His position gave him a clear view of the north gate, the one that led to the helicopter pad. He sat, patiently, enjoying the cool air in his nose and lungs, absorbing the grandeur of unobstructed stars, and he waited.

The boys returned, all stealthiness and skulking. The guard on duty opened the gate—just a little—and the boys slipped inside.

Sonny sat very still. Angus and Randy walked to the lab, passing within ten feet of his position. They were quiet as mice, but once inside the lab he could hear them stifling giggles. They'd found something tonight, that was for damn sure.

He stood and walked to the gate, as silent as a desert whisper. The guard didn't hear him coming.

"Hey, kiddo," Sonny said. "What's your game?"

Cho Takachi whipped around. Sonny found himself looking down a chrome pistol barrel.

"Ah," Sonny said. "In retrospect, maybe the whole sneaky-sneak thing wasn't such a good idea."

A wide-eyed Cho shook his head. At least he wasn't wearing sunglasses for once. He lowered his pistol.

"Goddammit, old man. You scared the piss out of me. How the hell'd you get so close without me hearing you?"

"Old prospector's trick, kid. Maybe I'll teach you sometime." Sonny thumbed toward the lab. "What's your game with Huey and Dewey in there?"

"Game? What game?"

Cho had an excellent *I'm innocent* face. Might be a halfway decent poker player.

"Cut the act," Sonny said. "I watched you let them out. I watched you let them back in."

Cho's head bobbed in a single, silent curse.

"It's three in the morning," he said. "What are you doing up at this time, anyway?"

Sonny pointed at his dick.

"If you reach my age, you'll find out. Can't sleep more than two hours without having to take a squirt."

"So your rebellious wang is somehow my fucking problem?"

"It's the prostate, not the wang," Sonny said. "But I'll save the anatomy lesson for another time. Don't worry, I won't tell Kirkland or O'Doyle that you treat this gate like a revolving door. *If* you tell me what's going on, that is."

Cho regarded Sonny for a moment, realizing he'd been caught red-handed. He holstered his gun and brushed long black hair away from his eyes.

"It's no big deal," he said. "Angus pays me to look the other way if they need to sneak out during my shift. The deal is they have to be back before my shift is over."

"So they'll do this again?"

Cho shrugged. "I'm guessing so, from the way they were talking."

"You know where they're going?"

"Not a clue. You can't blame a guy for making a little extra on the side, can you?" Cho flashed his most charming grin.

"Can't blame you at all. But if they head out tomorrow night, I'll be right behind 'em. And I ain't paying you shit. That's the cost for keepin' my clam-taster shut about your little game. Deal?"

"Fair enough," Cho said, clearly relieved that Sonny wouldn't tattle. "What do you think they're up to?"

"I have an idea or two. Greed, young man. It always comes down to greed."

"Bit of a greed fan myself. If you figure out what they're up to, think maybe you can cut me in on the action?"

Cho's loyalty didn't seem to stretch that far. He'd betrayed his job to take a payoff from Angus, and would betray Angus to take a payoff from Sonny? At least he was consistent.

"We'll see," Sonny said. "Let me make sure they don't do something stupid to put us all out of a job first. Now if you'll excuse me—" He pointed to his dick again.

"The meddlesome prostate, right," Cho said.

"That's what I like about you, kid. You're a fast learner. See you tomorrow night."

Sonny headed for the men's Quonset. Maybe he could get a couple hours of sleep in before the morning shift got rolling. If he was going to chase those two young bucks around this mountain, he'd need all the sleep he could get.

FOUR HOURS AFTER Angus and Randy returned to the lab, Veronica Reeves stood on a small plateau, staring out at the sprawling view of a desert awash in sunrise. Her eyes only half registered the morning's stunning beauty. She was over a thousand feet up the mountain. The dry landscape spread out for miles before her, but all she could think about was the opportunity presented by EarthCore's endless arsenal of technology.

She'd simply died and gone to heaven. Since she'd discovered the caves at Cerro Chaltén, her star had risen, and she'd been blessed with funding and the latest equipment. At least, she'd thought it was the latest equipment. The truth was that she'd been using Stone Age garbage.

The best ground-penetrating radar equipment she'd ever heard of measured to depths of five hundred feet, and only then if the ground conditions were just right. Angus's portable GPR array penetrated over *three miles* down, regardless of the ground makeup. It was also more accurate than anything she'd ever seen, especially inside three hundred feet.

And that *map*. When Connell had taken her to the lab, introduced her to Angus Kool, showed her the 3-D image of the caves ... Well, Veronica still hadn't fully recovered. If Cerro Chaltén had a similar network of tunnels, her work there hadn't even scratched the surface. From a computer in Denver, Kool had accomplished more than she had in three years of being on-site, either freezing her ass off in the mountain cold, or suffering heatstroke as she tried to go farther and farther down.

As if the digital map wasn't enough, Angus apparently also had a way to deal with the heat—something called a "KoolSuit." Veronica didn't know what that was, exactly, but she was willing to wear anything that would let her explore the lower tunnels.

A promise, from a guy like that? Probably not worth a bunch of slightly used toilet paper. But that had been the deal she'd made: for letting the dig continue, she got unlimited access to everything EarthCore found, full use of all tech and a healthy "research stipend." Maybe the amount he tossed out was peanuts to his company—it was more than her entire budget for the last three years combined.

And the *big* promise: if she demanded an area be left alone, EarthCore would leave it alone.

Money, technology, access. She had everything she could want and more. So why did it feel like she'd made a deal with the devil?

Because she had.

Kirkland was a reptile, a slug in a tailored shirt. He didn't care about history or human culture. All he cared about was the platinum. If push came to shove, he'd try to back out of the deal. Until that happened, though, there was *so much* she could accomplish, so much she could learn.

Angus's map had shown her where to begin. She'd seen a surface area speckled with abnormalities, bright spots of green that represented matter denser than the transparent colors of dirt and rock. That area on the map turned out to be a small, natural plateau. It would be a few more days before Angus's laser drill—a fucking *laser drill*, for crying out loud—punched a hole into the tunnel system. Until then, she planned to make the most of every minute available.

The plateau was about a mile from camp, a bit farther down the slope. EarthCore guards brought a small, wheeled GPR suite—there were no roads, they had to haul it here by hand—then worked it along a grid under her supervision. Connell insisted on providing physical labor. She and Sanji had carried little more than personal items.

"Ronni," Sanji said, "the data processing is almost finished."

Veronica turned away from the stunning view. Sanji was crouched in front of a monitor that displayed the newly compiled GPR results.

Her father, who'd spent his career as a brilliant laboratory and field biologist, was digging in the dirt and obviously having the time of his life. The walk here had been a gentle slope, save for a few boulders they'd climbed over, yet it had taxed him. He'd gained so much weight while she'd been gone. As if she didn't feel guilty enough for leaving him alone as it was.

Veronica stood behind him, looked over his shoulder. She expected to see the usual GPR shades-of-gray readout, but this was something far better—full color, in greater detail than she'd ever seen.

"Dad, just look at the *tools* EarthCore has."

Sanji nodded. "I know. This shows common readings—loose dirt, sand, gravel—in shades of brown. Rock and densely packed, undisturbed earth appears as shades of black and gray. The yellow marks are anomalies. Angus programmed this to highlight anything linear."

Hundreds of two-dimensional images appeared. Most were nothing more than a splotch of yellow, and yet she could clearly identify some objects: a human hip bone, a pan, a broken pickax, possibly half a double-crescent knife, even an old six-shooter. The GPR screen created a road map of where to dig.

"Amazing," she said. "Just amazing."

The edge of the readout showed a deep black that contrasted with the lighter brown surrounding the yellow artifacts. She pointed to the black edge.

"You said the black is undisturbed earth?"

Her father nodded. "It's denser, apparently, even compared to dirt that was dug up many decades ago."

Black graced only the plateau's perimeter—most of what they now stood on showed signs of disturbance. Veronica frowned, thinking of that first Cerro Chaltén site where she'd discovered the massacre's long-buried remains. Based on the yellow images that were clearly human bones, she had a bad feeling that they had found something similar.

"Well, it won't dig itself up," she said. "Let's get started."

16

August 24

CONNELL FOLLOWED MACK HENDRICKS into the adit, carefully echoing the Aussie's footsteps, ever conscious that a million tons of limestone hung over their heads. It had been a long time since he'd actually been inside a mine, and he'd forgotten how detailed the process was.

Finding a site was one thing. That was Connell's job. Find it, put the right people in place, fund it properly, then sit back and wait for the magic to happen. He was a pusher of paper. He was a manipulator of people. Although he excelled at those tasks, Connell held true admiration for the artists who really made a mine happen; people like Mack.

Mack moved through the safe areas of the shaft, constantly glancing back to make sure Connell stayed close. Connell marveled at Mack's ease within the stone cavern's confines. It was little things, mostly, like how Mack didn't watch the ground yet never stumbled on loose rock, or how his hard hat stayed naturally plastered to his head, while Connell's continually bobbled no matter how many times he adjusted it.

"Bit of gravel here, mate," Mack said, his voice echoing slightly off the rough stone walls. "Watch your step. The vertical shaft is just ahead."

Smells of oil and gas fumes filled the long, horizontal tunnel. The ceiling was only seven feet high. It was lined with many parallel grooves, like a rock-eating monster had moved along, taking thousands of big-toothed bites. Squat diesel tractors—designed for mines and less than four feet tall from tire-bottom to cab-top—hauled loose rock, equipment and supplies to and from the vertical shaft.

Normally, a mine required dozens of the strange-looking trucks to do that job. That was because in every mine before this one, loose rock came from both horizontal and vertical shafts. Thanks to Angus's invention, however, the vertical shaft produced no rock at all—only dust, which was blown out through thick tubes.

The growl of engines, the steady rumble of generators, the constant hum of blowers … the combined sounds made Connell feel like he was in the belly of some great beast, waiting to be digested.

"Here we are, Mister Kirkland," Mack said. "Welcome to the vertical shaft."

The cavern surrounding the vertical shaft spread out before them, a stone dome chewed out by the same many-toothed metal monster that had made the adit. Everywhere Connell looked the walls allowed just enough room for the machinery installed within. No extra space. It reminded him of opening a walnut and seeing how the inside of the shell perfectly mirrored the contours of the nut.

In the center of the dome floor, a strong, circular rail surrounded a twenty-foot-diameter shaft that led straight down. Metal framework perched over it, a crouching black spider forever frozen. A yellow crane sat close, hoist line connected to the eighteen-foot-diameter elevator deck—known as a "cage"—that was used to raise or lower men, supplies and rock. The cage wasn't in use, because the cables that led from the black spider far down into the hole were currently connected to the laser drill. Those cables and a thick hose rose up from the hole, into the black spider, then to massive, half-empty spools that sat in their own perfectly carved niches.

Mack stood at shaft's edge. He glanced down, then back to Connell.

"It's not going to bite, mate. Come on."

Connell realized he'd stayed back almost at the tunnel entrance, as if something might reach up out of that great hole and grab him if he came too close. He felt like an idiot. Mack was clearly enjoying Connell's discomfort. He could just imagine the Aussie's thoughts: *You're all big and bad when it comes to giving orders, but when it gets down to the real work, you wouldn't know the business end of a shovel if I stuck it straight up your ass.*

Or something macho like that, anyway.

Connell walked to the rail. He looked down into a bottomless pit.

Powerful lights burned every hundred feet along the shaft's length, a glowing line of giant pearls reaching farther than he could see, lighting up the cable and hose that—somewhere, down there—connected to the distant laser drill.

"How deep is it?"

His voice sounded small in here. He already knew the answer, as Mack updated him daily, but Connell needed to hear it. Things on paper were one thing—seeing this in person, it didn't seem possible.

It didn't seem *real.*

"This morning we passed thirty-two hundred meters," Mack said. Then he winked. "That's two miles for you Yanks."

Two miles down, a pulsed plasma laser array was hard at work. The laser array looked like a giant lawn-mower blade, ten feet on each side attached to a center rotor. One hundred and forty-four laser heads—each with a beam radius of one inch—were attached to the blade bottoms. Above the blades sat a compact liquid-ring vacuum pump. The rotor spun the blade, the lasers fired in a computer-controlled sequence that vaporized the rock in a level ring, and the vacuum instantly sucked in the vaporized limestone and pushed it up the tubes before the dust could damage the laser array.

The end result? A perfectly round shaft with sides as smooth as poured concrete.

Mack's walkie-talkie squawked harshly, a garbled version of his name between bursts of white noise. He pulled it out of his belt.

"Hendricks here."

"Mack, is Mister Kirkland with you?" the voice squawked.

"He is, Jerry. What's up?"

"You'd both better get back to camp fast," said the static-laden voice. "There's been an accident at the lab. Mister Kool and Mister Wright were hurt bad."

SANJI, SONNY AND TWO EARTHCORE guards carefully dug into the plateau's dirt and rock.

Veronica watched them. She needed a break. A girl could only take so much.

It was different this time. And not just because of the bodies. It was this mountain. It radiated a feeling, perhaps an *emotion* all its own. A dark emotion, one that draped over the sprawling rocks and sand as a shroud drapes over the face of a corpse. Veronica had felt that vibe right off the bat but mentally drowned it out in favor of the feverish excitement of exploration. Now, however, the sweet taste of discovery soured in light of their recent find.

Mass graves were nothing new to her. They dotted Cerro Chaltén like a giant case of measles. Five times Veronica had excavated such sites of violence and death. Many were far worse in scope than what they'd found on this Wah Wah Plateau — but this time it affected her in a way she'd never expected.

She was *furious.*

The Cerro Chaltén massacres were from a distant, exotic, ancient culture. Primitive people who were dead thousands of years before modern civilization even began.

The remains of the destroyed camp she had just unearthed, though, belonged to *Americans.*

Her people.

And just like that, like someone had flipped a switch, her perception changed forever. She now saw the Chaltélians in a different light. She had thought of them as highly advanced in technology, in art, in communication. Drastically ahead of their time. They were all of those things still, sure, but now there was a new layer – they were a savage, merciless tribe bent on murdering anything that crossed their path.

Once word of the mass grave filtered back to camp, Sonny McGuiness had come running. He helped examined the artifacts: a rusted pistol, a mining pan and the termite-ridden remains of what he said was a sluice, used to separate valuable metal from plain dirt. Based on old newspaper articles he'd found a week earlier, Sonny felt certain that the mass grave belonged to the William Benjamin mining camp, a camp that had disappeared in 1885.

Just 130 years ago.

The thought that descendants of her Cerro Chaltén culture roamed the plains and mountains of the southwestern United States should have thrilled her beyond imagination. Instead, it bothered her. It even scared her a little. It all hit a bit too close to home. According to her findings, the Cerro Chaltén civilization had ended around 1500 BC. The Utah version of that culture hadn't died out at all. It existed right up through the turn of the century.

The Chaltélians were *modern*.

Or at least part of a modern age. By no stretch of the imagination could she call such an incredible display of savagery "modern." Just as at the Argentinean sites, Chaltélians had cut the Benjamin party to pieces. The longest human remain discovered on the Wah Wah Plateau thus far was a piece of femur just over eighteen inches. Veronica even found thin scraps of fabric around some of the bones. One tough leather shoe still surrounded a mummified foot.

Sonny said eight people had gone missing from the Benjamin camp, but the remains were so chopped up Veronica hadn't been able to accurately count the number of victims. It was almost as if the attackers had carved up the bodies and made sport of their remains, tossing them back and forth until the plateau was covered with blood, bone and savaged body parts.

A few of the skulls were intact, but most had been smashed to pieces—literally "counting heads" wouldn't work. Sanji had struck on the idea of counting feet instead. So far they had found twelve feet: seven left, five right.

Just like the massacres at Cerro Chaltén, all traces of the mining camp were buried a good six to ten feet underground.

Americans. Not people separated by distance and time. Americans. Her people. Hell, as far as she knew, one of these victims could have been her great-great-grandfather.

"Ronni," Sanji called out, breaking her daze. "I found another foot. A right one, I think."

Veronica shuddered, suddenly wishing—for the first time in her career—that she wasn't digging up the secrets of those long-dead and forgotten.

She wondered if perhaps forgotten is where the dead should stay.

CONNELL HELD ON for dear life as Mack drove the Jeep through the camp, honking the horn madly to warn everyone away. Mack hit the brakes, skidding the Jeep to a dusty halt at the edge of the landing pad.

Both men jumped out and sprinted to the helicopter. Its long blades had already spun up to full speed, blowing up a cloud of dust and stinging sand.

O'Doyle and Takachi finished loading Randy into the chopper. Angus was already inside. Both men had bloodstained white gauze wrapped around their heads, their hands. Angus had a huge, bruised goose egg under his left eye. Neither man was conscious.

Connell leaned toward O'Doyle, shouted to be heard over the helicopter's roar.

"What happened?"

"Chemical tank blew," O'Doyle shouted back. "Static electricity ignited it or something like that. Both men were standing in front of it."

"Are they okay?"

O'Doyle grabbed Cho, pulled him closer, repeated the question.

"They should be fine," Cho said. "But they both had head wounds, and you don't screw with those. I'm sending them to Milford Valley Memorial Hospital for observation, just to be sure."

Connell hated to lose Angus and Randy for even a day, but Cho had been a combat medic and Connell wasn't about to argue with the man's expertise.

O'Doyle ushered everyone to the edge of the landing pad. The helicopter lifted off and headed west.

As it shrank away into the distance, the noise faded with it. Connell could speak normally again, although he heard the angry growl in his own voice.

"Check out the accident, Mister O'Doyle," he said. "Look for any sign of foul play."

O'Doyle nodded. "My thoughts exactly, Mister Kirkland. I'm on it."

Connell found it a bit too coincidental that a lab accident took out his top two scientists. What seemed more likely was that a rival company was onto them, trying to sabotage the camp and get to the Dense Mass from another entrance somewhere on the mountain.

If his suspicion turned out to be accurate, he was running out of time.

KAYLA MEYERS WATCHED the helicopter head west. This place grew more interesting every second. A small blast had rocked the lab, followed by thin black smoke that seeped out the roof. Cho Takachi rushed in immediately after the explosion. Bertha Lybrand was there seconds later.

Curiouser and curiouser.

Kayla slipped back into her tiny, camouflaged dugout and returned to cleaning her weapons. A cloth lay spread out on the sand, her Steyr GB-80 pistol on top of it, loaded and ready to go. She loved the weapon, mostly because it held eighteen rounds in the mag and one in the chamber for nineteen shots of 9 x 19 mm stopping power. Her Israeli-made Galil ARM submachine gun lay in spotless, well-loved pieces on top of the cloth. She, like many others, considered it the best subma-chine gun in the world. Like the Steyr, she adored the Galil mostly for its ammo capacity—a fifty-round magazine of 45 millimeter shells.

Clean weapons meant peace of mind.

She paid close attention to the process, guarding against tiny grains of windblown sand. Couldn't take any chances on weapon reliability out here. She had a growing feeling her babies would come into play before this little desert soap opera was over. She wouldn't mind using the weapons, not one bit.

She smiled as she finished assembling the Galil. She popped in a fresh magazine. Her smile widened.

Nope. Wouldn't mind at all.

THE SETTING SUN DANGLED just above the horizon. Its molten orange color shrouded the mountain range with a thick, smoldering glow. After only an hour of hunting, Sonny McGuiness had finally found his prey.

"Sonofabitch," he said. "And I thought Kirkland was a devious prick."

He'd spent the day with Veronica and Sanji, digging up that awful plateau. Calling William Benjamin "crazy" was like calling an aircraft carrier a "dingy"—the word didn't even begin to describe the reality. Benjamin had chopped those men to bits. That was a special kind of psycho right there.

And that Veronica girl. Come on. Nice ass and all, but she thought some lost civilization had gone all purée on Benjamin's crew? Sure. Right. If that's how they taught college kids to think these days, Sonny was damn glad he'd never gone. She was all right, though—anyone who would work that hard under a blazing sun all day long deserved some respect. Her and Sanji both—neither one of them shied away from breaking a sweat.

After they found that weird line, though, they were done for the day. Sonny had headed back to the Land of Air Conditioning to get some sleep and wait for darkness so he could follow Angus and Randy.

Then some thingamajigger in the lab had blown up.

Now the two nerds were in a shitty little hospital in Milford. No more skulking around for them, at least not until they got back. Sonny should have taken advantage of that to get some real sleep, but that wasn't how he was wired. The nerds were gone—whatever had dragged them out in the wee hours of the night was not.

Sonny had to know.

Curiosity: it was a real kick in the nuts.

He'd headed out an hour before sunset. No one stopped him, he had free rein to come and go as he pleased. Connell wanted Sonny to keep exploring, keep researching, keep looking for any and all information that would help the cause.

Angus and Randy knew nothing about covering their tracks. Sonny had found the secret spots, the hiding places, the hidden treasures of men who had mastered the desert—and who hadn't left a footprint behind in over a hundred years. Following a one-day-old trail left by a pair of corncob-up-the-ass lab rats was a comparative cakewalk.

He'd tracked them. He'd climbed. He'd found this.

"You two little turdballs really take the cake," Sonny said. "Serves Kirkland right, though—you treat people like shit, they shit on you right back."

While EarthCore spent millions to sink a shaft, Angus Kool had found another way in. A way he kept to himself.

Like the loose fist of some stone giant, a small projection of greenish limestone camouflaged a clearing. Little more than a flat slab of rock, the small clearing protruded from the mountain, ending in a fifty-foot drop straight to a jagged outcropping below. Surrounded on three sides by large, weather-worn boulders, the tiny mesa offered a stunning view of the sprawling desert. At the back edge of the mesa sat an irregular dark opening, about two feet high and three feet wide.

Sonny noticed something above that opening. Scratches, and not the natural kind. He stepped closer, and as he did he saw the lines were thin, jagged letters chiseled into the stone.

S. ANDERSON
D. NADIA
W. IGOE JR.
1942

Sonny's blood ran cold. That creeping feeling washed over him again—Funeral Mountain, caressing his skin, a cat lightly batting a mouse to keep it away from safety for a few torturous minutes longer.

The place Anderson wrote about in his last report…this was it. This was the entrance to his tunnel. This was where he'd found the platinum knife. Right in there. Had the three boys died here? Had they gotten lost? Had they knocked out a linchpin rock and been killed in a collapse?

Or, had something killed them.

First the Benjamin bodies. Now this.

Anderson had stood in this very spot. He'd been both younger than Sonny and older than him, born long before Sonny was, dead far younger than Sonny was now.

Sonny wanted to turn around and head back to the camp.

His feet wouldn't let him.

The tiny tunnel entrance beckoned, taunting Sonny's curiosity like a grade-school bully.

Come on, Sonny Boy. Don't be chicken. Don't you want to know what's in here? Don't you?

He wanted to know. He *had* to know.

Sonny slid his silver bracelet from his wrist. He held it with both hands, thumbs rubbing on the faded swastika.

"It's just a cave," he said. "Just a tunnel. Ain't nothing in there but bugs."

He slid the bracelet back on. He pulled a flashlight from his bag and aimed the beam into the darkness.

Sonny crawled inside on his hands and knees.

At first he had plenty of room to lift his head, but the tunnel rapidly bottlenecked to a space no more than fifteen inches from floor to ceiling. That feeling, that *funeral feeling*, it was stronger in here. He forced himself to breathe slowly, to stay calm.

Maybe he should turn back? Bring Cho, maybe, do this in the daylight?

No, that was stupid. Daylight would only help for the first thirty feet or so. And Cho or no Cho, Sonny knew that once he left this spot he would never return. No fucking way. If he wanted to satisfy his curiosity, it was now or never.

The tunnel narrowed even further. Sonny had to turn his head sideways to fit through. Twice he bumped his head on unforgiving rock overhangs, but he ignored the pain. Soft, flour-like sand lay under his chest, leftovers from an ancient river that once flowed through the passage, carving the tunnel from solid limestone and leaving the powdery sediment behind. Jagged walls closed in on either side of him, a limestone crypt made for an oh-so-snug fit.

No sound other than his breathing.

His flashlight clumsily played down the tunnel, and he thought he saw an opening in front of him. He pushed forward, fighting back the panic growing in his belly and balls.

After another twenty feet, the ceiling suddenly slanted up, almost high enough for Sonny to stand up straight. The tunnel continued on. He wiped sweat from his face, leaving a smear of cave silt.

Sonny played his flashlight around the cave, knowing three young BYU students had traveled this same path over a half century ago. Evil-looking white spiders sat motionless in their webs. Small crickets with long legs and even longer antennae moved slowly along the walls and ceiling.

He continued on.

No footsteps here. Odd. This far into a tunnel, there wasn't enough air current to blow sand, even powdery stuff like this. Any footsteps Anderson and his friends made should have still been here. Maybe water still flowed through here occasionally, surging up during an unseasonal rain, perhaps.

Sonny came to a massive pile of boulders, obviously the site of an ancient cave-in. A narrow, dark hole rested at the bottom. Just left of it, a small boulder that looked oddly like a limestone pumpkin.

This is where you boys stopped the first time. And when you came back here the second time, no one heard from you ever again.

He realized he was trembling. Shivering like a child just awoken from a nightmare. Maybe the evil that created this awful feeling lay just beyond this jumbled pile of huge boulders. Maybe Veronica's lost tribe or even Benjamin's demons waited for him just past the opening, waited for him to poke his too-damn-curious head through, waited to grab him and drag him off to some unknown horror.

Get ahold of yourself, you cowardly old fart. You've got to see what's past here or it's all you'll think about for the rest of your days.

He wanted to know. He *had* to know.

Without giving himself time to reconsider, Sonny flopped to the ground. He crawled past the pumpkin-shaped boulder and through the opening. He stood, shaking, his body telling him to leave, his brain telling his body to shut the hell up.

His flashlight beam traced across the tunnel walls, came to rest on a small charcoal drawing. Six curving sunbeams reached out from a central circle. A primitive sun, maybe? The drawing was simple enough, but there was something odd about it. Sonny couldn't place it, and at the moment he didn't give a shit.

He wasn't alone.

That feeling hit him all at once, irresistible, undeniable. His flashlight beam ripped across stone, this way and that, up and down and all over. Nothing but rock, nothing but shadows and darkness ringing a moving circle of light.

Sonny scrambled back through the cave-in opening, unforgiving rock punishing him for moving too fast, scraping at him, hurting him. Something was coming, the darkness forming up into a living thing that would drag him down and never let him go.

He pushed through, crawled past the pumpkin-shaped boulder.

Stooped over to keep his head from banging on the rocky ceiling, he sprinted up the tunnel slope, boots pounding into the fine, dry silt.

Up ahead: fading daylight.

Just like on the way in, the tunnel narrowed. Sonny dove to the ground. The flashlight clattered away, smashing against the wall. He crawled, breath coming as torn gasps that seemed to suck in as much dust and silt as they did air.

He banged his elbow, hard. He tuned out the pain, kept moving, and then he was out of the cave, back on the mesa.

Sonny stood. Chest heaving, stomach clenching, he stared out into the darkening sky. His elbow stung. So did his hands. He looked at them: three knuckles split open. Blood fell in small droplets against the sunheated rocks.

He turned, stared back at the cave opening, sure some horror would pour forth at any moment.

But nothing did.

It was just a cave. Just a small, dark opening.

Why had he been so afraid?

Claustrophobia, old-timer. Brought on because that cave reminds you of the coffin you'll be wearing before too long.

That's what he told himself. But somewhere inside him, inside the part that had taken to the land, the part that embraced the desert like a lost love, he knew it was a lie. Sonny sat on the cliff's edge, his feet dangling above the fatal drop, his eyes staring out into the sunset.

This mountain was death.

A war raged inside Sonny McGuiness's mind. His emotions and his intellect battled for dominance. To stay was to get rich. Rich enough to retire forever. To leave? To leave, he'd have to leave that wealth behind.

But at least he'd get to keep his life.

THE HELICOPTER TOUCHED DOWN. Katerina Hayes was glad the ride was over. Not because she minded flying—which was more than a little thrilling, kind of like being in a movie—but because Achmed had looked like he might throw up at any moment.

"Oh, my," he said, one hand over his mouth. "Have we stopped?"

"You can look now," Katerina said. "Terra firma."

For the first time in an hour, Achmed opened his eyes and looked around. The hand stayed over his mouth. She'd tried to tell him that shutting your eyes was about the worst thing you could do for motion sickness, but he hadn't listened.

A man outside the helicopter opened the side door, letting a wave of heat slip in and slap her. Oh, Lord, was it going to be like this all the time?

"Doctor Hayes, Doctor Frigbane," Patrick O'Doyle said. "Welcome to camp."

Him again. She should have known.

Katerina didn't like the big security guard. In fact, he scared the hell out of her. He'd killed people, or so the story went. Rumor had it he'd served in an Israeli commando unit and had once single-handedly slain four terrorists using nothing but a combat knife.

O'Doyle offered a hand to help her out. She took it, her skin already prickling from the heat. She stepped onto the landing pad's concrete, sand gritting under her shoes.

He looked back into the helicopter. "Doctor Frigbane? Do you need a hand?"

"Several," Achmed said. "And how many times do I have to tell you to call me *Achmed*?"

"As many times as times there are," O'Doyle said, reaching in to help the man out. "And it still won't work, *Doctor*."

Achmed stepped out of the helicopter, stood on weak legs.

"You, I take to your quarters," O'Doyle said to him. He glanced at Katerina. "You, I take straight to Mister Kirkland."

Had she done something wrong? Had Angus blamed her for something?

"Why does he want to see me?"

"I wouldn't know," ODoyle said. "I don't make a habit of questioning my boss's decisions."

"Can I clean up first?"

The big man shook his head. "No, ma'am. He said bring you straightaway."

She wasn't going to argue with him. She wasn't entirely sure he wouldn't kill her if she did.

They climbed into O'Doyle's Jeep. He drove off the landing pad— stopping just long enough for Achmed to finally throw up—then into the camp. People bustled about. Mostly miners, by the looks of it.

She didn't know any of them. She recognized a few people from the Denver lab, some scientists, some techs and assistants. They all gave her a welcoming wave. The camp looked neat and efficient, everything new and gleaming.

The Jeep stopped at a Quonset hut. Achmed threw up again. Poor guy. O'Doyle pointed to a trailer.

"That's Mister Kirkland's office, Doctor Hayes. Do me a favor and go straight there while I help your friend get cleaned up?"

A fair deal by any stretch, she figured.

Katerina walked to the trailer. Lord, *please* let that have air-conditioning. She reached out a fist to knock, then stopped.

Remember why you're here. Remember who you're doing this for.

She tugged a gold locket out from under her shirt. As the sun beat down on her, she popped it open. On one side was a tiny picture of herself with her husband, Harry. Their vacation in Puerto Rico, before the baby. Matching blue floral shirts. He had black hair, just like her. This was the only picture that made her agree with her friends' constant observation—that Harry and she looked like brother and sister. On the other side of the locket, their daughter, Kelly, smiling, sitting at the piano. Katerina was teaching her, on the same piano her mother had used to teach her.

She hadn't seen either of them in two weeks, not since this whole Wah Wah situation erupted. First, she'd worked incessantly in the lab with that bastard Angus, who never seemed to get tired and was never satisfied no matter how many hours the staff put in. Then, O'Doyle had told them all they were no longer *allowed* to go home, not until the camp was up and running, the mine was functioning and the company had full control of all land that needed controlling. Even her phone calls to her family were monitored, just to make sure no info got out.

She should have been furious at the invasion of privacy, but she wasn't. The people who worked in EarthCore's lab were far from stupid. Everyone saw the potential of this find. As people employed in the mining industry, they understood the find's potential ramifications. If word got out too soon, other companies—even other *governments*—might not play by the rules. People could get hurt. If everyone obeyed the law, that would be a nice world to live in, but it wasn't the *real* world.

Then came the call: Angus and Randy were injured. Connell wanted Katerina and Achmed to take their place. Immediately.

She had managed a quick phone call to Harry before she left, telling him that she was going to be on-site. No, she didn't know how long. No, she couldn't tell him where. No, she wouldn't be able to call him. No, she didn't know when she'd be able to call at all.

Yes, it might mean big things for her career.

That was all Harry needed to hear. He was so damn supportive. She often had to work late, as did everyone on Angus's staff, yet Harry never complained. Not once. Inside the fridge she always found a meal waiting to be microwaved. Outside the fridge she always found a new crayon drawing from her daughter.

Keep working hard Mommy.

I love you Mommy.

I'm proud of you Mommy.

She knew Harry coached Kelly to write those messages. He never let his daughter write things like *I miss you*, or *come play with me*, things that would have drowned her with guilt. Even after years of Angus's unending demands, there was nothing but support from her wonderful husband and her growing daughter.

Harry was the reason she still worked at EarthCore, where—despite her "genius"—she worked for a man who treated her like an imbecile. Harry had always told her someday it would pay off.

"For you guys," Katerina said. She closed the locket, slipped it back into her shirt.

She knocked.

"Come in," Kirkland called. She entered the trailer. She tried to look confident.

"Sit down, Doctor Hayes." He gestured to the two folding chairs that sat in front of his cheap metal desk. She sat, looked into his cold, gray, penetrating eyes.

"Thank you for getting out here so fast, Doctor."

She nodded. As if she'd had any choice *but* to come.

"Mister Kool and Mister Wright have been injured and will not be able to handle their duties for at least a few days," Kirkland said. "You're in charge while they're gone."

In ... charge?

"Wait, what? *Me?*"

Kirkland sighed. "Your first words as boss, and you're making me doubt my decision already. Do you not want the job or something?"

How had she just leapfrogged four, maybe five people ahead of her?

"Oh, no, no I want it," she said. "Absolutely. I'll tear this job a new asshole, Mister..."

Her voice trailed off. Had she just cursed in front of this man?

"That's better," he said. "I'll take that over *who, me?* any day of the week."

He smiled. A forced smile, no real humor behind it. She suddenly realized how exhausted he looked.

"I want it," Katerina said. "It's just that, well, Achmed has seniority on me. So do several other people in the lab."

Kirkland shrugged. "You have seniority on Angus, but he's been your boss for years."

She rolled her eyes. "I don't think you can count him as normal in any equation, Mister Kirkland. I might not like the man, but there is no denying he's special."

"That's one word to describe him." Kirkland tapped his phone, called something up. "And to answer your question as to why you're in charge, let me share several words he used to describe you. I quote, *Doctor Hayes has an impeccable work ethic and never complains when I assign her extra duties. I know that when others on my staff are past the point of breaking, she will get the job done. Because of this, I give her far too much work, and yet she completes every task I assign. I can only compliment her by saying that in five or six years, she could be almost as good as I am now.*"

He set the phone facedown on his desk. He stared at her.

Angus yelling, Angus insulting, Angus treating her like she was stupid. Her, *stupid.*

"He didn't say those things," she said. "He couldn't have."

Kirkland waved his hand dismissively. "I really don't have time for junior high melodrama, Hayes. The lab techs reported they are detecting some kind of unknown seismic spike. I want you to figure out what's causing it."

"A seismic spike? Could it be rock settling due to the new vertical shaft?"

Kirkland drummed his fingertips on his desktop.

"For someone of your intellect, Doctor Hayes, do I need to define the word *unknown* for you?"

Her face flushed hot. Apparently, there were *two* people who could make her feel stupid.

"No, Mister Kirkland."

"Good," he said. "You're in charge of the lab. The rest of the lab staff doesn't know this yet. You inform them of my decision. This will upset some of them, but I don't care. I want the cause of that spike identified within twenty-four hours. We have people in that shaft. Their safety is now your responsibility, got it?"

She nodded.

"Good." He gestured to the door. "That will be all."

Katerina wasn't really sure what had just gone down. She was in charge of the entire lab. She left the trailer, floating more than walking.

On-site at the biggest test dig in the company's history, and she was *in charge*. She wanted to rush to a phone and call Harry, but phone calls remained off-limits. Well, he'd find out soon enough; more immediate things demanded her attention. This was her chance to move up the ladder, her chance to be noticed.

If her coworkers thought Angus was a hard boss, they didn't know anything yet. She might only have a few days, a week, tops, to make the most of this opportunity.

She wasn't about to let it slip away.

17

August 25

THE EXCITEMENT HAD RETURNED in a big way, but it couldn't entirely eclipse Veronica's smoldering disgust. *Massive* was the only word she could apply to the discovery—the Wah Wah find was simply unmatched in depth and impact.

So why did she feel like a transgressor? Like a grave robber? She'd dug at dozens of sites, unearthed the remains of literally hundreds of human beings. So why was this plateau any different? Veronica couldn't answer that nagging question, but she wasn't going to let that stop her.

This would make her a household name. Carl Sagan. Jane Goodall. Neil deGrasse Tyson. Marie Curie. That kind of fame. That wasn't why Veronica had gone into science—that's not the trade you choose if mass popularity is your goal—but now that it was here, she was going to embrace it. The Cerro Chaltén find had given her a tiny taste of that fame. This? This was altogether on a different level.

The fact that a nine-thousand-year-old culture from Tierra del Fuego had migrated to North America (or perhaps the other way around, she didn't know) was stunning in itself. The fact that the mysterious culture remained alive in the late nineteenth century seemed shocking, unbelievable, the kind of story that belonged in supermarket tabloids rather than scientific papers. But at this point, there was no doubt: the burial of the Benjamin camp was so similar to the Cerro Chaltén massacres that Veronica knew the same culture was responsible for both.

With Sonny's help, she'd pieced together the story of the Benjamin camp massacre. Benjamin's crew had spent months blasting, hauling out rock, then blasting some more. The Chaltélians must have decided the miners were attacking, or perhaps had offended some aspect of their religion. Whatever the cause, the mining sparked an all-out assault. The Chaltélians even destroyed the mine, causing a cave-in that filled the shaft with tons of rock. To the outside world, no trace of the mine remained.

In addition to human remains, she and Sanji excavated pickaxes, dishes, tools, guns and a dozen other common implements of the Old West. They'd even found the remains of two horses. At least they *thought* there were two—dismembered, scattered bones made it difficult to be sure.

The carnage wasn't limited to just the plateau. Sonny had discovered an old trail leading from the plateau down the mountain. With the portable GPR suite, Sanji had scanned the trail and the area around it. About a hundred and fifty meters from the massacre site, he discovered another victim—and his horse—butchered and buried in rocky soil, presumably where they'd fallen while trying to escape.

The body count so far: at least eight. People, that was. She wasn't counting horses just yet.

Veronica brushed dirt off a human skull, careful not to disturb bits of mummified skin and hair. The skull had been split open, probably with a rock. Large scratch marks lined the interior of the brain case. It looked as if someone had jammed a knife in an open wound and violently stirred the brain. She sighed with amazement and disbelief at the violence of this lost culture.

She heard a commotion farther down the trail. She looked up from her brush and skull toward Sanji, who lightly slapped at the GPR monitor. He seemed confused. So did the two EarthCore men with him. They shrugged their shoulders as they tweaked the controls.

Veronica gently set the skull down, then carefully made her way down the rocky trail to the men.

Sanji looked up at her, perplexed.

"The machine appears to not be working," he said.

"No sir, it's working just fine," one of the technicians said.

"It doesn't go *straight down*," Sanji said. "That is not possible."

Veronica looked at the display, saw the reason for their confusion. Brown indicated disturbed earth: there was a vertical line of it going down, with solid black—the color for undisturbed earth—on either side.

Sanji was right. It had to be some kind of malfunction.

"Guys," she said, "what's the scale on this?"

The technician pointed to a scale icon at the bottom of the display.

"One inch of what you see here equals a half mile."

Sanji brushed dust from his hands, shook his head.

"Exactly," he said. "So according to that display, the brown line goes a mile deep, even past the bottom edge of this machine's range."

Veronica leaned closer to the display, scanning for any yellow anomalies. There weren't any.

"So according to this, we're looking at a shaft that goes down at least a mile?"

"No, not a *shaft*," Sanji said. "A meter-wide *line*. We're standing on it. According to the machine, the line runs straight out from us in both directions."

Had the Chaltélians dug a trench, maybe? Perhaps something symbolic?

Veronica stood straight. She looked down the slope for a moment, taking in the camp and its blue buildings below, the valley beyond, the heat-hazy Frisco Mountains beyond that.

She looked to her left.

She stared, not sure if her eyes were playing tricks on her, showing her an idea generated by the GPR display's line.

She looked right.

No tricks. It wasn't her imagination.

How could she have not seen this before?

A line. Not on the ground, but in the rocks that straddled that line. Big boulders looked like halves of the same rock, as if the line itself split them in two, letting the halves fall back on either side. In some places massive boulders simply stood tall like giant limestone bookends waiting for books, a meter space between them.

The display said the line beneath her feet was a mile deep. A mile or more. A mile *vertical*. As for the *horizontal*, it was longer than that. Much longer.

She looked down at Sanji, who also stared numbly along the length of the line. He saw the same thing. They stood there, two highly trained scientific minds, trying to come up with a single idea of what it all meant.

BY THE TIME CONNELL FINISHED up for the day, the sun had set, the moon had risen and the temperature outside his air-conditioned trailer was about the same as it was within. He stared up at the cloudless night sky. The moon blazed so bright it almost hurt his eyes. Stars sure didn't look like this from his Denver apartment. So bright. So clear.

He headed for the men's latrine. If it weren't for ol' number-one and number-two, he might not leave his admin trailer at all. Biology, man. No way around it.

The latrine was on the other side of the mess Quonset. As he approached the mess hall, he heard music and laughter coming from inside. Good. His people deserved it. When Mack had brought the good news that afternoon, Connell had placed an order for beer and booze. It was time for the staff to celebrate.

The primary vertical shaft was complete.

He'd canceled the evening shifts, called every building in camp and told everyone to stop working. Everyone except him, of course. And Katerina. Filling in for Angus Kool was a job that didn't have enough hours in the day as it was.

People had been surprised he'd called for a party. So had he, truth be told. He wasn't managing things from an office in Denver anymore. He was here. He saw firsthand the effects of stress and lack of sleep. He'd been there when Angus and Randy had been taken to the hospital.

He'd been there when that same helicopter had evacuated three injured miners after a small tunnel collapse.

Being in camp meant he couldn't tune people out as assets, as statistics, as pieces to be moved on a chessboard. He saw the pain. He saw the sweat. He saw the blood. He saw the effort. In person, people were ... well ... they were *people*.

It was beginning to dawn on Connell just what a mega-prick he'd become since his wife's death.

AC/DC's "Highway to Hell" blasted from inside the mess hall. Shadows bobbed as people moved by windows, making the light that hit the ground shimmer as if alive. Connell walked past without looking in.

As he approached, two men walked out, laughing with each other and swaying a little bit. The bigger of the two saw him. He thumped his buddy's shoulder, pointed at Connell. The smaller one nodded.

"Hey, Mister Kirkland," the smaller one said. "You coming to the party?"

Connell started to simply say no and keep walking, but he stopped. He didn't have to have a long conversation with these men, but he didn't have to blow them off, either. He'd done too much of that for too long.

"Just a bio-break," he said.

He was surprised that he recognized their faces; he'd seen their picture in their employee records. That shouldn't have surprised him at all, he supposed, considering how long he'd spent choosing the camp staff. He'd picked people based on their performance records and lack of filed complaints. He'd wanted hard workers, people who didn't bitch, people who didn't try to milk the system.

"You're Sherwood," he said to the little one. "And you're ... Hanson, is it?"

"*Jansson*," the big one said in a slight Swedish accent. He seemed delighted Connell had recognized him. The two men stumbled over, offering their hands. Connell shook them, already regretting his choice to stop and talk—how long would this take?

"Brian Jansson. Nice to meet you, Mister Kirkland," Jansson said. "I mean face-to-face and all. You really put in a lot of hours in that trailer."

"I suppose I do."

"Thanks for the party," Sherwood said. "Mack said you sprung for the beer and all."

"My pleasure."

Sherwood had a baby face. No surprise, considering he was the youngest person in the camp. Strong kid, though, with a wiry body built from a life of physical work. Jansson was Connell's age, but looked a decade older.

"Are you two done for the night?"

Jansson nodded sadly. "Yah, Mack kicked us out. Not because we're drunk, though."

"Which we are," Sherwood said. "Totally."

Jansson lightly cuffed him on the shoulder.

"We're the early shift," he said. "Mack wants us to have plenty of sleep. First thing tomorrow morning we blast into the natural tunnel complex. After that, he says we'll reach the Dense Mass in a day or two."

"That's what he told me as well," Connell said. "We're almost there. Well, gentleman, you get your sleep. Nature calls."

He nodded a good-bye and again headed for the latrine. He was almost to the door of the men's latrine when the women's opened, and Veronica Reeves stepped out, moving fast with her eyes cast down.

Connell stopped. She kept coming.

"Watch it," he said, the words coming out far harsher than he meant.

She looked up, surprised, reactively put a hand on his chest to keep from bumping into him. She removed the hand as if he were somehow repulsive to the touch.

"Excuse me," she said. "I didn't see you."

"That's because I'm not lying on the ground."

Her face scrunched in confusion.

He felt stupid.

"Because you were staring down," he said. "I was trying to make a joke."

Her eyes met his. He had the feeling she was more looking *through* him than *at* him.

"Remember when I told you you'd make a shitty comedian?"

He laughed. "Yeah, I do. How's the GPR equipment working out for you, Doctor?"

"Just call me *Veronica*, okay?"

She seemed upset, angry. She seemed ... *distant*, which was weird because he didn't know her at all.

"All right," he said. "How's the GPR equipment working out for you, Veronica?"

She looked off in the distance, up the mountainside, perhaps toward the plateau that held her discovery.

"Fine," she said. "We uncovered fascinating stuff. Achmed looked at the results, figured out there used to be a tunnel entrance at that plateau. It was destroyed, though. Someone must have used enough dynamite to level a building. Achmed figures a quarter mile of tunnel collapsed. He said the settled rock is too unstable to safely dig through."

Connell nodded politely. Achmed had told him the same thing earlier that day.

"Doesn't matter now that the vertical shaft is complete," he said. "We're in, we don't need another entrance. If you're happy with your results, I'm happy. EarthCore wants to take care of your needs."

She glanced at him, briefly, then her gaze again wandered back up to the plateau.

It had been so long since Connell had spoken to a woman about anything other than business. Too long, he knew. He didn't really remember how to do it anymore, but he felt compelled to keep talking to her, maybe find out what was wrong.

"All those bodies getting to you or something? I know they would get to me."

She nodded. "Everything's fine. I'm just a little distracted, that's all."

He thought of what she'd found, what Sonny had learned of the mountain's history.

"So strange an ancient culture could make it almost to the twentieth century, and they're unknown," he said. "In this area, I mean."

She pursed her lips, thinking.

"A little, sure. If the tribe mostly lived in the caves, perhaps only came out to hunt, they could have stayed hidden for a long time."

It seemed odd to think of primitive people hiding in caves while railways steadily snaked across the continent, connecting both coasts for the first time, while telephone wires were starting to spread across American cities, while the first vaccinations were taking place. And yet, based on what Veronica had found, that seemed to be the case.

If people had stayed hidden from the modern world through the 1880s, how long did they last after that?

He thought of the platinum knives, the double-sickle blades that stayed razor sharp for centuries.

"They couldn't still ... well, you know."

She raised an eyebrow. "Still be down there, you mean?"

He knew it was a stupid idea, but he nodded anyway.

"No chance," Veronica said. "In the caves there's no sunlight, and no sunlight means no food. To support a population of any size, they'd have to come out regularly to hunt and gather, yet aside from the massacre scene, there's no trace of them. You'd have to have a culture that completely hid their existence not only from miners, not only from the native tribes that dominated this area for centuries, but also the hikers, campers, climbers, hunters, mountain bikers, ecologists, surveyors, geologists and other scientists who study the area, and—"

"I get it," Connell said. "Lots of people."

She nodded. "And never a sighting or any sign of these people that someone might have reported along the way. Bigfoot has been spotted more, and he doesn't even exist, know what I mean? Once upon a time they could have stayed hidden, but there's just too many people now, too much technology. Plus, Angus's fancy-pants map doesn't show any current openings to the outside, so there's that."

He supposed that all made sense.

"Then what happened to them? Where did they go?"

She crossed her arms. "Well, well, well, Connell Kirkland—are you telling me that you're even the tiniest bit curious about something *other* than money?"

"Sometimes I get bored of visualizing myself as Scrooge McDuck swimming through pools of gold coins."

She smiled. "You'd look good with a top hat and a monocle, I admit."

Well hey, look at that. Maybe he wasn't so bad at jokes after all.

"So what, then?" he asked. "Did they just leave? Maybe they thought more White Men would come or something, so they headed out across the desert?"

"Possible, but those knives are so unique you'd have to think some would survive. If not intact, at least someone would have reported on them somewhere. Same thing at Cerro Chaltén—no knowledge of the knives anywhere." She tilted her head toward the mountain's peak. "What I think happened up there is they watched the miners for a while.

They saw what dynamite was, learned how to use it. Not exactly rocket science to light a fuse. They killed the miners, planted the dynamite, ran a fuse back into the tunnels, then blammo. They sealed themselves in."

It sounded almost cartoonish, like the Coyote getting blown up by a trap he'd set for the Road Runner. Sizzling fuses, boxes labeled *TNT*, and colorful, comedic explosions. Only there was nothing funny about a million tons of collapsing rock.

"What did they do then?"

"They *died*," she said. "From Angus's map, a good mile of that tunnel collapsed. Maybe it was more than they bargained for, I don't know. Maybe a bunch of them died in the cave-in, the rest starved to death. Maybe they sliced each other up with those knives." She glanced off, bit her upper lip. "God knows they loved to use them."

An awkward silence followed. The look in her eyes, it seemed... *haunted*. Connell felt compelled to say something, just to fill that void.

"You really think it's possible for a culture to kill itself off like that?"

"Has happened before," she said. "Many, many times in history. Trust me—I'm an anthropologist."

She forced a smile.

He forced one of his own.

"Well, if you'll excuse me—" he held up the first two fingers of each hand, curled them twice "—*Veronica*—" he lowered his hands "—I must use the little boys' room."

Her nose wrinkled.

"Did you just make air quotes for my name?"

"Yes."

"Why?"

"Because you asked me to call you that. I was trying to be funny. Again."

She shook her head, then the corners of her mouth ticked up, just a little. A smile. A tiny one, yes, but a *real* smile.

"When I said *you're not good at it*, I was wrong," she said. "You're horrible."

"You don't say."

"I do. I'm joining the party. You coming?"

He shook his head.

"Couple of hours' work left. No rest for the wicked."

"Too bad," she said. "Tomorrow's the big day. I guess I'll see you then. Later."

She walked away. He watched her.

He caught himself looking at her ass. Looking at her ass, and thinking of that little smile.

"Nope," he said quietly. "Nope-nope-nope. You haven't done shit in five years. Everything is on the line, so why start now?"

As he entered the latrine, he realized there really wasn't a good answer to that question.

BOOK THREE

FUNERAL MOUNTAIN

18

August 26

6:15 A.M.

For a man that planned every aspect of massive, multimillion-dollar mining operations, a man that controlled everything down to the last bolt, Mack Hendricks had registered an epic lack of foresight—he'd stayed up drinking until two a.m. with Sanji Haak and Veronica Reeves.

That, combined with a five thirty a.m. wake-up time, was an issue. When *also* combined with a mind-melting hangover, it became a problem, a nonstop reminder that stupid *always* carries a cost.

Felt like a bomb was going off in his head. Among an endless supply of beer, wine and booze, Kirkland had ordered four bottles of Jäger. Four. Who does that? Correction: Who over the age of twenty-five does that? And then Kirkland hadn't even shown up to the party, leaving Mack to do shot after shot of the stuff with his miners, a few lab techs, and the tag team father & daughter combo of Sanji and Veronica.

A pounding skull couldn't dull Mack's mood, though. He wasn't going to miss this, not for all the booze in the world. Pain or no pain, why shouldn't he be chipper? He was about to embark on the defining moment of his career—even if his head had been cut off, there still would have been a smile on his face.

At least he had some extra time to recover. The elevator shaft was so deep it took half an hour to go from the surface to the bottom, or vice versa.

As he traveled down the circular elevator with the morning crew, he reflected on what they had all accomplished together. They'd finished the 3.6-kilometer deep shaft (or, 2.27 miles for Those Who Refused To Learn The Metric System). Not a world's record, but that didn't matter. Once they entered the tunnel system and followed it to the Dense Mass, they would be right around 5.24 kilometers—3.2 miles—below the surface.

Deeper belowground than human beings had ever been.

Digging the vertical shaft would probably prove to be the easy part of this operation. Thanks to Angus's invention, it was a straight shot down. No crumbling, no subsequent collapses, no problems of any kind. The hard part was all the support structures that went along with it. Kilometers of air ducting and electrical cable, a massive temperature control rig, an elevator system capable of traversing the entire distance— the list went on and on. Angus had invented the drill head, but everything else? That was all Mack's design.

This mine was a masterpiece.

Twelve men in the morning crew with him. They all wore blue coveralls, yellow mining helmets, clear plastic eye protection. They stood in the flatbeds of a pair of squat battery-powered trucks: six on one, seven on the other. Two of the men had heavy drills at their feet, three-meter bits as thick as a man's thumb resting against their shoulders. The other men carried shovels, pickaxes, portable lights.

Mack felt pride looking at them: uniformed warriors heading into battle, about to make history.

Down and down the elevator went. Over and over again, they passed by the big lights mounted in the round shaft wall: a glow below his feet, then brightness on coveralls, helmets and tools as the elevator drew even, then strange shadows dipping and stretching as it continued down. They passed by air pumps every few hundred meters. Some pumped out cool air to fight the geothermal heat. Others were pulling air up from below. Cool air fell, of course, but in a shaft this deep, the hottest air was always at the bottom.

Mack checked his handheld air sampler. No traces of poisonous gas. Even with the cool air being pumped into the shaft, the temperature sat at thirty-eight point nine degrees Celsius. The lower they went, the higher that number would go.

Brian Jansson leaned in, trying to see the readout.

"How hot, chief?"

Mack told him.

The big man rubbed his face, spreading sweat. Everyone was sweating already and they were only three quarters of the way down.

"If we had some beer and some women we could call this a sauna," Jansson said. He looked around at his crewmates. "Get us another big party cooking, eh?"

Out of all the men in EarthCore's mining crew, Mack liked Jansson the most. He was a skilled and careful worker, and the only time he bitched was to be funny.

"A sauna's fine, Jansson," Mack said. "But only as long as I never have to see you naked."

Jansson did a shimmy like he was posing for the camera. The crew laughed along with him.

The elevator touched down on the shaft bottom. No more jokes; the crew got to work on making a horizontal shaft that would breach into the natural tunnel complex.

There were no permanent lights down this far. That had to wait until the area had been fully cleared. Men set up temporary floodlights that gave steady illumination. Helmet lights bobbed all over, moving in time with the crew's confident motions.

They drilled long burn holes into the wall, setting them in a pattern to blow rock downward and clear a three-meter space. They loaded the burn holes with explosives and a remote-activated detonator, then gathered up the temporary lights and returned to the elevator. Mack took a head count to make sure everyone was accounted for, then took the cage up a hundred meters. He made sure each man donned air masks connected to a central tank, did a second head count, then detonated the charge.

The blast roared through the mountain. Limestone dust billowed up the shaft like a plume of tan volcanic ash, blinding them for a bit.

Air-filtration units placed up the length of the shaft removed the dust within minutes. Mack watched his handheld monitor, waited until the readout said the air was clean enough to breathe. Then, the men removed their masks and descended again.

The blast had cleared a good ten meters of new tunnel. They had another three or four more rounds of blasting to go before they breached into the natural tunnel complex. Mack was on the bleeding edge of accomplishment, of etching his name in history. Despite the explosion and the heat, his head didn't even hurt anymore. Adrenaline and pure excitement proved to be a great hangover cure.

The men set to the backbreaking task of hauling loose rock back to the elevator platform. In teams, they lifted big chunks and set them on squat electric flatbed trucks. Smaller chunks were picked up one at a time, with the remnants scooped up on shovels. The trucks moved the rock back down the new tunnel and dumped it on the elevator. No vaporizing here, they'd have to take all of it to the top of the shaft, move it out, then come back down again. The men found spots on the platform among the rubble, either standing between piles or sitting on them. The elevator returned to the top of the shaft.

Each round—blasting, moving the rock to the shaft, riding up, dumping, riding back down—took over an hour.

Three hours after the first blast, Mack's men drilled the fourth series of burn holes. This would be the one, he knew it. They'd created a little over ten meters of new space.

Angus had provided a sturdy, plastic-coated map. Mack had expected something fancier, maybe a version of the 3-D map on a tablet computer or something, but Angus didn't have that. The plastic map was quite detailed, though. Figuring out orientation in the 3-D layout sometimes took a bit of time, but truth be told, Mack preferred having a map that couldn't run out of battery power.

They drilled. They placed the charges. Mack and his men returned to the elevator, did the head count, rode up a hundred meters, donned masks, did the second head count, then detonated the charges.

They heard the explosion, but this time there was something more—a billowing wave of heat roiled up the shaft along with the suffocating dust. Mack felt his skin prickle and burn in sudden, shocked complaint. A paralyzing wave of terror gripped him as the blast-furnace cloud baked him alive. Behind him on the platform first one man screamed in alarm, then another, and another.

The screams tapered off. No one had burst into flames. Still insufferably hot, but it felt like the heat had leveled out. Mack checked the temperature. He started to laugh.

"Hey, chief," Jansson said through his mask. "What's so funny?"

Mack held up the gauge for all to see. "Sixty-six point six Celsius, mates. Welcome to hell."

The men laughed, but not very hard. Behind those goggles, Mack saw scared eyes. He was sure they saw the same thing behind his.

A man held up his hand—Keith Sherwood, youngest guy on the crew. Mack nodded at him to speak.

"Six-six-six, that's funny," Sherwood said. "What's that in actual degrees? And by *actual*, I mean in American."

Jansson shook his head sadly.

"For you, that's about a hundred and fifty degrees Fahrenheit."

The ventilators cleared away the dust but made only a tiny dent in the temperature. The handheld unit said the new air contained plenty of oxygen, some hydrogen and higher levels of nitrogen, but no contaminants. Mack pulled off his mask and took a tentative, testing breath. He wrinkled his nose in disgust at a faint yet offensive smell. Something like a combination of rotting fruit and dog shit. He motioned for the other men to remove their masks. Their faces showed instant disgust.

Sherwood took a big breath through his nose, then gagged, then bent at the waist and threw up, much to the amusement of the older men.

Jansson patted him on the back.

"I love the smell of Hades in the morning," he said. "It smells like victory."

"You should love it, mate," Mack said. "It smells just like your breath."

The men laughed again, louder this time. They were getting used to the heat. Well, as used to it as a man could get. He'd have them clear out this load of rock, then they'd be too exhausted to do any further work. Only so much a man can do in an environment like this.

He lowered the elevator to the shaft floor. He led his men forward.

Together, through headlamp beams turned almost solid from whirling dust, they saw an amazing sight.

They had punched through.

A natural cavern, maybe four times the size of the space they'd created to hold the winch for the elevator and the laser drill. He stepped inside. Some of the men followed. Their lights played along rough tan-green walls, up to a flat sandstone ceiling, and across each other's sweat-drenched smiles. They all felt the pride of a tough job well done. At the back of this new cavern stood the opening of a natural tunnel. It loomed black and promising.

"Chief," Jansson said, "we going in?"

Mack wanted to, but this wasn't the time to rush things. Caution first, always.

"No, I'm afraid not. Kirkland already told me who gets to be first."

He turned to face the rest of his men.

"All right, boys, let's clean up this loose rock. Make sure you're drinking plenty of water, or you'll pass out down here. Get your job done, but don't be in a rush. Slow is steady, steady is smooth, smooth is fast. Get to it."

The men did. Heat like this changed the game; a job they could normally do for five or six hours without a rest now drained them inside of fifteen minutes.

It would only get hotter the deeper they went. The natural tunnel complex was far too large to cool with pumped air. Angus apparently had a solution to the temperature problem, although Mack didn't know what that was yet. He'd find out when he returned to the surface.

Time to begin phase two, and start exploring the largest tunnel complex known to man.

10:17 A.M.

Katerina didn't miss her family as much as she had figured. She simply didn't have time to think about them. She sat at a small desk that belonged to Angus, trying to cope with the pressure bearing down on her from all sides.

"It's been forty-eight *fucking* hours, Achmed," she said. "You're no closer to figuring out the cause of that aberrant spike. We have to figure this out, there are people in that shaft."

… and Kirkland will have my head if I go back to him with yet another shoulder shrug, was how the sentence should have ended.

Achmed glared at her. She realized, and not for the first time in the last two days, that he was glaring at her the same way he used to glare at Angus. It hurt her to ride Achmed like this, but she needed answers.

"I can't see through solid rock," he said. "How am I supposed to find out what it is? The damn computer keeps cutting out every six hours, how can you expect results with work conditions like this?"

She slapped the desktop.

"*No more excuses!* No one is going to die on my watch. If the computer is giving you shit and you can't solve the problem until it works, then start by fixing the goddamned computer. I've got other problems and don't have time to babysit you."

She could hardly believe those words were coming out of her mouth, but they were, and she meant them. Being in charge wasn't exactly the dream job she'd envisioned.

Achmed's face screwed tight with anger.

"I need *help*," he said. "You've taken the rest of the staff to help you study that meaningless line. If you want me to solve the problem, give me more resources."

Maybe he was right about that.

"Take Mitchell," she said. "And Rodriguez. Get it fixed."

He walked away, already shouting for those two to join him at the main computer.

Achmed had checked the spikes against Mack's blasting record – they hadn't been caused by any EarthCore activity. She feared the spikes meant cave-ins somewhere in the natural tunnels, something that would slow the project down and make Kirkland very unhappy.

She returned to her work. Achmed had one mystery, she had another. In addition to the seismic spikes, Kirkland wanted to know the cause of the strange line Dr. Reeves had detected. Katerina had assigned every free person to mapping that line, and the results were shocking.

Four miles downhill and a half mile uphill from where Reeves and

Haak had found the phenomenon, the line broke off into two lines that each a took ninety-degree turn south. Both of those new lines reached south for 3.28 miles. At that point, both took a ninety-degree turn toward each other, making a new line, a line that completed a rectangle—a 4.652-mile-long and 3.28-mile-wide rectangle, in which the mine shaft sat almost dead-center.

They had taken to calling it the "Reeves Rectangle." Who made it? Why? And how on earth did they do it?

Katerina didn't have any answers. She shuddered—Connell wouldn't like that, wouldn't like that at all.

11:52 A.M.

Mack and every miner on staff—even the morning shift—sat on folding chairs in the security staff's Quonset. They watched in rapt attention as O'Doyle held up a bright yellow formfitting jumpsuit. The suit, supposedly, would allow them to safely explore the caves.

"This is a *KoolSuit*," O'Doyle said, his voice bellowing like a drill sergeant's. "That's *Kool* with a *K*, as in its inventor, Angus Kool. The fabric is a microtubule material that accommodates the flow of coolant throughout the suit. This small backpack unit circulates fluid through the material to regulate your body temperature."

The morning-shift miners looked beat, drained by the heat. All except for Jansson and Sherwood, who watched O'Doyle's every move and seemed locked in on his every word. They'd quietly asked if they could pull a double-shift and go down with Mack. He wasn't crazy about the idea, but the two men were both experienced climbers. Having them along might help identify the safest path, help reach the Dense Mass faster.

O'Doyle gripped the suit in both hands and tried to pull it apart. The man's muscles bulged and twitched. O'Doyle had an old man's gut, but a young man's arms. There was no doubt he was trying his best to rip the suit—the suit stretched slightly, but refused to break.

"The material itself is very durable," he said. "KoolSuits are also coated with a layer of Kevlar, so they should hold up well while you're crawling through the tunnels. However, be aware of the dangerous environment. We expect the temperature to exceed two hundred degrees Fahrenheit, which means that if your suit rips in any way, repair it immediately with the patches stored in your backpack. Then alert your supervisor and head for the surface as fast as possible."

Mack raised his hand. O'Doyle nodded at him.

"That means no tough-guy stuff," Mack said, turning slowly to address all the miners. "Safety first, always. Any tear, no matter how small, and you get back to the surface. If I see anyone with a tear that they haven't reported, you are automatically fired. No second chances, no excuses, understand?"

Heads nodded. Mack gestured for O'Doyle to continue.

"Mister Hendricks threatens you with unemployment," O'Doyle said. "I'll threaten you with your life. Mister Takachi here has been a combat medic and understands what happens to the human body in dire situations. Mister Takachi?"

Cho Takachi stood up. He pushed his sunglasses up a sweat-sheened nose.

"At the temperatures we expect, any problem could prove fatal," he said. "Without a functioning suit, you will dehydrate and die in a matter of hours. Do *not*, I repeat, do *not* remove your gloves to touch *anything*. Not under any circumstances. The rocks in the lower tunnel are hot enough to cause second-degree burns on contact."

He sat. O'Doyle set the suit down on a table. He picked up a pair of yellow gloves.

"The most important parts of your suit are the gloves and the flexi-mask. That is why your suit pockets contain a spare pair of gloves and a spare mask. If a glove tears, undo the wrist seal, remove it, put on the replacement, and *make sure* the wrist seal locks tight."

He set the gloves down and picked up what looked like a flimsy piece of plastic wrap—the flexi-mask. He spread it out across his palms and pressed it to his face. It seemed to conform to him, almost to *hug* his cheeks and chin, eyes and forehead. He lowered his hands. His face looked a little duller, but other than that, he might have had nothing on at all.

"As you can see, the mask covers my face but doesn't block my mouth or nose. Air that would cook you from the inside out is lowered to breathable temperatures. Do not ask me to explain the tech, because I do not understand it. What I know is you get the benefit of not having to wear a re-breather, and trust me, that is a good thing. The KoolSuit hoods cover your head, neck and ears. This mask covers the rest and automatically locks in with the hood's material. Mister Hendricks, if you would be so kind as to let me guide you through putting on the suit while everyone watches?"

"I'd love to, mate."

He stood in front of the men, had no shame stripping down to his boxers while some of the miners hooted and made jokes. All in good fun. Mack did everything as O'Doyle told him to do, obeying every deep-voiced order to the letter. Mack wanted his people to be safe, of course, but O'Doyle also had a tone of command that could not easily be ignored.

As Mack donned the rubbery KoolSuit, careful to make sure every seal was secure, excitement began to wash over him. They had built the camp, they had drilled the shaft, they had blasted their way to the tunnel complex. Now he was preparing for the final step—to explore an area untouched by man. Granted, it was going to be mostly tight tunnels, nothing more to see than limestone walls eroded by millions of years of circulating water, but that feeling of discovery pumped adrenaline through his blood.

The suit felt cool against his skin, effortlessly chasing away the midday heat. He barely felt the mask but sensed the air that he breathed was cooler. He felt something hard in the seat—must be some padding in case people had to sit down on rocks.

"Fits great," he said. "A bit heavier than I thought, though."

O'Doyle took his right wrist, held it up for all to see.

"There is a built-in display woven right into the fabric," he said. "External temp, body temp, a clock with timers, air-quality measurements, it's all right there for you."

Jansson raised a hand. O'Doyle nodded at him.

"Pardon me for asking," Jansson said, "but I don't see a fly in those pants. How do we pee?"

O'Doyle pointed at Mack's crotch—Mack suddenly felt a bit uncomfortable.

"Inside your pants is a flexible tube," O'Doyle said. "Similar to the flexi-mask. Place your penis in the tube and leave it there. Women have a different fitting—you'll know if you get the wrong suit. I chose not to help Mister Hendricks with his tube, as we're not even on a first-name basis yet. Trust me, men, you do not want to be whipping out your tally-whacker in air that's two hundred degrees. EarthCore's health-care plan will not cover the subsequent sex change requests."

The miners laughed.

"If the suit feels a bit heavy, that's because it carries a gallon of water," O'Doyle said. "If you carried water in an external container, it would wind up being the same temperature as the hot air—which means it would boil away. Bad news. There's bladders throughout the material, so the water *in* the suit is kept cool *by* the suit. There's a drinking tube in the neck that slides right up inside the mask. Seeing as hydration is so important, the suit will filter your urine and add that water back to the mix."

The men groaned in disgust.

O'Doyle held up a hand to silence them.

"And now, let's have a serious talk about poop."

He grabbed Mack's shoulders, spun him around to show his backside to the miners. O'Doyle made a fist, rapped his knuckles against the hard pad in the seat of Mack's suit.

"So that you don't burn your precious little bungholes, Doctor Kool included a built-in feces processor," O'Doyle said. "Just squat and go. The suit will take your turds and put them through the world's smallest little airlock. Believe it or not, men, this suit will even clean up any fecal detritus left on your rectum. In other words, this is the closest I've ever been to being so rich I can afford to have someone else wipe my ass for me."

The men laughed again. Mack, though, did not. It hadn't crossed his mind, but it made sense: it could get so hot down there that taking down your pants to take a shit might cause skin burns.

The fun was over—time to get going.

"All right, men," he said. "Mister O'Doyle and Mister Takachi will help you suit up. Thirteen of us need to be dressed and on that elevator as soon as possible."

12:21 P.M.

Patrick O'Doyle could have crushed Connell Kirkland in a heartbeat. Both men knew it. Physical prowess, however, had little to do with their relationship.

"Two Koolsuits missing," Connell said.

Patrick nodded once. "Yes sir."

Connell stared. It was a stare worthy of a CO in any forward combat area, a stare that said, *I'm having a hard time processing what a stupid, worthless fuck you are—I trusted you and you let me down.*

Patrick had delivered an identical stare many times in his life. As far as "the stare" went, it was always better to give than to receive. Patrick was usually the giver. He was on the receiving end this time, though, and he deserved every miserable, skin-crawling second of it.

Eight years in the marines had taught him that authority was something you followed without question. Eight years, multiple tours and multiple combat engagements had riveted that rule into his soul to the point where it was never forgotten, never unlearned. The marines had also drilled home one more concept: there is no excuse for failure.

"Two KoolSuits missing," Connell said again. "When did you find out?"

"This morning, as Mister Hendricks prepared to take the first crew into the tunnels. There are twenty-six suits, enough for two full thirteen-man mining crews. We counted off the thirteen that outfit the men currently in the tunnels with Mister Hendricks. After the training session, we did a count on the remaining suits and discovered two were unaccounted for."

"*Unaccounted for. Is that some kind of bullshit military speak for I have no idea how to do my job?*"

Patrick winced.

"I'm afraid that's exactly what it means, Mister Kirkland."

No beating around the bush. No excuses. The buck stopped here.

Connell was a good boss. A demanding boss who told you exactly what he wanted, then let you figure out how to get that job done on your own. Need resources? He provided them. Needed ideas? He gave them. He was fair, but he also expected success in all things—if you didn't get the job done, it was your fault and no one else's.

It wasn't just failure. It was failing *him*, failing Connell Kirkland, the man who had basically saved Patrick's life.

Two years earlier, Patrick had been jobless, let go after twenty-one years of service to his country. Twenty-one years, his entire adult life. Jobless, damn near homeless. Unless you counted living in a flophouse as homeless, in which case he was that, too.

He'd been forgotten. He'd had nothing. He'd had no one. All that service, all that pain and sacrifice, and no one seemed to give a fuck about him. He wasn't good for killing anymore, so why bother? They had used him up, then discarded him.

He'd grown up an orphan. Never really knew his parents. Foster homes. Growing too big, too soon, with too much anger. Nobody could handle him. School wasn't his thing. Sports gave some outlet, wrestling, in particular, but he didn't have the discipline needed to excel. Graduated, but barely—no prospects for a kid with little education, no connections, no family. So, he'd taken the only route possible for many teenagers just like him: he'd enlisted.

The marines gave him the discipline he needed. And as far as anger outlets went, hard to beat hand-to-hand combat training, learning to shoot, burning off all the energy he had and then some. He'd grown up with nothing, but in the service he found his true calling.

Then came deployment.

The service changes a man. So does real combat. Killing. Seeing people you know get killed. The brutality of war, of trying to do your job and also stay alive at the same time.

Three deployments. Twenty-seven confirmed kills. Taking life bothered some of his fellow marines, affected them at a deep level. It didn't bother Patrick. At all. He didn't know what that said about him as a person, and he didn't really care. He was good at it. He was praised for it, rewarded for it. At eight years in he was ready to re-up for a third hitch, work toward his twenty, when his CO had sent him to Washington, D.C., to meet with a man named Murray Longworth.

What Longworth had to say didn't surprise Patrick. Sometimes, higher-ups in government needed specific things done, things that no one could know about, things that would never be reported on or recorded in any way. They called it "gray work."

Turned out Patrick was good at that, too.

Patrick O'Doyle became a nonperson. Longworth's people erased his past, removed all military records, fingerprints, dental records, anything that could tie his corpse—should he die while on mission—to the U.S. government.

He spent a decade traveling the world, killing who they told him to kill. He specialized in jungle work and urban penetration. On three separate occasions, Murray had asked Patrick to volunteer for missions instead of ordering him to go, because it was unlikely the operator would be able to escape after the target was hit. Patrick accepted all three. And all three times, he made it back.

The last of those missions, though, had ended badly. He'd been caught. Tortured. His captors had burned off his ear. Had he talked? He didn't remember. All he knew was that he'd gotten very lucky — a drone strike had hit the compound where he was being held, caused enough damage and chaos that he'd escaped.

Scarred. Disfigured. He stood out now. Couldn't blend in. Murray couldn't use him for gray missions anymore. Too bad, so sad, Patrick, but you're no longer on the starting squad. Murray had found work for him in the Department of Special Threats, a mostly off-the-books agency that handled crazy bioterror shit. The things Patrick had seen there. Belize. Saskatchewan. Black Manitou Island. A parade of death.

Then the budget cuts. Patrick O'Doyle and his twenty-one years of service were no longer needed. Thank you very much. Here's a pin and a ribbon, move on. Those eleven years you spent traveling the globe to wipe out the enemies of democracy? Yeah, those don't count toward your retirement. Have a nice life. Your grateful nation really appreciates your service, just not in a way that will pay the bills.

He had found himself without direction for the first time since he'd turned eighteen. Skills such as avoiding local police, jungle survival and how to kill a man from a mile away didn't translate into the civilian world. There were no missions, no commanding officers, no *orders*. He'd had no one to tell him what to do. He'd felt lost.

What did he do for a living? Bagged groceries. Mopped floors. Made barely enough to pay for food and a rent-by-the-month hotel. The indignity of it all. He'd been a soldier, a leader of men, a prized asset. From all that to nothing. A scarred, ugly, lonely nobody. Every day, eating a bullet seemed more and more like the only way out.

Then that woman had found him. So strange. A knockout blonde shows up at the flophouse. Perfect body, perfect face, eyes as soulless as black marbles. She had a plane ticket. Did he want work? Real work? Fly to Denver to meet with Connell Kirkland. Patrick had. The interview lasted about fifteen minutes. Connell hired him on the spot. Big salary.

Big responsibility. For the first time in his life, Patrick held a job where the paycheck didn't come from Uncle Sam.

Structure and purpose. That's what Connell had given him. And *pride*. Patrick belonged again. He had responsibility. Connell didn't care about his past, his scarring, didn't care about anything other than seeing that his company and his personnel were properly protected.

This man, this lanky, tall man with the dead gray eyes, he had given Patrick his life back. And a future. A *retirement plan*. Percentages.

All that, and he'd let Connell down.

"Those suits are expensive," Connell said. His voice remained distant, detached. "Do you have any idea of how much each suit is worth?"

"Yes *sir*, Mister Kirkland." O'Doyle snapped off the word *sir* crisp and loud, exactly as he would have done were he still in the service. "Each suit is worth thirty-five thousand, two hundred and thirty dollars. American."

Connell nodded. "Very good. As if the price wasn't enough to piss me off, there's the small fact that we're on the side of a mountain in the middle of a fucking desert. I know you well enough to assume that you accounted for all the suits both when we left and when we arrived. Am I correct?"

"Yes *sir*."

"As a security chief, you seem to be very good at misplacing things in the middle of a fucking desert, don't you?"

"Yes *sir*."

The air conditioner's hum and the slow thump of Connell's fingers drumming on the desktop—*ba-da-ba-bump, ba-da-ba-bump*—were the only sounds in the trailer. O'Doyle thought Connell looked like a grenade with the pin pulled, ready to explode at any second.

"And the lab accident," he said. "Tell me again what you found."

Patrick had already told him. Twice. When you were a failure, Connell liked to make you repeat things.

"A pressure valve may have been tampered with. Looks like something hit it. Could have happened a week ago, could have happened today. That probably let static electricity get into the tank, the tank blew."

Ba-da-ba-bump, ba-da-ba-bump.

"That happened two days ago," Connell said. "And you're no closer to finding out who did it?"

Patrick felt his jaw clenching, his teeth grinding. If he'd been closer to finding out, he would have said so, and Connell knew that. In many ways, this calm-voiced repetition was far worse than being screamed at.

"No *sir*. I've found nothing else."

"Then look harder. Now get out of my sight."

Patrick left. So humiliating. Someone was getting the better of him. Someone was making him look like a fool. Someone was making him *angry*.

He knew he wasn't the smartest man that ever walked the earth, but he was one of the most tireless and dedicated. Sooner or later he'd find the truth, he'd find the bastard responsible. When that happened, he planned on carving *Semper Fidelis* into the fuckwad's chest.

12:40 P.M.

Two missing KoolSuits. Two injured scientists. Sabotage. No, not just sabotage, *expert* sabotage, as if someone knew the equipment inside and out.

"They wouldn't," Connell whispered.

He picked up his cell phone, dialed.

"Milford Valley Memorial Hospital," a woman answered.

"Angus Kool's room, please."

There was a pause as the woman transferred the call. The phone rang five times before someone answered.

"Hello?"

"Angus?"

"No, this is Randy."

"Connell here. Let me talk to Angus."

"He's sleeping," Randy said.

"So wake him up."

"The doctor doesn't want him disturbed," Randy said. "He's still feeling a lot of head pain."

Randy wanted to protect Angus. That's what friends did for one another. Well and fine, but he was picking the wrong time to exhibit his misguided loyalties.

"I don't care if his brains are dripping out of his ears. Wake him up right fucking now."

"Fine, hold on a second."

After a brief pause, the phone rustled as it switched hands.

"Mister Kirkland, what's up?" said a sleepy Angus.

"How are you doing, Angus?"

"I was sleeping, that's how I was doing. What do you need?"

Could he be up to something?

"Just wanted to check up on you guys."

"Golly, Dad, thanks a bunch, but me and the gang aren't going anywhere."

"Fine," Connell said. "Sorry to wake you."

Angus hung up without another word. He and Randy were exactly where they were supposed to be. If they were, who had stolen the suits? Who had sabotaged the lab? And how were they getting in and out of camp so easily?

Connell knew the answer: someone in camp was on the take. Someone was getting paid off.

If he didn't get his people to the Dense Mass soon, that someone else would beat him to it.

And then all of this would be for nothing.

No matter what the cost, Mack Hendricks had to move faster.

12:47 P.M.

"Slow down, Jansson," Keith Sherwood called out. "You're descending too fast."

Brian Jansson looked up from his slightly swinging line, his light playing up the chasm and flashing brightly in Keith's eyes. Jansson dangled in a sea of black, like a yellow worm on a hook.

"I'll be sure to be careful, Mommy," he said. "Been climbing since before you were a single cell of annoying tickling the inside of your daddy's nutsack. I think I know what I'm doing."

"Asshole," Keith murmured under his breath.

He didn't want to be in this sliver of a tunnel. Rough limestone walls pressed against his body on every side. The suit kept him cool, but he felt the heat on his face, on his eyes. There was no turning around here; to get out you either crawled backward for thirty feet or descended into the chasm.

Keith panned his headlamp on a plastic-coated map. Mack had sent them here. According to the map, several thin tunnels branched off the chasm floor a hundred and fifty feet below. The steep vertical drop might provide a shortcut to the Dense Mass, so it had to be explored.

"Almost to the bottom," Jansson called up. Keith again looked down into the chasm, only his head peeking over the edge. Janson was farther down now, the equivalent of fourteen or fifteen stories. He looked like a wriggling yellow toy soldier.

"Seems okay," Jansson said, voice echoing off the dark chasm walls. "Jagged rocks, poor footing, but it looks okay. I'll—"

A cry of pain. A muffled, brittle *snap* that echoed up just as his voice had. Keith's light reached down: far below, Jansson lay on his side. So far away, so small.

"Jansson! You okay?"

A pause.

"Fine," Jansson said, forcing out the word. "If you don't count my broken leg."

Keith felt a new stab of fear. This dark place, so far below the surface, and without Jansson he would be alone ...

"Quit fucking around, man."

"Wish I was," Jansson said. "My foot slipped on this boulder. Leg's broken. Left arm might be dislocated, too. Mack's going to kill me."

"Hold on. I'll tie a new line and come get you."

Keith felt at the chasm edge, hands searching for the best way over.

"Don't be an idiot," Jansson said. "You know procedure. If you have rope problems, we're both stuck here. You can't pull me up by yourself—go back and get Mack, get help."

Crawling backward through this tunnel ... no one with him ...

"You're crazy," Keith said. "I can't leave you here."

Jansson laughed, a sound choked off by a grunt of pain.

"Goddamn, maybe a rib, too," he said. "Just go, kid. It'll take you maybe twenty minutes to crawl back to the others, so I'm looking at an hour all by my lonesome. The sooner you start, the sooner I'm out of here. Until then about all I can do is whack off. Good thing I hurt my left arm and not my right, eh?"

An hour down there, on his own. His batteries would last that long, easy, so he wouldn't be in the dark. Just the thought of it made Keith's skin crawl.

"What about your suit? Any rips?"

Far below, the yellow toy soldier felt at his legs, grunted as his good hand searched around.

"I think it's okay. Fuck, this *hurts*. Would you go get somebody?"

"Okay, just hold tight."

Keith closed his eyes, tried to focus. He couldn't think about himself— every minute he waited was another minute his friend would be in agony. He took a deep breath, then pushed away from the chasm's edge.

IN MINUTES, ALL SOUND of Keith's efforts faded away.

Jansson was truly alone.

He gritted his teeth against the pain, pushed himself to a sitting position. It hurt, sure, but he'd felt worse. What was this, the third time he'd broken his leg? The fourth? Just be cool. Sit and wait. Help would be there before he knew it.

He sat still, ears instinctively hunting for sounds, finding none. He hated the quiet, and caves were *dead* quiet. Not a sound at all, other than your own. You didn't notice how noisy the world around you was until you came to a place like this. No wind, no creaks, no squeaks, no honks... nothing. A weird feeling, like someone had grabbed nature's remote control and hit *mute*. Damn fool thing to get in a hurry and break a leg. He should have been more—

A sound. Something small, echoing.

click-click, click...

Metal on rock?

He flashed his light upward, toward the tunnel mouth a hundred and fifty feet above. Nothing moved. He waited for the sound to come again, but only silence met his ears. He looked around the chasm bottom, his headlamp following his gaze. Several tunnels, but all very small, probably too small to crawl through. The trip was a waste of—

Another sound. Different. Coming from one of the tunnels leading out from the chasm floor. A hiss, a rattling whisper... the sound of dry, rustling leaves sliding across open pavement.

1:20 P.M.

Mack leaned over the chasm's edge. His headlamp probed the depths below, illuminated only rock.

"Jansson! Jansson, answer me, mate."

Nothing but his own voice echoing back.

Keith was right behind him, the passage so narrow Mack couldn't even turn around to talk. "This is it, Keith? You're sure."

"Absolutely. He's down there."

Things were going from bad to worse. Once out of that initial natural cavern, Mack had discovered some of the tunnels leading from it were *not* natural—they'd been chiseled into the rock. So much for being the first people down here. The artificial tunnels seemed to line up with Veronica Reeves's claims—something that would not make Connell happy when Mack was next able to report back.

But that detail meant nothing compared to this: a missing man.

Mack pulled out the Marco/Polo device and checked the signals. The unit showed only two names:

MACK HENDRICKS
KEITH SHERWOOD

No man down there, no flash of yellow KoolSuit. Jansson's rope still hung over the chasm's edge. Mack gave it an experimental tug: it moved easily. That made no sense. The rope was Jansson's safety line, the way for rescuers to bring him back up. If he was hurt, why would he unhook it?

Mack reeled in the rope, curling the slack into a coil at his right.

He reached the end: the rope had been cut.

A neat slice, machine-press perfect. Something on the end of the rope, something wet.

Something red.

Keith nudged Mack's foot. "We going down to get him or what?"

Mack stared at the blood beaded up on the nylon sliced end. He leaned a little further over the edge again, letting his light scrub the floor far below. Nothing moved.

"He's not down there, mate."

"Of course he is," Keith said. "Where the hell else could he be?"

"I don't know. Could you see him after he fell?"

"Yeah, I could see him fine."

"He's not there now," Mack said. "Start moving back, and do it quick."

"We've got to go down and look for him!"

"No, we're going back to phone up for help. Now *move*, Sherwood, or I'll start kicking you in the face to *make* you move."

Mack slid backward, working his way out of the thin tunnel.

He hoped O'Doyle knew how to rappel.

1:32 P.M.

Katerina Hayes tried to rub the stickiness from her eyes. She hadn't slept a wink last night. Neither had most of her lab staff. They hunted for an answer regarding the mysterious, miles-long rectangle that surrounded the campsite and the mine. So far, no rational explanation.

They had hypotheses, sure. Crazy-pants hypotheses. The one that best fit the observed data? A high-powered laser fired from orbit. Ridiculous. When she'd heard that one, she'd been so desperate she actually hoped maybe there was evidence of melted rock, possibly millennia-old scorch marks.

They'd found none of that. She felt like an idiot for making people look.

On the surface, the line was nearly invisible. You could only see it if you knew exactly where to look. If not for the GPR suite, people might have walked over it a hundred times without noticing.

Most of the line's camouflage came from landslides, water erosion, windswept dirt and sand. Such natural actions had covered most of the line, leaving only split rocks on either side as the only evidence visible with the naked eye.

Extrapolating on a computer erosion model, they had generated an estimate of the rectangle's age—somewhere around thirteen thousand years old.

Calling it "science on the fly" was an understatement. She and her staff made it up as they went along, dubbing the new discipline "chronogeomorphology": judging a formation's age by the erosion on and around it.

And figuring out the Reeves Rectangle was far from her only problem.

She gave her eyes another rub, this one just as ineffective as the last. She wished she was back in Denver with her family. She didn't want to be in charge anymore, didn't want to face Connell Kirkland's disappointment any longer.

But if she had to eat shit, she wouldn't be the only one munching down.

"Achmed! What's the status on that latest tremor?"

He rose from his station and shuffled over. His normally dark and beautiful eyes were now just plain dark. Sunken cheeks showed the effects of a few scant hours' sleep over the past two days. Even his porn 'stache looked somehow tired and limp.

"*Tremor* is a bit of an overstatement, I think," he said.

"A pile of shit by any other name still stinks."

She was pushing him hard and she knew it. The tremors threatened the financial future of this operation, and the lives of the men working inside the mountain. A second aberrant spike on the seismograph, this time only a quarter mile from the main shaft, had thrown the lab into a tizzy.

"The epicenter of the latest occurrence happened closer to the surface, but it was still isolated," Achmed said. He sighed. "Again, no sympathetic vibrations anywhere."

Katerina scowled. It was the same story she'd heard before. Small disturbances, from deep underground. They kept happening, and only from the mountain below them—nothing like it from the nearby peaks, which they were monitoring for comparison.

"I need *answers*," she said. "You're the expert on this, and you've been working on it for two days. There's no way you don't have any ideas. I want a hypothesis. Now."

Achmed glared at her. Their friendship was gone. Vanished. Dissipated by her demanding position of power.

"You've seen the map of this place," he said. "You know that mountain is so riddled with tunnels it makes Swiss cheese look solid. You want my best guess, Katerina? It's the same as yours—that blasting has made the entire tunnel complex unstable."

She'd expected that answer. While they had drilled the main shaft without explosives, carving out the adit and breaching the tunnel complex had required blasting. Normally that would pose little threat to overall geologic stability, but with a massive network of caves anything was possible.

Achmed stared at her, his tired eyes a challenge to refute his idea. She couldn't challenge it. She looked down.

Kirkland would not be happy.

"What about the seismometer?" she said. "Is it still cutting out every six hours?"

Now it was his turn to look away.

"It is. Every six hours on the dot. And no, I still can't explain it. Or fix it. We've rebooted the computer a dozen times. We've recalibrated everything."

Three days straight of the unexplained malfunction. Settling, possible cave-ins, shitty equipment... she wished Angus had never been hurt in the first place.

"Find me an answer," she said. "Find it, or you're fired."

He shook his head, glared at her. "Don't worry, Kat. If you're going to keep being the boss, I'll save you the trouble and just quit."

He stood, gave her desk a solid bump with his leg before he walked away.

She was out of time. She had no answers. If she was going to do her job—and do it right—she needed to tell Kirkland to halt exploration entirely until these problems could be solved.

That thought made her sick to her stomach.

"A few more hours," she whispered to herself. "We'll figure it out, just a few more hours before I tell him."

2:23 P.M.

Patrick O'Doyle double-timed it to Connell's office trailer. This one wasn't his fault. Anyone could see that. How could he be held responsible for a man disappearing over *two miles* underground?

He opened the door without bothering to knock. Connell looked up from a pile of paperwork.

"Mister Kirkland, they lost a man in the tunnels."

Connell's eyes began to narrow, then relaxed. A strange look crossed over his face. Not a look of concern, exactly—maybe the look of someone who has finally figured out a frustrating puzzle.

"When did this happen?"

"About two hours ago. Mack did the search himself. Said the rope had been cut, and there was blood on it. No sign of the miner."

"Who is the missing man?"

"Brian Jansson."

Connell leaned back in his chair, looked up. Calm as calm could be. A thinking man thinking things over.

"Jansson's been with the company twelve years," he said.

Patrick wasn't sure if he was supposed to comment on that, so he kept to the facts.

"He was apparently hurt rappelling into a deep chasm. His partner, Keith Sherwood, went back, got Mack. By the time Mack reached the chasm, Jansson was gone."

Connell's fingers drummed the desktop. "I see three possibilities. All bad. The first is that Jansson was stupid enough to wander away after his partner went for help."

"Not likely, sir," Patrick said. "Mack is an excellent leader. He's drilled safety protocols over and over. His men would know to stay put."

Connell nodded. "I agree. The second possibility is that Jansson is working for the same people who sabotaged the lab. Maybe he faked his injury, and he's on his way to the Dense Mass, to help someone else drill in from another spot on the mountain. I'm sure you can guess the third possibility."

Patrick could.

"That the people who sabotaged the lab are already in the caves. They either have Jansson, or they've killed him."

Connell's expressionless face shifted, twitched. His lip curled into a brief sneer.

"Get your ass down there. O'Doyle. Find out what's happening. Who are the best three guards you've got?"

"Bertha Lybrand, Bill Crook, Lashon Jenkins."

"Get them suited up. You and Crook find Jansson. Missing man or not, Mack has to keep moving toward the Dense Mass."

A part of Patrick told him to keep his mouth shut, to just follow orders, but no matter how much he respected Connell, this wasn't the military. He had the right to speak his mind.

"Mister Kirkland, if we have potential threats in those tunnels, should we really still be worried about the platinum?"

"If someone took Jansson, they took him because they're trying to jump this claim. If they get there first, then all of this—" Kirkland waved his hand, gesturing to the camp and mountain outside the trailer "—is for nothing. That's not going to happen. We brought in armed guards for a reason. Are you going to protect the company's personnel and assets or not?"

He didn't salute, but Patrick felt his body stiffen, snap to attention. An automatic reaction. Connell wasn't military, but he was all leader.

"I'll get him back," Patrick said. "And we'll get there first, no matter what it takes."

He turned and reached for the door.

"One more thing," Connell said. "Don't say anything sensitive over the shaft phone. If we've been infiltrated, someone could be listening — we can't trust anyone or anything at this point."

2:31 P.M.

It made no sense.

Kayla had picked up a call from Connell to Barbara Yakely. Still using those idiotic "secure phones" of theirs. He suspected someone might be trying to jump the claim. He wanted Barbara to find out what company was buying up land around the Wah Wah Mountains. Connell felt positive a spy walked among the camp personnel, possibly working with operatives floating along the camp's periphery.

But one couldn't run a covert operation like that without at least *some* communication, and she'd picked up nothing. The only people on this mountain were herself and the EarthCore staff.

All her instincts told her Connell was wrong, but he was a very sharp man. She wouldn't dismiss his concerns out of hand. If someone else was working this mountain, her payday could be in jeopardy. She couldn't assume anything.

Sooner or later, someone would fuck up and she'd figure out what was going on. Patience was the key. The camp below buzzed with activity and confusion. People rushing everywhere. That night would be a good time to sneak in and snag a KoolSuit. She had to find a way down into those tunnels and take at least a limited peek for herself. Any intel she could provide on the tunnel system would increase the price she'd demand when she sold that intel to another company.

Judging by the level of activity, she expected the staff's fatigue to highpoint around one a.m.

She already knew her approach. A guard named Braxton would be working the north gate at that time. Braxton had a gut, was carrying about twenty pounds more than he should have. He got lazy about two hours into his shift. Instead of walking the north fence line from corner to corner, he turned at the generator and walked back eastward. That meant he didn't get a good view past the diesel tanks that were just west of the generator. Kayla could crawl close when he was walking away from her, and when he made that early turn she knew she'd have a good thirty seconds to quietly go up and over.

Once inside, she'd get what she needed.

2:54 P.M.

Connell stood next to the elevator cage, old-fashioned phone handset pressed to his ear.

"Don't think Jansson is a spy, mate," Mack said, speaking from a similar handset far down at the shaft bottom. "Haven't known him long, but he seems fair dinkum. Besides, your theory doesn't make any sense."

"Did Sherwood actually *see* the broken leg?"

Connell heard mumbled words: Mack turning to speak to someone else.

"He didn't. A hundred and fifty feet is a long way to see detail."

Jansson didn't seem like spy material to Connell, either, but it was too real of a possibility to ignore. He had to assume the worst while hoping for the best.

"So you've got a man who claims he broke a leg, which no one saw," Connell said. "And your procedure says he's supposed to stay put, but when you go to get him, he's gone. What does that tell you?"

Mack was silent for a moment, then answered quietly. "It tells me maybe he was lying. But we have to go after him regardless, Kirkland."

"Of course we're going after him."

Lybrand, O'Doyle, Jenkins and Crook walked onto the circular platform, carrying food, water, batteries, floodlights, even a portable battery-powered generator—everything needed to set up a base camp in the tunnels far below. On top of their formfitting yellow KoolSuits, the four guards had pistols strapped to their belts and machine guns in their hands.

"Guards are heading down now," Connell said. "O'Doyle will take over the search for Jansson."

"No," Mack said. "He's my man, I'll lead the search for him."

The winch rumbled. The cage started down. O'Doyle looked at Connell, gave him a thumbs-up.

Connell pressed the handset tighter to his ear and cupped his hand over the mouthpiece against the noise.

"Mack, listen to me. You have to keep moving toward the Dense Mass, you understand? We *have* to get there first."

Another pause. Connell waited. Mack was smart enough that it didn't need to be spelled out.

"I get it," he said, voice cold, angry. "No one is taking this from us, Mister Kirkland."

Connell hung up. He jogged back out the adit, heat-spawned sweat making his shirt stick to his body. He'd barely stepped into the sun before the secure phone in his pocket buzzed with an incoming call.

He answered.

"What have you got for me?"

"Ain't got squat, honey," Barbara Yakely said. "No bids of any kind."

Connell closed his eyes. The sun beat down on his face. The pieces refused to click.

"Check again," he said. "And keep checking. Someone has to be buying up rights in this area. Someone is making a move on us, Barb, I can feel it."

"No one has bought any rights in that area since 1945, honey. Ourselves excluded, of course. I had our people check with all of our corporate informants, too, and we can't find anybody who's even *looking* at the site. A few competitors are starting to get curious what we're doing there, but so far you're all alone."

Connell stared off into space. His theory had just gone down the crapper. "I'll call you if anything turns up."

He broke the connection. If the competition wasn't making a move, what was going on in the camp? And, more important, what the hell was going on down in that shaft?

3:11 P.M.

They built this.

Veronica Reeves didn't know how she knew, she just *knew*. Veronica sat cross-legged on one corner of the rectangle, turning her head slowly to look down each line. One line spread out and up the mountain, disappearing over the near ridge. The other line, one of the "short" ones, moved outward at a ninety-degree angle from its friend.

What had this meant to the Chaltélians?

The lab dated the rectangle between thirteen thousand and seven thousand years old. Precise figures didn't matter—the time span did. It was roughly the same time frame for the Chaltélians' dominance over the Tierra del Fuego area. Too close to be coincidence.

While hidden for millennia, the rectangle was an accomplishment greater than the pyramids and more impressive than Peru's massive Nazca lines. Egyptians built *up*. Chaltélians built *down*. Way down. *Impossibly* way down. Katerina Hayes—the head scientist now that Angus Kool was gone—couldn't explain how modern technology could carve a line that deep, let alone figure out how a primitive people did it.

Something extraordinary had happened on this mountain. A mystery worth the attention of Veronica's entire career, her entire life.

She needed to bide her time a little while longer. Connell couldn't keep her in camp forever. She wouldn't need Connell's funding, not once this story got out. Once the world knew of the rectangle, she'd shut him down faster than students clearing out after the last day of finals.

Then the mountain would be hers alone.

4:41 P.M.

Patrick O'Doyle let the rope hold most of his weight as his booted feet carefully felt out footing on the chasm floor's treacherous ground. Certainly looked like a good place to break a leg. Jagged rock stuck up all over, like spikes in a Burmese tiger trap. He kept one hand on the rope, the other on his EBR. The weapon's strap looped over his neck and around his back.

He turned his head, moving the headlamp light across the steep-walled chasm. He saw it almost instantly, a touch of wetness in the forever-arid area. Only a touch—most of it was already dry. Even in the strange lighting, there was no mistaking it.

Blood spatter.

About two feet off the ground and three feet long, horizontal with a slight angle, a center streak of red surrounded by a spray of fine droplets. The victim had been sitting four or five feet from the wall.

Patrick moved to the spot where he figured Jansson had been sitting.

More blood on the ground rocks, also dry. He carefully probed the area, then his light fixed on something pale and white.

O'Doyle picked it up, inspected it, then flashed his light rapidly around the chasm, looking for any threat. Nothing there except small, dark areas—the mouths of several tunnels. He started back up the rope with an expert's speed.

He wanted out of that chasm, and he wanted out now.

5:11 P.M.

News of Jansson's disappearance spread through the camp, falling on all ears as assuredly as the sun fell on the faces of anyone who stepped outside. When that news reached the ears of Sonny McGuiness, Sonny McGuiness decided he'd had enough.

Hard to spend your 2 percent if you're dead.

Kirkland had hired him to research, and he'd researched. He'd done a bang-up job of it by all accounts. He'd found several disturbing things that Kirkland chose to ignore. Well, they couldn't be ignored anymore.

One man was missing.

Angus and Randy in the hospital.

Three more miners hurt. Those didn't bother him so much, as it was a dangerous business and injuries were pretty much unavoidable. But add all those bad omens together? Too much. Too much by far.

Sonny knew if he said it out loud, it would sound crazy, so he didn't say it out loud. He knew what was going on—Funeral Mountain was waking up.

He felt it in his old bones. That awful sensation he'd felt on that first day atop this lifeless peak . . . it had steadily gotten worse. Maybe it made him a coward, but he couldn't stand it anymore. Something about that strange cave drawing still haunted him, something he couldn't put his finger on. It added to his unease, to his skin-crawling, asshole-puckering, *instinctive* desire to leave.

Besides, he still knew about the second entrance. He'd wanted to tell Connell about it, but hadn't. This was a business, after all, and you couldn't just give up a sweet tidbit of information like that for free. Connell wanted to play cutthroat? Sonny could do the same.

Maybe he could trade that info for the 2 percent he'd give up the second he left camp. If so, Sonny would find out via a phone call. No face-to-face meeting for that negotiation. Fuck that. He was getting the hell out of Dodge.

Sonny packed his bag. Tomorrow morning he'd talk to Connell, get permission to leave. Connell held the keys to Sonny's Hummer, just like he held the keys to every vehicle in the camp. Sonny didn't care; he'd get the keys one way or another. He had to get out. Hopefully, he could talk Cho into leaving with him. The kid had a lot of potential; Sonny didn't want to see him hurt. Or dead.

Whether Cho came or not wouldn't stop Sonny, for he knew in his soul that if he stayed much longer, Funeral Mountain would never let him go.

8:15 P.M.

The night air started to chip away the afternoon's heat but didn't stop Connell's sweat-fest. For the second time that day, he stood next to the vertical shaft, once again clutching the phone that ran all the way to the shaft bottom over two miles down.

With guards in the tunnels to hunt for Brian Jansson, Mack had continued toward the Dense Mass per Connell's orders. Mack had discovered a large cavern—and in it, found something completely unexpected. He'd trekked forty-five minutes back to the elevator shaft in order to call up to the surface himself.

"You've got to come down and see, mate." The excitement in Mack's voice didn't quite mask his exhaustion. "I'm not kidding. O'Doyle's here with me and he agrees. You'd best bring Reeves and Haak, too."

Connell tried to breathe slowly. He rolled his neck left, then right, trying to loosen muscle made rock-hard by the day's stress. Was everyone in this camp a fucking idiot?

"That's a bad idea, Mack. From what you've described, if Reeves sees it, she will insist we stop. Completely stop."

"They need to see it."

"I'll decide that," Connell said. "Get your ass back in those tunnels and keep moving."

"Mister Kirkland, I'm officially telling you that you can blow it out your ass. You made a deal with Reeves. I'm not moving a muscle until you live up to that deal."

His fingers squeezed the handset, so tight his knuckles hurt, so tight his hand shook. They were so close. Someone was trying to beat them to the prize, and his goddamn foreman was disobeying orders?

Yes. Because Mack had something Connell did not: ethics. Mack Hendricks was true to his word. The naive prick thought everyone else should be, too.

Connell was the boss, but right now, Mack had control. And, truth be told, Mack was right—Connell had promised Veronica she would be informed of any significant finds. From Mack's description, it didn't get much more significant than this.

"All right. If I come down and bring those two with me, will you keep moving toward the Dense Mass?"

"Not without some firepower, mate. I ... hold on a second." Connell heard mumbling voices, then Mack again. "O'Doyle says he'll send two guards with me, but he wants to wait until all the guards are down here."

If a goddamn tank would have kept Mack moving, Connell would have found a way to get it down there.

"That'll have to do," Connell said.

"Then I'll keep going. But just me and the guards, I'm not risking another one of my men until we know more. Fair enough?"

"Well, *fuck*," Connell said. "If you're going to give the goddamn orders, maybe you should have my job."

"I know you're pissed about the professors, mate, but trust me, you're doing the right thing. This is bigger than just money."

Bigger than just money. Maybe Mack should grow out his hair, roll a fucking fatty and reminisce about Woodstock. Money ruled the world—anyone who didn't understand that was either intentionally deluding themselves, too stupid to see reality or a fucking hippie.

"Let me talk to O'Doyle."

Connell waited while the phone traded hands.

"O'Doyle here. This is absolutely amazing, Mister Kirkland. I've never seen anything like it."

That tone of voice—childlike glee mixed with pure adult awe.

"I've already heard about the sights," Connell said. "What about Jansson?"

"Whereabouts still unknown. I rappelled into the chasm. I found blood spatter on the wall. Definitely not from someone just falling and bumping their head. Looks to me like a slash wound, one that cut deep. There's more, but I think it's best if I tell you in person."

Connell had warned him about saying sensitive information over the shaft line. What had O'Doyle found? Did he think Jansson was already dead? A *slash wound* ... had someone killed the man?

"Do you think it's safe to bring the professors down there?"

"Absolutely," O'Doyle said. "If someone did attack Jansson, there's a big difference between an unarmed man with a wounded leg and combat vets strapped with automatic weapons. Tell Cho to arm up Mateo Flores, Jimmy Cooper and Pete Braxton so they can come down with you. There's more than the cavern, sir. I found something else. You need to see it ASAP." O'Doyle paused, as if he didn't want to reveal more bad news. "Someone ... someone beat us down here."

Connell didn't answer. He gazed absently at a rock on the ground. The words didn't seem to register in his mind. A punch to the stomach. A kick in the balls. A knife in the back.

"Mister Kirkland? Did you hear me?"

"Yeah. How do you know?"

"You'll see when you get here."

Connell sighed and hung up. Anger fought defeat for dominance of his emotions. After all his work, all his speed, all his manipulation, someone—somehow—had gotten into those tunnels before EarthCore.

11:02 P.M.

"Katerina, wake up."

A man's voice. Someone shaking her shoulder. She lifted her head from the desk, blinking away much-needed sleep. She'd drooled on her paperwork. She wiped it away, got her bearings. Achmed, standing there. He'd woken her.

"What is it?"

"There's been another spike," he said.

He seemed more excited than before. No, not excited ... *agitated*. Agitated and afraid.

"I plotted the three most-recent spikes against Angus's map. I found something."

Achmed walked quickly through the maze of equipment, leading

Katerina to the display that constantly showed Angus's green and yellow tunnel map. Three red dots glowed softly.

"You want to tell me what..." A yawn paused her sentence. "... what I'm looking at?"

"The initial aberrant spike was 2.34 kilometers below ground zero, 3.02 kilometers away from the main shaft." Achmed tapped a red dot. It started to blink.

He tapped a second dot. It blinked in time with the first.

"This is the second epicenter," he said. "It was 1.78 kilometers down, and 1.25 kilometers from the main shaft." Another tap. "The third spike occurred while you were dozing, about a half hour ago. It's 0.58 kilometers down, 0.32 kilometers from the shaft."

Three blinking red dots. Katerina stared at them. A flourish of fear turned her insides cold.

"The tremors are getting closer to the shaft?"

"Not *tremors*," he said. "*Cave-ins*. No question at this point. Here's where shit gets crazy."

Again his fingertip tapped the display. A line representing one of the small natural tunnels glowed a brighter yellow than the rest. The line was very close to the first red dot, ended directly under the second. Achmed tapped again; another yellow line pointed away from the second dot, ending near the most-recent epicenter.

"So the cave-ins are occurring in solid rock *between* existing tunnels?"

Achmed nodded. "Judging from Angus's map, the space between those tunnels is between fifty and a hundred meters of solid rock. But that's not all, look at *this*."

He rotated the picture so that they were looking straight down on the mountain, as if they were in a helicopter a thousand feet above the peak. He tapped again—a green dot appeared.

She knew what it was. She didn't want to believe it. She asked anyway, hoping that her brain had made some ridiculous connection that simply didn't exist.

"The green dot." Her voice sounded distant, like a bad recording. "What is it?"

Achmed licked his lips. He didn't want to answer any more than she had wanted to ask. But he did.

"The green dot is the main vertical shaft."

Katerina's stomach dropped. The three red dots and the yellow lines weren't perfectly straight, but the path was clear.

They formed a line.

A line heading for the shaft.

"That's impossible," she said.

Achmed nodded. "I know."

And yet, there it was.

"Tell everyone to stop their projects immediately," Katerina said. "Everyone is on this, right now. We're running all of these figures again until someone figures out how you screwed this up."

19

12:11 A.M.

Connell Kirkland hated to be wrong. This time, though, the spectacle of what he saw chased away any annoyance—Mack had made the right call.

It had taken the better part of an hour for Cho to get Connell, Veronica, Sanji and the three guards into the KoolSuits and trained on safety procedures. Then another hour waiting for the elevator and riding it to the shaft bottom. Once there, O'Doyle ordered Crook to guard the elevator shaft, then led everyone else into the natural tunnel complex.

Moving through those tunnels proved surprisingly easy. There were a few places where everyone had to crawl on their bellies to get through bottlenecks, smooth material of the KoolSuits sliding across dirt and rocks, but for most of the long, constantly descending hike he walked only slightly crouched over, if not totally upright.

The hour-long trip from the elevator to what Mack wanted everyone to see was largely uneventful. Caves and tunnels, unremarkable limestone walls.

Their final destination, though, was a completely different story. Mack called it the "Picture Cavern." Far too simple a name for such a sight, but it had already stuck.

The massive space easily ran the length and width of a football field. The ceiling arched above, at least a hundred feet at the apex, as if the cavern were a small domed stadium. Something was embedded up there at the highest point, something not natural—a round object maybe the size of a beach ball. Powerful flood lamps lit up the cavern's mostly flat stone floor.

But no one cared about the ceiling or the floor. Everyone stared at the walls.

Veronica stood there, glassy-eyed, slowly turning in place.

"What do you make of it, Doctor Reeves?" Connell asked.

She didn't answer right away. When she finally spoke, it was with a voice so soft Connell had to lean close to make out her words.

"I saw drawings in the Cerro Chaltén tunnels, but nothing like this. The heat made it impossible to get this deep." She faced him, eyes wide. No arrogance, no authority, just the blank look of someone who was completely overwhelmed.

"I don't understand, Connell. How could people survive the heat long enough to create all of this?"

They stood shoulder to shoulder, staring in awe at the brightly colored carvings and paintings that covered every last inch of the sprawling cavern's stone walls.

O'Doyle approached. At his side, the skinny Lashon Jenkins, machine gun in hand. O'Doyle nodded toward Veronica, who was oblivious to anything but the walls.

"You stay with her," O'Doyle said. "And politely request that Doctor Haak stay with her so you can keep an eye out for them both."

Jenkins nodded. "Got it."

"Good man," O'Doyle said. He glanced at Connell. "Mister Kirkland, a word in private?"

The magnificence of this millennial old place would have to wait. Connell was about to find out what O'Doyle wouldn't say over the shaft phone.

"Lead the way, Mister O'Doyle."

12:27 A.M.

At Cerro Chaltén, drawings were sparse, spread so far apart through the endless tunnels that each one was like discovering a lost treasure. Every drawing moved Veronica a tiny bit closer to understanding Chaltélian writing. She was convinced they had a written language—not just pictographs, but actual words. Whenever her team found another crude, priceless image, she would rush to the find, hoping each time it would turn out to be the Chaltélian Rosetta Stone.

Down here, under the Wah Wah Mountains, things were different. An unbelievable amount of painted and carved pictures filled the walls. Up to a height of about twelve feet, art covered almost every square inch of space—not just once, but *twice*. The first set of pictures were detailed bas-relief carvings, some several feet high and wide, most a ten-inch-square tile. The second set were wild, multicolored, primitive images painted over the tiles, almost like graffiti. Chaos atop order.

And everything she saw reflected an image from real life. No *letters*, no *words*, but rather, *pictures*. Such a stark difference between the two sites. Why? What did it mean?

"Ronni, this is amazing," Sanji said, his voice a reverent whisper.

The carvings displayed a level of stone-working skill that defied imagination. Some tiles showed recognizable images, like juniper bushes, mountain ranges, animals, illustrated scenes from the desert above. Other images were unknown, their meanings lost—mythological monsters, perhaps, or creation myths chiseled into unforgiving rock.

She smiled at a large carving clearly illustrating the Wah Wah Mountain Range, a ridgeline view similar to what she'd seen when she first approached from the East. She made out several identifiable landmarks. Work that detailed, that exquisite—it must have taken decades to complete.

While the carving quality boggled the imagination, the paintings looked like Cro-Magnon cave drawings; primitive by any standard. Perfectly preserved in the dry cave, the bright, angry colors of the paintings were mostly unrecognizable—childlike images drawn during a paint-flinging temper tantrum.

Sanji reached out, delicately touched a carving of a deer. Black and red paint covered it.

"Why would they cover such wonderful carvings with such crude drawings?"

"Vandalism, maybe," Veronica said. "It's like there are at least two distinct cultures down here. One became very good at working stone, the one that followed possessed only rudimentary artistic ability."

Her father's fingertips gently traced the deer's antlers.

"But the low-quality work is more recent," he said. "The paintings are on top of the carvings. I would think the culture would get better as time wore on."

Some cultures did. Some didn't. Most of the time, though, primitive cultures didn't evolve—they were wiped out by something stronger.

"My hunch is that the Chaltélian culture was taken over by barbarians, for lack of a better word," she said. "Or, possibly, what I consider to be the Chaltélian culture is actually the barbarians, and another group, an older group, made these carvings."

"So the paintings are an effort to wipe out the history of the original tribe?"

That was a logical guess. And yet, the more she looked at the carvings and the paintings that covered them, the more she saw similarities.

"I'm seeing repetitive symbols," she said. "Possibly the succeeding culture incorporated elements of the predecessor."

Sanji turned his head this way and that, brow furrowing in confusion.

"I don't see what you're talking about."

Veronica pointed to a tile, maybe two-foot square.

"Look at this roundish creature with the tentacles. It's obviously some sort of a god or deity representation. If you look around, you'll see them everywhere."

Sanji turned, looking here, looking there. He started to nod.

"Yes, I see them now. You're right—they're all over the place. Maybe more of those than any other image, now that I think about it."

She took his hand and walked backward, gently pulling him along with her. As they moved away from the wall, a larger image started to dominate their vision. Some fifteen feet high, a bit longer across. Bold black outlines framed brilliantly bright reds, oranges, and yellows. The picture's angry vibrance resonated despite its primitive quality.

Sanji nodded. He pointed, his fingertip sliding through the air, marking the big image's outline.

"The same pattern of tentacles," he said. "If that's what those curly things are. Their god again?"

"One of them, anyway. I highly doubt they were monotheistic. The barbarians may have incorporated elements of Chaltélian religions, but who knows?"

She knew she was missing something, something that could make sense of all this. It bothered her, deep in the core of her being. But maybe that wasn't the mystery of carvings and paintings, maybe it was the same dank feeling of dread she'd felt up on the surface.

Sanji walked away to another image that caught his interest. Veronica continued to stare up at the large tentacle god. If that's what it was—a god—then she could understand the tribe's violent nature. The image on the wall radiated absolute anger, raw aggression. If it was a god in the pantheon of these lost people, then it had to be a god of war.

Or, perhaps, a god of evil.

12:30 A.M.

A darker spot in the picture cavern. Just enough light to see the sign in his shaking hands. Fury swept over him, clouding his mind. Only once in his life had he felt rage this pure—when he'd learned his wife's murderer had blown twice the legal limit.

The sign was simple; a small, thin piece of plywood little bigger than a sheet of typing paper. A stake pointed out the bottom. Painted on the sign was a curved, cartoon head of a little bald man, his nose peeking over a line that hid the rest of his body. His round fingers also hung over that line. Two expressionless black dots represented eyes. A simple message adorned the back of the sign.

KILROY WAS HERE.

"Where did you find this?" He kept his voice down, so as not to draw the attention of Veronica and Sanji. They were exploring the Picture

Cavern, rail-thin Lashon close by, his head always swiveling, his eyes always looking.

"Lybrand found it," O'Doyle said. "Dead center in the middle of the Picture Cavern, wedged into a crack in the rock floor."

The middle of the cavern, where it couldn't be missed.

"Anyone else see it?"

"Only Mack," O'Doyle said. "Lybrand was in the lead. She was the first one in the cavern. She hid the sign, told me about it later. Smart move on her part, sir."

A calling card. A fucking *message*. Someone rubbing Connell's nose in it: *hey, dipshit—we got here first.*

"Could Jansson have done it?"

O'Doyle shrugged. "Depends on how accurate Angus's map is. According to that, none of the tunnels from that chasm lead here. Besides, he couldn't have brought the sign with him, or Mack and the other miners would have seen it. There's not exactly any hiding space in these suits."

Connell looked at his own bright-yellow, formfitting KoolSuit. The thing clung so tight someone could tell his religion. He glanced back at O'Doyle, who looked like a muscle-bulging superhero in the tight yellow outfit; the Hulk with a beer belly. Black nylon equipment webbing hung around his waist, over his chest, but even that wouldn't have been enough to hide the sign. No way could Jansson have slipped it in past Mack.

Kilroy was here.

"The phrase seems familiar."

"It's from World War II," O'Doyle said. "Allied forces, especially U.S. troops, saw that image all over Europe as they liberated the continent from the Nazis. When they pushed back the Germans, sometimes that message would be waiting—on bridges, walls, that kind of thing. Someone was so bent on being a joker he actually crept across enemy lines and painted graffiti. No one ever found out who was responsible."

O'Doyle looked over his shoulder, made sure no one was near. "Got something else." He reached into an ammo pouch and pulled out a small, pale object.

At first glance it looked like a strange stone, or maybe a piece of dried fruit.

Then Connell recognized it: a human thumb.

The nail looked remarkably undamaged. Just behind the nail, however, where the first knuckle starts, the thumb stopped. Dirt, sand, and even one small pebble stuck to the stump. A thin piece of bone protruded past the flesh, dull white in the cavern's poor lighting.

"Where did you find this?"

"Jansson's chasm," O'Doyle said. "He's dead, I'm sure of it. Someone slashed at him with a wicked-sharp blade. He probably held his hand up defensively, blade sliced right through bone. The attackers obviously removed his body, but didn't get all the pieces."

O'Doyle had always been so reliable. Smart, efficient, levelheaded. But this? How could the man have been such an idiot?

"You should have sent everyone up," Connell said, focusing on keeping his voice calm. "Why did you bring down more people?"

"You said it was urgent we continue toward the Dense Mass. Don't worry, Mister Kirkland. We have plenty of firepower down here, and Lybrand is under specific instructions not to let Mack and the miners out of her sight."

Connell stared at the thumb. Could he really blame anyone but himself? O'Doyle had said there was blood spatter from a slash wound. Connell had wondered if Jansson had been murdered, yet he'd sent people down anyway. But still, a fucking *severed thumb*?

He glanced at O'Doyle. The big man was looking all around the cavern. Eyes narrow. Eyes *hungry*. With a sinking feeling, Connell finally got it. Whoever these saboteurs were, they had made O'Doyle look bad—he wanted payback.

Slashed at him…

Wicked-sharp…

In his mind, Connell heard the *thump* of Veronica's platinum knife hitting his desk.

"O'Doyle, where are our people?"

"Crook's at the elevator shaft. Flores and Cooper are with a few miners in the chasm where Jansson vanished, seeing if they can find any sign of him in the tunnels there. Lybrand and Braxton are with Mack, moving toward the Dense Mass."

"How far away is Mack? Can you reach him?"

O'Doyle nodded, pointed to a walkie-talkie in a pouch hanging from his webbing. "Lybrand has one. She's dropping battery-powered signal repeaters every thousand feet or so. She and Mack are maybe twenty-five minutes out."

"Flores and Cooper are closer to the shaft than we are?"

O'Doyle nodded again. "Maybe twenty minutes from it."

"Call Lybrand. Tell her to bring her group back."

"Mister Kirkland, I don't think that's necessary."

Connell thrust the severed thumb toward O'Doyle, so close the big man flinched back a bit.

"You not thinking is the fucking *point*." Connell's words came out as a low hiss. "We'll wait here for Mack's group, so we head back together with three guns instead of two. Call Flores and Cooper, tell them to take every last miner to the surface immediately, then send the elevator back down. We're getting everyone out of here until we can figure out the best way to keep everyone safe."

O'Doyle's eyes narrowed.

"Everyone *is* safe," he said. "That's what you hire me for."

Was this giant moron *offended*?

"Call them, right fucking now, or you're fired. Understand?"

The narrowed eyes widened, briefly, and the man's lip twitched—a strange combination of anger and fear.

"Yes *sir*, right away."

O'Doyle turned away, pulling his walkie-talkie out as he did.

Connell glanced at the professors. They were still walking around, gawking at the cavern's endless pictures.

12:32 A.M.

Mack moved in a half crouch, helmeted head scraping lightly against the stone ceiling. KoolSuit or no KoolSuit, he'd never felt so exhausted. Going back up would have helped, but it was a one- to two-day hike to the Dense Mass—someone had to suffer the effects of this endless heat. If he'd dropped out, one of his men would have gone in his place, and that wasn't acceptable.

He stopped. He heard the two guards behind him stop as well. Mack turned his head slightly, letting his headlamp beam play out into the tunnel's darkness.

A hand on his shoulder, a woman's voice near his ear.

"What is it?"

Lybrand. She was always just a step behind him, surprisingly agile in the narrow tunnels.

"Thought I heard something," Mack said.

"Like?"

He started to speak, stopped. He wasn't sure what he'd heard. The rattling of someone's equipment, maybe.

"Probably an echo from us," he said.

He hoped that's what it was. There were only two explanations for Jansson's disappearance, and neither were good. The way Kirkland painted the picture made sense. Jansson had either betrayed Mack, Connell and EarthCore, or someone had taken him away. If it was the latter, that *someone* was in the tunnels and willing to do whatever it took to reach the Dense Mass first. Having Lybrand and that other guard, the chubby one—Braxton, his name was—along helped, but it didn't chase away the fact that there might be killers down here.

Maybe killers with more guns than Lybrand and Braxton.

"Mister Hendricks," Lybrand said, "if we're going to stop, I need to call back and let them know."

He shook his head, tried to chase away thoughts of bullets bouncing off the narrow limestone walls. Maybe there was danger, sure, but the payoff was enough to bear a little risk. More than enough. *Way* more.

"No worries," he said. "We'll keep going. And would you call me *Mack* already?"

He took one step, then the noise came again.

click-click ... click

Not an echo. Coming from ahead of them, somewhere in the tunnel's darkness.

"I heard it," Lybrand said.

She slid ahead of him, knelt, put her rifle to her shoulder and aimed it down the tunnel.

"Mack, get down," she said. "Braxton, get up here."

Was this really happening? Three miles underground, and someone was coming after them?

Braxton slid past, knelt next to Lybrand.

Three headlamps lit up the tunnel, played off the walls, the rock-strewn ground.

Up ahead, something *moved*: whip-thin legs, a round flash cutting through the light before vanishing behind a shin-high rock.

His brain fished for a word to describe it, came up with a rather unpleasant one: *spider*. As close as he could get, but it hadn't had eight legs. Had it?

"Mack," Lybrand said. "What the fuck was that?"

He shook his head for a few seconds before remembering he was behind her, that she couldn't see him.

"I don't know."

"Some kind of big-ass insect," Braxton said, his words clipped. "Nobody told me there'd be two-foot-long crawly silver bugs down here."

"There aren't," Mack said, even though there obviously were. "Nothing that big lives this deep."

Braxton glanced back. "Tell that to the fucking silver bug hiding behind that rock."

"*Eyes forward,*" Lybrand snapped.

Braxton did as he was told, aimed his rifle down the tunnel.

"Maybe it's metal," Lybrand said. "A robot or something?"

Mack shook his head. "You ever seen a machine move like that?"

No one answered. He certainly hadn't, anywhere outside of a movie. The speed, the fluidity—only an animal had that kind of motion.

A sudden burst of walkie-talkie static made everyone jump.

With smooth motions, Lybrand slung her rifle, drew her pistol and aimed it down the tunnel as she pulled the walkie-talkie from her belt.

"Lybrand here."

The answering voice was so thin and full of static Mack could barely make out the words.

"*This is O'Doyle. Report back to the Picture Cavern immediately.*"

"Roger that," Lybrand said. "We saw something moving. An animal of some kind."

Whatever the thing was, it adjusted its position behind the rock; Mack saw the briefest reflection of something dull and curved, then nothing.

"*Leave it,*" the thin voice squawked. "*Get back here on the double.*"

"On our way," Lybrand said.

She shoved the walkie-talkie back into its pouch, rose to a half crouch. She gripped Braxton's shoulder.

"Take point, move fast," she said. "Everyone else, keep up with Braxton. I'll bring up the rear."

Braxton slid by once more, heading back up the tunnel.

Mack was only too happy to turn and follow.

12:34 A.M.

When it clicked, it clicked all at once, an instant congealing so final she would never be able to see it any other way again.

"It's a textbook," she said, loud enough that her words echoed off the ceiling.

Sanji looked at her. So did Lashon, for once not flicking his eyes toward every corner and shadow.

"Sorry," she said. She glanced across the cavern, seeing if O'Doyle and Connell were looking as well. They weren't. O'Doyle was on his walkie-talkie. Connell was mostly in the shadows, his back turned, staring down at something Veronica couldn't see.

She looked about the room, wondering why she hadn't seen it immediately. If she ignored the graffiti, bas-relief carvings covered the majority of the Picture Cavern's space. Thousands of them tiled the walls with even rows of perfect illustrations. A juniper tree. A tribesman with a spear. Cactus. Grasshoppers. Tentacle gods. Mountains. A wolf. A bow. Arrows flying. Everything that could possibly make up life in this area of the world was represented on one tile or another.

Sanji looked around slowly, nodding as he did.

"I see it. My goodness, Ronni, you're right. This is a classroom."

Lashon had been little more than armed background decoration thus far, but he finally spoke up.

"If you don't mind me asking, ma'am, what are you talking about? How is this a classroom?"

"Think how deep we are inside the mountain," she said. "I think the people who lived down here visited the surface very rarely. Maybe some never went outside at all. I think they used these carvings to teach their children what things looked like up on the surface."

Sanji shook his head, made a *tsk-tsk-tsk* sound he'd made when she'd been a little girl. Oh how it had driven her bat-shit crazy back then. Now, it called up warm memories of a happy time.

"That doesn't make sense, Ronni," he said. "The only reason we're able to function right now is because of the KoolSuits. How could people spend their entire lives down here? It's one hundred and seventy degrees Fahrenheit. You know the roasts I used to make you? Guess what temperature I slow-cooked them at?"

Lashon raised his hand.

Sanji smiled wide. "Yes, Mister Jenkins?"

"One hundred and seventy degrees," Lashon said. "Fahrenheit."

Sanji reached up, clapped the man on the shoulder.

"Very good. When we get to the surface, I'll dig up my gold stars."

"Funny," Veronica said. "Quite hysterical when you look at how much time people had to spend down here, carving away at solid rock. Know what I mean?"

Both men took another slow look around, eyes lingering on some of the larger carvings.

"I see your point," Sanji said. "Maybe it wasn't this hot down here back then. Or they had some simple but effective technology for lowering the temperature. Maybe an irrigation system to bring water from the surface to cool things off."

Lashon raised his hand again.

Sanji nodded at him, the joke already old the second time around.

"Maybe they were muties," he said. "Like the X-Men or something."

Sanji managed to not roll his eyes. "A genetic mutation might allow them higher heat tolerances, but only within the laws of physics. Cow meat, chicken meat, pig meat, people meat—when the temperature gets high enough, everything cooks."

Veronica doubted they were mutants. An irrigation system made the most sense, but in a desert? The water would have had to come from an underground river. She couldn't think about that now. There had to be some kind of pattern to these carvings, something to make them work together to tell a larger story.

She walked to the wall. The men came with her. She gently touched a tile representing a tentacle god. Her fingers cast strange shadows from the light of her helmet lamp, making the tentacle god seem to wriggle with life.

Sanji also touched the wall, but at the tile's border rather than the bas-relief carvings itself.

"Ronni, look at this pattern of dots. It makes a box around these four, no, these five tiles."

She saw the slightly raised bumps beneath Sanji's fingers. She took a step back, saw that the bumps did, indeed, form a box that contained five tiles.

"Holy shit," she said. "Nice work, Pops."

"Gold stars for me as well," Sanji said.

The first tile showed a tentacle god standing at the mouth of a cave. The image to the right showed a running tribesman carrying a spear. In the third image, the tribesman was snarling, the blade of his spear plunged deep into the tentacle god. The fourth tile made her shudder: three tentacle gods holding double-crescent knives, hacking away at the tribesman, cutting him to pieces. Such detail; a severed hand flying through the air; tentacle gods waving the knives; the expression of pain and horror on the tribesman's face. Moving headlamps made the small shadows flutter, made it all seem like a bit of real life semi-frozen in stone. The final tile showed the tentacle gods burying the tribesman's remains.

Veronica felt as if she'd been punched in the stomach. A piece of the puzzle she'd labored on for five years was finally answered—she now knew why the Chaltélians wreaked such havoc.

"It's a punishment," she said. "The tentacle creatures, they represent some supernatural being. This carving is a warning of what happens if you go against the gods." She thought of the Americans dead on the plateau above, the skull with the gouge marks on the inside. "I wonder what law Benjamin and the miners broke."

"That one seems obvious." Sanji had walked a few feet to the right. "Look at these rows over here. All of the picture groups start with a tribesman or animal at the mouth of a cave. The next picture shows that individual moving into the caves, and then, good day, sir—I say *good day.*"

The final tiles in each group showed the tentacle gods butchering the transgressor, deer or rabbit or human—Utes or Hopis, maybe, people that had lives and hopes, families and dreams—then burying the remains. It made sense: this was how the Chaltélians stayed hidden for so long.

"These tunnels were sacred," Veronica said. "If you weren't from the tribe, it was sacrilege to come near them. The punishment for transgressors was death."

"Gives me the willies," Lashon said. "If the mountain is holy ground, aren't we transgressors, too?"

She didn't answer. Neither did Sanji.

O'Doyle strode toward them, pistol in hand. Why was his gun out? Lashon straightened up and stood at attention.

"Professors, we have to go," O'Doyle said. "Mack and Lybrand are almost back. We're joining up with them and heading back to the elevator."

He wanted to rush them out of here? Connell was pulling a fast one, show them the cavern so he could say he tried, then, *oops*, we accidentally drilled right through it.

"We're not leaving," Veronica said. "This is a monumental find, do you understand?"

O'Doyle nodded. "Of course. But there's danger down here and Mister Kirkland wants everyone out."

Veronica's hands went to her hips. "Well, I really don't care what *Mister Kirkland* said! He can't just boss us around, you know. He can't make us leave."

The scarred man's lips pressed into a tight line, the very image of someone who was almost finished trying to be nice.

"Maybe Mister Kirkland can't make you leave, but I can. And I assure you, professor, you won't enjoy it."

Lashon moved to stand shoulder to shoulder with O'Doyle. Both men stared, hard-eyed.

Veronica felt a hand on her elbow.

"Ronni, I don't think a hammer is all that effective against guns, do you?"

She glanced at O'Doyle's pistol, at Lashon's machine gun.

O'Doyle pointed to the other end of the Picture Cavern. "Go join Mister Kirkland. Please."

Veronica wanted to punch him but doubted she'd hurt anything other than her hand. Even if she had a hammer—the literal kind rather than a figurative one—it would probably just bounce off that too-thick skull.

She stormed toward Connell, Sanji a step behind.

12:37 A.M.

The figures danced across the computer screen in front of Katerina and Achmed. Both scientists stared in bewilderment, then shook their heads.

"That's impossible," Achmed said.

Katerina shook her head in denial of what her eyes told her. She thought for a moment, pondering the results and what it meant if they were accurate. It was mind-boggling and entirely unacceptable.

"How long did it take us to run that equation?" Katerina asked.

"Thirty-five minutes."

"Can we shorten it up at all?"

"We can't," Achmed said. "If we think there's a mistake in these results, we have to reenter everything from scratch, assume we made an error in the entry somewhere."

Katerina pondered that option. If the data was accurate, she needed to alert Connell immediately. But it just didn't make *sense*. There was no way the data could be accurate. It was a mistake. It had to be. "Run it again," she said. "And let's make sure we do it right this time."

1:01 A.M.

Kayla slid through the shadows. A strong breeze carried sand across the camp, made waves roll across the canvas covering the Quonset huts.

She adjusted her bag, moving it to the small of her back as she knelt next to the miners' hut. She sat perfectly still, eyes slowly scanning the area. People were moving, but they were all preoccupied with their tasks. They'd been here long enough that no one bothered to look around anymore—the camp had become familiar to their eyes.

Kayla stayed still for another five minutes, watching carefully, then slid to the hut's rear window and peeked through. A dozen miners inside, every last one of them sleeping so soundly they might as well have been passed out. Expensive KoolSuits sat in limp piles on the floor or draped over tables.

Amazing. Without O'Doyle and Connell around, discipline slacked off considerably. If O'Doyle hadn't been in the tunnels, she wouldn't have come into camp at all—there was *risk*, then there was *pure stupidity*.

She watched for a few more minutes. Nothing moved. She slowly opened the hut's back door and slid inside. All those sleeping men. She could have killed them all if she wanted to, one at a time, silent and sure. But she wasn't there to kill anyone.

She quietly gathered up a KoolSuit and slid out the door. They'd certainly miss the suit. This time O'Doyle might even search the hills and find her warren. But she needed only a peek into the tunnels, and that was the last bit of information she needed before selling to the highest bidder. She'd try to penetrate the tunnels in a few hours, perhaps at three or four a.m., her last action on this mission. If she could get in, great; if not, she was still in her Land Rover and out of the area by six a.m.

And a few hours after that, the bids would start rolling in.

1:17 A.M.

Achmed hadn't screwed up.

"But it doesn't make any sense," Katerina said.

No one answered her. The entire lab staff—all bleary-eyed from the constant stress, the lack of sleep—stood around her, staring at Angus's map display. The red dots and yellow lines remained. People had double-checked Achmed's calculation, then triple-checked them.

"The same results, all three times," Achmed said. "I guess you should have believed me from the start."

Katerina nodded slowly, still staring at the map. She should have trusted him. Instead, she'd assumed he was wrong, because she didn't want to deliver news like this to Kirkland.

She glanced at the display's clock: 1:18 a.m.

Wait... had they really spent an hour rechecking his work? More than an hour?

They had.

Three spikes. Three cave-ins. Her eyes traced the yellow lines and red dots. If the pattern continued, the next red dot would likely occur at...

She ran for the door.

"Achmed, come on!"

Katerina burst outside and screamed for a guard to bring a Jeep.

1:19 A.M.

Kayla had the KoolSuit up around her hips when she saw the woman run out of the lab building, screaming something at one of the guards. The guard heard her, sprinted for the hangar where they kept the vehicles.

Kayla sat, the KoolSuit's top hanging limply from her waist. She watched the scene through her binoculars.

A Jeep roared out of the hangar, slid to a stop. The woman got in, as did a man who had followed her out of the lab. Nice-looking guy, but what was with the porno 'stache?

The guard spun the wheel and gunned the engine, whipping the vehicle around so fast the man and the woman lurched to grab whatever they could lest they be tossed out. The guard floored the Jeep and headed for the west gate. He steered with his left hand only. His right hand pressed a walkie-talkie to his ear.

Things were getting interesting.

1:24 A.M.

Sonny now understood how a rabbit felt just before the bobcat's bite. He lay on his cot, shaking. Fear festered in his gut like a Mezcal worm come back to life: wiggling, soft, disgusting.

That creeping sensation—the one that had grown steadily worse ever since he'd arrived at Funeral Mountain—was now so intense he could barely stand it. But he was safe inside the camp. Wasn't he?

The image of the crude cave drawing popped unbidden into his thoughts. It *meant* something, but what? Had Anderson and his friends seen it back in 1942? Sonny wondered if the students had ever felt as he did now. He wondered if Benjamin's people had felt the same way. Maybe they had.

And, maybe, they'd ignored it.

Just like he'd been doing for weeks.

Maybe they'd ignored it until it was too late, until they wound up butchered, hacked to pieces and buried where no one would find them for over a century.

But Sonny wasn't ignoring it, not anymore. Tomorrow morning he was out of there.

Unless … unless Connell wouldn't let him leave.

Armed guards. Fences. Concertina wire. Those things could keep someone *in* just as well as they could keep someone *out*.

Sonny sat up.

"Fuck this," he said.

He wasn't waiting for morning. If Cho was working one of the gates, Sonny could be out of the camp and be long gone before Kirkland had anything to say about it.

Sonny didn't need a car, didn't need someone to drop him off. If he left now, he'd reach Route 21 before the sun came up. Someone would come along after that, a trucker or something, someone would give him a ride to Milford. That road didn't have a lot of traffic, but it was far from abandoned.

He dressed quickly, almost fell over while pulling on his pants. He grabbed his canvas backpack out from under his cot.

Screw the percentage. And screw that sonofabitch Kirkland.

Sonny quietly walked to the door, thumb rubbing a hard circle against his bracelet's swastika.

1:29 A.M.

Cho Takachi didn't mind late-night duty. He'd actually requested it. Who wanted to stand in the fucking desert heat all day? Not him, that was for sure.

And, it had proven quite lucrative.

He didn't know how much money Angus Kool had, but it was obviously enough that he didn't bat an eyelash at paying four digits just to be let out of camp a few times. Too bad about that guy's injury—Cho would have liked a few more of those paydays.

The stars burned bright above, pinholes punched into a deep black sky. It was gorgeous out here. Boring as hell, sure, but gorgeous.

"Hey, kid."

Cho whipped around and crouched simultaneously. He almost started to bring up his rifle but stopped when the voice registered.

"Sonny. God*dammit*."

The little old man stood not even four feet away. How had he snuck up like that? The camp lights made his white beard shine, even while his dark skin blended into the night. White beard, white eyes, almost floating by themselves.

"You're shitty at this job," Sonny said. "Why don't you quit?"

Cho rolled out his neck, tried to shake off the blast of adrenaline coursing through his body.

"Bad time to be sneaking about, Raisin. That missing miner maybe was taken out. We people who carry guns are on edge, you know?"

Sonny shrugged. "Open the gate. I'm leaving."

The way he said that, different from before.

"What, you mean . . . for good?"

Cho felt an unexpected pang of loss.

"The place won't be the same without you."

Sonny adjusted his backpack. The thing was almost as big as he was.

"Come with me," he said. "Some bad shit's gonna go down here."

Cho started to ask if that was some kind of joke, but the look in Sonny's eyes showed, quite clearly, that it was not. Cho had never seen the old man this morose, this serious.

"I can't leave. I have a job."

"Then quit, like I said."

"What, and just walk out of here?"

Sonny nodded. "That's right. I've been working this desert for forty years. I know what I'm doing. We'll be fine, probably be in Milford before noon tomorrow."

This dude would get 2 percent of the entire operation if he stayed, and he was walking away?

"You leave now, you're as crazy as Benjamin," Cho said.

Sonny's left hand rubbed at his right, thumb circling that weird swastika bracelet. His mouth moved a little, the way old men's mouths do—like he was chewing on something that wasn't really there. His eyes blazed, hard and all-knowing. For the first time, Cho felt the difference in their ages—he felt like a little boy being lectured by a much older, much wiser man.

The kind of man little boys should listen to.

"That's the thing," Sonny said. "I'm not so sure Benjamin was crazy at all."

Chilling words, said with total conviction. But part of being nuts was believing in the stories you invented, right?

Cho reached out and lifted the gate latch. He slid the gate back on its track, just enough for a little old man to slide through.

Sonny's lips pursed. His nostrils flared wide as a great sigh left his body. That hard edge vanished, as did his air of wisdom and authority. His shoulders slumped.

"You coming with me, kid?"

Cho shook his head.

"Guess I'll go it alone," Sonny said. "Be safe, kid."

The old man headed down the road.

Cho quietly slid the gate shut, then faced back into camp.

No one watching. No one had seen.

"Be safe, old fella," he said quietly.

Once again, he stared up at the stars.

1:34 A.M.

It had taken forty-five minutes or so to walk through the tunnels that led from the shaft elevator to the Picture Cavern. Connell had assumed it would take the same amount of time to get back, but in all the stress he'd glossed over a rather basic fact—those forty-five minutes had been *downhill.*

Walking back was an unexpected ordeal. It was easy to put your butt on a boulder, kick your legs over and drop lightly to the other side. Climbing those boulders was another story. The steep incline, the loose footing...an hour's worth of ascent had drained everyone. Even O'Doyle was breathing hard.

Mack led the way. The foreman was almost sprinting, going up the slope so fast Lybrand had yelled at him twice to not get ahead of the group. Mack seemed driven—he wanted out of the tunnels, and he wanted out bad. Whatever animal he'd seen had spooked the hell out of him.

But he wasn't the only one in a hurry. Connell fought back his own fatigue to urge everyone on. He didn't know what was happening in these tunnels. What he did know was that his people weren't safe, that *he* wasn't safe and that—maybe—Veronica Reeves had been completely wrong about the "lost tribe" still being lost.

An impossible thought. A stupid thought. A thought he didn't have time for, but in the few moments his mind wasn't occupied by his screaming legs, his burning lungs and a stomach that seemed ready to rebel, he couldn't make that thought go away.

Finally, the walls changed from natural tunnels to a man-made one. A few seconds later, Connell and the others arrived at the elevator shaft that had no elevator, just a wide circle of empty sand surrounded by the shaft's smooth walls.

Crook was there, waiting, both hands on his machine gun, his normal pale face even paler behind the clear, paper-thin mask. He scanned the group for a moment, making sure there was no threat, then grabbed the shaft phone handset and held it out toward Connell.

"Mister Kirkland, its Katerina. She says it's urgent."

Of course it was urgent. Everything was urgent. All Connell wanted to do was sit the hell down. That's exactly what most of the others did as he urged his exhausted body the final twenty feet.

He took the phone, held it against his chest as he leaned into the shaft and looked up. Far, far above, he saw the cage coming down. A tiny circle, *too* tiny, not getting bigger fast enough.

"Crook, how much longer?"

"Cage should touch down in about fifteen minutes, Mister Kirkland."

Fifteen minutes. Not so bad. They'd all be headed up to the surface soon, be safe and sound within the hour.

He put the handset to his ear.

"This is Kirkland."

"You need to get everyone out of there, now!"

He winced, tilted the handset away a couple of inches, but her urgency fueled his fear.

"The elevator is on the way down," he said. He spoke quietly, not wanted to further agitate the others. "It only moves so fast. Calm down and tell me what's going on."

He heard her take a deep breath, let it out right into the phone.

"All right," she said. "Sorry. Remember those seismic anomalies you wanted me to look into?"

Connell closed his eyes. From panicked screaming to questions that didn't need to be asked.

"Of course I remember."

"There was another one since you went below. Achmed and I ran some numbers on the readings. The time between the epicenters and the readings match data for tunneling through that same amount of rock. We're almost sure the anomalies were cave-ins caused by natural fallaway, maybe some kind of open-face blasting. The path heads straight for the top of the shaft. There's no question, it's not a natural occurrence."

Connell paused. "Tell me that again so I know I heard you right, Doctor Hayes. And this time in English."

Katerina took another deep breath, blew it into the phone again, then answered.

"The cave-ins weren't natural. They were man-made. Someone is digging their way out of the mountain, and they're coming straight for the shaft."

1:40 A.M.

The winch hummed along. The thick black cable went down and down and down, uncoiling from the massive spools.

"This is ridiculous," Achmed said. "Why are we waiting here?"

It was just them and two miners in the small cavern. Less than ten minutes for the elevator to finish lowering, then another thirty minutes for it to make the return trip.

Katerina leaned against the rough wall, trying and failing to get comfortable. She could have sat on the rail surrounding the vertical shaft, but getting within even ten feet of the edge gave her a rush of vertigo that made her head spin.

"We're waiting because Kirkland wants to talk to us when he comes up. Do you need another reason?"

Achmed squatted down on his heels next to her, rested his back against the wall. God, he looked so exhausted, so beat. He stared down.

"I guess not," he said.

"Then stop fucking asking me."

She didn't know why she was being mean to him. Well, she did— she'd doubted Achmed, and that embarrassed her. For some insane reason she didn't fully understand, she was taking that out on *him*.

Great logic, Kat, that makes a ton of sense.

She'd fucked up. She needed to own that.

"Listen," she said, "about what happened in the lab, I—"

She felt it against her back. So slight, so faint, but there … a tremble.

"Did you feel that?"

He glanced up at her with sunken eyes, not understanding.

A second vibration.

Achmed stood bolt upright.

"It's happening," he said. "They're here."

Sudden fear drove through her, compressed her, immediately drowned any sense of denial. She wanted to scream *who's here*, but she knew Achmed didn't know who "they" were. First the missing miner, then someone impossibly digging their way toward the shaft—and now that dig was almost complete.

Whoever it is, they're going to kill us.

Her daughter. Her husband.

"Let's get out of here," she said.

She moved to the adit, stopped when she saw Achmed wasn't following her.

"Kat, where the fuck are you going? We have to stay. If something goes wrong with the elevator when they're coming up ..."

He didn't need to finish the sentence to paint the picture, but even if he had it wouldn't have mattered to her.

She pointed to the two miners. One stood at the elevator's controls, the other was slowly circling the railing, alternating between looking up at the winch mechanism and down into the shaft.

"They've got it handled," she said. "Come on."

Achmed stared at her. He shook his head.

My daughter ... my husband.

Humiliation joined fear, mixed with it, created an altogether new emotion that overwhelmed her. She couldn't wait here under all that rock, she just *couldn't*.

Katerina turned and sprinted down the adit.

She ran as fast as she could, legs churning even while her brain told her the footing wasn't safe, that she might trip and hurt herself and be stuck here when it all came down and—

The floor lurched beneath her—no small tremble this time, but rather a shudder that might have moved the whole mountain. When her right foot came down the ground wasn't where it was supposed to be. It twisted over, and for the split second before the pain hit she had the strange sensation of both the side of her foot and her anklebone touching stone at the same time.

She fell hard, bouncing, skidding. The unmistakable grinding sound of falling rock reached through her ears, made her body lock up tight. She covered her head, a ridiculous but automatic gesture—as if it could stop tons of death about to smash her bones to paste.

A scream ... a *man's* scream.

The echoes of falling rock ceased.

She opened one eye, almost afraid to look, as if daring to do so would finally bring the mountain down. Spinning dust, driven by air coming from behind her, from the winch cavern. No fallen rock around her, but there assuredly was back there.

Back where Achmed had been.

My husband ...

She had to move, had to move. She started to stand, but her right ankle screamed at her, told her she wasn't going anywhere.

My daughter…

Katerina pressed her palms to the rough stone floor, managed to rise up on her left foot alone. She had to keep going, had to get out of there.

One hand on the wall, she hopped along.

From back in the winch cavern, or whatever was left of it, she heard a new sound.

Dummm… dummm… dummm…

C-flat. A ringing, deep C-flat that caressed the stone around her, filled the adit as if it were God himself striking a key on the world's largest piano.

She kept moving, trying to ignore the fire in her ankle.

Dummm… dummm…

Rhythmic, repeated. What could that noise be?

Dummm… ping!… dommm… dommm…

That *ping*, was it snapping metal? The pitch had changed, from C-flat to C.

More snapping, more *pinging*,

Dimmm… dimmm…

D-flat.

She realized what was happening.

"God help me," she said.

She tried to hop faster, heart and soul screaming at her to move faster, *faster*, ruined ankle refusing to help.

Then, another sound. A scraping, a hissing.

The sound of dry leaves blowing across a sidewalk.

1:42 A.M.

Dimmm… dimmm…

Connell leaned into the vertical shaft. He looked up, craning his neck, trying to make out detail of the approaching cage's circular bottom.

"What the hell is that ringing?"

Bill Crook shook his head. "Dunno. It's never made that sound before."

A rhythmic thrumming, like the *gong* of a big grandfather clock reverberating through the shaft. Every three or four strikes, the pitch increased slightly.

It was close now, only a few minutes away, the black bottom lit up with a slow-motion strobe effect as it lowered past one light, then the next.

Dimmm…dimmm…twang!

Connell kept staring for a few seconds, his brain unable to process what his eyes showed him. Not a slow strobe anymore—a *pop-pop-pop-pop* of flashing black. Because it wasn't *lowering*, it was *falling*.

"No," he said, shaking his head as if that might change the fast-forward horror he simply couldn't accept as real.

He had to turn. He had to run. He had to warn. He couldn't move. Fear rooted his feet to the ground, gripped his insides and pinched his brain.

A scraping sound, the screeching of metal grinding against stone, echoing through the shaft—the hateful roar of a dragon.

Like a rubber band stretched too far, fear's grip finally *snapped*.

He pushed away from the shaft, bellowing a roar of his own.

"*Run!*"

Frozen people staring at him, wide-eyed. Why weren't they running? Only Veronica, pulling at Sanji's wrist, trying to yank the fat man to his feet, but how could she move that slow?

Connell's feet took him to her, his hands reached out on their own, grabbed Sanji's other wrist, grabbed and *pulled*.

Any second now the elevator would hit, shatter, tear the shaft to pieces. That *sound*, the screech of a wounded demon dragged into hell, getting louder closer *louder closer*.

A slurring moment between Sanji sitting and lurching to his feet, pulled along by two people, away from the elevator shaft, and then the choke hold on time slipped away.

In the last moment, the demon's ear-piercing scream made Connell wish he'd been born deaf.

Five tons of metal hit at terminal velocity, smashing like a bomb blast. The ground trembled beneath Connell's feet. Bits of rock crumbled from the carved ceiling. Sanji fell and Connell fell over him—or maybe it was the other way around.

A rock crashed down on his right, hit another rock, bounced up spinning through the air.

Shouts of pain from behind. Connell looked back as he scrambled to his feet. Lashon, on his back, face twisted in agony, knee pulled to his chest. His lower leg dangled like a limp sock filled with jelly.

Connell moved toward him, then Braxton was at Lashon's side, bending, grabbing, lifting. A *crack-pop* like a thin pane of glass fracturing down the middle. All three men looked up in time to see a chunk of the ceiling the size of a minivan drop on top of Braxton and Lashon both, hitting so fast no one had time to scream, falling so hard it shook the ground when it smashed the two men beneath it.

Connell didn't think, he turned, his body dictating the action. More *crack-pops*. Rocks of many sizes dropped from the ceiling. A fist-sized chunk fell, hit a bigger boulder and bounced up fast at an angle — Connell barely saw it before it cracked into his temple.

The world blurred. The world spun.

He sagged, felt rock against his side. He heard screaming. Sanji, maybe? He heard rocks falling. He opened his eyes for a moment, saw a storm of dust billowing around him, a storm that grew darker and darker until all was black.

1:43 A.M.

A woman's scream, single and lonely and thin, echoed up to Kayla's position. It had come from the adit, or somewhere near it, the kind of scream that made goose bumps prickle.

Kayla trained her binoculars on the adit mouth. No night vision needed, thanks to the one light that hung over the entrance, illuminating the dirt and rock beneath in a dull, almost green shine.

Movement.

A woman, stumbling, limping out of the adit mouth ... the woman from the lab ... bleeding, cut bad, *so* bad ... blood spraying from a neck wound—a wound Kayla knew was fatal from just a single glance. Dead woman walking, only seconds left.

The woman dropped to her knees, then fell face-first onto the gravel-strewn rock road. The wound let out another spray, weaker, and then just a small spurt.

She didn't move.

Kayla tingled all over, especially down low, down *there*. What was happening? Who had murdered that woman?

Something scurried out of the adit mouth, a blurring-fast, dull-gleam of legs. It crawled on top of the woman, stopped there.

Was that... a *spider*? A big-ass, round spider with four legs?

There was a moment where she realized something spectacular was about to happen, something that would change her life, change *everything*, then she saw flashing colors playing off the adit's walls. Dim at first, barely noticeable, but quickly growing in intensity. Colors, so many colors...

The spider moved aside.

What came next jarred Kayla, made everything she knew, that she had *ever* known, crumble and disintegrate.

The adit mouth vomited forth a stream of bizarre, glowing creatures. Each about the size of a man, although it was impossible to tell because they were packed so close together, the pulsating lights of one lost in the thrumming incandescence of those behind it, around it. They didn't walk or run, they *flowed*, round bodies carried by extensions that seemed to squish out of them to the ground below, then suck back in when they moved past.

How could they not have arms? How could they not have legs?

Boneless bodies, fluid and graceful.

Her head spun, brain half-stunned into thoughtlessness, half-consumed trying to find words that defined what she saw: sea urchins with soft, waving spikes; jellyfish firm enough to move, to roll; deflated beach balls with whipping squid limbs.

They were multicolored amoebas lit up from within. A silent, flashing mass pouring down the steep road toward the EarthCore camp, their colors brilliant and electric against the night's blackness.

Black spots on their skin, or hide, or membrane or whatever the fuck it was, on the round bodies, on the extruded, here-then-gone tentacles, black spots that remained consistent while red and orange flowed one way, yellow and green another, while brown-ringed blue circles expanded and contracted, purple and lime and gold and turquoise and pink and maroon all fighting a mad war across tendrils that squished out, gripped the ground, then seemed to draw back into the body like a video of squirting toothpaste being played in reverse.

Hundreds of the creatures. Halfway to the camp's west gate.

Almost fluid, nearly formless, their bodies changing constantly, but one thing remained consistent, remained fixed and firm and final—every last one of them held a strange, double-crescent knife. Their changing colors gleamed off the weapons' polished surfaces. So strange to see those bits of hardness among a rushing tide of soft dough.

Kayla couldn't think: she could only watch.

A sharp burst of gunfire made her jump, the reports echoing off the mountainside. A guard, the only one manning the west gate, opening fire with his EBR. He stood just inside the fence.

One thought climbed to the surface, a strange thought: could these things flow *through* the chain link?

The guard fired again. An alarm Klaxon blared through the camp.

The column of squishy creatures hit the gate. No, they couldn't flow through it. They didn't have to. Gleaming blades—now reflecting the camp's lights as well as the ever-changing colors—came up and down, up and down. The chain link rattled and bent as the blades sliced through it.

The creatures poured through.

The guard had waited too long. He turned to run. A double-sickle knife whizzed through the air, the spinning blades hypnotic in that one second of travel before a point drove deep into his back, sent him stumbling forward to fall hard to his hands and knees.

He reached behind him, grasping, desperate. Kayla saw him clutch the blade, saw his severed fingers flop to the ground.

The man vanished under a crashing wave of glowing nightmare. More knives—up, then down, then up again, trailing great arcs of blood that glinted in the camp lights.

Down again.

Up again.

The river of living color split into vibrant streams that flowed through the camp.

1:48 A.M.

At the east gate, Cho Takachi slowly squatted down, then lay flat on his stomach. Elbows on the dirt, he tucked the Mark 14 EBR to his shoulder. One eye closed, he sighted straight down the road that led to the west gate.

The west gate, where something beautiful was hacking Frank Hutchins to pieces.

Blood.

Those knives.

Glowing bodies flashing with angry colors.

Why hadn't he listened to Sonny? The old man had said something bad was going to happen. Had Sonny known it was this? How could *anyone* have known it was this, when Cho couldn't even process what *this* was?

Frank's hand ... sailing through the air, hitting the dirt road and rolling a few times before flopping to a halt, three fingers curled loosely, middle finger sticking up as if Frank had been trying to flip his killers the bird before they gutted him.

The creatures—*so beautiful, so impossibly angelic*—kept coming through the ruined west gate, flowed north toward the separator, toward the administration trailer, south toward the hangar and the fuel tanks.

And straight down the road, toward Cho.

Had they seen him?

If they did, they would cut him, pile on him like they had on Frank, slice him to pieces with those heavy knives. Cho knew how sharp the knives were. He'd held one in his hands.

Benjamin's demons.

The man hadn't been crazy, not at all. He'd been telling the truth.

Cho felt like he'd been transported into a movie, teleported there by some spell, a monster movie where all would die, all but one, because someone had to live on or how would you get people to come see the sequel?

He glanced to his left, to the armory building. Lots of ammo inside. More guns. Could he hide there?

One of the creatures rolled/flowed/stretched to the separator building's blue walls. A platinum knife whipped up, down, slicing a screeching gash in the sheet metal. Other creatures rushed over, did the same, slashing over and over, ripping free great shreds of metal.

Nope, not going to hide in the armory.

He heard a woman screaming. He heard gunfire. Both sounds came from the north, where the Quonset huts were, where people had been sleeping until the Klaxon's shrieking call. Cries of shock, of alarm. Of pain. Of death.

The lab door opened. A man walked out, coffee cup in hand. He was halfway between Cho and the glowing angels of death slicing into the metal wall. The man took three steps before he saw them. He stopped, stared, his back to Cho.

The coffee cup slipped from the man's weak fingers.

The angels of death stopped hacking the wall.

A sound like the screeching of hot tires on hotter asphalt. Cho saw new colors explode on their strange bodies, amber spots and circles of seafoam green (how the *fuck* did he know what seafoam green looked like?). Boneless arms stretched out and the creatures rushed in. If the man had a thought to turn and run, that signal didn't make it from his brain to his feet before they were on him.

A purple and emerald snake-arm stretched out, brought down a double-crescent knife in a whipping curve. The blade *crunched* into the man's skull, slicing through bone and eye alike until it wedged into the upper jaw. The man had a second to shudder, or maybe twitch, and then two more glowing limbs snapped out. The first blade sliced horizontally, cutting clean through the man's stomach. Stuff burst out of him, blood and bits, severed intestines hanging down, wiggling like cut eels that reflected the many colors of his killers. The third blade came up from underneath, hitting him in the armpit, sending his arm spinning away (he's already dead isn't that overkill a dead man doesn't need an arm) to skid across the dirt.

Blades rose and fell, so fast, *so fast.* Blood splattered against the lab wall, stretched in great arcs across the dirt road. Legs came off, were then hacked to pieces as if each now-useless limb might be the angels' ultimate enemy. Arms and hands and the head, crushed and sliced into a hundred pieces. In a few seconds, the man went from a walking human being to a wet pile of chopped meat.

The three glowing angels left him. They flowed into the open lab door.

From inside came screams. Men and women both.

Cho slowly rose to one knee. He reached up and lifted the gate's latch. It didn't make a sound.

"Thank you, Sonny," he said, the words little more than escaping breath.

Still crouched, he slid through the open gate, then gently rolled it closed behind him.

The latch clicked shut.

EBR clutched tightly in his hands, Cho duckwalked down the road. He moved that way for a few meters, rose to a crouch, kept going like that for another few meters, saying a silent prayer of gratitude for the shadows that seemed to welcome him in like the embrace of long-lost family.

He couldn't take it anymore. He stood. He ran down the sloping road.

It was only a few flashes of red, yellow, and orange that let him know something was behind him. That, and the *smell*. The smell of dead things, the smell of rot. Still running, he threw a glance over his shoulder but couldn't get a good look at it.

Cho stopped and turned, firing on full automatic. Screaming, he emptied the magazine into the glowing thing, but it kept coming. A yellow and brown tentacle curled back then whipped forward—a metallic flash sailed through the air.

Something hit his left shoulder, filled it with fire.

The angel kept coming.

Cho dropped the Mark 14, drew his pearl-handled .45 and squeezed off three rounds, *boom!-boom!-boom!* The thing shuddered each time. Fluid sprayed, dark shadows backlit by the creature's light.

It dropped in a lifeless heap on the dirt. The colored light faded, faded, then was gone. It seemed to *deflate*, like a waterbed with many holes poked into it, until it was nothing more than an empty sack.

Cho turned and ran. He ran and ran and ran.

He started to slow. He felt weak, cold.

He holstered the .45, felt at his left shoulder. Blood. Lots of it.

"Oh, fuck," he said.

He swayed to the right, feet sliding through the gravel at the road's beveled shoulder. Momentum turned him, had him stumbling in reverse as he fought to keep his balance, then his heel caught on something and he fell backward.

He heard the *thonk* of his head hitting a rock and was out before he felt the pain.

1:51 A.M.

They swarmed over the camp, a throng of color-changing, shape-shifting lightning bugs pouring between, around and over buildings. Screams, both male and female, filled the night air along with the creatures' odd sounds. Odd, angry, *aggressive* sounds—the noises reminded Kayla vaguely of an 18-wheeler locking up its brakes, but with many different pitches and tones.

The things were cutting at anything they found: canvas, wood, sheet metal, light poles...people. So many people.

She watched, detached, feeling oddly like she was standing over a fish tank of piranha into which someone had just dropped a handful of goldfish. The few people who were outside had no chance—they were trapped, blocked by fences topped with concertina wire. Nowhere to run.

The door to the guard Quonset burst open. Three men came out in a tight group. Front and rear men with Mark 14s up at high-ready, the middle man with his weapon over the shoulder of the point man. Trained soldiers. They weren't as tight as Kayla would have liked, but she knew the security personnel had been drawn from all over EarthCore—they probably hadn't practiced stacked tactics.

"Come on, boys," she said, zooming in with the binocs. "Come on."

She wanted them to make it out, wanted at least *someone* to make it out. She didn't know why; these people meant nothing to her.

The men turned right, headed straight for the oncoming mass of flashing creatures belching forth from between the separator and the admin shed, pouring down the road in front of the Quonset huts—two streams of horror flowing together, joining like tributaries forming a relentless river.

The men fired in short bursts.

"That's it," Kayla said, her hands squeezing the binocs tighter.

Somewhere in her mind, it surprised her that the things could be hit, could drop in a still heap like a beanbag tossed through the air to land on the floor. But those behind poured over the fallen: the psychedelic wave crashed on.

They were too fast. There were too many. The middle man turned to run and the line fell apart. The creatures swarmed over them like army ants.

The hacking began.

Human screams, so prevalent in the first few minutes of the conflict, quickly died out.

The hangar door ripped outward, folded around the hood of a Land Rover that turned hard right, back end skidding as it headed for the east gate. Three creatures clung to the sides and top, ropy arms whipping, platinum knives spiderwebbing glass, gashing metal. Camp lights flashed off the vehicle's green paint.

A few of the creatures had circled fast along first the north fence, then down the east—they spilled out around the corner of the lab building into the main road, rushed toward the oncoming Land Rover. The vehicle swerved, corrected, already losing control when it slammed into them. One splattered against the grille like a water balloon dropped from twenty stories up. Another went down under the front right wheel, squishing out a great gout of yellow fluid. The Rover swerved again, too far this time, back end coming around in a wide skid until it was sideways—it rolled twice before it smashed into the lab's wall, knocking a huge, crumbling hole in the cinder block.

Color flowed into the wreck. If the driver and passengers had survived the crash, they were already dead.

A light pole twitched, then fell, blinking out when it smashed into the ground.

Kayla felt numb. So much carnage.

She panned around the camp, hoping to see survivors. Just one man, sprinting south with rolling multicolored beasts a few steps behind. The man ran headlong between two trucks, moving so fast he didn't notice the chain-link fence behind them in time. He smashed into it, bounced off, fell on his ass. He scrambled up again, ran to the fence—the mindless, unthinking act of a panicked animal. Instead of running left or right, instead of climbing, he gripped the chain link, screamed in frustration and gave it a single, rattling shake before his pursuers caught up with him.

Another light pole tilted, fell, blinked out. Just one more, and the camp would be dark.

Kayla panned west. The creatures were attacking the hangar, carving up the sheet metal like leafcutter ants tearing apart a tree. What was left of the roof started to sag under their weight. They were also hacking away at the fuel tanks there; diesel gushed out of big holes, flowed east following the camp's natural slope.

And at the northwest corner, the same thing: blades punched into the camp generator's big fuel tanks. Diesel poured from multiple holes— ten thousand gallons of gas flooded through the camp.

She wondered if it might ignite.

The last light pole fell. When it hit the ground, the Klaxon alarm finally ceased.

Night's dark claimed the camp, but not for long.

The *whoosh* of orange flame started at the generator, sailed across the flowing fuel. Finally, something glowed brighter than the creatures.

They let out shrieks and other strange noises. A few were caught in the flames, died in a whipping frenzy of forming/unforming tentacles, but most rushed clear, far faster than the fastest man she'd ever seen, stretching out glowing limbs to eat up the ground or scurry over the chain link.

The generator building started to burn. So did the separator, the women's Quonset, the administration trailer. Flames rose higher, whipping and angry, orange tongues licking the sky, lighting up the billowing smoke. If the creatures were still screeching, Kayla couldn't hear it over the fire's roar.

She sat in her camouflaged warren, paralyzed, unmoving. But the show was far from over.

Bits of burning paper or cloth flitted up, over the road that ran between the east and west gates, landed in the spilled hangar fuel. That, too, flamed to angry life. Fire raged through the already ravaged building. The tanks of the Jeeps and Land Rovers caught, sending their own orange pillars towering into the air—the skyline of a city made from flame.

The camp burned. She watched blinding orange rising high, crowned by billowing black, the surrounding desert lit up in a shimmering circle.

She didn't know how long she watched. Maybe minutes. Maybe hours.

Fuel spent, the inferno finally started to die down. Some areas burned out completely, just sat there, smoldering. Pyramids of flame lowered, lowered, until just a few hot tongues danced: maybe fuel, burning, maybe wood ... maybe corpses.

The glowing creatures finally seemed to rest. They surrounded the camp. She lowered the binocs. From this distance, they looked like a loose circle of Christmas lights wrapped around a dying campfire.

The circle broke. As a unit, the shimmering, flashing horde moved back up the road toward the adit mouth, much slower than it had poured down. They were tired, maybe. The intense battle had taken its toll.

They dragged their dead along with them, at least the ones that hadn't been burned to a crisp in the fire.

Into the mouth they flowed, steadily vanishing from sight. A few stragglers brought up the rear. The last one entered, was out of sight for a second, then came back out. A tentacle arm reached up, slashed at the light above the entrance. The light blinked out, leaving the mountainside as black as the night.

Kayla set her binoculars aside, flipped down her starlight goggles.

The creature was gone.

The mountain was still.

She turned her attention back to the camp.

But there was no camp.

The last of the fires flickered out.

Every building had been torn down, sheet metal warping and twisting in the inferno. The lab's north wall, and just a bit of the west wall, were the only parts of that building still standing—what had been the camp's heart not thirty minutes ago now looked like an ancient ruin.

She sucked in a sharp breath: in a rush, what she had just seen played back through her thoughts. She hadn't been able to think while it happened, but now it was over.

Opportunity? She'd come to the desert looking for it, and now here it was. More opportunity than she'd ever dreamed. Screw the South Africans. Screw the Russians. Screw EarthCore. Hell, screw the platinum itself. Those things offered only money, and money couldn't buy her what she wanted most in the world.

She didn't know what, exactly, she had just witnessed, but she knew damn well no one had ever witnessed anything like it before.

Whatever those things were—unknown animals, monsters, aliens, maybe even demons, because she wasn't ruling *anything* out—they were her ticket back into the NSA.

Kayla flipped on the COMSEC unit and jammed all frequencies. She programmed it to break jamming every fifteen minutes and do a five-second scan—if someone made it out of camp, they'd probably call for help.

She couldn't have that. She couldn't have people coming out here to rescue any survivors.

Kayla Meyers had to make sure no one got away.

BOOK FOUR
THE TUNNELS

20

11,307 feet below the surface

A FILM OF DUST LINGERED in the still air, seemingly suspended by magic, defying gravity's pull.

Headlamp beams swerved back and forth through the dusty tunnel, feeble attempts at illuminating the endless darkness.

A hundred yards away from the shaft bottom, the survivors sat in the horizontal tunnel Mack and his crew had created not even twenty-four hours earlier. They waited for Mack and O'Doyle to return from the ravaged vertical shaft.

Connell Kirkland sat on his ass, elbows on knees, face in his hands. Dull, unending agony inside his head. He'd never felt pain like this.

Veronica sat on his right, arm around his shoulder, left hand gently pressing gauze against his temple. That hurt, too, but it was such a paltry splinter of pain compared to the war raging inside his skull that he barely noticed it.

Sanji sat on his left. He wasn't consoling anyone. A rock had fallen on his hand, smashing his left pinkie and ring finger. Bones broken, probably, but the suit itself hadn't torn or split—Angus Kool made durable stuff.

Sanji didn't complain about the pain. In fact, he said nothing. He held the left hand to his chest, tightly covered by his right.

Lybrand stood close by. Uninjured, at least as far as Connell knew. She held her machine gun, her headlamp light pointing first left, toward the shaft, then right, toward the natural cavern opening that led into the tunnel system. Back and forth. Over and over. She was serious about her business. Her eyes were hard, but also wet; tears rolled down her cheeks, leaving thin, shining trails across her dusty skin.

Footsteps, coming.

Lybrand snapped the rifle butt to her shoulder, spread her feet, dropped into an athlete's ready stance. She aimed the barrel toward the approaching noise.

"Knock it off," Veronica said. "You know it's Mack."

Lybrand ignored her, kept the barrel level and steady.

"Oh, for fuck's sake," Veronica muttered. "Because *that's* what we really need right now, to shoot each other by accident."

Headlamp beams sliced through the dust. Mack and O'Doyle returned.

Lybrand lowered her weapon, angled it down across her chest.

"Lashon?" she said. "Braxton?"

Connell didn't know why she was asking. He'd already told her he'd seen the two men die. Their bodies remained hidden beneath a slab of rock too big to move.

O'Doyle held a machine gun in his hands, another slung over his shoulder.

"They're gone," he said. "So is Crook."

The throbbing in Connell's head swelled, pushed at his brain. When Mack had helped him here, he'd seen Lashon but not Crook. He'd hoped desperately the man was still alive.

Veronica gently took Connell's left hand, put the bloody gauze in it, then pressed hand and gauze both against his temple. She stood.

"Did falling rock kill Crook?"

Mack shook his head, making the headlamp beam jiggle.

"Piece of the cage," he said. His voice was a dull thing, as alive as the rocks above him. "Shot out when it crashed, punched right through him. He bled out. He didn't have a chance."

Silence once again filled the tunnels. Someone coughed. Dust swirled.

Connell closed his eyes tightly. More dead men. Gone, because of his obsession. What would Cori think of him now? He wanted to curl up in a ball and die. Or maybe have Lybrand put that rifle barrel in his mouth, then ask her all nice and pretty-like to pull the trigger.

No. If he'd ever had the balls to kill himself, he would have done it five years ago.

Three men dead. And Janssen, still missing, probably gone as well. Six people still alive, including himself. He was the boss. These five survivors were his responsibility.

He shifted his feet, trying to rise. O'Doyle stepped in quick, strong arm lifting Connell the rest of the way.

"Take it easy, Mister Kirkland. Head wounds are serious business."

Connell's first reaction was to say something like, *No shit? Wow, I would have never guessed by this fucking nuclear bomb exploding inside my fucking skull.* But what good would that do?

"How bad is the shaft?"

Five headlamps swung to light up Mack's face. He coughed, spit on the ground. He licked his lips, worked his tongue in his mouth like it was full of dirt and dust.

"We're in a world of shit," he said. "The area we carved around the shaft bottom is damaged, obviously. It's unstable. I think we don't go back in there, for anything. Even to bury Jenkins, Crook and Braxton."

Three headlamps panned down. Lybrand, Sanji and O'Doyle, maybe taking a moment of silence. Connell's headlamp, however, stayed fixed on Mack's face. So did Veronica's.

"We don't go in there until they repair the shaft, you mean," she said. "That *is* what you mean, right? Tell me that's what you fucking mean."

Mack worked his tongue in his mouth again. Probably nothing left in there, he was just looking for a way to not say what everyone already knew.

"The shaft is full of fallen rock," he said. "At least a hundred feet deep. Probably deeper. Much of that rock came from the shaft itself."

Sanji stood, damaged hand still clutched protectively against his chest.

"But they'll dig that out, come get us," he said. "How long will it take them to dig us out?"

Mack sighed. "The rubble included a few parts from the winch mechanism. It wasn't just the cage that came down, it was the whole elevator assembly. Considering the frame I engineered for it, I highly doubt it just *fell*. The winch room itself must have collapsed. The entire shaft is compromised. Remove the rock that's packed in there now, more rock will likely fall in and they'll have to start over. If they come and get us, they'll have to sink an entirely new shaft."

Veronica glanced at Connell as if he could wave some magic wand and make this all go away. She and Sanji both had no idea how fucked everyone was.

Her headlamp swung back to Mack.

"*If* they come and get us? What the hell do you mean *if*?"

Mack looked up, looked at Connell. Both men knew the financials. The operation had taken every cash reserve EarthCore owned. Barbara would have to sell off everything, every last asset, to generate enough money to fund a rescue operation.

Other companies might help, might volunteer time and men and equipment, but only if they knew there was hope. Connell and the others were deeper than any human being had been before, cut off from communication. It might take a week for someone just to get a message down here, to try to find out if anyone had survived.

But those details wouldn't help anyone right now. He needed time to think. He needed to give these people at least some tiny degree of hope.

"Angus has a drill prototype in Denver," he said. "Barbara will probably ship that out immediately, but it will take three days or so to get here."

He saw Veronica nodding.

"Yeah, that's what I'm talking about." She looked around at the others, headlamps swinging wildly. "Another drill. Sink a new vertical shaft, come and get us."

Lybrand slung her rifle.

"Wait a minute," she said. "It took a *week* to drill the first. Does that mean it will take a week to rescue us?"

Mack looked down again. "Plus three days to ship the drill here. A day or two to build a new adit, another two days to install a new winch mechanism. If everything goes perfectly, without any delays or mistakes, we're looking at two weeks. At best."

If Connell could have walked without falling over, he would have kicked Mack in the nuts. Apparently the man hadn't got the mental memo about creating hope.

"Two weeks at best," Sanji said. His voice was a whisper, but in a place where the only sound is someone breathing, a whisper can hit like a shout. "And at worst?"

Mack said nothing. His headlamp lit up his dirty left boot, then his right, as if he'd found something so utterly fascinating with his feet that he couldn't look away.

Hope. What was Connell thinking? Call a turd a rose and it still smells like shit. There was no room for hope down here. There was barely enough room for reality. They deserved to know the real deal.

"At worst, we die here," he said. "Let's get our heads around that right now, because my brain hurts bad enough without having to listen to people bring up ideas that won't work. Mack's two-week estimate is if things go perfectly, and in this business things *never* go perfectly. This isn't some standard rescue operation. My best guess is three weeks, probably four. Mack, how long do the batteries in these headlamps last?"

"About two days," he said. "We have extras in the Picture Cavern. We have a small generator there to run the floodlights, but only enough fuel for a few days. There is no other power, no hope of getting power. If we ration, we have enough light for maybe a week, total."

"Oh my God," Veronica said. "We're going to be stuck down here in the dark? For *weeks*?"

"We'll manage," O'Doyle said. "We need to know about food and water. Darkness can't hurt us."

Veronica glared at him. "Thanks for the platitude, you fucking idiot. In your experience with sensory deprivation—which I'm sure is quite vast—how long before we start to hallucinate? Huh?"

Lybrand's light snapped around, made Veronica's eyes squint.

"Shut the fuck up," Lybrand said.

O'Doyle held up a hand toward Lybrand, the gesture telling her to stop.

"Food," he said again. "And water. How much is stored in the Picture Cavern?"

Connell wanted to know that himself. He knew Mack had been setting up a base camp but had been so busy he'd paid no attention to the details.

"Well, there's six of us down here," Mack said. "Which means we've got enough food and water to last about three days, if we ration strictly. From then on, we're all on the underground diet plan."

No one laughed. In three days, they'd be thirsty, hungry. In seven, they'd be in the dark. The reality of the situation began to sink in, even to Connell.

And he was about to let them know it was even worse than they thought.

3:17 A.M.

Veronica felt the weight of the mountain bearing down on her. She had no idea how much that weight actually was (millions of tons of rock, maybe?), but it was enough to kill her just like it had killed Lashon. She was in her crypt. Her father, too. Her world would be pitch-black when the thirst came, when dehydration-driven confusion, dizziness and lethargy overcame her. At some point, she would fall unconscious and never wake up again.

"I know this is bad," Connell said. "But there's more."

Veronica stared at him. Wasn't a slow, painful death already as bad as it got?

Lybrand held up her palms in a *hold on a second* gesture.

"We're in a tomb here, Mister Kirkland," she said. "How can there be more?"

Veronica said nothing, but she wanted to know why that woman was even talking. Lybrand was just a grunt, just a stupid soldier or guard or whatever. Smart enough to point a gun, to solve problems with her fists, and probably nothing more.

Five headlamps swiveled to light up Connell's face. If the light was blinding him, he didn't show it. He had the same blank expression he'd worn every damn minute up on the surface. Every minute, that was, except for that moment outside the party, when he'd smiled.

Was he enjoying all of this? Fucking corporate piece of shit. Was it his greed that had made this happen?

Veronica didn't want to die. She *didn't want to die.*

"Before the elevator crashed I talked to Doctor Hayes," Connell said. "It appears EarthCore may not be the only ones down here."

"No shit, mate," Mack said. "I already told you about that silver spider."

"Wasn't a fucking *spider*," Sanji said.

He sounded pissed off. Maybe it was the pain, building up inside him, giving him a need to vent at any opportunity. Veronica could understand that feeling, and she didn't even have broken fingers.

"You don't know that," Mack said. "You didn't see it move, mate."

Sanji huffed. "I don't have to see it. If it looks like metal and lives where there is no life, then guess what? It's a robot of some kind. No arachnid that size could live down here—there's no food."

Veronica laughed, a fast, barking thing. "Well, if it *is* a spider, I guess it's got something to eat now, right?"

"Enough," Connell said. "Everyone, be quiet for a moment, just listen."

He took in a slow breath. When he did, Veronica knew that he was going to make things even worse. Worse than being trapped miles belowground with some kind of crawly thing. Oh, that's right, she'd forgotten about the crawly thing—because that would make dying insane in the dark so much better.

"There were some seismic anomalies that our science staff couldn't explain," Connell said. "That's not a major red flag. Those things happen all the time in a deep mine. I had Hayes keep studying them, though, and she found something disturbing."

He paused. He blinked too fast. Whatever he had to say, he was trying to find the right words to make it sound not as bad as it actually was. He shook his head—apparently, there was no way to put a happy face on this one.

"She discovered that someone else was in the mountain, digging toward our main shaft," he said. "Whoever that was, at this point, we have to assume they reached our shaft, and are probably the reason the winch cavern collapsed."

Lybrand unslung her rifle, once again held it in both hands.

"So someone did this on purpose," she said. "Someone wants us dead? This is just fucking pristine."

O'Doyle's headlamp beam snapped to her.

"Be quiet," he said.

Lybrand said nothing more.

O'Doyle was ugly enough in a normal setting. In the dusty spotlights, the side of his face made him look like a monster that belonged in this underground cemetery, a lich or a wight, an eater of the dead.

His headlamp slowly swung back to Kirkland.

"What else did Hayes say? Do we know who it is? How many people are we're up against?"

"Good question," Mack said. "Who the hell did this to us?"

Before this, Mack had spoken in almost a monotone, the voice of a man resigned to an inevitable end. Not anymore. Now there was fire in his words. Hatred.

"She didn't know," Connell said. "My guess is that another mining company is trying to jump this claim. As crazy as that sounds, it still happens. We've had other incidents. Jansson's disappearance. Two KoolSuits that came up missing. And..."

Veronica saw him glance at O'Doyle, a here-then-gone look.

"And the people that did that might be down here with us," Connell finished.

"The camp," Sanji said. "Sonny and the others. If these people want the platinum so bad that they would try to kill us, wouldn't they attack the camp as well?"

Veronica closed her eyes, shook her head. They already had no hope. If the camp had been hit, then there wasn't even a shred of a chance at rescue. They had *less* than no hope.

"Possible, but not likely," Connell said. "Hitting the elevator and damaging the shaft puts EarthCore out of commission long enough for someone to dig another entrance to these tunnels. The tunnel complex is huge. I don't know how they found out about it, but they did. While we're dead in the water, they can get to the Dense Mass first. We have mining rights for our area, but we can't buy an entire mountain range. No one can. Basically, it comes down to the first company to reach the ore and develop a working mine gets it all. So targeting the elevator was a surgical strike. Hitting an armed camp outright would be another story entirely, don't you think, Mister O'Doyle?"

The scarred man nodded. "With the firepower we have up there, taking out the camp would require a paramilitary unit and the intention to commit mass murder. Burying a few people beneath a mountain is one thing—taking on armed, trained men in the open is much riskier. And even if that operation succeeds, it's going to leave a lot of evidence. You can't just make seventy people disappear. Trust me, the camp is still up there. Everyone is fine and they're already working on ways to get us out."

Well, wasn't that just all fucking fancy? Connell's thug thought everything would be fine. It wasn't enough that Veronica would die down here, she'd die side by side with a Cro-Mag that believed manna would fall from heaven and Jesus would fire up Santa's sleigh for a nice midnight ride to safety. If O'Doyle thought...

Connell's words bounced around inside her head.

"Wait a minute," she said, her voice quiet and thin. "You think someone else is going after the Dense Mass?"

Connell nodded. "Mining laws are meant to protect the people or company who first generate value from a claim, so—"

Veronica waved her hand dismissively, cutting him off.

"Not *that*. I don't care about your legalese business bullshit. You said they want to reach the Dense Mass first. Our shaft is ruined, so they'd need another way in. Right?"

She held her breath. Could it be that simple? Could the people who had caused this tragedy wind up—in a twisted way—being the possible saviors?

He stared at her, his headlamp beam in her face. Then Mack's beam joined it. Then O'Doyle's. Then Sanji's.

"Ronni, you are one smart cookie."

Connell nodded. "Goddamn right she is."

Lybrand's beam bounced from face to face, hitting them all before settling on Connell.

"I don't get it," she said. "What's that got to do with us?"

Connell held Veronica's gaze for a moment longer. Then, he smiled.

"Because their way in is our way out," he said. "If there are claim jumpers, they're heading for the Dense Mass."

O'Doyle nodded, grinned an evil grin that made Veronica want to shrink away from him.

"We can follow Angus's map of the tunnels to the Dense Mass," he said. "Once we're there, we find these claim-jumping, murderous motherfuckers. Then, we'll make them show us the way out."

Veronica's held breath rushed out, making dust motes swirl and dance. They had a chance. That chance lie with people who wanted them dead, with people who were probably as well armed as O'Doyle and Lybrand, but at least it was something.

Hope had returned.

4:12 A.M.

Through the starlight goggles, the adit mouth looked large, glowed an eerie green. In years past, Kayla wouldn't have given that color a second thought. But now colors weren't just *colors*, they meant something else altogether. They meant danger. They meant *death*.

Her hand hurt. She was holding her weapon too tight. She let go with the left first, shook it, then the right, shook that as well. Gripping so tight, as if this was the first time she'd ever held the Galil.

Jesus Lord and Savior, but she was scared.

She'd seen them move. If one or two came, she could kill them. But if a horde spilled out of there, like before? She wouldn't even make it a hundred yards before they brought her down.

Brought her down, and started cutting.

Why was she doing this? Was she really going to go in there? From her camouflaged nest, it seemed so simple: just slip into the adit, take a look around, slip back out. But plans made from afar sometimes crumble when you get close.

She was standing right where the woman from the lab had fallen. Where she'd died. Nothing here now other than a few smears of blood, dried on the rocks. Something small and white blazed in the starlight vision. Kayla knelt, pressed her gloved fingertip to it, lifted it.

A tooth.

No, *part* of a tooth. Cracked down the middle. All that was left of the woman.

Kayla brushed the tooth away, let it fall back to the ground.

Why was she doing this?

She knew the answer—because she wanted her life back.

When she reached out to the NSA, she would need more than just a story that would make her sound like she was strung out on meth. She needed real information.

One foot after another, slowly, so slowly, she moved into the adit. A long tunnel of black and green, straight out of a horror movie.

Hey, gang, let's go check out the house where that guy butchered a hundred people. It'll be a gas!

That's why movies sucked, because only a fucking idiot would do something like that.

And yet, here she was.

She kept moving in. Her hands were shaking. She double-checked that her finger was against the trigger guard and not the trigger itself. Not the time for trigger discipline to fail, send a couple of rounds to ricochet off rocks and bounce around in this narrow space.

"Keep going," she hissed. "Things we want come at a price."

She kept going.

When she saw the rockfall that blocked the adit, that made an impassible dead end, she wasn't sure if she should be angry or elated. She felt relieved, though, that she couldn't go further. There was no denying that emotion.

Some of the boulders must have weighed ten tons or more. It would take army engineers at least a week to clear the tunnel. She knew she was close to the elevator shaft, which meant the shaft was likely filled with fallen rocks as well.

Not good.

Without a way into the tunnels, all she could do was give the NSA this location. That, and her meth-head-sounding story. Would that be enough?

Yes. It will be enough. They HAVE to let you back in.

She'd never get another chance like this. She had to make it work.

4:22 A.M.

Sonny McGuiness had never felt quite so terrified. His balls, his stomach, his chest…everything pulsed, tried to wrinkled in on itself, maybe make him fold up and vanish, slide through this dimension to some other place, some other time.

When he'd been a little boy, his mother had let him see a flick called *The Werewolf*. He'd gone into that theater thinking he loved horror movies. He'd been wrong. The images burned into his seven-year-old brain, and for years after he had dreams of werewolves that chased him. He'd fall and couldn't quite manage to get back on his feet. He'd shout for help, knowing that the monster was closing in, knowing he would be torn to shreds. That sublime, pure fear, the moment just before the claw ripped the small of his back... that moment stretched out forever and all he wanted to do was get away, to wake up, to *wake up please God wake up*. When the sting hit home, he did wake: sweating, screaming, sometimes pissing the bed.

That had been the worst fear he'd ever known. Until now.

He was squatting beneath a scrubby juniper tree, the thin trunk between him and the camp. The fire had died down, but the flame god that had snaked up from the camp still danced a Ghost Dance in his eyes. Or maybe that was in his thoughts. He wasn't sure.

No more lights. Blackness. The camp was once again an indistinguishable part of the mountain.

The mountain, *Funeral Mountain*... it had come alive.

Sonny had made it to the end of the new road—where it met the horrible, existing dirt road about a mile and a half from the camp—before he heard the faint echo of gunshots. He'd turned and watched. Too far away to see anything, but he'd watched all the same. Then came the Klaxon. And after that, the fire. Not much at first, but it had grown into a massive column of flame, as if Satan himself had reached up from beneath the camp to drag everyone down to hell.

Sonny had made it out. *Just* made it out. By how long? Twenty minutes? Thirty?

If he had waited until morning, he'd be dead. Burned alive.

Had anyone escaped? If so, were they hurt?

He'd been asking himself that question for two hours now. He wanted to get closer, to see if anyone needed help. He wanted to, but he could not.

Because if he moved—either toward the camp or father away from it—the mountain might know he was there.

And it would come and get him.

No cell phone. Connell had taken it.

If anyone had got out, they might be hurt. Burned by the fire, injured by falling on rock. And, Sonny had heard gunfire. Faint echoes, but no mistaking it.

People could be hurt, even dying. If Sonny went to Route 21, or hiked due east to Milford, those people might die before he came back with help. If he found wounded people, though, and they were too injured for him to help, not going to Route 21 could mean their deaths just as well.

But why was it up to him? There were radios in the camp. Walkie-talkies. Kirkland had that cell phone. And there had been people in the adit, the shaft, who wouldn't have been caught up in the fire. They had radios, too. Someone had already called for help.

Help would come soon. They had to.

Either way, Sonny wasn't moving.

He rubbed at his bracelet. He rubbed and rubbed and rubbed. The skin started to flake away from the pad of his thumb, but he didn't notice.

Daylight. He had to stay in this spot, this *lucky spot* until daylight came. When it did, he'd head back up the new road and see what he could see.

That gunfire...

Had it all been from EarthCore guards? Kirkland thought someone was trying to jump the claim. Maybe those people had come, maybe on their own, maybe drawn by Funeral Mountain's evil, Sonny didn't know. What if they'd killed everyone? Or, worse, what if more claim jumpers were coming? If they were, they'd come on the roads.

Just like the road he was near now.

And if he walked along the dirt road toward Route 21, and more of the bad guys came...

If they'd killed everyone in the camp, they would kill him, too.

He made up his mind. Shortly before dawn, while there was still some cover of darkness, he'd circle southwest. The EarthCore camp was in a little plateau. He could climb up the peak south of the camp, though, to look down into it. He'd be out of sight and off the roads. He could see what he could see. If there were bad guys, he could stay hidden.

If there weren't, maybe he could figure out how to help.

His thumb moved faster across the engraved silver.

6:34 A.M.

They'd made it back to the Picture Cavern without incident. Mack wasn't sure whether that counted as a miracle or not, but considering how things had gone so far, he'd take it.

Even though time was of the essence, O'Doyle had insisted everyone get a few hours of sleep. The tunnels were going to get demanding, get dangerous—no place for people who had been awake for over twenty-four hours. Mack had laid down on the Picture Cavern's rock floor. He hadn't thought he'd be able to sleep, but when O'Doyle shook him awake, two hours had passed like magic.

Mack busied himself preparing backpacks. The portable flood lamps gave plenty of light. He wanted to enjoy that light, because in an hour or so the only illumination would come from headlamps and a few flashlights.

He stuffed the packs with batteries, food, water, climbing gear, KoolSuit repair kits, first-aid kits, all evenly distributed. A little more climbing gear for himself, of course, because he knew what he was doing. And a little more food, too, because he was the one doing the packing.

He wished he knew what to think, but his brain seemed to be missing gears. He'd built a masterpiece of a mine—now that was gone, destroyed by some motherfucker even more greedy and more cutthroat than Connell Kirkland. Which was saying something.

As if the mine mattered. Those three guards: dead. Jansson: probably dead.

Mack had to be honest with himself—more people would likely die either on the way to the Dense Mass, at it or on the way up. So much travel still to go, in caves where no one had ever set foot before. Maps were great. Maps didn't tell you what the footing was like, though, didn't show what areas might be weak, might collapse the first time someone bumped into a wall or accidentally kicked a rock.

And then there was the fact that the only way out was to find people who had no problem murdering to get what they wanted. Somehow, Mack didn't think those same people would now extend a helping hand.

The only good news was the KoolSuits themselves. According to Angus's specs, the things would work for three or four days without a recharge. As long as no one got cut, as long as the suits didn't tear, then

Mack didn't have to worry about people dying from the heat—just from cave-ins, falls or the saboteurs who had already tried to kill them once.

Off to the right, Kirkland was out cold. Mack would have found that as evidence of the man's callousness, but Mack had slept just as hard. Everyone was drained. Even O'Doyle was getting a few minutes' sleep, trusting their safety to Lybrand, who stood in the cavern's center.

Mack glanced over at Sanji and Veronica. She'd put splints on his two fingers, then taped the splints together. The man was in a lot of pain, which was only going to get worse once the climbing started. Mack hoped Sanji made it, but he didn't know the man, had no connection to him. If Sanji got into real trouble? Well, Mack wasn't going to die for a stranger.

Things were a real shit-burrito, all right. Low on batteries, low on food and water, bastards trying to kill them, and then there was that creature he'd seen.

No, of course it wasn't an arachnid, Sanji you know-it-all fat fuck, because arachnids have eight legs.

Maybe Mack didn't have a biology degree, but he could fucking count to four. But maybe Sanji was right—maybe it was a machine. That made sense—so hot down here people couldn't come down without severe temperature regulation, but a robot or a probe of some kind wouldn't have that restriction. If it was a robot, though, it was so advanced that there was nothing like it. Anywhere. Could it be a rival company had their own version of Angus Kool? Angus invents the suit to explore the tunnels, the rival invents the crawly machine?

How many of those things were down here? Did they bite? They didn't need light, obviously … when the batteries ran out and the darkness took hold, would the crawly things attack?

Which brought up a question so basic it made Mack's nuts shrink up into his belly: had the crawly things attacked Jansson?

Braxton had called them "silverbugs."

Braxton. Dead as shit. He and Lashon both, crushed by a rock so big O'Doyle couldn't even retrieve their weapons. And Crook, with his guts torn out by a piece of cage that hit him so hard it broke his damn pistol, shattered his hips, cracked his spine. Maybe Mack didn't know what a miracle was, but he knew a blessing when he saw one—Crook being knocked unconscious so he couldn't feel all that agony before he died.

Mack's right wrist buzzed softly, the wrist display's alarm going off. He finished the last backpack, then walked over to wake up O'Doyle. Soon it would be time to go.

6:49 A.M.

"This isn't Kirkland's fault," O'Doyle said quietly. "He's still the boss. We're going to follow his orders unless his orders will put people in danger, understand?"

Bertha Lybrand didn't understand, not even a tiny bit, but she nodded anyway. She had her own opinion about that dead-eyed piece of shit. How much had Kirkland known before the elevator came down? *Seismic anomalies.* Bullshit. Even if Mack said it was okay, what kind of a man sent people down here while there were little earthquakes going off, or whatever those signals meant?

This wasn't the army. People weren't expendable. *She* wasn't expendable.

She and O'Doyle stood at the edge of the Picture Cavern, away from the others. Bertha had her back to the wall. She didn't like that, because the wall showed a giant painting of what that mouthy bitch Reeves called a "tentacle god." The fifteen-foot-high monster painted in orange and red and green was evidence of some kind of sick culture. You could tell just by looking at it.

"It's *someone's* fault," Bertha said. "If not Kirkland's, then whose?"

He frowned at her. "Stop with the blame game. None of the people down here sabotaged the elevator. You know that. We need to focus on the job at hand, and that job is getting these people to safety. You're not like them. You're a soldier. I need your help. I know this situation is bad, but can I count on you to stay cool?"

From anyone else, it would have been a bullshit motivational pep talk. *Can I count on you? Can you be all that you can be? Can you strive for excellence?* From anyone else, sure, but Patrick O'Doyle wasn't just *anyone else.*

She didn't know if she loved him. If she didn't, she sure as hell wasn't far from it. He was more than a decade older than she was, but he was everything she could have ever wanted in a man. Strong. Disciplined. Reliable. And, above all, he *understood.*

Bertha stared at him, admiring the hard lines of his face. He was so solid, so beautiful. She even liked the scar that stretched across where his ear had once been. The others probably thought that made him ugly. They probably thought she was ugly, too. She'd been told as much enough times in her life.

Patrick thought she was pretty. He'd said so, several times. She believed him. Maybe if he was trying to get her in the sack that might have been just a line, but he hadn't tried. Not yet, anyway. Maybe that was because privacy was so hard to come by out here. Or, maybe it was because he had that thing so rare these days, especially in men—Patrick O'Doyle had class.

She'd asked him how he got the scar. He'd told her it was classified. When he'd said that, he had this look in his eye, this sense of betrayal about him. She didn't know the details yet, but she'd seen the same thing happen to some of the few friends she still had from the service, and it had happened firsthand to her—his country had fucked him. He still couldn't come to grips with that. He was older, sure, but she'd had her own bitter moment of acceptance long ago. Maybe she could help him.

If, that was, they didn't die down here.

No, he hadn't told her much about himself, but at least she'd learned about that strange white and blue tattoo on his bicep. The Argentinian flag. In a personal tradition born of youth and foolish, macho pride, he said he'd adorned his body with the flag of every country where he'd killed someone. She'd asked why the U.S. government had sent him to Argentina to kill. He'd said that was classified, too. Bertha wondered how many more flags he had tattooed on his body. And, in what places. She intended to find out—state secret or no state secret, she was going to get that man naked.

If, that was, they didn't die down here.

Cheated. That's how she felt. She'd been in love only once, way back in the tenth grade. She and Billy Rasmussen had passed notes in history class. They'd cut school to walk the littered streets of Paterson, New Jersey, holding hands and being young. Juvenile love, to be sure, but she still treasured the memories. She'd joined the army at eighteen, shortly after Billy died of a heroin overdose. Six years she'd served, until that day in a desert not unlike the one far above where she now stood.

That man's face. She could never forget that man's face.

Maybe that face was part of the reason she'd never found love again.

She'd had flings, of course. And a few one-night stands, but nothing that stuck. Hard to imagine that at thirty-two years old, Billy Rasmussen was the only serious boyfriend she'd ever had.

All that time, and out here, in the middle of nowhere, she'd finally found someone.

It had happened fast. Something between Patrick and her just clicked.

No, not *something*. That was romantic bullshit. She knew exactly what it was, knew the thing that let them connect so deeply—they'd both killed people. Up close and personal, where you could smell the fear on a last breath as your knife punched through a heart, as you heard the gurgle of lungs filling with blood. Those moments changed a person forever. She never thought she'd find a man who understood what it was like to carry that feeling around, endure the memory of watching life seep away from another human being. O'Doyle understood. He knew. When she talked to him, she felt complete. For the first time in her life, she felt whole.

His gloved hand rose, rested on her shoulder, squeezed.

"We're not going to die down here," he said.

Well, that put that thought to rest, now didn't it?

She wondered what his eyes looked like to his enemies, to his targets. Because he certainly didn't look at them the way he was looking at her.

Bertha had waited her whole life for someone to look at her that way.

Only it wasn't just *someone*: it was Patrick O'Doyle.

"You can count on me," she said. "I won't cause any problems. I'll help you get everyone out of here alive."

He smiled. His gloved hand touched her cheek.

"Thank you," he said. "Keep an eye out. I'm going to show Kirkland how to use the EBR."

Bertha snorted. "I bet that silver spoon fucker's never fired a gun in his life. You're not going to let him actually shoot it, are you?"

"No, we don't have enough ammo to waste even a single round." He gestured to the floor, the walls, the ceiling. "Besides, this place isn't exactly a safe firing range."

"All right. Just make sure *he* knows that. Kirkland's all-powerful in that little trailer of his, but down here he's just a schmuck that can't make it on his own."

Patrick frowned at her again.

"He's not as bad as you think."

He walked off, leaving Bertha to ponder how a man as experienced and smart as O'Doyle could fail to see through someone as selfish and transparent as Connell Kirkland.

7:02 A.M.

Connell hefted the weight of his backpack. Thirty pounds? Maybe thirty-five? Not so bad now, but they had more than a day's hike ahead of them. That extra weight would add up.

Mack fastened the backpacks straps, tugging on them to make sure everything was tight and secure.

"Be careful about bending forward," he said. "If you want to squat or pick something up, bend your knees, don't bend over. On the decline, the backpack's weight will land you flat on your face."

Connell felt a little ridiculous: Mack adjusting the straps like Connell was in the kindergarten grade being sent off for his first day of school.

"Got it," he said.

Mack patted him on the shoulder. "All set, mate. How's the head? That Motrin help?"

"A bunch," Connell lied.

"Good on ya, mate."

Mack walked to Veronica and Sanji, started adjusting their packs. *Good on ya.* What the hell did that mean, anyway?

O'Doyle stepped up, one rifle in his hands, another strapped over his shoulder. He had the biggest backpack. He wanted to carry most of the load. Figured. He had a knife sheath attached to his chest webbing, black handle sticking up almost to his shoulder.

The scarred man held out the rifle.

"Here you go, Mister Kirkland."

Connell sighed. He'd never fired a weapon in his life.

"Just because you showed me how to use it doesn't mean I'll be worth a squirt of piss if the shit hits the fan. You sure someone else shouldn't carry it?"

O'Doyle spoke quietly.

"Mack needs his hands free, so he gets my sidearm. Haak's fingers are broken, so I don't want him carrying anything. And between you and me, Reeves seems a bit too pissed off to be carrying a firearm."

Connell glanced over at her. She slapped Mack's hands away when he tried to adjust her straps, started tightening them herself.

"Yeah, I guess I can see the logic in that," Connell said. He took the weapon. Even though they were three miles belowground, in heat so bad they'd die without the suits, holding the gun somehow seemed like holding doom itself.

O'Doyle pulled two magazines out of his webbing, handed them over. Connell stashed one, held the other.

"Should I load it now?"

"I would prefer you didn't," O'Doyle said. "I'll be up front with Mack, Lybrand will be in the rear. If there's trouble, you'll have time to load it. If either of us tell you to *lock and load*, though, just drop the backpack and focus only on the weapon. One of us will tell you where to go and what to do. Remember, we only have six magazines total, including your two, so no matter what happens, you keep your fire selector on single-shot. One pull of the trigger means one bullet. Got it?"

Connell nodded, then instantly wished he hadn't.

"Yeah, got it."

"How's the head?"

"It's fine."

"Liar," O'Doyle said. "Just hang tough, Mister Kirkland. I'm going to get you out of here."

Connell wasn't sure he'd ever heard nicer words. He believed O'Doyle. The man had made mistakes, sure, but that didn't matter right now. This was a survival situation. Connell had never met anyone so obviously adept at survival as Patrick O'Doyle.

"Call me Connell, okay?"

O'Doyle stared for a moment, seemed almost confused.

"I'll try," he said, then walked away.

I'll try? That was as odd as *good on ya.*

Mack raised his hand for everyone's attention. He got it.

"Time to go," he said. "Same order as we discussed. O'Doyle takes point. I'll be twenty paces behind him with the map, guiding us down. Kirkland, twenty paces behind me." He pointed at the gun slung over

Connell's shoulder. "And since you're behind me, be careful with that, eh?"

Connell nodded and again immediately wished he hadn't.

"Good," Mack said. "Twenty paces behind Kirkland, Veronica and Sanji. Lybrand brings up the rear. Any questions?"

There weren't any, which wasn't surprising. Six lives had boiled down to one common denominator: reach the Dense Mass, or die.

"All right," Mack said. "Let's make good time."

Around six hours after the elevator plummeted to the shaft floor, the party set out down the tunnels. They knew roughly where they were headed, but nothing about what they'd find along the way.

21

14,100 feet below the surface

10:32 A.M.

In three and a half hours, they'd moved nearly three thousand vertical feet below the Picture Cavern. All things considered, Patrick O'Doyle thought they were making good time.

They moved steadily downward through switchbacks and criss-crossing tunnels, sometimes crawling hundreds of feet down ancient rock slides, using massive boulders like misshapen ladders. When the tunnels were wide open and the footing sure on some ancient stream bed, it felt like they moved quickly; but they wanted to move *downward*, not *horizontally*. Twice, Mack stopped the group at drop-offs too steep to climb. Those caused delays, because the man insisted on using climbing harnesses and there were only two harnesses available. They had to descend in shifts.

Patrick hated to wait, but safety was more valuable than speed. As Mack kept saying, *slow is steady, steady is smooth, smooth is fast.* Patrick had heard that phrase a million times while in the military, and he agreed with it. If someone was injured bad enough that they had to be carried, that would slow their progress to a crawl. A severe enough injury, and he'd have to make the call to leave that person behind, come back with help if he made it out.

Which was one extremely big *if.*

Hostiles were involved. They had destroyed the elevator shaft, killed Crook, Braxton and Jenkins. Those same hostiles had broken into the camp, stolen KoolSuits, sabotaged the tank that injured Kool and Wright. These people were willing to do whatever it took to steal the claim from EarthCore. That included murder.

For the most part, Patrick and the others said little. Because of the seriousness of the situation, sure, in part, but also because of the surroundings. The endless expanse of tight, unforgiving stone tunnels alternating with brownish-tan caverns soaring high overhead seemed to humble everyone. In the midst of such grandeur, speech seemed somehow childish and ineffective.

Patrick watched the walls, the ceiling, the boulders and the rocks, but mostly he watched the ground—one wrong step could prove disastrous.

That was why he saw it.

His subconscious mind noticed it first: something about the sand bothered him. He kept moving, kept watching, waiting for his brain to figure it out.

Then, he finally recognized a pattern.

"Mack, hold up."

The foreman stopped, turned, waited.

Patrick waved Kirkland forward, then knelt. He reached his fingertips toward the silt but didn't touch it. Tiny double indentations, as if made by a fork with only two outside prongs. If there had just been a few, he might have spotted the pattern earlier, but there were hundreds of them, so many it almost looked like beach sand after a drizzle.

Kirkland came up, stood behind him.

"Are those tracks of some kind?"

Surprising: the desk jockey understood almost immediately.

"I think so," Patrick said. "Too many of these for it to be anything else. I should have seen it sooner."

"I'm amazed you saw it at all," Kirkland said. "The rest of us could have walked forever and not noticed them. Mack's silverbugs?"

"Based on Lybrand's description of the things, I would guess so."

"Oh, for fuck's sake," Kirkland said. His headlamp beam played slow, widening circles across the silt. "How many of them would there have to be to make all these tracks? What do we do now?"

Patrick stood. "We keep moving, Mister Kirkland. Hopefully, they'll steer clear. If not, we'll handle it."

Kirkland licked his lips. His eyes glanced left and right.

"If you say so. And it's *Connell*, remember?"

"Connell, right." Now wasn't the time for bonding, but the guy was the boss, and Patrick wasn't going to argue with him. "Shall we move out?"

Connell gestured down the tunnel. "It's your show, big man."

Patrick looked at Mack, pointed down the tunnel. Mack nodded and walked on.

11:15 A.M.

He was burning alive. Fire searing his face, his hands, his neck. Frying like a piece of meat in a pan. Skin, melting … eyes heating, *popping*.

And through the flames, something coming after him, a heat-haze shimmering horror. Flashing colors, glowing, tentacles aflame themselves, stretching toward him, ever closer …

Cho Takachi opened his eyes, then they shut by themselves, a reaction to the blinding light. He started to raise his left hand to block that light, but that brought a new pain, a *deep* pain in his shoulder. He shifted, raised his right hand instead, tried to blink away brightness that sent stabbing pains through his squinting, blinking eyes.

His skin … it *burned*. His face, his hands, his neck.

Something *stank*. Rotten garbage … dog shit.

So thirsty.

The sun, the day, too bright. The one time he actually needed his sunglasses more than ever …

He finally forced his eyes open just enough to look around.

The desert. He was in the desert. Scrub brush off to his left. A couple of scraggly junipers behind it. Shade. Not much, but some.

The sun, not directly overhead but close to it. Not quite noon. What was he doing here?

Lying on his back. The pain. His skin, his left shoulder ... his *head*.

Cho turned to the side just as he threw up, acrid bile filling his mouth, spilling out on to the rocky sand.

What was going on? His skin *burned*. He was being boiled alive.

He had to move, get to that shade.

Cho rolled to his right side, trying not to jostle his left arm. He couldn't do anything about jostling his head, though.

The desert. The camp.

Memories rushed back. Glowing creatures. Frank. Blood. The chase. Firing the Mark 14 ...

A surge of adrenaline. He pushed himself to his feet, stood on legs that threatened to abandon him at any moment. He felt like he'd been hit with a giant mace.

Over there. Discoloration in the sand. The source of the stench. Brown. Deflated.

Dead.

Cho shuffled to it, trying to ignore his screaming skin. He stood over it. Flies buzzed. Looked like a pale brown garbage bag. Thicker than most ... like a deflated football, maybe. Where were the tentacle-things? Maybe they shrank back in when he'd killed it. In the dark it had been a demon, a nightmare. Now it looked like nothing—dried-up, crispy nothing. If he hadn't killed this thing himself, in this very spot, he would have walked by thinking this was nothing but a bit of old trash. At least a hundred flies swarmed on it already. Maggot food.

He glanced up the road to the camp. *Gone*. Some blackened cinder block. Scorched, twisted sheet metal curled up on itself. All that remained. Frank had died. That lab guy with the coffee cup. How many others? *All* the others?

The attack had come at night. Cho had fallen, hit his head. He must have laid in the desert sun for hours. Took a lot for him to get a sunburn, but four or five hours without moving ... that was a lot.

He felt weak.

Where were his weapons?

Sun beating down hard, he turned in place. There, his .45.

He shambled to it, moving with all the grace of a career drunk. How much blood had he lost?

It wasn't easy bending over to pick up the pistol, but pick it up he did, and he instantly felt a little bit better holding it. The metal was hot to the touch.

At least he had something.

And he also had ...

He holstered the .45, then felt at his belt. There it was: his walkie-talkie.

No one left in camp to get the signal, but the unit was powerful. Maybe he could get someone to come help him.

Shade. He had to get out of this sun. It was killing him, cooking him.

Cho focused, used what little strength he had to walk to the junipers. He stumbled through the scrub, then sat down beneath a tree. Not full shade, but better than nothing. Maybe it would be enough.

He switched on the walkie-talkie. Static. He scanned the frequencies. Static, static and more static. Was it broken? Didn't seem like it. Maybe he was too far out.

He wasn't up to walking, wasn't up to moving, was barely up to breathing. He settled on one channel, then pressed the "talk" button.

He released. Waited. Static, static and more static.

Cho switched to the next channel and tried again.

22

14,980 feet below the surface

2:47 P.M.

If he never saw another tunnel in his entire life, that would be just fine.

In the corporate world, being six-foot-four was a great thing. He wasn't blind to the way things worked: being a tall, white male brought with it a boatload of advantages, even before he did a lick of actual work. In narrow caves with low ceilings, though, his height flat-out sucked. Even in the biggest caves he was walking half bent over.

His back was killing him from the backpack and all the stooping. His legs burned from seven hours of hiking across unsure footing, so much so that he almost forgot about the steel hammer throbbing deep in his head.

Almost.

He wasn't going to make it much farther if he didn't stop and rest, but he couldn't bring himself to ask. Sanji hadn't complained yet. He was forty pounds overweight. And had two broken fingers.

Their lives were on the line: Connell didn't want to be the weak one.

Maybe if he just toughed it out a bit longer, Sanji would ask for a rest. Or Veronica. Those were his best chances: Mack didn't seem tired in the least, and Connell suspected O'Doyle and Lybrand were capable of marching for days.

Connell focused on where he walked. O'Doyle had said that one wrong step could spell doom. Connell had listened. As long as they were down here, he was going to listen to anything that man had to say. Connell was so fixed on watching his feet land in the right places that he took three or four steps into a cavern before he realized he could stand.

Mack and O'Doyle were waiting for him.

"Twenty-minute break," the guard said. "Get off your feet, everyone."

Connell didn't have to be told twice. He found a rock, sat. His body rejoiced at simply *not moving*.

Veronica and Sanji emerged from the tunnel, saw everybody resting. They practically collapsed on the silt-covered floor. Lybrand was the last out. She found a rock and sat, breathing hard. Well, what do you know? Even the super soldiers can get tired.

Mack and O'Doyle came over to Connell. Mack knelt, held out his plastic map so all three of them could see it.

"We're not doing bad," he said. "Pretty good pace, considering, but it gets harder from here on out."

"*Harder?*" Connell's word came out as a surprised squeak.

Mack nodded. "I'm afraid so. The closer we get to the Dense Mass, the steeper it gets and the more tunnels there are. We have to be careful to not get sidetracked."

He moved the map closer to Connell. Connell looked at it, trying to make sense of the three-dimensional tunnels. It was like looking at a picture of a tangled fishnet. So many side passages, so many connectors.

"If we're getting closer, is there any chance we'll run into the opposition?"

The opposition. That name just come out. Such a strange word for *murderers*, for *saboteurs*, for *killers*.

O'Doyle nodded. "The closer we get, the more likely we are to see them."

Connell supposed it was a pipe dream to think they might reach the Dense Mass, find the way out, and escape without any violence. The three dead men he'd left behind were evidence of the opposition's ruthlessness. He had to be realistic. There had already been blood. There would be more.

"O'Doyle, maybe you should be up with Mack? Twenty paces back might not be enough if someone attacks us."

The big man's eyes narrowed, and he looked off. His mouth twisted a bit to the right.

"That's smart," he said. "I supposed I should have thought of that."

Yes, he should have. Connell's urge to trust O'Doyle, to take his word as gospel, took a bit of a nosedive. As the experienced caver, Mack had to be up front, obviously, but if he'd gotten into sudden trouble, would O'Doyle have been able to help in time?

With a sinking feeling, Connell realized that maybe this situation—as fucked-up as it was—was like everything else in his life: he couldn't trust other people to make the decisions.

Sometimes, you want someone else to be in charge: at all times, that turns out to be a mistake.

Mack clapped O'Doyle on the shoulder. "It'd make me feel a whole lot better to have you up with me, mate. Got a feeling you've seen action before."

"Some," the bigger man said. He glanced at Lybrand. "Any issues from the rear?"

She shook her head. "Nothing that I've seen or heard."

O'Doyle nodded. "Good. Let's hope it stays that way. Twenty-minute nap, everyone. That means you, too, Lybrand. I'll stand watch."

"Thank *God*," Veronica said. She curled up, dragged her backpack beneath her as a pillow. "And I don't even believe in God."

Either Sanji fell asleep instantly or he was already out, because he began to snore.

Connell mimicked Veronica. He wasn't sure if he could trust O'Doyle to take care of things anymore, but he would have to for at least the next twenty minutes. Right now, even twenty minutes of sleep was more valuable than the platinum they'd come for in the first place.

3:02 P.M.

"Hello, is anyone there? I'm hurt. I need help."

The sun was on its way down. That couldn't happen soon enough. Wouldn't make much of a difference, though—unless someone answered him soon, Cho Takachi knew he was going to die.

Maybe he was dead already. If so, being dead hurt.

He'd gone through all the walkie-talkie's channels. He'd heard nothing but static. He'd thought about getting up, walking out, but he knew he wouldn't make it far. So, he'd gone through the channels again, one by one. Then again. Then again.

Dehydrated. A big laceration on his left shoulder that needed probably fifteen to twenty stitches. A concussion, for certain. Maybe Cho didn't know much in this world, but he knew wounds. Without help, his were fatal. The longer he sat there, doing nothing, the longer he would live.

Which, all things being equal, really wouldn't be that long.

All he could do was keep trying.

He switched channels.

"Hello, is anyone there? I'm hurt. I need help."

Static, static and more static.

It made no sense. The walkie-talkie should have picked up *something*. The nearest town was just over twenty miles away—there had to be radio traffic in the area. Had to be. So why wasn't he picking up anything?

So hot. So *dry*. Next time he saw a glass of water, he'd want to whack off to it. Well, drink it first, ask for another, *then* whack off while waiting for it to arrive.

He switched channels.

"Hello, is anyone there? I'm hurt. I need help."

Static, static and...

"I read you, go ahead."

A woman's voice. Scratchy, but there.

He started to shake.

"This is Cho Takachi from the EarthCore mining camp in the northern Wah Wah Mountains. We've been attacked. I'm wounded and need immediate assistance."

"*Attacked?* That's crazy. How's the rest of the camp?"

"I...I think they're all dead. I might be the only one left."

"Jesus Christ," she said. "Is this a joke? Because if this is a joke, it's not very funny."

"It's not a joke." Cho barely stopped himself from screaming at her. "Please, *please* come help me."

A pause. Then, static.

"No," Cho said. He slapped the radio against his thigh. Triggered the "talk" button. "Hello? Are you there?"

She came back almost immediately. "I'm here. Where are you?"

He tried to remember coordinates, couldn't.

"East side of the South Wah Wah Mountains," he said. "Maybe six or seven miles south of Route 21."

"You said there's a camp. Any company signs? Landmarks?"

Cho glanced up the slope. Nothing but a black spot, really. The camp was tucked into a little plateau, not visible from lower elevations.

"Camp is about a mile north of the highest peak in the range," he said. Look for a new road due east from there. It's only been up for about two weeks, should stand out. When you come up that road, I'll come out and wave. Gotta stay in the shade until then."

"Smart," she said. "Okay, mile north of the highest peak, due east, new road. My name is Maggie. You said yours was Cho?"

"Cho, that's right."

"All right, Cho. I'm coming. I've got water and a first-aid kit. Don't leave that spot. I'm on my way."

"Thank you," he said. He heard the pleading tone in his voice but he couldn't stop it. Didn't *want* to stop it. "Thank you so much. How far away are you?"

No answer. Just that static again.

Cho keyed the "talk" button several more times, asked if she was there again and again but received no response. He tried the other channels, but the static dominated.

It didn't matter. She'd repeated his location back to him. She was coming. She'd said so. She had to come.

He set the walkie-talkie down, and he waited.

3:11 P.M.

Patrick O'Doyle's headlamp spotlighted Mack Hendricks. Mack's light lit up the plastic map.

The expression on Mack's face. Patrick knew that look. He'd seen it on men before. And a few women. On some of his missions, if he'd had a mirror, he would have seen that look on himself.

"Mack, are you lost?"

The Aussie glanced up, eyes wide like he'd been caught exposing himself to orphan children in a monastery.

"Uh…" He shook his head, perhaps more to clear it than to say no. "I'm good. I'm just trying to figure out the best way for us to go, that's all."

His light lit up the map again. He turned it ninety degrees. He stared. He turned it another ninety degrees.

"Fantastic," Patrick said.

He'd decided to let Connell and the professors sleep a little more. The tunnels were getting more complex, so he'd gone with Mack to get a head start on the next leg. They'd stopped at a triple branch in the tunnels. One branch led off at ninety degrees to the left, another went steeply up and about fifteen degrees to the left, and the last headed gently down at about thirty-five degrees to the right. Mack was obviously trying to orient their position.

He'd rotated the map three times so far. It looked upside down, but Patrick reminded himself there was no upside down on a three-dimensional map. Mack knew what he was doing. He had to know.

Patrick turned away from him and looked down the tunnels, his light probing the passages' dark depths. He wasn't happy that Mack might be lost, but he wasn't about to take over map duties—all these tunnels looked the same to him.

He thought about what Reeves had said, about the lights going out. *Sensory deprivation.* The lack of noise alone was enough to drive someone batty. If they didn't make it, if the batteries ran out, who would die first? Maybe that person would have it the easiest. The last person to die would find out what real silence was like. No noise, no light, absolute darkness.

If there was gunplay coming, put himself between the enemy and his charges. Or, if he was *really* lucky, and some numb-nuts wanted to play with blades, he'd be the first in line with a smile on his face. Killing a guy with a knife? That was something rare and special. He'd love to cut up the assholes who'd murdered his men. Just love it to death.

Guns and knives, he'd face without thinking twice. But dying alone, in the dark, where the only sound was your own voice, your own breathing? No chance of survival? That gave him the willies. Big-time. Mamma O'Doyle's youngest was made to go out with a bang, not a whimper.

He panned far left. Maybe that way? He panned to the middle tunnel. Maybe they had to go *up* to go *down*? Jesus, he hoped Mack knew what he was doing. So confusing with all the —

click-click, click-click

Mack jerked back, dropped the map, started grabbing for his pistol.

"No," Patrick said, snapping his hand at the man palm up, like some kind of human stop sign.

Mack froze, hand on the pistol's grip.

The last thing they needed was bullets fired by a panicked hand.

"That's the noise," Mack said. "That's what we heard before we saw the silverbug."

Patrick scanned the floor, left tunnel, middle, right. Mack's beam echoed the path: left, middle, right.

click-click, click-click, click

The tunnel amplified the small sound, made it seem to ooze from the stone itself.

Mack's beam picked up speed: left, middle, right, left-middle-right. "Where the *fuck* is it?"

He was already on the edge of hysteria?

Leftmiddleright *leftmiddleright.*

"Mack, calm the fuck down," Patrick said. "And pick up the map."

click-click-click, click, click-click

The noise sounded random, halting, like something starting then stopping, starting then stopping.

A reflection from the far-left tunnel.

Patrick's headlamp beam snapped to the ceiling, lit up a long-legged, silvery sphere not even fifteen feet from his face.

3:17 P.M.

Mack stared in disbelief.

A silverbug. Round body about the size of a softball, four long, pencil-thin limbs. A misshapen, dull metallic daddy longlegs.

Sanji had been right: dull metallic, because it wasn't a spider—or a *bug*, for that matter—it was a machine.

A long, wedge-shaped protrusion stuck out from the round body, pointed toward O'Doyle's head. Other chunks and baubles broke up the outline, made it more *sphere-like* instead of perfectly round. This close, this *still*, Mack saw it was metal—a thousand tiny scrapes, scratches and dents had taken off the sheen, made it look burnished, made it look beat-up and used.

Four legs stuck out from the ball's equator, one every ninety degrees. The first segment of each leg jutted up from the body at a sharp angle, although *up* was actually *down*, since it was clinging to the tunnel ceiling. The second segment paralleled the ceiling. The last segment was actually a pair of even thinner rods, about half the diameter of the first segments. They each ended in a strong little hook, giving the silverbug eight contact points with which to cling to the rock.

The silverbug's body stood stock-still, but some of the sphere-body parts moved with small whirring and buzzing noises. From end to end, the silverbug looked to be about fifteen inches long. With the segmented legs stretched out flat, it might be as long as four feet.

O'Doyle slowly adjusted the position of his machine gun. He didn't point it at the machine but moved it so that all he would have to do was raise the barrel and start shooting.

"Go get the others," he said.

"I can't leave you here alone with that thing."

"*Do it*," O'Doyle hissed, managing to yell without raising his voice. "We don't know what this thing is and I'm not letting it out of my sight. Go get the others, now!"

Mack hesitated only a second, then turned and ran back up the tunnel, moving as fast as he could over the rough footing.

3:31 P.M.

Connell blinked, hands still clutching the steering wheel. A dull throb pulsed in his neck. A stabbing pain lit up his right knee. His mind finally centered on a single word: accident.

He turned to look at Cori. Faint light strayed from the lamps surrounding the driveway. She was sitting next to him, far closer than she should have been, pressed near by a mangled monster of plastic and metal that had once been the passenger door. Snow blew through what was left of the window, melting where it hit blood.

She stared out at nothing. Her beautiful blonde curls clung to her face, held fast by glistening red. Flecks of glass glittered in her hair. Blood sheeted her scalp, her cheeks, her chin, pulsing down to stain her white coat.

His dying wife turned, looked at him.

"Get out, Connell." Something liquid and gurgling masked her smooth voice. She sounded weak, fractured. "You have to get out."

He shook his head.

"No, I need to stay with you."

Her broken hands reached up, grabbed his shoulders. He could smell her blood. She shook him, shook him.

"Get out, my love. Get out. Wake up. Wake up, Kirkland."

The dream drained away, but not the sleep, and not the hands. Someone held his shoulders tight. He blinked his eyes open, saw Lybrand standing over him.

"Wake up, Kirkland," she said, and gave him another little shake.

"Wha ... what is it?" He struggled to come all the way out of it, to get a grip on what was happening. The fatigue in his body didn't want to relinquish its hold.

"Patrick has a silverbug," Lybrand said. "He's alone with it now."

That chased the sleep away. She walked to the still-sleeping Veronica. Mack was trying to rouse Sanji.

Connell stood, trying to ignore his body's rather vocal complaints. He hefted his backpack, then picked up his rifle from where he'd leaned it against a rock. He felt ridiculous with the weapon in his hands. Was he supposed to load it now, or not?

Lybrand had barely given Veronica a good shake before she walked back to Connell. She pointed to the empty magazine chamber.

"Thing works better as a firearm than a club, Kirkland. Load it, then bring everyone. Make it fast."

"Right, of course." He started to reach for a magazine, but both hands were full. He slung the rifle over his shoulder, where it hit the backpack and started to slide off. He caught it just before it hit the floor.

He glanced up, assuming Lybrand would be staring at him like the idiot he was, but she was already running down the tunnel, her yellow suit flashing in his headlamp beam.

"*Wait*," he yelled, his voice bouncing off the stone walls. "We need you!"

If she heard him, she didn't show it. She was already gone.

He pinched the rifle stock between his chest and arm. With his free hand, he finally fumbled the magazine out of his belt. He slid it in as O'Doyle had showed him, slammed it home, pulled back on the lever and let it go. The lever shot forward, locked into place.

That was it. It was loaded. In his hands he held a weapon that could kill people, either on purpose or by accident.

Mack and Veronica had pulled Sanji to his feet.

Connell strode to them, the EBR in his hands, feeling simultaneously ludicrous and kind of badass for carrying it.

"Mack, Lybrand said you saw a silverbug?"

He nodded, making his headlamp bounce. "Clinging to the fucking ceiling. Sanji was right, it's a little robot or something."

"Told you," Sanji said. He clutched his splinted hand to his chest. He looked like he was half-asleep or half-drunk. Or both.

"Lybrand went after O'Doyle," Connell said. "We have to catch up to them. Get your packs on."

Mack picked up Sanji's pack, helped him into it while Veronica took care of her own.

Lybrand gone. O'Doyle gone. The people Connell had paid to protect them weren't there anymore. Until this moment, a cell phone had been the most effective weapon he'd ever used. Now he was armed and dangerous.

Veronica looked at him, waiting, as did Sanji. It wasn't until Mack looked at him the same way that Connell realized he'd assumed the Aussie would take over. Mack was all manly—taking over seemed like the manly thing to do.

But Mack just waited.

Which meant Connell had to call the shots. Awesome. Just what everyone needed.

"Professors, stay behind me," he said. "Mack, bring up the rear, make sure nothing comes up behind us, okay?"

Mack's headlamp bounced.

"Let's go," Connell said, and moved down the tunnel after Lybrand.

3:33 P.M.

Help hadn't come.

No helicopters. No cars. No sirens. No nothing.

It had taken Sonny hours to circle southwest, to work his way up the next peak. He'd started just before dawn, when the hidden sun started to light up the sky. His old body hadn't moved as fast as he'd hoped. He was still hiking and climbing at noon when he decided to stop for a couple of hours, ride out the worst of the heat in the shade of a limestone outcropping. At two p.m., he'd started up again, all the while waiting to hear someone coming.

No one had.

He'd found a spot about a half-mile south of the camp, higher up on the ridge. He used his binoculars to look down at the blackened ruin, kept waiting for some sign of life.

Nothing moved.

He watched the adit, too, hoping to see someone stroll out of there.

No one did.

What he saw barely made sense. The fuel tanks had caught fire, obviously. But where were the bad guys? If there had been gunplay, shouldn't there have been a winning side and a losing one? Where were the survivors?

There was enough scrub brush and little trees around, and he was far enough away that there were places to hide, sure, but he'd been watching for over an hour and there was no movement at all.

Sonny took a small swig from his canteen. Enough water to last him a day, maybe a little more. Come nightfall, he'd have to decide if he was leaving this place for good. He wanted to help, he really did, but where *was* everybody?

Maybe it hadn't been claim jumpers. Maybe his first instinct, no matter how crazy it seems, had been right—people hadn't done this, Funeral Mountain had.

Benjamin's demons. Maybe they were real. Maybe everyone really was still down there, just chopped into little bits and buried.

Why don't you go down there and see for yourself? Don't you wanna know? Don't you?

No. He didn't. Not this time. No amount of curiosity could outweigh his fear, his revulsion. He'd already done the best he could. There was no one left that needed his help.

The EarthCore staffers were dead. Just like Anderson. Just like Benjamin.

Sonny had no intention of adding his name to that list.

Coming up here, seeing what he could see? His version of *bravery*. That bravery was all used up.

As soon as the sun set, he was out of there.

3:34 P.M.

How had it come to this?

A few weeks ago, Veronica Reeves had been on another continent. She'd been doing the work she'd been born to do, the work that had made her career, brought her some small degree of academic fame. She'd had her assistants and her staff, people who had also been her friends.

She'd been *happy*.

Now she and Sanji were a few steps behind a corporate stooge who had no business carrying a fucking machine gun. They were *miles* underground. People were trying to kill them. She was no mathematician but knew the odds of surviving this were less than good, and *less than* was getting ready to leave town.

She was afraid. She was angry.

Veronica wanted to blame Connell, but she couldn't. Not really. She'd forced him to let her research the site. She'd forced him to let her come *down here*, for fuck's sake, to make sure she was among the first to see anything significant.

She had gotten her wish.

No, it wasn't Connell's fault, it was hers. Plain and simple.

She really didn't give a shit about the Chaltélians anymore. Screw that culture. Dead and gone forever. If she got out of here, she could get a teaching job, she could write a book. Hell, she could wait tables, for that matter, anything that would get her away from mountains, from tunnels, from strange knives.

Connell stopped suddenly. Veronica and Sanji did as well, just a few feet behind him.

"O'Doyle," Connell hissed. "We're here."

"No need to keep quiet," O'Doyle called back, not whispering, but not yelling, either. "Whatever this thing is it knows I'm here. Bring the professors up."

Connell turned, faced her, tilted his head down the tunnel. She was about to tell him to go fuck himself, that she wasn't going anywhere near this robot thing, but before she could Sanji walked forward. Veronica had an instant to be mad at her father, too, then she followed right behind him.

She found herself in a small space, ceiling barely high enough for Connell to stand upright. One tunnel behind her, three in front of her. O'Doyle stood there, broad shoulders seeming to stretch the yellow suit material to its limits. Off to his right, hugging the wall, stood Lybrand: rifle at her shoulder, barrel aimed and steady. And clinging to the ceiling of the center tunnel, the thing she aimed at—a nightmarish, junkyard-metal version of a bizarre cave spider.

Sanji seemed fearless. He slowly walked forward, stood at O'Doyle's left.

"It's bigger than I expected," Sanji said.

Veronica couldn't argue there. Those long, thin legs—they could easily wrap all the way around her body. She shuddered at the thought.

"Ronni, come closer," Sanji said. "See what you think."

Maybe she could tell her father *and* Connell both to go fuck themselves at the same time, cut her workload in half. But she didn't. She walked forward, slowly, stood on O'Doyle's right, between him and Lybrand. Lybrand adjusted her aim slightly, maybe to make sure Veronica wouldn't take an accidental bullet.

The machine moved. Not all of it, just a wedge-shaped protrusion. Like an arrow pointing the way, its tip moved from Sanji to her.

Did it know she was there?

She took a breath, tried to let go of her frustration and fear. The metal thing sat there, unmoving. It didn't look like the robots she'd seen in documentaries or in online videos. It looked … kind of *alive*. More like modern art than a machine.

"Can't see," Mack said. "Sanji, move to your left a little."

Mack stepped forward. That one little movement was apparently one movement too many.

Without warning, the silverbug dropped from the ceiling, or maybe jumped, because it was on the ground in the blink of an eye. It landed on its eight splayed-out feet or toes or whatever they were. Veronica wasn't sure if it had flipped over or merely reversed its legs.

The machine perched on the tunnel floor for one more second, unmoving and dead, then it scrambled back into the shadows to the tune of rapid-fire *clicks*, thin legs nothing more than blurs, moving as fast as any animal Veronica had ever seen.

They stood quietly for several seconds, not knowing what to think, not knowing what to say. On a collective level, they all knew their situation had suddenly changed, although they didn't know exactly what that meant.

Connell broke the silence. "What the hell was that thing? I've never seen a machine move like that, have any of you?"

Their ears filled with the still, impossible silence of the caves. No one moved, save for darting glances into every dark area, every nook and cranny. Everyone was on the lookout for a flash of silver.

Connell spoke softly. "Anyone ever seen anything like that before?"

"Maybe I have, in a way," Mack said. "I was at a conference a few years back on the future of mining. NASA had a display, showing explorer robot concepts they hoped to use on Mars. The explorers were similar insect-looking machines, only much bigger. Long legs let them cover all kinds of terrain. Craters. Mountains. That kind of shit. Someday we could use the machines to go to places too dangerous for men. Robots could dig holes, blast tunnels, haul rock. But the ones I saw didn't move like that. The ones I saw walked like *machines*."

Mack didn't have to explain the analogy. The silverbug had moved with an animal's natural, fluid grace.

"I've been to MIT's robot lab," Sanji said. "And Boston Dynamics. I've seen the state of the art. I've seen videos of dozens of military robots. We probably all have. Even the best in the world don't run that smoothly, not even close. It had to be moving twenty-five miles an hour before we lost it in the dark, and I think it was still accelerating."

"It's a recon unit," O'Doyle said. "Whoever attacked us is using these things as scouts, most likely. The machine's head—if that's what that weird wedge was—aimed at each of us in turn. It probably has a camera."

"A *camera*?" Veronica suddenly had to pee. "So those assholes know where we are?"

Mack shook his head. "Probably not. Not yet, anyway. Hard for signals to travel very far down here. But if it has a camera, it has a recorder. So the opposition might not know where we are at the moment, but if that silverbug runs right back to them, they'll know soon enough."

It just kept getting worse. Every moment, her life—or at least what remained of it—got more and more insane.

"Then we should move," she said. "Move *fast*."

Connell nodded. "Good plan. O'Doyle, Mack, lead us out."

Mack pulled the plastic map from his belt. He stared at it, looked down a tunnel, stared at it some more.

"This way," he said. "I'm sure of it."

Veronica thought he didn't sound that sure at all.

3:58 P.M.

A car engine. Not a normal one: a deep, throaty gurgle. Something with power.

Sonny heard it echoing off the mountainside. He looked east, along the new road that led out of the camp, but he saw nothing. It took him a moment to realize why—the sound wasn't coming from the east.

He looked west. Between his position and the camp, a big, dark blue Jeep was slowly descending a streambed so thin and long-since dried up that small trees grew up from the middle of it. The vehicle drove over these, inched up on and then over the boulders in its path.

Had someone finally come?

Sonny glanced around the blackened ruin of the camp. Still no movement. If someone had called for help, they weren't in any rush to come out and greet it.

Why was the Jeep coming from that direction? There weren't any roads there. It would have had to drive up from the West—and no way a car could get up that slope, over the ridge and down to the spot it was at now. If that was even drivable, which Sonny doubted, it would have taken hours.

He should have heard the Jeep long ago. But he hadn't.

The vehicle seemed to be angling for the camp, though, headed for the road that ran between the adit mouth and where the west gate had once been.

This was one strange turn of events.

He scanned the camp again. His heart surged with a stab of surprise: this time, he saw movement. A man, walking out from a small cluster of junipers, not even a quarter of a mile from the ruined east gate. He was waving toward the vehicle coming from the other side of the camp.

Sonny stared, disbelieving. Had that man been hiding there all this time?

Something about that man…

Sonny squinted, looked closer. Hard to tell from this far away, but did he recognize that black hair?

He did.

"Sonofabitch," he said. "I'll be goddamned if that isn't Cho Takachi."

4:02 P.M.

Oh, thank God, thank God, *thank God*.

Cho Takachi watched the Jeep inch its way down the mountain on the other side of the camp. Dark blue, more beautiful than any jewel, than any painting. The sound of that engine: like a symphony or something.

Must have been an old trail up there, maybe a creek bed that stayed bone-dry until rainy season. Did Utah even *have* a rainy season? He didn't care.

Rescue had finally arrived.

The Jeep reached the road that led to the adit. Big tires let it climb up onto that road, then it turned toward the ruined EarthCore camp.

He'd expected help to come from the other way, to drive *up* the road rather than *down*. Maybe there was a trail up from the flats west of the mountains. That Jeep definitely looked like it could handle rough roads, though, even drive where there were no roads at all.

It drove through the blackened camp, wheels crunching on cinders, twisted sheet metal and other wreckage. Cho wondered if it crunched on the burned bones of Frank Hutchins, or that guy with the coffee cup. It rolled past the charred, overturned Land Rover still embedded in the lab's broken cinder block wall.

Then out through the remainders of the east gate, the same gate Cho had escaped through.

Closer it came, until he could see the driver. A woman. A redhead.

Cho laughed. "Just my luck," he said. This would probably turn out to be the one time in his life where a porno flick could unfold in real life, and he was in too much pain to even get a hummer, let alone actually screw. *H-Two-Ohs* before *hoes*, as they say.

He reached the edge of the new, well-packed dirt road just as she reached him. The Jeep slowed, stopped.

The redhead got out. And, of course, she was hotter than the sun that had burned him to a crisp. Figured. She quickly came to him, green plastic squeeze bottle in hand.

"Wow, man." Her eyes flicking from his face to his shoulder and back again. "Oh my God, let me help you."

She stopped cold. She stared at the pearl-handled .45 in the holster at his belt.

"No-no, it's okay," Cho said. "I was a guard up there, we were attacked, like I said."

The woman glanced up to the camp's remains, then back.

"I drove through that just now," she said. "Looks like someone dropped a bomb on it."

She kept staring at the pistol. Maybe he should toss it, or maybe just hand it to her. But those creatures might still be around. Maybe the noise of the Jeep would bring them. He desperately needed to stay armed.

"Lady, I'm harmless. Honest. Do I look like I'm in any condition to cause trouble? Please, help me." He nodded toward the squeeze bottle. "And please tell me that's water in there."

She looked at it, almost surprised to find it in her hand.

"Yeah," she said. "It's water."

That seemed to break her fixation with his pistol. She came closer, gave him the bottle. He squirted a long stream into his mouth. Cool, clean, magnificent. He swallowed it down, squirted again.

"Take it easy," she said. "I don't want you to wind up drowning."

The coolness spread down his chest to his stomach. He'd never felt anything so amazing.

She took the bottle from his hand, slid her shoulder under his good arm.

"Let's get you in," she said.

She led him the six or seven steps to the rear driver's-side door. If he'd seen the four-doored vehicle from a distance, he might have thought it a child's toy. The oversized wheels seemed too big for it, made it look unusually high off the ground. Thing looked like the baby brother of a monster truck.

"Jesus, lady. One hell of a ride. That a custom job?"

The redhead nodded.

"Goddamn right," she said. She kept talking as she opened the door, gently helped him up and in. "Wrangler Rubicon. Five-point-seven liter Hemi. Long-armed suspension, thirty-seven-inch tires, lots of bells, more whistles than you'd get from a beauty pageant parade marching past a construction site. Just picked it up a few days ago."

Which might explain the plastic sheeting draped over the seat and onto the floorboards. So she was a neat-freak. So what? Cho wasn't about to complain.

She stood on the side rail, leaned in over him.

"Just lie down, my friend. We'll get you where you need to go."

"Sure. Drive easy though, okay? I ain't doing so good."

"No problem, brother."

She sounded like a hippie. *Dammit.* Hot like fire, and a free-love type to boot? What a time to get attacked by monsters, get cut, bleed all over the place and pass out under a blazing desert sun.

He slowly lowered himself, butt near the driver's seat, head behind the passenger seat. He closed his eyes. A bench seat offered far more cushion than the hard ground. He heard her open the Jeep's rear door, fish something out of the back. She shut it.

A moment later, the rear passenger door opened. He looked up. The redhead stood over him, left forearm leaning on the Jeep's frame.

"You gave me quite a scare," she said.

"Yeah? Why's that?"

The woman took a step back. Her other hand came out from behind her back, aiming a pistol with a long silencer attached.

"Because I thought you were going to blow it for me, you piece of shit."

Cho heard the *whuff* first shot, felt something slam into him. He didn't hear the next three shots, because he was already dead.

4:06 P.M.

Sonny couldn't move. Not a muscle. Nothing moved save for his heart, kicking in his chest, making him wonder if this was the big one. His heart, and his hands, which trembled, shook so bad his old binoculars rattled against his eyes.

That woman killed him.

Just like that.

She shot Cho in the head, like he was *nothing*.

The twitching binoculars made the image blur. Or maybe that was from the tears.

The woman stepped to the Jeep, reached down: Cho's arm had draped out. She lifted it, tossed it back inside, slammed the door shut. She looked around, maybe making sure no one had seen. She pulled at her red hair: it came off. A wig. Blonde underneath. She shook that out, then climbed into the Jeep.

She wheeled it around, drove back into the camp.

Even though a mile separated them, he waited until she looked to her right, away from him. When she did, he dropped to his back so fast a rock punched into his ribs. Lying flat there was no way she could see him—he was safe.

For now.

He'd been afraid to use the roads. That fear may have saved his life. Had she seen him, she'd have assuredly killed him.

Sonny had wondered where the bad guys were. No more wondering.

Had anyone else survived the fire? Had she been lurking in the night, killing them one at a time?

Claim jumpers, not demons. Kirkland had been right. But it didn't really matter, did it? Demon or human, Cho was just as dead.

Who was that woman? Was she working alone? Had she destroyed the camp all by herself?

Whoever she was, she'd murdered Cho Takachi. For that, the bitch had to pay. He was a good kid. A vet. He'd survived whatever had destroyed the camp, and she'd shot him down like a dog.

She had destroyed the camp, yes, maybe killed everyone in it, but people would still come here. Resupply trucks, maybe helicopters carrying more EarthCore staffers. If she stayed much longer, someone would see what had happened here. The cops would come. She had to know that.

Which meant she wasn't planning on staying long.

If she left today—maybe even as late as tomorrow night—she might never be found out. Cho's killer would never be punished.

"You're not going to get away with it," Sonny said. He said it quietly, on the off chance that a strange wind might carry the words a mile across the mountains to that killer's ears.

"I'm going to find out who you are. You're gonna pay."

He decided to stay right where he was until dark. Sonny McGuiness lay there.

He waited for the sun to set.

He waited for the crying to stop.

4:08 P.M.

Piece of shit. Piece of goddamn *shit*.

She'd almost missed him.

It amazed Kayla that anyone had made it out of the camp alive. But that was why she'd set the COMSEC to jam everything. If she hadn't, the guy with the newly ventilated skull in her backseat might have already gotten word to the powers that be.

She'd picked off his signal during one of the COMSEC unit's periodic break-and-sweeps. Fucking OCD freak trying every damn frequency. Maggie had seemed like the best match for him. Maggie was the outdoorsy type, liked hiking and camping and all that backwoods garbage.

Well met, well dead.

Had anyone else made it out? If so, they could be to Milford by now. Even if no one escaped, this big black cinder on the side of a desert mountain stuck out like a whitehead zit on prom night. It wasn't going to go unnoticed for long. If the po-po came while she was here, she was screwed.

And the fucking Jeep. She'd dropped eighty grand on the thing. She'd covered the seats in plastic sheeting, but had forgotten two things: *one,* to cover up the Jeep's interior roof and, *two,* that sometimes a 9 millimeter can send up an awful spray of blood and brains. Add *one* plus *two,* you got *three*: she had to burn the Jeep. Not yet, but soon.

Eighty grand down the crapper. Goddammit.

A heavy question tore at her thoughts: *Had anyone else made it out?* She'd missed this guy. Who else had she missed? She needed an inventory of some kind, see if the rest of the staff was accounted for. She wasn't sure how this would play with Vogel and the NSA, but she'd been around the block enough times to know the fundamentals—for her to have negotiating power, the NSA needed "exclusivity." There couldn't be anyone left to talk about what had happened.

Barbara Yakely would want to find out, obviously, but that old bitch's money wouldn't make any difference if the U.S. government cordoned off the area. Free country? A belief for fools. The people with the most weapons ran things. The government had more weapons than anyone else.

There had to be a way to find out who was accounted for and who wasn't.

Angus Kool.

Kayla stopped the Jeep. She reached under the seat, pulled out a box of surgical gloves. She snapped them on, then twisted in the seat and reached for Cho. He stared out at nothing, head broken apart by four rounds at point-blank range. She pulled at his shoulder, making him flop facedown. A glob of brains slid off the seat, flopped down onto the floorboards.

Kayla brushed his thick hair away from the back of his neck.

There it was: a tiny dot of metal and plastic.

She pinched it between thumb and forefinger, pulled it free with a little tug. She faced forward, eased back into the driver's seat, staring at her new prize.

"Perfect," Kayla said. "Doctor Kool, you've helped me more than you could ever know."

23

15,439 feet below the surface

6:04 P.M.

While it wasn't a place where sympathy mattered, Mack felt sorry for O'Doyle.

Mack was having trouble crawling through a tunnel so narrow it reminded him of a sewer pipe, or one of those ventilation ducts movie heroes always seemed to find themselves in. If pipes/ducts were made from solid rock, of course, complete with bumpy bits that dug into shoulders and legs. And why, oh *why* hadn't Angus installed some kind of cup in these things? Mack had racked his beanbag at least a half dozen times already.

If it was painful for Mack to get through, it was agony for O'Doyle. He was thirty pounds heavier and a lot wider. There were places Mack thought the man wouldn't fit through at all, but he did.

It wasn't just the confined space that was getting to them: there was the constant fear of tearing the suit. A rip too big for the repair kits and sayonara, sucker. Mack could only imagine how shitty a death that would be. The suits had kept them all alive so far — not a tear in the bunch — but he feared they were creating a false sense of security. In his head, he *knew* how hot it was, but his body felt so comfortable it was effortlessly easy to forget he was in a place where he could literally cook to death.

Mack crawled. Hand reach, forearm down, knee slide up, push. Repeat. Over and over and over.

His body wanted a break. Even when he could walk, it was at a half-crouch, a position that made his back ache and his thighs scream. Human bodies weren't meant for this. Fatigue was beginning to take its toll – making his concentration slip. He'd need more than just thirty minutes of sleep, and he'd need it soon.

Hand reach, forearm down — right on a rock he hadn't seen.

"Ah, *fuck.*"

"Mack! You all right?"

O'Doyle's voice from behind, oddly muffled by Mack's own body.

"Just dinged my elbow, mate. I'm fine. Gimme a minute."

O'Doyle said nothing. The man wouldn't admit it, but he needed a break even more than Mack did. What did they *do* to American boys in the service to make them so tough?

Mack rubbed at his elbow. The rock had dug in there real good. It felt nice to stop, though, to just sit for a moment, to . . .

He heard something. Faint, but steady.

A quake?

A collapse?

He held his breath, waited.

The noise continued.

"Mack? You okay?"

"Fine," he said. "You hear that?"

A few seconds of silence.

"Kind of a rumbly sound?" O'Doyle said. "Sorta echoey?"

Mack wasn't sure if *echoey* was a word, but it matched what hit his ears.

"Hold on a minute," he called back.

He pulled the map from his belt, stared at the confusing web of tunnels. This coffin-tube ended in another fifty meters or so, opened up somewhat to give a little more space. Maybe three hundred meters after that, it intersected with a large tunnel.

Larger than any they'd seen yet.

Large, and *long*.

"O'Doyle, my friend, whatever you do, don't quit now. We're coming up on a tunnel you're going to absolutely love."

"Why's that? Because I fucking *hate* tunnels, Mack. I hate them and want to shoot them."

Mack laughed, stuffed the map away. "Not this one, mate. It winds its way through that big kidney-shaped cavern, goes aways, then right through to the Dense Mass Cavern. And it's tall enough that you can go the whole way standing up."

O'Doyle sighed, almost sagged.

"Mack, I've never wanted to kiss a man more than this very moment."

Mack laughed. "Sorry, O'Doyle. You aren't my type."

The pain in his elbow seemed far more tolerable.

Hand reach, forearm down, knee slide up, push.

Repeat.

6:25 P.M.

The sun had set. The last of the day's light was draining from the sky, thin clouds turning from glowing reds and oranges to duller shades, soon to be dark blues and grays, then invisible as the night's blackness swallowed them up.

Don't you wanna know? Don't you?

He didn't. He did. He couldn't. He had to.

Some goddamn song wouldn't leave his head. *Should I stay or should I go now?* No idea who that band was. Not bad for a bunch of white boys, though.

His whole body ached from stress. He felt like a paperclip bent forward and back, forward and back, slowly heating, weakening. How long until he snapped?

Down in the camp's ruins, Cho Takachi's murderer walked through the blackened rubble. She had a gadget in her hands. He couldn't tell what it was, but it looked like she'd cracked open a remote control or maybe an old radio: plastic, colored wires, bits and pieces of electronics too tiny for him to make out.

She was completely unaware that he watched her every move. *Hopefully* unaware, anyway. Because if she found out he was up here, just one peak away, just *one mile* away, he'd end up like Cho.

The woman had a bag slung over her shoulder. Reminded Sonny of his own bag. He wondered what a psycho like her might carry in there. She also had a nasty-looking machine gun slung high across her back. He didn't recognize it. The only ones he probably *would* recognize would be an M16, AR15 or an AK47. Sonny didn't know shit about guns.

She'd left Cho's plastic-wrapped body in the camp, along with a long canvas bundle and a blue jerrican. Then she'd driven her Jeep back the way she'd come. He'd watched her the whole time. About a mile and a half from the camp, she pulled in to a narrow space between two boulders and under a bit of an overhang. She'd draped camouflage netting over the Jeep's exposed rear, the color perfectly suited to the Utah desert's brown and tan tones. She'd placed a pair of cut-down junipers in front of the net. *Presto chango*, the Jeep was damn near invisible. Even with the binoculars, if he hadn't seen her drive in he wouldn't have known the vehicle was there.

Bitch knew her business. Knew it well.

He'd then watched her walk another half mile or so, along the mountainside, still well above the camp. She'd ducked behind a boulder, vanished. Sonny waited for her to show herself. After about forty-five minutes, she did, the rifle slung over her shoulder, the cobbled-together device in her hand. He understood: that was her hiding spot, where she had probably sat and watched the camp, just as he was sitting and watching her now.

She moved through the wreckage, the char, slowly sweeping the device from left to right. Every now and then, she'd stop, kneel, pick up something small. He couldn't see what those things were.

The woman stood. She looked to the west, stared for a few moments. Then, she walked to Cho's body. She grabbed the plastic, stood and yanked. *Voilà!* A magician's flare, and a dead body rolled into the cinders. She knelt, opened up the brown canvas bundle, picked something up, stood.

She held an axe.

"Oh, sweet baby Jesus," Sonny said in a whisper. "Don't do it. Don't you do it, don't you—"

She raised the axe like she'd done the motion a million times before, brought it down hard and fast. *Chonk*: Cho's forearm came off. She raised it again. *Chonk*: into his neck, but the head didn't sever. She put a foot on his shoulder, wrenched the axe free, stepped back. *Chonk*: Cho's head rolled twice, lay on its side, ruined eye staring up into the darkening night.

6:26 P.M.

Kayla Meyers lowered the jerrican. She wiped sweat from her forehead, then backed up slowly, pouring a trail of gas that led to the pile of stacked body parts. Satisfied she was far enough away, she set the can down. She lit a match.

"Piece of shit," she said.

She dropped the match. The gas trail *whuffed* to life, flame crawling to the pile, setting it aflame. Clothes and skin instantly started to blacken and curl.

Dark enough now that people wouldn't see the smoke from a distance. If anyone did come near, they'd see what they thought was a small campfire. But since the camp was on a plateau inset between a trio of slopes, she didn't think anyone would see anything at all. In a few hours, Cho's body would be a torched-up dismembered mess—just like all the other bodies.

One piece of shit down.

Twelve more to go.

So many body parts... there was no way she could have done a head count on her own. Not in small part because sometimes there weren't heads. *Ba-dum tsh*, thank you, I'll be here all week. But she didn't have to play CSI and reassemble dozens of butchered, burned people, because Angus Kool's "Marco/Polo" tech solved that problem for her. A simple RFID chip on each person. All she'd had to do was assemble a "Marco" receiver to ping those chips and capture their transmitted data.

Props to that little bastard Angus, though—he engineered quality stuff. His little "Polo" transmitters worked just fine, even after the bodies they were attached to burned to cinders.

End result? She had her inventory, a small pad of paper neatly listing the twelve people still unaccounted for:

POSSIBLE SURVIVORS:
Veronica Reeves
Sanji Haak
Bertha Lybrand
Patrick O'Doyle
Mack Hendricks
Sonny McGuiness
Connell Kirkland
Lashon Jenkins
Bill Crook
Pete Braxton

And, of course, the last two names: ANGUS KOOL and RANDY WRIGHT.

Except for Angus and Randy, she assumed the people on that list were dead. Most of them had been in the mine when the monsters attacked. Even if the survivors had somehow avoided the bloodthirsty creatures, they were trapped under miles of rock with no way out. Kayla didn't want to assume anything, but at this point she felt confident she could write off Connell and the others.

She watched Cho's body burn. She was almost out of time. Connell didn't talk to Barbara Yakely every day, but he talked to her enough that soon she would send someone out here to see why he didn't respond.

Angus or Randy—or both—could get out of the hospital in Milford at any moment, want to come back to work, wonder why they couldn't reach anyone at the camp. Milford wasn't even two hours away. A quick car rental and boom: they'd be pulling up to the east gate, gazing at the carnage.

That made the two men a complication.

Kayla couldn't do anything about Barbara Yakely. She could, however, do something about Angus Kool and Randy Wright.

She was running out of time. She had to be the one to bring this to Vogel. He'd balk at something as simple and logical as killing survivors.

How a man so weak had been put in charge, Kayla really didn't know. Vogel was good at politics, though. If she gift wrapped this for him, he'd be able to take it straight to the president.

And if that happened? Kayla would have what she wanted.

To get her life back, she needed to end the lives of Randy Wright and Angus Kool.

After all, they were only a short drive away.

24

15,512 feet below the surface

6:31 P.M.

Connell stood with the others. What the hell were they going to do now?

"So much for walking in standing up," O'Doyle shouted.

Everyone had to shout to be heard over the river's roar.

The big man alternated between looking at the violent river and glaring at Mack. Mack chose to not look back. He wasn't looking at anyone.

Six headlamps played across the roiling surface of an underground river, a band of angry onyx maybe seventy feet wide. The river ripped through a chasm that had towering vertical walls reaching up at least a hundred feet. The walls showed sandwich lines of various petrified sediments, all in shades of gray or red or tan. Up at the top, where their headlamps cast only a dim illumination, a flat sandstone layer sparkled with pristine white gypsum. About fifty yards downstream, the water sprayed up and over and off jagged rocks before vanishing into the cavern wall.

Connell looked at Mack. "Suggestions, Hendricks?"

Mack licked his lips, let his light play off one end of the river, then the other.

"Fucking map didn't say there was water," he said. "Dammit."

He pulled the much-maligned map from his belt, knelt and spread it out across slime-coated stones at the water's edge.

O'Doyle joined him. Connell walked over as well, limping slightly. Too much time on his feet, too much hard ground had aggravated his old knee injury, the one he'd suffered in the accident that killed Cori. It had acted up before from time to time, sure, but when it did, he popped a few Motrin, then stayed off his feet as much as he could for a few days. The latter wasn't an option down here.

He grunted as he knelt next to the other two men.

Mack's yellow-gloved finger tapped a spot on the map.

"See? Doesn't say it's a river. Angus should have labeled the damn thing."

He seemed more interested in avoiding blame than solving the problem.

"That doesn't matter," Connell said. "Try to figure out if another tunnel goes over it, or under it."

Mack stared some more. His fingertip followed this line of tunnels, then that, then came back, then repeated the process. He sighed, took off his helmet, tried to scratch his head through the suit.

"We have to cross," he said. "There's tunnels on the other side that will take us to the Dense Mass."

"Is that right?" O'Doyle said. "Funny, I've heard that one before."

Mack snatched up the map, held it toward O'Doyle.

"If you're so fucking smart, mate, then why don't you take over?"

"Maybe I should," O'Doyle said. "I have no idea how to read that thing, and I'm still probably better at it than you are."

Connell grabbed the map out of Mack's hands, slapped it down hard on the rocks.

"Stop talking shit, both of you," he said. "We have a problem. So let's *solve it.* Mack, make sure we need to cross this thing. See if there's another way."

Mack nodded, went back to work tracing tunnel lines with his fingertip.

O'Doyle glanced downstream.

"We should rig something so we can go downriver," he said. "The map says it will take us right to the Dense Mass."

Connell felt O'Doyle's desire for that simple answer. Shared it, even—the river was moving so fast they'd reach their destination in hours, if not minutes. But what they both wanted didn't jibe with reality.

"Those rocks at the mouth would kill us. Look at that current—we'd have no control."

A continuous, vibrating sculpture: water ripping downstream, hitting those rocks, spraying up high, arcing back down. Hypnotizing in its consistency. Frightening in its power.

Mack nodded. "Kirkland's right. We have to cross." He looked up. "We could go back, but I think we'd lose all the time we've made so far. And it looks like the other paths we'd take would still bring us to the river, just at a different spot." He pointed across the water. His headlamp lit up a dark semicircle set into the wall. "The tunnel we were just in continues there. We reach that, and we're good to go."

O'Doyle looked up, shook his head, exasperated.

"For fuck's sake. Mack, give me a climbing harness, then get some rope ready."

"You got it," Mack said. He tore off his backpack, clearly relieved that he could do *something* that would be of use. He removed a climbing harness, tossed it at O'Doyle's feet.

O'Doyle unsealed his glove, knelt, put his hand in the dark river. Froth splashed up around his arm.

"Like bathwater," he said.

He stood and started unfastening his KoolSuit.

Lybrand rushed over, face twisting into an angry scowl.

"Just what the *fuck* do you think you're doing?"

He pulled his right arm free. The limp material hung at his side. His muscles twitched with every movement, fluttering beneath skin marked with a dozen rectangular tattoos—flags. Connell recognized a handful of them: Brazil, France, Iraq, South Korea.

"Crossing the river," O'Doyle said to her. "I have to tie off a rope so everyone can make it across."

He pulled his left arm free: Argentina, Kuwait, Saudi Arabia, Egypt. He pushed the suit down to his waist. More tattoos on his back: Turkey, Australia, Russia, Colombia, Algeria, Afghanistan. The black flag of ISIS. Pakistan. Libya. Others Connell didn't know. Flags lined up in regimented rows and columns, covering his entire back from below his neck down to his waist and even spreading to his upper arms.

Lybrand stood there, mouth open, a shocked look on her face.

"So many," she said, her words mostly lost in the river's roar. "So *many.*"

Veronica came closer, looked O'Doyle up and down.

"What are you? Poster boy for the United Nations?"

O'Doyle laughed. "Something like that, Professor."

Mack sprinted to the cave wall, trailing rope. He started hammering a bolt into a crack.

O'Doyle took one of the climbing harnesses and held it under water, cooling it down. Then he stepped ankle-deep into the stream, pushed his suit down to his ankles. The fact that he was now fully naked—save for his there-but-not-there face plate—didn't seem to bother him in the least.

"I'm into a little T & A as much as the next girl," Veronica said. "But do you really think now is the time for a striptease? Without your suit, you'll cook in this heat."

This heat. Connell blinked at the words. The suits worked so well he'd forgotten about it. He called up the temperature on his wrist display: 200.1 degrees Fahrenheit, 93.3 Celsius. Almost to the boiling point.

O'Doyle stepped into the wet climbing harness and started fastening it.

"Look at the rocks in this river, Professor," O'Doyle said. "If I hit any of them, it could rip my suit wide open. Fuck me, it's *hot.*"

Sweat already covered him head to toe. He'd been naked all of thirty or forty seconds, and it was already dripping off him.

Connell knelt next to the water. He unsealed his glove, just as O'Doyle had done. He felt the heat on his hand instantly, as if he'd reached into an oven. He dipped his fingers in. It looked like it would be freezing cold, but it wasn't.

"This water is probably a hundred and thirty degrees," he said.

"You won't last long in there. You don't have to do this, we can find another way."

O'Doyle flashed a reassuring smile. "We have limited supplies, Mister Kirkland. We can't afford to backtrack."

Mack returned, coil of orange rope in tow, the end of it reaching back to a carabiner attached to the bolt. He started to hand it to O'Doyle, but Lybrand snatched it away from him, gave him a glare that made him back up a step.

She handed O'Doyle the rope. She stared up at him, eyes wide and full of worry.

He touched her face, smiled at her.

"It'll be fine," he said.

He held up the rope for everyone to see, as if he was teaching a class of children.

"This is my lifeline. It's attached to the wall, but that anchor is a last resort. You need to hold on to it, tight. Play out the slack, but if I'm sucked downstream and I don't make it across, you need to reel me in just like a big fish."

He clipped the rope to his harness.

Connell stepped to the water's edge, picked up the rope. Mack fell in behind him, then Lybrand, then Veronica, each taking some of the slack.

"I'll be anchor," Sanji said. Sanji was the last, started wrapping a long loop of rope around his waist.

O'Doyle waded into the stream, arms out to balance against the current. Five headlamps tracked him, his painted body brightly spotlit against the lightless chasm's blackness. He dropped lower in the water with each slow step, as if descending a steep staircase. The river roiled up around his body.

He looked at Connell. "You ready?" Connell nodded.

O'Doyle's powerful legs launched him into the river. Connell realized that O'Doyle wasn't aiming directly for the far side, but rather upstream, well past a rock that jutted out of the river like a shark's fin breaking the surface just before attack.

The big man shot downstream, arms pumping hard. He tried to turn his body to catch the shark-fin rock, but the current was too fast, too strong—he slammed into the jagged stone like a bird hitting a window pane. He bounced off a bit, stunned, then rolled past the far side.

The rope snapped taut in an instant, yanking the party, sending them stumbling into the shallows. The river, *so powerful*, they weren't prepared. Veronica lost her footing on the wet silt and hit the ground hard. Sanji lost his balance, feet sliding on the slimy ground and dropping him on his ass.

The rope pulled Connell, took him two steps in, then three, then four. The river swirled around his shoulders. Mack splashed directly behind him, the water up to the Aussie's waist. Lybrand grunted and strained. Mack's feet slipped in the slick silt and he fell face-first into the water, splashing madly as he fought against the shallow's insistent current.

Less than four seconds after he'd jumped in, O'Doyle's life lay in the hands of Connell and Lybrand.

The current's pull yanked Connell another step into the river. Water swirled around his head, in his mouth, up his nose. He coughed, inadvertently relaxed his hold just enough for the rope to whiz through. He clamped down: before the rope stopped slipping, he felt it tear through his KoolSuit gloves, through the skin of his palms and fingers.

He tilted his head back to keep his mouth out of the water. His boots found purchase against an invisible rock. He leaned back, pulled. The river raged against one side of his head, splashing his helmet free, sending it spinning downstream.

Behind him he heard Lybrand growl with effort. Primitive instincts screamed at him to let go of the rope, to get back to shore, but he ignored them. His muscles howled in protest. Something in his back popped with a banjo-like twang of pain: he ignored that as well.

Veronica stood and threw herself on the line, pulling back as hard as she could. Her strength gave Sanji a chance to recover as well; the fat man dug his heels into the silt and rocks with a snarl of fury. He started walking backward, one strong step at a time.

Out in the river, the taut rope began to pull O'Doyle back, the shark-fin rock acting almost as a pulley. He coughed water, splashed to keep his scarred head above the surface.

With the weight of the others behind him, Connell was able to back up a step. Mack tried to stand, but again slipped and fell. His helmeted head bounced off a round rock with a splash and a dull *thonk*. He instantly went limp and started to float downstream.

Connell left one hand on the rope, desperately reached out with his other, snagged Mack by the collar just as the current started to suck the Aussie toward the river's powerful middle. Mack's helmet stayed glued to his head.

O'Doyle reached the shark-fin rock. He crawled atop it. The rope sagged. Connell let go and used both hands to pull Mack toward the shore. Lybrand rushed in and helped. Together they pulled Mack clear of the water, dropping his limp body on the slimy rocks. Ignoring the pain from his back and bleeding hands, Connell again picked up the rope.

Water sprayed up around O'Doyle's feet. He struggled to keep his balance on the rock, bent legs twitching, shoulders jerking. He paused for a moment, then launched himself toward the far shore. He splashed in. Long strokes of his thick arms brought him to the river's edge, where the current once again slammed hard into jagged rocks.

Still in the shallows, O'Doyle rose on hands and knees, white ass pale in the glow of headlamps.

"Hurry," Lybrand shouted across the river, fighting to be heard over the endless roar. "Your suit!"

If he heard her, he gave no indication. He tied the rope around a boulder sticking up from ankle-deep water, pulling it taut a foot above the surface before he tied it off.

Lybrand didn't wait for orders. She scooped up O'Doyle's suit and stuffed it into her webbing. Into the water she went, backpack and all, not caring in the least as water splashed up around her and her slung rifle alike. One hand over the other, she pulled herself along the rope.

Veronica came next, guiding Sanji. He managed well despite his broken fingers.

Mack regained consciousness. He was groggy and weak, but was able to make it across with help from Connell.

Connell was the last one across. The current sucked at him, wanted to take him and smash him, but with the rope getting across wasn't that difficult. The hardest part was having no light of his own: the river had taken his helmet, and he wasn't going to get it back.

As he stepped from the roiling water onto the rocks, his knee and back throbbing, Connell saw that he wasn't the only one in pain. O'Doyle had his suit back on, but hadn't put the gloves on yet. He must have smashed his hands against the rocks—a bleeding gash lined his right palm, and the knuckles on his left hand looked like raw hamburger.

O'Doyle leaned close.

"Lybrand told me what you did, Mister Kirkland," he said quietly. He held out his hand. "Thank you."

Connell extended his own hand, noticing that his palm—raw and bloody from the rough rope—spilled red droplets onto the wet rocks. They shook hands, ignoring the other's wounds as well as their own, their blood running together. Connell looked up into the big man's eyes, realizing this was the first time he'd ever shaken O'Doyle's hand. Connell also realized, quite suddenly, that it was the first time in years anyone offered him a hand in friendship, not as some business formality.

"You're welcome. Now, can you finally call me *Connell?*"

O'Doyle nodded. "You got it."

Lybrand bandaged their wounds. Connell replaced his torn gloves with the spare pair in his belt. O'Doyle moved the crew farther down the tunnel, until the river's rage faded to a dull murmur. They found an alcove resplendent in dull brown flowstone glistening with a sheet of slowly trickling water.

"We need a rest," O'Doyle said. "Two hours. Lybrand, take first watch."

He lay down and was out instantly. Sleep nabbed them one at a time, all except for Lybrand. Connell nodded off last, watching her stand over the body of her sleeping man, EBR clutched in her hand. Her eyes flicked attentively down one end of the tunnel, then the other.

And up at the ceiling.

Always at the ceiling.

9:01 P.M.

Kayla hated being away from the mountain. Anything could be happening back on that dark peak. An EarthCore helicopter or car, bringing people out, some mountain biker taking a random road simply because it was new…any number of possibilities that could ruin her chances.

Make this quick. Get back as fast as possible.

She got in on the tail end of visiting hours. Milford Valley Memorial Hospital looked clean and well run, despite its small size. Kayla approached the reception desk, behind which sat an overweight nurse with a beehive hairdo and horn-rim glasses. From the look of her, she might have been working that job back in the sixties, when she would have been the epitome of fashion.

The woman—her name tag read "Alice"—glanced up at Kayla but didn't smile. "May I help you?" she asked.

"I'm here to see Angus Kool."

The woman's eyes widened slightly, then returned to normal.

"I'm sorry. We're not allowing any visitors for Mister Kool."

"Fine. Then let me see Randy Wright."

"He's in the same room," Alice said. Now she smiled, forced and fake and apologetic. "Doctor's orders, you see."

Kayla reached into her purse, fingers tracing along the inside pockets, gracing over multiple IDs.

"I'm Agent Harriet McGuire, FBI," she said, flipping open her ID badge. "This is a matter of national security. You will take me to that room immediately."

The beehive woman's face turned ashen. Her eyes widened, and this time they stayed that way. She looked at the badge, then back up at Kayla.

"But...but you can't, ma'am."

Kayla leaned over the desk.

"Take me to that room, or you'll spend the night in jail."

The woman's mouth opened, then closed, then opened again.

"Right now," Kayla said. "*Move* it, Alice."

Alice hopped out of her chair, grabbed a key from a pegboard. She smelled like baby powder and potato chips. She moved quickly down the hall. Kayla followed.

"I assure you, Agent McGuire. I'm only acting on orders from the doctor."

Alice turned down a left-hand hall, looked back once, then inserted the key into a door marked C-2. Just as she turned the handle, Kayla shoved the woman in her back, sent her stumbling. Kayla reached into her purse, had the little Beretta Nano out before Alice hit the flecked linoleum floor.

Kayla walked in, shut the door behind her.

Two beds, both empty.

Angus, you little prick.

Kayla looked at Alice. "When?"

Behind the horn-rim glasses, the eyes went wider still.

"I...I don't know what you mean."

Kayla knelt and reached in the same motion, grabbed a handful of beehive and yanked it down, pulling the woman's head back. Alice opened her mouth to scream but froze when the cold barrel of a gun slid past her teeth and rested against the back of her throat.

"You fucking sow," Kayla said. "Thought you'd make a little extra money, did you? Now it's time to pay the piper. Talk to me."

Kayla slowly pulled the gun from the woman's mouth. A thin strand of saliva swung from the barrel.

"They were only here for a few hours," Alice said in rapid-fire delivery. "We admitted them into this room then he told me to shut the door and he offered me ten thousand dollars to play along and told me to go get the doctor and he paid him, too, and I didn't think I'd get into trouble and—"

"Shut up," Kayla said. "When did they leave?"

"Two days after they arrived. He did something to the phone."

Kayla walked to the phone, which sat on a small rolling table between the two beds. There was no cord in the phone's jack. Behind the table, she found the phone cord. It ran from the wall jack into a small metal-and-plastic contraption no bigger than a toaster.

You little prick. You little fucking prick. You routed the calls.

"So am I in trouble?" Alice asked quietly.

"That depends. All you have to do is help me." Alice nodded as Kayla wrote down a number on a scratch pad next to the phone. She handed it to the woman.

"If they come back, you call that number."

Alice looked over the top of her glasses. "That's it?"

Kayla nodded. "That's it."

"But what about..."

"What about the money? Keep it, just call me if they come back."

Alice nodded. She stood and held the scrap of paper with both hands, pressed it to her chest.

Kayla left without another word. It was all she could do to keep herself from sprinting to her Jeep.

That little prick Angus was more than she'd bargained for.

9:28 P.M.

The small shovel bit into the stony ground with the sound of metal scraping against unforgiving rock. An inefficient way to dig, but that wasn't the point.

"Oh, *lawdy*," Angus said, shouting the words. "I been diggin' all the livelong day. Won't somebody come and help me?"

He glanced at the KILROY WAS HERE sign lying on the ground next to him. Another inch of digging or so, and he could plant it. He wished he could see the look on Connell Kirkland's face when this sign was discovered. Would have been priceless.

Well, *priceless* was a relative term. Especially considering how much Angus had spent on all of this shit. First paying Cho to look the other way, then triple that amount for the man to put on fake bandages and a little fake blood. Then, bribing a doctor and that fat, smelly nurse to seal off his room. Any of those things could have gone south, but none had.

Money was a wonderful thing.

He and Dirty Randy had stayed in the hospital for a couple of days, in case anyone from EarthCore showed up. No one had. The fuckers. During that time, Angus set up a relay on his hospital room's phone, routing any calls to a cell Randy had stashed along with the other equipment.

When Kirkland finally called, Angus had been up on the mountain, two miles north of the camp. The relay had worked like a charm.

That arrogant prick might still be calling, for all Angus knew. He and Randy were too far down to get any signals from the surface.

He knew now that he wasn't the first person in these tunnels. Some of the tunnels weren't even natural—they had been chiseled into solid stone. It was disappointing he wasn't first—even if the last people in them had died off hundreds if not thousands of years ago—but the mystery was still every bit as intriguing. Maybe Reeves's "Chaltélians" were a real thing after all. Maybe they'd carved out these tunnels with primitive tools. It would have taken *centuries*. And there was the problem of how those people had managed the heat, but that was the least-important question concerning Angus at the moment.

The most important? What the hell were all those amazing little robots doing down here?

Randy had dubbed them "ALs," short for "artificial life-form." The silvery creatures lurked everywhere. The things seemed to be *watching,* sometimes even *tracking* Angus and Randy. Angus didn't know what to make of their behavior, but there was only one way to see what made such clearly advanced machines tick.

Take one apart.

AL tracks dominated this area of the tunnel system, ubiquitous wherever a patch of dry silt covered stone. The tracks were far thicker here than anywhere else they'd seen so far. It seemed like the perfect place to catch one.

Randy would do the catching. Angus was bait. They'd already established that the four-legged robots reacted mostly to movement and noise. Randy lay half-buried under dirt and rocks, motionless, about twenty yards down the tunnel from Angus. They'd rigged a blanket from the ceiling and hoped to use it as a net.

Angus looked at his handheld monitor. It weighed less than a pound but gave an excellent readout with its four-inch display. The unit picked up data from the tiny, five-ounce motion sensors they'd placed about thirty yards down the tunnel. Angus had planned to use the motion sensors to keep tabs on EarthCore personnel, but the devices turned out to be invaluable for gathering observational data on the ALs.

The readout showed a scale map of the tunnels, covering a one-hundred-meter-diameter sphere. Angus stood at that sphere's center. On the screen, a red dot slowly moved closer. Angus banged the shovel against the wall three times, letting Randy know the system had picked up an approaching AL. They had decided not to use walkie-talkies, as they had no idea how the robots communicated. Radio waves might give away Randy's location.

Clearly, the ALs were the most advanced robots Angus had ever seen. He theorized they wandered in a loosely programmed pattern, probably utilizing some form of fuzzy logic to maneuver through the tunnels and collect data. Once they had enough info, the ALs likely returned to the surface to pass the info on to their masters—probably for the purpose of creating detailed maps of the tunnels.

Which meant that EarthCore wasn't the only company after this particular pot of platinum at the end of the rainbow.

Angus wondered if Kirkland knew. If so, Angus hoped it pissed Kirkland off. A lot.

The red dot came closer. Angus gripped the shovel, waiting patiently. *Just a few more feet … that's it … annnnnnd … now!*

He slammed the small shovel twice against the wall, *tink-tink*.

The blip moved a little more, then stopped.

"I got it!" Randy's voice echoed down the tunnel. "Get over here!"

Angus felt a rush of adrenaline in his chest. He sprinted down the tunnel, feeling oddly like some primitive cave dweller deep into the hunt.

Randy stood over a blanket that seemed to squirm and kick with a life of its own. Long, thin whipping legs poked through the many slashes they'd cut into the fabric. Angus heard the whine of machinery.

"Help me," Randy said. "Watch out for those feet, they have hooks that look sharp."

Angus took a step forward, then a step back. He had no idea where to go from here.

"What do we do?"

Randy carefully snatched up two corners of the blanket, lifted them. The AL seemed to know it was in trouble: its wild kicking increased.

"We jump on it," Randy said. "On *one*. Three, two—"

"Randy, I—"

"*One!*"

Randy threw himself into the squirming blanket. Angus did the same before he even knew he was doing it. They rolled the AL tighter in the blanket.

Randy bunched all four corners together, then stood and lifted it.

"Holy *cats* this is heavy!"

Angus grabbed the bunched-up corners, hefted it. Randy wasn't kidding—the thing weighed a ton.

"Didn't expect this much mass," Angus said.

Randy nodded in agreement. "The way they crawled on the ceiling I assumed they were made from some alloy, maybe aluminum." He smiled at Angus. "Well, we got it. What do we do with it?"

They both looked at the bag, listening to the whirring sounds emanating from within.

Angus smiled.

"Come on, buddy. You've had a biology class before, haven't you? I think it's time we had ourselves a good old-fashioned dissection."

25

15,521 feet below the surface

9:43 P.M.

"Professor Reeves, wake up."

The hand on her shoulder shook gently. Sleep danced enticingly around her head, calling to her to slip back into slumber. She felt the hand's gentle strength squeeze firmly, pressing for her attention.

"Professor, we're in danger."

Her eyes were already stinging before they even fluttered open to see Connell's face. He returned her look only for an instant, then his eyes flicked down the tunnel. He was tense, alert—and pointing a machine gun in the same direction. The gun's barrel reflected the light of his headlamp in a thin, lethal, metallic line.

She sat up slowly. She reached to wipe sleep from her eyes, ground them against the thin face shield before she remembered it was there.

Connell wore Mack's helmet. Veronica glanced around, saw Mack. He was still asleep. She suspected he'd suffered a concussion back at the river.

"I'm up. What's wrong?"

"Silverbugs," Connell said. "A bunch of them. Their behavior is making O'Doyle nervous."

A *bunch* of them? The thought of even that single machine sent a shiver down her spine. It had moved so *fast*, like a big metal spider buzzed up on a highball of Red Bull and crack. And now there were more of them?

She reached over, pushed at her father's gut.

"Pops, wake up."

He grumbled, started to stir. She gathered up her helmet, flicked her light on, placed the helmet on her head and looked down the tunnel.

What she saw almost made her scream.

Past Lybrand—who stood at the ready, rifle in hand—was a line of silver bugs stretching along the floor of the rocky tunnel that led back to the river. One burnished body after another. At least forty of them in Veronica's line of sight before the tunnel curved away, cutting off any view. But it wasn't the number that chilled her as much as their actions.

The silverbugs bobbed in a sickening, snap-motion *jerk* toward the ground, paused for a moment, then popped back up. A choreographed nightmare, moving as one, as if they were on a unified timer, or—even more disturbing—parts of the same brain, the same organism.

"What the hell are they doing?"

"No idea," Connell said. "We're not sticking around to find out. You help Sanji with Mack so I can keep my gun ready."

Her father had come fully awake, saw what they were facing. The two of them quietly roused Mack. The Aussie's eyes were glassy, unfocused. Sanji dragged the man to his feet. Veronica slipped under Mack's left arm, Sanji under his right. Their KoolSuits brushed together with rubbery squeaking noises.

Up ahead, away from the silverbugs, O'Doyle and Connell hovered over the map. Connell said something. O'Doyle nodded, his eyes flicking back every few seconds to check on Lybrand and the line of twitching machines.

Connell folded the map, put it in his belt. He jogged to her.

"We're moving out," he said. "About a hundred yards ahead, we're taking a tunnel to the right. Looks like a steep vertical climb, but at the end it takes a sharp descent and moves us toward the Dense Mass."

The fear in his voice didn't do a whole lot to comfort her.

Sanji nodded at Connell. "We'll take care of Mack. What about the silverbugs?"

Connell's tongue peeked out for a moment, the tip hitting the inside of his plastic face shield, leaving a small dot of wetness.

"O'Doyle doesn't want them following us. Let's go."

He headed down the tunnel, hands tight on the rifle.

Veronica and Sanji followed, moving as fast as they could under Mack's weight.

9:48 P.M.

Patrick stared at the bobbing line of silverbugs stretching down the tunnel's length. The machines' clicks and whirs played off the rough stone walls, filling the tunnel with a light but persistent din.

"You ready?"

"I am," Lybrand said.

He couldn't think about her as a woman right now, as someone he cared for, wanted to love. She was a soldier, like him. It was up to the two of them to discourage pursuit.

What did these damn things want?

He slung his rifle.

"Use your sidearm," he said, drawing his Glock 21. "You cover our backs. Don't forget Connell and the others are up there. Keep your hand on my back so I know where you are. I won't take my eyes off them unless we have to run, so you let me know what turns are coming up. Once the firing starts, we won't be able to hear anything. Pat my left shoulder and I'll go to my left, right shoulder and I'll go to my right. Keep an eye on me—if I turn to run, you need to already be three steps ahead of me and booking it. Understand?"

"I understand," she said.

Not *sir*, or *O'Doyle*, or even *Patrick*. Maybe she wasn't sure anymore what she was supposed to call him. Maybe he wasn't, either. He was calling the shots, but he wasn't her boss. Not down here. They were more partners than anything else, the two people who could get everyone out alive.

He took a deep breath to steady himself. "Let's see what happens."

Lybrand put her hand between his shoulder blades, letting him know she was there.

Patrick aimed at the first silverbug. He let his breath out slow. When it was gone, just before he breathed in, he squeezed the trigger: the gun kicked in his hand.

The bullet ripped through the sphere with a spark and a pop. A smell like burning chocolate instantly filled the cave. The silverbug fell to the ground, two of its legs curling in while the other two twitched violently in random directions.

He fired again, aiming for the next in line, but the swarm was already in full retreat, scattering like enraged ants. His bullet missed the mark. A madly flashing blur of faceted reflections, and in seconds, they vanished behind the bend in the tunnel.

Was that it?

"They're smart," Lybrand said. "They made the decision to haul ass in like, what, half a second?"

"If that."

She walked past him, toward the still-twitching silverbug.

"Don't," he said, the word coming out sharper than he would have liked. "Could be booby-trapped. Let's move back, just like we planned."

She got behind him, again put her hand between his shoulder blades. She tapped twice.

Patrick started backing up.

Far away, right at the tunnel's bend, he saw a silverbug lurking. Patrick kept moving. He waited for a clear shot.

9:53 P.M.

When the killer had driven off, Sonny had watched her. He watched her drive through the camp, down the new road. He watched her head north, toward Route 21. He watched until he could see her no more.

Then, he'd moved.

Don't you want to know? the insufferable little voice had asked. *Don't you?*

He didn't. He did. He couldn't. He had to.

Not sure what he was doing or even why he was doing it, he'd left his spot. Walking down a mountain at night wasn't the brightest choice even in normal times. He'd countered that dumb thing with a smart thing, which in itself was dumb: he'd used his flashlight.

Every step he waited for a shot to ring out. Was she really working alone? He didn't know. Yet he kept going anyway. Kept going, and soon he'd felt that creeping tingle of the place he'd sworn he would leave behind forever.

He was back on Funeral Mountain. He had to do it. For Cho.

Sonny had meant to go through the killer's hidey spot, but when he'd got there, he couldn't do it. If he did, she'd know. She'd search for him. She'd find him.

By the time her headlights played across the camp ruins, Sonny was settled into a perfect spot about twenty-five yards away from hers. Boulders surrounded him, gave him a narrow peephole through which to watch her.

He needed something to identify her.

Maybe he'd get lucky.

10:23 P.M.

Kayla stomped toward her warren. She didn't care about being quiet anymore. Screw that.

That little prick Angus Kool had thrown a major monkey wrench into her plans, but he wasn't going to stop her. No way, no how.

What were *Snoopy & Motherfucking Woodstock* up to? They'd been dicking around with that underground mapping system. Were they looking for another way into the mountain? Maybe to steal some platinum for themselves? Had they gone in before the attack? If so, were they dead? Chopped to bits by crazy fucking acid-trip stretchy color-monsters?

She didn't know. She couldn't wait anymore. If those two jagoffs were still alive, if they saw the camp and called for help, her chance was gone.

Kayla slid into the camouflaged little space that had been her home for the past two weeks. She started punching numbers into the Harris COMSEC unit. To properly disguise her location—and that's what this was all about, like some real estate agent's wet dream, *location, location, location*—she needed to create a web of bounced signals and coded relays. As far as the NSA was concerned, her call would originate from a pay phone in Duluth.

She wished she could find Angus and Randy, put a bullet in their heads, but there wasn't time to do things right. She had to act now, before the sunrise brought yet one more fuckup.

About an hour of programming, then she could make the call.

10:47 P.M.

Veronica Reeves could hike for miles. She could handle mountain trails with ease, leave bigger and stronger men in the dust. She often had, making her assistants at Cerro Chaltén beg her to take a break, to take it easy on them.

But when she'd done those things, she hadn't been carrying a 180-pound man.

The incline itself would have been enough to exhaust her. Lugging Mack's weight had wiped her out inside twenty minutes. She'd hated to ask for help, but she was slowing them down, and the sound of gunfire coming from the tunnel behind them removed any need for pride.

Connell had switched with her; she got the map and moved up front, he got to help carry Mack. He kept the rifle, though. She wasn't sure how she felt about that.

Veronica tried to watch both her footing and the map. Maybe there was another way they could go. She had more sympathy for Mack now, though—this map seemed to make no sense. Why hadn't Angus—

Another gunshot from behind made her jump.

Veronica kept going. The tunnel split in two: she could go up to the left, or down to the right. She studied the map, anxiety building as Connell, Sanji and Mack came up behind her. Connell and Sanji were exhausted, breathing hard, bodies sagging under Mack's weight. Mack had his eyes up, though, which was a good sign.

"Ronni, which way?"

Left and up. No, right and down.

She pointed.

"That way," she said. "Go, I'll catch up."

They took Mack into the tunnel. She noticed he looked a little stronger, was finally carrying some of his own weight. She hoped he could carry it all soon, or her dad might have a coronary and drop dead.

Their lights faded out.

Veronica knelt, started forming loose rock and sand into an arrow pointing to the right. That would tell Lybrand and O'Doyle which way to go.

A glimmer caught her eye.

She snapped her head up, fear gripping her—she was alone. No weapon if the silverbugs poured down the tunnel to the left, swarmed over her, long legs crawling, hooks tearing...

Nothing there. Veronica let her headlamp beam play around the tunnel walls. No movement. No reflections.

She bent her head toward the arrow—again, that glimmer. She looked up. Nothing there.

Suddenly it hit her: she reached up, snapped off her headlamp.

It took a second for her eyes to adjust—total blackness, then there it was far down the tunnel. Faint but unmistakable.

A tiny line of light. Yellowish. Still. Like being in a dark house and seeing daylight through a crack in the wall.

Veronica screamed down the tunnel to her right. "Connell! Get back here now!"

Another gunshot made her lurch, made her foot scatter the half-formed arrow.

A bouncing light from her right: Connell, running to her.

"What is it? What's wrong?"

"Where's Sanji and Mack?"

He jerked his thumb behind him. "I left them up there. Why is your light off?"

In answer, she gently reached up and turned his lamp off, then pushed the side of his face to make him look down the tunnel.

"Holy shit," he said. "What's up there?"

She switched her headlamp on again, pulled out the map.

"It looks like a huge, kidney-shaped cavern. It's huge, even bigger than the Picture Cavern. Looks like the bottom is far below our current elevation. The tunnel might lead to a cliff on cavern's side."

"Is there a way down to the cavern floor?"

"I don't know," she said. "It's hard to tell."

"Well, we're going to find out," he said. "Go get Mack and Sanji, bring them to this spot and wait. I'll run back for Lybrand and O'Doyle."

If there's a light, that means someone is there. We may have found our silverbug owners."

10:51 P.M.

"Platinum," Randy said. "The whole thing?"

Angus nodded. "Yeah, dude. I think so. Except for the innards."

A pair of tiny portable halogen lamps flooded the tunnel with light. The AL lay on a flat rock, its spindly legs sticking motionless into the air. Angus had found small catches built into the body, catches that had let him remove the bottom of the sphere. What had been a fast-moving robot a few hours ago would now make one helluva bowl for chips and salsa.

Randy lifted one mangled leg, tapped at the heavily dented spherical body.

"Wish we hadn't smashed it up so bad," he said. He let the leg drop. "We damaged the internal structure."

Which Angus regretted, but it wasn't like they'd had a choice. With no suitable equipment on hand, they'd used that most primitive of research techniques—smash the thing with a big rock until it stopped moving.

Angus was a smart man. One of the smartest in the world, he wasn't too shy to admit—yet the technology in this machine blew him away.

The legs were thin, hollow straws made of the same material as the shell. Angus didn't exactly have a mass spectrometer in his pants, so he couldn't be sure, but he suspected the material was the same platinum/iridium compound that made up the Dense Mass.

Long strands of a fibrous black material stretched through those leg tubes, anchoring at various points inside. Artificial muscle, he figured. Contracted to apply force, just like the real thing. The stuff had to be very powerful to make the ALs move so fast.

The first two sections of every limb were identical, each about a quarter inch in diameter and eight inches long. The last section was actually two thinner tubes, about an eighth of an inch in diameter and, again, eight inches long. Those last two tubes—Randy had dubbed them "split feet"—ended with a cluster of tiny retractable hooks or claws, perfect for gripping any type of rough surface.

The shell itself was a hollow ball about seven inches in diameter, packed full of fascinating items. The black muscle material coated the interior, obviously providing locomotion for various external gadgets whose purpose remained a mystery. Angus figured a large blue chunk of glassine material in the center served as some kind of battery. Randy thought he identified an irregular, faceted crystalline lump as the CPU, the AL's computer brain, but that was only a guess — the structure differed from anything the two men had ever seen.

About the only things they *could* identify were a pair of tiny pneumatic pistons mounted behind the wedge-shaped head, and a cluster of orange lumps that Angus had identified as a simple radio transmitter and receiver, not so different from the RFID chips of his Marco/Polo System.

Randy tapped his finger against the orange lumps.

"You really think these machines operate independently? No one is controlling them?"

"Radio waves aren't going to travel that far down here," Angus said. "Certainly not from the surface, so I doubt they're remote-controlled. I bet the ALs use the transmitters to talk to each other more than with their owners."

"Ah, like a distributed intelligence," Randy said. "A colony of ants working together as opposed to individual bugs wandering around."

Angus nodded. "Makes sense, doesn't it? If these things are made for exploration and mapping, you don't waste energy by having them covering the same ground. A simple algorithm makes sure they each take an area, stay a certain distance apart. I bet we could jam their communication. Fix our walkie-talkies to transmit static at that frequency. Might mess them up pretty bad."

It would at that. The ALs didn't seem to pose any danger, but jamming was a good card to hold back in case it was needed.

Angus squatted on his heels, looked closely at the leg they'd opened up. Something about it didn't seem right.

"No wires," he said. "Look how the artificial muscle groups don't connect with each other. No connection between them, no continuous signal with the brain. How do they get the signal to contract?"

Randy rapped his knuckles on the dented, scratched shell.

"The platinum itself does the work, I think. I bet the main processor sends signals through the entire shell, but specific muscles only react to specific commands."

Angus should have thought of that. Made perfect sense. Platinum's high conductivity would help. The metal didn't corrode, either, and wouldn't be affected by the high temperatures down here. No wires to break, no fuses to short out. The ALs looked durable as all get-out.

"Dude, Kirkland is going to shit egg rolls when he sees one of these."

"Yeah," Randy said. "That guy hates competition."

"That, and the platinum itself. There's over half a million bucks worth of metal in this one alone. That's before all the crazy tech. And we've seen *dozens* of these little boogers scurrying about."

Randy glanced around, as if the talk of money might bring some unseen enemy.

"Who could afford to make such a thing? And who could keep tech like this secret? No one has stuff this good, Angus. Not even the military."

"Well, *someone* has stuff this good," Angus said. "And money to burn, too. Or we wouldn't be looking at it."

"But it's *so much* platinum. Just in the ones we've seen, we're talking maybe three hundred *pounds* of the stuff. No one can afford that kind of investment for a simple exploration."

"Not with the known supply, no." Angus pointed down. "But if you have enough raw material, cost isn't an issue."

Randy's jaw dropped.

"You think someone is already mining the Dense Mass?"

"Must be," Angus said. "No one is going to make machines like this out of platinum unless they've got tons of it. The people who made these ALs must have found the Dense Mass and already mined it. A portion of it, anyway."

"Doesn't make any sense." Randy played with the AL's leg, moving it up and down like it was part of his favorite toy. "If someone got to it first, how come Kirkland didn't know? And how come the platinum market isn't flooded?"

Ah, Randy... so naive.

"King-Shit Kirkland doesn't know *everything*," Angus said. "Looks like someone is smarter than he is. And the market isn't flooded because scarcity determines price. Just because people possess a resource doesn't mean they want to sell it all at once. How do you think the Saudis got so rich? If they put all their oil on the market, the stuff would be cheaper than Kool-Aid. Or the De Beers with diamonds—they hoard that shit so that stupid women make stupider men pay crazy prices for a shiny rock. Sell something all at once, it's worthless. Sell it over decades, it's priceless."

Randy frowned. He nodded, frowned deeper, then shook his head.

"But if this mystery company already reached the Dense Mass— which we think they *had* to do to build the ALs—then why would they build the ALs at all?"

Randy had a point.

"I don't know," Angus said. "Maybe—"

A soft beeping from the tablet: the motion-tracker app. Randy picked it up.

"Uh, Angus? I think you better figure out how to jam those radio signals. And fast."

He turned the tablet so Angus could see the screen: on it, some twenty red blinking dots were coming closer.

10:56 P.M.

Patrick O'Doyle cursed under his breath. He didn't know how many shattered silverbug bodies he'd left in his wake, but the damn things kept popping up all over the place. He was down to his Glock's last magazine, and only five shots remained. The silverbugs had quickly learned his effective range and stayed beyond it, far enough that he missed most of the time, but still close enough for the light of his headlamp to reflect off their twitching legs and burnished bodies. They scurried across the tunnel floor and up the walls, moving away from the light as it flashed back and forth. The collective noise of their whirs and their feet clicking on rock filled the tunnel with an eerie, constant chatter. It sounded like a million windup toys packed into a small steel box.

The silverbugs increased their distance even more when Lybrand started shooting—her aim proved to be far more accurate than his. He felt a surge of pride each time she pulled the trigger and another machine erupted with a shower of sparks and that sickening smell of burnt chocolate.

Patrick switched aim, targeting one creeping out just past the tunnel's far bend. He fired, saw rock chip away—a miss. The silverbug scurried out of sight.

He swept left, looking for a new target, but nothing moved.

"Cease fire," he said. He brought the Glock to his chest, angled down in the SUL position.

He kept moving backward, Bertha's hand still firmly between his shoulder blades. She tapped his left shoulder. He turned, able to take the bend without looking away.

"They gave up," she said. "I'm down to two rounds. There were dozens of those things, maybe hundreds. Why didn't they just swarm us?"

He didn't have an answer. Maybe they didn't attack at all, maybe that wasn't their purpose.

She tapped his right shoulder. He turned, grazed the wall, corrected, kept moving backward, kept looking for targets. His beam played off the ceiling and floor, a thin spotlight fighting a losing battle against the endless darkness.

A new voice hissed out.

"Don't shoot! It's me!"

Kirkland, screaming at the top of his damn lungs.

Patrick turned, sprinted down the tunnel. Just as he'd asked, Lybrand was already three steps ahead. They reached Connell in seconds. He had the EBR in his hands. If he'd been gripping it any tighter, he might have broken it in half. Patrick would have to get the man to relax a little. At least he had proper trigger discipline.

"We saw a light," he said. "Something fixed, like a crack in a wall. Not sure what it is. I came to get you so we could all check it out together."

"Good call," Patrick said.

A light. The assholes who'd killed his men?

Connell looked down the tunnel, back where Patrick and Bertha had come.

"We heard shooting," Connell said. "More silverbugs?"

"A fuck-ton," Bertha said. "We shot a bunch, they kept coming. Then they stopped chasing."

"Let's move before they come back," Patrick said. "Connell, lead the way."

He did. He moved quickly, but was clearly favoring his right leg. It was slowing him down somewhat.

Patrick saw a light up ahead, bodies silhouetted. Unmoving. Rigid. Reeves and Sanji, Mack leaning heavily against the tunnel wall.

Then he realized the light wasn't coming from them.

And, it wasn't white.

Reds, blues, greens, yellows, flashing and pulsing.

Connell sprinted, his pain apparently forgotten. Patrick was only a step behind.

What was that *smell?*

He and Connell reached the others, stopped.

Far down the tunnel, Patrick saw the light Connell had described, a glowing crack in the wall.

Between him and that light, the source of the flashing colors.

A tentacle god.

10:59 P.M.

What Connell saw hammered him, jarred him, *sheared* his thoughts as hard as if another rock had cracked into his skull.

He remembered the last vacation he'd taken with Cori before her death. A driving trip of California. San Diego. Highway One. Big Sur. Cannery Row. Amid a hundred touristy things, they'd visited the Salk Institute to see an exhibit by the artist Chihuly—crazy sculptures of colored glass, twisting tentacles that seemed like living things flash-frozen in a moment of mad motion. They'd seen it at night, the sculptures lit up from within, glowing against the night sky.

Then, and now.

Now, something that looked like a Chihuly sculpture come to life. The size of a basketball, maybe. Undulating tentacles touching the tunnel floor, sticking out to the side, sticking up, all swaying like cobras poised to strike. It wasn't only the body that moved, it was the colors—spreading and shrinking, expanding and contracting, *flowing*, all the hues the world had ever known cascading and coursing. Loose patterns, flowing lines … hypnotizing in their complexity, stunning in their simplicity.

The curling tentacles, they weren't fixed. Some shrank into the body, some extended out, a kaleidoscope sun birthing slow-motion solar flares, casting incandescent radiance against the surrounding walls.

Within the shimmering colors, he saw black spots of various sizes. Thousands of them, spread all over each there-then-not tentacle, throughout the shapeless body. Small, polished onyx jewels embedded in strange flesh.

All the art in the Picture Cavern—carvings and paintings alike, the flawless and the mad—it all made sense. Not gods or demons, not visions. *Living creatures.*

The assault on his eyes, his thoughts, and his nose as well: the pungent reek of dog shit mixed with the sickeningly sweet waft of rotting fruit. Strawberries, perhaps. Maybe apples.

The still moment stretched on, as permanent as the mountain itself. Endless and disturbing. He couldn't think. He couldn't speak.

O'Doyle slowly pushed his pistol toward it, two-handed grip firm and unforgiving.

Connell reached out, put his palm atop the gun.

"Don't shoot," he said, the voice that creaked out of his throat somewhere between a hiss of command and a cry of confusion. "We don't know what it is."

The thing didn't come closer, didn't move away. It stood there, tentacles waving softly.

"*Kill it.*"

Two words Connell would have expected from O'Doyle or Lybrand—but they came from Veronica Reeves.

"We know exactly what it is," she said. "We all saw those carvings in the Picture Cavern. We know what these things do to people. The *knives,* Connell. Now we know what happened to Jansson."

Those carvings. The stone-still images of horror flashed through Connell's thoughts: cutting, slicing, severing.

Jansson's thumb.

Slashed at him …

Wicked-sharp …

But that strange, amorphous creature in front of him seemed so small. Couldn't have weighed more than ten pounds. How could something this size have killed a grown man? One kick would send it flying. The knives were almost as big as the creature itself.

A hand on his shoulder. Lybrand, leaning close, whispering.

"It's seen us," she said. "Whatever the hell it is, it's seen us. What if it wasn't another company that attacked us—what if it was these things?"

Her voice carried steel, the sharp edge of a sword. It made him shiver.

Was she right? No, the Kilroy signs … someone had done that to send a message. A message to him. Creature or no creature, other people were down here.

O'Doyle slowly adjusted his stance, dropping his hips a little lower.

"Say the word," he said. "I'm ready."

Connell had to decide? This wasn't mining, this wasn't business. How did he have the right to make a call like that?

Motion from a thin fissure in the wall to the creature's right, up near the ceiling.

Connell felt himself take a step back, sensed the others doing the same.

Two yellowish-brown globs squeezed out of that crack, accompanied by a hissing sound of dead leaves blowing over concrete.

"Lybrand," O'Doyle snapped.

"Got it," she said. She aimed at this new threat, while O'Doyle remained locked on his.

A second small creature slid out of the fissure like pudding pushed through a strainer, its body swelling as it left the stone confines. No glow, no colors. Yellowish-brown skin flecked with those spots of onyx.

Limbs squished out. It positioned itself between the people and the first creature, which had yet to move.

"This one isn't glowing," Sanji said. "Ronni, why isn't it glowing?"

"You're the fucking biologist, you tell me," Veronica said, more scared than angry, but still plenty angry. "I don't give a ... oh, *shit*, there's another one."

A third creature slid from the crack. This one glowed a soft fuchsia, pulsed through with spots of wavering orange. Connell had never seen such beautiful colors: deep, rich, luminous. The creature extended, flowed to the first one—which was still a wild shimmering shift of tones—wrapped tentacles around it, pulled it toward the crack.

So many limbs, all boneless, flowing.

"Like an octopus."

The voice surprised Connell, pulled his attention away from the light show—Mack, leaning against the wall, that immovable stone surface the only thing stopping him from falling on his face. Mack lifted an arm toward the creatures. His hand hung limply, like he was trying to point but didn't quite have the energy.

"All those arms, but no water," he said. "Rock octopuses."

Connell again looked at the creatures. The original one seemed clumsy, its movement not as precise as the two who had come after.

The creature that wasn't glowing at all came closer.

O'Doyle twisted, snapped his aim toward it. Lybrand did the same.

"Don't," Connell said, the single syllable sharp and firm.

The yellow-brown creature stopped moving. It grew arms, shrank them back. Tentacles waved softly. Connell saw some of the onyx spots vanish into the body, only to pop up again. The spots alternated this action—there were hundreds of them, some shrinking back while others stayed visible, like twinkling stars in a clear night sky.

A single, thick limb seemed to bubble out of it, shooting straight up until the tip touched the tunnel's roof. The new extrusion pulsed three times with a bright light, the pulses starting at the body, moving up to the end, then disappearing, a *whump-whump-whump* of yellow. The creature stood motionless.

The cave filled with a surreal stillness. No one spoke. No one *breathed*.

Lybrand finally broke the silence.

"What the fuck is it doing?"

"It seems like it's waiting," Sanji said. "It wants us to do something."

Another *whump-whump-whump* of yellow light.

It let out a high-pitched screech that made everyone jump, a sound like old razors scraping a chalkboard.

"Rocktopuses," Mack said, sounding groggy and delirious. "Aye-aye, rocktopi. God, my head hurts. Anybody got any aspirin?"

Sanji took a step toward the creature. Lybrand reactively angled her pistol down.

"Get the fuck out of my way," she said. "What are you doing?"

O'Doyle took a step to his left, changing his angle.

"I have a shot," he said. "Connell, I am telling you, let's kill these things and move on.

That seemed to jar Sanji. He turned his back to the creature, spread his hands wide.

"I think it's trying to communicate with us. Don't shoot."

Without waiting for a reply, Sanji turned to face the creature again. He slowly lowered his helmet and turned off the light. He raised his right arm up, pressed his palm flat against the ceiling. With his left hand, he rested his helmet's headlamp against his right biceps, then quickly turned the light on and off three times.

A *whump-whump-whump* of yellow KoolSuit.

The creature's extended limb *whump-whump-whump*ed—the exact same color as the KoolSuits, the exact same color it had flashed before.

"Holy shit," Connell said.

Sanji answered with another *whump-whump-whump* of his own.

The creature squeaked, screeched, pulled in the extended limb. It spun in circles even as it extruded new tentacles, waved them, pulled them back—a frantic display of energy and action that didn't really do anything.

"I don't believe it," Veronica said. "It's ... it's *excited*."

Sanji paused, unsure of what to do next.

"Don't stop now," Lybrand said. Her tone had changed, from forceful to amazed. "If it wants to do-si-do, then do-si-do."

Sanji turned in a circle, moving his arms in and out in his best mimicry of extending pseudopods.

The creature squealed again. Its body pulsed a deep orange, then, almost as if it had lost track of what was going on, corrected to KoolSuit yellow. It cavorted through a series of antics: rushing up the side of the wall; thrusting up a new limb and dangling from the ceiling like a ball of jiggling yellow Jell-O; tapping one snakelike limb on the ground three times, then repeating the pattern with another.

Sanji mimicked as best he could. In seconds, he was already breathing hard—the exhaustion of lugging Mack around caught up fast.

"I'm doing my best," he said. "But I don't understand what it's trying to say."

Veronica shook her head, clearly blown away by the surreal scene.

"I don't think that's language, Dad. I think it's *playing*, like a child."

Connell had no idea what any of it meant. These creatures ... he'd never seen the like. No animal similar to it, not anywhere, and yet he was already adjusting to what he saw: the impossible was already becoming normal.

A flicker of movement caught his eye, high up on the wall, in the crack that had spawned the second two tentacle gods. A new limb oozed through—but this one was bigger. *Much* bigger. So big it seemed to jam, to squish so thick it clogged the crack and could go no further.

A new shriek: a sound like tires burning on asphalt, so loud Connell's hands shot to his ears.

Sanji stepped back, stepped away from the quivering mass that undulated in the crack like a glowing worm pushing against rotted wood. Lybrand stepped aside, let him back up, then she stepped in front of him and raised her weapon.

Sanji's dance partner pulsed a bright purple. It stretch-flowed to the crack in the wall. The fleshy mass there seemed to sense it: two smaller buds protruded out, pinched down hard on the purple one, then pulled back, *hard*—the small creature shot into the crack like a glob of pudding sucked through a straw.

"Veronica," Connell said quietly, "what's on the other side of that wall?"

He didn't take his eyes off the crack. He heard the plastic map rattling as she fumbled with it.

"Looks like the wall is pretty thin," she said. "There's another tunnel on the other side."

A deep, deafening screech stabbed the air, made everyone wince.

The two small tentacle gods moved to the fissure, the second one that had come out tugging at the first one, which still moved in an odd fashion...like it was drugged or something.

"I don't like the looks of this," O'Doyle said, his weapon leveled at the crack. "I think that's an adult, an adult pulling children away from danger. Reeves, is there a connection between this tunnel and that one?"

Like bread dough hurled against a slat fence, the bigger creature curved out of the crack—trying to force its way through, maybe, but it was still too large to fit. Crazy colors raged across the visible surface: electric blues, neon greens, smoldering reds.

"Don't see one," Veronica said. "I don't know, this fucking map is a hot mess."

The two small tentacle gods stretched limbs up to the crack. Electric blue buds formed, pinched, and they were both yanked through, leaving the humans alone.

With no light but the headlamps, the tunnel seemed stale, the air seemed thin.

click-click, click-click-click ...

Five headlamps whipped around like a sweep of Broadway spots swinging toward center stage.

Fifty feet back down the tunnel, a line of silverbugs slowly closed in, convulsing in rhythm, snapping toward the ground with sickly speed and then slowly rising back up, only to snap down again.

Headlamp beams angled farther down the tunnel—silverbugs as far as they could see.

And far away, something else as well. Something unrecognizable. The tunnel seemed to *flow*, to *convulse*. What the hell was that? Was the tunnel wall *moving*?

"Oh, fuck me," O'Doyle said. He jammed his pistol into its holster, whipped his rifle into firing position. "Everybody, *run!*"

Veronica grabbed Sanji's arm, pulled him so hard the man stumbled.

"Head for the light in the wall," she said, her voice more a desperate scream than a command. "There has to be something there, come on!"

Lybrand grabbed Mack, threw him over her shoulders in a fireman's carry, then pounded after Veronica and Sanji.

Connell couldn't bring himself to run. What was that? It wasn't possible for the walls to . . .

Then he saw it, saw the individual parts amid the moving mass.

He ran then. Oh, hell yes, he *ran*.

11:04 P.M.

Randy Wright felt very much like a worm on a hook.

He cupped his hands to his mouth, shouted up the tunnel: "Nothing. Keep trying."

He walked slowly. The secret exploration with Angus had been a thrill, an actual adventure. For once in his life, Randy had fully flaunted authority and embraced doing something daring. The joy of discovery, the thought that he was putting his mark in the history books. All fun and games.

It wasn't fun anymore. He was scared.

He didn't like the way the ALs tracked his movements, adjusting themselves to keep their wedge-shaped protrusions pointed in his direction as he walked back and forth through the stone passage.

Angus's voice called back: "It's probably a low frequency. Better to travel through the tunnels that way."

Angus was still in the small cavern where they had dissected the silverbug. He was tinkering with the walkie-talkie, trying to find a way to scramble the machines' communication.

Randy of course, had been sent out to draw the silverbugs' attention. He hadn't wanted to. Angus had insisted.

"Don't really care about theory right now," Randy called back. "Just figure out what frequency they're using."

The ALs tracked his every step. A single AL had fascinated him—twenty-odd ALs clinging to the walls and the ceiling made his skin crawl, made him wonder if these machines might be meant for more than just exploration.

Randy took another step. The ALs watched him.

He took another.

ALs scattered down from the walls and the ceiling, going from still to full speed so instantly that he froze. He wasn't just *scared* anymore, he was *terrified*.

The clicking machines rushed to form a straight line on the tunnel floor. They started to bob in a coordinated, herky-jerky fashion. Something about the movement looked insect-like ... *predatory*.

Randy didn't want to be part of this experiment anymore. He didn't even want to be in these tunnels—he wanted out of there.

"Angus, you'd better hurry! They're up to something."

Then, just as suddenly as they'd started bobbing, the ALs broke ranks and moved randomly, walking in loose circles, even bumping into each other.

"That did it! That's screwing them up royally!"

Randy sagged with relief, felt the tingle of adrenaline coursing through his veins. He took a moment to catch his breath, to put his hand on his chest and feel his heart raging within, then jogged back up the tunnel to where Angus sat next to the dead AL. A walkie-talkie—which looked just as broken and dissected as the AL itself, wires exposed and circuit boards hanging off—stuck up from the hollow body.

"Frequency is at 300 kilohertz," Angus said, smiling. "I rigged the radio to broadcast alternating blasts of static and random data at that frequency. What did it do to them?"

"They're wandering all over. They look drunk."

Angus stood, stretched. "That's because they use communication with each other as part of their sensory system and navigation ability. Kind of like a moving computer network. I was right—they act like a communal life-form, like an insect hive."

Randy had suggested the machines were like ants, not Angus, but that really didn't matter at the moment. He stared at the mess that was once Angus's walkie-talkie.

"We can't exactly carry that pile of junk around with us."

"Of course not," Angus said. "I had to fiddle a bit to find out what signal would be best. Give me yours and I'll modify it."

Randy handed it over, wondering if Angus really knew what he was doing.

"Will we still be able to send and receive after you modify it?"

Angus shook his head as he sat and got to work.

"No, I have to hard-wire the circuit board. The signal has to stay on, we can't switch back and forth."

Exactly what Randy had been afraid of.

"Then what the heck happens if we need the radio?"

Angus glared up, irritated. "Would you rather have ALs following us around?"

No. No he would not. Better to be incommunicado than to see that sickening AL conga line again.

Randy shook his head.

"Thought so," Angus said. "Now that we know it works, let's turn it off and see what they do."

"Turn it off? Are you crazy?"

"Jesus *Christ*, Dirty Randy, you are a *serious* pussy. I scrambled them. We turn it off, they probably reconnect with each other, recalibrate. It will be like you just vanished." Angus reached to the gutted walkie-talkie and switched it off. He pointed to the map screen. "Pick that up, see what they do."

He cracked open the case of the unbroken walkie-talkie.

Angus hadn't asked Randy what he thought about turning off the scrambled signal. Angus never *asked,* he just *told.* Maybe it was high time for Randy to stand up to him. There were *two* people doing this, not one and an assistant.

"*Randy!* Didn't I just tell you to pick up the fucking map?"

Randy snatched it up, a knee-jerk reaction. He felt ashamed for his response. Maybe he would stand up to Angus, but later—this wasn't the right time.

The map showed the loose line of blinking red dots. They were moving again, steadily passing out of the range-motion sensor range. Randy expanded the map, encompassing a larger view of the tunnel system.

"Looks like they're heading for that big kidney-shaped cavern," he said. "They seem to be making a beeline for it."

That cavern was only about four hundred meters away. They'd already planned on exploring that cavern next. It was the second-largest area in the complex—only the space surrounding the Dense Mass was larger.

"Sah-*weet*," Angus said. He pressed the walkie-talkie case back together with an audible *snap*. "Those little fuckers followed us, so now it's our turn to follow them."

Follow them? That was ridiculous.

"Wait a minute," Randy said. "We shouldn't risk—"

Angus grinned and turned on the walkie-talkie. It filled the small space with static.

"What's that, Randy? I can't hear you, this thing is too loud!"

Randy took a deep breath. "*I said, we shouldn't—*"

Angus cranked the volume all the way up. He shook his head, made a confused face and mouthed, *I can't hear you*. He did all of this without losing that smug look that sometimes made Randy want to punch him in the mouth.

Angus turned the volume down. "Let's go, right now," he said, then turned it back up before Randy could reply.

26

15,506 feet below the surface

Bertha Lybrand focused on moving.

Big breath in, step left, step right, big breath out, step left, step right…

She carried Mack uphill, a flood of horror on her heels. Patrick was somewhere behind her, letting off short bursts with the EBR that echoed through the stone tunnels like rolling thunder. Her legs had wanted to give up hours ago—she hadn't let them then, she wouldn't let them now.

Kirkland caught up to her.

"Let me help," he said.

He pulled at Mack; the shifting weight made her stumble.

She shoved Connell in the chest. Too hard. His shoulder smashed into the wall. He spun off, skidded, almost fell.

"Get up front," Bertha said. "You have to cover Reeves and Sanji!"

He had the wide eyes of a deer in headlights, eyes she had seen years ago when tracer rounds lit up the desert. When men screamed. When men died.

Kirkland nodded hard, his helmet bobbling. He sprinted ahead, EBR held in a white-knuckled grip.

Up ahead, she saw it, saw the light. Not like the light of the creatures, not colored and flowing, but fixed and steady. Like *daylight.* That was impossible, they were so far belowground—a small part of her wished desperately that the maps had been wrong, that they were close to the surface and about to break out of this hell.

Behind her, Patrick fired off another three-round burst, then another: *Ba-da-da! Ba-da-da!*

Pain-filled screams riddled the air. Not human screams—the impossible earsplitting squeal of those *things.* She'd never heard anything like it, not even in nightmares.

Big breath in, step left, step right, big breath out, step left, step right...

The breaths weren't *big* anymore. Her stomach clenched. Lungs burned. Legs cried out for rest. The light, getting closer, stronger.

"Rocktopi," Mack said.

"Mack, shut...the..."

She didn't have the wind to finish.

Step left, step right, keep going, soldier, you stop and you die.

It wasn't the first time she'd run for her life. The IED tearing through the troop transport. Sergeant Cole's guts spraying across the roof. Parnell's leg, torn off, accidentally sent flying when Kalb kicked it. Blood everywhere. Screaming. The crash. Out into the night. Rounds pouring in. Firing back at nothing, just pulling the trigger so she could do *something.* The order to run. Sprinting, sprinting, sprinting after someone she thought was Lieutenant Berg, but it wasn't Berg, it was Alhassen, just another grunt like her, no idea what to do or where to go. Her legs, burning, *burning* until she couldn't run anymore. Stopping. Puking. Hiding. Waiting for death, waiting for what they would do to a woman. Knowing she had to save the last bullet for herself.

Mack's feet skidded off the side of the tunnel, bringing her back to the now. His feet hit the side because the tunnel was narrowing, funneling her toward that growing light. Ceiling, lowering. Sides, pinching in.

"Goddammit, Lybrand, *move!*"

Was that from the *then* or the *now*? The *now*, because it was Patrick, shouting at her even while he defended her back.

She had to squat. How the fuck could she run and squat at the same time? Her legs were going to catch fire and burn her alive.

Patrick fired off another burst. More screeches, *closer* screeches, so close they had to be right on top of her.

The ceiling lowered further. Duck-walking now, and a new memory, that ridiculous drill she'd done in boot where she carried a fucking chunk of telephone pole while squatting, refusing to quit until at least one of the men in her unit quit first. She'd thought that duck-walk shit was just like high school algebra—when would she ever use it in real life? Drill Sergeant Petty with the last fucking laugh.

Up ahead, Sanji crawling, because the ceiling was too low to even squat. His big body blocked the light like an eclipse of the moon.

The moon... his big ass in that tight suit... hey, girl, that's funny.

She stumbled. Her knees ground against stone. She fell forward, pushed Mack ahead of her. He hit, groaned. Something stomped down hard on her ankle—they had her, they *were on her.* Patrick fell on his ass next to her.

He turned, looked at her, eyes wide, lip snarling, spit string from lower lip to upper teeth. The look of a human monster, a *killer,* and in that moment she knew this was him, the *real* him behind the sweet talk and the compliments and the desire to be a better man.

At his core, this barbarian was the essence of Patrick O'Doyle.

"*Get your ass up, Lybrand! Move or die!*"

He looked down the tunnel. Spit flying, he screamed the pure truth of rage, then squeezed off three bursts: *Ba-da-da! Ba-da-da! Ba-da-da!*

Bertha was back up even before the second burst finished. Patrick's screams chased away the fatigue and the self-pity, made her heart pound in her ears and eyes and feet and hands. She crawled past Mack, grabbed at his neck, squeezed up a handful of KoolSuit and started dragging him along the stone floor.

"Get up, Mack! *Get up,* you motherfucker!"

Patrick screamed at her, she screamed at Mack, good for the goose, good for the gander.

The ceiling lowered to not even two feet: light filling all of that space, blinding, bottom to top and left to right. No more Sanji—he had to be through.

She crawled, two legs and one hand, dragging Mack along. He moved a little, tried to get up, tried to help.

Jagged rocks dug into her knees and shins, stabbed at her hand. The rough ceiling pushed against her backpack, tapped at her slung rifle, knocked on her helmet, and then she was through, rolling onto her left shoulder.

Light everywhere now, bright as day (it's not day just stop it but what if it is the sun what if you're *out*) she stood—lots of clearance, at least higher than her head and thank *God* for that—she reached back in, grabbed Mack's hand, dragged him through the opening like a dead fish sliding across ice.

Sanji, next to her. "I have him!"

He grabbed Mack.

Bertha stood, unslung her rifle, shrugged off the backpack and let it drop. She meant to kneel and aim down the tunnel, give supporting fire to Patrick, but before she could, something caught her eye—something that *made* her look, a giant's hand palming her head and turning her.

Sky. Sunlight.

It couldn't be.

Bertha stood in a cave. Not a *tunnel*, but a *cave*, because this one *ended*, it opened up to a bright cavern so large she couldn't quite comprehend it at first. The light held a strange blue tinge that seemed to cast a dull pallor on everything. She looked to the cavern's ceiling, had to shield her eyes against a brightness so intense it might as well have been the sun itself.

Fifteen or twenty feet away, the cave's edge. Veronica and Kirkland standing there, staring out. Sanji, dragging Mack to join them.

In a dream, a vision, Bertha walked forward on rubbery legs, the muscles in them long since drained of all strength.

The cliff ended at a drop-off, two hundred feet, at least, a fall that would stop suddenly on hard-edged boulders. The cavern floor, far below, filled with strange, clumpy orange things that might be trees. A glistening river meandered through fields of multicolored plants laid out in regimented rows.

Farmland?

Ba-da-da!

Behind her, Patrick's weapon.

What the fuck was she doing?

"Kirkland, with me, *now!*"

She jogged halfway back to the squat opening, saw Patrick crawling through. She sprinted the last few steps, threw herself down on her belly, aimed through the opening.

Seventy meters in, flashing monsters, a wave of color.

What had Mack called them?

Rocktopi.

Too many to count. A wall of glowing sickness, pushing forward like brackish water rushing up a rusted pipe. Her helmet light gleamed off double-crescent knives, their solidity and hardness a lethal contrast to soft bodies and boneless tentacles.

Fifty meters and closing.

Bertha squeezed off a three-round burst, then another as Patrick scrambled to his feet.

"Get up," Patrick said as he scrambled to his feet. "Run, goddammit!"

"Nowhere to run, sir," she said. "Cliff."

"Cliff? *Shit.* Hold this position."

The sound of his boots rushing away.

She fired again: *Ba-da-da!*

A creature fell, but the psychedelic wave washed over the top of it, not slowing. Their rough skin scraped against the rock: the rattling rasp of a million paper-dry leaves.

"Lybrand, *fall back!*"

She pushed to her hands and knees, then her feet, shuffled backward, stock tight to her shoulder, and her vision focused down the length of her weapon, toward the tunnel's dark opening.

A hand between her shoulder blades, stopping her. A *big* hand.

"Hold here," Patrick said to her. "Free fire."

She dropped to one knee again, waited for the horror to pour out of that crack. Behind her, Patrick screamed at Kirkland.

"We have to run, now."

"There's nowhere *to* run," Kirkland said. "Look at this fucking cliff!"

Kirkland was on the edge of hysteria. Lybrand wasn't that far from the same. But Patrick, his voice was stone itself, rigid and unbendable.

"Then break out the climbing rigs," he said. "Move, man!"

The tunnel opening started to flicker with color.

"*Too late*," she shouted. "They're here."

She ejected her magazine, popped in a fresh one, set a second full one on the stone in front of her.

"God*dammit*," Patrick said. "Kirkland! On my left! Reeves, get Mack's sidearm and his two magazines. Lybrand, give your sidearm to Sanji, now!"

Bertha shifted the rifle stock to her left shoulder so she didn't break aim, drew her Glock with her right, held it up above her head, where it was instantly snatched out of her hand.

"Reload it," she said.

"Got it," Sanji said.

Patrick knelt on her left. He popped in a fresh magazine.

Down the tunnel, the disco glow grew brighter.

"Reeves, Sanji, stand behind us," he said as he shouldered his weapon, aimed. "Do not fire until I tell you to. Kirkland, *short bursts*, you understand?"

"I…I…" The man's words were more breath than voice. "I don't think I can do this."

"*You will fire when I tell you to fire*," Patrick screamed. A war cry. The voice of a god, a god that could do the impossible and get them through this if they just listened to him. "Short bursts, Kirkland—aim, squeeze, release, *do you understand*?"

"Yes, yes I understand!"

"Safeties off," Patrick said. "Fire on my command. Pick a target, put it down, pick another target. Maybe it's a good day to die, but it isn't *our* day."

Bertha choked on a sudden laugh, and then it was out of her, uncontrollable and ridiculous.

The glow brightened. The monsters were almost there.

"Something funny, Lybrand?" Patrick asked without moving his gaze or his aim. The war scream was gone—he sounded calm, measured.

"Depends," she said. "Did you stay up at night to write that corny shit, or did it just pop out?"

"Shut up," Reeves said. "For fuck's sake shut up both of you no jokes how can you make jokes?"

"Kind of wrote it," Patrick said, ignoring Reeves. "Came up with it when I was twenty-two, taking a shit in a ditch in Panama. You don't like it?"

She didn't have time to answer.

A sickening, flashing mass squeezed out of the opening, seven or eight of them at once, mashed together like lumps of glowing Play-Doh. They sprang up, from a condensed mass to full-size individuals, black-spotted skin shimmering in blood red and lava orange. So much bigger than the little ones—these stood as tall as a man, taller if you counted waving tendrils that held deadly, double-crescent blades.

Just fifteen yards away. They screeched, and they flowed forward, new limbs squishing out like toothpaste shot full-force from a new tube.

A tentacle as thick as a python reared back, whipped forward—a knife whizzed through the air, straight at Lybrand's face. She flinched right, felt something slice into her left cheek.

Their screeches rang loud—Patrick's rang louder.

"Front row, *fire!*"

Three Heckler & Koch HK416s opened up. The cave's air trembled with the roaring report of automatic fire, one tight three-round burst indiscernible over the next.

Bullets punched through soft bodies, kicking up a spurting rain of pale yellow fluid. The front row sagged, fell, and those behind poured over the top.

Bertha sighted, squeezed off a burst. Her target quivered, twitched, stopped. She angled to the center, found another, squeezed again. Sprays of yellow. Orange and red light blinking out, leaving the yellow-brown black-spotted skin, but it kept coming. She hit it with another burst. It shivered, shuddered, made her think of the man she'd killed, how he'd kept twitching after he'd died.

She angled right for another, fired before she noticed it wasn't coming toward her, it was running away, squishing its body back into the opening.

"*Cease fire!*"

The gunshot echo pulsed through the huge cavern behind them, slowly fading out.

Dead, wounded and dying rocktopi littered the cave floor, spurting thick, oily, yellow fluid in all directions. Some lay still. Some shuddered as if caught in a freezing wind. Still others reached their long tentacles toward the funnel mouth, pulling themselves slowly forward inch by agonizing inch. Even in an unknown creature, Bertha recognized the obvious struggles of the wounded desperately trying to escape.

O'Doyle stood, switched his EBR back to single-shot. He turned and offered it to Sanji.

"Trade me," he said.

Sanji took the rifle, handed over the Glock.

Bertha watched Patrick reach to his chest, pulled the Ka-Bar from its sheath. He held the knife in his left hand, the Glock in his right.

He looked at her.

"You okay?"

She nodded, remembered the crescent blade slicing her. She reached up, felt at her cheek. It burned. Her fingers came away bloody, but not that bloody.

"I'm fine," she said.

He nodded once. "We have to finish the job, and we have to conserve ammo. You ready?"

His eyes bore the remorseless look of a cold-blooded killer. How could she have thought herself in love with him? But she understood: this had to be done. No way of knowing what else those things were capable of. Cut off from the surface, Patrick wasn't taking any chances, even if that meant he had to brutally dispatch the wounded.

She handed her rifle to Reeves, who stared, stunned, shocked. Bertha reached out and took the Glock from her hand. No snotty comment from Reeves this time. No, not when she saw what life was really like.

Bertha held the Glock in her right hand. With her left, she drew her own Ka-Bar.

She looked at Patrick, nodded.

He stepped close to the nearest rocktopi. A half-stuffed, yellowish-brown garbage bag, still moving. Faint colors flickered across skin that had blazed like a lighthouse beacon only moments earlier. He aimed his Glock at it, stretched out his foot until his toe rested on a double-crescent knife. He slid that foot backward, pulling the blade away, metal scraping loudly on gritty stone.

Bertha suddenly wanted him to leave it alone, let it crawl away, or die, or whatever. Wasn't this awful enough already?

Patrick crouched, closed in, blade out in front of him.

The creature let out a soft noise, a hiss more than a squeal. It sprouted new tentacles, tentacles that gripped the stone slab and tried to pull its body away from Patrick—an amoeba reaching out, desperate for life.

Patrick slashed, a flick of the wrist, opening up a long line that spurted thick yellow. Tentacles spasmed, vibrated, quivered. The thing *deflated*, lifeblood gushed out onto the stone.

A pulse of yellow—KoolSuit yellow, she noticed—waved across its skin, then faded out.

It squeaked, a tone that would have sounded cute if it were made by a cuddly animal or a dog toy.

A thick smell billowed up: rotting meat mixed with hot tar.

O'Doyle gagged, convulsed once, covered his mouth with the back of the hand that held the Glock.

Bertha heard Sanji vomit: once, twice, a third time.

The creature fell still. No noise. No light.

Patrick stepped toward the next one, stopped, turned to Bertha. He gestured to one close to her, still twitching, and with one word told her it was time.

"Well?"

She nodded. They were fighting to survive. She wasn't going to leave him hanging, make him do all the black work.

Time to step up.

Bertha walked to her victim. Yellow globs bubbled up from bullet holes. The skin glowed *black*, something she wouldn't have thought possible until now. It wasn't crawling for its life, because it couldn't— tentacles half formed, shrank back, half formed again.

In her younger days, she'd had a bumper sticker on her car: *Join the Army! Travel to foreign places, meet exotic peoples, and kill them.*

Didn't get more exotic than something that wasn't even a person at all.

She gave her head a hard shake. Not a time for a crisis of conscience. They were three miles underground in a place so hot they'd die without these suits. Three of her fellow guards were dead. And these things had thrown a knife at her—if she hadn't moved when she did, that blade would have punched into her face.

Bertha sighed, stepped toward the creature.

"Sucks to be you," she said.

She raised the Ka-Bar.

Before she brought it down, the rocktopi started to squeal.

Bertha Lybrand would never forget that noise. It would echo through her thoughts for the rest of her life.

11:18 P.M.

Angus crouched low, by the tunnel wall. Randy was in front of him, also down low—just as shocked, just as surprised.

"I think that was gunfire," he whispered.

The rolling echo had finally faded away. Thirty meters ahead, a boulder that mostly blocked the end of the tunnel. Beyond that boulder, *light*. Not a halogen, not portable of any kind, but something stronger. Something bigger.

Something that shouldn't be there.

Randy turned, leaned close. *Too* close, like he always did.

"Angus, do you think that was gunfire?"

"I don't know," Angus hissed. "How the fuck would I know?"

Sometimes Randy asked obvious questions. And he always—*always*—thought Angus had all the answers. Most often, Angus did. Not this time, though.

Randy seemed as freaked-out as Angus felt, although Angus wasn't going to show it. Randy glanced to the boulder and the light beyond.

"Should we go up there? We have to see what that light is, don't we?"

Just once Angus would have liked the guy to make up his own fucking mind. No matter what happened, Angus always had to make the decisions.

If that had been gunfire—and Angus was sure it had been—then who was firing? And who were they firing *at*?

"Oh, shit," he said. "Randy, give me the tablet."

Randy slid his pack around, handed it over.

Angus tapped the Marco/Polo app. The app activated the RFID ping. He watched the screen, waiting for results.

Six names popped up, with six corresponding soft *dings*.

"*Six?*" Randy said. He reached for the tablet. "Who is it?"

Angus slapped his hand away, quietly read off the names.

"Reeves, Haak, Lybrand, O'Doyle, Hendricks and Mister Giant Cock-Face himself."

Randy sucked in a hiss of breath.

"*Kirkland* is down here? This far?"

For such a smart man, Randy asked so many stupid questions.

Angus tapped the screen, looked at the vital signs. Randy leaned in to look.

The pulse and heart rates of Kirkland and the others were racing, all except for O'Doyle, who was normal in both categories. Temperature steady across the board—the suits were working fine, of course.

"They're excited," Randy said. "And look at the beta waves—aside from Mack, everyone's readings are through the roof. Like they were in a fight. Maybe they were the ones doing the shooting?"

Or being shot *at*, although only an incredibly stupid person would shoot at Patrick O'Doyle.

Angus understood Reeves and Haak being down here, and Mack, of course. Maybe even Lybrand and O'Doyle, to protect the staff, but Kirkland? Angus had fantasized that Kirkland might be the one to find all the KILROY WAS HERE signs. Now, Angus didn't want that at all, because it seemed that Kirkland had reached the kidney-shaped cavern *before* he had.

That wasn't how this was supposed to go. That mother*fucker* could not have been the first one down here. He just could *not*.

"Let's move up," Angus said. "But be real quiet."

Randy crawled toward the boulder, Angus close behind. Together, they slowly rose up and peeked over the top.

Angus Kool was a man of science. He'd seen many amazing things in his years, even discovered a few that no one before him had ever known. He'd walked in places no human being had ever walked. If anyone on Earth could have been prepared to witness something this unprecedented, he knew it should have been him. And yet, staring over that boulder, he had trouble comprehending what his eyes showed him. His logic failed him, as did his vocabulary.

"What the fuck?"

Randy nodded slowly. "Yeah," he said, which wasn't any kind of an answer at all.

They were at one end of the massive kidney-shaped cavern. It curved slightly off to the right, growing wider and taller before bending back to the left. The walls arched high overhead until they met at the center, but the zenith couldn't be seen due to the blazing light there that illuminated the cavern with a strange, bluish hue. The cavern stretched away so far they couldn't make out details at the far end. Acre upon acre of never-before-seen plants grew in orderly rows. A river curved softly, water rippling but mostly calm. Near the cavern's center, a small village of dilapidated stone buildings, crumbling like the ruins of some ancient Aztec temple.

That bluish light reflected dully off small, moving bits of metal — silverbugs, crawling through the crops, along the riverbanks and down ... were those *paths*? Yes, paths that wound through the strange fields and around the strange trees. There was even a bridge over the river, a bridge that gleamed with the soft warmth of precious metal.

A bridge of platinum.

"Angus, what is all of this?"

Angus shook his head, not caring, for once, that Randy was asking yet another stupid question.

And then, he forgot about the question, forgot about Randy, forgot about *everything*, because the "villagers" showed themselves.

They came down the path, shapes that didn't make sense. Limbs forming, extending ... living, pulsing, moving like multicolored fractals. Soft bodies flowing in a way that mammals could not, that insects could not, in a way that made Angus think of jellyfish or a swimming feather star, of the pulsating, hypnotic patterns of a hunting cuttlefish.

"I don't ..." Randy said.

"It's, can't ... they aren't ..." Angus answered.

"But aren't they ..." Randy said. "How can it?"

In the tiny parts of his brain still capable of rational thought, Angus knew that he and his best friend had just set the bar for the stupidest conversation of all time.

Some of the creatures moved quickly, tentacles stretching out at crazy speeds. Others moved slowly, assisted by others.

"Wounded," Randy said. More rational now, perhaps he was regaining the intelligence smacked away by an eyeful of the impossible. "Maybe from the gunfire."

Angus nodded absently.

The column of creatures flowed across the bridge and into the village. They spread out. The slower-moving ones were helped into buildings. Still more of the creatures spread out, occasionally piping up with a screech reminiscent of a diamond saw slicing through a core sample.

"Angus … are we looking at aliens?"

Angus nodded absently again, although he wasn't sure if he was *still* doing that and hadn't stopped from before.

"Maybe," he said. Definitive, and with authority. Because that was how a genius rolled, right?

He tore his attention away from the bizarre visage, looked around the cavern. Past the trees and fields, stone walls sloping up at steep angles. In those walls—and not just at ground level, but all over, some two or even three hundred feet off the ground—were hundreds of dark spots.

Tunnel entrances.

The metallic flashes came faster—the silverbugs were moving, moving fast. They formed a line from the village toward the bridge, the same way the boneless beings of light had come. Angus expected them to do that jerking thing, the up-and-down thing, but they didn't. The flashing creatures reacted though, their patterns shifting from dozens of colors and patterns to pulsing waves of orange and red.

"Those squid-things are holding something metallic," Randy said. He reached into his webbing, pulled out a small pair of binoculars. He focused in.

"Oh my God, those are *knives*," he said. "Some kind of double-bladed thing. I don't see any guns. These creatures must have attacked our people. That's the only thing that makes sense."

Angus felt numb. Numb, and *stupid*—a feeling he was most unfamiliar with. *Our people?* What the hell was Randy talking about?

"There's more silverbugs," Randy said. "They're carrying something."

He pressed the binoculars against Angus's chest, hard enough to make Angus take a step back to maintain his balance. Randy pointed off at an angle to the right.

It was ridiculous to get angry at Randy, especially *now*, of all the times, but he was getting angry nonetheless. Aliens or monsters or whatever they were, Randy was being … well, he was being *pushy*.

Angus needed to let that go, needed to be logical. He looked through the binocs in the direction Randy wanted.

Silverbugs, *hordes* of them, all pressed together, platinum liquid flowing between the crumbling stone buildings. Like an army of cartoon ants pilfering a picnic basket, they carried what looked to be long, thin sheets of steel.

The red and orange creatures swarmed in, lifted the sheets away from the machines.

The line of silverbugs leading to the bridge started to jerk, to twitch — that sickening down-up-down dance.

Angus had seen enough. He didn't know what was going on, and he really didn't want to find out. This wasn't *discovery*, this wasn't *science*, this was Cthulhu nightmares carrying big-ass knives, this was high-tech platinum ALs jerking away like dogs humping a leg. It was wrong, all of it, and he didn't want to deal with it for one moment longer.

He slid back down behind the boulder. Randy didn't follow. What an asshole. Angus grabbed his webbing, pulled him down.

"We need to get back to the surface," Angus said. "I mean like right fucking now. Let's get the hell out of here."

Randy's lip curled up, and this time, he wasn't looking through binoculars. He was looking right at Angus. Not *near* Angus, not at the floor, but eye to eye, *hard* — something Randy just didn't do.

"We have to get the others," Randy said. "You know we do."

The *others*? It took Angus a second to understand what he meant.

"No," Angus said. "*Fuck* no we don't."

Randy leaned closer. Behind thick lenses, his eyes narrowed. Angus leaned away.

"We are going to *help them*," Randy said. "Understand me? You and me, together, we're going to help them."

The tone of voice, the intensity … this wasn't Randy, not the Randy he knew. This was like a completely different person. He was serious about helping those stupid fucks?

Angus tried to stare back, tried to overpower Randy the way he had done so many times before. The effort lasted all of a second, then Angus felt his face flush hot as he looked away.

He, looked *away*, from fucking *Dirty Randy*.

The heat, the stress, seeing those crazy things. Randy was wigging out, that was all. Angus could manage that. Get Randy back to the surface, everything would be back to normal. He wanted to help? Okay, Angus had a way to do that.

"There's a thumper update coming up in a few minutes," Angus said. "We can use the portable thumper to send a message back, have the surface system broadcast one of our pre-programmed SOS messages."

Randy's eyes softened slightly.

"Which message?"

There, that was more like it.

"Well, I didn't happen to program a message for *Hostile Tentacle-Creatures Swinging Big Knives,* but situation fourteen seems to be the best."

Randy thought, nodded.

"Armed claim jumpers," he said. "That will get the authorities out here on the double. The surface should be crawling with SWAT teams and Utah State Troopers inside thirty minutes. Good call."

"Goddamn right it is," Angus said. "So get it done."

Randy scrambled to do just that, whipping off his backpack and pulling out the small portable thumper.

Control. Angus had control again. He clung to the emotion, took strength from it. The situation was insane, but at least having control felt familiar, *normal.*

He slid the tablet into his backpack, then rose up slowly, leaned an elbow against the boulder, watched through the binoculars as Randy started setting the portable thumper up on its collapsible tripod legs.

The boneless creatures, the glowing fractals … they were along the line of twitching silverbugs. A hundred of them, maybe, carrying three of four sheets of the steel. They carried them to a tunnel entrance.

Randy, at his right, again taking the binoculars, again *not asking for them.*

Angus watched the column sweep into that dark space, briefly lighting the entrance with oranges and reds, until they vanished inside. The dark shadow returned.

Through the elbow leaning on the boulder, he felt a rhythmic vibration: the portable thumper's hammer banging out a rapid, complex dance—sending a message instead of just receiving one. The vibrations lasted only seconds.

"Packing up," Randy said. He handed the binoculars over. Angus took them, looked at them oddly, as if they were somehow responsible for this bizarre situation.

Randy started collapsing the portable thumper.

"Good," Angus said. "Now we can get the fuck out of here."

He turned back to the boulder. He stared through the binoculars for a few more seconds. The few squishy creatures that remained were lying in the village, either twitching slightly or completely still.

Angus felt a tugging at his backpack. He spun around, but Randy already had the tablet in his hands.

"We're not leaving," Randy said. His fingertip tapped madly at the screen.

"God*dammit*. Enough of this bullshit. Give me the fucking tablet, *right now*."

Randy paused in mid-tap. He glared over the black rims of his glasses.

"Angus, I'm going to tell you something I should have told you a long, long time ago," Randy said. "If you don't shut your motherfucking mouth, I'm going to hurt you."

Randy held that stare another moment, until fear blossomed in Angus's chest, until he imagined Randy's fists smashing into his mouth, his nose, his throat.

Angus sat down.

Randy started tapping the screen again.

The rage didn't build inside Angus, it exploded all at once. Rage and frustration and humiliation, because Angus wanted to kick that asshole in the balls but he couldn't do it, because Randy would then *get up*, and he would beat Angus, just like the kids in school had beat him, over and over and over again. Angus hated them, hated feeling weak, hated *Randy*.

In that moment, that flush-faced moment where he felt small and weak and helpless and stupid, felt like a *loser*, he wanted Randy Wright to die. He wanted it with everything that he was.

"Got it," Randy said. "I mapped the Polo signals. Kirkland and the others are about two hundred feet up. That tunnel the glowing creatures went into, it's part of a series that may lead to Connell and the others. I think the creatures are going after them."

He looked up from the screen, stared down at Angus. This time, Angus couldn't look away, even though he wanted to.

"We're going to help them," Randy said. "You and I. Together."

Angus felt like a worm, a crawling worm that wanted to burrow away from the light. He hadn't felt like this since high school. And the reason for that feeling was Randy Wright, his supposed *best friend*.

Had Angus really been whining about wanting someone else to make the decisions? Because Randy had just made one, and Angus didn't like it.

Not one fucking bit.

Randy reached down, offered his hand.

"I know you're scared," he said. "I'm scared, too. But we have to do the right thing. We have to help. Are you with me?"

No, I'm not with you, you backstabbing asshole. You'll pay for this shit. I gave you everything and you bully me? You'll learn.

Angus clasped the offered hand.

"You know it, buddy," he said. "With you all the way."

Randy smiled. He pulled Angus to his feet.

11:19 P.M.

On the surface, the thumpers' sensitive seismic sensors picked up the tiny repetitive throbbing from below. All six of the thumpers processed the message, read the instructions contained within.

As a unit, they beamed a sync signal to cue up their efforts and began broadcasting the pre-programmed *Situation Report No. 14* on all radio frequencies.

11:23 P.M.

After three rings, a groggy-voiced André Vogel answered the phone. "Hello?"

"André, did I wake you?"

A pause.

"Who is this?"

"You don't recognize my voice?"

Another pause. Kayla smiled, trying to picture the look on the man's face.

"Meyers," he said. No more grogginess. "I don't believe it. You know damn well that using restricted access codes to reach me is a federal offense."

Kayla's anger bubbled just from the sound of his voice, but she stayed calm.

"I've got a matter of national importance," she said. "Please hear me out. I only need two minutes."

André Vogel had come up through the ranks, starting out as a computer analyst, eventually moving into the field and finally earning the powerful role of NSA director. Vogel answered to only one person: the secretary of defense.

"You've got a lot of balls calling me, Meyers," Vogel said. "But then you always did have balls. Since this is the only chance you're going to get, go ahead."

"I've found something that will make your career."

A huff, the sound of a man who was already in a top position of power and didn't need any help.

"And that is?"

"It's not that easy, André," Kayla said, trying hard to keep her tone respectful. "There are conditions."

"Well, give me an idea of what this wondrous piece of information is and we'll haggle over a price. I can't believe you wouldn't go through normal freelance channels on this."

"It's not about the land of sand and oil or any of that penny-ante bullshit," Kayla said. "This is the biggest thing you've ever heard of."

"Of course it is." Vogel was fully awake now, that familiar growl back in his voice. "I'm assuming that since you didn't go through the usual channels, this isn't your usual price."

"It's not," Kayla said. "This is big, beyond anything we've seen before. It's not money I want."

She heard a rustling sound, wondered if he was rubbing at the corner of his squeezed-shut eyes with thumb and forefinger, the way he did when he got pissed.

"You're wasting my time," he said. "If you don't want money, what do you want?"

"I want back in."

"Back in what?"

Kayla looked at the handset as if *it* were stupid. She had to be patient, see this through. Not the time to get angry. She took a deep breath, put the handset back to her ear.

"I want my life back," she said. "I want to be reinstated to the NSA."

Another pause, this one so long she wondered if he'd just hung up without a sound. She found herself chewing at her thumbnail.

"That will never happen," he said, his words clipped. "You don't know how lucky you are to even be alive."

Her frustration welled up, started to bully her thoughts around. So hard to focus, to keep kissing this fool's ass. She had to keep playing the game.

"So I sold some information to a corporation," she said. "So what? It didn't hurt anything. No harm, no foul."

"You know damn well that's not why you got the boot."

The anger, the frustration, the humiliation, they all combined forces, rushed up from her lungs through her throat and out her mouth.

"*Yes it is*, Vogel. Because I'm a woman. When *men* did the same thing, you didn't kick *them* out. You think I don't know what it was really about? Your damn boys' club couldn't handle that I was better than everyone else!"

She heard him clear his throat—something he did when he was even angrier than when he rubbed his eyes, something he did when *he* was trying to control his temper. The sound chilled her, made her feel like she was ten years old again, hiding in her room, waiting for her father to come punish her for some trivial offense.

"I'm going to tell you this one time, and one time only," he said. "Because I don't think you're ever going to get it, but when I write you off for good, I want to know in my heart that you *know* the truth. You didn't get kicked out for selling secrets to Genada, Meyers. No one gives a shit about that. You got kicked out because of those children."

She blinked, not comprehending.

"What children?"

Whatever control Vogel had, it disintegrated, shattered by his roar.

"*The children you tortured,* you sick fuck! I saw the pictures. You and those goddamn *pliers*. What state secrets did you think a *nine-year-old girl* would have? You're a psychopath. They wanted to put you down like the animal you are, and you know what? I'm the one that stopped them. And every night when I go to sleep, I see those pictures in my head, the girl and her seven-year-old brother—fucking *seven years old*—and I know I made a mistake."

Was Vogel drunk? Did he think she was really stupid enough to believe this was about that mission in Kiev? Ridiculous. She'd got the information she'd been sent to get, so what else mattered? She vaguely remembered hearing something about "the children" when he shit-canned her, but that was just smoke and mirrors to hide his real reasons.

She felt a sharp pain in her thumb, pulled it away from her mouth. Blood trickled down. She'd bitten the nail, torn it down to the quick until it split the skin.

Think, girl, think. She had him on the phone. She wouldn't get him back, not ever.

"I found a new species," she said. Not what she had wanted to say. Not what she had practiced saying. The words had just come out.

When he spoke again, it was the worst of all his voices. With André Vogel, Director of the NSA, anger came in three phases: exasperation, then yelling, then the quiet monotone.

"A new species," he said.

He wasn't asking a question, he was simply repeating it as if to make sure he'd heard her correctly.

"Yes, I know, but listen." Her words rushed out like she was trying to say something—anything—to stop Cyrus from getting the belt. "It's an *intelligent* species. I've never seen anything like it, no one has. They attacked a camp I was watching. They killed people, they killed *Americans*. It's a new discovery and a threat to national security. You can take this straight to the president."

The COMSEC unit's soft beep drew her attention. It had just completed its periodic frequency sweep—it had isolated a clear transmission signal.

"I've known you for a long time," Vogel said. "You're a psycho, but you don't bullshit. Do you have proof?"

She stared blankly at the COMSEC unit, checking the readout and not believing what she saw. At the same time, she realized she'd watched that entire attack and hadn't shot any video. Not a single frame.

"Meyers, you better have proof. You don't just—"

"I'll get your fucking proof," she said, then broke the connection.

Everything was falling apart.

She reread the message on the COMSEC's display.

"Angus," she said. Now it was her voice that came out as a monotone. "Angus Kool, you fucking little prick."

Kayla shut down the COMSEC unit, detached the main controller. Built that way, built to be portable. Without the extra power and signal amplifier, the range was much shorter, but she didn't need a lot of range for what came next.

She knew exactly where to begin.

27

15,506 feet below the surface

11:29 P.M.

Mack shook his head. "Honestly, for inexperienced climbers, it's a recipe for disaster. If we use all the rope, tie off the harnesses, we *could* descend two at a time. But even if we make it safely, what are we going to do when we get down there?"

Patrick looked out at the sprawling cavern. Mack had a point. They'd seen the creatures—"rocktopi" everyone had taken to calling them—massing in that village. Few visible now, though. They were either hiding or, more likely, massing for another attack.

If Patrick and the others descended the cliff's vertical face, they'd be visible the whole way. The rocktopi would see them, probably be waiting at the bottom.

"All right," he said. "Go keep watch at the tunnel mouth for a while. Tell Lybrand to take a break."

Mack nodded—slowly, still suffering the effects of that blow to the head—then walked off.

Patrick mulled over the party's situation. This cave made for a defensible position—the narrowing walls acted as a funnel, forcing the rocktopi together, making it easy to mow them down. A good spot to wait while his people recovered. In the tunnels, though, it would be a different story. The enemy could come from the front, or from behind, or from the *sides* if there were big enough cracks in the walls.

Still, he had to get his people out of there. The enemy knew where they were. But the choices sucked: either back into the tunnels or down that cliff face.

Kirkland was sleeping. Good man. He'd lost his shit at the beginning of the firefight, but he'd done fine once the bullets started flying. Patrick would make a warrior out of him yet. Kirkland was favoring that knee, though. And that seemed to be getting worse.

Veronica and Sanji were in the process of examining a dead rocktopi. They crouched over the mutilated carcass. Sanji had cut into the creature, peeled the hide back. Rocks weighed down the thick skin, exposing multicolored guts.

Patrick was dreading this talk. Reeves had studied this culture for years. She'd hit the jackpot, as near as Patrick could figure; she'd want to talk to the creatures, work out a way to communicate. And Sanji, a biology professor—without question, he'd want to preserve life, do anything possible to avoid more killing.

This was a fight for survival: not the time for liberal sympathies.

Patrick walked to them. The *smell* of those things. Bad enough when they were in one piece, far worse with holes cut into that weird skin. He peered over Sanji's shoulder at the strange creature's body. Patrick had seen countless combat wounds in his day, men torn to pieces, organs everywhere ... but nothing like this. Rocktopi guts were thick and stringy, punctuated by colored lumps. The yellow blood had congealed, then started to separate—pale yellow fluid with chunks of darker yellow globs, like rancid cottage cheese.

"You two find anything that will help us?"

Sanji's wide eyes never left the corpse, but Veronica looked up. Fatigue pulled at her face. Thick streaks of goo covered her hands and forearms.

"I don't know what good this will do," she said. She sounded beaten, both mentally and physically.

"Every little bit helps," Patrick said softly. "We need to know as much as we can."

She sighed and looked over at Sanji. He was oblivious to anything but the rocktopi's innards, sifting through slime and unknown body parts.

Veronica lifted a chunk of hide and tossed it to O'Doyle. He stared at the ragged cube of flesh. It felt thick and firm, yet pliant, like relaxed elastic. It stretched easily, with all the resistance of a rubber band. The outer skin appeared to comprise many tightly packed fibers.

"No bones, obviously," she said. "That membrane is both skin and support structure. Poke a big enough hole in it—" she gestured to the flattened rocktopi dotting the cave floor "—and that's all she wrote."

Patrick noticed a thin film on the skin, slightly sticky to the touch. "What's this slimy stuff?"

"Rot," Sanji said. "The tissue is already breaking down. That could explain how we didn't find any remains of them in the old burial site, or at Cerro Chaltén—their bodies dissolve before any kind of natural preservation can take place."

Patrick dropped the chunk of skin. He wiped the tacky slime off on his pants leg.

"We've identified a stomach," Sanji said. "Full of fibrous plant material. And the equivalent of intestines, as well as an anus and a mouth, although I only know that because one orifice has teeth. The brain appears to be at body-center, and it is quite large, but I'm sure you guessed that based on the fact that they use advanced weapons and have developed agriculture."

"First thing that crossed my mind," Patrick said.

"We're not sure if they have a heart or they circulate blood via tension from their whole body," Sanji said. "The rocktopi are basically big bags of liquid. Most of the organs escape known classification."

Up until that moment, Patrick hadn't considered the creatures' origin. They were trying to kill him and his people, so he was going to kill them first. That was how he'd lived much of his life, so why was this any different? Survival first, everything else, second.

"They're so different," he said. "Are they aliens or something?"

Veronica stood, wiped off her hands.

"Of course they're fucking aliens," she said. "What else could they be?"

Sanji lifted a bit of flesh that looked half-blue, half-translucent. He closed one eye, squinted at it like a jeweler examining a rare stone.

"Aliens come to earth, bury themselves three miles belowground and never make contact with humans," he said. "Even when human culture travels to the stars? An advanced race that brings a knife to a gunfight, so to speak. Sounds rather unlikely, don't you think? Another possibility, also unlikely but *less so*, is that these creatures could be extremophiles."

Veronica rolled her eyes. "And I could be Marilyn Monroe."

"Extremophiles," Patrick said. "What is that?"

Sanji tossed the bit of flesh away, started digging for more. The finger splints made his motions awkward. He winced repeatedly, but didn't slow.

"Life that lives in extreme environments," he said. "Mostly, in places science once thought no life could exist. It's possible these creatures evolved along some divergent branch and we have never seen them because they live so deep underground. Remember that humans have never been this far below the surface before."

Veronica pointed to the cavern roof, to the blazing light up there. "They evolved on Earth. Right. With no known species even remotely resembling them. And they developed technology for artificial light that lets their *also* never-before-seen plants undergo some form of photosynthesis? And then there are the silverbugs—advanced robotics, yet those, too, have never been seen? Do you have an answer for that, Pops?"

Sanji shrugged. "I don't. But just because that tech is here doesn't mean they made it. Who is to say the government didn't discover these creatures long ago and set all this up to study them? Maybe someone found this primitive-but-intelligent life-form, at the level of Denisovans, perhaps, or Idaltu."

Patrick blinked.

"How about we pretend I have no idea what you brainiacs are talking about, and use words we working stiffs can understand?"

"*Cavemen*," Veronica said. "My father wonders if someone found the squid version of cavemen and tried to slowly bring them up to modern standards."

Sanji sorted through the body parts, found another chunk of skin. He held it up for all to see.

"They appear to fight among themselves," he said. "In many places the membrane, which has a rough, fibrous pattern, as you see, is criss-crossed with random straight lines."

Patrick leaned closer, saw the lines.

"Scars?"

Sanji nodded. "Probably. Could be indicative of infighting, perhaps even tribal warfare. An indication of a primitive culture. Perhaps some-one discovered this species, kept it secret, tried to help them advance until they were at a level where people could meet them?"

Veronica rolled her eyes.

Sanji might know science, but he knew jack shit about how the real world worked. If the government had been behind this—or any private enterprise, for that matter—EarthCore would have never been allowed to set up shop.

Nothing made sense.

"If only we could ask them," Sanji said. "A simple dialogue would help so much."

And there it was. Time to address the elephant in the room.

"Professors, I want you to understand what we're up against. We're not going to risk anyone's safety to try to talk to them. We're not even going to give up ground. If they come close enough to kill, I'm killing them."

Sanji and Veronica seemed confused.

"Wait a minute," she said. "Do you think we want to sit down and have a powwow with them or something?"

She said it like it was the dumbest thing she'd ever heard.

"Well, yeah. I just assumed you'd want to communicate with them."

"You assumed wrong," Sanji said. "We can worry about communi-cation when we're safely on the surface."

Veronica shook her head. "Thought we'd be Hollywood professors and say something like *don't you dare kill another one of them?* We want to live, dummy. You watch too many movies."

He felt relieved. He also felt a little silly.

"Good to know. Any other info?"

Sanji gestured to the deflated corpses.

"Just that they seem far from healthy," he said. "Even with a brief glance, every one of these creatures appear to have lesions, internal growths that might be some form of cancer, probable skin diseases, et cetera. I don't know enough to make an educated guess, so my *unedu-cated* guess is congenital defects."

Patrick glanced at the yellow cottage cheese and old spaghetti mess spread across the stone, wondering how Sanji could make sense of any of it.

"Congenital? You mean birth defects?"

Sanji nodded. "Difficult to tell with a creature never before studied, of course. Could be caused by radiation exposure, or viral or bacterial infections, but my hunch is that these are congenital defects caused by excessive inbreeding. They've been down here for thousands of years with no apparent contact with outside members of their species. Unless they have a way of reaching other populations, or the population in this complex is *much* larger than it appears, the gene pool would eventually grow stagnant. If their reproductive strategy is at all like the vast majority of species on this planet, regular breeding with close relatives increases the chance that offspring will be affected by recessive or deleterious traits."

Patrick held up a hand. "Working stiffs, remember?"

"Fucking your cousin is bad," Veronica said. "Sisters and brothers, worse. Do that over repetitive generations, people get dumber and more diseased. Like in Kentucky."

"I'm from Kentucky," Patrick said.

Veronica nodded. "Well, there you go."

"You're a real asshole, Doctor Reeves."

"You're not the first to say that," she said. She turned to Sanji. "Come to think of it, those first three we saw were kids—could the one that acted slow, or oddly, could that have been some form of intellectual disability? Maybe caused by inbreeding?"

"Very possible," Sanji said. "But if that young one *was* handicapped, the others were caring for it. That indicates a culture where they look out for each other. Fascinating."

Patrick tuned out the pair's babble. He glanced at Lybrand. She was sitting near Mack. She saw Patrick looking at her, looked away quick, pretended to busy herself with her sidearm.

What was her problem?

The action, of course. She'd fought fucking *monsters*, that was her problem, that was everyone's problem. Combat against people was stressful enough. Against these things? Another level.

Best to give her space. She'd be fine soon enough. As for Kirkland, though, Patrick didn't know.

"Doctor Reeves, could you do me a favor and go talk to Connell?"

She glanced at Kirkland. "He's asleep."

"He needs to wake up," Patrick said.

"What am I supposed to talk to him *about*? Who the Lakers are going to pick up in free agency?"

Patrick glared at her. "He was just in a battle. He killed squid-cavemen, or aliens, or whatever they are, and he helped keep us alive. He's never fought before, never even fired a gun. So how about you stow your shitty attitude and see how he's doing?"

Veronica bit her lip. A wash of emotions caressed her face: wide-eyed fear, mixing with some internal rage.

"Yeah, sure," she said. "Sorry."

She walked over to him.

Unlike Kirkland, Patrick had plenty of combat experience. He'd seen people break under stress more times than he could remember. It was just a thing you developed a knack for, a way of knowing who might become a liability, who you could count on if you wanted to stay alive. He'd survived hundreds of missions—that knack was a key reason for his survival.

And that knack told him Veronica Reeves was damn close to the edge.

11:34 P.M.

Veronica had no idea what to say to Connell, but if she could do something to actually contribute to their survival, she had to do it. Her knowledge was useless down here. A life pursuing this exact culture, yet nothing she'd learned had any application at all.

For fuck's sake, she'd thought the Chaltélians were *human.*

If she did get out of here, she was going to be a laughing stock. Well, she deserved to be.

She knelt next to Connell. She glanced back out at the cavern, taking in the crops, the houses ... and entire culture, waiting to be explored. The artificial sun made her squint against the brightness. That thing in the Picture Cavern ceiling ... that must have been a sun that burned out. Maybe that's why the monsters had abandoned it—some places are too dark, even for creatures of light.

She gently shook Connell.

He sat up in a snap, eyes wide, hands grabbing for his rifle.

"It's okay," she said. "It's okay, they're not here."

She was surprised to find her left hand grabbing his shoulder, her right cupping his cheek.

He blinked, confused. Recognition slowly set in. Chest heaving, he looked around the cave, out at the cavern.

"Sorry," he said.

"Don't worry about it. O'Doyle said you need to wake up."

Connell nodded. He slid to the wall, rested his back against it. He clutched the rifle tightly against his chest, like a child holding a teddy bear against the night's shadowy demons.

She scooted over, sat next to him.

"How do you feel?"

"Like I killed something," he said instantly. "Like we saw something wonderful and amazing, and I killed it."

She put her hand on his knee. "So it wouldn't kill you. Or me. Or any of us."

He looked at her, eyes hollow and haunted. He wasn't on the verge of tears but wasn't far from it, either.

"I guess so," he said. "Do you have any water?"

She got a bottle from her backpack, handed it to him. He drank, long and deep.

"Thanks," he said. "What about you? I know we're in a shitty situation and all, but aren't you at least a little excited? Seems like this is the discovery of a lifetime."

She nodded. "It is. Just not *my* lifetime. Seems kind of obvious now, doesn't it? The caves, the depth, the heat, the lack of human remains. I thought it was just some lost tribe. Pretty stupid, eh?"

Connell snorted. "Because the evidence just screamed *boneless neon creatures from hell*, right? Give me a break, Reeves. That's like me saying I should have known pursuing this find would have me paranoid about robot spiders, petrified something will tear my suit so I'll cook to death, and shooting these . . . *things* . . . just to stay alive."

Veronica looked at him. Really looked at him. He'd always been clean-shaven. Now a day's growth of stubble lined his jaw. Made him look more rugged. Even more handsome. She'd watched him open fire on the rocktopi. Two days ago, she would have thought a guy like Connell Kirkland would fold at the first hint of danger. She'd been wrong.

There was more to him than she'd thought. Probably more than *he* thought, too.

She put her arm around him.

He tensed up, then his body seemed to deflate as if someone had pulled a plug and let all the stress flow out of his body. He sagged against her, head resting heavily on her shoulder.

Mack's voice—loud, urgent—broke her reverie.

"O'Doyle, we've got problems!"

She looked up at Mack, who knelt before the tunnel mouth. Then she heard it—heard the sound that in a few hours had become synonymous with fear.

click click, click-click-click . . .

11:36 P.M.

Kayla read the dial on the portable SIGINT unit.

She looked around for any sign of movement, for strangely colored lights. The monsters had struck without warning—would they do so again?

No sign of them.

Kayla moved the unit slowly from left to right, the signal needle swinging to the red when it pointed toward the as-yet-unseen transmitter. She turned back again, making sure she had the direction correct, then walked forward.

That fucking little prick.

She came around a small boulder, and—finally—she found it. A metallic, pyramid-like device maybe ten inches tall: a stainless-steel hydraulic piston that had already pounded a three-inch-deep hole into the rocky ground; a trio of seismic sensors, one mounted at the base of each tripod leg; a small, rubber-encased industrial computer; and, of course, a motherfucking radio transmitter.

If anyone had received his message, if the police or rescue teams or—God forbid, the media—found out about the monsters, well, then she was screwed. Everything hinged on secrecy, on André being the one who controlled the information.

Angus, you fucking little prick.

How could she have missed it for this long? The answer was obvious—until a few hours ago, Angus's device didn't stay on all the time. It cycled, signaling every six hours and then only for a few seconds. A hard signal to catch, but that didn't make her feel any better. When it came to signals intelligence, she was the chosen one. At one time the U.S. government considered her the *best in the world.* To be outfoxed by a cock-sucking scientist was simply too much.

Angus Kool had invented a way to communicate with the surface from who knew how far underground. The system also probably served some mapping function, like an underground GPS with the pyramid devices taking the place of satellites. If that was the case, there were more of these things, at least two more for triangulation purposes. And she'd have to track down every single one. How long would that take?

Kayla had underestimated him.

She reached into the pyramid and yanked the antennae from the transmitter. Maybe the device would yield some information. She would take it back to her warren, examine it, but later—first, she had to find the rest of that fucking little prick's handiwork.

11:42 P.M.

Mack Hendricks lay on his belly, staring through the narrow opening. Lybrand on his right, rifle in her hands, her headlamp beam glinting off the line of convulsing silverbugs that stretched down the tunnel.

He pointed to the nearest robot, not even five meters away. "Shoot it. Make them run."

She shook her head.

"We can't waste the ammo."

Before he could argue, he felt a big hand on his shoulder.

"Get to the cliff," O'Doyle said, calm but firm. "You're in the firing zone."

A place Mack certainly did not want to be. He pushed himself up, felt his head swim with a new wash of dizziness and thick agony. He stumbled, stayed on his feet only thanks to O'Doyle's help. The world swam.

"We have him." Sanji's voice. More hands.

"Mack, sit down, take it easy." Veronica's voice.

Mack sat. His head cleared. He sat a meter shy of the cliff's edge. Veronica knelt next to him. Sanji stood close, pistol in hand.

Lybrand hadn't moved. O'Doyle knelt on one side of her, Kirkland on the other. Three people dressed in dirty yellow suits and combat webbing, rifles in hand, blue helmets on their heads.

From his position, Mack could see past them down the tunnel—the darkness was already giving way to flashes of color.

"Thirty meters," Lybrand said.

The clicks and whirs of the machines. The scraping, dead-leaf sound of the rocktopi, like the dry hissing of a poisonous snake. Screeches poked at the air, needles punched into his eardrums. And that *stench*— runny dog shit blended with rotting kiwi.

Kirkland turned to O'Doyle.

"Firing line?"

"Not yet." O'Doyle sounded as calm as if they were all sitting around a card table on a summer afternoon, drinking beers. He reached down, patted Lybrand's shoulder. "One shot. Give them something to think about."

She adjusted her position, sighted.

The rifle's sharp report, and in almost the same instant, a *clank* of metal on metal.

Had she hit a silverbug?

The colors grew brighter, flashier. Mack saw the creatures now, but something was different. He could only see bits and pieces, their light silhouetting darker rectangles.

The headlamps of Kirkland, Lybrand and O'Doyle caught one of those rectangles, reflected from it, and in that moment, everyone understood.

"Shields," Mack said. "They have *shields?*"

Like a three-man-wide phalanx of Roman soldiers, the rocktopi moved forward, a wall of metal that ran from one side of the narrowing tunnel to the other, the plunger of a syringe slowly squeezing forward.

"Twenty meters," Lybrand said.

Kirkland backed up a few steps, hands death-clutch-tight on his rifle. "Goddammit. What do we do now?"

O'Doyle didn't answer.

And why would he? What was there to say? Mack and the others were stuck between a bottleneck of rocktopi and a two-hundred-foot drop.

"We've got to go down the cliff," Kirkland said. "We have to go *now*, take our chances."

Without turning around, O'Doyle shook his head. "Not enough time. Mack's in no shape to climb, and your knee is for shit."

"Fifteen meters," Lybrand said.

Kirkland looked back at Mack. The man's mouth was open, like he was in the middle of a word that would never be spoken. His eyes softened for a moment, an almost apologetic look.

"Then give Mack a gun," he said. "We'll hold them off while the rest of you descend."

"The *fuck* I will," Mack said, shouting the words so hard the pain raged up again. He put both hands to his head, as if that might stop his brains from leaking out his ears.

He wasn't going to die for these people.

"Ten meters," Lybrand said, her voice quavering, getting louder.

O'Doyle stood. "Firing line! Same as before."

"No," Kirkland said. "Let me do this, I'll—"

The big man turned to face him, leaned closed, roared.

"Get on the fucking firing line, now!"

Kirkland flinched. Hell, even Mack flinched. Shocked, confused, Kirkland ran to the same spot he'd manned for the last attack. He knelt—the tunnel mouth fifteen yards in front of him, the cliff edge fifteen yards behind.

Lybrand grabbed O'Doyle's arm.

"If he wants to die, let him," she said. "Either him, or *all* of us!"

Colors flashed madly from the tunnel mouth, but O'Doyle seemed oblivious. For a few seconds, a pause that dragged into eternity, he just stared at Lybrand, his face creased with a look that could only be described as *betrayal*.

"We fight," he said quietly. "Get on the line."

She did. So did he. O'Doyle stood between Kirkland and Lybrand. He waved Veronica and Sanji forward.

"Stay close," he said. "Be ready to hand me your sidearms if I ask for them. Don't fire unless I give the order, but if we go down before that, you're armed and you're on your own. Survive."

O'Doyle faced the tunnel mouth. He knelt.

The professors said nothing.

Mack said nothing.

Silverbug clicks, creature shrieks, the sound of leaves blowing across concrete and now the sound of big metal plates scraping against stone. The funnel was pushing them closer, so that only one or two could come out at a time.

Mack thought of those platinum knives. Whipping blades, slicing into his belly, his muscle. Once the cutting started, how long before death? Would he still be alive when they started cutting him to pieces?

A flash of metal, just inside the narrow opening. Reflections of the headlamp beams, the artificial sun, the visual cacophony of rocktopi colors. Glowing bodies and the onyx-colored spots peeking out from the spaces between shields.

"Hold your fire," O'Doyle said, the command devoid of emotion. "Single shots only. Take time to aim, every bullet has to hit center mass."

A shield slid sideways through the opening, mostly blocking the glowing tentacles that pushed it.

"Hold," O'Doyle said.

The tentacles brought the shield upright. Mack saw a creature flow out of the rock behind it.

Kirkland fired: a clang, the whine of a ricochet.

"*Hold your fire!*" O'Doyle, far louder than the gun.

Kirkland had four shots left. So did Lybrand. O'Doyle had five. That plus the bullets in the two pistols was all that stood between Mack and those monsters, those blades.

A second shield slid through.

What was O'Doyle waiting for?

"Fancy meeting y'all here."

A voice from behind. Mack whipped around, first forgetting the sudden movement would make his brain scream, then not caring about the pain, because there, dangling from a rope just in front of the cave, was a smiling, yellow-suited Angus Kool.

11:46 P.M.

"Connell!"

He turned when Veronica shouted his name, an automatic reaction even though death was fifty feet away, pouring out of that tunnel mouth. He turned, and what he saw stunned him.

Angus Kool, dressed in full rappelling gear atop a dirty KoolSuit, hanging down from some unseen point. A rope dropped down on either side of him, harnesses attached.

Mack said something Connell couldn't hear. Veronica and Sanji handed their pistols to him, then they grabbed at the harnesses.

Angus's eyes met Connell's. Angus smiled.

"Hey, boss. Glad to see me?"

The sound of metal grinding across stone, pulling Connell's attention back to the danger. A third shield sliding through the cave mouth.

"O'Doyle, Angus is here! We have to back up!"

The big man turned, paused, taking in the new situation.

"Angus?" Lybrand said, her eyes and the barrel of her rifle still locked forward. "Where the hell did he come from?"

"Heaven," O'Doyle said. "Firing line, fall back ten steps, be ready for my order."

Connell shuffled backward, making sure he stayed even with Lybrand and O'Doyle. Why was O'Doyle waiting to fire?

They stopped ten feet from the cliff's edge. Veronica and Sanji were already on the way up. Still hanging there, swaying slightly, like a spider on the end of a strand of silk, Doctor Angus Kool.

"You're Kilroy," Connell said.

Angus smiled. "You didn't really think I'd let someone else be the first to see all this splendor, did you? Randy is twenty feet above us, Veronica and Sanji will send the ropes down once they're up." He glanced past Connell, toward the shield wall, and his smile faded. "Uh, are you guys going to shoot those fuckers, or what?"

O'Doyle knelt.

"Firing line, get ready."

Connell pulled the rifle stock tight to his shoulder, aimed, knelt, felt his knee scream out in complaint. He ignored the pain, knowing there would be a price to pay later—if there *was* a later.

A silverbug scurried out from behind the shields, legs a metallic blur as it crossed in front of them, then it vanished behind again.

The shield wall slowly came forward. Metal scraped against rock, a ringing sound like three church bells dragged across gravel.

The bell tolls for me, Connell thought crazily.

Through the spaces between the rough-hewn rectangles, he saw more rocktopi pouring forth, scurrying silverbugs on their left and right.

Almost like...like the robots were *herding* the glowing creatures.

Connell felt sweat between his skin and the KoolSuit. His stomach twisted with sour complaint.

He sighted down the barrel, just as he'd been taught. He tried to find a space between the shields, one eye squeezed so tight it hurt.

Metal grinding on stone. Screeches. Closer. *Closer.*

"God*dammit*, O'Doyle," he said. "What the fuck are we waiting for, them to hand us a fucking invitation?"

"Shut up," O'Doyle said. "Lybrand, pick a space between the center and right shield. Take out the middle carrier. Kirkland, when that shield drops, I fire, then you fire after me. A *single shot only.* We repeat the order—Lybrand, then me, then you. Got it?"

Only fifteen feet away now, grinding closer. So close he saw his reflection in the battered rectangle of metal before him. His heart in his throat. The bells, ringing. Clicks and hisses and small screeches.

"I got it, would you *just fucking do it already?*"

"Shut up," O'Doyle said. "Lybrand, take your shot."

Somehow, Connell heard her breath slowly easing out. He remembered what O'Doyle had taught him—breathe out, and in that brief pause before you breathe in again, squeeze the trigger. Don't pull... *squeeze.*

Connell felt a strange calm wash over him. He saw the onyx spots peeking out from between the shields. That was his key, *the spots,* not the ever-flashing, ever-shifting colors.

The metal rectangles slid forward, only ten feet now, shifting slightly with the motion of their carriers.

Lybrand fired.

An inhuman screech of agony.

The front shield angled backward. It didn't fall, just tipped, exposing a slim window of flashing color on either side.

O'Doyle fired. The left shield twisted slightly, opening more space. *Out, out, damn spot.*

Connell's world shrank to one gleaming bit of black, dead-center in a wash of orange and yellow. He breathed out. He squeezed.

The rifle kicked hard against his shoulder, but he stayed locked on his target, saw the black spot blink out, saw a squirt of yellow replace it.

He heard another shot, knowing it was Lybrand, then O'Doyle

fired while Connell was sighting in on a new spot. He breathed out. He squeezed.

The right shield tipped forward, an ancient drawbridge dropping, hitting the stone floor with a *gong* and a billowing cloud of dust, so close Connell breathed it in, coughed to clear his nose and mouth. In the space where the shield had stood, a rocktopi whipped and thrashed, like food half in and half out of a whirring garbage disposal.

The rocktopi advance halted.

Lybrand fired. The right shield fell back, pinned a dying monster beneath it. O'Doyle fired. A rocktopi twitched, squirting a long gout of yellow. Connell fired.

He had two shots left.

The rocktopi moved backward, only one shield standing.

"Kirkland, hold your fire!" O'Doyle bellowed.

Lybrand fired: another rocktopi dropped. O'Doyle fired: the bullet clanged off the last shield. He fired again: the shield spun, almost fell, but another rocktopi grabbed it, steadied it.

The creatures stretched and reached and flowed back to the cave mouth, retreating, colors now purples and greens and blue instead of yellows and reds. Colors of panic?

Just one shield left, and finally Connell understood O'Doyle's strategy. Two shields lay on stone, a good twenty feet from the narrow tunnel mouth—twenty feet of open killing ground the rocktopi would have to cross to recover them.

Lybrand fired again.

"Out!"

O'Doyle fired. He slung the rifle in a fast, smooth motion.

"Out! Mack, sidearms!"

Mack handed O'Doyle one of the Glocks, handed Lybrand the other.

Screeches and shrieks: the rocktopi poured forward again, brushing past the last standing shield, a tidal wave of angry color bursting forth.

O'Doyle and Lybrand leveled their pistols, held them with both hands. They squeezed off rounds, *pop-pop-pop*, firing even faster than when they'd held automatic rifles.

Rocktopi dropped. More rushed over the fallen. O'Doyle and Lybrand fired. Connell lost count of the shots. The rocktopi slowed, stopped, retreated fast, again sliding into the tunnel. The last shield turned sideways, like a thick door dropping on its side edge, blocking most of the opening.

Lybrand ejected her magazine, stared at it, shook her head.

"Out," she said.

"Two rounds left," O'Doyle said.

Connell didn't know what to do. Was it over? He stood there, rifle in his hands, two rounds remaining in the magazine.

Rocktopi bodies littered the cave floor, some leaking fluid in all directions, some already drained flat. A small landscape of gore and grease, of dropped shields, quivering tentacles and fading colors.

"*Two more*," Angus called out. "Move, dummies!"

"Lybrand, Mack," O'Doyle said. "Get your gear, *move*."

Lybrand snagged her backpack, threw it on and grabbed the rope. She went up, arm over arm, not even bothering with the harness. Connell had a moment to wonder how strong that woman was—then he noticed Mack, fumbling with the harness, his movements clumsy.

Connell slung his rifle.

"Angus, get up there, fast," he said. "Drop your harness down, get everyone ready to pull Mack up."

Angus was ascending before Connell even finished the sentence.

Connell got Mack's right leg into the harness, then the left. He fastened the waist an instant before the Glock fired.

He turned, saw that lone shield, upright and sliding forward. Three rocktopi single-file behind it, the rest of them cowering in the narrow tunnel mouth.

A flash of spinning reflection and a hiss of air—a knife hit O'Doyle, sailed past him out into the cavern trailing an arc of blood. He turned away, eyes squeezed shut, hand pressed to his face.

The shield kept coming.

Connell stepped toward it, unslung his rifle and aimed in the same motion. Before he could squeeze off a round, another spinning reflection. He ducked—the knife whizzed past.

He heard it hit.

Or, maybe he just heard Mack's scream.

Something inside Connell *snapped*. Fear vanished. Rage erupted. Primitive and explosive, the need to protect his own, to fight, to *kill*.

He rushed at the jagged rectangle, turned his shoulder, threw himself forward with all his weight and strength. He slammed hard into the metal—it rocked back, fell, him on top of it, rocktopi underneath.

He rolled off, rolled right, fast, rifle clutched to his chest, knowing that every second would bring the tip of a knife punching through the back of his neck, his belly, his balls. He lurched onto his right hip, saw movement, brought the barrel up and pulled the trigger twice, not *squeezed* because fuck that he *pulled* and the stock pounded into his chest, *wham-wham.*

A rocktopi twitched in front of him, spinning in death throes.

He saw a second monster slide out from under the shield, yellow and red and orange, saw it rush toward O'Doyle.

The third creature was up, stretching and *leaping* toward Connell, one long pulsating snake-limb holding a gleaming, double-crescent blade.

Connell lurched left as the blade arced down.

Lightning and fire laced through his left shoulder, the blade point digging deep through muscle and bone and arteries and he was going to die and be slaughtered, chopped to pieces.

He was on his feet. He saw nothing but the knife, the blade slick-red with blood, *his* blood. It came toward him, almost floating on its own, a magical blade carried by a cloud of color.

Rifle, still in his hands. He flipped it, gloved fingers clasping around the barrel and the forestock. He brought the rifle butt up to his ear, stepped forward, twisted his hips and *swung.*

The rocktopi tried to pull back, but it wasn't fast enough. The rifle butt *cracked* into the knife, sent the double-blade flying across the cave floor.

Connell reared back for another swing—the rocktopi surged forward, leapt on him, *enveloped* his chest and head, pinned his left arm to his body. He fell back, landed hard on his ass.

He twisted, rolled his weight on top of the creature. He punched with his right fist, over and over, but it was like punching a waterbed.

Reeking skin molded against his face. Pliant and raspy, like rubbery sandpaper. He couldn't *breathe.*

A lurch, a shift, and he was on his back again, the creature's weight on top of him. Something around his right wrist, pinning it against the cave floor.

Can't breathe, *can't breathe.*

The weight, ripped up and off him.

Air, rushing back into his lungs.

A roar, the roar of primitive man that once lived in caves like these, the *thonk-thonk-thonk-thoung* of a knife blade punching home again and again.

Something screeching, a sound so close and horrible it made reality twist and bend.

O'Doyle, enraged face sheeted with blood, mask gone, KoolSuit shred hanging against his neck, another flapping from his bloody right thigh, the rocktopi squeezed under his left arm like some oversized pillow, his right hand driving the big Ka-Bar knife down again and again and again.

The hiss of dry leaves on concrete.

Connell looked to the cave mouth—they were coming, *again*.

He saw his rifle. He grabbed it, aimed it at the oncoming creatures, and they flowed away like vampires retreating away from a cross, sliding back into the cave mouth.

A hand on his shoulder.

"Come on," O'Doyle said.

Connell walked backward, rifle still aimed.

He turned, saw Mack—one crescent blade curving down and away from his stomach, the other buried in his sternum. Blood covered his KoolSuit, from his chest down to his crotch, along his left leg, pooled beneath him, mixed with the yellow fluid leaking from a quivering rocktopi that O'Doyle must have just killed.

Mack's half-lidded eyes stared out.

Dead.

O'Doyle reached up, sliced through the rope. Mack sagged to the ground, a marionette with the strings cut, as boneless as the things that had killed him.

"Drop the rifle," O'Doyle said. "Take the rope, hold on tight."

Connell did, standing over Mack's dead body, clutching the rope with both hands.

O'Doyle cupped his hands, shouted up. "Pull!"

Connell felt himself lifted. His body dragged along rocks, but he focused only on holding tight, on enduring the pain of his shoulder, his knee. And why was he so hot all of a sudden?

Hands grabbed him, dragged him onto another flat stone cliff. People asking him if he was all right. He tried to talk, couldn't.

Then, someone lying next to him. O'Doyle, all blood and muscle, mumbling.

"So hot," he said. "So hot."

Yes, so hot, *scorching*. What was going on? Connell struggled to draw a full breath. Every square inch of his body prickled and burned with a million tiny bee stings.

"Their suits," he heard Lybrand yell in a dreamy, far-off voice. "They're losing all the coolant!"

Connell again tried to speak, again failed. All he could think about were those chips of onyx he'd aimed at.

Out out, damn spot…

The spots didn't go out—*he* did.

BOOK FIVE

THE ROCKTOPI

28

August 28

5:21 A.M.

Kayla found herself somewhere between admiration and rage. Squatting on her heels, she stared at the last of the pyramid-like devices Angus had scattered all over the mountain. She appreciated the genius that had gone into building the object but at the same time wanted to slice open the builder's belly.

She stood, took two steps back, fired her Steyr GB-80. Angus's device shattered into a dozen useless pieces of smoldering, twisted metal and ripped wires.

Now he was completely cut off. Tracking down and destroying all of his hidden machines had cost her six precious hours.

You fucking *little prick.*

She had to get to him. Did he have any other little tricks he could use to call for help? Hopefully, the first unit she'd found could provide some information, maybe even a way to track him.

Angus Kool would get the pliers. And this time, Kayla wouldn't stop with just a knuckle or two.

29

5:34 A.M.

Randy Wright felt like a real piece of crap.

A pair of small portable lights lit up the small cave. Randy sat next to Connell Kirkland, keeping an eye on the sleeping, wounded man. Angus, Veronica, Sanji and O'Doyle slept as well. Lybrand remained awake, watching over O'Doyle, but she looked exhausted.

This whole thing had started out as an adventure. Not anymore. Mack Hendricks was *dead*. Killed by those strange animals.

If Randy and Angus had been up front with their technology, and with their alternate entry point into the tunnel complex, would Mack still be alive? Maybe. Randy would always wonder if he could have prevented a man's death.

But at the same time, if he and Angus had sat back, done nothing, then Veronica, Sanji, O'Doyle, Lybrand and Kirkland would be dead as well.

Angus was a *hero*. Sure, he'd been scared at first, but Randy's friend just needed some encouragement. When the guns started roaring, Angus—the more experienced climber—had done the right thing and gone down to get the others.

Connell lurched, screamed, sat up suddenly. Randy grabbed his arms, careful to avoid the wounded shoulder.

"You're safe, Mister Kirkland. It's all right."

A wide-eyed Connell stared at Randy, then at the sleepers, then all over the small cavern, every move a hard twitch. He took in a sharp, deep breath, let it out in a *whuff*, seemed to calm himself.

"Gotta stop waking up like that," he said. "Where are we?"

Randy let him go.

"We're in a cave that Angus and I sealed off with rocks. We're safe. For now, at least."

Connell started to get up, winced sharply, stayed where he was. His right hand felt gingerly at his left shoulder. He looked at the KoolSuit material there—stitched together, just like the skin beneath it.

"I was cut," he said. "How bad?"

"Twenty-one stitches. Looks like it missed ligaments and tendons. Sanji stitched you up while I followed behind, repairing your suit. Lybrand and Angus did the same for O'Doyle. We used up all the KoolSuit patches, though, so we have to make sure no one else gets cut."

Connell's gaze flicked around the cavern again, landed on O'Doyle and Lybrand.

"He was cut, too."

Randy nodded. "Fifteen stitches on his face. Another ten on his leg. Sanji thinks he'll be okay as long as we don't move him for a day or so."

Connell grimaced. "We don't have a day."

He started to rise. Randy tried to help, but Connell pushed him away.

So *different*. Whatever had happened in the past few days, it had changed Connell Kirkland. Made him harder. Gave him the air of a man Randy would cross the street to avoid.

"Wake everyone up," Connell said. "We have to figure out our next step."

5:36 A.M.

They sat in a circle at the small cave's center. The people he'd spent the last twenty-four nightmarish hours with looked exhausted, defeated. Just like Connell felt. Even O'Doyle—tireless, indestructible—seemed broken, drained of his confidence. He leaned against Lybrand, so much so that she was the only thing stopping him from sliding onto his side.

Randy and Angus, though, seemed fine.

Connell started with them.

"Tell me how you two got down here."

Randy looked at the ground. Angus did not. He stared right back, with that goddamn *smirk*.

"We faked the lab accident," he said. "Hope that didn't cause any grief."

A bit of intensity returned to O'Doyle's eyes. A nasty line of stitches ran from his left upper lip to his temple. Now both sides of his face were mangled. He glared at Angus, who didn't seem to notice.

"That got you out of camp," Connell said. "How did you get down *here* without anyone knowing?"

"I found another entrance. Don't worry, it wasn't suitable for mining, the adit had to be dug regardless. I believe it's the same entrance that Sonny talked about in his report, the one where the geology students disappeared."

Veronica pulled the plastic map out of her webbing, held it up.

"I've been over this a dozen times," she said. "There's no second entrance."

Angus shrugged.

Connell felt an echo of the cold rage that had made him rush the rocktopi.

"You hid it," he said. "You took it off the map entirely."

The smirk became a grin.

"*Duh.* I knew you wouldn't let me in the caves until they'd been explored, despite my notable experience in the field." He tapped his pointer finger against his sternum. "*I* mapped this system. *I* deserved to be the first person down here. We knew Mack's path would lead to what you call the Picture Cavern, so we left a little calling card there."

Connell glanced at Randy, who kept his gaze fixed on the floor.

Randy knew he'd done wrong. At least he knew it now, anyway. But Angus? Not even close.

"Being the first wasn't enough," Connell said. "You had to let everyone know you were first."

Angus nodded. The look in his eyes spoke volumes: it wasn't about *everyone* knowing, it was about *Connell* knowing.

"The signs prove we got there before anyone else."

"Cocksucker," Lybrand said. "This is a game to you? A goddamn dick-measuring contest?"

Sanji shook his head. "That is wrong, Bertha, because Angus clearly has no dick whatsoever."

Angus rolled his eyes, as if anything those two had to say was insignificant.

Connell's shoulder screamed, steadily fanned the flames of anger burning in his chest.

"Randy told me we're safe," he said, working hard to keep his voice level. "Tell us why."

Angus pulled a walkie-talkie from his webbing belt.

"Because they network with radio signals. I modified this to jam them. They come near us, they get all scrambled. They can't even walk, let alone spot us."

Connell looked around. "Who has a walkie-talkie?"

"We do," Lybrand said, indicating her and O'Doyle. "Mack had one, but I sure as shit ain't going back down there to get it."

Connell wished he'd insisted everyone carry one. Too late for that now.

"Angus, when you modify one to scramble, can you change it back so it works normally?"

The little man shook his head.

"One-way street, brah. If I make it a scrambler, that's all it will do. You want me to modify the others?"

Two functioning walkie-talkies. Those might be vital if they needed to reach someone close to the surface or had to split up. But if the group did split up, and had only one scrambler, wasn't that also a risk?

"No," Connell said. "Communication might mean the difference between life and death. We'll stay close together."

Veronica's face wrinkled with confusion.

"I'm still not getting this. You use a hacked walkie-talkie to give the monsters a cheap buzz?"

Angus closed his eyes, gave his head a small shake.

"No, *Doctor* Reeves, and I use that term loosely, it scrambles the artificial life probes, not the living creatures." Another small shake, showing it was so beneath him to educate dumb people.

If Veronica was supposed to feel diminished, she didn't know it.

"Artificial life," she said, glaring at him. "What the fuck are you talking about, you arrogant dickless piece of shit?"

"He means silverbugs," Sanji said.

The word seemed to amuse Angus. "Silverbugs? That's quaint, considering how they're made from platinum, but I'll roll with it."

Connell knew he should have felt surprised the probes were made from platinum, but the truth was he no longer cared about the metal. Or money. Or anything other than getting these people out alive.

O'Doyle gently pushed himself upright.

"The silverbugs aren't the ones trying to kill us," he said. "The rocktopi are."

Angus glanced at him. "*Rocktopi?* You guys are so cute with all these little names. Yes, the rocktopi are trying to kill us, when the silverbugs *tell them* to. Randy and I saw the machines bring those shields that almost cost you your asses."

Connell thought of the silverbugs on either side of the rocktopi phalanx, herding them, maybe even encouraging them to attack.

"You think the machines control the creatures, and not the other way around?"

"It's obvious," Angus said. "Well, to anyone with half a brain, anyway. The monsters use knives against firearms. I doubt anything that stupid can work advanced machines. I think the ALs—" he held a hand against his chest, looked at Sanji "—oh, excuse me, learned sir, I think the *silverbugs* tell the creatures where to go and what to do."

Around the circle, people glanced at each other. Connell knew what they were thinking—the long lines of jerking silverbugs, and the attacks that followed along those paths.

"So say you're right," Connell said. "Say the machines call the shots, and you can scramble the machines. We still need to get the hell out of here. Can you tell us how to do that?"

Angus sighed again—the dumbest question he'd ever heard. He reached into his backpack and pulled out a tablet computer.

"I invented a kind of GPS for underground exploration. The map updates every few hours, triangulates our location so we can't get lost."

He tapped the screen. A map of the caverns flared to life. He held it up for all to see.

Connell stood. He stared, stunned, as Angus turned the tunnel system, rotated it, zoomed in and out.

Veronica leaned forward, reached across the circle and snatched the tablet from Angus's hands.

"You had a *perfect* map of these caves," she hissed. "And you didn't tell us?"

He crossed his arms, sneered. "The map I gave Mack was already a feat of genius. If you idiots can't figure out how to read that, then I—"

Connell took a step toward him. Angus looked up just as Connell kicked out, drove the toe of his boot into the smaller man's mouth.

Angus fell to his side, hands covering his face.

Connell kicked again, wildly, this time his boot caught Angus in the thigh. He reared back for a third, but strong arms wrapped him up, knocked him off his feet. Connell landed hard on stone, looked, expected to see O'Doyle, but he'd been tackled by Sanji.

"Stop this," Sanji said, still holding Connell tight. "We need Angus, so stop it."

That cold feeling, the need to hurt... it didn't vanish, but it receded somewhat.

Sanji got up, once again clutching his fingers to his chest, his face wrinkling with pain.

Connell stood. O'Doyle and Lybrand were smiling at him. Veronica stared at Angus, who was still curled up in a ball.

They'd been lost, and because of that they'd been *slow*—this piece of shit had a map that could have fixed that, that could have kept Mack Hendricks alive.

Connell took a step toward him.

Randy Wright hopped to his feet, stepped between them, his hands balled into fists.

"That's *enough*," he said.

Connell stopped. He pointed a finger at Randy's face.

"It's your fault just as much as his. You two are going to get us out of here. You'll tell us everything from now on. Understand?"

Randy's fists remained clenched. He looked like the kind of man who'd never been in a fight, yet here he was, ready to defend Angus.

"We were wrong," he said. "We'll make it right."

Simple. Honest. Intense. Randy didn't shy away from the blame. Did he know how much better of a man he was than his supposed *best friend*?

"Good," Connell said. He tilted his head at Angus. "Now get to work, both of you."

7:05 A.M.

The industrial computer's small display showed a detailed map—an entrance into the tunnels. Something Angus had labeled "The Linus Highway."

He'd found a second way in. A way he'd kept all to himself.

You little fucking prick.

The bastard *wanted* her to fail.

Kayla downloaded the map into the COMSEC handheld unit. She put the unit in her backpack along with her Marco/Polo device, food, water and ammunition. She slid into the KoolSuit, then strapped on her shoulder holster.

It wasn't too late. She could still pull this off. She could get *proof*.

The monsters were down there, but she only needed one. Hell, she only needed a *piece* of one. Get down there, get a sample, get back to the surface, call André.

And maybe, if she was lucky, she could find the survivors. She could kill them.

If she was *really* lucky? She could get some alone time with one Doctor Angus Kool.

She checked her bag, made sure that her favorite things were inside. They were. She slung that over her shoulder, holstered the Steyr, picked up the Galil, then headed up the mountain.

7:21 A.M.

Angus and Connell knelt next to each other, staring at the tablet on Angus's upraised knee. Everyone else stood behind them, watching

Angus's finger trace patterns on the map, illustrating the way out of the tunnel complex.

Patrick stood behind them, Sanji on his left, Bertha on his right, both helping him to stay standing. He couldn't get comfortable, not with his thigh wound barking at him.

He was lucky to be alive. He'd been in a knife fight with a damn glowing monster, and he'd come out on top. Still couldn't remember exactly how it had gone down, only that he'd looked up, saw the thing coming, tried to avoid the first slash—tried, and failed, as his leg would attest. He'd panicked, thrust out with all his strength.

But that one strike had been true.

He'd punched the blade deep, pulled out, stabbed again. And again. He'd kept stabbing until he saw that flashing blob suffocating Connell.

Angus finished his explanation, fingertip pressed firmly against the map's largest feature.

"The Dense Mass," Connell said. He sounded doubtful. "But you and Randy came in another way."

When Angus spoke, his voice no longer rang with arrogance. The swollen, split lip Connell had delivered seemed to have done a world of good. Like most assholes, Angus Kool had needed an ass-whoopin' to straighten him out.

"We came down the Linus Highway," Angus said, fingertip tracing a thin line that reached almost to the top of the mountain. "It's pretty much a straight shot to the Dense Mass, but we branched off about halfway down so we could follow another path and reach the Picture Cavern before Mack did."

Connell stared at the map. Everyone waited.

"Then you haven't seen it," Connell said finally. "You haven't seen the Dense Mass?"

Angus shook his head.

Connell glanced up at Randy, who also shook his head.

"We have two choices," Randy said. "We go down to the Dense Mass Cavern, go around the big ore deposit and then up the Linus Highway. The highway is uphill, sure, about a thirty-degree grade, but it's pretty much a straight shot. And the ceiling averages six feet in height, so no crawling."

Crawling. The word made Patrick shudder. His leg wound sliding across unforgiving rock, over and over. The suit could handle it, but would the stitches beneath hold up to the repetitive abuse?

"Some positives there," Connell said. "I assume the other choice is to go back the way we came?"

Randy nodded. "Correct. Not all the way to the Picture Cavern, but close to it. Which means we go *up* all the obstacles that you went *down* to get here."

Lybrand glanced at Patrick's leg, a snap-look, then she reached down over Angus's shoulder, tapped the Dense Mass on the screen.

"We're going *that* way," she said. "Decision made."

Connell held up a hand, telling her to be quiet.

"We don't know what's there," he said. "Could be more risks, more creatures, more silverbugs."

Lybrand's lip curled. She started to speak, but Patrick gave her elbow a light squeeze. She looked at him, wanting his help making her case. She wasn't going to get it.

"Let Connell talk," he said. "This isn't just about me."

Patrick wanted to live. Of course he did. But he'd been a soldier most of his life. If he had to stay behind so everyone else could survive, he was willing to pay that price.

Lybrand was a soldier, too—she should have understood that. But maybe she didn't. She'd been willing to leave Connell and Mack behind to save herself. Well, not *herself*, to save Patrick, too. They barely knew each other, yet he knew he would die for her, and suspected she would die for him if need be. The problem was, she would let others die for him as well.

Patrick didn't know how to feel about that.

"The route to the Picture Cavern is longer and harder," Connell said. "But we've been through it. We know what we'll face. We have to consider that. What about rocktopi and silverbugs, can this map show where they are?"

Angus tapped icons. The map zoomed in. An orange dot appeared in the center of a small cavern. All through the tunnels around it, blinking red dots.

"Our position on this map was updated at five a.m.," Angus said. "The orange dot is us. The red dots are silverbugs."

Patrick looked for the scale, saw it, realized that dozens of silverbugs were only four or five meters away. Others saw the same thing; a wave of fear rippled through the group.

Randy held up his hands, looked around, a *take it easy* gesture. The guy was calm and cool. O'Doyle was starting to like him.

"They don't know we're in here," Randy said. "We planted motion sensors all over this area before we dropped down to rescue you. When we brought you here we had the scrambler on. We sealed up the entrance, turned off the scrambler. They didn't see us."

"How do you know they didn't?" Lybrand said.

"Because they were just wandering," Angus said. "When they know someone is present, they exhibit very structured behavior."

Veronica huffed. "Yeah, we noticed. But why not leave the scrambler on?"

Angus started to answer, but Randy spoke first.

"Batteries," he said. "And, it would be an anomaly in their normal behavior. If we leave it on, we're worried they might map the dead zone, so to speak. If they have enough time, they could figure out the center of that dead zone and know where we are anyway."

Connell stood. He rubbed at his knee. The line of KoolSuit patches up and over his shoulder looked just like the line across Patrick's thigh. Maybe Connell was a desk jockey, but after this, he and Patrick were blood brothers. A bond forged in battle is not easily broken.

Veronica looked at Patrick. So did Sanji and Angus. They were waiting for him to make the decision, just like Lybrand was, but the decision wasn't his to make. He was wounded: only one path gave him any hope of making it out alive. For the good of the group, someone else had to make that choice.

"Connell, your call," Patrick said. "I stand by you either way."

Patrick felt Lybrand's glare. He ignored it.

Connell thought for a moment.

"If we take the Dense Mass route, how long to reach the surface?"

Angus tapped the screen twice. "If we aren't stopped, we can be at the Dense Mass in twenty-five minutes. From there, a three-mile hike up the Linus Highway."

Patrick winced at the thought. A helluva climb, but far better than the alternative.

Connell rubbed at the stubble on his chin. "Took us a day to get here from the Picture Cavern. So a day, at least, to get back. Randy, how long from there to the way you came in?"

Everyone looked at Randy, but Patrick watched Angus. The little man glared at Randy, glared *hard*.

"Another half day," Randy said. "But that was Angus and me, moving fast."

The implied meaning: *that was without a wounded man who can barely walk.*

Connell took a deep breath. He nodded.

"We don't have two days' worth of batteries," he said. "Or food. Or water. Let's get our gear together. We head for the Dense Mass in twenty minutes."

7:30 A.M.

Kayla Meyers eased past the pumpkin-shaped boulder and through the small opening. She stood, brushed off her KoolSuit, donned her starlight goggles.

Footprints in the fine sand. Several sets. All small. Some of them had to be from Angus Kool, others from Randy Wright. A few more, maybe. She didn't know who the others might be, didn't care. In these caves, footprints probably lasted forever.

She followed the footprints. In just a few yards, only two sets remained.

Angus and Randy.

Snoopy and *Woodstock*, butt-buddies for life.

According to the map, this tunnel branched off in places, made a few minor turns, rises and dips, but basically angled straight down for about three miles. It ended at the Dense Mass Cavern.

She walked. No sound here. No wind, no breeze, no cars, no nothing. Creepy.

A quick check of the Marco/Polo unit. No signal. Angus, Randy and the others—if any others remained alive—were out of range.

Of course they were. Because Angus wanted to make it hard on her. Because Angus thought he was *smarter* than she was.

Fucking little prick.

Kayla stowed the Marco/Polo unit.

She followed the footsteps.

7:38 A.M.

Angus Kool wanted to murder Connell Kirkland.

Not *beat him up*, not *kick his ass*. Murder him. End his life. No way to put a nice face on it. No need. Kirkland was a bully. Bullies deserved to die. Ergo, Connell Kirkland *deserved* death.

While the others prepared to leave, Angus and Connell sat side by side, backs against the small cavern's stone wall. Kirkland had the tablet, was poring over the map, trying to plan the best way to the Dense Mass and the Linus Highway. When he had a question, he wanted Angus there to answer it. Angus played along. Oh, *yassah*, I can follow orders! I've learned my lesson!

The exercise was ridiculous. He should have just asked Angus the best way to go, then followed that plan. Like this lanky idiot had any idea what he was doing.

Connell moved the map, zoomed in on a spot.

"This is a river we crossed. We went there because Mack thought it was a big tunnel that led through the kidney-shaped cavern, then through the dense mass."

The kidney-shaped cavern where I saved your worthless life? And my reward for that was you kicking me in the face?

"That doesn't help us much," Angus said. He reached across, zoomed the map out to show a larger perspective of the complex. The Dense Mass Cavern loomed large: a solid blob of yellow. "As you can see, that tunnel—which may continue to be the river, or it could be where the river *used* to flow, and the water now goes somewhere else—is far to our left. The path I already planned follows these straight tunnels and puts us in the Dense Mass Cavern just south of the ore body."

Connell nodded. "Your map won't show us what's *in* the Dense Mass Cavern?"

Sure it will, massah! Why, it's had that detail all along, you just never asked!

"No, it can't tell you what's inside."

Connell changed the scale, zooming in on that cavern.

"You said this updated every six hours," Connell said. "When was the last update?"

"Twelve hours ago. One might have come in about five thirty, but my face was occupied at the time because of the appointment with your boot."

Connell didn't take the bait. Of course not—like that dude gave two wet shits about what he'd done.

"You said we had to go *around* the ore body to get to the Linus Highway?"

Oh, dear Jesus, please strike me down if I have to answer one more obvious question from this imbecile.

"Yes," Angus said. "Since the Linus Highway is on the other side of the ore body, we will have to go *around* the ore body."

He heard the condescension in his voice, couldn't help it. Connell, thankfully, either didn't notice or didn't care.

Connell tapped a point on the tablet screen. "According to your path, this is where we come in." He tapped a spot west of that, a yellow line, thicker than most, that ran south from the yellow glob of the Dense Mass Cavern. "That's the tunnel Mack talked about, a river when we crossed it, the same river that flowed through the kidney-shaped cavern, right?"

What are you going to point out next, that air has oxygen? That gravity is the reason we don't float off into space?

"That's right," Angus said. "So?"

Connell pointed to a spot on the north side of the big yellow blob—the thick line again.

"The river, or the tunnel that was once a river, comes in on the south of the cavern and exits on the north," he said. "Is it reasonable to assume that tunnel goes *through* the ore body? If we could follow that, it's a half mile or so from where we come out to the Linus Highway, instead of three or four miles around. Right?"

Angus stared at the tablet. No, the map didn't show anything *in* the Dense Mass Cavern, but one glance showed that Mack had been right—that thick tunnel ran through it. Angus had missed that, and that made him even angrier.

"Seems possible," he said. "But if it is the river, can we traverse it?"

Connell shook his head. "I don't know. We couldn't get through it before, it ran underground. But as bad as O'Doyle is hurt, we need to shorten our trip any way we can, so we'll have to check. If we can't use that path to get to the other side, we'll have to cross and go around the ore body."

"If we *can* cross it," Angus said. "Otherwise, we turn around and go back the other way and lose maybe—" he eyeballed the map "—thirty minutes. Fifteen there, fifteen back to where we first entered the cavern."

Kirkland zoomed in further, blowing up the southern spot where the thick yellow line met the cavern. "What are these little semi-circles at the cavern's edge? They're too perfectly shaped to be natural formations."

How about you ask the fucking monsters that built the place, you stupid piece of shit? Or better yet, why don't you kick the tablet, push it around, hurt it, so it does what you want it to do?

"I don't know," Angus said. "Alcoves, maybe. They don't seem to have exit tunnels."

Kirkland hunched over the tablet again, kept touching, kept zooming.

Angus wasn't sure if he wanted Kirkland to die in these tunnels or to make it out alive so Angus could kill him. Tie him up. Slice him. Kick him in the face over and over, until his nose smashed, his teeth fell out, until—

"And this?"

Kirkland tapped a yellow line pointing down from the center-bottom of the Dense Mass itself until it faded out. Not down toward the bottom of the screen, but deeper into the earth.

"Not sure," Angus said. "A vertical shaft of some kind, obviously. It goes beyond the map's bottom range of almost four miles."

"Could we go down that shaft if we had to?"

And lo, another stupid question, Sweet Baby Jesus, and yet still I live. It's almost as if you don't really exist.

"No, we couldn't," Angus said. "That far down, the geothermal heat is too much even for the suits. You'd cook."

Kirkland bent over the table again, leaving Angus to sit there and think that, yes, *cooking* Kirkland might be an even better way to murder him than kicking him to death.

7:40 A.M.

She still hadn't come back.

Sonny stared through the binoculars, watching the place where the murderer had vanished behind a ridge. She'd practically sprinted up there. And he knew where *there* was, knew where she was going—the other entrance, the place that had made Sonny almost piss himself with fear.

Would she go beyond the place where Sonny had freaked out? Would she go deeper?

And if so, how long would she be gone?

He lowered the binoculars, licked his lips. He glanced toward her warren. Invisible, but he knew where it was because he'd seen her go in, seen her come out. Had she left any info behind? Could he find out who she was?

Don't you wanna know?

He did. But if she came back while he was in there...

Don't you wanna know?

He did. But he wanted to live more.

Sonny raised the binoculars again. He'd watch.

Another half hour. Just to make sure.

7:43 A.M.

A quiet moment before they headed out. Bertha wiped a bead of sweat from Patrick's face. It wasn't because of the heat; the suit controlled his temperature.

He was sweating from the pain.

"How do you feel?"

Patrick grimaced, almost snarled. "Doesn't matter how I feel. We're doing this."

Even if Randy's first-aid kit had contained serious painkillers, Patrick wouldn't have taken them. This wasn't the time to be fuzzy, to have slow reactions.

The wounds didn't matter. They didn't. Patrick was going to make it out. She'd destroy anything that got in his way. Silverbugs, rock-topi...even Angus Kool.

Or Connell Kirkland.

Patrick nodded toward her backpack.

"Really wish I could pull my own weight, carry something."

She shook her head, wiped away another bead of sweat.

"Don't worry about it," she said. "I'm fine."

A lie. She was beyond drained. And still a three-mile climb ahead of them? Maybe halfway up—when she was sure they'd made it—she'd ditch the pack, but for now she wasn't going anywhere without what little food and water they had left.

He winced, sharply and suddenly, which pulled at the long line of stitches across his cheek, forced himself to instantly *un*-wince.

To see him in this much pain … it gutted her. Maybe he was a cold-blooded killer, not the man she'd built up in her head, but she wasn't sure that mattered—whatever he was, she loved him.

"I wish we had some morphine," she said.

He huffed. "Not much into the hard stuff, but if we get out of here, let's look into that."

She squeezed his hand, trying to reassure him that everything would be all right. She looked at their clasped fingers, how similar they were; big knuckles, dozens of small white scars—the hands of people who'd known violence.

Bertha had often looked at her ugly hands and wondered if anyone would ever want to hold them. Patrick wanted to. He didn't care what they looked like.

"We're getting out of here," she said. "I promise you that."

She lay her forehead on his solid shoulder, and he gently stroked her hair.

7:48 A.M.

No ammo.

Low on food and water.

Miles yet to hike, most of it uphill.

Monsters that wanted to kill them.

Two people badly wounded, including himself.

It seemed hopeless.

And yet, Connell felt different. He felt *focused*. These people were down here because of him. He would get them out, no matter what it took.

"All right," he said. "Let's go over it again. Angus and Randy far out front with the map and the scrambler. If they see rocktopi, or anything blocking our path, they run back and warn us. We change our route if we have to. Lybrand and O'Doyle, you're in the middle, go as fast as you can. Sanji and Veronica, about twenty feet behind them. The scrambler's range is about fifty meters, so Angus and Randy, don't get too far ahead of O'Doyle and Lybrand, got it?"

"We got it," Randy said. Angus wasn't to be trusted, but something had changed in Randy.

"I'll bring up the rear," Connell said. "When we get to the Dense Mass Cavern, we're going west. We think it's about a fifteen-minute walk to Mack's river. We'll see if we can follow that river through the ore body. If that works, it comes out right at the Linus Highway. We go up, we get out. If we can't navigate the river, we have to go around the ore body. Everyone understand?"

Heads nodded again.

It was time.

No guns. Two knives.

The thing they counted on to keep them safe? A hot-wired walkie-talkie.

If the rocktopi attacked, the battle wouldn't last long.

"Okay," Connell said. "Open it up."

Sanji, Randy, Angus and Veronica started clearing rocks from the cave entrance.

30

15,798 feet below the surface

8:09 A.M.

Her fingers traced detailed carvings. Such delicate work, such masterful beauty from such a savage race.

"Veronica, we *can't* keep stopping," Connell said. "If Angus gets too far ahead of us, we lose the scrambler's effect."

He sounded pissed, on the edge of screaming at her. She couldn't blame him. She *wanted* to move, understood that she was causing a problem, but the carvings might hold the answers that she'd sought for seven years at Cerro Chaltén.

When they'd left the small cavern, Veronica understood what Randy and Angus had been talking about. Silverbugs, yes, all over the place, but they had walked erratically, bumping into the walls, stumbling over one another. Many didn't walk at all, their round bodies resting on the tunnel floor, legs waving randomly.

They looked *drunk*.

Angus and Randy had set an aggressive pace. Everyone kept up, even O'Doyle.

After only a few minutes of walking, though, Veronica saw occasional rocktopi graffiti on the tunnel walls and ceiling. The same disturbing paintings of boneless limbs and furious colors, all the more horrible now that she knew what those images represented. The closer the party moved toward the Dense Mass, the more packed together the paintings became.

Halfway there, the tunnel stopped looking like a rough cave and started looking like a tube, a masterpiece of carving that rivaled the stonework of medieval churches, even the Egyptian pyramids. Smooth walls curved up into a smooth ceiling. The floor became flat as a pancake. Wild paintings covered every inch, even more chaotic than before.

A few hundred feet further, storytelling tiles lined the tube's smooth walls, tiles similar to what she'd seen in the Picture Cavern. Up there, the image of the mountain appeared over and over, a backdrop to most of what the Chaltélians had been trying to communicate. In the tube, the mountain was nowhere to be seen — another shape seemed to have replaced it.

Shortly after the tiles started, the paintings became sparse again. Then faded out altogether.

Why? Why would the graffiti stop? It was almost as if... as if the vandals, for lack of a better word, were unwilling to go further down this tunnel. Were they *afraid* of what lie in the Dense Mass Cavern?

She ran her fingertips over a tile featuring that shape, wondering what it meant.

"Ronni, snap out of it," Sanji said. An edge in his voice, maybe even more so than in Connell's. "We have to go. Lybrand and O'Doyle are getting ahead of us."

Veronica glanced down the hall; O'Doyle, leaning heavily on Lybrand, but farther ahead than they should have been. Couldn't they wait a few seconds? No, no they couldn't. With his wound, they had to keep moving.

She turned back to the wall. "I just need a second, Dad." She pointed to the group of tiles in front of her, at a specific shape she'd been seeing. "See this image? It's everywhere."

To their credit, both her father and Connell looked. Connell touched it.

"This kinda fountain-pen-shaped thing?"

Sanji shook his head. "More like a cartridge with a bullet on each end."

Both descriptions were in the ballpark. Long, thick, widest in the middle, ends tapered down to rounded points.

"Everywhere we see that shape, it's at the start of a sequence," Veronica said. "When we see the bullet shape, the next panel in the sequence shows hundreds of tiny rocktopi."

Connell leaned closer. "Tiny. Maybe they're children, like the ones Sanji danced with?"

Sanji nodded and tapped a fingertip on the image.

"What if the shape is an egg sac of some kind? Or even a nest. We've seen almost nothing of these creatures. They could secrete something that hardens, like spiders and silk. Or maybe these are ritualistic nurseries of some kind that they build with their own hands."

"*Tentacles*," Connell said. "Own *tentacles*."

Sanji nodded. "Own tentacles. I give you that the rocktopi probably didn't build the silverbugs, but if they can use knives, they can use tools."

Veronica wondered if the bullet-shaped symbol was representative of a physical thing or a metaphorical one. Even though the robots were advanced tech, these carvings seemed to have a mystical feel to them, perhaps indicative of a primitive culture.

"Wait a minute ... I recognize the year," she said. "Not *our* year, I mean the date within their culture. The images coincide with their zero year. That means the egg-sac image could be connected to their origin story, their equivalent of the Garden of Eden. Maybe..."

Her words trailed off. She heard something in the darkness behind them.

click-click ... click-click-click.

Three headlamps swung back fast, landed on burnished metal. A silverbug, round body on the ceiling, spindly legs spread out, hooked feet clinging to carvings. The wedge-shaped protrusion pointed at Sanji, then Connell, then her. Movements firm, precise.

If it had been drunk, it sobered up in a fucking hurry.

Another silverbug scrambled across the ceiling, stopped shortly behind the first.

They began to jerk up and down.

A third joined the line.

From far down the hall, Veronica heard the sound of dry leaves scraping against concrete.

"We fell out of the scrambler's range," Connell said. *"Move."*

Veronica ran down the hall, the two men close behind.

8:12 A.M.

Angus started to step over the twitching silverbug, then changed his mind. He picked it up by a long leg, lifted it. It was a little like picking up an Alaskan king crab—it dangled there, legs curling slowly, randomly.

"Put it down," Randy said. "We have to keep going."

Angus glared at him.

"Oh, I'll put it down, all right." He whipped the silverbug against the wall. Randy winced at the sound of metal ringing against stone. Angus whipped it again, cracked a graffiti-covered bas-relief tile, sent half of barbell-shaped carving flying. On the fourth strike, the thin limb tore free. The now three-legged silverbug fell to the floor, even more wobbly than it had been before.

Randy looked worried.

"We're making too much noise," he said.

Sometimes, that guy wore on Angus's last nerve. And those stupid Rec Specs—get eye surgery already. They made Randy look like a retarded bug.

"Know how we'll make less noise? If you have a nice cup of *shut the fuck up.*"

Randy shook his head, pulled out the tablet and checked the map.

Oh, he wanted to show off, did he? Wanted to rub it in that Connell had given *him* the map instead of Angus? Connell Kirkland was a selfish, manipulative cocksucker. His asshole actions were predictable. They fit a pattern of privileged bully douchbaggery. But Randy's behavior? Disappointing, and more than a bit mystifying.

Randy had always been easy to get along with. Not as smart as Angus, but smart enough to know good sense when he heard it. Now? Now the guy was talking all the time, talking out of turn. Far worse, he was listening to the wrong people.

Listening to *stupid* people.

"We're almost there," Randy said.

Angus sighed. "Wow, so glad I have a *genius* reading the map I made, otherwise I'd have never figured that one out."

Randy ignored the comment.

The two men moved down the hall. Not a "tunnel" anymore, not with this craftsmanship. Stone carved so smoothly Angus almost wondered if someone had created a laser drill before him. Yet that made no sense, because these halls were made centuries ago. No, this was likely the result of generation after generation of master craftsman chiseling perfect paths through solid limestone.

An intersection. Angus and Randy stopped. A hallway curved off to the left and to the right, walls decorated with graffiti-painted bas-relief tiles. In the hallway to the left, a pair of scrambled silverbugs seemed to be trying to drunkenly crawl over each other.

Angus pulled a motion sensor from his bag, set it next to the wall.

"Only three of these left," he said. "How are Mister Giant Cock-Face and the others doing?"

Randy zoomed in the map, frowned.

"Lagging behind. Looks like Connell, Veronica and Sanji fell out of scrambler range, but they're in it now, and running to catch up."

"Un-fucking-believable," Angus said. "They fell out of range? For fuck's sake, how dumb do you have to be?"

Randy said nothing. Yeah, he knew it was stupid, wasn't bothering to defend them.

That was better. That was the *old* Randy, the one smart enough to listen. Maybe he would listen now.

"Those gimps are slowing us down," Angus said.

Randy's eyes hardened. "They're *hurt*."

"Cry me a river. Ever heard of survival of the fittest? I'm not going to die down here waiting for them to catch up."

Angus glanced back up the hall, made sure O'Doyle and Lybrand were out of earshot. They were far back, limping closer.

He turned back to Randy.

"We saved them once. Let's haul balls and get out of here. It's not like we didn't tell them the way out. They don't need us to find the Linus Highway. They don't need the map, either."

Randy squared his shoulders. The look on his face—so different from the man who'd always been eager to appease. Now he looked disgusted. Even worse, *dismissive*.

"If you want to go, *go*," he said. "But you'll go without me. And without the map."

The map Angus had fucking *invented*?

He felt his hands clench into fists.

"Give me that map, or I will kick your ass."

Randy sneered, and in that moment, Angus thought he looked like Kirkland. Looked like every bully that had ever pushed Angus around.

"I'm tired of your crap," Randy said. "I was wrong about you. Maybe I've *always* been wrong about you."

He turned and walked down the hall.

Angus stared at his back.

That motherfucker. That *cocksucker*.

So angry he couldn't think, could barely *see*.

He heard Lybrand and O'Doyle, coming closer.

Angus jogged to catch up to Randy.

8:14 A.M.

Such a tiny little nest.

A big boulder with a cracked notch at the bottom, creating a shadowy overhang. She'd dug into the stony ground, making it deep enough to lay down in and not be seen, just wide enough for a canvas cot, a half-empty case of water bottles, a few boxes of military rations.

And a sealed plastic bin.

Don't you wanna know what's in there?

He didn't. He had to.

Sonny tried to open the lid's plastic latches, but his hands shook so bad the fingers rattled together. Was this what he could look forward to in the years to come? Be palsied like Gramma McGuiness?

If he didn't hurry, he wouldn't live long enough to find out.

He ripped at the latches, a burst of rage and panic that twisted one, bent it.

"Oh, shit," he said, looking at where the blue plastic had folded with a white line. No covering that up. When Miss Murder came back, she'd know. She'd *know*.

He opened the lid. Inside, boxes of ammo, a gun-cleaning kit, bits of electronics. Energy bars.

And ... a purse.

Sonny grabbed it, opened it

He stopped, scanned the horizon. No sign of her.

Inside the purse: lipstick, keys, single stick of Wrigley's gum, some lint, car keys.

A small, spiral-bound pad of paper. He flipped the cover open, read.

Possible survivors. Connell. The science lady and her Indian dad. O'Doyle and a bunch of guards. Angus. Randy.

All those bones and body parts in the camp ... could that many people still be alive? Maybe. Maybe they were all down in the mine when the attack hit.

Sonny put the pad back in the purse. When he did, his fingers felt something in the liner. A tug opened up a hidden pocket. Inside were ID badges: Carrie Thomas, private investigator; Melissa Wilson, detective, Salt Lake City Police Department; Harriet McGuire, FBI; Maggie Smith, reporter, *MiningWorld* magazine. And driver's licenses: Miriam Van Doren, Vermont; Connie Browning, California; Kayla Meyers, Texas.

Were any of these identities real? They all looked perfect, legit. Who the hell *was* this woman?

She'd hiked up to the other entrance. Was she going into the tunnels, to kill the survivors just like she'd killed Cho?

A sudden thought: Sonny had to go after her, save those people.

"No fucking way," he said, the reaction powerful, instant, shaming. Even in the prime of his youth, he probably wouldn't have had the balls to go after her. And he wasn't young anymore. Not even close.

If there were survivors, Sonny wasn't brave enough to help them.

At least, not *down there* he couldn't.

One last look through the binoculars. Sonny scanned the landscape, looking for any sign of Miss Murder.

Nothing.

He put fake IDs in one pocket. He put the car keys in the other.

"Fuck you, you psycho bitch."

He put the purse back in the bin, put everything back in place, then he quietly slipped out of her warren.

Sonny knew where she'd gone: up the same trail he'd taken to the mesa, where Anderson and his friends had gone in. He could move the Land Rover closer to that spot, find a place where he could watch the mesa. If Kirkland or any of the others came out, Sonny could pick them up halfway down the trail. If that woman came out? He'd be far enough away to drive off before she could get anywhere near him.

"Get them out of there, Kirkland," he said. "Get them out of that mountain, I promise you, I'll be waiting."

8:16 A.M.

The Linus Highway went down.

The footprints did not—they went *left*, into a tunnel that was little more than a crack in the wall. She'd barely be able to turn around in there. Not even enough room to use the Galil.

If she was wedged in there, and those living lava lamps came after her...

Kayla holstered the Steyr, pulled the little industrial computer from a pouch and examined the map. This branch to the left, one of many between here and the Dense Mass. Other tunnels, too, branches off branches off branches. Hundreds of ways to go, if not *thousands*. This tunnel system...staggering in size and complexity. The biggest maze the world had ever seen.

No telling how old these footprints were. The Little Prick & His Bestest Butt-Buddy could have been here minutes ago. Could have been here *days* ago.

Another very real possibility—what if those two weren't even in the caves anymore at all? She might follow their tracks for days and never lay eyes on them.

Only two exits on the map, and one of them—the shaft—completely destroyed. Angus and Randy had come in via the Linus Highway. Odds were they'd come out the same way.

And, the Highway led straight to the Dense Mass—the goal of Connell Kirkland and everyone who might be with him.

Angus and Randy weren't the only ones she needed to kill.

She put the map away, checked the Marco/Polo device. Still no signals.

Those footprints, so enticing. But following them, that wasn't the smart choice.

Kayla stowed the Marco/Polo device. She drew the Steyr.

She continued down the Linus Highway.

8:24 A.M.

The noise: loud, echoing off the stone carvings and flat floor. It reminded Randy of a phrase he'd heard in college—*give a thousand monkeys a thousand computer keyboards and an infinite amount of time, and they'll produce the works of Shakespeare.* Something like that.

He didn't care about monkeys. Or Shakespeare. He didn't care about keyboards, either—just the sounds they made.

The *clacks.* The *clicks.*

So loud it was almost deafening. How many silverbugs would it take to make that much racket?

He'd find out in just a few more feet, when he reached the next intersection—because it sounded like the noise was coming from there, from the hallway on the right.

Angus, tugging on his arm.

"Dude, fuck this. We'll find another way."

Randy pulled his arm free. He didn't even want that bastard touching him.

"No, we're almost there. Straight is the shortest way. And the scrambler's working. Isn't it?"

Angus pulled out the walkie-talkie. Nodded.

If the scrambler was working, did they have anything to fear?

Randy moved closer. If Angus didn't want to come, he could stay behind.

How had he been friends with that man for so long? Followed him around. Made excuses for him. Randy had wanted a friend, a *real* friend, so bad that he'd ignored what his eyes showed him, what his ears told him.

Not anymore.

A silverbug stumbled out of the hallway that led right, half crawling, half rolling. Randy's headlamp beam played off the burnished shell.

He watched it for a moment. There could be danger here. He had to know if it was safe for O'Doyle and the others. He took a big breath, then stepped forward and peeked around the corner.

His headlamp beam showed something that didn't make sense.

The walls, they were *moving*. The ceiling, too. The floor looked like a shimmering wave of metallic snow.

Silverbugs. *Everywhere*. Packed in so tight he couldn't see the stone beneath them.

Angus came up, also peeked around the corner.

"Holy *shit*," he said. "What are they doing?"

Randy shook his head. "Maybe they were doing something specific before the scrambler hit them. Something coordinated."

The hallway dead-ended about fifty feet in, shimmered with a thick coat of the robots. Was this an alcove? Or maybe a hall that hadn't been finished yet?

A silverbug dropped from the ceiling, dangled by one long leg, then fell, crashing into others. Its round body rolled down. It started to crawl, or tried to, sliding over the silverbugs below it.

"Let's go," Angus said.

No. Not yet. Randy wanted—*needed*—to know what they were doing. There was one way to find out.

"Shut off the scrambler."

Angus stood, appalled. "Are you fucking *insane?* I'm not shutting the goddamn thing off, not for a second. What the fuck is wrong with you, Randy? You better pull your head out of your ass, *pronto*, Kemosabe, or—"

Randy turned, grabbed Angus by the throat and squeezed lightly.

Angus froze, stared, wide eyes blinking.

"Things aren't like they used to be," Randy said. "From now on, *I* tell *you* what to do, and you do it. Understand?"

Angus tried to shake his head, but Randy squeezed tighter. Tears filled Angus's eyes. He was afraid. Afraid of Randy. It was…exciting. It felt *good*. Angus had treated him like shit for so long. Randy had eaten that shit with a spoon and begged for seconds.

Not anymore.

He reached to Angus's belt, pulled out the walkie-talkie. He let go of the smaller man's neck. Angus took a step away, rubbing at his throat.

A wash of guilt—that was no way to treat someone, not even Angus. Randy had been bullied enough times in his life to know there was no excuse to do it to someone else. He would make it up to Angus. Later. There were good people down here—Randy needed to do whatever it took to make sure they were safe.

He pinched the volume knob between forefinger and thumb. He turned it past zero, felt the click as it shut off.

A thousand monkeys stopped typing. Dead silence. The silverbugs didn't move.

Randy looked at the walkie-talkie, made sure he'd actually turned it off. He had.

"They're recalibrating," Angus whispered.

The noise hammered back all at once, someone hitting the power on a TV that already had the volume maxed out. The machines burst into action.

"Turn it back on," Angus said quietly. "Now."

Randy started to, then stopped. The silverbugs didn't seem to notice him. No wedge-shaped heads pointed his way.

A few seconds more…

The living sheet of platinum writhed with activity, machines moving so fast he couldn't focus on a single one for more than a second. A new sound joined the familiar clicking—the rapid-fire popping, chipping sound of breaking rock.

So much movement, a swimming pool full of ants.

On his left, a cluster of them pressing their wedge-shaped heads to the wall, to one of the carved tiles. The wedges moved so fast they *blurred*, smashing into the rock, kicking up a cloud of stone chips.

Down on the floor, silverbugs scurried over one another. Their wedge-shaped heads did something different, they pecked at the loose stone, and every time they did the loose stone was no longer there.

"The machines built this place," Angus said. "The tunnels, maybe the caverns… all of it."

A silverbug stopped chipping. It rotated—the wedge pointed toward Randy. Then another silverbug turned. And another.

The scrambler was ripped from his hands.

Angus turned it on, cranked the volume knob all the way up.

"I'll just hold on to this," he said, and jammed it back into his belt. "Randy, I used to think you were smart, but you know what? You're a fucking retard."

"That's not a cool thing to call someone."

"*Now* is the time to be politically correct? *Double-fucking*-retard. Like that better?"

The silverbugs, drunk again. The one that had first looked at Randy slipped from the wall. Two split feet reached out, grabbed the legs of others to try to stay up, but all three fell to the floor, exposing the tile they'd been carving.

Randy stared at it in disbelief. Not a carving of rocktopi or tribesmen or deer or anything else. Modern people, wearing mining helmets.

Seven of them.

"Oh my God," Angus said. He pointed. "Randy, those carvings…"

They were stylized, but their likenesses unmistakable: little Angus, tall Connell, muscular O'Doyle, Veronica's ponytail, Lybrand's bulk.

And there, on the very end: Randy's wraparound plastic glasses.

The carvings were like a sentence, reading left to right. He looked at the next panel: blank. The two after that, blank as well. The sequence wasn't finished, but that didn't matter. Veronica had explained that the tiles were like a sentence. Randy had seen similar sequences up in the Picture Cavern—knew how that sentence was supposed to end.

Over the noise of a thousand monkeys typing, another sound … a woman, yelling.

Randy and Angus turned, saw Lybrand helping O'Doyle hop down the hallway. Not that far behind them, Connell, Veronica and Sanji.

"*Run,*" Lybrand shouted. "The rocktopi are coming again!"

31

15,967 feet below the surface

8:26 A.M.

"Light...up ahead," Bertha said, each word a heavy breath out, each pause a gasping breath in. "It's...gotta be...Dense Mass Cavern. Keep going."

She carried most of Patrick's weight, a burden that made each step punishing, from her heels to her knees to her back, through legs that begged her to stop, to a stomach that threatened to spew if she didn't.

Eyes scrunched tight, he shook his head.

"I can't," he said. "Just leave me."

"The fuck I will. *Come on.*"

Bertha took another step. Almost dragging him now.

From behind her, she heard the hiss of leaves on pavement and the sound of heavy footsteps—both coming closer.

If she could just get him to the Dense Mass Cavern. Then what? She only had a knife, and she was sucking air so bad she didn't know if she could even wield that. Maybe find a place to hide. Something. Anything. She would not give up.

Veronica raced by at a full sprint. Rage blossomed, made Bertha want to drop O'Doyle, pull her knife and cut the bitch. Bertha had looked back a few times, seen Veronica dawdling, fucking around with carvings or paintings. Maybe she'd dropped out of scrambler range. Maybe she was the reason Patrick was about to die.

His leg gave out: he slid to his left, started to fall, taking her down with him—Sanji was there, catching them both, kept them upright.

"I've got you," he said, grunting under their weight.

Bertha regained her balance. "I have his right, get on his left."

Before Sanji could adjust, Kirkland slid under Patrick's left arm.

"Sanji, go," Kirkland said. "Catch up to your daughter."

The Indian man hesitated, glanced at Patrick, then after his daughter. He nodded at Kirkland, ran down the hall.

The brief pause made her body think it was done, and when she started moving, that body rebelled. Her stomach heaved, sending bile down her chin, onto her webbing and KoolSuit. Her legs cramped.

She ignored both things.

One more step. One more step. One more step.

Up ahead, the hall ended in light.

"Almost there," she grunted. She didn't know if she was telling Patrick or her legs.

His weight lurched against her. She glanced left, saw Kirkland limping, favoring the knee—but he didn't let go.

"O'Doyle, you fat *fuck*," she said, forcing the words out through pain-clenched teeth and snarling lips. "Walk, goddammit, *help us!*"

Patrick said nothing. His head lolled, bounced with each step.

Passed out.

She and Kirkland were carrying all of his 250 pounds.

A rocktopi screech echoed through the hall, a drill bit driving through steel.

They were so close she smelled their billowing stench.

Memories of her childhood sprang up, unbidden, unneeded. A camping trip with her father. Him teaching her how to shoot. Hunting deer. Him explaining *life feeds life,* that in the end all creatures wind up as food. Her letting herself believe him, so that she could pull the trigger, kill an animal that had never threatened her.

Now she was the target.

This is what it feels like to be prey.

Kirkland yelped—that was the only word for it—and limped so badly he almost fell. Still, he refused to let go.

"Ten more steps," he said. "We're almost there!"

The rocktopi were right behind them, so close she waited for a blade to slash into her calves, her thighs.

Nine steps.

Eight.

The end of the hall, bright, blinding, bouncing.

Seven steps.

Six.

A crash to her right, the ring of metal, a knife skittering down the hall in front of her, rolling and bouncing like a quarter thrown across a table.

Five steps.

Four.

Kirkland, screaming, falling, skidding.

Three steps.

Bertha's left arm around Patrick, her ear on his chest, her right arm thrown between his legs, the back of her head on his ribs, still reaching, grabbing Kirkland's wrist, standing, all of Patrick's weight on her shoulders.

Screeching. Hissing. Colored lights playing off the wall carvings.

They should be on her by now, they should be slicing, chopping.

Two steps.

Dragging Kirkland. Carrying Patrick.

Her body giving up.

One step.

Blinding light.

Falling.

Bertha Lybrand tucked into a ball. She waited for the cutting to begin.

32

16,000 feet below the surface

Connell rolled to his back, clutched his knee. Such *pain*. Something wrong in there.

Chest heaving, lungs burning, every muscle giving up the fight.

No screeches.

A new sound, unmistakable—the sound of a waterfall.

His eyes opened: pain forgotten, a rush of horror—flashing rocktopi filled the hall, just five feet away.

Oh God gonna die I hope there's a heaven I might see Cori should have lived a better life so I could have gone to heaven and be with her…

"Get up, *slowly.*" Sanji's voice. Quiet, calm, the kind of voice you use if someone trips and lands near a poisonous snake.

Connell stared. The rocktopi … they had stopped at the end of the hall, a mass of forming and shrinking tentacles, platinum knives, pulsing purples and coursing blacks.

Hands, helping him stand. Veronica.

Connell didn't understand. "They're not attacking. Why?"

"Not sure," she said. "Maybe coming in here is taboo for their religion."

Randy and Sanji, struggling to rouse O'Doyle. Angus, helping Lybrand to her feet. Everyone slowly backing away from the rocktopi.

It didn't make any sense. He should be dead. They should all be dead.

"Religion? What are you talking about?"

Angus answered. "Holy ground. And these motherfuckers build one *hell* of a church."

He tilted his head behind him.

Connell stopped, looked—and felt the bottom drop out of his world.

Gigantic. So big he couldn't process it, half-buried in the cavern floor.

The Dense Mass.

He'd seen the map. He'd known the dimensions of this cavern: four miles long, a half mile wide. He'd known those dimensions, been prepared for them. Nothing, however, could prepare him for the vastness that spread before his eyes.

Monstrous.

Colossal.

Really, really fucking big.

Up above, in the ceiling, a string of artificial suns like the one in the kidney-shaped cavern. They cast a bluish tint down onto the metallic behemoth below.

A *fountain pen with the cap on.*

A *cartridge with bullets on both ends.*

The mystery of the caves, the creatures, the silverbugs, *everything.* The rocktopi's "Garden of Eden" wasn't a myth, wasn't the creation of some primitive religion.

As unbelievable as it was, the evidence towered in front of him, real and undeniable and massive beyond comprehension. Blue-white light gleamed off an all-too-familiar color.

The rocktopi were aliens after all.

Their Garden of Eden?

The ship that had brought them to Earth thousands of years ago. A ship made of solid platinum.

8:30 A.M.

Still holding Connell, helping him stay on his feet, Veronica Reeves stared at the ship. So did everyone else.

Everyone except Lybrand.

"We need to move," the woman said. "Those creatures might change their mind and come in after us."

Veronica glanced to the hallway entrance she'd just left. Such a crazy, panicked run to get here, she hadn't looked at anything—and now she couldn't help *but* look.

The rocktopi packed into the round hallway entrance. They shimmered with colors they hadn't displayed before. Blues, greens, coursing grays and blacks.

The cavern walls around that entrance: dense with carvings, intricate shapes, curved columns, stonework of the highest caliber spreading left and right as far as the eye could see, and *up* as well, rising with the wall until it curved far overhead.

Spectacular, but *broken*. Cracked in a thousand places. Chips and chunks had fallen away, some as big as cars or buses, to crash and crumble on the floor beneath.

And the floor itself. Big, sprawling tiles of bright, colorful patterns. Enamel, maybe, or some other material. She didn't know. Miles and miles of what must have once been flat and perfect, but like the walls, thousands of cracks ran through them, making the floor uneven like a sprawling concrete parking lot after a severe earthquake. Craters, some small, some the size of swimming pools, filled with and surrounded by jagged boulders, smaller rocks and gravel—ejecta from parts of the ceiling dropping down from over a thousand feet above.

Breathtaking. The scale, the scope the grandeur. An ancient ruin that dwarfed Angkor and Tikal, Teotihuacán and Pompeii, Vijayanagar and Persepolis.

"Hey, *dumb-asses!*" Lybrand again, yelling this time. "In case everyone forgot, the extra-fucking-terrestrials that want to butcher us are standing right over there."

Veronica came back to the moment, saw that the others had also been staring at the impossible scene: the ruined ship, the walls, the endless floor.

Extraterrestrials. Yes, no question about it anymore—creatures from another planet. A partial answer to the larger puzzle, an answer that created far more questions.

"Lybrand is right," Sanji said. "We need to move."

Everyone looked to Connell. He was sitting on a knee-high rock, head hung, legs spread out, the very picture of exhaustion. Spots of orange on his shoulder—red blood from torn stitches soaking through the KoolSuit's yellow microtubule material.

He realized everyone was staring at him, waiting. He shrugged.

"I'm not up to this anymore," he said. "I hurt. So bad. Randy, can you take over for a bit? Lead us west, to that river?"

Veronica was surprised by that. Surprised and annoyed.

"What am I, chopped liver?" she said. "Why him? He leads because he's a man?"

Connell shook his head. "No, because Sanji has to help carry O'Doyle. And you..."

His voice trailed off.

"*And me* what?"

"Because you're a selfish bitch," Lybrand said. "You could have helped us, but you care only about yourself." She tilted her head toward Angus. "You're as bad as him."

Veronica looked at Angus, expecting him to be just as angry as she was, but he wasn't paying attention. He stared at the ship. Doe-eyed. Mouth open. Like a little kid staring at the biggest Christmas tree he'd ever seen.

Randy nodded. "Sure, I can lead us. For now."

There was a strength to the eyes behind those glasses, strength that hadn't been there before. Lybrand was right—Veronica knew she'd run right by them, so scared she hadn't even thought of stopping to help. With Connell and O'Doyle hurt, maybe the once-mousy scientist was the best choice after all. From zero to hero. All it took, apparently, was some bloodthirsty aliens.

"Everyone up," Randy said. "I know we have injuries, but we have to move. It's fifteen minutes to the river. If we're out of sight of the rocktopi, we'll stop there for a bit."

Sanji and Lybrand again helped O'Doyle. The brief rest had let him catch his breath, somewhat. Connell limped so badly that Randy came back, slid under Connell's shoulder, helped him along. Angus could have done it, maybe, but he was still oblivious to anything save for the ship's hull passing by on their right.

As they walked, the waterfall's roar grew louder. Despite the vastness of this ancient place, no one talked. What was there to say, really? Should they ask questions to which no one had answers?

Veronica gawked at the massive ship, at the cavern wall towering up on their left, at the floor. Once upon a time this must have been a grand place, the equal of anything the world had produced. Now it was a crumbling ruin, as ravaged by time as any of the ancient cities she'd seen in her youth.

A *clink* under her foot. She stopped, picked up a chunk of gleaming platinum, twisted and warped, almost like metal-colored melted wax.

Angus pointed to the wreck.

"Look at that hole," he said. "Internal explosion, probably."

A gaping void in the central shaft. Big, maybe a hundred meters across, but it was hard to gauge the scale. The hull seemed to have sagged in, a sheet of wax dripping from a flame held below it.

"Must have been a serious blast," Randy said. "Could that have been what made it come down from space?"

Veronica held up what she'd found. "I don't think so. Whatever it was must have happened after it was already down here. A big enough bang to splash molten metal all the way to where we're standing."

She noticed the others looking down, around. There were splashes of the metal all over the place.

Angus laughed. "I'd drop that if I were you. Platinum melts at seventeen hundred degrees Celsius, and this alloy is probably a lot higher than that."

Veronica shrugged. "So?"

"So an explosion that can rain molten platinum across hundreds of meters could have been nuclear. You know, there's the whole radiation thing. But do what you want."

She tossed it away, wondering if it had felt warm in her hand.

"Let's move," Randy said. "I think I can almost see the waterfall."

As Veronica walked, the mist thinned, seemed to recede in front of her as if she was walking into a fog.

Finally, she saw the waterfall.

She stopped. So did the others.

Once upon a time, this spot must have been beyond spectacular. From two hundred feet up, water poured down, flowing over the remains of the biggest rocktopi that had ever been.

"Holy shit," Lybrand said. "Hey, Angus—that one must have liked himself even more than you do."

Carved from the mountain itself, maybe. At least two hundred feet tall. The rounded body and strange extrusions of that species. Smooth reaches of stone that ended in jagged chunks: tentacles that had long since snapped free to crash down and smash the beautiful floor below. Only two extrusions remained unbroken, reaching out and out and out; like huge, curved construction cranes stretching across the wide streets of some surreal city. Rushing water coursed over the sculpture. Millenia of erosion had carved at the stone, grinding it down. Some colors remained—bright patterns here and there in spots and chunks— but most of the exterior had been worn away by chunks of ceiling, the water, or perhaps just time itself.

The waterfall crashed down into a wide pool filled with fallen rock. One broken tentacle stuck up from the rippling surface at a shallow angle, a few streaks of green and gold still spotted with chips of black.

The river didn't stop at the pool. It raged out into a winding chasm that cut through the cavern floor. Smoothly curved stone rose up from the edges of the roiling surface, terraced layers showing the ancient river's previous paths. Here and there she saw chunks of broken, flat rock topped with thick platinum—perhaps it had once been an engineered riverbed, like the concrete spillways of Los Angeles. Whatever design this place once had, it was long gone, the victim of erosion, falling rock and lack of repair.

When had the rocktopi left this place to crumble under its own weight? Was it already empty when Christ was born? Even older than that? When Ahmose united Egypt? When Sargon of Akkad carved out the world's first empire?

The hungry river wasn't satisfied with the stone rocktopi and the cavern floor. Oh, no, there seemed to be no end to that monster's appetite. The river raged into a hull crack that spanned nearly a hundred meters. Over thousands of years, the silt-filled water had acted like a slow and steady buzz saw, each change of the river's course taking a chunk out of the dead ship. Clanks and plinks constantly filled the air: the sound of current-powered gravel smashing into metal.

At some point, the undercut area had collapsed. The ship's hull arced high up on either side of the hundred-meter break. At the top, the two reaching sides almost touched, forming a mist-filled, shadowy canyon.

Like a cross section on some architect's drawing, the river's erosion exposed the ravaged hull's interior. Circular hallways with gleaming rings on the ceiling. Circular room after circular room. Wherever she saw undamaged walls, there were no edges—only curves.

Randy pointed to a flat spot at the edge of the waterfall's pool.

"Put O'Doyle there. We all need a rest."

Veronica left Connell, ran to the spot, got down on hands and knees. She swept aside gravel, broken bits of colored masonry, a few fist-sized rocks, clearing a space for him to lie down. It didn't make up for her earlier selfishness, but at least it was something.

Lybrand and Sanji set O'Doyle down, then collapsed on either side of him. Veronica wondered how much longer they could keep carrying the man. Hopefully, a short rest would let O'Doyle support some of his own weight.

Connell limped over to the trio and sat. He pointed to the near side of the waterfall.

"Angus, there's those alcoves."

Veronica saw them. Three on either side of the ancient rocktopi statue, set far enough back that the water hadn't eroded them. Half domes set into the wall. Protected from falling rock as well. Whatever was inside, perhaps it had been protected from the ravages of age.

Randy raised his hands to get everyone's attention.

"Seems like the river goes all the way through," he said. "But we don't know for sure. We don't want to get caught inside and not be able to get out. So while you rest, I'm going to walk along the shoreline, see what I can see."

Angus raised his hand. "I'll go with you."

Randy looked at him for a second, doubtful. "Really?"

"You know it, buddy," Angus said. "I won't let you go alone."

"Okay," Randy said, and he smiled. "Cool. Thank you."

Angus nodded once, the pursed-lip *no problem* nod of a bro. Maybe he'd changed, too. Probably not. At least someone was going with Randy, because Veronica sure as fuck wasn't about to do it.

Randy turned to Connell. "I know you wanted to keep two walkie-talkies working, but Angus and I should have one if we go into that ship so the silverbugs can't make the rocktopi follow us if there are rocktopi inside. And we should leave O'Doyle without one, because he can't even run. I want Angus to modify Lybrand's walkie-talkie."

Connell nodded tiredly.

"As long as we still have one to contact the surface, if we get close but can't get out, I guess so. Do it."

Lybrand tossed her walkie-talkie to Angus. He knelt and got to work on it. It took him only a few minutes to crack open the case, make whatever adjustment he made, then put the thing back together again. Angus tossed it back to Lybrand, who set it next to O'Doyle.

Randy looked at his wrist display.

"It's eight forty-eight in the morning," he said. "Our wounded need some rest if we're going to make it. Twenty minutes is all we can spare. Angus and I will be back at eight minutes after nine, sharp. Then, we head out. Angus, let's go."

The two men jogged toward the sprawling ship.

Veronica watched them go for a moment, then looked toward the alcoves. She could see inside a little. She focused. A carving, like the others, but this one was round. No, a half sphere.

A planet.

8:50 A.M.

Kayla didn't move. She didn't breathe. She had never been this still in all her life. Not when men with guns had been coming to kill her. Not when her father had been stumbling down the hall, trying to figure out which daughter's room he would enter next. She stood in a tunnel branch that was no more than a fissure, so thin she barely fit.

Steyr in hand, she watched the silvery four-legged spider walk past her up the Linus Highway.

Smooth strides of long metal legs, so thin they didn't look strong enough to support the round body. She knew state-of-the-art technology. She knew what her country was capable of building, knew what other countries were capable of building.

No one could make a machine that moved so smoothly.

When it was ten feet past, she eased out of the fissure just enough to aim. She fired. The bullet slammed into the round body, denting the metal and knocking the spider to the far wall.

It took a staggering, wobbly step. Kayla fired again. This bullet punched a neat little hole in the shell.

The machine stopped walking. The round body dropped to the silt, legs twitching spasmodically.

Kayla fired one more round.

The thing stopped moving.

She carefully lifted it by one thin leg. Heavy, far heavier than it looked.

"You wanted evidence, André?"

It *was* evidence—but was it *enough* evidence?

Kayla stashed the dented robot in the fissure. She'd retrieve it on her way out.

She checked the map—only about forty-five minutes to the Dense Mass. No other spiders in sight. None of those squishy killers, either.

Kayla slid a fresh magazine into the Steyr, then continued down the Linus Highway.

8:52 A.M.

Above him, a sprawling arc of platinum that mostly blocked out the artificial suns high above. A few feet below him, a river that had gouged a hole in an alien ship.

Randy Wright stood on a thin ledge of platinum that stuck out over the rushing water. The ledge connected to a narrow, flat, highly polished area that must have once been the river bottom before the unforgiving water cut deeper.

As dangerous as things were, as many obstacles as they had yet to cover, this was so thrilling. People needed help—he was helping them. People needed a leader—he was leading them.

Him. *Leading.* Dirty Fucking Randy.

"How's it look?" Angus asked from behind him.

"Pretty good, actually," Randy said. "Current is swift here, but doesn't look dangerous. As long as people can stay afloat, they're fine."

Back where the raging torrent entered the ship, there were dangerous spots: rapids made from chunks of rock and shards of metal sticking up from the surface. Fifty meters in, however, the river took a bend to the right, out of sight, bleeding away some of that current. And the water leveled out, bleeding off even more.

At some point in the distant past, this part of the ship had collapsed. Torn hull all around, twisted hallways, warped rooms. The material that had fallen to the bottom was long gone, steadily carried away by the river's constant erosion.

This would work. This would carry them through. They were going to get out alive.

Watching his feet, Randy slowly turned.

Angus was right there, smiling, closer than Randy had thought—almost blocking the ledge.

"You think they can make it," he said.

Randy wished the man wasn't standing so close. The ledge was so thin there was no way around him.

"Yeah, I do."

"That only took us five minutes to figure out," Angus said. "Come on, let's check out some of this ship before we head back." He pointed behind him, to his right. "We can get in through that hallway, looks like."

A bent tube stuck out slightly, the once round shape contorted into a tight oval angling down. Randy could see through that oval to the area beyond—a round hallway. It looked straight. Angus was right: that would lead into the undamaged areas of the ship. They could spend a few minutes and . . .

No. As much as Randy wanted to see this place, this wasn't the time for that.

"We can't," he said. "We have to get back. If we go in there and get hurt, we—"

"What are we, seven years old?" Angus laughed, spoke in that tone he'd always used when he wanted to do something risky, when he wanted to make Randy feel like a chicken. "We're not going to *get hurt*, for fuck's sake. We'll never get a chance like this again. We have to grab it."

Of course Angus wanted to explore. That's what he did. The chance to see something no one else had seen. Not just that, the technology that might still exist inside the ship, things that could fuel Angus's imagination for inventions. He hadn't wanted to come for friendship or support, he'd wanted to come for himself.

Randy should have known.

He shook his head. "No exploring. There's the rocktopi, and the silverbugs, and this wreck is thousands of years old. There could be all kinds of dangerous things in there, stuff we haven't seen yet."

Angus still hadn't moved, still blocked the way off the ledge. He seemed so eager, so excited.

"Danger this, danger that, blah-blah-blah," he said. "This is an *alien ship*. After we get out of here, this place will be locked up tighter than a nun's cooter. The security here will make Area 51 look like Grand Central Station. You'll never get a chance like this ever again. Come on, man, all I'm asking for is ten lousy minutes."

Randy licked his lips. The river burbled on below him, the sound of the waterfall echoed in from outside.

Angus was right.

But what if this once-in-a-lifetime opportunity ended up costing someone else's life?

"We're going back," he said. "We just can't risk it."

The smile drained from Angus's face. The helpful friend was gone: the arrogant ass had returned.

"You used to be a cool guy," he said, sneering. "You turned into a loser. You want to waste this chance? Fine. Be a loser."

Angus turned, scooted off the ledge to polished metal that lined the river's path. He ran for the twisted tube.

"Angus, don't!"

Randy chased after him, but it was too late. An agile and an experienced caver, Angus easily slid into the tube and was gone. Randy stopped at the tube, shouted in.

"Get your ass back here!"

"Ten minutes," Angus called back, his voice already fading away. "Come on, man, don't leave me by myself. What if I get hurt?"

That cutting laugh of his, echoing off metal.

Randy's gloved hands clenched, unclenched. He couldn't leave the man. And he couldn't deny it—every last bit of him wanted to see more, wanted to see the inside of the ship that had brought the rocktopi.

Ten lousy minutes. That was all.

"Hold up," he called into the tube, then crawled through.

8:57 A.M.

"*Get out, Connell.*" *Something liquid and gurgling masked her smooth voice. She sounded weak, fractured.* "*You have to get out.*"

He shook his head.

"*No, I need to stay with you.*"

Her broken hands reached up, grabbed his shoulders. He could smell her blood. She shook him, shook him.

"*You'll die here. They're going to cut you open.*"

A glow behind her. He knew what it was, but he couldn't know, he'd never seen anything like it before.

A tentacle rose up, shimmering with coursing patterns of red and yellow. The end of it wrapped tightly around the center ring of a double-crescent knife . . .

Connell woke, pushed himself up on one elbow. Heart kicking, he looked around, expecting to see her, Cori, coming for him.

She wasn't there, of course. She never was.

He groaned as the exhaustion reclaimed his body. The waterfall's roar. Sanji, sleeping. O'Doyle, also asleep, his head in Lybrand's lap.

She was looking right at Connell.

"You dream a lot," she said. "Nightmares."

He nodded. "I do. You?"

She glanced off. "Yeah. All the damn time. Hate 'em."

Was there anyone that liked nightmares? Maybe. Crazy how a nightmare about Cori could actually scare him when the waking world provided all-too-real terrors.

Connell looked at his wrist display: just ten minutes since Randy and Angus had left? He'd been asleep for, what, five minutes?

He looked around again.

"Hey, where's Veronica?"

Lybrand jerked a thumb over her shoulder.

"She went to check out those alcoves."

A new layer of fatigue. How could someone that smart be so stupid?

"Can you go get her? We need to stay together."

Lybrand shook her head.

"I don't give a shit about Blondie. I'm staying with Patrick."

Connell couldn't blame Lybrand for that. He pushed himself up, put some weight on the knee. Not as bad as before, but also stiffer. Maybe the trick was to keep moving, as long as "moving" didn't involve sprinting at top speed or carrying O'Doyle's weight. Something grinding away in there, though. Not a good thing.

He limped to Sanji, shook the man's shoulder.

"Wake up. Randy will be back here in ten minutes, and your dumb-ass daughter went off on her own."

Sanji blinked a few times, then the words hit home and he was on his feet in seconds. When this had started, he seemed like a jovial guy, the very picture of fat and happy. Now his eyes were sunken, the skin below them darker, the wrinkles more pronounced. He seemed like a person who had never known real danger. Now that he'd experienced it, some of the light had gone out of his world.

"I'll get her," he said. "Which way?"

"I'll go with you. Got to keep this knee loose. Lybrand, you okay here?"

She shrugged. "Does it matter if I'm not? Either way, you're still going after that bitch."

"Hey," Sanji said. "That's my daughter you're talking about."

Lybrand glared at him like she wanted to bury a knife in his throat, then that expression softened.

"Yeah, okay," she said. "Whatever. Just hurry back. Don't make us wait to leave."

Connell and Sanji walked across a floor that once must have been spectacular. Still was, really, even with the damage. The giant stone rocktopi on their right, splashing water sparkling from the blue-white light above.

"Your daughter always this bullheaded?"

"She is," Sanji said. "But I am worried about her. Not just her physical safety. I think this is getting to her mentally."

"It's getting to all of us."

Sanji shook his head. "Yes, but look at the decision she just made, to go off on her own. She's not thinking straight. Will you help me keep an eye on her? Please?"

A father, worried for his child. An emotion Connell could empathize with, imagine, but could never really know. Cori's accident had stolen that bit of his life, just as it had stolen her.

"Sure," he said. "I'll keep an eye on her."

They reached the alcove, a semicircle some fifteen feet high, set into the cavern's carved walls. Inside, a round room with a curved ceiling, the apex some twenty feet high. Like the Picture Cavern, detailed carvings completely covered the walls.

Sanji strode toward Veronica.

"Ronni, what's wrong with you? You can't go off on your own!"

She spoke without turning around.

"They were running away."

Her voice sounded distant, tired … maybe a bit disturbed. It stopped Sanji in his tracks.

"Running away from what?" he asked.

Veronica pointed to a carving just to the right of the alcove's entrance. Connell came closer.

The carving showed a long, narrow, evil-looking shape, bristling with many sharp protuberances and jagged spines. It made Connell think of paper wasps, with their thin bodies and dangerous demeanor.

Sanji reached out, let his gloved finger play along the shape.

"Looks almost biological," he said. "Another alien of some kind?"

"I think it's a spaceship," Veronica said. "I believe this was their enemy in some ancient war. Follow the sequence of tiles."

The tile to the left of the wasp ship showed a familiar image: the same tapered cylinder that had been on the hallway tiles, the same shape as the real-life version sitting cracked and broken out in the cavern. Engraved lines had to be weapon fire of some kind, reaching out from the tapered hulls and into a pair of wasp ships, both of which were breaking up into pieces. The next square showed a planet surrounded by wasp ships. In the middle of the planet was a detailed rocktopi. The next square chilled Connell—the planet breaking into pieces from a wasp ship attack.

"Their planet was destroyed," Veronica said. "Looks like the Garden of Eden out there was part of a navy but had no home to return to."

Connell wondered what that must have felt like. A planet destroyed, a species suddenly without a home. The rocktopi stranded in their warships, left with nowhere to turn.

"That wasn't the end of it," Veronica said. "Look at this one."

Her gloved fingers traced the curves and lines of another tile. Hundreds of the wasp ships, surrounding three of the rocktopi's tapered, cylindrical forms.

Connell shook his head, feeling actual pity for the ancestors of creatures that had tried to kill him.

"They were being hunted," he said.

Veronica nodded. "Looks like they were highly outnumbered. Maybe those three ships were all that remained. No reinforcements. They fled. They came here. Oh, for fuck's sake … their Year Zero—it's the year they *landed*. How could I not have figured that out?"

"That doesn't matter now," Sanji said. "Do these carvings show where they came *from*? Obviously, they can breathe our atmosphere and survive in our gravity, but how did they know Earth would be a suitable habitat?"

Connell looked around for carvings that might answer the question. He found none. Neither did Sanji or Veronica.

"We'll never know," she said. "Maybe they didn't know ahead of time. Maybe they searched until they found a suitable planet. Could have taken centuries. Millennia, even. Hundreds of generations born on ship, living their lives, dying. A self-contained culture."

Connell knew nothing about physics or space travel, other than what he'd learned from watching movies and TV. Had that ship out in the cavern been able to travel faster than the speed of light? It must have—the nearest star other than the Sun was some insane distance. More than twenty *million* miles, if he remembered right.

"Ronni, look at this."

Sanji was off to the right, examining a series of large tiles, each about four feet square. At the bottom of the first tile, the definitive outline of the Wah Wahs. Above that outline, a large, rectangular chunk of the mountain range floated in the air, leaving a gaping hole beneath. A tapered cylinder shape was half in, half out of that hole.

"The rectangle," Veronica said, her voice cold and flat. "It wasn't a trench. They lifted the entire fucking mountain and set the ship inside. That rectangle is thirteen thousand years old. That's how long these bastards have been down here." She rubbed at her temples. "Thirteen *thousand* years ago. The Mesolithic Period. People hunted with sticks and stones. Flint spear points were our highest level of technology. There might have been less than a million people on the entire planet, and very few in North America. So why bury themselves? The rocktopi could have easily wiped out humanity and taken over Earth for themselves."

"Perhaps the surface is too cold for them," Sanji said. "They seem to thrive in these high temperatures. I wouldn't be surprised if even a mild winter could kill them."

That made sense, but Connell knew that wasn't the reason. His eyes flicked across the sequences. The history of a species spelled out in carved stone. One image after another—the battle, the planet's destruction, the overwhelming odds—connected in his mind, and the rocktopi story became perfectly clear.

"It's not about temperature," he said. "I mean, sure, they like it hot, and cold might kill them, but if they can engineer that huge ship out there they could have made buildings to keep them warm. They didn't want to conquer, they wanted to survive. They're down here because they are *hiding*. Hiding from that wasp-ship enemy that wants to wipe them out. That's why they're so deep. That's why there's no trace of them on the surface. That's why they bury all remains of anything they attack—they don't want any evidence, not even a shred, that they're here. Because that way, even if the wasp ships find Earth, it's possible they might *not* find the rocktopi."

Sanji rubbed at his face.

"Then why are the ones we've fought so primitive? Their ancestors built starships. They must have built the silverbugs, too, designed that cavern with the food that has kept their descendants alive for thousands of years. So, why are their descendants seemingly no smarter than cavemen?"

Connell said nothing. He didn't have answers.

Sanji checked his wrist display. "Five minutes until Randy returns. Quickly, let's see if the next alcove has any answers."

He and his daughter rushed out, went left. Connell wanted to tell them to stop, to go back to Lybrand and O'Doyle, but he wanted answers even more.

Just a few more minutes.

He ran after them.

9:01 A.M.

In here, the artificial sun's light couldn't reach. In the ship, his headlamp beam was the only illumination.

Angus ran from room to room, feeling shocked and giddy and amazed. He might as well have been a medieval farmer suddenly zapped forward in time and dropped onto the deck of an aircraft carrier—did he even understand the *concepts* of what he saw?

Another room, bigger than the last few. Round, with oval doors like all the others. Curved walls, shallow dome ceiling. The floor was flat, except at the edges of the room, where it curved up into the walls.

Randy entered the room.

"We have to go," he said, but he said it without conviction. He turned in place, looking at everything, just as amazed as Angus was.

"Sure," Angus said. "Just a few more minutes."

A musty, archaic odor filled the air, the smell of abandoned industrial machines combined with buildings left mildewy by receding floodwaters. River mist drifted lightly inside the ship, collected on the curved walls and dripped down to collect in little stagnant pools. The dark alien vessel felt dungeon-like and dangerous, as if it might spring to life and swallow them up at any moment.

How many rooms had he looked at so far? Six? Seven? Too excited to keep count. All the rooms had been empty. No wood, no plastic, no materials of any kind other than platinum, really, save for some ceramics embedded in the walls. Whether those bits were art or control interfaces, Angus didn't know.

And with each room he left, he wondered if the next one he entered might be a treasure trove packed with ancient yet advanced technology. It couldn't just *all* be empty, could it? He wasn't expecting a teleporter or anything, but was it too much to ask for a few gadgets and gizmos? Something he could spend years studying, taking apart, reverse engineering, then patenting?

He was already smarter than everyone he'd ever met. If anyone deserved to get a boost from a dead alien ship, it was him.

"This is so unreal," Randy said. "Every room is like a squashed bubble. All curves. I haven't seen one straight edge yet."

He'd been pissed Angus had gone in, but that had lasted about thirty seconds. Randy might be a backstabber, but he was smart enough to appreciate just how *un-fucking-believably awesome* all of this was.

Angus shook his head in pure amazement. He'd done that in every room, would probably keep doing it.

"An entire ship made of platinum-iridium," he said, sliding his hands across the curved wall. "*All* of it. To think, if not for that river eroding it, grinding bits of it to dust, and some of that water making its way to Sonny's spring, this would have never been found."

Randy knelt, rubbed his palms on the wet floor, held them in front of his headlamp beam.

"No corrosion, no decay of any kind," he said. "Must be why they chose this alloy. It doesn't break down unless acted upon by something, like the way the cave water erodes it. This hull will last *forever,* until the damn tectonic plate this mountain rests on slides back into the mantle." He stood, wiped his hands on his thighs. "But I don't see any wiring, any ducting. There's no access panels. Everything is *solid.*"

Angus thought of the silverbug he'd dissected, torn apart on top of that rock.

"Platinum is a great conductor," he said. "Signals could go through this entire hull—all three miles of it—with almost no degradation. It's just like with the ALs. You don't need wires when the shell itself is the wiring. I wonder if this was a warship? The alloy is strong, conducts well, can withstand intense heat. Imagine the kind of damage this beast could take and still keep kicking. Blowholes in it, signals still go through. No wires to sever. No wireless signals to jam. It's ..."

No *edges.* No *lines.*

Angus walked back into the strange corridor. A tube, yes, but not a straight one. It twisted subtly, up a little, to the left a little. So ... *organic.* Up above, curved metal bars blended seamlessly with the ceiling, a horizontal ladder running the length of the corridor. The long spine of some dead metal monster. He imagined the rocktopi swung from those, like a long-armed gibbon, one extrusion after another shooting out.

But even with those bars there were no seams. Everything was a curve. Nothing had an edge. Every room like a bubble ...

"Holy *shit*, Randy. This entire ship, they *cast* it, somehow."

Randy stepped to the door. "Calm down, you're yelling."

"*They cast it!* Somehow, I don't know, they take millions of tons of molten metal, they form it, inject it with air and control the, I don't know, the *air shapes* to make the rooms and the halls, then just let that shit cool and you have *the entire ship.*"

"Angus, did you change the frequency on the scrambler?"

"I mean this is *fucking titties and beer,* man! It's ..."

The flat, quiet tone of Randy's question hit home. Something was wrong. Very wrong. Randy stood in the curved entryway. His wide eyes stared down the corridor, headlamp beam catching swirls of floating river mist.

He was scared.

"I didn't change it," Angus said. "Why?"

Randy slowly raised a hand, pointed in the same direction as his headlamp beam.

Angus turned. There, maybe twenty meters away, a silverbug hung from one of the curved ceiling bars. His and Randy's headlamps blazed off a polished shell and off its perfect, unmarred legs. The shape was the same as they'd seen before.

But that *gleam* ...

This one wasn't burnished by hundreds of tiny scratches. No dents. No big scrapes.

It wasn't *old.*

More important, it wasn't milling about aimlessly. The wedge-shaped protrusion aimed at Angus, then Randy, then Angus, then Randy.

"I don't get it," Angus said. He heard the whine in his whispered words. "The scrambler doesn't affect it?"

Randy slowly stepped into the hall.

"They must have made a new one. With a new frequency, to get around our scrambling."

Angus felt like a fool. A *terrified* fool. Why had he gone searching through this ship? He should have stuck to the river, not gone into the darkness, screaming his head off like that. Had his yelling drawn the thing?

"We're missing something," he said. "The rocktopi are fucking primitives. They *couldn't* have made a new silverbug."

"If they didn't, that leaves only two possibilities. Either something we haven't seen yet made it, or the *new* AL was made by *old* ALs."

Artificial life. He'd thought of them as a collective organism. Artificial, sure, but still operating like an ant colony. Except ants were limited by biology: they couldn't engineer new kinds of themselves to deal with new threats. Artificial life — *robots* — didn't have the same limitations.

The silverbug let go. Two headlamp beams tracked it as it dropped to the floor, long, thin legs reaching out first, touching down with metal-on-metal *click*s. The round body slowly settled.

A sharp sound made Angus jump, a ringing, a scraping that echoed through the metal hall before quickly fading away.

From just under the wedge shape, a nasty-looking blade stuck out. Six inches of sharpness, curved forward like the horn of a charging rhino.

"We're in trouble," Randy said. "Now they've got soldiers to go along with the workers. The rocktopi aren't building the silverbugs, Angus — they're building themselves."

The machine didn't move. It was as still as the ship itself.

As still as death.

9:03 A.M.

Veronica stared at three carvings. Ten feet square, they were the largest she'd seen yet. Inset deeper than the others, and *rough*. It looked like the rocktopi had long ago chiseled out the tiles that had been there and carved new images in the space beneath them.

More of their story, more clues to the mystery … So why didn't she feel excited?

Not just about these tiles, why didn't she feel excited about *any* of it.

This was way more than some lost tribe. This was a game changer. This was beyond the first explosion of the atom bomb, beyond the Wright brothers, beyond Edward Jenner or Louis Pasteur, beyond Watson, Crick and Franklin. Beyond *anything* humanity had known.

As cliché as it sounded, nothing would ever be the same again.

And she was *there*. As it happened. Her earlier work had helped make this possible. She had every right to claim this as her discovery.

So, again, the question — why didn't she feel excited?

A familiar hand on her shoulder, a squeeze she would know with or without these suits.

"Ronni, what is it?"

She turned. Those big, brown eyes. The same eyes that had looked upon her as a child, the man who had taken her in, made her his own.

"Nothing," she said. "Just trying to figure these tiles out."

He held her shoulders.

"You can't lie to me. You know this."

She let herself be distracted by Connell, who was walking along the wall, looking at the tiles.

Sanji gave her a little shake, just enough to make her look at him again.

His stare bore into her. She felt like she was in high school again, coming home three hours after curfew, trying to come up with a lie so she didn't have to tell him she'd been drinking, that she'd had sex with a boy she barely knew.

"Dad it's … it's just that it's *extra-fucking-terrestrials*, as Lybrand so eloquently put it. I missed it completely. I should have seen it."

He sighed.

"How could you have seen it? They hid themselves well. And is that really something to worry about right now?"

It wasn't. She knew it wasn't. They had to worry about staying alive, getting out.

He pulled her in, hugged her. He smelled like a man that hadn't showered in days, but she didn't care. He was her father. Wherever he was, it was home.

"I know I'm not much of a fan of the sports," he said. "But their terminology is best right now. I love you, my daughter, but you need to get your head in the game." He held her at arm's length, pierced her with those brown eyes. "People are dead. We need to make sure we don't lose anyone else. Focus on that, you understand?"

She did. Everything was so fucked-up, but he was right—she could worry about it later. As long as he was here with her, that was all that mattered.

"I understand."

He forced a smile. "Good. Now show me what you're looking at, we're almost out of time."

She gestured to the carvings.

"These seem like they were an afterthought. Something else was taken out, these were carved instead. We've seen graffiti, but not replacement."

Three squares.

The first showed hundreds of rocktopi, a teeming mass of intertwined tentacles. If aliens had their own version of souls twisting and burning in hell, it would look like that. While the carving was rough, it was detailed. Half the rocktopi seemed more bloated than the ones she'd seen in the tunnels. About a quarter of the carved aliens were splitting, *popping*, the work so intricate she could easily imagine yellow fluid splashing in all directions. Another quarter were flat, deflated—the way the creatures looked after death.

"Disease of some kind," Sanji said. "No question. A plague." He pointed to the base of the carving. "Aren't those marks Chaltélian numbers?"

He was right. Yet another obvious thing she'd missed. She quickly counted, working her way through their strange base-12 system.

"Looks like … five thousand, eight hundred, sixteen."

"That's the dead?" Connell asked. "They lost that many."

Veronica realized there were two sets of numbers. One she recognized from her work in Argentina—the zero year, the beginning of their calendar.

"No, the number on the left is a measurement of time," she said. "I think what happened in that carving happened in their year five thousand, eight hundred and sixteen."

Connell huffed. "This makes my brain hurt. Fifty-eight hundred years *after* they landed? And that was like seven *thousand* years before now. Crazy."

Sanji stepped closer. His gloved fingertip poked at a splitting rocktopi.

"The other number," he said. "Maybe it's a death toll."

She counted.

"Looks like … twenty-four thousand … three hundred and five."

Her father turned, looked at her. "Twenty-four thousand? How many did they start out with?"

Veronica remembered that number from the hallway images, the ones she had thought represented their Garden of Eden.

"Thirty-two thousand," she said. "I think that was their original crew complement."

Connell let out a long whistle. "That means they lost three-quarters of their population, all at once."

Sanji turned to the carvings again. "Possibly. Five millennia after they landed, the population could have been much smaller or vastly larger. No way to know. But a massive number nonetheless. It could explain why they're so primitive. Who knows how much of the leadership and knowledge died in the plague."

"They can move mountains," Connell said. "And we're not talking some motivational poster in the break room, we're talking about literally *moving a mountain*. If they can do that, surely they have supercomputers or something that can store all their knowledge, right?"

"You are thinking short-term," Sanji said. "When the plague hit, they'd been down here for over five thousand years. How long can any computer last, even one from an incredibly advanced civilization? Surely all things break down eventually."

Connell grunted in agreement. "As often as I have to replace equipment, I guess you've got a point." He reached up, lightly slapped his palm against the second carving. "This is the wreck."

It was, obviously. The detailed carving showed the ship exactly as it looked in the cavern, with one key exception—an explosive cloud in place of the gaping hole.

"Kaboom," Connell said. "It's been seven thousand years since our last accident, but that last one was a doozy."

Veronica looked closer. More flat rocktopi. Thousands of them, very small because they were in scale with the ship.

Sanji pointed to the number marks at the bottom edge.

"Another cataclysm," he said. "When did it happen, and how many dead?"

She counted. It came easier this time.

"Just over a century after the plague hit. Another six thousand dead."

Had they been inside the ship when the explosion hit? Or perhaps in the cavern surrounding it? Could some of them have died from radiation after the fact?

Maybe it was all three things.

Connell moved to the last big tile, while her father rubbed his eyes through his thin mask.

"They could have been down to a few thousand survivors," Sanji said. "And if the blast was radioactive, some of those who survived could have suffered damage to their genetic material. Think if that happened to a fixed population of humans. The gene pool might stagnate. We thought we found birth defects in the rocktopi—that fits the idea of a limited breeding pool."

Her father spread his arms, turned in a slow circle, taking in the whole room.

"We've called the rocktopi *primitives*, even described them as *cavemen*. Everything we've seen points to a logical idea—they have devolved. Once a brilliant, spacefaring race, their homeworld destroyed, so they fled for their lives. They hid down here, possibly flourished for thousands of years until disease and tragedy gutted them, left them with a genetic pool so small inbreeding was inevitable. Imagine if that explosion also wiped out what tech they had left, or if they couldn't come into their ship until the radiation died down. How long would that take? A century? *Ten* centuries? How many generations would it take before they lost their technological knowledge altogether?"

A horrible concept. It almost made her feel sorry for the creepy crawlies. To think that a sentient race—one far more advanced than humanity—could decline like that. It was scary.

"They went out with a whimper," Veronica said. "Not a bang."

"I think their *bang* is right here," Connell said.

He pointed to the third carving. Like the second, it showed the shipwreck but at a smaller scale. A line extended down from its center. The line was five times as long as the ship. It ended in a clear representation of an explosion, one that seemed to be shattering pillars of some kind.

Sanji stepped closer. "What is that line?"

"Don't know," Connell said. "But I saw the same line on Angus's tablet map, so it's still there. That map said it goes down over four miles, but from the looks of this, it's more like twenty miles. I feel like this is important, so—"

Veronica heard a buzzing sound.

Connell looked at his wrist.

"Shit, we're supposed to be back." He looked to the alcove exit, then back at the third carving. "We'll go in a second, just see if you can help me figure this out real quick."

9:06 A.M.

They had rushed through the ship, seeing what they could in the little time they had. Those minutes had seemed like seconds.

The minutes spent silently staring at the soldier silverbug, those passed like hours.

It remained on the corridor floor. Motionless. More abstract sculpture than working machine.

Randy hadn't been trying to wait it out, he'd just been too terrified to move. That blade, the way it curved forward like a stubby scimitar. The flat gleamed. The edge showed two shining dots, each on a reflection of the two headlamp beams locked onto it.

He'd seen how fast they moved. Maybe fifteen feet away—it could close that distance in seconds.

"Randy," Angus whispered, "we have to do something."

Angus was right. They couldn't just stand there. What if new silverbugs were forming lines out in the cavern, leading rocktopi against Connell and the others? The alien creatures acted like it was forbidden for them to come in, but could their little metallic masters convince them otherwise?

"You're right," he whispered back. "The longer we wait, the more the others are at risk. We have to get back to them."

Out of the corner of his eye, he saw Angus look away from the silverbug for the first time, glance at Randy, then back to the silverbug. Angus had to be afraid, too.

That meant Randy had to be brave enough for both of them.

"Okay, here's what we do," he whispered. "We back away slowly. Maybe it will stay where it is."

"What if it doesn't? What if it follows us, or attacks?"

That whine in Angus's voice again. He had always been so full of himself. Not here. Not now.

"If it follows, we keep going," Randy said. "Our chances are better with all of us together. If it rushes us—" he licked his dry lips, felt the icy swirl of fear prickle his guts "—we grab it. We can't outrun it. It has four legs—you grab the ones on its right, I grab the ones on its left. We pull tight, like a tug-of-war. We go back the way we came and throw it into the river."

A pause.

"Like a tug-of war," Angus said.

"That's right. We just pull tight. It can't use the knife on us if we pull tight."

A bigger pause. Angus's breathing, rapid, ragged. Was he mustering his courage or hyperventilating?

"All right," he said. "Fuck it, man—let's do this."

Randy nodded, making the headlamp beam bounce along the machine's gleaming curves.

"On three, take a single step back," he said. "One ... two ... *three*."

Randy gently picked up his left foot, leaned back, stepped down.

The silverbug shot forward.

Randy raised his hands, had a moment to mutter *"ohshitohshit"* then his eyes locked on the machine's legs. The thin straws of metal had always seemed like a blur, but in that instant he saw their every movement, reaching forward, grabbing, pushing back, metal claws slipping slightly on the wet metal floor. Not like it was moving in slow motion, but rather like he was processing what he saw faster than he'd ever done before.

The silverbug closed, gathered, leapt, knife point leading its charge. Randy sidestepped, reached out, fingers splayed like two fleshy nets. The knife point slid past, into the air where his body had just been. Thin legs hit his palms—his fingers clamped down *fast*, so fast, and he held the thin metal in a stone-tight grip.

Randy's gaze flicked past the still-moving machine, to Angus ...

... but Angus wasn't there.

A flash-moment of not understanding, a moment where Randy's thoughts ceased working but physics did not. The silverbug's momentum whipped him around, twisted him to the right, off balance. The metal body *clang*ed into the corridor wall just as Randy stumbled to the left, his body out too far for his feet to catch up. He landed hard on his side. His helmet bouncing up, then off.

A *crack* when it hit the floor.

His headlamp beam winked out.

Randy blinked, eyes trying to adjust to the almost total darkness.

A rapid-fire burst of *click-click! click-click-click!*

He rolled to his back just as the silverbug sprang, its four thin arms outstretched like a pouncing spider. Hands shot up, grabbed the front arms, but the ball of platinum was moving too fast to stop. The knife point shot forward, punched through his mask, into his cheek. Fire lance through his face.

Metal hooks clawed into his arms, his hands, dug in deeper as the machine used the footholds to lurch its heavy body forward again.

Can't see can't see —

"Angus! Grab it!"

A flash of blinding light, a headlamp beam gleaming off the silver-bug's side.

A reflection—Randy's own face, distorted by the curved metal shell—staring back at himself, Rec Specs askew, blood sheeting his cheek.

The light angled away … and it was gone.

The weight, pushing him down. Claws digging into his flesh. Another *lurch*: a stabbing pain deep in his neck. The metal—*inside* of him—felt hot against the back of his throat.

He struggled for a few more seconds, pushing with all his strength, then his strength gave out. His grip relaxed. Thin metal arms slid out of his hands.

The hot metal slid out of his neck, then stabbed home again.

Randy lay on his back. Something poked at him, over and over, but he didn't feel the pain, just the pulling, the jerking, the jostling.

Coldness spread over him.

His eyes were wide open, but he couldn't see anything. Was that because there was no light? Or was it because he was bleeding out, and just like in the movies, everything was going black?

That question would be his last.

Randy Wright would never know the answer.

9:08 A.M.

A buzzing on her right wrist. The display read 9:08 *a.m.*

Bertha twisted, gently, so as not to disturb Patrick, who was asleep with his head in her lap. She looked back to the alcoves. Connell, Veronica and Sanji were still in one of them, apparently.

She looked toward the massive shipwreck.

No sign of Randy or Angus.

"Fuck all of you," she said, her voice a growl. "If you dick around and Patrick dies because of it, I'll hurt you like you can't even imagine."

O'Doyle twitched in his sleep. His scarred face wrinkled, winced.

He had nightmares, too, apparently.

Bertha watched him. Despite his KoolSuit, sweat beaded on his forehead beneath the formfitting mask. He didn't have a fever, at least according to the display on his right wrist.

She would have liked to feel for herself, to take off her glove, peel back his mask and put her hand against his cheek. She couldn't do that, though, not unless she wanted him to breathe in a surprise lungful of two-hundred-degree air.

The suits stayed on. The masks stayed on.

It was almost cruel to be this close to him, to hold him and yet not be able to actually touch his skin. She let him know she was there, though, her gloved hand gently stroking his hooded head.

Spots of dried blood dotted his thigh. She didn't dare check that, either, for fear of ruining Angus's KoolSuit repair job. In Patrick's current state, Bertha doubted he could handle another blast of heat.

Bertha stroked his head. She watched his face. She watched it so intently she didn't see a pair of spidery, metallic shapes emerge from the ship and crawl along the curved terraces of the river's former paths.

9:09 A.M.

"Those pillars are in a chamber, I think," Sanji said. "They look like they're supporting a great weight."

They did look like that. Sort of. But Connell didn't think that made sense.

The line—thin and straight—reached down some twenty miles from the ship until it hit what appeared to be a miles-wide chamber with hundreds of tall pillars. An explosion was breaking those pillars. For what purpose? To collapse the entire mountain? No, that didn't make sense, with seventeen miles of rock between the chamber and the mountain, it would hold up just fine.

Veronica pointed to the bottom of the square.

"Look at this series of smaller carvings. They seem to be related."

The first tile showed a rectangular console, with buttons of different shapes. The second showed a sphere dropping into the long shaft. The third was almost the same as the big one above it—an explosion, shattering the pillars. The last frame in the series illustrated some kind of flood. Liquid filled the tunnel. Rocktopi appeared to be bursting into flames.

No, not liquid…

The truth hit Connell so hard he leaned away from the carvings, as if they might hurt him.

Veronica looked at him quizzically.

"What is it?" she asked. "What does it mean?"

"It was a doomsday device," Connell said. "I think the sphere is a bomb. A big one. They would have lowered it down to that pillar chamber, detonated it, and magma would have rushed up the shaft, filling the entire tunnel complex, killing everything inside."

She stared at the sequence. She shook her head.

"Those crazy motherfuckers. They'll do anything to avoid losing."

Sanji glanced from Veronica to Connell, then back again.

"I don't get it," he said. "How is burning up in molten rock going to help them defeat their enemy?"

Veronica reached up, tapped the carving of the wreck.

"I said *avoid losing*, not *defeat*. That's a warship out there, which means the rocktopi culture was military in origin. Maybe it's remained that way. Looks like the original crew would rather have their descendants die before admitting a final defeat. Death before dishonor or some bullshit like that."

Connell tried to imagine the power of an explosion that could punch a hole deep enough to create a volcano.

"If we find any random buttons, let's not go pressing them, okay?"

Sanji shook his head.

"There is no way such a device would work after all this time. I do not think—"

A shout cut him off, a shout from the cavern.

Lybrand, screaming for help.

9:09 A.M.

A kick to his shoulder, a woman's shout. Panic in that voice.

An attack… the Colombians found us, coming to gut me and string me from a tree like they did to Matty…

Without moving a muscle, Patrick opened his eyes, instantly aware of every injury, every limitation. He expected to see dense greenery above him, or the black of a jungle night, but he saw neither.

Blue-white light. High above ... was that *stone?*

He wasn't in a jungle. Or a city. He wasn't in the desert, either, but far beneath one.

And it wasn't the Colombians who wanted him dead.

"Patrick, get your ass up, *now!*"

Bertha on his right. He rolled to his right, onto hands and knees, careful not to jar his leg. She stood there — on his left, now — knife extended in the direction of a beached leviathan that had once soared through the universe.

"I see them," he said.

Two silverbugs, only yards away, creeping with the smooth, steady motion of cats closing in on prey. Impossibly bright, shiny platinum legs and mirrorlike body reflected the artificial light from above. On their curved bodies, he saw a warped reflection of the rocktopi waterfall behind him.

The machines looked new.

Ten-inch blades jutting out from a dark slot in their round body, curving up like a long kerambit. Bad news.

He moved his hands until each sat atop a loose rock the size of his fist. He pushed himself up, stood in a fighter's stance, adrenaline rush already drowning out his pain.

They crept closer. Two meters now, split feet reaching out slowly, a moving crouch of potential energy. They looked so *alive.*

"Put your knife away," he said. "It won't hurt them and you need both hands when they attack."

Bertha slowly slid the Ka-Bar into the sheath on her chest webbing, clicked it home.

Patrick reached out his left hand, pressed a rock against her thigh. She took it from him, shifted it from her left hand to her right palm, felt its weight before her fingers closed on it.

"Rocks," she said. "Rocks against robots with knives. That's just awesome."

He started to tell her how he wanted to attack, but she was already moving, left foot reaching forward, right arm stiff and pointed straight at the silverbug, then windmilling up and backward. Her left foot planted as the fist-gripped rock passed her right thigh—a softball pitch, and a violent one. The rock shot out of her hand so fast he barely saw it, *gonged* as it smashed into the closest silverbug, sent it tumbling.

The other silverbug rushed at her, a gleaming crab-spider instantly moving at full speed.

Patrick hurled his rock, a hurried throw that didn't have Bertha's speed or accuracy—the stone cracked into the ancient tile floor inches shy of the target, bounced, sailed just over the metal shell.

He stepped toward it, reached, wasn't fast enough.

The silverbug leapt, arms outstretched, split feet splayed wide.

Bertha crouched, snarled. Her hands popping up in a defensive posture.

She tried to grab the machine in midair.

The curved blade flashed.

Two fingers on her left hand fell to the ground as if they'd never really been attached at all.

The metal body slammed into her, sent her stumbling back.

Patrick took another step, kept reaching.

The world moved so *slowly*.

Split feet curled around her right arm. The blade flashed again, from left to right across her face.

Blood flew.

A third step. Patrick's palms on either side of the round body. He lifted hard, stretched his hands up. Hooked feet dug into her flesh and suit, tried to hold on, slashed long, dragging lines in both as he ripped the machine off her.

He twisted and stepped in the same motion, taking it *away* from her, even as his eyes spotted a boulder. The kerambit pointed away from him. Patrick heard himself roaring, *screaming*. He brought the silverbug down with both hands, with all his strength, smashing it into unforgiving stone.

Metal dented. Rock shards flew.

Legs reversed. Sharp claws pierced his forearms.

He lifted high, arched, brought it down again.

Another dent. Rock chips.

Lift, arch, *smash*.

Lift, arch, *smash*.

Lift, arch, *smash*.

"O'Doyle, *stop!*"

Lift, arch, *smash.*

Lift, arch, *smash.*

"O'Doyle!"

Arms wrapping around from behind, encircling his chest.

"*Stop,* it's dead!"

Lift, toss the enemy away, turn fast, left elbow back, the feel of it hitting home, the grunt of another enemy, that enemy letting go, falling away. Reaching down, grabbing a shard of colored tile. The enemy hitting the ground, stepping forward for the kill ...

Patrick stopped.

Not an enemy. Connell. On his side, his hands pressed to his mouth, blood on his yellow gloves.

Patrick turned again, toward the ship, eyes searching for the silver-bugs. One a few feet away, round shell smashed like a wrecked car, three legs motionless, one twitching. The other one, a few feet farther away. Only one big dent, but lay still.

Bertha.

He spun, saw Connell lying there, saw Sanji and Veronica on top of Bertha.

Two fingers on the ground, still encased in KoolSuit yellow.

Blood, *everywhere.*

"Kirkland, get up and watch for more silverbugs!"

Patrick stepped over him, not knowing if he'd heard, not even caring.

He knelt next to Bertha, shoving Veronica and Sanji out of the way.

Bertha's good right hand covered the mauled left, unable to stop the blood that spurted forth from the stumps. The sleeves of her tattered KoolSuit dangled from her forearms. Blood sheeted the right side of her face. She'd rolled on the ground while writhing in pain—bits of rock and sand stuck to her blood-drenched skin, as did a few flecks of colored masonry.

"I'm here," he said. "Baby, I'm here."

Bertha's eyes alternately pinched shut and stared with wide-eyed disbelief at the two yellow fingers laying a few feet away.

He had to stop that bleeding. He pulled Bertha's knife from its sheath.

"Sanji, backpack, *now.*"

It was at his feet before Veronica could stand.

Patrick slashed at it, cutting off two long strips of nylon fabric.

"Hold her good arm," he said.

He expected Sanji to do it, but Kirkland was there, hooking her right arm, pulling it away, locking it up tight. Blood covered his mouth, dripped down the inside of his thin mask.

Bertha fought weakly, kept staring at the severed fingers.

"Those are mine," she said. "Patrick, I need those."

She was in shock.

He dropped the knife, pinched her forearm between his elbow and body, heard her cry out, ignored it. He fumbled with the strips he'd cut, but they were already bloody, too slick to manage.

Sanji snatched them. He looped one around the stump of her missing pinkie.

Bertha yelped, pulled the hand back—not far, but enough that the bloody strip fell away.

"Hold her *still,*" Sanji barked.

Patrick gripped Bertha's wrist, suddenly at home because someone was giving an order and he didn't have to think.

Sanji looped the strip again, then pulled it tight on the stub with a *snap* of his wrists.

Bertha threw her head back and screamed.

"*Shut up,*" Patrick said. "Bear down and *shut up.*"

Blood streaming down her cheek and slashed mask alike. Her lip curled, her eyes widened. She glared at him. With hate and pain at first, then just pain.

"*Do it,*" she said.

Sanji looped a strip around her ring finger, *snapped* it tight.

She threw her head back again and her eyes scrunched, but she clenched her teeth and grunted instead of screamed.

In that bloody moment, Patrick knew he couldn't possibly love her more.

Bertha coughed. She stuck out her tongue, like she had something caught in her throat.

"Can't...so hot."

She gagged.

Her mask. The silverbug blade had partially sliced through her upper lip, must have broken the breather.

Veronica, shoving her way in, hands pulling at Bertha's belt.

"Take it easy," she said. "We have to get your spare mask on."

"Her cut," Patrick said. "We have to stitch her first, she—"

Veronica pulled the mask out of a pouch. So thin, little more than face-shaped plastic wrap.

"Her lungs are cooking," she said. "Air first, the cut second."

Sanji ripped off Bertha's ruined mask, tossed it away like so much trash. Veronica pressed the new one to her face, used fingers and thumbs to smooth it tight.

Bertha struggled, gagged.

Patrick held her tight.

Another gag, a cough, then a deep, desperate heave in.

She twitched. She calmed.

She could breathe again.

9:11 A.M.

He sprinted down the riverbank, the water rushing past on his right. Out of the darkness of that horrible place, back in the blue-white light. The giant rocktopi statue, warped by eons of erosion. Below it, his people, huddled together by the waterfall pool. Near them, on the ground … more soldier bugs? The bugs weren't moving. Had O'Doyle smashed them, somehow?

Angus felt an urgent need to be with Kirkland and the others. The shit was hitting the fan now—machines with knives, the rocktopi still somewhere out there … he needed the safety of the group.

He didn't want to be alone.

The backpack lurched with each step, threatening to throw him off balance. He grabbed at the buckles, unfastened them, stumbled as the backpack fell away and then he was sprinting again.

Tug-of-war? What a fucking idiot.

Randy, dead. His friend. Murdered by that psycho machine.

Everything shimmered. Eyes, stinging. Angus pressed his fingertips through the thin mask, tried to wipe away the tears.

I could have saved him … I could have thrown that thing into the river … I let Randy die.

No, that was stupid, stupid, stupid—the soldier bug would have killed one of them. Should Angus have died so someone else could live? Fuck no. Survival of the fittest, of the smartest.

Lying there, terrified…that knife driving into his throat, slicing…

Lungs burning. Angus kept sprinting.

Everyone huddled together. There was O'Doyle's big back, Sanji, Veronica…and Connell, blood all over his face. On the ground… Lybrand?

Veronica looked up, was the first to see him coming.

"Angus! Where's Randy?"

Yes, two soldier bugs, gleaming in their newness, but broken, unmoving.

Angus pointed to one of the dead, gleaming silverbugs. "One of those got him. The scrambler doesn't work on the new ones. Randy is dead."

Veronica looked away.

Connell glared at him, eyes narrowed in disbelief.

Sanji shook his head, closed his eyes. "Dammit. We have to get out of here, or we're all going to die."

O'Doyle shouted over his shoulder.

"Angus, Lybrand's suit is cut, fix it!"

His back was so big Angus almost couldn't see her. Almost.

Blood, everywhere.

The sleeves of her KoolSuit.

Torn to shreds.

Yellow fluid leaking out on to the cracked floor.

If the rest of her suit was intact, she wouldn't die right away. She *would* die, though. It would be slow. Agonizing. Better to kill her now. Less cruel that way.

"I can't fix it," he said. "We don't have anything left to fix it with."

O'Doyle reached to the ground, picked something up. He stood. He turned.

He held a knife.

His chin was near his chest. He glared out from beneath that ridge of bone he called a forehead. The red slash line and fresh stitches made him look like a monster, made Angus stop in his tracks, made his balls shrink.

"Find a way," O'Doyle said. "Come up with something, fast, or she'll be wearing *your* KoolSuit."

The others snap-glanced at the scared man, all took small steps away from him. They looked shocked.

Back in the hotel room, that day all of this began, Angus had feared Patrick O'Doyle. Even in the lab, Angus had kept his distance, because there was something deep inside the man that just wasn't right. Whatever camouflage O'Doyle used to hide his real self, he wasn't bothering with it anymore.

He stood there, knife in hand.

He was finally being himself.

A killer.

Well, fuck this. Fuck ALL *of this.*

Angus ran for the river's edge.

O'Doyle screaming his name.

A step down to a former path, then the edge that dropped away. Stepping, leaping, hands forward, splitting the water, a *thud.*

Dizzy. Sliding along.

He'd hit the bottom.

Up, have to breathe…

A thud in his back, the current throwing him right, spinning him. Under again, hot water in his mouth…

He popped up, splashing, coughing. Facing upstream. Far off, he saw Patrick O'Doyle limping along the bank. To be that far away, Angus would have to be near the shipwreck.

Oh God…

He whipped around just as the water angled down, sped him on like a dipping roller coaster.

The ship canopy blocked out the light, and he was sucked into the rapids.

BOOK SIX
EXODUS

33

16,000 feet below the surface

9:15 A.M.

So hot.

Not all over. *Warm* all over, yes, but hot only on her hands and arms. Sunburn hot.

Bertha heard voices, understood what everyone was saying, although she couldn't really put things together, wasn't really sure what was going on.

"We have to go after him!"

Patrick. Screaming, so loud his throat had to hurt. Why was he yelling like that?

"Silverbugs! They're all over the place!"

That was Veronica. Selfish bitch. Bertha didn't like her.

"The old kind," Patrick said. "Still scrambled when they get close. Ignore them."

"Up in the waterfall! Around the statue!"

That was Sanji. Bertha didn't know what to think of him. Seemed like an okay guy, although the apple doesn't fall far from the tree—if his daughter was a bitch, that meant he wasn't much of anything. Right?

Around the statue … what was he talking about? Oh, right, the two-hundred-foot-tall rocktopi. Kind of amazing, really. Colossus of Rome or whatever. The stop-motion Sinbad movies she watched with her dad. Or that big statue from the *Game of Thrones* show, the one that straddled the harbor so all the people on all the boats had to look up at his cock when they passed beneath.

She opened her eyes. Seemed too bright. Her face burned, but in a different way from her hands and arms.

The rocktopi statue … was it glowing? No, it couldn't, it was stone. So what were those colors? She blinked, squinted up. Something moving up at the top, in cracks in the walls around the statue. Angry colors, lighting up the waterfall mist. Glowing little clouds. Like flashing angels. *Hundreds* of flashing angels.

Would they come down?

"Empty the backpacks! Put the dead silverbugs inside of them!"

That was Kirkland. Such a dick. All of this was his fault. Patrick, barking words more than speaking. He sounded like her old drill sergeant.

"Everyone, get that rope around you! We can't lose anyone in the rapids. Move your asses, they look like they're coming soon!"

Someone moving her, jostling her, looping something around her chest. Rope, they said *rope*. Tie everyone together.

She looked away from the waterfall angels. It was Patrick, so close to her.

That nasty cut on his face. The stitches. She wanted to kiss those stitches, take away his pain. Maybe he thought he was ugly, but he wasn't. He was a beautiful man. A killer, but was that his fault? They'd told him lies. She knew. They'd told her the same lies. *For country. For your mates.* All bullshit. She could help him. She could make all his days—from this one to his last—so much better.

"I love you," she said.

He stopped moving. Their faces, so close, separated by a couple of inches, separated by the thin faceplates. A killer's eyes: analytical, remorseless. But something else in there, too. A good man who wanted to claw his way out. A man who wanted to live in peace.

"I love you, too," he said. "You're hurt. I will get you out of here. Can I take your knife?"

How ridiculous he was even asking her. She nodded.

He worked it free of her webbing, put it in his own. He leaned closer, touched his forehead to hers. Then, he went back to tying her up.

Bertha closed her eyes.

So *hot*.

9:18 A.M.

He washed up on a beach made of platinum dust.

Angus hurt. The blow from hitting the river bottom, then a couple of good smacks while going through the rapids. Lucky he hadn't drowned. Had probably come close.

River must have changed course here. Gravel and gleaming sand, reflecting the light that filtered through from the break in the ship far above. Rooms and hallways all around, reaching up hundreds of feet. Wreckage from when this area had collapsed.

No, that wasn't quite right.

Some twisted metal, but not much. He could see into bubble rooms, see the Swiss-cheese composition of the ship, but most of the edges that faced the river looked defined, cut. More like planned viewing decks, like designers had sliced away this part of the ship to let the river flow beneath. Not accidental ... *engineered*.

A few feet up the beach, he saw worn limestone blocks. An old wall that the river had mostly eaten away before the water changed course. Glittering platinum dust, long since dried in place, showed where the waterline had once been.

At some point, the rocktopi had *wanted* the river to flow through their ship. Maybe it had been some kind of acceptance they were here forever, that they were never going to leave. The Dense Mass Cavern's carved walls were obviously meant to be permanent. Perhaps the ancient shipwrecked crew had wanted to make the most of what they had. Make their home ... *nice*, for lack of a better word.

Angus glanced up, to the canyon far above, where two curves of hull almost met. Light filtering down. Where was he, exactly? About halfway through the ship? Couldn't be that far to the Linus Highway.

He was almost out.

click-click … click-click …

The sound came from his right, from one of the bubble rooms. Silverbugs. Burnished and scratched, not new. Staring right at him, evaluating him. If they were the old ones, why weren't they scrambled?

He pulled his walkie-talkie from his webbing. Water dripped from the cracked plastic shell.

Ruined.

Well, *shit.*

One of the silverbugs crept closer.

Angus pushed himself back into the river. He didn't take his eyes off the silverbug, even as the water rose to his hips, his chest.

The current carried him downstream again.

9:20 A.M.

The waterfall roared on, the sound almost background noise now.

Connell shoved the second silverbug into the empty nylon backpack. He tied the top tight. Not waterproof, but it would work for a little while. The first silverbug—the one that would go to Lybrand—was dented, but there weren't any breaks visible in the round shell. It would float just fine. Probably. This one—the one O'Doyle had smashed against a rock over and over again, screaming and snarling the whole time—had several gouges in the shell. Water would leak through the backpack, then fill the sphere. Eventually, it would sink. For the short-term, however, it would help keep someone afloat.

"Kirkland!" O'Doyle, bellowing. "Stop fucking around with that thing and *tie off!*"

Connell set the backpack down, picked up the rope, looked at it. He had no idea how to tie a knot.

Whether it was the rest, Lybrand's injuries, seeing Angus run away or a combination of all three, O'Doyle was in charge once again. He had some of his strength back. *Some,* not *all.* He limped along, occasionally stumbling a bit. Fresh spots of orange spread across his thigh. Connell knew the man didn't have long before he collapsed again—hopefully, they would be back to the surface before that happened.

Fucking rope…what was he supposed to do, tie it like he'd tie his shoes?

Small hands took the rope away from him. Veronica. She moved fast, looping it under his armpits.

"O'Doyle," she called over her shoulder even as she started tying it tight. "What if we get tangled up in this?"

"A chance we'll have to take," he said. He was busy tying the silver-bug-stuffed backpack to Lybrand. "We don't know how rough the water will be when we exit the ship. If the current takes someone away, we can't go after them."

Translation: once through the ship, O'Doyle wasn't waiting for anyone. He was getting Lybrand to the surface. If Connell, Veronica or Sanji was swept away? Well, that was just too bad.

Connell didn't dig the idea of being tied to others while in the rapids. Veronica clearly didn't dig it, either, but—like him—they were obeying O'Doyle's orders.

The sound of a hundred simultaneous screeches tore at the air, the battle cry of a demon army. Connell looked to the ancient rocktopi statue. At the top, all around it, cracks in detailed wall carvings, places where the ever-changing river had once flowed. Those old channels left tunnels, tunnels the rocktopi now filled. Their murderous oranges and psychotic reds lit up the spraying waterfall, set the river mist ablaze. Stoplights in the fog.

Too many to count.

Far too many to fight.

Whatever their hesitation to enter the Dense Mass Cavern, they were working up the courage to get past it.

O'Doyle, pressing something into his chest.

"The scrambler," he said. "Keep it out of the water, keep it safe. It's our lifeline, Kirkland, understand?"

Connell looked down at the walkie-talkie. He took it, looked up.

"If we're going to die, can't you call me by my first name?"

O'Doyle stared, then his new scar twisted with a slight smile.

"We're not going to die. Trust me, Connell, I've been through worse and lived to tell the tale."

Connell stared back, and then, of all things, he laughed. It sounded ridiculous, and maybe more than a bit insane.

"You've been through worse than being trapped three miles underground, chased by robots and fighting hand-to-hand with alien cavemen that want to slice you to pieces?"

O'Doyle shrugged. "Maybe you've never been to Colombia."

A screech, then a sound like a hundred pounds of bread dough dropped from ten stories up.

On one of the big rocks at the waterfall pool's edge, a rocktopi lay mostly flat, its body conforming to the stone below it. Yellow goo leaked from ragged tears in its thick skin. The creature flashed—blue, then green, then a pale red—then its light flickered out.

"They're coming," Sanji screamed, still fumbling with his own rope. "Time's up! Everyone in the water!"

Connell looked to the top of the rocktopi sculpture. The beasties were moving faster, making more noise. It wasn't until one jumped through the mist and plummeted down to splash heavily into the pool below that Connell understood what was happening—the first one had tried the same thing and missed the water.

He remembered the scrambler in his hands. If it was on when it got wet, would that ruin it? He didn't know. He switched it off.

A tug on the rope tied around his chest.

They were tied in a chain, about fifty feet of slack between each of them. Veronica to Connell, Connell to Lybrand, Lybrand to O'Doyle and O'Doyle to Sanji. Veronica stepped down to a lower terrace, the former bottom of the old river, then down another terrace and stood at the river's edge. She hopped off and slid feetfirst into the water.

O'Doyle and Sanji helped Lybrand down the first terrace.

Connell glanced back to see if that diving rocktopi was coming. It floated in the middle of the waterfall pool, bobbing slightly. No light. *Dead.* Either from the fall or from drowning. Maybe they wouldn't give chase after all.

An army of silverbugs scrambled up the soaring wall, up the statue itself, oblivious to the water crashing down on and around them. Free of the scrambler's effects, they coalesced into lines that led from the broken floor up to the mist-shrouded rocktopi high up on the wall.

Something hit hard near Connell's feet, sent chips of rock against his leg. His eye followed the movement: a bouncing wet rock. He looked back to the top of the sculpture, saw a long, orange and red arm *snap* like a whip—a rock sailed through the air.

*Crack*s and *thonk*s: a rain of stone began.

"Connell!" Veronica, screaming at him. "Come on!"

He hefted the backpack turned flotation device and ran to the river. Down a terrace, then another, then he leapt into the water near Veronica. He sank to his chin before his feet hit bottom—it was shallower than he'd thought.

Splashes all around him as the rocktopi assault continued.

O'Doyle winced as he slid over the edge, into the water, then reached up for Lybrand. Sanji helped ease her in.

Veronica let out a grunt, like she wanted to scream but had choked on it. She pointed, found her voice.

"They're climbing down!"

In the waterfall's mist, long arms drooped down like glowing cake batter, formed around cracks or rocks below, then the rest of the rocktopi body flowed after it—real tentacles clinging to the statue's broken versions. Flashing amoebas reaching and flowing, reaching and flowing. One slipped, a colorful blob rolling free, instantly flashing a pure, deep cobalt, then it slammed into the floor, guts splashing everywhere.

Screeches and squeals. The waterfall's endless bellow. Rock missiles smashing down on floor and water alike.

Another tug on the rope, harder this time—Veronica, out in the water, being pulled at by the strong current. Connell felt that same current pulling at him, at his floating backpack, saw Lybrand start to come downstream toward him.

O'Doyle pushed out into the river.

Sanji sat his butt down on the ledge, feet in the water. He turned to put his hands on the stone so he could slide in—a softball-sized rock bounced off his head, cracking his helmet in two. He slumped sideways, onto his shoulder.

If he had rolled toward the river, he would have fallen in, floated away.

He didn't.

Disoriented, hurt, he rolled *away*, onto his back on the terrace's flat stone.

Connell heard Veronica screaming, but her words didn't register, if she was even saying words at all. His mind could only process two things: Sanji, rolling slightly, head gushing blood, and the wave of angry rocktopi descending the wall, reaching the floor and flowing forward, platinum knives reflecting the artificial sun.

O'Doyle tried to move toward Sanji. The river pulled at Veronica, and Connell, and Lybrand, the weight of three bodies dragging O'Doyle away. The rope between him and Sanji snapped taut. O'Doyle grabbed it, tried yanking hard, but couldn't get any leverage in the neck-deep river. He started to pull himself—and everyone behind him—arm over arm toward Sanji, who lay there like an overweight yellow anchor.

It was over. Dozens of rocktopi rushed toward Sanji. They'd kill him, then reel everyone in like fish on a line.

Connell saw O'Doyle reach underwater. When his hand came up, it held the big knife.

"*Noooo!*" Veronica, screaming, pleading, and Connell understood that single word just fine. He heard it even as his heart surged with both hope and shame.

Cut it, cut that fucking rope, Sanji's a dead man anyway, CUT IT.
O'Doyle did.

A slice up, a slice down, a slice up—
And through.

Connell shot backward, ripped along by the current, every sense sparkling and poking, his body electrified, filled with a savage need to survive and a matching need to stop, go back, to *help.*

He treaded water, not caring what might come up behind, unable to look away.

At the river's edge, the rocktopi swarmed in.

Sanji rolled to his hands and knees. Blood poured from his head, a dripping tap of crimson water. He looked up, saw the others rocketing downstream, away from him.

Connell was still close enough to see the expression on Sanji's face when the man realized both what had happened and what was about to happen.

The rocktopi crashed over him. Furious yellows, raging oranges, the mass of bodies glowing brighter than ever before. Boneless limbs went up and down and up and down, until arcing red join the collage of colors.

The light above seemed to blink out. Connell fell backward, the river pulling him down into the rapids.

9:22 A.M.

Angus slid into shadow. Not pitch-black, but as his eyes adjusted he could see nothing at all. The current carried him on.

Not much farther now. Couldn't be.

He saw light up ahead, stronger than before. The river carried him out of the shadows. Blinking against the brightness, he saw a wall of limestone blocks ahead. The water started carrying him to the right—a course change clearly caused by those blocks—he kicked hard, reaching for the wall's edge.

He reached up, grabbed it. Holding on by one hand, body against the wall, he looked around.

These blocks...they weren't eroded. Some of them even looked new. Finely fitted together. Were the rocktopi maintaining this wall or something?

The river bent off to his right. A few hundred feet on, it bent back to the left. The bend seemed to bleed the current, slowing the river down to a calmer pace.

His eyes finally adjusted. He saw the same Swiss-cheese rooms arcing to his right, the same curving ship sides above, almost meeting at the top.

To his left, the source of the new light.

It burned bright from the top of a dome-shaped, cathedral-like structure. The limestone wall wrapped around in front of that dome, protecting it from the water that had eroded so much of the ship.

Angus pulled himself up with both hands. A level stone floor reached away from the top of the wall, into the dome.

In the dome's center, fifty feet from the breakwater, dangling like a low-hanging chandelier, hung a large, polished orb, about ten feet in diameter. Between it and him, something that looked like a waist-high altar. The orb hovered over a metal-rimmed hole in the stone floor. Angus remembered his map, remembered the strange line Kirkland had pointed out that plunged deep into the earth.

What was that orb? Maybe some kind of bathysphere, so rocktopi could descend past the point where geothermal heat would cook them to a crisp?

Movement caught his eye. Up on the curving dome, near the light. A silverbug, crawling across the inside of the dome wall...the *bumpy* dome wall.

His breath froze. Silverbugs, thousands of them, still as stone, coating the dome's interior. Metallic termites packed in tight. He sat very still, studied them. A wash of relief when he realized they were all burnished, a little beat-up. No shiny new ones here.

The one he'd first seen kept moving, crawling over its fellow machines, reached the cable that supported the sphere and scurried down. It walked across the sphere's curved surface. The wedge-shaped head pressed into a small hole: a circular panel popped open. Angus watched the silverbug crawl half inside that hole, saw its rear legs jiggling. It crawled back out. A split foot shut the panel; Angus heard it click home.

That panel... the diameter just a bit larger than the diameter of the silverbug.

A perfect fit. An *engineered* fit.

"Well, fuck me," he said. "Maintenance. That's what these things were originally made for... maintenance."

Goddamn repair robots.

Maybe the rocktopi—their long-dead ancestors, anyway—had made those machines. As the rocktopi got dumber, maybe the machines took over more and more responsibilities. If their programming was to serve the rocktopi, keep that race alive, maybe the machines *had* to become smarter in order to fulfill that mission.

click ... click-click ...

Coming from his right.

He slowly pushed back into the water. As the current took him, he looked to his right: two silverbugs on top of the wall.

Angus swam to the middle of the river, where the flow was the strongest. The current carried him around the next bend, leaving behind the cathedral with its dangling orb.

Up ahead, Angus saw the dimness of the canyon-like breach give way to the full, blinding light of the cavern's artificial suns. He was almost out of the ship.

He kicked hard, swimming for the shore. Just before he broke free of the ship's shadow, he waded into the shallows, exhausted, drained, but smiling with success. An almost proper beach, sparkling platinum dust so thick it was like mud. His feet sank in up to his ankles as he finally left the water behind.

Plenty of partial bubble rooms here, just like everywhere else in this ship. He moved to the one closest to the edge. Platinum silt covered the floor.

He listened. He heard nothing.

Finally, Angus peeked around the corner.

The Dense Mass Cavern was the same here as it was on the other side of the massive wreck: a huge wall stretching for miles in either direction, covered in chipped colors and cracked designs; the ship's platinum hull curving up on his right; an ancient tile floor battered by falling rock.

And fifty meters ahead of him, across that shattered field of tile, an arched entrance to a tunnel.

The Linus Highway.

He had made it.

Newfound energy filled him. He ran for the entrance, aches and pains forgotten. Screw Randy, screw O'Doyle, screw Kirkland—he was getting out.

Through the entrance. The incline started immediately. Angus attacked it. Nothing could stop him now. Up and up and up he went, one foot after another. No silverbugs. No rocktopi. Rough walls, a tunnel that looked natural even though he knew better.

Just keep going, keep going… only a little bit more and you're free.

9:27 A.M.

Not much farther now. Maybe two hundred yards to the Dense Mass Cavern. Downhill was easy—Kayla knew that coming back up this constant slope would be a grade A bitch.

The Marco/Polo unit beeped softly, startling her. Making her body spike with excitement. She stopped, pulled the device from her webbing. As soon as she looked at it, the beep vanished. A fluke signal, maybe, already gone, but she'd seen the name:

ANGUS KOOL

In these stone tunnels, a signal could bounce a long way, bounce a *certain* way that instantly changed and that signal would be lost. But to get any signal at all, he had to be close.

Got you now, you little fuck.

Kayla kept moving downhill.

9:28 A.M.

"You *motherfucker!* You *let him die!*"

Veronica's anguish raged forth, slapped off the rushing water, bounced off the ship that arced above them.

Patrick heard her words, felt them deep in his soul. Yes, he had let Sanji die. Patrick wanted to live, desperately wanted it, of course he did, but he hadn't sliced that rope for himself—he'd done it so Bertha might live.

No man left behind.

An admirable phrase, but this wasn't the military. Hell, this wasn't even *sanity*.

So tired. Tired to the bone, to the marrow. Tired in his heart. His soul. His leg, on fire. Muscles, weak, like old cloth, saggy and useless. His body was trying to shut down. It was all he could do to stay conscious.

How much more could he take?

Sanji had been a good man. Through it all, he hadn't complained. He hadn't been selfish. A good man. That vision of flashing death sweeping over Sanji … that would stay with Patrick for a long, long time.

One would think a man's memory could fill up with horrors, fill to overflowing so that no new hauntings could lodge in the nooks and crannies, jam their way in there so deep they wouldn't leave until the brain itself decomposed. One might think that; one might be wrong.

Just another piece of playback to make Patrick afraid to close his eyes at night.

Sanji was gone. Patrick had to make sure that sacrifice was worth it. He had to get Lybrand out. Hopefully, Connell and Veronica as well. Hopefully.

He swam, clumsily pulled on the rope at the same time. He pulled closer to Bertha. She was floating, the silverbug backpack clutched to her chest. Water splashed against her face, slid inside her mask, dripped down red.

Still bleeding.

He held her, letting the backpack keep them both afloat.

"The rapids," he said. "You hit anything?"

Heavy eyelids blinked. A slow shake of the head.

The river carried them along. Splashing sounds, someone swimming toward them: Connell, his broken nose streaming blood.

"O'Doyle, you okay?"

His words sounded pinched, like they were forced through a filter of intense pain.

"No," Patrick said. "Need a rest. You get hurt in the rapids?"

Connell started to answer, winced, took in a hissing breath.

"Back," he said. "Hit it on something."

Quiet again. Just the sound of the river: flowing water, echoing *plinks* and *pops*. The ship sailed passed on either side.

More splashing noises—Veronica, this time, coming closer.

"You *cocksucker!*"

Her mouth a twisted snarl, her hands claws reaching for his face.

Connell grabbed her arms, held them.

"Stop it," he said, firm but not angry. "Sanji's gone, this won't help."

"Because *he* is a fucking *coward*." She pointed a finger at Patrick. "A goddamn *coward*."

Of all the horrible things Patrick had done in his life, he'd never been accused of that. Maybe if you live long enough, you'll commit every sin there is.

"He had to do it," Connell said. "If he didn't, we'd all be dead."

Veronica fell quiet. Her anger shifted to pain, and she started to sob.

Patrick closed his eyes. So weak. Could he sleep the rest of the way through this ship?

"A beach," Connell said.

A beach...a chance to rest?

"Have to stop," Patrick said. "Gotta rest."

Connell said nothing.

Patrick opened his eyes. Yes, a beach, on the right, gravel and sand all gleaming with platinum. Eroded limestone blocks. Dark spherical rooms beyond.

And all over that beach, silverbugs.

"Hold on a little longer," Connell said. "Let's see if there's a better spot, okay?"

Sure, there's a better spot—six feet under, which is where Patrick knew he was heading.

He closed his eyes again.

One arm holding the backpack, another holding Lybrand, he floated on.

9:30 A.M.

One foot after another. Up the slope. Legs burning, but that didn't stop him.

Just keep going, keep going... only a little bit more and you're free.

The echo of a long *beep* made him stop cold.

Up ahead ... a small light ... moving.

"Doctor Kool, are you there?"

A woman's voice. A *rescue party*.

"I'm here!"

Another burst of energy. He attacked the slope as if it were downhill rather than up, each step effortless and easy.

Seconds later the light of her headlamp filled the tunnel. She strode into view, holding a nasty-looking machine gun.

Web gear covered a yellow silt-smeared EarthCore KoolSuit. Dirty blonde hair spilled out from beneath an EarthCore mining helmet. A pair of thick night-vision goggles hung around her neck.

"Doctor Kool, are you all right?"

He didn't recognize her, and that didn't matter.

"I'm fine. Holy *shitballs* am I glad you're here! Who are you?"

"Barb Yakely sent me," she said. "We're here to get you all out. Where are the others?"

Angus suddenly found himself out of breath. The climb, catching up with him. He bent, put his hands on his knees.

"Rocktopi killed them," he said. "I'm the only one left. Get me out of here."

He didn't care if his lie was soon discovered, as long as he made it to the surface before O'Doyle came hopping up the Linus Highway.

"*Rock, toe, pie?*" the woman said, sounding it out. "You mean those glowing monsters?"

Angus stood, nodded impatiently. "More of them back there, so get me out. Right now."

He started up the slope again, brushing past her—she grabbed his arm, yanked him to a stop.

"I'm here to get *everyone* out," she said. "Where's Kirkland and the others?"

What was this stupid bitch's problem? Angus pointed to his ear.

"Are you fucking *deaf*? I told you, they're all dead. You obviously know who I am, so you know how important I am to EarthCore and Yakely. I'm *ordering* you to take me to the surface right now!"

The woman cocked her head to one side. Through the paper-thin mask, Angus watched her eyes narrow, her upper lip twitch slightly.

A chill washed through him—something about her reminded him of O'Doyle.

Angus saw the woman whip the rifle butt up, didn't even have time to flinch before the wood cracked into his cheek.

He sagged, started to fall. Someone caught him. Everything spinning…a knife in his cheek, or maybe a metal spike. Coppery taste in his mouth. Blood?

His tongue poked at the inside of his teeth. One missing. Incisor. Left. Still in his mouth. He started to spit, swallowed instead, felt it scrape his throat.

On his stomach. The smell of the cave silt: earthy, like wet stone. Someone moving him. The woman. She had his wrists. Jerking motions. Pain there, too, but nothing compared to the fire coursing through his face.

Fingers on his cheeks, digging into his jaw, the agony so screamingly intense it killed all thought, all movement.

Something else in his mouth now, filling it…he couldn't bite down. Mouth open so wide his jaw felt like it was being ripped off. The pain in his cheek…his head throbbed…it hurt to *blink*.

Facedown. The parts of him that didn't scream felt completely numb. Except his hands. No, not his hands, his *wrists*, stinging…behind his back…he couldn't move his hands.

He was tied up.

"Mphmh," he said. Couldn't form words. What was in his mouth? Tasted like rubber. His lips flapped wetly against it when he breathed.

"Hush, darling."

The woman. Her voice, cold, drawling like in those old Mae West movies.

"I don't have as much time to spend with you as I'd like," she said. "So it's important to establish my credibility right out of the gate."

She squatted in front of him. Smiling, knees wide. Something in her left hand. She held it out toward him. A rust-speckled pair of pliers.

He hurt so bad he could barely see. He looked at the pliers, the evil smile on her face, the pliers again. Chipped red fingernail polish gleamed in her headlamp beam. She pushed the pliers together, pulled them apart—they made a noise like that of a hungry baby bird.

Angus lurched to get up ... and went nowhere. Hands bound behind his back. Ankles, too—when he tried to kick, it pulled his wrists.

He was hog-tied.

An explosion of agony in his face, burning and piercing in his cheek, the numb weight of his brain throbbing.

"Oh, stop," she said. "I'm a professional, little man. You're not going anywhere."

She stood, leaving him staring at her boots.

"I have some questions to ask you, Doctor Little Prick."

She stepped over him. Couldn't see her boots. He couldn't see her at all.

"You're going to answer them."

That baby bird sound again.

Weight on his ass ... was she sitting on him?

"You might not *believe* that I'm good at what I do," she said. "I don't blame you, sugar plum—you're a scientist. Such a *smart* scientist, too, aren't you? And you know what you scientists just love?"

Strong hands on his, gripping a finger. He tried to clench his fists, but she pried his right pointer finger free.

"You love *data*, buddy boy."

Her voice, growing angrier.

Those pliers, what was she going to do with those *pliers*?

Angus lurched, twisted, tried to rise up on his left knee, shake her off. She seemed to match his every move. She weighed too much ...

"You wanted to keep me out of the NSA," the woman said.

She was crazy what did she want with him he didn't even *know* this woman he'd never seen her in his life she—

"You wanted to make me look like an idiot. You need some *data* to properly understand who you're dealing with. You're just like him, you little prick, you *fucking little prick*, you think I'm stupid and worthless, do you? Just like Dad thought?"

Angus started to scream, tried to shout *no I don't!* but couldn't get the words out past the ball jammed in his mouth. Yes, *a ball*, that's what it was, some kind of rubber ball ...

He felt hard steel close around the last knuckle of his finger, felt the metal teeth digging in.

"Mpphh! Mmmhph!"

"*Shhhh*, honey. Be a good boy."

The pliers crunched down.

9:36 A.M.

Veronica reached the wall first.

The river bent off to the right, but no one was looking at that. They all stared at the gleaming orb, and the strange altar in front of it.

"My God," Connell said. "It's still here."

She floated there, one hand on the wall, the other on the silverbug-stuffed backpack Connell had given her. Thing was already half sinking. It wouldn't be of use much longer. She didn't care.

Her father was dead.

Hacked to pieces, *butchered*, like an animal. Murdered by things that should have died off thousands of years ago.

She'd seen his hand come off.

She'd seen his blood spraying.

Just before she slid backward down into the rapids, she was almost sure she'd seen them cut off his head.

O'Doyle's fault.

No, she already knew that wasn't true. There was no helping her father. Not really. She wanted someone to lash out at. She needed a target, but not some*one* ... some*thing*.

The rocktopi.

Connell swam up next to her, steadied himself with his hand on the limestone blocks. O'Doyle weakly pulled Lybrand to the wall, Connell pulled them in.

The four survivors stared into the open dome, stared at the orb. A giant Christmas ornament dangling over a shaft that ran straight to the depths of hell. *Hell.* That was where she'd send the rocktopi and their vicious little machines. Straight to hell.

"Silverbugs all over," O'Doyle said. His voice sounded thin, drained, like that of a dying old man. "Connell, you better get the scrambler out."

Connell shook his head, winced when he did. "Screw that. We have to be close, we have to keep going."

"I need a rest," O'Doyle said.

Veronica tore her eyes away from the orb and looked at the man. One thick arm held Lybrand's head, making sure her face stayed above the surface. She hung limply; the float tied to her chest the only thing keeping her from sinking.

"Yeah, Connell," Veronica said quietly, just loud enough to be heard over the river's metallic, plinking echo. "I need a rest, too."

Connell closed his eyes. He floated there a moment, taking deep breaths. He nodded. He reached up one long arm, grabbed the top of the wall. Grimacing, he pulled himself out of the water, the toes of his boots pressing into the limestone. He turned, sat on top, dangling legs dripping water down to the river.

From all sides, silverbugs converged toward him. The entire dome seemed to shift, to move—what Veronica had thought was a solid wall was anything but. The machines scrambled across the stone floor, skittered along the top of the limestone wall. An angry chorus of clicks and whirs filled the air.

Connell stayed calm. He carefully pulled the scrambler from his webbing. He shook it hard, twisted his wrist as if to force out any water.

"Here goes nothing," he said, then he turned it on.

Almost instantly, the silverbugs' coordinated movement collapsed into a jumble of wandering confusion.

Veronica reached, gripped the top of the wall. She hauled herself up. She and Connell helped pull Lybrand up onto the wall, then helped O'Doyle. Veronica looked at her companions: all exhausted, all wounded, all doomed. She knew none of them would make it out alive. Too many rocktopi, too many injuries, too far to travel.

They were all going to die.

Just like Sanji.

Just like Randy.

Just like Mack.

Just like that miner, just like those guards.

Veronica wouldn't let those deaths be for nothing. She walked along the wall, then onto the chamber's stone floor toward the altar, stepping over drunken silverbugs, her hands working at the knots she'd tied in the rope around her chest.

She was almost to the altar when a hand gripped her arm, stopping her.

"Stay close to the river," Connell said. "If those new silverbugs show up, we may have to move fast."

Veronica shrugged his hand away.

"It doesn't matter," she said. She was close enough to see the altar. Made of platinum, smooth and curved, waist high, flat top covered with colored ceramic dots and shapes—a control panel.

"It *doesn't matter*," Connell said, echoing her words. "Why doesn't it matter, Veronica?"

He must have been just as tired as O'Doyle. Connell spoke slowly, softly, like he was talking to a child.

"It doesn't matter because I'm staying here," she said. "I've got to destroy them." She waved her hand, gesturing to the chamber, the ship. "Destroy *all* of this. It doesn't belong here. They're not a part of this reality."

If Connell couldn't see that, it wasn't her problem.

"You're upset," he said, even quieter than before. "Understandably so. But Sanji's gone, and you can't sacrifice yourself. It won't bring him back. Besides—" he pointed to the altar top "—how could you figure all of this out?"

He wasn't going to talk her out of it. She tapped her temple.

"Because I'm smart, remember? Cover of *National Geographic* and all that. Little ol' thing like a ten-thousand-year-old alien bomb shouldn't faze me a bit."

He grabbed her again, by the shoulders this time, spun her around to face him, leaned in close.

"You can play crazy some other time," he said. The voice a growl now, no longer quiet and understanding. "I've had enough people die in this godforsaken place. You're coming with us."

His fingers dug painfully into her muscles. She knew he meant it. If he had to, he would drag her back to the river. He was injured but still much stronger than her.

Was he right? Was she being crazy?

To want to kill an alien race, for revenge . . . yes, she was being crazy.

Veronica nodded.

"Okay. You're right. I don't know what I was saying."

Connell gripped her right arm, pulled her to the river's edge.

"O'Doyle, your rest is over," he said. "We go now."

The big man lifted his hung head, gazed out with eyes that looked like they wanted to close forever. He glanced at Veronica, then back to Connell. He nodded.

"Yes sir," he said.

He tried to rouse Lybrand. She didn't respond. O'Doyle gently rolled her off the wall. She splashed into the river. He slid in himself, held her, kept her head above water.

Would either of them make it? Were they already as good as dead?

Connell held Veronica at the river's edge, just a three-foot drop into the water below. He let her go, turned off the scrambler, carefully stuffed it into his webbing.

The silverbugs suffered a collective shiver, then returned to their coordinated activity.

Connell stared hard at her, pointed down to the water's surface.

"After you," he said.

She nodded, stepped off, plunged in feetfirst. He followed her in.

O'Doyle guided Lybrand to the middle of the river, where the current pulled at them. In seconds, her rope pulled taut on Connell. He, in turn, pulled at Veronica until she swam for herself. She had been the first in the rope line, now she was the last.

Veronica chanced a look back over her shoulder. The silverbugs wandered across the orb's polished surface, keeping it perpetually prepared to fulfill its role. Over ten thousand years they'd been down here, under this mountain, older than any human civilization, older than any human religion. How long would the rocktopi continue to exist? A poisoned, dying race, barely hanging on to intelligence, barely above the level of animals, kept alive only by their caring machines.

It was all just too much.

The current pulled at her exhausted body.

"Connell," she said softly, then closed her eyes and stopped fighting.

Veronica Reeves slipped below the surface.

9:40 A.M.

Connell watched O'Doyle and Lybrand, wondering if either of them would make it. They were fifty feet ahead, the rope between Connell and Lybrand already tight enough to be a mostly straight line some fifty feet long. O'Doyle's rally back at the rocktopi statue had faded away to nothing. The man had all the drive of a limp piece of bacon.

If those two were going to live, it was up to Connell to make sure it happened. Well, good fucking luck with that. His back felt like there was a screwdriver jammed in his spine. He couldn't move his arm that well anymore, thanks to the shoulder wound that was now more numb than painful. How much blood had he lost? The lack of sleep, the endless fight-or-flight.

A cloud in his head.

Hard to focus on anything.

But he could do it. He had to do it. He would make sure O'Doyle and Lybrand got out.

Them, and Veronica. She just wasn't all there. Use that bomb to kill the rocktopi? Connell knew the pain of losing someone you loved — knew it better than most — but he wasn't going to let Veronica's grief get her killed.

Up ahead, the river banked to the left.

Connell twisted in the water, looking back for Veronica — but she wasn't there.

"Veronica?"

He looked to the limestone block wall passing by on his right, then to the orb-dome room already fading away in the distance.

"Veronica!"

He twisted in place, looking down as if he might see her yellow suit close by, just under the surface.

The rope that tied him to her... his eyes followed it... there — a few feet back upstream, a blob of yellow below the surface... fading... *sinking.*

Connell threw himself toward her. Searing agony replaced the numbness in his shoulder. The stabbing pain in his back made his movements jerky, twitchy. He fought on, gritting his teeth, forcing his body to ignore those things. American crawl — he'd learned it in summer camp as a little boy. Left, right, turn to the side to breathe in, face down in the water and breathe out, keep kicking.

He reached her in seconds. He gulped in a big breath, held it, dove. Disorienting, the feeling of being pulled backward and swimming down at the same time. Kick, kick, *kick*. Already exhausted body quickly starving for oxygen. Can't see ... water inside his mask, *hot* water, can't open his eyes what if they cook they—

—his hands found her limp body. He pulled her in, wrapped one arm around her waist. Lungs screaming, he kicked for the surface.

She suddenly thrashed, came alive all at once, pushing and pulling. Air, he needed air. He let go of her, clawed for the surface ... hands grabbed his leg, yanked him down deeper.

Connell's thoughts fled, any semblance of intelligence vanished— the fight to reach the surface, only that and nothing else, not the hands pulling at his waist, tugging at him.

He punched unseeing, trying to hit her, to *kill* her, whatever it took to be free, but the water slowed his fist—it glanced off something.

The hands let go. He was *free*.

Lungs *screaming*, had to breathe, kick and swim and kick, couldn't hold it anymore couldn't—

—he broke the surface, breathing in so loud the gasp echoed through the ship canyon. Water slipping into his mouth, his throat. Coughing.

A tug on the rope around his chest, from behind ... Lybrand and O'Doyle's weight, pulling him downstream. The rope ... again, the rope ... he grabbed at the rope tied to Veronica, started reeling it in ...

No resistance.

Hand over hand he pulled, reeled it all in, knew what he would find ... the end of the rope.

She had untied it.

Connell felt the current start to take him around the bend.

Far upstream, she broke the surface, gasping just as he had. She swam for the limestone wall. Strong strokes, but something in her right hand made her movements awkward.

He started toward her again—American crawl, children, the basic stroke of swimming—but his arms wouldn't obey. They kept treading water, those small, automatic motions were all he could manage.

He had nothing left with which to fight.

The current pulled at him, both the water surrounding his body and the rope around his chest.

Veronica reached the wall.

She looked back at him as the current took him around the bend. Before she vanished from sight, she raised one hand and waved good-bye.

9:44 A.M.

"*Please,*" he said, the word a huffing breath of near madness. "*Please...* I told you everything. *Don't hurt me any more.*"

Kayla nodded. He had told her everything. As bat-shit crazy as it all sounded, she'd seen enough with her own eyes to know it was the truth.

She still straddled him, still felt that lovely buzz down below.

His left hand clutched spasmodically. She'd left that one alone. The right, however, was a mangled mess. Broken lumps within the yellow fabric. Twelve swollen lumps, to be precise.

She'd gone through the six knuckles of his pointer and middle finger before even taking out the ballgag, before asking him a single question. After that, the little prick had been only too happy to babble away, answering whatever she asked.

His ring finger and pinkie? She'd broken those knuckles as well. One at a time. Just to be thorough.

Five people left alive: Connell, O'Doyle, Lybrand, Veronica Reeves, Sanji Haak. At least they were alive when Angus had left them, run away like the coward that he was. He'd let his best friend die. Now why wasn't she surprised at that?

Just five people left. No weapons except for a couple of knives. And Kayla was only a few minutes' walk from the Dense Mass Cavern and the alien ship. Angus had told her the survivors would wind up there. All good intel.

But the rest of what the little prick said... so staggering. An alien ship. A goddamn *alien ship,* with *goddamn aliens.* This went *way* beyond mere reinstatement. If she pulled this off, she might get far more than Vogel's approval—she might very well wind up with his job.

She had yet to break the knuckles of his right thumb. She looked at it, caressed it, wondered if she should make it an even fourteen, get *all* the knuckles on that hand. It would be fun. But, no... no need to be greedy. She'd taught the little prick an important lesson. Time to move on.

"*Plea-eee-eease*," he said, his sobs chopping the word into bits.

Maybe if she came back this way, she could have a little more of him.

"All right, honey," she said. "It's all right."

Kayla picked up the ballgag from the tunnel floor. She didn't bother to clean off the silt clinging to the spit-covered rubber, just jammed the whole thing into his mouth. He *mmpf*ed and *hmmpf*ed as she fastened the straps. She put her palm on his head, fingertips at his eyebrows. She pulled back as she leaned over him, forcing him to look up at her. Face and mask smeared with snot. Eyes red and puffy from crying.

She stood, adjusted her gear. Angus had a real Marco/Polo device, with a bigger screen. Not cobbled together like the one she'd made.

"You do good work," she said. "Maybe you can tell mama all about it when I come back for you."

She bent, kissed his hood-covered forehead, heard him whimper when she did.

Kayla left him there.

She headed down the tunnel.

9:47 A.M.

Connell crawled through the shallows, hands and knees sinking into platinum muck. He reached O'Doyle and Lybrand, collapsed next to them, cheek slapping into mud worth millions.

The three of them. All that was left.

They had traveled miles. There were miles yet to go.

"O'Doyle," Connell said without looking up, "you guys still alive?"

"Yeah," came the answer. Every word a heavy breath. "But don't know for how long."

Connell grunted. Lybrand's slashed suit wouldn't have much coolant left. Was she already cooking? Time to go, but it was so nice to just lie there. A rest, a short one … what could that hurt?

"We have to go up," O'Doyle said, although he sounded like he wanted to do anything *but* move. "Right now, Connell. I'm sorry, but if you're going after Veronica, you're on your own."

Veronica. She was back there, in the belly of this incomprehensible ship, this ancient relic of a dead race.

Connell gazed upstream, back into the ship's deep, misty, jungle-esque shadows. Was he going back for her? She was grieving, crazy … she needed help. But how long would it take him to reach her? He couldn't swim upstream. Could he walk along the river? He wasn't sure he had the energy for even that, let alone bringing her back here and then the final hike up the Linus Highway to the surface.

More important than his fatigue, though, was the reason she'd stayed behind. She wanted to use that orb, blow this entire place to kingdom come. Had she already started that process? How long would it take? Was the clock already ticking? How long before the silverbugs led the rocktopi to her?

He remembered her grabbing him, yanking him deeper into the water, pulling at his leg, his waist…

His hand shot to his webbing—the scrambler was gone.

She had faked drowning to steal it from him so she could work on the orb, uninterrupted by silverbugs.

Connell shook his head. If that orb was still a functioning weapon, he had to assume she could make it work.

His soul dragged, fractured, hurt even more than his body. He knew she wouldn't make it out alive, and if he chased her, he'd die as well.

"She made her choice," Connell said. "I'm not going back. The three of us are getting out of here."

He forced himself up. His muscles didn't want to function. He made them. He pleaded with them, cut deals with them: *just do this for me for a little bit longer and I swear we'll all sit on a couch and watch cartoons for the rest of our existence together.*

He and O'Doyle and Lybrand had washed up in a bubble-shaped room, one of thousands spread through the ship. Maybe forty feet in diameter. The river had eaten away some of one side, exposing the dark interior. Beyond the room's left edge, the open space of the Dense Mass Cavern. Blue-white light beat down from above.

They had made it.

"Linus Highway has to be close," Connell said. "Stay here while I look."

He had to step over O'Doyle and Lybrand. They lay on the platinum mud, legs still in the shallow water. Only their chests moved.

Footprints. Already mostly gone. Filled in by the thin, lapping ripples of the river's edge, but clearly, footprints. Angus. He'd made it this far.

With each step, Connell's feet slid before sinking in. Had to be careful here. So close to the way out, wouldn't do to add a pulled hammy to his list of injuries. He walked the last few feet along the slick shore, reached out and gripped the room's edge to steady himself.

Beeeeep.

He froze. The sound had come from outside the ship.

Connell glanced back at O'Doyle—head up, now, exhausted but alert.

Someone was out there. Was it Angus? Maybe Randy, if Angus had lied? Was that a sound from a silverbug?

Or, could it be something they hadn't seen yet ... something even worse than the rocktopi.

O'Doyle quietly stood. Half-hidden by the bubble room's shadows, he drew his knife.

Connell leaned close to the ship's edge. Slowly, so slowly, he leaned out, peeking past with just one eye.

The muck gave way to the same tile floors they'd seen on the other side of the ship. A few hundred feet away, the arched entrance of a tunnel.

And in the middle of that arch, a Marco/Polo unit in her hands, stood a woman wearing a KoolSuit, a machine gun slung over her shoulder.

Kayla Meyers.

9:51 A.M.

Three signals, flickering on and off.

CONNELL KIRKLAND
PATRICK O'DOYLE
BERTHA LYBRAND

Kayla looked at the ship, and just as quickly, she looked away. Nothing could be that big. How many stories high? And off to her left, the end of it, she had to crane her neck to see the top of that. Higher than a skyscraper. So big, *too* big. This whole place ... a *miles-long* room, under a mountain ... a fucking alien spacecraft all beat-up and shot to shit, with a river flowing through it ... none of this was right.

This place, she didn't know how to handle it ... it made her *afraid.*

She wanted out of here. But no, not yet.

The signals didn't lock on. Interference from all the platinum? Angus had given a clear signal because he'd been in the tunnel. Connell and the others, they were close, but they could be anywhere.

Maybe she could account for the interference, just enough to give her a clear direction as to the source of those signals.

Kayla started to adjust the controls.

9:52 A.M.

The scrambler worked.

Thank God.

She held the walkie-talkie tightly, clutched it to her chest as if it were a crucifix that could ward off vampires.

Water still dripped from her as she walked toward the platinum altar. Silverbugs occasionally dropped from the domed ceiling, bouncing off the stone floor with a *clank*. Sometimes their little legs bent or even snapped off. The few of them that had been on the orb's polished shell slipped away, one by one, dropping noiselessly into the shaft below.

Her muscles twitched. Her entire body tingled, as did her face, her brain, a feeling she remembered from pulling all-nighters back in college. *So tired.* Her muscles, just sludge oozing between skin and bones.

This room ... it was *spotless*. No dirt on the stone floor, not even a speck of platinum dust. The orb, the altar, the dome itself, all perfect, as if this room hadn't seen a day of the eleven thousand years it sat waiting for the rocktopi's genocidal enemy, waiting for doomsday.

That enemy was nowhere to be seen, but she was ready to usher doomsday in with a warm welcome.

She would kill them, just like they'd killed her father.

His hand, flying ...

His blood, spraying ...

His loss *hurt*, physically. She tried to breathe, felt the tears welling up. She hadn't thought of him for the past few minutes, and now that she did it was like an avalanche coming down to crush her. He'd been her everything.

And now he was gone.

Because of *them*.

The rocktopi had truly died out in a planetary holocaust countless millennia ago, unknown light-years away. This group, this Wah Wah tribe, had escaped, but to what end? Look at what they had become. The entire race should have gone extinct long ago.

The time had come for the Wah Wah tribe to join their ancestors.

More *clonks* of falling silverbugs. Almost raining now, shells smashing every few seconds. She kept an arm over her head in case one came down on top of her. Silverbugs wandered down the walls, walked aimlessly across the stone floor.

Veronica stood in front of the altar. She recognized it from the alcove carvings. Doubt welled up—had she made a mistake? She didn't understand the controls. She'd spent years trying to crack the Chaltélian language and had failed. What made her think she could understand this?

She closed her eyes. She felt her father's hands on her shoulders.

Think, Ronni. You can't give up. You have to think it through.

She couldn't talk back to him, but she could do what he asked. She could *think*. She could honor his memory, finish the fucking job and obliterate these abominations before they took more human lives, broke more hearts, shattered more families.

Veronica again looked at the altar's flat top. Think things through. Something jumped out at her—no pictoglyphs here. In the Picture Cavern, nothing *but* pictures. And the walls as well, just carved images. Not glyphs at all. At Cerro Chaltén, those had been true glyphs, images that were words as opposed to a literal representation of an animal, plant or place.

A key difference between the Wah Wah tribe and the Chaltélians. The Wah Wah rocktopi ... they were *dumber*.

Maybe when they landed, they had been a fully functional culture. Maybe the original crew had taught their children language, math, science, even the arts. Generation after generation that could have continued—until the explosion that tore a huge hole in the ship. Until the radiation that followed. Until the plague.

Five thousand years ago, give or take, maybe the Old Rocktopi had been advanced enough to see their gene pool degenerating. Could they have known their species would soon decline? Could they have *planned* for that, or at least tried to?

A silverbug smashed into the altar, bounced off. Just missed her. Not many remained on the dome walls. The drugged-out machines covered the floor now. She glanced over them, looking for a gleam, a shine... Nothing. They were all old. None of the new ones that had attacked Lybrand. A few stumbled to the river's edge, fell in, were swept away.

The rocktopi could have programmed the silverbugs to handle everything. Farming, tunnel construction and maintenance, maybe taking care of the ship until the radiation faded away. To make sure customs were passed down, laws and religious beliefs were carved into the stone, in case things got so bad their written language faded from memory.

For ten thousand years, this race had lived in these caves. Had stories of spaceflight become the quaint tales of old fools? Then something only taught in history classes? Without technology or computers to show images, maybe those stories faded to legend, then myth, then faded out altogether. Ten *thousand years*. America was only two and a half centuries old, yet much of the nation's history was already gone forever. Even in the age of technology, with movies and unassailable historical records, some people believed that the Holocaust had never happened, that the moon landing was a hoax.

Once the makers of history die, perhaps it's only a matter of time before history itself changes.

At one time, the silverbugs might have been no more than servant machines catering to the rocktopi's every need. Thousands of years passed, countless generations, and gradually the silverbugs became part of the environment, as common as air or the stone walls of the rocktopi's tiny universe. Eventually, perhaps *hundreds* of generations after the plague, the rocktopi's intellect faded away. Wracked by ignorance and genetic deterioration, they regressed to little more than savages, kept alive only by the efforts of the silverbugs.

The servants became the keepers.

Veronica looked at the altar's controls in a new light. Aside from the artificial suns, this was the only piece of working machinery that remained. *Priorities*. The silverbugs were programmed with priorities, instructed to keep the most important devices functioning at the expense of all else. How important was an educational computer if the artificial suns ceased functioning and no food could be grown? The suns were an obvious first priority, and by appearances, this doomsday device ran a close second. Whatever that mysterious enemy was capable of, death was far more desirable.

And if such a death was an ultimate priority for the race, then the Old Rocktopi must have provided for its use. Veronica doubted the silverbugs were programmed to destroy their masters, no matter what the situation. Most likely, the orb had to be set off by a rocktopi.

If death was preferable to the enemy and if the orb had been kept functional for this long, then the Old Rocktopi intended its eventual use—there had to be simple instructions somewhere. Simple, like the carvings in the Picture Cavern.

She ran her hands across the control panel. She circled the altar, looking at the sides, at the base.

No pictures.

An unbidden memory of driving to the EarthCore camp, telling her smiling father he needed to lose weight. A fresh wave of grief. She shook it away, forced herself to concentrate.

But it was no use. She'd spent years trying to understand the Chaltélian language, and she was going to figure this out in a matter of minutes? Ridiculous.

She had failed.

Veronica jumped as a silverbug hit the floor next to her, bounced into her leg. She scooted away, but it wasn't trying to get her. She looked up to the ceiling to see how many of them remained.

The ceiling … all the silverbugs were gone.

For the first time, she could see the curved walls.

Her grief flowed into fury.

Veronica Reeves smiled.

9:56 A.M.

O'Doyle helped Connell drag Bertha across the platinum silt, deeper into the bubble room's shadow.

"But she came down from the surface," O'Doyle said, just loud enough to be heard over the river's constant sounds. "And she's worked for you. She's got to be here to help us."

Connell's brain felt like mud. Thoughts slow, plodding. Maybe he wasn't thinking clearly, but his IQ hadn't dropped sharply since this all started—Kayla Meyers was *not* there to help.

"I never told her where this place was," he said, still pulling, dragging, fighting against the agony in his back and knee. "That means she hacked our systems or she turned an EarthCore employee. If she's here, she's working for someone else. The Russians or the South Africans, maybe."

"She armed?"

Connell huffed. "She's a killer—she's always armed."

A killer...something Connell knew firsthand. Maybe this was some kind of karmic payback. The assassin he'd hired to murder his wife's killer, standing in the way of escape.

Two grown men, but both were so drained it was all they could do to haul Lybrand across the silt to the room's edge, as far away from the river as they could get without searching for a way that led further into the ancient ship.

O'Doyle fell to his ass next to Lybrand. She didn't move. He leaned over her, gloved hands gently caressing her face through the thin mask.

Connell had probably known what his plan was the moment he laid eyes on Kayla. Now, watching O'Doyle worry over Lybrand, that plan solidified. It was what had to be done.

O'Doyle looked up.

"If she's armed, then we have to run," O'Doyle said. "This ship goes on forever, we can hide somewhere inside."

Deeper into this strange ship, where rocktopi might be, where silverbugs might be. No, not when the way out was so close.

"If you run, she'll hunt you," Connell said. He wasn't sure how he knew that, he just *knew*.

Barbara Yakely didn't know how to contact Kayla. Kayla wore a KoolSuit and carried a Marco unit, two things that were only available in the EarthCore camp. Connell hoped he was wrong, that through some fluke of the fates Kayla had found the alternate way in and that she *was* there to help, but he also knew that was a naive fantasy.

She was there to kill anyone she saw, either hired to do so, or so that she could sell this location to another company.

If Kayla Meyers saw O'Doyle and Lybrand, Connell knew damn well she would kill them both.

He couldn't let that happen.

Once upon a time, Connell had been in love. Losing that love had destroyed his life. Now he had a chance, one *last* chance, to save two people perhaps as in love as he'd once been with Cori. O'Doyle and Lybrand might make a future together. And what future did Connell have to look forward to? Endless work. An empty apartment. Nightmares of the evening his entire world had crumbled into nothing.

And, there was that long-ago sin to atone for.

Connell had no illusions—he had pissed his own life away.

If here, at the end, he could do something good with it, wasn't that worth dying for?

"Turn Lybrand on her side," he said. "I need that Polo unit on her neck."

O'Doyle was just as tired, just as hurt, his mind probably just as muddy. It took him a second to understand. When he did, his sleepy eyes widened. He shook his head.

"No way," he said. "There's two of us, Connell. We can take her. Don't do this."

Honorable words that rang hollow. O'Doyle wanted to fight, but he knew full well he was in no shape to do so.

"You don't know Kayla," Connell said. "Hurry up before she comes in here. Roll Lybrand over."

O'Doyle did.

Connell unfastened his glove, slid it off. The heat hit his skin in an instant, like he'd dipped his hand in scalding water. He felt at the back of Lybrand's neck for the seal to her hood. He opened it slightly, reached inside, felt for the little dot of her Polo sounder. He pried the bit of plastic off like it was a scab. He put it in a pocket of his webbing, pulled the glove back on and sealed it up.

Then Connell held out his hand, palm up, to the scarred, sagging man before him.

"Your turn," he said.

O'Doyle stared at the hand.

Connell instantly understood what O'Doyle saw—not the yellow glove, but rather the cut on the palm beneath it.

The same cut that had let their blood mix together.

"We can set a trap," O'Doyle said. "Something. Anything."

It hit Connell—there, of all places—just how much he'd tuned out since his wife's death. The only relationship he had was with his boss. He'd been around O'Doyle for a few scant hours, but they had fought side by side, fought for each other, saved each other's lives.

This man was a friend. A true friend. Connell's *best* friend.

"You don't know her, Patrick. She's as dangerous as you are. If you want Lybrand to live, this is the only way."

The look in O'Doyle's eyes. Desolation. The knowledge that he couldn't do the one thing he'd been born to do. He nodded, stripped off a glove. He bent his head, opened the seal of his hood and pried the little dot free.

He offered it up.

"I won't forget this," he said.

Connell took the dot. He put it in the webbing pocket with Lybrand's, careful to make sure both bits of plastic were safely in there before he closed it.

He knelt, started scooping platinum dust on Lybrand, hurriedly covering her legs, hips and chest. O'Doyle did the same to himself, scooping armfuls on top of his suit's yellow fabric.

Connell took a step back. In seconds, the shadows combined with millions of dollars' worth of platinum to make the pair look like lumps of silt. If Kayla's headlamp panned this way, she'd see them instantly, but out of the corner of her eye she probably wouldn't notice a thing.

Especially if she was distracted.

Connell turned to walk away.

"Wait," O'Doyle said.

The big man held out his sheathed knife.

"If you get a chance, you stick her," he said. "In the belly. You *keep* sticking her until she stops moving. Got it?"

Connell nodded. He took the sheath, stuck it into the webbing belt at the small of his back.

So many dead—this was his one chance to help two people live.

At least someone might make it out.

He walked to the edge of the ship.

10:02 A.M.

On the Marco/Polo unit's controls, three names stopped flickering, suddenly glowed steady and strong:

BERTHA LYBRAND
PATRICK O'DOYLE
CONNELL KIRKLAND

Kayla looked up and saw Connell standing at the edge of the ship canyon, where the river flowed out of it—a mere fifty yards away.

"Connell!"

It was almost over. She didn't have to fake her smile.

Kayla stuffed the Marco unit into her belt, leaving both hands free. The Galil hung at an angle across her chest and stomach.

She walked toward him.

"Oh my God, I'm so happy to finally find you. Are you all right?"

He reached out his right hand, grabbed the edge of the ship, took a half step closer to it.

"Stop right there," he said.

She did.

"It's okay," she said. "I'm here to rescue you. Where are the others?"

Tension in his body. His hand gripped the ship's hull, ready to pull him behind the edge, out of her line of sight.

"And how did you know we needed rescuing? How did you know where we were?"

That look on his face … she should have known he was too smart to not know why she was there.

Oh well—as long as he died, it didn't really matter.

Kayla snapped-grabbed for the Galil. Connell ducked behind the ship's hull. Kayla fired anyway, a quick burst, but he was already gone and the bullets clanged off platinum.

She sprinted after him and entered the ship canyon's steamy shadows.

10:03 A.M.

It would be easy.

Just follow the instructions etched into the cathedral ceiling. Even for the self-destruction of their entire race, the Old Rocktopi relied on simple pictures.

And that made sense.

She didn't know much about rocktopi communication, but she knew that of her own species. Without some central cultural reference, such as television or radio, human languages fractured, split and mutated into countless regional dialects. In just decades, a language could change so much that people who spoke the original tongue might not understand the new form.

How much could a language change over the course of eleven thousand years?

It was funny to think that this race—a race that had once traveled among the stars and had the power to move mountains—now communicated at a level equal to that of primitive humans. She wondered if the same fate lay in store for her own race. Perhaps in the end, the *very* end, mankind would be left with nothing more than crude pictures.

The instructions: an engraving of the control panel, step-by-step pictures showing what buttons to press, what knobs to turn. Simplicity itself.

That same concept explained the Picture Cavern. The carvings there were instructional, filled with the one message rocktopi understood all too well: *If it comes from the surface, kill it.*

Like they had killed her father.

Now it was their turn to die.

Veronica took a deep breath. She double-checked the first instruction, then pressed a yellow square.

10:04 A.M.

Patrick lay still.

The woman Connell feared so much came around the corner, rifle in hand, the river on her right, the room in which Patrick and Bertha hid on her left.

Kayla Meyers. *Farm Girl.*

Patrick knew her from his service days. She was the real deal, would put a bullet in you as soon as look at you. He had an urge to rise up, move quietly through the shadow toward her, put her down—but he knew he'd never reach her.

Kayla crept forward, stepping carefully through wet platinum sludge. She couldn't stop herself from looking up, craning her head left and right.

If she looked into the room...

She continued along the riverbank.

Her movements: steady, strong, graceful. Kayla moved like a big cat. But she also looked afraid, overwhelmed by the strangeness that surrounded her.

She moved past the room, out of sight.

Connell had a brief head start, but with his knee, how long until she caught him?

Patrick counted to ten. He shook Lybrand. Her eyes fluttered open.

"Baby, if you got anything left, we need it now," he said. "We got one chance to get out of here."

The skin of her forearms and hands almost glowed red. Swollen, covered in blisters. Her lips were cracked and dry. A crusty film caked her eyelids.

"Go without me," she said. "Please. Survive."

He shook his head, brushed platinum dust off them both.

"If you don't make it, I don't make it," he said. "You want me to live? Then you have to help."

Patrick pulled her to her feet. She could barely stand.

One last sprint, a three-mile hump, and he could save her. He lifted her in a fireman's carry. Every atom of him wanted to stop, to quit, to sleep.

Just a few more miles.

He carried her out of the bubble room. He glanced left, upstream—Connell and the woman both were already lost in the mist.

Patrick gritted his teeth, stepped through ankle-deep silt and exited the ship canyon. He carried his love to the tunnel entrance.

Lungs already burning, muscles already begging, he started up the Linus Highway's steep slope.

10:05 A.M.

The mist-filled ship rose up on either side, towering above ... so many rooms, *hundreds* of them, all the wrong shape. Everything about this place was wrong, wrong, *wrong*.

Kayla caught a glimpse of Connell up ahead in the mist. Limping. Hurt, or faking? Trying to lure her in?

She raised the Galil, squeezed off a burst. As she brought the gun down, her right foot slid in the deep mud. A ripping pain in her left ankle. She hopped on her right foot, trying to slow her momentum, but she slipped—she fell to her side, splashing in the river's shallows.

Kayla scrambled to her feet, kept moving. The left ankle, twisted. Maybe a light sprain. Not enough to stop her from chasing him.

Or, should she just leave?

Leave this fucked-up place behind forever?

No. If she did that, she was saying good-bye to her dream, right when she was *so close* to getting it.

Kayla kept moving down the riverbank, moving as fast as she could.

10:06 A.M.

Bullets whined off metal somewhere ahead. How close had they come to hitting him, to ripping through skin and muscle and bone?

He was going to die here, miles underground. Kayla was going to shoot him in the back.

Keep running, as long as you can, lead her away from Patrick...

Connell fought through the fire in his knee, the spear point in his back. A fast hobble more than a sprint, each step sheer agony that pierced the last of his adrenaline rush.

Up ahead, the river bent to the right.

He knew where he was: not far from the orb room...not far from Veronica.

If he went that way, Kayla would follow, he'd lead her right to Veronica.

Shit, shit, *shit, SHIT!*

Had to find a place to hide.

It hit him: he *couldn't* hide from her, not with the Polo unit on his neck.

Dammit *dammit*, why hadn't he taken that off before? He could have tossed all three little dots aside, kept running, maybe that would throw her off.

He scanned the rooms on his left. Just ahead, an oval one that looked like a corridor, leading deeper into the ship's darkness. Get out of sight for a moment, get that Polo unit off, then maybe he could keep moving while she tracked it down, circle back somehow...

A *bap-bap-bap* of Kayla's rifle: heat exploding through his right thigh.

He screamed, stumbled, hands clutching at his leg.

Connell landed hard, instantly scrambled to hands and knees. He crawled through the silt and dust toward the shadowy corridor.

10:08 A.M.

A second set of gunshots echoed through the ship canyon, fading away into the river's roar.

This set sounded closer than the first.

Connell, Lybrand and O'Doyle didn't have any bullets left, so who the fuck was doing the shooting?

Maybe rescuers. Maybe *soldiers.*

They would come down here, take control of the ship. They'd keep it a secret, keep everyone out.

And … they would keep the rocktopi alive.

Her father's butchers. *Alive.*

Veronica was almost finished with the instructions. Just one last button to push, a blue one with a spot of red in the middle.

A drunken silverbug stumbled into her leg. She kicked it aside.

As near as she could tell, the orb would descend anywhere from forty-five minutes to an hour. Maybe a little more. When it reached the proper depth, it would detonate, blow this place to bits.

"You don't get to live," she said.

She reached for the red-blue button, stopped just before pressing it.

If it only took forty-five minutes … was that enough time to reach the surface?

A chill rippled through her. In her hatred and anguish, she hadn't thought about the most-important part of her plan—getting out alive.

A gleam of metal at the river's edge caught her eye. There, two silverbugs, water beading up and dripping from their smooth shells.

Smooth, flawless shells.

Veronica didn't move. She didn't breathe. Where had they come from? Had they swum here? Had they—

She flinched at the metallic sound of spring-loaded metal: a gleaming, curved blade jutted out from each of the silverbugs.

Blades pointed right at her.

The machines stood between her and the river.

She hadn't seen another way out of the room.

10:10 A.M.

Alone.

No light.

His nose, clogged shut. Angus had to suck in air in big, fast gulps when he sneered his lips away from the ball, then feel those lips flap when his breath shot out again. The ball forced his mouth open so far the mask wasn't properly aligned—some breaths came in cool and normal, some so hot they seared his lungs.

His hand... *his hand.*

Wrist still tied behind his back. The ruined fingers, mostly numb but still enough bubbling misery to remind him over and over and over again of what she'd done to him, one knuckle at a time.

That *cunt.* If he got out of here, he'd kill her, slice her into pieces and make her *hurt* so bad for so long oh yes he would he—

A sound. Something other than his breathing.

Was it a *click?* Silverbugs coming for him. On his stomach, unable to move, barely able to breathe.

Wait... a light?

The rocktopi, flowing toward him, coming with those knives to slice him, to hack him...

No, the light bounced... a mining helmet.

Oh no ohno*ohno, that woman,* coming back for him like she'd said she would.

Angus started to scream. He couldn't stop it. He screamed for help, prayed for a miracle, for someone other than that woman to come, *anyone* but her.

The light came closer, filled the tunnel.

Not the robots.

Or the monsters.

Or that evil bitch.

Lybrand over his shoulders, lungs heaving, legs wobbling, Patrick O'Doyle stopped and smiled down at Angus.

"Hello, coward. I was hoping I'd run into you again."

10:11 A.M.

Patrick set Bertha down as gently as he could.

The man on the tunnel floor, Angus Kool... he was nothing. He was the difference between Bertha living and dying. Patrick didn't want to kill him, but that was up to Angus.

Ballgag. Hog-tied with copper wire. Brutal work. And that hand... fingers so swollen it looked like a yellow Mickey Mouse glove.

Crying. Screaming. Eyes scrunched. Body shaking with sobs.

Patrick knelt in front of him.

"I'm taking your suit. If you fight me, I'll kill you."

He stepped behind Angus as the man screamed louder.

Patrick gripped Angus's left forearm, squeezed it tight as he unwrapped the wire. Angus fought. Of course he did. Patrick let go of the wire, grabbed the man's swollen fingers and *squeezed*.

More screaming, the kind that tore vocal cords, the kind that made throats bleed—but the fighting stopped.

Patrick finished unwrapping the wire, stripped off the man's gloves. He pulled apart the seam that ran down the middle of the back, pulled one arm free, then the other, ignoring the muffled, helpless pleas. The man's skin instantly sheened with sweat. Patrick yanked the suit off Angus's hips, down the little man's legs, leaving him naked save for the hood. Finally, Patrick undid the ballgag.

"It's so hot don't do this gimme the suit I'll die I'll die I invented it it's mine IT'S MINE!"

Patrick tore off the hood. He stood, stepped back.

"The higher you go, the cooler it gets," he said. "You want to live? Run fast. I see you again, and I kill you."

Angus scrambled to his feet, cradled his mangled hand to his chest. Still crying, still shaking, snot dripping from his nose, spit dangling from his lip. He looked at the lime KoolSuit in Patrick's hands.

"Please," he said. *"Please."*

Patrick shook his head. "Last chance."

Angus drew in a big breath—it came out as a scream of rage, pain, terror. He sprinted up the tunnel, naked ass bouncing in the helmet's lamp.

Patrick knelt next to Bertha and started stripping off her ruined suit.

"Hold on, baby," he said. "Hold on a few minutes longer."

10:13 A.M.

A trail of blood: red splattered across platinum sand.

The trail led into an oval corridor steeped in shadow. Even in this sprawling canyon the ship felt claustrophobic, pressed in on her in a way that the Linus Highway had not. The corridor would make things even tighter, promised to suffocate her, drag her under.

But she had to get this done. Connell was in there. O'Doyle and Lybrand probably weren't—Connell had led her away from them. He would know where they were.

Her Marco/Polo unit let out a new *beep*. She checked it, found a new name flickering on and off:

VERONICA REEVES

Somewhere around here, somewhere close. Kayla would take her out as soon as she could.

But first—Connell Kirkland.

Galil aimed before her, Kayla stepped into the corridor.

The shape, all wrong. Oval. No edges. Strange, curved bars in the ceiling, perpendicular to the corridor's slight bends. A few meters of light that quickly took her from full illumination to complete darkness.

At the edge of that darkness, almost past a bend in the corridor, there he was.

Connell had both hands pressed hard against his right thigh. Blood covered the yellow fingers of his KoolSuit gloves, smeared across his leg. Sallow complexion, face seemed almost as yellow as the material framing it. Nose looked broken. Dots of blood—orange and red both—across his shoulder. The guy was in bad shape, but those *eyes*... deep with exhaustion yet burning with a fierce determination.

"You fucking *shot* me," he said.

She nodded. "Can't put one past you, can we?"

He sneered, a mixture of pain and hate.

"Fuck you, Meyers. Just put a bullet in my head and let's get this over with."

"In a hurry to die?" She kept a good meter of distance between them, the gun lowered at his chest, her finger firmly on the trigger. The canyon's half-light barely filtered this deep into the huge hallway, casting the scene in a surreal twilight. "Want to wind up like your buddies up top?"

The sneer eased.

"The camp? You killed them?"

"Wasn't me," she said. "Those flashing creepy crawlies. Carved your coworkers into wee little chunks."

He seemed to deflate, to sag in place.

"You have O'Doyle and Lybrand's Polo dots on you somewhere," she said. "Nice trick, that. Surprised I fell for it, but even a blind squirrel finds a nut once in a while. Where are they?"

He glared up at her, some of that fight back in his eyes. He shook his head.

"They're hiding in the ship," he said. "But you don't have time to find them if you want to get out of here alive. Reeves is about to blow this whole place sky-high. You stay, you die."

She stepped forward, snap-kicked his leg. The toe of her boot cracked into the fingers clutching the wound—she heard the light *snap* of a small bone.

He grunted but didn't scream. He released his thigh, bloody left hand clutching his bloody right to his chest.

That sneer flared up again: hateful, arrogant.

"Fuck you," he said.

She aimed the Galil, pulled the trigger.

The leather boot atop his foot burst open in a cloud of meat, bone and blood. He fell to his back, hands clutching the mangled foot. *Now* he screamed, oh yes he did, a delicious sound magnified by the oval corridor.

Two bullet wounds. A lot of pain. That would dilute the effect of what came next, might even make him pass out. But he wasn't little Herbert Darker—wounded or not, Connell was a man, and men were dangerous.

She slung the Galil. She pulled the pliers out of her pouch.

"Look at me, Kirkland. Look at me."

He did. Chin on his chest, he looked down his abused body at her, eyes filled with tears, mouth twisted into a grimace that almost looked like a grin.

She slowly opened and closed the pliers.

"Usually I start with the knuckles, but I'm in a hurry. So, I'm going to start with your balls. I'm going to crush your right nut unless you tell me where the others are."

He groaned, sobbed a deep-throated sob.

When he drew in a shaking breath for another, she heard a new sound. *click-click ... click-click click ...*

She whipped around, drawing her 9 millimeter in the same smooth motion. The contrast between staring into shadow and looking toward the light made her squint slightly, slowed her reaction.

On the floor, a long straight line of the long-legged, silvery probes, leading back out the corridor and to the left, upstream. In unison, they snapped down, then up, then down again.

The ship was wrong, this corridor was wrong, but that jerky motion ... she felt the acidic tickle of fear spurt in her stomach, instantly spread to her chest.

"What the fuck are they doing?"

From behind her, Connell croaked out words.

"Means ... monsters ... are coming."

10:15 A.M.

One chance.

Kayla had the pistol straight out in front of her, both hands holding it firmly, her feet a little more than shoulder width apart. She moved her aim from one silverbug to the next, to the next.

In that moment, she didn't know what to do.

One chance.

He hurt so bad, so deep. His shoulder, his thigh, his broken finger, the raging firestorm in his foot. He'd never imagined something could hurt so bad.

"How much time," she said. "How long before they come?"

Her voice, still calm, at least somewhat. For a moment, he imagined the two of them fighting side by side, against the silverbugs and the rocktopi, just like he'd done with O'Doyle and Lybrand.

Then his left hand slid behind his back, gripped the handle of O'Doyle's knife, and he remembered what that *one chance* was.

He rolled to his knees, drew the knife, then lunged toward her.

The blade's point drove into the back of her right knee. He felt it sink in, felt it jar when it hit bone, skidded, sink even deeper—he felt the crossguard slap against her KoolSuit.

Her scream made him wince, despite the agony rolling through his body. She twisted as she fell, half collapsing, half aiming. In the partial light, he saw the pistol barrel swing toward him. He let go of the knife, flailed a hand at the gun, caught her wrist. She landed hard, trying to angle it toward him.

Explosion of pain as he pushed off his ruined foot.

On top of her, straddling her. Her wrist, held tight.

Kayla, screaming, shouting, other hand grabbing at her waist—a knife, she was going for a knife, was going to stick him in the belly over and over until he didn't move.

Connell looked into her eyes: the eyes of an animal, the eyes of a woman, the eyes of a lost little girl.

He reared his head back, threw himself forward, smashed his forehead into her face. She grunted, twitched, kept fighting but not as hard. He reared back again, smashed again, felt a dull ache in his head.

She sagged back.

He did it again, just to be sure.

10:16 A.M.

Screams echoing through the river mist. Someone was out there, but too far away to help her.

The two new silverbugs, just sitting there, thin legs spread wide, those knives curving forward.

Veronica hadn't moved. Neither had they.

Her body began to tremble.

Maybe she could change the frequency on the scrambler. Had to try something. The walkie-talkie was sitting on the control panel's flat top.

She grabbed it.

As one, the two new silverbugs rushed toward her, scurrying over their beat-up, burnished brethren or just knocking them out of the way.

The first silverbug sprang at the altar, hit it, launched toward her face. She brought her hands up instinctively. The machine crashed into the hot-wired walkie-talkie, smashing it to pieces. The attacker fell to the ground, but before Veronica could react the second scurried around the altar's base, sprang, sharp claws fixing fast on her hips and ribs.

The curved blade drove deep into her stomach.

She beat at the machine, screaming. This couldn't be happening, it *couldn't*.

The blade slid out, drove back in again.

The *pain.*

Veronica's fists rained down on the round shell. Knuckles split, smearing blood across gleaming metal.

Something on her back, sharp little claws digging in—a stabbing explosion in her back.

Veronica spun, thrown off balance by the weight.

A moment of stillness: this was it. She would be dead soon. More pain to come first, more horror, but this was it—her life, at an end. A strange calmness mixed with absolute fear. Was she wrong about death? Was it really just *over,* or was there a God, an afterlife?

In that instant, she hoped there was, so she could see her father again.

Her father.

Another thrust into her belly, another into her back.

The taste of blood.

She stumbled.

Her father.

His hand, flying...

Veronica fell, caught herself on the altar. Arms and legs, so weak, nothing left...

More thrusts, agony enveloped her, consumed her.

Her father.

His blood, spraying...

They had butchered him.

They were butchering her.

She started to fall, caught herself at the last moment.

Her gaze landed on the red and blue button.

She fell forward against the control panel. Vision fading. Pain. Cold.

"Die," she said. "Just fucking *die* already."

Veronica fingered the button, then pressed it home.

She sagged to the stone floor.

The silverbugs kept on stabbing.

Above her prone body, ancient but well-cared-for machinery started to move. The dome trembled as mechanisms unused for eleven thousand years finally rumbled to life. Metallic groans, grinds and squeaks. Gears turned in complaint, engines hummed to life.

The noise seemed to awaken the countless silverbugs covering the cathedral room's stone floor. They stopped wandering or rolling about.

They paused, motionless, but only for a moment—they came alive as a unified flood. Hundreds of them dove for the river and followed the current downstream, answering some unseen call. More of them, *many more*, crawled from room to room, using what little shore there was, moving *upstream*.

They had to make their masters listen.

Somewhere up in the ceiling, out of sight, ancient machinery shuddered. A massive spool started rolling out its miles-long cable. The orb lowered three feet, stopped, bobbing ever so slightly from the sudden movement.

And then, it dropped.

The spool whined as cable lowered, and the orb plunged into the earth.

10:18 A.M.

Patrick worked the water tube from the KoolSuit's neck, put it to Lybrand's lips, squeezed.

She swallowed weakly, then coughed, spit.

He checked the body temp readout on her wrist: 99.8.

Just like that, almost back to normal.

She blinked, looked up at him. An instant where she almost smiled, then her eyes widened, her face scrunched.

"*My hands*," she said. "*My arms!*"

Now covered by the KoolSuit sleeves, yes, but the suit did nothing for the scorched skin, the weeping blisters.

Her arms shook. She stared at them as if they were alien to her.

"I know you're hurting, but we have to move," Patrick said. He wanted to carry her. He simply could not. He wasn't even sure if he could walk himself. "I'm tapped out, you have to rally. Can you move?"

She shook her head, shook it hard.

"My arms, *my arms*."

click-click, click

The noise made them both freeze, and for a second, made them both forget their pain. Patrick looked back down the tunnel: his headlamp beam lit up a single silverbug crouched motionless on the wall. Far off along the slope, he saw glimmers of other silverbugs scurrying up to join the first.

"I can move," Bertha said.

Patrick nodded. It was that, or die.

He helped her to her feet, being careful not to touch her arms.

Leaning on each other, they headed up the Linus Highway.

10:20 A.M.

Every step: Excruciating pain. Stepping on jagged glass.

The knee, the back, the foot, the thigh, the finger, his nose.

Losing blood. So weak. When he opened his mouth to breathe in, he felt the skin stretch on his face. It was getting warmer—must be losing coolant.

Muscles felt like they were made from rusted barbed wire.

Bones, forged of chipped razors that sliced against nerves.

How was he still alive?

And why did he keep moving?

For God's sake, he had nothing, *nothing*—with all this agony, why did he want to live?

Just lie down. Just rest. Just *quit*.

He couldn't.

The beast inside him wanted to live more than the man he was wanted to die.

He'd led her away, expecting she would murder him. It was what he deserved. But he'd fought her … he'd *beaten* her. He'd cheated death, and that had rekindled a fire inside of him.

Connell carried her pistol in his left hand. With his right, he used her rifle as a cane.

He ignored the silverbugs, moved past them, *thump*-dragging one sliding step at a time.

He'd left Kayla alive. The silverbugs would lead the rocktopi to her, and that would be that. She might even buy him a little time. With that knee, she was even worse off than he was, and she certainly wouldn't catch him.

Connell had even left her the knife. She wanted to kill? Let her kill a few rocktopi, if she could.

10:21 A.M.

Rocktopi swarmed out of the river, following the string of silverbugs that lined the shore, jerking spasmodically. Long limbs flowed over the limestone wall, onto the cathedral room's stone floor, pulled the rest of the alien bodies up behind. Purples, blues, deep shades that shimmered and flowed. They stayed close together, clustering, as if afraid something might reach out and snag stragglers, drag them to an unseen doom.

There, by the altar they had seen only in carvings—one of the yellow-skinned, stiff-moving monsters that had murdered so many. Cut into pieces, red fluid in a pool beneath the ragged chunks.

A few rocktopi wandered to the control panel, a few skirted the edges of the room and a few more peered down the shaft. The orb dropped steadily downward.

As it descended, ancient lights surged to life, or at least tried to. Some flickered uselessly. Most didn't turn on at all, their function long since claimed by the persistent fingers of time. A few managed to sputter fully awake. They cast dim reflections on the orb's polished surface.

These rocktopi were on one side of the river. On the far shore, another group moved fast along the riverbank, following a line of silverbugs that urged them on.

10:23 A.M.

Kayla crawled past silverbugs. They scurried out of her way, circled back to rejoin the line, sometimes walking *on* her in their haste.

She crawled toward her knife, which Kirkland had left lying at the corridor mouth. The naked blade reflected hazy light filtering down from far above the artificial canyon.

Her face felt like he'd hit her with a sledgehammer. He'd head-butted her. Could you believe that? That skinny, stuffed-shirt desk jockey. Stabbed her in the knee, then *head-butted* her. Connell Fucking Kirkland had done that.

And she'd thought him weak.

The world shimmered. Kayla blinked away tears, only to have more flow into place. She'd taken one look at her knee, instantly thrown up all over herself. Kirkland had stabbed all the way through, from the back out the front. The joint was ruined forever: tendons, ligaments, muscle, cartilage, the important shit that made it work all sliced halfway to Fuckville and beyond.

She didn't want to kill anymore, and that surprised her. She didn't want to hurt. There was enough hurt already. All she wanted to do was get out of this place.

Why hadn't she trusted her instincts? She should have never come down here.

Kirkland had escaped. So had O'Doyle, Lybrand and probably Reeves.

All of this—the hacking, the destruction, days of cooking in the desert sun—it had all been for nothing.

Kayla crawled.

A silverbug scurried over her back.

She reached for the knife, held it.

Why had Kirkland let her live? Left her with a weapon?

Maybe he was toying with her. Maybe he was the kind of sick fuck that enjoyed the misery of others. People like that were destined to burn in hell. She could at least take minor satisfaction from that fact.

Kayla crawled.

She gripped the corridor's smooth edge, grunted as she rose to stand on her good leg. Every motion sent shattering pain through her knee, reminded her of the long reconstruction efforts to come.

If she was lucky.

Downstream. In the river, the water would carry her weight. That was the way to go. Just had to hop through this wet platinum sludge, hop *carefully*, then—

—movement on her left: movement, and *color*.

The burst of horror hit her all at once, made her atoms tingle.

Kayla Meyers looked to her left.

A wall of glowing monsters poured down the riverbank toward her, the mist magnifying their flashing red and orange bursts like stoplights illuminating the morning fog.

So, *that* was why he'd left her alive.

"Clever boy," she said.

Kayla shifted her balance, hopped slightly, and turned to face her attackers.

10:26 A.M.

Say one thing for Kayla Meyers—that woman sure could scream.

She'd saved her best for last. It echoed through the ship canyon.

Defiant at first, a scream of rage, then of pain, and, finally, a guttural plea that faded to nothing. Not words, really, but sounds any human being could understand.

Connell took no joy from her death. Maybe he should have left her a gun … maybe she would have held them off longer.

He kept moving, each struggling step his own personal Spanish Inquisition. *Confess! Confess!* He would have, gladly, to anything, just to make this pain stop for even an instant.

And yet, he kept on.

Hard to breathe. Heart, hammering.

He saw the bubble room where he'd left O'Doyle and Lybrand. He moved past that, unable to keep himself from whimpering when he slipped, when he reactively put his ruined foot down to stop from falling.

Past the ship corner, out of the canyon.

There … the entrance to the Linus Highway.

He didn't know if he could make it.

He also knew he had no choice but to try.

The animal inside understood one thing and one thing only: survival.

Connell Kirkland limped toward the tunnel entrance.

Three miles to go.

Three miles.

10:35 A.M.

The orb descended.

A few more faint lights flickered to life. The reflections glowed like soft pearls, first appearing on the bottom, increasing in size as they arced up the curve, then shrank again as the orb descended past.

Down and down and down.

Reflections of massive, rough-hewn pillars, each larger than the Eiffel Tower, thicker than a skyscraper, each a monument of engineering and long-dead technological prowess, glided over the polished platinum. For several minutes, the pillars' images alone covered the orb's sides, until a new reflection arced across the metallic surface, gradually growing larger and more defined.

That reflection? A fish-eye distortion of the shaft bottom.

10:48 A.M.

This was what madness felt like.

Bertha wanted to strip off the suit, find a rough-edged rock and scrape the skin from her arms. Scrape it right off, because even that agony would be nothing compared to what she felt now.

Second-degree burns? Third? If she'd shoved her arms into boiling water and held them there for hours... that's what this was.

She leaned heavily on Patrick. He leaned heavily on her. A four-legged whole greater than the sum of two-legged parts.

He stumbled, started to fall.

Without thinking, Bertha grabbed him around the waist. He stayed upright, thanks to a fresh wave of scorching agony ripping up her arms.

"Can't make it," he grunted. "You go."

She shook her head. She would be dead right now if not for him. Bertha vaguely remembered seeing Angus Kool. Patrick had taken the man's suit. Patrick found a way to save her, she would do the same for him.

Bertha looked back—a line of silverbugs behind them, more flowing up the tunnel to take their place.

"Patrick, we go together," she said. "You don't make it, I don't make it. Do you want me to live?"

He glared down at her, like he hated her. Maybe, in that moment, he did hate her. Maybe he still would once they got out of here, but she didn't care—as long as he *did* get out.

"Move," she said.

He gritted his teeth, winced—from which injury, she did not know—then let her help him on.

10:55 A.M.

Heat.

Pain.

Connell stumbled, fell to his knees in the cave silt.

Silverbugs all around. He couldn't hear them. He didn't bother to see if they were shiny or burnished—if they were the kind with knives, he'd find out soon enough.

How far had he climbed? A mile? Maybe more? Maybe less?

The animal inside clawed and bit, hissed and spat.

The man leaned his weight on the rifle, tried to rise.

The world slipped. The world spun.

His face hit the cave silt, a small rock digging into his right cheekbone.

Where was he? The car … an accident … someone T-boned the car. Cori.

His fingers tingling. Toes, too.

That sound … metallic clicking, clinking. The engine, cooling from the winter's cold.

Connell blinked, tried to see. Everything blurry. Was that … a rock wall?

He pushed himself up on hands and knees. No, not a car accident. He was in the tunnels.

Silverbugs.

The rocktopi were coming.

His stomach, queasy … he might throw up.

Have to move. Have to move.

Connell picked up the rifle. He put the butt firmly in the silt, tried once again to rise. His arms trembled. His legs groaned. His foot howled.

Come on, come on …

He focused, begged his muscles to just do this one more thing. Inch by inch, he started to rise.

Then, he slowly started to sink.

He didn't even have the strength to stand.

So, he crawled.

Hand after hand, knee after knee, Connell Kirkland kept moving up the Linus Highway.

10:59 A.M.

Twenty miles below Connell's feet, the orb's descent slowed.

The air temperature was that of hell itself, raging at just over 1,900 degrees Fahrenheit.

The curved, polished platinum came to rest on the shaft floor, settling into a perfectly fitted depression made of the same metal.

An internal computer processed data on air pressure, heat and distance traveled.

Finding those readings suitable, the computer triggered the detonator.

34

121,440 feet below the surface

11:00 A.M.

The orb shuddered once, then disappeared in a nova of light brighter than the sun. Shockwaves lashed out at supersonic speeds, disintegrating the countless support pillars in a billowing burst of evaporated stone. A great rumbling and shaking began as millions of tons of rock, now without support from below, began to settle into the newly created void.

Devastating heat from the blast raced up the deep shaft, melting rock along the way. Within seconds the blast erupted into the Dense Mass Cavern, spurting upward like a geyser in an expanding cloud of destruction. The orb's cathedral room, which sat in the center of the immortal metal hull, sagged like cheap wax, collapsed in on itself, in seconds going from a magnificent technological monument to a white-hot sea of molten metal. Silverbugs erupted like popcorn, then melted in place to join the boiling pool of metal. Like a ring rippling from a pebble in a pond, the explosive heat reached out from the ship's center, melting the timeless vessel in a quickly expanding wave.

The shockwaves also traveled downward, winning the battle between the irresistible force and immovable object. Rock simply ceased to exist as starlike temperatures evaporated everything within reach, creating a huge bubble of superheated gas.

The orb didn't punch a hole through the earth's mantle. It didn't have to. The cold, calculated, precise science that once carved out the pillars had placed the shaft's bottom a geological hair's width from the swirling mantle. For millennia, the earth's internal pressure pushed against the shaft floor, obeying the laws of physics and seeking the easiest way out. But the shaft floor's precise design had held just enough strength to keep that incalculable force at bay, just enough to keep things as they were meant to be.

The orb, however, melted another half mile's worth of crust, a calculation as fixed and precise as a surgeon's stroke. At the bottom of that newly created bubble of plasma, the earth's pressure—so long held in check by the thinnest of margins—finally broke free.

Magma rocketed upward with tidal-wave force, pushed ever higher by the liquid core's grinding, pulsating pressures. The magma filled the new pocket and continued up the shaft, pushing the ten-thousand-degree gas bubble before it.

11:01 A.M.

O'Doyle and Lybrand crawled on their bellies, urged on by the unmistakable smell of fresh, outside air. The ground shuddered beneath them, pouring fuel on their desperate effort to escape the mountain.

The low rock ceiling scraped at O'Doyle's back. He grunted as he worked his thick trunk through the narrow opening, jagged limestone tearing his KoolSuit to shreds.

He wiggled past a pumpkin-shaped rock and continued on.

11:02 A.M.

At the waterfall, the temperature soared a thousand degrees. Two thousand. More. The river instantly boiled to superheated steam. The rocktopi clinging to the ancient, tentacled sculpture died quickly, the fluid in their bodies boiling, making them swell like water balloons before erupting with audible *pops*.

11:03 A.M.

The ground beneath Connell shook and lurched, knocking him about so violently that he couldn't even stay on his hands and knees. He fell to his chest. Cracks raced up the tunnel walls like bolts of splitting lightning, the sound of grinding rock following like thunder. Thick, swirling storm clouds of dust seeped into the air.

He looked up to see a fist-sized piece of rock fall from the tunnel ceiling, dust trailing behind it like a comet's tail. The rock bounced off the wildly shaking floor, settled against the tunnel wall.

The entire ceiling gave way.

Boulders crashed down.

11:04 A.M.

Magma exploded up from the shaft floor, a great gushing pillar of molten rock jetting against the tunnel ceiling more than two thousand feet above. There it licked against an artificial sun, which sputtered once and then fell dark. A great rain of magma sprayed across the cavern, rained down to splash into the hellish pool of bubbling, liquefied hull.

Confused silverbugs scattered everywhere, rushing pell-mell in all directions. Some scampered headlong into the boiling pools and melted in a fraction of a second. Some scattered up the walls, only to be peeled off by the torrential cascade of scorching lava. Some fell motionless where they stood, internal mechanics baked to death in heat rivaling that at the earth's center.

Swirling magma covered the ancient tile floor, forming a hell-spawned lake that rose slowly up the cavern walls. Boiling rock poured like water, flowing into the countless tunnels connected, splashing orange-hot and destroying everything in its path.

The Dense Mass Cavern trembled. A slight shake at first, then harder, then rattling as if held by the fist of a planet-sized giant. The floor cracked and jumped, torn apart by billions of tons of settling rock. The ceiling collapsed, dropping boulders the size of city blocks into the soupy mix of melted ship and liquid rock.

The orb's burst of energy created a void that nature had to fill. The mountain slowly fell in on itself as the column of magma continued to jet upward, pushed by the pressures of the world itself.

11:05 A.M.

The Land Rover rocked wildly on its shocks, bouncing like some child's toy as the ground shook and rumbled. He leaned heavily against the hood, trying to keep his balance on a jumping trampoline made of rock and dirt.

The world shuddered. The ground lurched. He wondered if the sky itself might fall.

Sonny McGuiness had never known fear this profound, this all-encompassing. He was down at the base of the mountain, but would that matter? Everything threw itself back and forth so violently the entire state might be breaking up.

And yet, he knew this place of death was, itself, dying, and that knowledge electrified his soul, filled him with joy beyond measure.

He raised a gnarled fist, shook it at the towering mountain.

"Now it's *your* funeral, you sonofabitch!"

The peak seemed to fold in on itself, a massive circus tent with the center stake kicked out. Unfathomable mounds of rock dropped backward out of sight—the mountain started *collapsing*.

It was impossible for the ground on which he stood to move this much, to kick like a mule, to lift the Land Rover and drop it down over and over. Sonny held on against the shockwaves, transfixed as the cursed place tore itself apart.

He held on tight, stared up the path that led to the mesa. If he saw the woman, he'd get in and drive off, earthquake or no earthquake.

But he couldn't leave, not just yet.

Because Sonny McGuiness wanted to watch a mountain die.

11:06 A.M.

For millennia, the big river had flowed down through the wide tunnel. Now water boiled away as magma flowed into it, flowed *up*, pushed higher by immeasurable pressure.

Liquid rock shot into the kidney-shaped cavern, pushing a wall of superheated steam ahead of it. Rocktopi died, but a little slower than their brethren in the ship and at the waterfall. These rocktopi had time to feel the temperature spiking. They had time to scream. Some even had time to flee.

Lava flowed across the fields, wiping out crops in a hiss of smoke.

The orange mass flowed into the village, swelling up and over buildings. It flowed inside, submerging dead and dying children.

And with those deaths, the last of the Utah tribe vanished forever.

11:07 A.M.

Pure darkness.

He wasn't hot anymore.

Cold, actually, his hands and feet growing numb with chill.

Connell coughed. Blood in his mouth, and on the rock pressing down on his chest, pinning him.

Pain everywhere, he was *made* of the stuff, yet it seemed distant, as if it were a photo, a memory.

Couldn't move his arms or legs. So much weight on him, trapping him like an insect kept in place by long pins stabbed through limbs and into wax.

Cold body, but the air in his mouth, his lungs, that felt hot. His mask had either come off or was broken. He didn't know which.

It didn't matter.

He tried to breathe deep, but the weight on his chest kept him to a shallow sucking, to tiny, rapid gasps.

It was over.

No one left to rescue him. No hope of rescuing himself.

He was dying.

What would it be like?

Kind of sucked, really—he should have died in a car accident so many years ago. He'd wandered through life, awash in selfish misery, spreading that misery to others. And here, miles below ground, when dying would have been the easiest thing to do, he'd rediscovered the primitive need to go on.

It would have been better to die when he didn't want to live.

Cold all over now.

The ground trembled beneath him.

The boulders on his chest, pressing down, settling, making each breath a tiny bit shallower than the one before.

A faint light flashed through the cracks between the boulders that were his tomb. Lybrand or O'Doyle? Please, no... he'd given his own life so that those two could escape.

Please, don't let them come back for me ... too late for me ...

The light, flashing brighter.

Was it rocktopi? Maybe death by blade would be better than this slow, exhausting suffocation, better than lungs compressed until they could draw air no more.

No, that light... no reds or oranges, blues or greens. Just *white*.

And then, a voice.

"Connell?"

He knew that voice. A voice from his past, from his dreams. A voice that could not be.

He started to speak, coughed blood again. He spat out a mouthful, drew a shallow breath, just enough to say one word.

"Cori?"

"Yes, my love. I'm here with you. Don't be afraid."

Blackness, then the light again.

He could *smell* her.

Was this a vision? Was this real?

He didn't care. Cori was with him again. Her light filled him, erasing his agony, relaxing his devastated body.

He felt something warm and tender gently lift his crushed hand. He instantly recognized her touch. He didn't mind the pain, as long as he could feel her again.

Connell's hand slowly grew cold in hers, and with a tiny smile on his face, his half-lidded eyes faded away into a blank stare of stillness and peace.

11:09 A.M.

Bertha and Patrick stumbled out of the tunnel mouth and onto a small mesa. They clung to each other, had to stay standing upright on stone that bucked beneath them.

A cliff, a sheer drop ... was there any way down? Yes, there, between those boulders ... a path.

A grinding rumble, louder than anything she'd heard in war. It froze her in place, her and Patrick both.

The mountain, rising up at a slope behind them. Several hundred feet up the rise, the rock simply *fell away*, a towering sand castle undercut by the coming tide.

A hundred feet of stone, *gone*.

Then another hundred, crumbling back, out of sight.

Bertha couldn't move. She clung to Patrick, tried to stay standing as the universe trembled and lurched.

More mountain above them, falling back, the slope vanishing as if some unseen demon was ripping the rock away to get at them.

Another grinding crack...and she saw light coming from inside the tunnel.

The mountain stilled.

No...that wasn't light coming from inside the tunnel...she saw *through* the tunnel—fifty feet in, the descending Linus Highway ended, opened to daylight, to air.

And past that new crumbling edge, she could see down into a void that moments ago had been an immortal mountain.

"Sweet mother of God," Patrick said.

In that void, boiling magma: orange and yellow and white-hot heat blazed with a light of its own, as if the souls of dead rocktopi had flowed together, merged, become a titan ghost rising up to take revenge. Lava swirled, a typhoon of molten rock, bubbles the size of garbage trucks rising and bursting, throwing death into the air.

The very center of that hellish whirlpool lifted, became a glowing dome that lasted all of a second or two, then the top ripped open and a jet of magma tore apart the afternoon sky.

Bertha watched, hypnotized, unable to move, as a shifting column of molten rock shot a thousand feet into the air, until it could rise no more, until it spread, the spray arcing...then began to rain back down.

Back DOWN...

She grabbed Patrick, drag-shoved him toward the mesa's edge.

He needed no such urging.

Together, their burns and cuts and breaks and bruises forgotten, they sprinted down the path as lava bombs crashed around them.

The mountain began to shudder anew...

11:10 A.M.

"Well, I'll be dipped in pig shit."

The trembling had died down enough for Sonny to stand without bracing himself on the Land Rover. He'd started for the driver's door, then stopped, remembering his quiet promise to Kirkland.

Sonny had raised his binoculars for one final look.

Coming down the side of the mountain, or what used to be a mountain, he saw two figures in yellow KoolSuits rushing along the very same path he'd taken to reach that mesa where Samuel Anderson, Douglas Nadia and Wilford Igoe Jr. had seen daylight for the last time.

Sonny had laughed at Funeral Mountain's death, but it wasn't over. Magma sprayed high into the air, higher than any skyscraper he'd ever seen—the flicking tongue of the devil licking out to suck down souls. Huge, snaking globs of half-cooled molten rock arced down, exploding like shrapnel bombs when they landed.

Whoever those two survivors were, they had no chance. Sonny needed to get in that Land Rover and drive the fuck off, *away* from the new volcano and its thousand-foot spire of lava—not *toward* it.

Sonny adjusted the binocs, focused in on the two survivors.

A man…the big security chief, O'Doyle.

And a woman…Bertha Lybrand?

Even at this distance he could see they were in bad shape, limping more than running, faces fixed with grim determination and also etched with fear. God, but they were a mess.

O'Doyle fell, landed hard, rolled for a bit before he stopped. The woman knelt by him. A magma glob hit close by—she shielded his body with her own.

So goddamn brave.

Sonny lowered the binoculars.

Could he get to them in time?

Don't you wanna know? Don't ya?

He sighed.

"Well, fuck it. You only live once."

He gave his bracelet a quick rub, thumb tracing the swastika, then he scrambled into the driver's seat.

11:11 A.M.

"Get the *fuck up, you asshole!*"

She kept pulling on his arm, yanking, but he refused to rise.

Artillery raining down around them, each impact launching a horizontal spray of black shards and burning rock. So close to escape, and they were going to die here?

"*Get up … GET UP!*"

She stepped back, and she kicked him. Right in the ribs.

"*Getupgetupgetup!*"

She kicked him again. He caught the foot, lifted hard. She stumbled back, fell herself.

The ground shuddered beneath her, so strong it was all she could do to get on her hands and knees and stay there.

A crack/splash beside her—spots of fire on her face, her chest.

Bertha rolled to her side, beat at her burning skin. She smelled her own cooking flesh.

Big hands on her shoulders, yanking her to her feet.

Patrick.

No more words, just movement.

A boulder smashed into the path in front of her, only a few feet away from crushing her to a pulp. She and Patrick skidded, let the rock bounce on down the path, then they followed it.

Lava splashing down around them, killing rocks flying through the air, the two soldiers searched for and found that last bit of primitive need.

They ran downhill.

11:13 A.M.

A rock the size of a boot smacked into the windshield, turning the glass into a web of cracks. Still embedded there, the rock was surrounded by a corona of the sun's light fractured into a million tiny rainbows.

"Sonofabitch!"

Sonny lowered the window, reached a hand down to brace himself on the outside of the door, leaned out.

Up ahead, Lybrand and O'Doyle.

A crunch on the hood, hot splatters kicking all over. Something burned his cheek. He slapped it away, leaned out the window again.

The Land Rover hit a rock, lurched upward—the door drove hard into his armpit, made him bite his tongue.

Blood in his mouth, but he wasn't stopping.

The geyser of magma continued to spray into the air, only not as high now. Volcanic bombs crashed down, as did rocks that hit and bounced.

A building-sized chunk of rock slammed down, point first, embedded into the trail with a thunderous shudder and stuck there like the spear of a stone giant. Sonny wheeled hard right, off the path. Rocks dug into the Rover's undercarriage, threw the vehicle left and right.

But he kept on.

He passed the stone spearhead, corrected. The Land Rover caught air as he drove it back onto the path and continued uphill.

11:14 A.M.

"I don't fucking believe it," Patrick said. "Sonny McGuiness to the rescue?"

He saw the little man's body half hanging out the driver's-side window, black skin framed by the blazing white beard. The old man was screaming ... he was *laughing*.

Patrick jerked his left leg, shook it, a sudden reaction to burning pain.

Ash poured down. The end of the volcano, or just the beginning?

He looked up: the Land Rover skidded to a halt, not even ten feet away.

Bertha ran for the front passenger seat.

Patrick opened the rear driver-side door, fell in more than climbed in, heard the door shut behind him.

"Hold tight," Sonny said.

Things got blurry. Patrick couldn't see that well. All the damage, catching up with him, trying to drag him under.

Plinking sounds, like hail hitting the Land Rover.

Lurching forward, then sideways, then pressed hard against the seat cushion. The car, spinning.

Impact from below—he was thrown into the air, so high he hit the roof, then fell back down, off the cushion, onto the floor.

Lybrand, screaming: *"Drive, goddammit, DRIVE!"*

Sonny, laughing, a cackle straight out of a bad movie.

Bouncing, rocking, thrown about in the tight space, unable to brace himself.

Then, *speed.*

"Patrick! Are you all right?"

He loved that woman, but damn if that wasn't the stupidest question he'd ever heard. All right? Hell no. He'd seen enough men die in his day to know he might only be minutes from joining them.

But he pushed himself off the floor, the last of what little strength he had shifting his body back onto the seat.

She was next to him in an instant, pressing against him.

Together, Patrick and Bertha looked out the Land Rover's rear window.

There, a new volcano bellowed a column of thick ash into a darkening sky. The mountain that had vanished was already growing again — what had once been limestone and granite was now the dark black of volcanic rock, a darkness streaked with steaming, snaking trails of rocktopi orange.

Patrick could barely move, but he managed to lift his left hand up to the window. He made a fist, then extended his middle finger.

"Fuck you," he said.

Lybrand collapsed against him, chest heaving. She nuzzled her head into his neck.

Sonny McGuiness just kept on laughing.

EPILOGUE

Five weeks later

PATRICK FINISHED his story.

Bertha quickly added a few details that Patrick had forgotten, or maybe didn't want to remember. When she finished talking, they both looked to the old woman sitting behind the desk in front of them, waited for her to speak.

Barbara Yakely said nothing. She looked off, as if trying to process the insane tale she'd just been told.

The eyes behind her glasses were red and swollen, puffy bags beneath them hanging darkly. She'd held a burning cigar the entire time Patrick and Bertha had been there, yet hadn't taken a single puff.

Patrick glanced at the framed pictures on the wall. A man in a suit and tie, the typical painted image of a company founder. Next to that painting, another, a younger man who was the spitting image of the first.

And, finally, a painting of Connell Kirkland. Dead eyes stared out. Suit and tie, of course. Patrick wondered if—after all they'd been through—Connell would have preferred to instead be immortalized in a KoolSuit and holding a weapon.

When Yakely finally spoke, her voice sounded like gravel mixed with heartbreak.

"So these...*things*...they killed my Connell?"

My Connell. Much more than a boss-employee relationship there. Not surprising considering the picture on the wall, its place of honor alongside one man Patrick assumed to be Barbara's husband, and another he assumed to be her son.

"Yes, ma'am," he said. "They were responsible for his death, although, as I told you, he sacrificed himself to save Bertha and me."

The old woman lifted the cigar, finally put it in her mouth. She tapped it a few times with her teeth, lowered it without taking a puff.

"Your story sounds like science fiction bullshit," she said. "How convenient there's no evidence of any kind. No way to find any evidence, either. Other than your face and her missing fingers. No offense."

Bertha bristled, but Patrick gently put a hand on her back.

"I wasn't exactly a male model before this shit happened," he said. "All the burns didn't help—thanks for noticing. Our story does sound like bullshit. No argument there. But we didn't make up a new volcano. You've seen the news coverage, the pictures. And what's more, you strike me as the kind of person who can spot bullshit a mile away. Tell me, do you think I'm lying?"

She stared at him. Stared hard. He held her gaze, calmly waiting. She would either believe him or she wouldn't, and either way, it didn't matter. Patrick was honoring his friend by telling the story to perhaps the only person who had cared about him.

And, hopefully, honoring him one more way as well.

"No," the old woman said. She set the cigar in an ashtray, rubbed at her eyes. "No, I think you're telling the truth."

Yakely picked up a folder from her desk, a folder that Patrick had provided. No tablet, no computer file, just good old-fashioned paper.

"You're sure," she said. "You're sure he couldn't have made it out alive?"

Bertha nodded. "Yes, ma'am. No one was behind us, and there was only one way out. The mountain collapsed. If that didn't kill him, the lava would have. He's gone."

Her tone was hard-edged, as usual, but Patrick heard a hint of uncharacteristic softness. Bertha had never liked Connell—still didn't—but she knew what he had done. For that, Connell Kirkland had earned Bertha Lybrand's undying respect.

Yakely sniffed.

"All right," she said. "He's gone. And now you want, what...*revenge?*"

Patrick nodded. "That's right."

The old woman leaned across the desk. Her eyes bore into him.

"But *why?* Everyone in that camp is dead. You two made it out alive. Lucky, from the sound of it. Now you want to put yourselves in harm's way again? Why don't you two ride off into the sunset together? If my Connell died so that you can live, why throw that away?"

A good question, one Patrick had asked himself a dozen times, one Bertha had asked him a hundred. Patrick was too old for this shit. He knew that. And when he healed completely, he'd still carry injuries from Funeral Mountain that would pain him for the rest of his life, slow him, make him feel even older than he already was.

Connell had died so that he and Bertha could escape.

So, yes, the question: *Why throw that away?*

The answer always came back instantly, and it was always the same.

"Because Connell Kirkland was my friend," Patrick said. "He was my friend, he's dead, and someone has to pay."

A spark in those sad, old eyes. A connection. In that moment, Patrick knew Yakely wanted revenge, too.

She opened the folder.

"And this Argentina thing, this is how you get your payback?"

"That's right," Patrick said. "If there any of those creatures left, we're going to wipe them out. They don't belong here, ma'am. We're going to make them extinct."

Yakely turned a page, read.

"This looks expensive," she said. "Is it dangerous?"

"*Very* dangerous," Bertha said, spitting the words out before Patrick could answer.

Bertha didn't want to do the mission. She wanted that same sunset Yakely had asked about. Patrick wanted it, too, but not yet. He would never rest until this was done. Even though Bertha said it was stupid, risky, and a waste of Connell's sacrifice, she wasn't going to let Patrick do it alone.

Yakely closed the folder, set it down.

"I'd have to sell off several assets to fund this," she said. "I'm willing to do that, but you're talking about taking an armed force of mercenaries into Argentina. Last time I checked, that's a sovereign nation. What makes you think the local authorities are going to allow this to happen?"

Patrick unconsciously rubbed his right biceps, massaging the rectangle of skin tattooed a light blue crossed by a horizontal white stripe, with a radiating sun in the middle.

"I've done business there before," he said. "I know what palms to grease."

Yakely raised the cigar—now half burned away—and finally took a long, slow puff. The end glowed the color of flowing lava. She held the smoke, turned her head, let it out slow.

"A lot of people died at our mine," she said. "Not just Connell. I had to call their families, tell them their husbands, wives, mothers, fathers, sons and daughters were dead. Do you know what that's like, Mister O'Doyle? Do you know how it feels to make those calls?"

He nodded slowly. "In my younger days, I made those calls myself. More times than I care to remember."

Bertha leaned forward, set her left elbow on the desk. She stretched out her fingers, or at least the two that remained. Nasty lines of stitches covered the two stumps. A tattoo encircled the stump of her ring finger.

"I can't wear a fucking wedding ring because of what happened to me down there, but Patrick and I were just married," she said. "That's his name inked on what's left of my finger. I love him. He's going to do this with or without your support, Missus Yakely. If you fund it properly, he's got a much better chance of coming out alive."

Yakely looked at the mangled hand, then up at Bertha.

"You're going with him?"

Bertha nodded. "I won't leave his side."

Yakely glanced to the wall, to the picture of the company founder. Her eyes softened. She licked her lips.

"I'll pay you *not* to go," she said in a whisper. "I'll give you a million dollars if you leave this madness behind and start your new life together."

Patrick was shaking his head before she even finished her sentence.

"Thank you, ma'am, but we're going," he said. "Nothing can change our minds."

Barbara sighed, wiped at her eyes. She nodded.

"I knew you'd say that. I can see it in you, O'Doyle. Stubborn. And idealistic. Two qualities that get people killed. But... if you want this, then I want it, too. It will take me a while to raise the money."

She wrote a number on a blank piece of paper.

"Call this number in the morning. My man Harvey will handle things from here on out. You don't call me, you don't come here, ever again. None of this can be traced back to EarthCore, you understand?"

Patrick nodded. "Of course, ma'am."

Yakely waved her cigar hand at the door.

"Thank you for the visit," she said.

Patrick and Bertha stood. Like a gentleman, he let his new bride exit first. He stepped out the door, then Yakely called to him, stopping him.

"O'Doyle?"

He looked back into the office.

"Yes, ma'am?"

Yakely's old hands clenched to fists. The cigar stub in her fingers crumbled, spilling smoking ash onto her desktop. She couldn't put on the brave face any longer—tears flowed down her cheeks.

"I want you to kill them all," she said. "Kill every last one of those motherfuckers."

Patrick nodded. "That's what I do."

He and his wife left. Soon, they would have the money they needed. Until then, though, there was still much to do to prepare.

Prepare for the trip to where Veronica Reeves had made her name.

Prepare... for Mount Fitz Roy.

BIBLIOGRAPHY

Allison, M. Lee, ed., and Sharon Wakefield, ed., *Energy and Mineral Resources of Utah*. Salt Lake City, UT: Utah Geological Association, 1990.

Carter, William, *Ghost Towns of the West*. Menlo Park, CA: Lane, 1971.

Lamb, Susan, *The Smithsonian Guides to Natural America: The Southern Rockies*, Washington, D.C.: Smithsonian Books, 1995.

Moore, George W. and G. Nicholas Sullivan, *Speleology*. Trenton, NJ: Cave Books, 1978.

Shawe, Daniel R., ed. and Peter D. Rowly, *Guidebook to Mineral Deposits of Southwestern Utah*. Salt Lake City, UT: Utah Geological Association, 1978.

Vogel, Shawna, *Naked Earth*. New York: Plume, 1996.

Watkins, T. H., *Gold and Silver in the West*. Palo Alto: American West, 1971.

Wharton, Tom and Gayen Wharton, *Utah*. Compass America Guides, 1993.

Whelan, J. A., *Geology, Ore Deposits and Mineralogy of the Rocky Range, Near Milford, Beaver County, Utah*, Salt Lake City, UT: Utah Geological and Mineral Survey, 1982.